Centa Isla

(sen-tah-ees-lah)

by

Jack Hale

Grosvenor House
Publishing Limited

This book is published by
Grosvenor House Publishing Ltd
Link House
140 The Broadway, Tolworth, Surrey, KT6 7HT.
www.grosvenorhousepublishing.co.uk

This book is a work of fiction. Any resemblance to
people or events, past or present, is purely coincidental.

A CIP record for this book
is available from the British Library

ISBN 978-1-83615-206-4

*To my love, Amber, who has read
this book a thousand times already and
heard about it a thousand more.*

1

She was so young, yet already so tired. Her mind felt languid, as though the spiders that filled the derelict properties around her had spun their webs into her mind. Rissa could feel it, a heaviness behind her eyes that weighed down her thoughts and plunged her into a deep malaise. It had become harder to shift that feeling. It was as though a pervading numbness had hollowed out her mind and filled it with apathy.

Even her favourite place no longer provided a welcoming few hours of escapism. Rissa felt the wind buffet her as she aimlessly watched clouds of smog drift across the sunless void that consumed the horizon. Behind her sat the grey, smoky streets of Centa Isla, sulking in a grey, oppressive smog. Even now, those claustrophobic streets waited patiently for her to return, but she would put off their suffocating embrace for as long as she could. This rusty old scaffolding was by far the best view Downtown had to offer. For a sight so chaotic and devastating, it was surprisingly serene and quiet, a pleasant break from the droning chaos of the city. She could clear her head up here and watch the smog drift across the endless horizon.

As the rain began to fall quicker and harder, the first signs of a storm began to fester. She reluctantly picked up her heavy backpack, clumsily manoeuvring the straps onto both shoulders. She would have to return sooner or later and staying out any longer would be asking for trouble. Rissa left the abandoned building site. The radio had forecast a dry night, though this was not the first time it had been wrong, nor would it likely be the last. In a matter of seconds, the downpour came down harder as the heavens opened, dangerously slickening the steel scaffolding beneath her as she steadily guided herself back down to ground level. The tall towers and apartment blocks once again captured her beneath their dwarfing shadows. Even at the very southern edge of Downtown, the tallest shadows of the City Centre could cast their leering embrace over her and the entire district.

As she descended, a shadow caught her eye. It flitted across a rooftop in an instant, so quick that she swore she had missed it. A mantle of grey shadow,

1

mired in the clotted darkness of the city, shambling across a distant rooftop. It was gone before she could properly see.

Returning to the ground always made her realise how much more she preferred to be higher up. To be back down among the oppressive towers and narrow alleys brought with it a tightness in her chest that she could not shift. This close to the edge of the city was perilous and rarely travelled. It was unpatrolled by the CIPD who prioritised the safety of the turbulent City Centre rather than the Synth-addicted dregs who lived this far out. The darkness that set in with the clotting rain was to her advantage.

The sunken, boggy earth of the derelict construction site quickly gave way to potholed roads and a network of twisting, labyrinthian alleyways. With the rattling of the old supports in her ears, Rissa looked back. She had often wondered what they had originally planned to build here. The earth magic that had raised the foundations had long since turned to dust, leaving the old scaffolding wobbling in place without a purpose. It had been there for as many of her twenty years as she could remember. It was a remnant, one of many, of promises left unfulfilled by the cataclysmic events of the Reckoning that put this city into the state of decay it found itself in.

An empty crushed can tumbled across the street as the wind and rain blustered through Downtown's corridor-like streets. It scuttled erratically across the old, cobbled roads, tripping in potholes as a drunk might in the early hours of first light. Her clothes were drenched through. Navy jeans glued to her legs and her white coat was so waterlogged that it began seeping freezing liquid down her back. Despite it all, Rissa enjoyed the rain for its gentle ambience and mistral beauty, every cold drop on her pale skin a reminder she was still alive. Her hair – blue as the sunlit oceans that once covered the planet – dripped with water, sticking in clusters to her scalp. Even with the weight of the water, her wild hair wouldn't lie still; jagged and resistant, as if it had been trimmed with a blunt knife and washed beneath a waterfall. Blue wasn't the normal colour of hair for a citizen of Centa Isla. That was made clear by the ominous cold stares she was receiving from the other side of the street. She could feel dagger-like eyes stabbing into her, tracking her as she walked slowly home. Rissa appraised them in an instant. Hoods, streetwear, the flash of concealed steel that typified the usual thugs that roamed Downtown after dark. These were an organised gang known as Empty Eyes, marked by the distinct eyepatch or bandage they wore. To earn your place among them, Rissa had been told that you were required to surrender the eye that had become blind to the suffering of the people. Hence the symbolic eyepatch. They preached toppling the current monarchy, doing so with indiscriminate acts of random violence and arson solely orchestrated to scour at people's faith in the leadership of the city. They gathered the lowest the city had to offer, lining their ranks with psychopaths, addicts and the transient population. They preached change, but Rissa was certain they were just enjoying causing chaos.

Centa Isla had once been a grand monument to the achievements of mankind in their golden age forged from a union of magic and technology. But now it was a decaying, claustrophobic prison with shelves of food that would empty and never refill. There were harsh restrictions and harsher penalties on all magic outside of Grandmaster that had left the city drab and lifeless. She was too young to have seen the Reckoning that had sown such devastation and incurred all these laws, but was old enough to feel the worst of the impact. The cataclysmic event that had shattered the world and condemned the city of Centa Isla to float alone in the abyss had been wrought by the mistakes of their forebears – punished for their abuse of magic following its inception. On the outskirts of Forge Town to the east, the air was still thick and lethal with smog that had been produced from that time of industry. Rissa had long since had enough of it all. She felt just as rotten as the stale air that now clogged her lungs. She just wanted out. From atop her rusted perch she had wished so often for there to be something more beyond the horizon that was lit by the exposed planet's core and smothered by industrial smoke.

Suddenly, a voice from across the alley interrupted her thoughts.

"Horrible night to be stranded Downtown, ain't it?"

Her tone was mild, but she knew that her intention was anything but. Rissa knew that Empty Eyes loathed her kind. Versorcerers, practitioners of The Algarethan Verse, holding the endless potential of magic in their very blood. The genes extended to her appearance, washing her hair the colour of the missing sea itself. Favoured in all aspects of life, most Versorcerers were nobles who resided within the lavish City Centre. Besides herself, there were precious few who lived Downtown.

Rissa watched the reflection in the shop window as after being ignored, the thugs began to cross the road after her.

"I was talkin' to you." The same one spoke again, clearly the brains of the operation. "No need to be rude."

A glance into a rippling puddle revealed to her that they had gained ground. For every step she took, the trinity of thugs had taken two. They muttered obscenities among themselves. Nothing she hadn't heard a thousand times. Her hands dropped into her pockets. Inside one of them, she found cold steel. But it was no blade that she carried but rather, a ring. It was a Conduit – a direct link to the magical blood she had inherited from her late mother. And the tool needed for mortals like her to perform magic.

Sure, she could have dyed her hair or concealed it. All of this unwarranted attention could have been avoided. But then, where was the fun in that? There was no doubt that these thugs expected her to be compliant with the restrictions on magic, perhaps expecting her Conduit to be gathering dust on the bedside table.

Rissa had grown up in Downtown and knew every nuance of it. This was her advantage. Just ahead a corner approached – a sharp turn onto The Blades. A main road in many respects, but not at this time of night. Rissa turned the corner and ran, timing three seconds between them as she heard their footsteps grow louder and heavier behind her. They were quick; potentially faster than her, especially with her cumbersome backpack compressing her spine into a right angle with every step. But she couldn't ditch it. She needed what was inside for later. Making a jaunt to the right, she scurried down one of the many arterial backstreets, narrow hazardous obstacle courses marred with overflowing bins, jagged pipework, exposed vents, and a scurry of rats. It would be easy to trip and fall.

Just then, another shadow flashed overhead. The adrenaline that blasted through her helped her turn quick enough to see the trailing ends of a grey cloak flying overhead, disappearing over the lip of the building.

Distracted, a pipe snared her leg and she almost stumbled. Her palms felt cold in the puddled water as she broke her own fall in a tidy handspring. Upon landing, she pulled her Conduit from her pocket and slipped it over her index finger. A powerful rush of endorphins surged through her veins the instant the steel touched her skin bringing with it the simultaneous impulse to destroy and create all at once. This was The Algarethan Verse, magic. Rissa had studied for two years at Grandmaster Academy before losing her place and in that time she had learned so much that she was excited to share with these lowlifes.

As her Conduit responded to her bloodline, Rissa became acutely aware of the water around her. Every droplet on her skin; the very storm that simmered in the sky; every ripple in every puddle that swamped the alley. It all felt within her reach. The heel of her trainer dug into the slick concrete, and she spun. Her arm extended, bearing the Conduit towards the thugs who were rushing frantically towards her. She watched in delight as the eagerness in each of their exposed eyes turned murky with the captured emotion of surprise and fear.

Her palm touched the floor.

I invoke the Missing Sea. Geyser, broiling and churning beneath the earth. Knock these idiots off their feet.

And it did. Her contact with the floor created a radiant circle of magic on the ground beneath where the onrushing thugs trod. From it, the very geyser she imagined burst forth. Rissa made the water cold. As close to freezing as she could as not to leave them with burns that could trace the use of magic back to her and then watched as the forceful jet propelled two of the three Empty Eyes into the air. They flipped, landing painfully with a loud crunch. The third – quicker on her feet than the rest, shuffled through the rushing water, a glint of steel in her hands.

Rissa kept her hand on the ground, recalling the spell from the textbook she had once run her hands across. She remembered the embossed runes that filled the page, the way the complex patterns had tingled the parts of her mind necessary to create the spell. Using that memory to create the skeleton of the spell, she then willed her intent into it, seeing the outcome in her mind's eye.

Coat this floor with a Path of Frost. Keep that blade away from me.

The circle of magic returned and the ground ahead of her turned to ice, as thick and lethal as the fiercest frost of Rainsturn. She raised her hand up and pressed it against the adjacent alley wall.

Vapour, blind her. Put doubt into her tiny mind.

A blast of steam exploded from the wall as though a pipe had burst. All of this in a matter of seconds. The onrushing thug's brow raised in surprise as she was blinded by a gullet of thick water vapour, her footing betraying her as she thudded to the ground with a loud crack.

"Damn you!" The mild-mannered tone had become a brittle growl. A knife suddenly swung blindly through the blanket of steam, nicking the flowing end of Rissa's jacket. Recoiling, her eyes darted up to a fire escape that loomed overhead. Rissa pointed her Conduit towards it, threading a weave of magic between two points: the wall of the fire escape and the brick wall beside her.

Vortex – portal me out of here.

Between these two points a swirling maelstrom of water magic formed, seafoam splashing and churning. Through the frothing gateway, she could see her destination. She felt no fear, only excitement as she stepped through the Vortex, emerging up onto the fire escape. It closed behind her immediately as to deny her pursuer a means to follow her.

Rissa felt her stomach churn against her as she displaced herself. Heaving with vertigo, her brain quickly adjusted, and she found her footing on the hatched metal floor.

"I can hear ya!" A thrown knife clanged against the steel floor beneath her before falling harmlessly into the alley. A sliver to the right and it may have slipped through the grids and caught her.

"You missed, by the way!" Rissa called down into the steamed-up alley, taking enjoyment out of the aura of frustration rising from below. There was a joy to dictating the direction of small encounters like this that made her feel as though she had a degree of agency in this dark city. She must have done this hundreds of times. It was a wonder they hadn't learned to leave her alone yet.

"Cocky wretch," she seethed. "You'll get what's coming to ya'. All of ya' will."

Rissa could picture her waving her fist. Moments passed as she mulled over a response but before she could there was a cry followed by a crunch as the sheet of ice claimed the thug on the way back. Rissa laughed loudly. She left the cacophony of curses and vitriol behind, choosing instead to ascend the steel steps to the roof where she took a moment to shake the numbness of magic out of her arms and fingers. Removing the Conduit from her finger, she unfurled her backpack and unzipped it. Her lower back throbbed from the constant impact of it striking her when running. It was a heavy thing, weighed down by a single item.

A brick. But not an ordinary one.

It had paved the tall walls of Grandmaster once upon a time, protecting those studying magic. Rissa had saved up a small fortune from work to get her hands on one of these from an old contact. It was incredibly illegal. But it wasn't mere sentiment that had her lugging the chunk about. These bricks were created by exalted Earth Versorcerers for the purpose of emitting a small field of magic, invisible to the human eye. Whilst others in her presence were oblivious, Rissa could feel a quiet heat from the brick – like a candle at the end of its wick. It was this magic field that allowed her to use the Conduit in the first place. Her ring was the equivalent of stabilisers on a bike – a practice model given only to students – and only active within the walls of the academy. It was a plain strip of polished steel embedded with a small blue crystal devoid of inscriptions or carvings. Her early expulsion had prevented her from having her own forged and inscribed. They were the real deal, requiring no brick to be used freely. It was one of many regrets she held from her time at the academy. She was younger, less disciplined. If she'd only put her head down a little more she could have a very different life. Maybe one more like her mothers.

The rain suddenly felt cold again and the small joy she had experienced in putting the Empty Eyes into place washed away, as did her smile. She remembered her mother's Conduit. It had been a brilliant bronze, laden with intricate inscriptions and metalwork. But she hadn't seen her mother nor her incredible ring in a very long time. Life had not been the same since her death. The city. Downtown. None of it. Her disappearance had marked the beginning of a downward spiral. She'd felt more in control of her life when her family was whole. In the eight years since, everything had gone off the rails. Rissa needed something to distract her. Something more long term. Something more than petty street fights. She'd go mad otherwise, she was convinced of it.

Her eyes snapped onto movement. Grey robes drifted across the distant rooftop, merging with the dark overcast, visible only when coloured hair spilled from beneath the dark hood. Before she could so much as squint in their direction, the entire city was suddenly lit up as the heavens themselves opened.

The sky turned violet, pulsing with colour like a flare, sending visible streams of foamy purple energy rippling through the air like a wave lapping at a distant shore. It mesmerised her. Such colours were normally only seen on the turn of the year when the planet's exposed core expelled all the magic that it no longer needed. Yet these past months, it felt like a regular occurrence, a sign perhaps that humanity's cursed run on this earth was coming to a violent end. Whether it was the blinding rain that caused her to squint or madness finally taking hold, Rissa wasn't certain whether the two figures falling from the sky were real.

She spotted one of them first. Its immediate size was not apparent until she had noticed the smaller one falling with it. They were close, mere streets away from where she perched. They disappeared behind a silhouette of a tall building and Rissa waited for the crash. Nothing. She would have rued herself mad were it not for the sudden impact that followed. Louder and more violent than it had any right to be, she felt the entire city wobble as the floating empire reacted to the impact. She crossed the rooftops in a matter of minutes by Vortexing herself across gaps that she couldn't cross with a sturdy leap. The rain poured heavily, dampening but not completely removing the stench of sulphur and sewage that had permeated the area.

Rissa peered over the rooftop to see that the street had caved in completely – the impact site burrowing deep enough to reveal the network of sewage tunnels that ran beneath the city. She had been so distracted by the mysterious hole that she had failed to notice the body that lay just inches from it.

"Oh no." Rissa created a Vortex from where she stood to a metre or so away from where the body lay still and then stepped through it. The repugnant smell of sulphur emanating from the pit stung her nostrils. The sounds of hammering rain failed to disguise the distant sound of husky breathing that sounded more like the compressions of a deflated tyre than a human being.

"Hey," she whispered to the body, immediately feeling foolish. A fall from that height would kill anybody, let alone this emaciated man. Against her better judgement she edged closer. The man looked young – far too young to be a stain on the concrete. As she got closer, he looked very un-stain like. In fact, the steady rising and falling of his chest made him very much alive. Rissa held her hand over his mouth, feeling the steady but faded breath pushing out of dried lips and sunken cheeks. He wore a torn grey robe and frayed black linens beneath. A hunk of scratched armour covered his chest. To touch his clothes felt … different. There was a willingness to show age in the fabric, tiredness, and signs of mistakes. Not at all like the synthetic, imitation materials that Centa Isla had become accustomed to churning out. They were probably worth a fortune if she would just-

A rattling distracted her. Her gaze drifted to the man's waist where a silver chain rattled. She followed it, feeling a surprising heat rising from the steel to find a small, curved blade, no larger than the key to her apartment, attached to it. Curious, she followed the chain as it snaked upwards, disappearing beneath the hem of his shirt. Upon lifting it, she found the chain violently pierced the man's flesh and disappeared into his body. She pulled away in disgust at the mangled wound. Yet, despite the stillness of the body, the weapon pulled at the man like an ant towing a giant, scratching at the concrete, desperate to reach the hole in the street where the smell of sulphur rose so strongly.

Rissa reached out and touched the blade.

The blade touched back. And it burned.

Thoughts and memories that were not her own invaded her mind. Emotions of love, loss, grief, guilt – all of it at once. She cried out and retreated, her palm burning in pain. Scalded upon her misadventurous palm, Rissa found a deep scar. The pain was brief, before turning to numbness. Tears had welled in her eyes and she promptly wiped them away on her sleeve.

Yet even as the pain faded, there remained a foreign presence still with her; something that had stayed beyond than the rush of emotion and incomprehensible memories. It was a word, spoken in her voice and in her mind, yet was distinctly not her own.

Run.

Perhaps she should have listened. But with the weight of her Conduit on her finger, there was very little in this city she was willing to run from. To run out of fear was to show weakness. The city had beaten that into her. The Algarethan Verse was her confidence, her backbone. It gave her control over any situation this city could throw at her, granting her the power to stand her ground and find brief sparks of energy in a lifeless, grey city. As the signs and vitriol that filled the city were quick to remind her, every spell cast brought Centa Isla toward a second Reckoning, but she had decided a long time ago that a bit of magic here and there couldn't do much harm. After all, what had the city ever done for her?

Excitement stirred in her chest as she stepped over the body of the man and approached the gaping maw that had formed in the middle of the street. She could never have imagined what she would find there. It took her a moment to realise that whatever it was had found her first. Poisonous crimson eyes, bloodshot and strained, glared at her from behind a steel mask. Its torso was enormous, humanoid in appearance yet afflicted by some sort of gigantism; skin grey and torn, as though there wasn't enough flesh to cover the whole skeleton. Most noteworthy however were the absence of its limbs for it bore only two stumps for arms. There were no legs at all. The creature simply lay in a bed of rubble, immobilised by concrete that had piled upon its massive chest. Heavy rain fell upon it, evaporating with a hiss against its body that radiated intense might and power. The air was so thick with the heat from its infernal body that her lungs burned as she swallowed the humid air. Rissa dropped into the hole, keeping her eyes fixed on the strange entity.

"Well, what are you?" She had read many books within Grandmaster. Many accounts of history and animals long lost to time. Nothing in those dusty tomes had compared to whatever lay before her now.

Suddenly, the creature began to disappear before her eyes. The limbs sizzled and hissed like they were being held to an invisible flame. It made a noise that drew pity from her. A pathetic gurgle, one of deep pain. In its eyes was the fear of an existence come and gone, erased with nobody to remember it. Flesh, bone, skin, it all began to dissolve into a flaky ashen dust, vanishing until all that remained was a thin veil of smoke that dissipated in the stormy winds. She stood there for what felt like an eternity, trying to keep the image of the beast fresh in her mind. Perhaps madness had taken her already.

Her thoughts were jolted by sudden peripheral movement. Rissa switched gears instantly and whirled around. A figure stepped out of the darkness, the light peeking out of the hole illuminating the familiar gaunt cheekbones of a man who should have died from his fall, yet was now wide awake.

"You need to forget what you saw here." He spoke directly. Not a request but an order. His gaze was intense, violet eyes piercing the dark to bore into her.

Rissa took a moment to find her words: "What was that creature?"

"It was nothing. Forget about it. For your own good."

"How can I?"

The man eyed her warily. He turned to leave, only for his legs to betray him. Rissa watched as he buckled, a grimace of pain crossing his face as he sought a wall for support. Rissa got to him first, supporting him down to a kneeling position.

"You fell from the sky. How are you even walking?" She looked him over for any visible injuries. She found none.

He ignored her. Despite his current weakness, his eyes turned steely. "There were others that fell before me. Did you see them?"

"No, just you, I think."

"Are you sure?" He seemed confused, frustrated. Whatever else he had to say on the matter he was keeping to himself as he sat there and stewed. Suddenly, his body buckled and convulsed before he hacked up bile into the flowing stream of sewage ahead of them. He groaned, coughing violently before eventually going quiet.

Rissa waited before speaking. "... Do you need to go to the hospital or anything?"

He squinted up at her. "Hospital?"

"Yeah. Not to labour the fact but you did just fall from the sky."

"I'll be fine. I just need a moment."

Then sirens. Distant but approaching quickly. No doubt the rest of the city had been woken up to the noise that the impact had created. It was only a matter of time until this area was swarming with CIPD. With her at the scene of the crime and a nice influx of magic residue decorating the nearby alley, this was not an ideal place for her to be.

"That sound, what is it?" The man asked, looking around warily.

"The end of your moment I'm afraid. You should come with me." She offered him a hand. Caution flashed across his face but finally he held out his hand. Helping him to his feet, she pointed further into the dimly lit sewer. "We can go this way."

"No…" He pushed her away, collapsing onto his hands and knees. "Please. You can't… get involved."

"Trust me." Rissa glanced up as flashing sirens lit up the city above them. "You'll prefer my company to a night in the Compound."

There was a pause before he spoke, as though he sought counsel from a force she could not behold or hear. "Fine. Lead me."

As she led him through the dark, dimly lit tunnels he was slow at first, but his pace gradually quickened. The walkways that ran either side of the stream of effluence were narrow and coated with slimy moisture. They could only walk in single file. Hanging lanterns lit the way but they were so spaced out that there were moments of total blackness where you could not see one foot in front of the other.

"I'm Rissa, by the way." There was a monstrous echo, so she spoke reservedly.

"Gault."

"Nice to meet you." Her curiosity brewed in her stomach, twisting it into knots with excitement. There was an aura of mystery around the young man that had her hooked. "Do you fall from the sky often?"

"My first time. Hopefully, it will be my last."

"A height like that is usually the last for anybody." She eyed him curiously, inspecting his clothing and how he carried himself. "Are you… a Versorcerer?"

"I am not."

"Okay, are you-"

"Look." He interrupted her, his eyes sharp in the dark as he stared at her. They stopped walking. "Thank you for your aid, but the less you know the better."

"I won't tell anybody."

"That isn't what I'm worried about."

The backpack was starting to chafe her shoulders, the weight of the hefty Grandmaster brick trying to drag her down while she supported Gault through the sewers. She repositioned the straps and continued, growing irritated by the lack of information she had been provided so far. As they moved, she felt Gault's burden upon her lessen as he took up more of his own weight.

They walked on until the sirens were just a faint echo through the tunnels and she pushed them to go further, stopping only when she heard the unexpected stomp of footsteps ahead. Through the clotting darkness, Gault stepped in front of her as though he knew what was coming.

"Gault! What is-?" Rissa could see only darkness.

A shiny untainted steel blade suddenly flashed in the light of a nearby lantern. Gault acted instantly, demonstrating inhuman reflexes as he materialised a weapon seemingly from nowhere and parried the blade away. It wasn't until Rissa felt her scarred hand burning did she realise that his weapon was the very same key-sized blade that had pinched her. It had exploded in size, becoming now a great scythe, like the sort of tool farmers of old would have used before the last fertile soil had died. It had a violet trim to its curved, spotless blade and boasted a textured steel that she had never seen before.

From the darkness emerged a hooded man, a greasy mane of dark, untamed red hair hanging in thick strands from beneath the hood to conceal any distinguishable features except for a black eyepatch crusty with dried blood. Even without properly seeing his face, Rissa knew that he was smiling.

"So glad you could join us, Gault." There was something else present behind the words; a reverb of some sort caused not by the echo of the tunnel but by something else. Something powerful. A long, grey robe trailed behind him and Rissa realised she may have seen this man before.

Gault's weapon spun, the curved steel emitting an ethereal violet glow that lit up the tunnel in a brilliant yet fleeting light as it whirled. In that flash, Rissa spotted more robed figures lurking in the thick darkness of the city's underbelly.

"There's more!" She called out to him, but surprisingly, he ignored her and instead charged towards the hooded man. They disappeared into the darkness as the sounds of their blades colliding filled the tunnel, Rissa backed away, priming her Conduit. It wasn't the CIPD that had found them, that much was clear. It only took her two steps backwards to bump into something. A hand touched her shoulder and a mild-mannered voice spoke softly in her ear.

"He never was a good listener."

Rissa yelped and hopped forward as a figure loomed behind her. Adorned with another frayed, grey robe, the hood came down for her to find a tall dark-haired man with bronze skin like fine sand, his complexion unerringly perfect even in the horribly unflattering light of the sewer.

"Who are you?" She demanded, already aware of shadows gathering on the other side of the tunnel.

"Jace. No friend of yours, I'm afraid." The man reached behind him and brandished a sword with a tidy flourish that wafted the sewer air towards her. "I don't know how you two met so quickly, but... You probably should have just stayed at home."

To her surprise, Jace then dropped his weapon to the floor, steel echoing through the tunnel upon impact. With a black boot, he slid the weapon across the scratched stone floor to her feet. Confused, she looked up.

"Maybe, don't arm the girl?" Another voice, warm in delivery yet poisonous in tone, drifted through the darkness.

Rissa caught a glimpse of green hair spilling from another grey robe as she flitted through the shadows. Who were these people?

"She deserves a chance to defend herself," Jace fired back. "Don't you have somewhere more important to be?"

The green-haired woman just laughed; her pitch pleasant if heard in a bar but terrifying down here in the murky dark. Fortunately for her, she seemed more interested in tracking Gault than wasting time with her. From behind his intricately woven jacket, Jace drew another sword and pointed its tip in her direction. "Forgive me, I like my opponents to be armed."

Rissa picked up the sword. Her wrist ached from merely trying to support its weight. Magic was her forte, not swordsmanship and it seemed that the gentleman hadn't yet got wise to the Conduit around her finger. She raised the blade to him.

All he needed was one swing followed by a deft flick and the hilt flew from her hands. Pirouetting, the blade landed with a noisy splash into the stream of sewer sludge.

Rissa grimaced. "That wasn't your favourite was it?"

"Having a favourite weapon is barbaric."

"Oh. Well, let me show you mine." She drew power to her Conduit.

I invoke the Missing Sea. Cresting Wave, protect me from his blade.

A wave of static water rose in front of her, apexing at the ceiling of the tunnel. As it appeared Jace lunged the sharpened tip towards her heart, but upon impact with the wild current the blade surged upwards, throwing him off balance. Rissa eased her palm slowly forward, coaxing the wall of water to press in, ushering Jace backwards. He staggered, pushed to a sharp bend in the walkway where even his nimble footwork wasn't enough to prevent him from slipping on the sludge and toppling backwards into the grimy water. He emerged seconds later, cursing and retching.

Rissa laughed. What a day she was having! She turned and ran as fast as she dared deeper into the sewers, listening for the distant clashing of steel. But when she turned the next corner someone was already waiting for her.

The menacing figure blocked her way. Sickly, pale skin and glazed white hair defined the tall and slender man. He stood as still as death. But there was something about his eyes that caused her to freeze. They were as black as the night itself, absorbing light like a void. Hollow and ominous, they stared at her as though she was a filthy sewer rat or scum beneath his boot. Quickly, her fear gave way to grit, and Rissa summoned the wall of water once more, making the water boil this time. He did not so much as flinch in the face of the scalding stream and instead held out his hand, palm upwards. Upon contact with his flesh, he did not burn as she had expected. Instead, her spell disappeared, dispersing into a thick cloud of vapour with a pathetic gurgle.

"What?" Rissa stood paralysed. Her fingers still tingled with the spell that had been cast and yet it had disappeared so quickly. What she had seen should have been an impossibility. Had she made a mistake? To lay a hand upon a spell and simply remove it was… impossible.

Yet, it seemed it was not. Rissa felt her legs lock in fear as his pale hands reached through the cloud of mist and wrapped themselves around her throat. His fingers twitched in quiet anticipation of watching the light fade from her eyes. He tightened his grip, pushing his thumbs into her trachea, her body lifting upwards off the slippery concrete. She grabbed his hands to try and release them, a deathly cold chill instantly coursing through her body. The spirit to fight that was always inside her was ebbing away. How could a mere hand gesture destroy her magic like it was swatting an insect? She clung to that failure as life left her. In desperation, she plunged her thumbs into his eyes, feeling them squash and roll harmlessly beneath her. She sought to pry his icy fingers from her neck, but his dark eyes just stared into hers, inhumane and unblinking and he tightened his grip further and watched her struggle in vain. Her peripheral vision went black. Her lungs began to strain, begging for air or for death – caught between the two desires in this moment of torture.

Tears stung her eyes. She'd led a pointless life.

It happened quickly. The chain that she had seen grafted to Gault's body flew through the cloud of vapour, coiling itself around the pale man's arm and pulling him. The grip around her throat was mercifully released as he was pulled backwards into the pervading mist. She fell to the floor, violently gagging and inhaling the rancid sewer air like it was the last source of oxygen in the city. Her arms hung off the walkway into the cold sewer sludge, jolting her to her senses. Adrenaline got her to her feet and fear got her thinking. Whatever was happening here was well and truly beyond her. All the swagger and confidence she'd built up across her last two encounters was gone and had been replaced by cold fear that gripped her chest in a vice.

Rissa moved warily towards the striking of metal, the deafening sounds of combat growing stronger until even the echoes pained her ears. Rounding a corner, she saw Gault duelling with her pale-faced attacker. He had saved her. Three of the grey robes surrounded him, yet he was the only one doing the attacking. His swings were wild, laced with desperation and fatigue. Unsure of how to help, it started to seem like she was watching the final stand of a cornered rat; the prey patiently waiting for it to run out of stamina before taking the kill.

She saw the pale skin and white hair. The mere sight of him causing a throbbing in her neck. All her logic told her to run as the voice in the back of her head grew stronger and louder. She was outnumbered and outmatched. Who were these people? Why were they here?

A glint of moonlight dappled the murky sewers. Rissa caught the luminous flash through a ridged grate above her. She aimed her Conduit, seeking to thread a Vortex through the gap in the iron and escape with her life. Just as she did so, she felt hesitation claw at the back of her mind. Her eyes fell to Gault and the battle he was very quickly starting to lose. They attacked him now, striking his weakening body with blades that drew blood upon his robe. There was something happening here far deeper than simple gang crime and there were powers in play the likes of which she had never seen nor heard of in her time in Grandmaster.

Vortex. Prepare our escape.

She weaved a thread of magic through the gap in the grate, watching as the small whirling mass of water appeared on the wall of a building across the street. It sloshed patiently, waiting for a partner to link to. She could have placed it beneath herself then and there and escaped unnoticed, but leaving Gault to die here didn't sit right with her. Whatever was happening, he seemed the only one who might know.

Her mysterious ally fought well but was quickly losing ground. With the slick sewer floor beneath him, his frequent, almost artificial lapses of strength allowed the blades of the grey robes to slip through his guard, nicking his flesh with slices of sharp steel. His legs gave way and Rissa watched, feeling her fist clench white as her Conduit brimmed upon it. She thrust her arm forward, emerging from the clotted darkness to create a Vortex beneath where Gault landed. The foaming maw of water opened and Gault fell directly through, disappearing from sight. Closing the Vortex before any of the robes could follow him, she felt her blood turn to ice as their frigid stares whirled on her all at once.

Vortex. Now it's my turn. Get me out of here!

She spun a repeat spell, feeling the massaging of her mind as she triggered the sequence for which The Algarethan Verse would allow her magic to exist. She opened the Vortex directly beneath her feet and fell down just as the figures surged towards her. One of the grey robes, crimson hair trailing through his hood, was quicker than the other two. As Rissa fell through the Vortex, she could feel the sting of his steel searching for her as she was spat out the other side and landed in a tidy roll on street level not far from where Gault should have emerged. She ended her spell quickly, the portal snapping shut in a violent guillotine of time and space.

A scream filled the air. Rissa turned. The grey hood had fallen, revealing a mane of blood red hair and a thick black eyepatch. The flesh on one side of his face looked burned, as though he had fallen upon a lit forge. He looked like an Empty Eyes thug, yet she had never encountered one of their kind with such fearsome power before. A fleshy, bleeding stump remained where his right arm should have been. Blood stained the brickwork of the wall she had placed her Vortex upon. For as fast as the red-haired man was, it seemed he was a second too slow to make it through entirely intact. His severed arm likely sat in the sewers where she had stood moments prior.

"You bastard!" He seethed, dropping to his knees.

"That's what you get." Rissa panted at him, breathless. Her legs were trembling from the adrenaline. "That was your fault, not mine!"

It took for a moment to realise that she felt lighter. And as that realisation set in, so too did the red hair part, to reveal the grimace of pain slowly shifting in a wicked grin. In his one remaining arm, he clutched her backpack. Within, she could still sense the Grandmaster brick warbling.

"Give that back." Rissa thrust her Conduit towards him, but the man only laughed.

Quickly however, the laugh broke away into a hacking cough. What she had assumed to be a burn on his face turned into much more. It glowed, bursting into life with the colourful rush of blood. The man winced, buckling over as the glowing spread down his body, pressing his veins against his flesh. The power snaked down his neck, disappearing beneath the collar of his robe for a moment before appearing upon the stump that remained of his right arm. A guttural, inhuman growl filled the air. There was an explosion of gore, further staining the brickwork with viscera as the missing limb was suddenly replaced by something larger and far more terrifying. Emerging from the stump that was left, a giant, fleshy limb grew, bearing musculature three times the size of the man. Jagged claws and leathery grey skin reminded her of the monster she had caught a fleeting glimpse of in the sewers earlier. The wicked claws that adorned it were the size of her forearm and clutched within them was her backpack. With little strain, he crushed the pack and the Grandmaster brick within, reducing it to rubble along with any power she may have had.

"No!" Rissa hissed, immediately feeling her connection to her Conduit fade as it lost its link with the brick. Now she was truly defenceless. Fear coursed through her and she turned to run.

Cruel laughter filled the air as the mound of clawed flesh reached for her only for a flash of violet to pierce the night. The whoosh of a blade flew past her and the monstrous arm that reached out suddenly fell to the floor, sizzling and steaming in a pool of its own demonic blood. The man screamed once more, losing the same arm twice in the span of two minutes. Gault towered over him, preparing his blade for the killing blow.

Then, the flash of red and blue sirens pelted around the corner. The roar of a magical engine, blasting fire crystals at full power as they ripped down the distant stretch of road towards them.

"Stop!" Rissa grabbed Gault's arm and pulled him away. Despite his momentary victory, he had little strength with which to resist her, his limbs weak and legs wobbly as she pulled him around a corner. She didn't stop there, pounding down the street until the shrill shriek of the CIPD sirens were getting quieter.

The tall apartment blocks of Downtown and derelict storefronts flitted by. Practically dragging Gault behind her, Rissa rounded one more corner, only to come face to face with a crimson uniform. A CIPD Officer. She came to a halt immediately, glancing at the patrol car that was parked by the side of the road. A shortsword swung from the hip of the officer, his palm wrapped around it in surprise. His eyes, light blue and dappled with fear, swept over her first, before fixing Gault with his gaze. Quickly, that hand fell from the hilt, a breath of relief falling from his lips.

"You need to be careful, ma'am." The officer addressed her. "There's Versorcerer's running wild tonight."

She could feel his gaze searching her. Behind her back, she flicked her useless Conduit from her finger and allowed it to drop into her back pocket.

"I know, sir!" She pointed back down the street they had come. "There was one back there!"

Those blue eyes sharpened and Rissa watched him carefully. A hand came up to touch his chin, fiddling with strands of facial hair that had sprouted. The officer was young, probably the same age her father had been when he started on the force. His crimson uniform was clean, free of cuts or blood. No service medals decorated the breast pocket.

"I'll check it out, ma'am." His hand fell to the hilt of his blade. Rissa could see him shaking. "You should get yourself home."

Behind her, Gault suddenly hurled. His body convulsed and he dropped to his knees, hacking up bile on the floor.

"Is he okay?" The officer asked.

Rissa quickly spoke up with an effortless lie. "He is very drunk."

"Right." The officer smiled at them. "Well, get him home safe."

"Thanks. Good luck out there."

Relief flashed through her as they left the officer behind. She practically carried Gault east as his condition worsened. They travelled towards her home, twisting and winding through the backstreets to avoid the public eye as he took time to hack up yet more sickness. She stopped for no-one until they reached the shadow of the apartment block she called home. Every shadow made her jolt with fear as she felt vulnerable now without the security of her magic.

Even now, she could feel the phantom touch of the pale hands around her throat. She had felt so powerless, her magic, the thing that gave her any sense of freedom and control in this cursed city had been dismissed with as little as a wave of the hand. The Grandmaster brick was destroyed and as far as she knew, the city was slowly filling with powerful people who seemed to command magic far greater than The Algarethan Verse. Whatever was happening was like nothing she had heard of before.

Suddenly, something in her shifted.

Her perception was still stained with fear, but the longer Rissa went with the grip of terror in her chest, she realised equally that there was a vestige of excitement that had come with it. It was little more than a glimmer, easily missed when her life was seconds from ending. But now, away from the danger, Rissa couldn't help but feel the adrenaline pounding through her system, the smashing of her heart against her ribs, dispelling the webs that had been spun in her tired mind. This was a new feeling to her and she couldn't help but feel like this was something she had been missing her entire life.

A smile dared to cross her face. Perhaps there was hope for her yet.

2

With time at her mercy, Lachesis waited patiently on top of one of Downtown's many apartment blocks. From the rooftop, she stared at the vast cityscape that dominated the horizon. An old rattling vent blustered hot air through her emerald tresses, making them wave like a grassy field in a warm storm. Even from here, the boastful shadow of Monument dwarfed her. It was the tower within which the King-Regent, his council and servant force all resided. Quietly, she marvelled at it, inspired by the way it stood proud and majestic, towering over all other buildings to enjoy the exclusive privilege of piercing the smog to reach for the softer clouds within the heavens.

A sudden distant trill of sirens drew her gaze. She watched, amused, as flashes of red and blue coursed through the city like little rats in a playpen. They scampered, bewildered, scrambling their garrison of fancily dressed officers and their noisy motor-powered carriage-like constructs. A young officer had discovered them as she had been trying to clean up the gory mess Kren'shal had made above ground. A facade of coy ignorance had granted her ample time to slide a dagger into his back. He was now dead; his body flung from the edge of this floating city. She had left his badge and his boots by the edge, ready to be discovered and declared as suicide. Such was her role here, patting down the soil to hide the bodies left by the fools under her wing.

"Watcher." A familiar voice called to her.

Twisting down her back, the Brand of the Watcher tingled with the presence of fellow Omens. She hissed quietly, painfully recalling the agony of its application, feeling the chafe on her wrists from where she had been bound for what had felt like eternity.

Lachesis turned to a familiar voice. Before her, were the aforementioned fools. Brand of the Sorcerer, Jace, carrying the stink of sewer in every step and Kren'shal, the Brand of the Demon, nursing a bloodied stub where his arm had once been.

"Boys." She greeted them, unable to hide the smile of amusement at their respective plight. "That went well, didn't it?"

"I don't get it." Jace replied, water dripped down his handsome face. Her heart jumped with pleasure as she watched his perfect complexion twist in confusion. "He had help so soon. How?"

"He got lucky." Kren'shal interjected. His words were unconvincing. He looked weak, his cheeks sunken and face heavy. His single eye, isolated by an eyepatch across its twin, looked dim. The usual bloodlust that lingered had faded, his long hair matted and clumpy as it hung heavy over his face like a pair of curtains left in a dragon's den. "Let me go. I'll make him wish the fall had killed him!"

Lachesis shook her head. "I'm afraid that won't be happening."

Confusion and anger. Same word, two different tones. "What?"

"You leave the seeking to me." Lachesis explained to them, approaching her two finest lackeys. "Return to task and stay the course. The Brand of the Scout will no doubt come to you, so beware."

As she approached Jace, she wrinkled her nose to the offensive whiff of sewage. "You should have just gutted the girl."

His pretty face stretched into a regretful grimace. "I know."

"I'm glad you do. Now shower." She gave him a disparaging look as though he were a misbehaving child. "Then, return to Grandmaster... lest your mistress notices you've gone."

Jace bowed his head, departing the rooftop. The air felt cleaner with him gone. She turned next to Kren'shal, gesturing for him to show her the arm that nursed a wound. He did so, shuffling his body to face her as he proudly showed off a raw wound with exposed bone, sinews, and muscle. Cauterised by the absolving flame of Jace's fire magic, the bleeding had stopped.

"That was a waste, wasn't it?" She asked him directly, peering beyond the thick veil of blood-coloured hair, through the eyepatch and past the sadistic exterior to the deeply fearful manchild behind it.

"You won't even let me get revenge."

"You'll have your revenge. There's beauty in waiting." She stroked the injury, tracing a manicured finger across the exposed bone, watching his body flinch and his face curdle with every touch. "Keep those thugs of yours aggressive. Skirt the City Centre, but do not enter. Kill no-"

"Kill no nobles. Put pressure on the King-Regent." Kren'shal hissed. "I know."

She just smiled at him. "Good. Now run along."

As the Brand of the Demon slunk away to the safety of his brigands, Lachesis mused once again over the city. As she did so, a rustling from among the alley beneath her drew her viperous gaze down. A rodent, a sweet little thing, sifted through discarded rubbish that filled the arterial alley like a clot. Lachesis dropped from the rooftop. As the ground rushed to meet her, she whipped a dagger from her boot and buried it into the old brickwork with enough force to soften her fall. Her shadow fell over the rodent, a lowly rat. It shrunk before her, too paralyzed to even flee as she wrapped its tiny, furry body in one hand. It squirmed in her grip, little snout sniffing frantically as its little pads pressed into her skin. Lachesis brought the rat up to her eyeline and waited patiently for it to finally look at her. When it did, she ensnared its gaze. The Brand of the Watcher on her back burned as she instilled the rodent with her will. It squeaked and squirmed as a green mist descended upon it, washing over its tiny black eyes until suddenly, everything was back to normal.

Holding the rodent, Lachesis closed her eyelids and sought the rodent in her grasp. Her brain tingled and she felt it answer her call. Upon opening her eyes, Lachesis saw herself, a giant in the eye of a city rat. She watched herself smile, controlling her body as she lowered the rat to the ground.

"Welcome to the coven, little one. You know whom I seek."

She felt acknowledgement from the tiny creature as it scurried away. Before it took her vision with it, Lachesis removed herself and slammed back into her own body. A smile crossed her face.

Another for her network of spies.

———

"You're eager." He said warily. "You shouldn't be."

Rissa had coped by taking a sip of coffee every time her perception of the greater reality of the world and universe had come under threat. Her third mug was empty. She felt her heart twitching as she rose, reigniting the fire crystal on the hob to boil the kettle.

The figures in grey robes were called Omens. Gault had explained their purpose to her already. They were humans, just like she was, yet sworn agents of a great evil. They would integrate themselves into the foundational structures of a society and identify weaknesses and exploit them for one singular cosmic goal: to usher in the great evil named Galleo et'al, so that it may unmake the world and feed on it. How they were going to go about that, well, neither of them had any idea. They could be anywhere in the city, planning anything.

"They want to bring it here?" She asked. "And destroy everything?"

"The very same way they destroyed mine." Gault paced around the clutter of her apartment. He stepped over unpacked boxes, discarded clothes and old books.

"This is a lot."

"You wanted to know." He smiled at her, warily. "Despite my warnings."

Gault took small sips of water and allowed himself only tiny mouthfuls of food, picking curiously at a bowl of synthetic crisps as though nourishing his body was a loathsome chore. He carried himself like his adrenaline was permanently on standby, unable to spare a bubble of oxygen where it might be needed to fuel a fight. He hadn't thrown up since they had returned home, the cause he had cited as a bout of sickness caused from his sudden transportation to this new, foreign world. Rissa could scarcely believe it. He'd be picked apart on an operating table if Verscience ever found out an otherworldly being had arrived overnight.

"Please help yourself!" She ushered the bowl across the coffee table, closer to his prickly fingers. "You should probably eat something proper. Sorry it's just this."

He eyed the bowl, still crunching the flaky, flavour in his mouth. "Potato. But it's... wrong."

"It's Resynthesized, if that's what you mean." She gestured around her, to the wood that lined her shelves, the food on the plate, the fabric that stitched her jacket. "Everything is."

"Resynthesised... with what?" She watched his brows furrow.

She smiled like it was the most obvious thing in the world. "Magic."

"What?" His violet eyes peered around the place as though seeing it all for the first time. His dark eyes glowed and the mark that had been scorched against his eye began to glow a radiant purple.

Rissa shrugged. What more was there to say? It seemed like a reasonable solution to having no farmland. She wasn't privy to the exact science of Resynthesis. Just that it was possible with the collaboration of magic and science to produce artificial properties that would have otherwise been lost to Reckoning. The city would have been long dead without it.

"That's just how it is. I couldn't imagine it any other way." She watched him, curious. "For you to not know that is... well, lucky, I suppose."

"All this magic. It's little wonder Galleo et'al wishes to come here."

"And what, destroy it?"

"Perhaps that was the wrong word." Gault took a moment. His eyes dimmed as though for a moment, he wasn't entirely present. "Consume. May be better suited."

"I don't suppose we'd be around to see that."

"Not if Galleo et'al has its way."

Galleo et'al. A name that Gault had provided her. It belonged to a dark, cosmic force. As the kettle began to sing with steam, she spun the name around her mind over and over. The name was so foreign to her she could barely fumble it out of her mouth. But perhaps that was for the best. Even so much as thinking the name made her shiver, like a horrific impulse had crossed her mind. Her mouth was numb and her lips were dry and cracked despite downing all that liquid. She could feel her heart hammering in her chest and reverberating in her ears like a drum.

Rissa couldn't help but observe a less than passing similarity between Gault and the grey robed Omens who they had encountered beneath the city. The strange marking over his eye looked darkly similar to the mark that the now-armless man had bore. The robe looked similar, although Gault's seemed to have been reinforced with steel plates, wearing it open as opposed to closed. Had she made a mistake trusting him? Was she the sort of weakness they would exploit?

Her mind flitted to the leathery, brittle skin of the monster that she found in the sewers. Even now, the poisonous eyes still bore into her from her memory. "That thing that came with you? Was that Galleo et'al?"

"No." Gault smiled almost in dark amusement. "It was a demon. One of many in service of the Dark One. They will be the first sign of this city's destruction."

"That doesn't sound good."

"No." His grave look told her that she was correct. "The Omens must be stopped before that can happen."

At the very least, they had time. Gault believed they had arrived at the same time as he had, meaning that for the time being; they were on equal footing. It was for once favourable that Centa Isla was no longer the sprawling kingdom history proclaimed it to be. Instead, it was a floating husk of its former glory. A floating husk that Rissa happened to know very well.

Humans, Omen or not, she could handle. But their master…

Galleo et'al. The Dark One, was another of its names it seemed. Even the thought caused the hammering in her chest to multiply, as though the name itself bore some unfathomable power to incite panic. Rissa pictured the city burning, the skyscrapers of the City Centre crumbling to the ground. It was a surreal thought but for some reason, guiltily preferable to the slow, malaise-ridden life that was waiting for her otherwise.

There was a part of her denying this truth even in the face of everything she had seen. But this threat did not scare her. It excited her. Her entire twenty years she had desperately been seeking a life of significance. Dangerous as it may be, she finally felt as though she was seizing control of her life, free finally from the vicious life cycle of Centa Isla.

Rissa had arranged her small apartment to face the single, tall window so that she was able to sit with light in her face and a book in her hands and watch the city go by. She had been an avid reader as a child and was always curious, always asking questions. Rissa still owned all her books, having added many new ones over the years such as those about plants that used to decorate the earth before Reckoning, drawings and hearsays of animals besides rats and roaches that had once roamed the planet. Now they merely gathered dust, sitting on her shelf as idle mementos, or scattered lazily across the floor with no place to be. But for the first time since she had been forced to leave Grandmaster, Rissa felt a returning twinge of curiosity and intrigue. There was more to the universe than just Centa Isla and Gault was her ticket to see it.

"You'll be dealing with dark entities." Gault warned. He had observed her staring out the window, catching a troubling glimpse of the excited light in her eyes. "There will be dark deeds and they will warp you. This is not a game."

"I know." Was her reply. She didn't know. How could she? But she wanted to leave no room for doubt in both Gault or her. "I'm not afraid."

Gault looked at her. She couldn't discern the emotions on his face, but for a moment she thought she saw pity in his tired eyes.

"Very well." He spoke at last. "We'll find the Omens, eliminate them one by one before they sink their teeth in too deep."

"Sounds easy enough."

"It won't be." Gault ran his gloved fingers through his dusty hair. "I am all but a stranger to this city."

Rissa thought for a moment. She replayed the images of the Omens in her head, still feeling the cold hands of the palest one around her throat as she recalled staring into the empty blackness of his eyes. With a monstrous shudder, she dismissed the image and thought instead of the hooded man who had unexpectedly sprouted a monstrous, malformed arm.

"The red-haired guy." She could still picture his face, one crimson eye barred by an eyepatch. She remembered his face lined with pain and then victory as her Grandmaster brick had been reduced to dust in his hand.

"Kren'shal." The name rolled off Gault's tongue, yet she couldn't even fathom how to pronounce it.

"Did he always wear an eyepatch?"

Gault's brow furrowed. He went quiet again, as if rolling through a secondary database to confirm his forthcoming word. "No."

"That'll do it then." Watching a brow raise in curiosity, Rissa went on, "Empty Eyes. Local gang. Part of the Initiation is having an eye removed. Eyepatches are very much their thing."

"That's extreme."

"For sure." She left out that in her late teens, Rissa had once debated joining them. Still grieving her mother and afflicted with a growing anger at the city itself and the systems that ran it. If a beleaguered wave of apathy hadn't come to wash away her rage at the last moment, she could well be one eye short now.

If her father thought she was a waste now, she didn't even want to think what he would have thought back then.

"Where do they congregate?" Gault asked, fixated on the Empty Eyes.

So desperate to be useful to him, Rissa grimaced. "I don't know a specific place. Downtown at least, that's for sure."

It was a rare thing, but she thought again of her father. A CIPD Officer of many years, he was proficient in obsession and neglect. He had no doubt committed days of his life to approximate the location of their den based on their recent activity. That was how logical, sequential, and methodical he was and his bizarre attention to detail nearly always paid off. Part of her was begrudgingly impressed that he had progressed so far into his career despite not having a drop of magical blood in his body. He had achieved a rare feat through his unwavering commitment, unpaid overtime and the distinct lack of fatherly presence. All this in return for his mediocre salary which barely afforded him a Band B apartment Downtown.

"I know how we can find it." Rissa said at last, spoken like an admission of defeat more than a triumphant idea. Her father's apartment wasn't too far from here, she just hoped that he wouldn't be home when they visited.

Gault gave her an expecting look and she begrudgingly rose, her sleepless night held together by caffeine and adrenaline.

She lived in Ocean's View, a Band D block of apartments. Home was Floor fifteen, Apartment sixty-five. The building was raised by Earth magic some seventy years ago, well before Reckoning had taken the ocean away back when Downtown was considered in history as an affluent area.

Things sure had changed. She rattled her rusty old key in the door, searching for the sweet spot where it actually bothered to lock before shoving the key deep into her pocket. The stairs twisted down thirty levels, each of the floors an exact duplicate of the one before save for the numbers carved by blade into the wooden doors. The occupants were less than savoury. The closer to the ground floor you lived the more Synth-addled addicts blocked the stairs with their comatose bodies. The higher up you lived, the more stairs you had to go down. You were at least removed from the Synthheads who openly used in the stairwells. Rissa had scored a happy medium if such a thing existed. There was no lift. Such a luxury reserved for Band A apartments that bordered Downtown and the upmarket City Centre. But her rent was affordable, paid weekly to The Crown who owned pretty much every building in the city. She worked night shifts at a sleazy City Centre bar to make her way. Where her rent money went she had no idea, as she hadn't seen even a sniff of maintenance around Ocean's View since she moved in a year ago.

She guided Gault down the stairs, stepping large strides over their first drug ravaged body sitting on the fourth floor. The victim was motionless and in the trademark catatonic state of Synth use; eyes glazed over but with a silly smile on their face. It took over the city a few years ago, allegedly a powerful mix of old-world herbs used to treat Smithy's Lung and a captured element of raw magic. It was inhaled using repurposed respirators that the workers used to wear in the smog-ridden factories to the furthest east of the city. It falsified users with grandiose feelings of being powerful, surrendering the body to visions of grandeur, wealth and glory. It granted the belief that you could raise buildings and shatter mountains. It was like having the world in the palm of your hands. In reality they held nothing but grime, dirt and the emptiness of a pathetic existence. Rissa watched as the Synth addict swayed slightly on the steps, a giddy smile still on her face. She looked young, with matted black hair hanging over her eyes and ripped dirty clothes. Whatever she was seeing now was clearly better than her reality. Rissa silently wished the young girl the best, for the side effects of Synth use were all too well documented. It was the instilled essence of raw magic that was responsible for the rush of power and might, however, it had the adverse effect of slowly rotting away the body from the inside. The flesh of mortals born without the superior genes of Versorcerers were unable to harbour the power that came with the primal elements and after repeated exposure, bodies were known to have "explosive" consequences. Quite literally. Rissa noted the dried, crusted red stains on the white tile walls of Ocean's View, the sort you could scrub for centuries and never see come out. They stepped over a succession of bodies on the way to the ground floor, exiting into a pleasant, windy morning. Fabric tarps were strung over loose pipes, billowing in the wind as the transient population of Centa Isla slept on the streets, nestled between the chokingly narrow alleys between each block. The city was busy with morning traffic. Depressed, bleary faces commuted, keeping the wheels of the city spinning in whatever direction it was heading.

It was a short walk. Her father lived directly north of her, up The Blades and onto a street that connected the City Centre to Downtown. It was a stone's throw away from his daily commute to the CIPD Station. Rissa knew the area well for she had lived with him for a couple of years. Venture, his apartment block, was far nicer than Ocean's View. There was still no lift, sure, but with no walking corpses and a significantly more upmarket interior, it was a clear winner. Yet Rissa liked Ocean's View more. She enjoyed a part of the grunge and the chaos she could glean from the safety of a window. From as close to the City Centre as they were, Rissa could hear the hustle and bustle and the distant thumping bass of a party just ending in the early morning hours.

She caught Gault looking at the cityscape. He seemed fixated on the tallest tower in the entire city by quite a margin. Monument. The heavily fortified tower that housed the royal family, their servants and their personal Kingsguard military force. A clock face clunked atop it.

"King-Regent Grayson Clovis." Rissa said quietly.

Gault lofted a brow at the title. "King-*Regent*?"

"Complicated family. He's in charge, that's all I know."

Gault stared at Monument a little longer. "They'll target this King-Regent. Find his weaknesses and exploit every one of them."

"They won't get in without a summons." Rissa explained, although not believing it entirely herself.

At that, Gault snorted. "They don't need a summons."

They left Monument's shadow and arrived at her father's apartment block. Rissa felt the twinge of anxiety gnaw at her chest. The chance of her father being home was miniscule as he was a workaholic only using home as a base to grab a few hours of precious sleep and to eat. Rissa remembered the loneliness of spending eight aching years sitting at the front door waiting for him to come home. He'd leave her money to go and buy something from the shop and he would make sure to leave sandwiches and easy dinners in the fridge for her to heat up. She had always appreciated that, but it wasn't what she wanted. She would have chosen starvation just to have spent a day in the old park with him. Walking. Talking. Anything. That park had since dried up and been turned into a cemetery. Once the soil became a mire and the trees turned bare and ashen, it became clear that nothing natural could grow in the industrial air that poisoned the sky around Centa Isla.

She stood outside the door and stared for an indeterminate amount of time until Gault cleared his throat, jolting her back to the present. Rissa had a spare key but had never intended on using it again. She had many a time debated dropping it over the scaffolding on the edge of town just to watch it disappear in the core of the world. Thankfully, she hadn't. The lock clicked and she let herself in, instantly greeted by the fresh, pleasant scent of sea spray. Her mother's favourite perfume. Rissa felt her chest heave with grief. It reminded her why she had to leave this place, why she chose to work a wretched job to pay for a horrible apartment. It reminded her of what her father had become since her mother's death. The smell of her perfume, once so pleasant, was now just a tormenting memory. She had chosen to run from it, while her father had immersed himself in it. Obsession, grit, madness. He believed she was still alive and everything in this apartment was designed to make him believe it. Her clothes were still hung up in the wardrobe, her favourite recipes still pinned to the fridge. A visitor who knew nothing would assume she was still living here. And the photos. So many they were impossible to avoid. Aryssa Rawdon's face, so much like her own yet pointier and somehow more refined. The same blue eyes and blue hair. Rissa had her nose, her mouth and even her magic. It was no wonder her father neglected her. She was the spitting image of the love of his life for whom he had given everything he had in this world and more. Even seeing her must have wrenched his heart in two. A pang of rage. There it was. The feeling that made her feel like the worst person in the world. The anger and selfish upset at her own mother for doing this to her family. For dying without a word and for throwing the life she had built for them into the void.

Resting on the mantelpiece of an ornate, faux fireplace was a photo that caught her eye. An old photo of her parents. Its age was revealed by looking at the backdrop of the city for it showed the remnants of the old park, a pleasant green hue on the horizon in front of which stood Donnel and Aryssa Rawdon. His hair was brunette and wild, a young man with nothing who had dug his heels into a hostile city and somehow gained the affection of a young noblewoman. They held each other close, smiling as the sun waned; splashing the hues of romance and passion over their faces. They were so happy in that photo. When waiting for her father to come home she would often look at that picture and wonder if it was her fault. At what point did the bags beneath her father's eyes start to grow? When did the wonderful head of hair recede and grey?

"Are you okay?"

Gault spoke. It brought her thundering back to reality so hard that she hadn't noticed tears welling in her eyes. One blink and they would have cascaded down her face. She held them back, surreptitiously drying her eyes with her jacket sleeve.

"Yeah."

She left him in the lounge and entered the room adjacent. It was his office, where on the rare occasion he was home, she would find him. It was a mess. A jarring contrast with the spotless lounge. It was like peeling back the layers of his psyche to see the carnage within. Folders, paperwork, newspaper clippings. They were everywhere, covering the desk, the walls and even parts of the floor where she trod. It looked like a disorganised mess, but Rissa knew her father too well - this was all organised chaos. Overlapped by nonsense newspaper articles of various crime reports she found a map of Centa Isla, slightly outdated but accurate enough for her. She didn't own a copy of a map for she knew this city as well as she knew the back of her hand. Her father had made various marks on the fragile surface as she had hoped. Coloured circles, mapping crime scenes in an attempt to correlate a headquarters. He had coded each circle with a colour corresponding to which gang was causing the chaos. She took the map to Gault and laid it out on the coffee table. He squatted in front of the table while she hunched over on the comfy sofa.

"Empty Eyes here." She pointed to the various red circles, their heat map ventured bravely out of Downtown and encroached frequently upon the fringes of the City Centre. "In red."

Gault nodded. "How recent are these?"

Rissa read the dates annotated above the rings. "Last couple of weeks by the looks of it. Look. They seem more aggressive than ever."

To that, Gault shook his head, creases of frustration on his brow. "He couldn't have had this much influence on them so quickly. Unless-"

He froze so suddenly that Rissa looked over her shoulder. Dread etched itself upon his weathered, yet youthful face.

Rissa blinked at him. "What?"

Looking as though he wanted to speak, Gault's eyes glazed over and once again she felt like an outsider to his internal monologue which compounded the crease in his brow to a right angle.

"That's not ideal."

"What isn't?"

"They've been here much longer than I thought." Gault started, his tone mounting with concern. "I knew something wasn't right. They were waiting to ambush me when I arrived."

"So, what does that mean?"

"I was a second behind them." Gault rose abruptly, startling her. He strode to the window, staring out at Monument which had suddenly taken on a menacing silhouette on the horizon. "Yet here, that second became days. They regrouped, recovered, and waited for me to show up."

Rissa didn't like the sound of all this. "So how long have they been here?"

"Before those, probably even earlier." Gault shook his head, pointing at the map and to the increased crime rates. "Your King-Regent will already be their puppet."

Rissa checked the dates. The first inklings of increased activity were over one hundred days ago, the entire ninety-one days of Landfall plus more.

"We should get a move on." Was all she told him. She was relieved to push the soft smell of sea spray from her nostrils as they swiftly exited the apartment and locked the door behind them.

She led Gault deeper Downtown, leaving the rumbling bass of the neighbouring City Centre behind. With her father's apartment disappearing into the cityscape behind them, Rissa had somewhere she needed to go before getting into another fight. Since leaving her apartment without the comfort of the Grandmaster brick weighing her down, Rissa was acutely aware of her fragility and intended to put that right as soon as possible.

Burrowing into the shallow earth was a network of transportation known as the Subrail. Carriages ran across several lines, taking full advantage of the depth of earth that drifted through the air with them while stripping the dense traffic from the streets and roads. Downtown Central was their nearest station, offering a quick ride across to the west of Downtown where her father's tracking of Empty Eye activity had highlighted. But there were more than just common thug gangs out there, Rissa had the pleasure of knowing one in particular.

The descent into the station was congested. As the early hours of light still bleached the city, haggard bodies moved with little regard for others, pushing and jostling their way through. She felt Gault tense as the crowd washed over them, as though he was expecting a blade in the back. He drew his fair share of eyes; tall, brooding, his torn robe and plated armour certainly an eyesore for the modern day. But nobody cared enough to say anything. The air was thick below the earth, the underground station terraformed into two separate platforms, tracks disappearing into dark, lightless tunnels. It was all grey concrete, the only dab of colour used to distinguish one rail line from the other. Bodies gathered around the platforms, waiting in an eerie silence broken by hacking coughs or the occasional confrontation.

Considered the last great creation of Centa Isla, the Subrail was implemented shortly after Reckoning, before the restrictions on magic and science came down hard. Ever since, it only seemed to receive the bare minimum of upkeep to maintain the system and integrity of the carriages themselves. The scream of "upkeep" rang through the tunnels as the crowds began to shuffle and idle in anticipation of the door swinging open.

"What is that noise?"

"That's our carriage. Come on."

Rissa didn't even need to look at the rail map. She shepherded Gault towards the left-most platform, marked orange for the Downtown Line. She skirted the back of the crowd as the mass of synthetic steel rumbled into the platform, brakes screeching and singing with strain. As it came to a halt, the doors hissed open with a billow of steam. Bodies met in a rumbling crossfire of entrances and exits. Rissa grabbed Gault's sleeve, keeping him in range as they edged their way on board. Once inside, the sterile interior filled quickly with warm bodies, pushing them progressively further into a corner. From so close, she could see the discomfort in his wide eyes. They darted left to right, suspicious of every nudge and every bump. He was going to have a lot of things to get used to, but in truth, Rissa was just happy to not to be the one who was surprised all the time. Beleaguered faces surrounded her, staring blankly into people's backs or through the dirty windows at the concrete tunnels beyond. Flashes of light broke through the carriage, stinging her eyes as they passed lanterns that illuminated the tracks. The tracks screamed an horrific, ear-piercing symphony as they careened through the labyrinthian underbelly.

"Next stop. Fishmarket." A droning voice, laced with apathy filled the carriage from a crackling speaker. The frequency dipped and warbled as interference broke up the voice. "Please change for the Coast Line."

The carriage suddenly jostled. Beside her, she felt Gault coil like a spring as the brakes roared, sending vibrations reverberating through her feet and up her legs. The relief on his face as she led him out Fishmarket and back up onto street level was palpable.

"How was that?" She couldn't contain a smile. It was nice to not be the one surprised for once.

"I felt like cattle."

She laughed, whether he intended to be funny or not she had no idea. "How did you expect to travel?"

"The right way." Was his curt reply. "Horseback."

"You've ridden a horse?" She felt the spell of curiosity upon her tongue. Rissa had never seen a horse, but she had read about them. Extinct beasts of burden who bore riders into combat, towed carriages and took part in races.

"Many times."

The urge to ask more overwhelmed her, but she contained herself. He didn't seem too keen to humour her, his steely eyes focused on the path ahead. Moving west, further from the city, centre the quality of the streets began to degrade. They traversed uneven, century old cobblestone roads, past abandoned storefronts and desolate homes with the smell of dry rot from the boarded-up windows. Bodies lined the streets. Alive, yet catatonic, just as she had seen outside Ocean's View. Synth was rife once you left the main roads. The CIPD rarely ventured their patrol cars beyond the freshly laid tarmac.

Gault was looking at them with a mix of pity and disdain. It was clear that he somehow didn't understand the depravity to which some people fall when faced with the brutality and indignity of life's hardest moments.

"I've taken it." Rissa told him as they walked.

He suddenly looked at her. His eyebrows shot up in repressed surprise and for a moment she could sense his judgement. At her giving up, at trying to hide from her problems.

"I was fifteen." She went on quietly. "Still three years away from packing my bag to Grandmaster."

She cleared her throat. The place she had gone to back then was a horrible state of helplessness - the crushing misery upon the realisation that she had no say over how her life was going to go.

"Three years was a long time back then. I couldn't hack it at home, so I turned to something that someone said would help."

Gault nodded slowly, as though to understand. "What happened?"

"Nothing."

"What do you mean?"

Rissa smiled, wondering how best to explain. "Synth is made in part from magic. The effect on someone whose very body is designed to handle it... nothing."

"Maybe it was for the best. Maybe not." She laughed weakly. "Either way, the worst three years of my life followed."

"Giving up is never the right decision." He looked at the comatose bodies wobbling in the alley as he spoke.

"Well, sometimes you can't always help it."

They arrived outside at a seemingly abandoned shop. Like many others, the windows were boarded up and thick drapes guarded the inside from prying eyes. Rissa knew this place well. She ratted a knuckle against the old wood, feeling the wet rot sink beneath her fist. Patiently she waited until someone knocked back. Gault remained quiet and glanced at her, confused. She offered a reassuring smile to him and spoke a password into the old decaying wood. "Only Dawn Will Follow."

Time passed. Enough for doubt to begin to creep in. Suddenly bolts clicked and latched, the wooden door rattled with age as it was swung open by a rough-looking man. His head was shaved and his face lined with piercings. Most defining was a mouth adorned with radiant golden teeth. His smile upon seeing her was dazzling.

"Look who it is, my favourite paper peddler." He stepped back and gestured grandly for them to enter. "And you've brought a friend. Didn't know you had it in you."

"Rand." Rissa greeted him, stepping inside the old store.

She had known Rand for many years. He was a major leader in Downtown's second most predominant gang - Eclipse. They were a quieter, far more subtle alternative to the mindless thuggery of the Empty Eyes. Eclipse offered an alternative for those with nothing left, offering a chance to belong without having to steal and murder. That wasn't to say that Eclipse wasn't dangerous. Rissa found them scarier than the Eyes who at the very least were transparent in their intentions. She had no idea how many people were in Eclipse and by some of the items they sold to those they trusted; they were entrenched deeper in the politics of the city than many believed. You never knew whose ears your words would reach.

As a teenager, Rissa had fenced Rand's newspaper: *The Dawn's Herald* in the streets of the City Centre for some quick cash. From there, she had found a friend in the dark underbelly of Centa Isla. He had sheltered her from the worst the life had to offer and provided a place for her to hang out while her father worked and she rotted at home. He had rejected her desperate pleas to join Eclipse more times than she could remember. This old, withered storefront had looked much healthier when she was younger. To the public, it was derelict, to those streetwise to know otherwise; it was a front for the Eclipse's smuggling operations.

"I assume there's something you're after." Rand asked, discreetly closing the door behind them and bolting it. "You never visit otherwise."

"Oh, now you miss me?" Rissa crossed her arms playfully. "Well, then you should have let me join up when I asked."

He laughed her off, flashing his golden teeth. "What I miss is the Wreaths. Nobody moved the Herald like you did."

The Dawn's Herald was a newspaper published by Eclipse themselves that promised the truth of the city. It contained information that it absolutely should not have, leveraging the contacts Eclipse held within the highest circles of the city. It had garnered a reputation during her stint for leaking secrets and she had used this to secure a sale many a time to sell copy after copy for as little as a single Wreath.

"Still not replaced me? Really?" Rissa recalled her days spent standing in the pouring rain of the City Centre. Traffic, bright lights, cigarette smoke. Selling papers to the drunk and desperate, hiding from the CIPD. There was a glaze of joy to the old memory, but she definitely hadn't been happy back then.

"What can I get for you?" Rand vaulted over a desk. His piercings rattled as he moved.

Rissa watched as Gault retreated to the back of the room and leaned against the wall closest to the door. His eyes scanned around the old interior as though he was searching for assassins. They were safe here, but it reassured her to be around someone so alert, especially in these times where she had the cold steel of a training Conduit in her pocket but no brick to use it with.

"Do you have any more bricks?" Rissa rubbed her temple. "I... broke the last one."

"Hm. Wait here." Rand gestured for them to wait and headed into the back, disappearing behind a set of dusty velvet curtains that guarded the rest of the store from the foyer.

Catching Gault's eye, she stayed his wary expression with a smile.

Rand returned promptly, laying a sheet white brick on the table. Immediately, she felt her Conduit respond to its presence. How Eclipse was getting their hands on things like this was still beyond her, even in her years spent hanging around their hideout. "This may be to your liking."

"That's perfect! How much?"

"Six hundred Wreaths."

"What!?" Rissa baulked. That was just short of her rent plus living expenses for an entire quarter of the year. "But the last one-"

"Was a favour." His curt response was as a businessman, not an old friend. "These are not acquired easily."

"Payment plan? Credit?" She tried. "Come on, we've done that before."

"Six hundred. Up front." Rand gave her a cynical smile. "We're not selling packed lunches."

"OK. Cheque?"

"I don't fancy that conversation with the bank."

"Come on Rand, who carries that much? You know me!" Rissa emptied her coin pouch onto the counter. The embossed surfaces clinked together as they crashed against the surface. Roughly one hundred or so Wreaths, made up of various embossed gold coins.

"The people who know the value of what we sell here would carry more than that."

Rissa had a stare down with Rand but knew there was no way she was walking out of there with a means to use magic.

Gault stepped to the counter. "We don't have time to haggle with you."

"Then you should have come earlier." Rand carried himself like no slouch. He was slim yet carried more weight than he let on. His torn shirt hugged his biceps and shoulders, grown from a childhood spent around a forge and anvil. He wouldn't single man a shady operation like this alone if he wasn't backing himself in a fight. Rissa knew that as a member of Eclipse, assuming he was alone was likely the first mistake someone could make.

"Easy guys." Rissa stayed with them with raised arms. "We can figure this out."

"No." Gault said to her. His eyes were cloudy suddenly, unfocused yet terrifyingly sharp. "We've wasted enough time."

Across the counter, Gault reached for the brick, gripping it in one hand. Just as he touched the goods, there was a flash. A blade flew into Rand's grip. As the blade came down, Gault reacted immediately. He moved, seizing Rand's wrist and pinning it to the counter before driving his shaved head into the brick. Blood exploded over the imbued concrete and Rand put his free hand up, surrendering the blade to Gault who knocked it to the floor out of reach.

"Gault, what are you-!"

"Alright! Alright... Easy..." Rand interrupted her, both hands now raised in surrender. He spat out one of his golden teeth, watching it splatter the counter in a glob of blood. "I can respect a show of strength."

Gault grabbed the brick from the counter with one hand and pushed it into her hands. "Come on."

He turned to leave, unbolting the door and stepping outside. Rissa turned to Rand, desperate to salvage their relationship. "Rand, I am so sorry. I will pay for this, just give me-"

"Just take it, kid." With his sleeve to his bleeding snout, Rand sat back on a stool and waved her away. "Just don't break that one."

With a last look of apology, Rissa took the brick and placed it into her backpack. It felt good to have some weight on her shoulders again. She left the storefront and found Gault waiting outside.

"What was that?" She questioned him immediately.

"Why are we negotiating with thugs?" Gault stared at her. With a chance to look in his eyes, she could feel his distance suddenly. Something slight had changed in him. "The Omens have a head start. We're wasting time."

"Rand is a friend."

"It won't matter." Gault whirled on her. His voice was calm, yet hard and pressed with intent. "Not if we don't find Kren'shal."

"You can't just do whatever you want!" She snapped. "You don't know this city. Not like I do."

Rissa watched his face carefully as he took in her words. Anger burned in his eyes, yet his face remained placid and neutral.

She continued. "I'm setting a boundary. No more wild cards. Not without checking with me."

"... So be it." He conceded, more eager to move than to argue. "Lead on."

Muting all conversation, she led him away from the Eclipse storefront and deeper southwest, where the street quality continued to degrade. At first, there was no sign of much activity. Lights flickered in the apartment blocks above them, but the streets were otherwise empty. Empty chip packets tumbled through the dark streets as the cold wind of early Rainsturn blew in. Just as she began to doubt the location on her father's map, they encountered the first gathering of Empty Eyes congregating outside an abandoned corner store. Immediately, they sauntered over, six eyepatches in total. One of them was familiar...

"You've got nerve showing up around 'ere." One of them pushed to the front. A familiar face, although now missing teeth. The same thug who had chased her into the alley before she encountered Gault. "After what you did."

"What happened to your teeth?" Rissa mused wryly, rubbing her chin.

"You! Ya' wretch!" As though to emphasise, the thug opened her mouth, revealing several missing teeth.

"Don't be too happy to see me." Rissa let out a low whistle at the damage done. "Pretty sure they're still in the concrete if you want them back."

"You'll pay for doing this to me!" The words suggested violence, but of the six Eyes, she drifted cowardly towards the back.

Gault stepped in front of her. "We're looking for your boss."

"Yeah?" One of the Eyes spoke up, the largest of the group, a barrel-chested male. "He ain't tryin' to be found."

Knives flashed into their hands as the six thugs slowly approached them. Rissa felt her Conduit in her pocket and slipped it discreetly onto her finger. Having the weight of the brick in her bag made her feel invincible once again. She shared a brief glance with him; her look telling him that this was the kind of fight he could pick. As the first of the thugs advanced towards Gault, he bore a knife in his hulking grip. Gault's response was explosive. With terrifying speed, he snatched the wrist that bore the weapon and broke it with a cruel movement, driving the knife into the wielder's shoulder. The broad chest heaved in a scream and before he had even hit the ground, Gault was attacking another Eye, kicking their knee in and inverting their leg with a devastating crunch. Rissa realised fairly quickly she wasn't even going to need to take part as he moved between them in a flash, punches hitting like hammer blows. He buried them with several, easy strikes, making sure to return to the toothless one, grabbing her by greased black hair and hoisting her up from the ground.

The violence brought Rissa trepidation, but equally also relief that he was on her side. Looking at the man there was no suggestion of such monstrous power in his deceptively slim physique. Where did it come from? His body was practically emaciated.

"Your leader." Gault demanded, speaking into the single working eye of the Empty Eye thug.

"Abandoned apartment block. South side. Graffiti all over." She hissed through cries of agony, distinctly more teeth absent than when they had started. Tears streamed down her cheek. "Don't even go lookin'. Boss'll string you up!"

Gault's gaze bore into her. "With one arm?"

There was enough information in the way her face fell to confirm to her that it could well be Kren'shal who was leading them and that if they could find their hideout, they'd very likely find the Omen.

Gault looked at her. A question on his lips. "Well?"

Rissa felt her brow furrow. "What do you mean?"

Gault's grip tightened on the thug's hair, and he pulled, drawing a scream. Dead or alive? He was asking her judgement on whether to kill these thugs. It was a heavy-set question. Rissa felt a responsibility to get the answer right. Killing them was insane, wasn't it? They were just thugs, now thugs with broken legs. Leaving them alive could draw vengeance, sure, but she didn't have that ruthless streak in her. Almost instantly, guilt started to overcome her. Guilt that she would even consider killing them in the first place. She wasn't a murderer.

"Let them go." She tried to say it nonchalantly, afraid of exposing her hesitation.

To his credit, Gault obeyed. He dropped the thug to the floor and stepped away from the pile of writhing, broken bodies.

"Stay out of trouble guys." Rissa left to a cacophony of curses and vitriol. "You don't want to make him come back."

And so, they left them, heading due South towards the edge of the city where so many projects and homes had been abandoned and left to the whims of the elements. It didn't take them long to find the building. It had been plastered in graffiti and left utterly disgraced and ransacked. The approach was ominous and quiet. A large party loitered outside the abandoned block, laughing over some cruel, pointless story. Quietly, Rissa gestured to the buildings above them - to the flat, unmaintained rooftops that led up to the disjointed apartment. If they were to get high enough, she could Vortex them a couple of floors up without needing to try the front door. It took her a moment to realise Gault hadn't been paying attention. His eyes were glazed over again, staring off down a dark alley.

"Gault?" She snapped her fingers at him.

He jumped, startled. "I-I'm here."

"Good. Let's get a look at this place." She gestured above her, to a rooftop vantage point, accessible via a fire escape.

Without another word he bent his knees and jumped, acquiring with ease three times the height of anything she could manage. He grabbed onto a fire escape; the aged and rusted steel groaning with strain as he hoisted himself up.

"Alright, show off." Rissa made things easier. First, a Vortex into the wall in front of her; another in the wall leading onto the fire escape. She stepped through effortlessly, offering a faux-dainty smile to him as though it was some sort of competition.

They climbed the steel staircase up onto the roof and dipped behind a snaking formation of corroded vents.

"Wait." Gault held out a hand for her to stop. She did, although she wondered why.

He took a moment, but the strange marking over his right eye began to glow. It thrummed with power, vibrating tiny ripples through the air in front of her. It was like standing in front of a speaker, yet it was deathly silent. She could feel the reverberations in her ribcage and skull. It ended abruptly. The power left the Brand like water down a drain. In that split second, something changed in his eyes; something that she couldn't immediately place.

"What was that?" She asked.

"I'm sorry." Gault muttered. He was already rising, vaulting over the ventilation shafts as he answered. On his face was a terrifying deadly calm, his eyes as vacant as a corpse.

"Wait! What was that!?" Rissa hissed before scampering after him. Gault was fast, insanely fast. He cleared the rooftop obstacles and had a stretch of a couple of metres to generate speed. He did so, surging forward and leaping from the rooftop without so much as a word. The gap between the building and the apartment block was a good couple of metres. He impressively landed a few floors beneath where they had intended, crashing through a window with a violent roll before disappearing into the building.

"What the hell?" What had just come over him she had no idea. It was as though a switch had been flipped. "This isn't what we agreed!"

Calling after him was useless, so she followed him. A Vortex was enough to get her in through the window he broke. But, upon arriving, she found herself following a trail of destruction. A twisting path of death led higher into the tower, paved with blade-scoured walls and broken bodies, missing arms and limbs. Distant cries of pain continued above her. Bile rose from her stomach, cresting at the back of her throat. Were they…? She put a finger to the pulse of one of the still, face down bodies. Silent. It took her a moment to spot the pool of blood slowly forming around the body. Horrified, Rissa pulled away.

What was happening? She followed the trail of carnage all the way up the winding stairs. Her trainers slipped on pools of blood and she put her hands out to catch herself, finding her palms soaked with crimson gore. Wiping them on her jeans, she tried not to look as she stepped over bodies, following distant cries of alarm. She reached the top floor where an apartment door had been kicked down. Running inside, she found another broken window leading onto a rooftop. From this high up she could see Gault, locked in combat with the one-armed man whom she now recognised as Kren'shal. The same Omen who had destroyed her first brick. This wasn't how she had expected things to go.

She leaped from the window, the brick in her backpack carrying her flying down toward the surface. Her Conduit hummed with energy as she pointed it towards the roof that rushed up to meet her.

I invoke the Missing Sea. Geyser. Break my fall.

Her spell manifested as a torrent of water. Blasted onto the rooftop beneath her, the sheer downforce was enough for her to land with a tidy roll yet otherwise remaining unharmed.

"Gault!" Calling his name did nothing. She got as close as she dared without getting taken down by stray blades.

Their fight was intense. Kren'shal, even with one arm, was proving a worthy opponent and yet every step he took in combat was away from Gault. They crossed rooftops with stunning agility and inhuman guile, their fight carrying them closer and closer to a main road that Rissa knew ran just a few streets away. If their fight reached that street they would have the CIPD bearing down on them for a second night in a row and a public audience to whatever execution was going to follow.

She couldn't let that happen.

As she got closer she saw the fear on Kren'shal's face. He looked gaunt; his mane of hair had been tied back, revealing a scarred face that was unbefitting of an expression of such terror. His body seemed weak and frail, his grey robe hanging loosely over him as though he had dropped several pounds overnight.

"Leave me!" Kren'shal seethed. Fluster and spittle flew from his mouth as he swung his blade in wild, violent crescents. There was no method nor technique, just madness. His single pupil had dilated to a dot that trembled with the precipice of madness.

Gault had explained to her that the burn mark across Kren'shal's face was a Brand. His was called The Brand of the Demon, a variant of dark power bestowed by Galleo et'al upon its Omens. It required him to take a life a minimum of every twelve days, else he would entirely transform into something akin to the demon she had glimpsed in the sewers. The longer he left it, the stronger he became. Kren'shal harnessed his power for "special occasions" it seemed, such as last night in the sewer.

They'd found Kren'shal at his weakest, having expended much of his power to sprout the demonic arm just last night. He had gone to ground, seemingly not expecting Gault to find him so quickly. Rissa felt a twinge of guilt for the role she played in all this. Gault would never have known how to find this place without her. The dead bodies littering the halls of the abandoned apartment block were as much down to her as the blade that killed them. They were not innocent thugs, but surely they didn't deserve to be butchered.

The sounds of traffic grew louder, only a street away over the lip of the building where they were fighting. Quickly, she caught on to Kren'shal's plan to get into plain sight where he would be all but invincible. It seemed that Gault had noticed this too. His attacks increased in aggression that only forced Kren'shal to retreat quicker. Rissa watched as Gault lunged, seeking to grab and maim the elusive Omen. He was able to grab hold of the robe that Kren'shal wore but with only one arm to get caught, Kren'shal was able to slip out of his clothing and make a mad dash for the edge of the building.

"Rissa!" Gault yelled.

She acted on instinct.

I invoke the Missing Sea. Crest. Prevent his advance.

She felt the weight of the brick on her back and the power of the Conduit on her finger as she touched the floor and brought her imagination to life. Water exploded out of the ground, rising and cresting in a semi-circle that blocked the Omen inches from the edge of the building. Trapped, Kren'shal turned and gave her a look that turned her blood to ice. Terror, fear, the look of a man about to die, captured in his gritted teeth and the despair that stung his eyes. His gaze bore into her, damning her a murderer. Even as Akor'shaki pierced his heart he did not look away, ensnaring her gaze in his powerful eyes as the light slowly faded from them as if he wanted her to know that it may as well have been her holding the blade.

Gault turned to her, nonchalant, as though nothing had happened. He was speaking before Kren'shal's body had even properly hit the floor. "Good work."

Good work? Rissa couldn't look away from the bleeding corpse. An Omen, supposedly, a harbinger of Galleo et'al had just been slain by her doing. By all accounts this should have been a victory. Yet she felt nothing but a churning pit deep in her stomach, like the beginning of a hurricane was whipping her stomach into a frenzy. Was she truly so shallow? This mission had swept her away, distracting her wide eyes with fresh experiences, new worlds and cosmic forces. While she'd been privy to murder.

For a fleeting moment she had felt like she had purpose in this world, that fate had brought Gault crashing down a few streets away from her to make something of her life. Instead, the reality was clear to her. She was just a murderer. Killing for good or evil was killing all the same. Frankly, she wasn't even certain if she was on the right side.

Had she made a mistake?

3

The timepiece fell heavy upon the eleventh hour. A bell began to chime, echoing through the tall chamber. King-Regent Grayson Clovis stood at a large, sprawling glass window. Even from the middle floor of Monument, the council chamber still offered a stunning view of the city he ruled. Industrial smoke and heavy-set fog lingered over the towers. Once, that smog had signified the progression of mankind into an industrial era – but now taunted him, clotting the air and the lungs of his people.

As a child, he recalled the Council Chambers being larger when he had roamed the tower. The ornate stone table that bore a seat at each distant cardinal had been imposing and he had never truly understood the practicality of being seated so far away from the people you were supposed to be talking to. But as he grew older, packing on muscle and size everything had suddenly seemed so much smaller and the nuance of tradition had made more sense as he found comfort in the familiar and stable. Still, he had wrangled with wild, impulsive thoughts for a long time that he should just simply abolish the old echo chamber for something more personal and modern. Yet, in the same vein wanted to respect the traditions that had held this city together for years – traditions introduced by his father who he had replaced as King-Regent. The true King, whom the crown truly belonged to, lay comatose in his chambers a few stories above him. So long as his father breathed, Grayson was nothing more than a King-Regent. Without the true authority to pass laws and make decisions as he pleased, he had been forced to appoint a small council of the most influential noble families, elevating them to holding Seats upon his Elemental Council.

The Crown he wore had been a poisoned chalice, a representation of potential power and nothing else. He adored his father; a powerful and capable man who never second guessed himself. His brazen eyes had always been fixed on the future for as long as he remembered him, even seconds before the brick thrown during a riot sent him under. He was not a beloved King by any degree but had never shied away from tough decisions. Grayson admired him for that, at least. Given the impossible job of guiding a steadily starving city without resources or farmland, there were no accolades granted to him for merely stopping the rot. All the while, their excessive use of The Algarethan Verse had reared the danger of a second Reckoning wiping them out once and for all. Laws were sanctioned and harsh restrictions were put in place, further damaging his reputation while protecting the public from the dark truth that Centa Isla was a doomed vessel.

The Resource Crisis or a second Reckoning. One of the two was going to kill them. It was these two monumental plates that Grayson had found himself spinning in his father's place. Already, his blond locks had begun to thin.

But he would be better than his father. He was determined. For all the right decisions he made, his father had failed to make a genuine attempt to better the life of the people. His irreverent will had destroyed the economy by absolving wealth to the nobility and cutting power to entire streets just to power the City Centre's parties for a little longer. Stupid laws had been created just for a day's entertainment.

The name Clovis had been driven so deep into the dirt that the riot that had put him into a coma had been inevitable. Now Grayson had to salvage the remains; a young man at only twenty-seven. If he knew one thing about ruling it was not to be anything like his father. The moment the title King-Regent had been passed to him he dismissed his father's advisors, relegating them to the Monument kitchens or back to the noble family they had spawned from. He wanted to reform the way things ran around here but was frustratingly limited in his influence despite wearing the ornate golden crown on his head.

As the bell continued to chime, the heavy wooden doors to the chamber creaked open, spilling light into the dark room. Four bodies entered, dressed regally. They were swarmed by a small group of servants who scurried about the chamber, drawing the giant curtains shut and lighting braziers. They left immediately as the figures seated themselves upon the four cardinals prompted by the table. Grayson made his way to his pedestal, up a small angular set of marble steps and into his position of domination, casting his muddy brown eyes down upon his council.

He waited until the servants had left in their entirety, dragging the doors shut behind and bathing the chamber in dim torchlight and silence. He bid the four figures to take down their hoods. "Introductions, then."

At the north cardinal facing yet the furthest from him, the figure rose confidently. The hood fell to reveal a strong-featured man. His hair was white and fanned, as though he'd arrived through a wind tunnel and his skin was dark and soothing like a gentle summer's breeze. "Marco Barrett. Seat of Air."

Grayson smiled softly, seating Marco with a gesture. "The Crown recognises you."

Marco was seated, back straight and legs crossed. Grayson went around the table, introducing the East and South cardinal.

"Theora Eculaire. Seat of Water."

"The Crown recognises you."

"Like I give a damn."

Grayson had the patience that his father lacked and would use it. He had yet to win over all of his council yet would not falter to their mindless cynicism.

"Kiara Harrington. Seat of Fire."

"The Crown recognises you."

Grayson turned his attention now to the West cardinal where the final figure had already risen. There had been a… change in the assembly of his Elemental Council. Even as they entered, tension had arrived with them. Flitting gazes and suspicion pervaded the table. He was so used to seeing the stocky shadow of Davin Freid, Seat of Earth filling the chair that to have such a gaunt figure filling his seat now was quite a disparity. It seemed that the others had caught onto this too. All eyes were on the newcomer.

"Rise and introduce yourself to The Crown."

Pale hands lowered the hood. Jet black eyes, sheet white hair. Grayson couldn't help but think the man looked like a corpse that had been reanimated. His comatose father had more life in his eyes than the man who bowed before him.

"Azrael. Seat of Earth."

A shout from the East, Theora Eculaire was on her feet as though she had been waiting for this moment to speak. "By the missing sea, who is this? Where is Davin Freid?"

Intending to at least finish the traditional introductions, Grayson stayed her with a hand. "Let me finish-"

"As if I'll let you finish. You surely don't recognise this stranger you've let waltz into our council chambers?" She was an old woman but had plenty of life left to give. Grayson knew he had a great mountain to climb to win the stoic noble over. She had little respect for the Clovis line of rulers and was not afraid to make it known. It was a wonder she had survived his father's reign without losing her head.

Azrael was looking at him. Grayson could feel the black eyes scouring his peripheral, demanding his attention. When he looked back, there was a silent message in those lightless eyes that he somehow knew.

Defend me.

He took a breath. "The Crown recognises you."

"Heavens help us." Theora sat down, exasperated.

Her silence gave way for another speaker, the Seat of Air, Marco Barrett who maintained his perfect posture all the while. "To see Theora's question answered - what has become of Davin?"

"Davin Freid succumbed to smithy's lung two days ago." Grayson lied. He maintained eye contact one by one with his advisors, injecting a faux melancholy into his voice. He felt no pity for Davin Freid, a gluttonous wealth-hoarder who had previously sat on this council to do nothing but object to anything that threatened to remove money from his deep pockets. No wife, no children. Only servants that were glad to be free of his demands. It had been an easy choice to decide who Azrael was going to replace among his council. He did what he had to do for the good of this city. To him, no life was greater than the salvation of Centa Isla and the restoration of his family name.

"And so, you replaced him with some transient?" Theora spoke up again, gesticulating toward the still and silent Azrael. "Did you not think to consider us?"

Marco Barrett spoke first. "He is the King, Lady Eculaire."

"King-*Regent*." She practically spat the second half of his title out. "The boy has let it go to his head."

Grayson sat and listened as they squabbled on about who had a right to do what. He had called this meeting for a reason and intended to waste no more time in getting to it. His fist thundered down on the table as hard as a hammer on steel. "That's enough."

To their credit they fell quiet, even Theora, who seemed to appreciate a show of strength over any pandering. "I have not called you to these chambers to bicker."

"Then pray get on with it. The clock is soon to chime for midday and we have achieved nothing beyond pointless salutations."

"I propose an end to the Resource Crisis." He spoke firmly, gesturing to Azrael. "Courtesy of the Seat of Earth. A great mind that I was fortunate to find."

Theora audibly huffed. Marco leaned forward. At the south of the cardinals, Kiara had still yet to speak a word or show any kind of interest toward the discussion. He felt the demanding gaze of Azrael upon him once again and gestured toward the black-eyed man. "I give you the floor, Seat of Earth."

Azrael had no need to explain the Resource Crisis. Everybody in this room knew it intimately. Contrary to the public belief that Centa Isla had at least several years left before resources dried up completely, Grayson knew the dire reality. They had mere months. They had been scrambling, mobilising the greatest minds in Grandmaster and Verscience to come up with a string of solutions. Every time they met with failure and the dread of famine and doom only grew within the elite circles. The store shelves were emptying quicker than they could fill and he feared that the public would soon catch on.

When Reckoning had fractured the planet, it had upset the ecosystem of magic that existed in the world around them. With mineral deficient soil no longer able to support crops, Centa Isla had been forced to artificially create these compounds and resources through an arduous process, known as Resynthesis. A tremendous feat of collaboration between the warring forces of magic and science that, at face value, was the solution to all of Centa Isla's problems, allowing them to simply recreate what nature had taken. But they had discovered that in order for any kind of matter to be Resynthesised - it had to first draw magic from the atmosphere around them to form the item, which only destabilised the planet further. They stood at the precipice currently, monitoring the levels of magic in the air via probes that were spotted around the city. If they Resynthesised too much at once, stealing too much magic from the already unstable atmosphere, they could incur a second Reckoning which would well and truly finish them off. It was as though they juggled balls of flame with one arm and a blindfold. Grayson had sprouted grey hairs over this matter. The basic needs of supply and demand were simply not attainable. It was good fortune that he had stumbled upon Azrael, despite not initially trusting the man for his dead-eyed stare and monotone voice. It was that very voice that spoke of the salvation of Centa Isla now. He held his reservations, of course, but thus far there had only been good ideas.

"All your efforts have been truly commendable." The gaunt figure rose from his stone seat and began to circle the large round table. His voice was like silk scrubbed with sandpaper, laced with intent and force of will. "But you have been misguided. You seek to inhibit your use of "Resynthesis" when you should be addressing the core problem."

Grayson watched his council. There were words desired to be said, yet for someone so lacking in charisma and energy, the languid movements of Azrael captured the attention of all present, as though he commanded a hidden power that nobody could truly ascertain.

"You must broaden your horizons and banish the fear of what you don't yet understand." Azrael continued. He reached beneath the stone table and planted a small, wooden chest upon its smooth surface. The locks snapped open, and the wood groaned as the lid was lifted and from it a chunk of rock was pulled.

"A rock?" Theora Eculaire sounded none too impressed.

From the south cardinal, Lady Harrington finally spoke. "No. It's... different."

Azrael planted it on the table. Even from his raised platform, Grayson could feel the air in the chamber begin to shift, like a window had been opened in a stuffy room. The air felt fresher, the Versorcerer's genes in him reacted to an increased concentration of magic in the air as the hairs on his arms and the nape of his neck stood up on end. The rest of the council surely felt it too. "The mere presence of this is your salvation. Even in this small quantity it will slowly restore the lost magic taken from us by Reckoning."

There it was. Their salvation. The reason he had allowed this upstart a seat upon their sacred chamber. Grayson felt his fingers ache with the desire to take the rock for himself.

"There is more of this mineral?" Marco Barrett asked. The wild hair swayed as he rose, leering at the rock as if he couldn't get too close.

"Infinite. But not within reach." Azrael replied. "It exists in the void beyond this shattered core. A construct of my design, a Obelisk, will pierce the heavens and grant us that reach, affording us all the resources we could ever need to thrive."

Grayson allowed himself a small smile as the council humoured the prospect Azrael offered. He had told no lies when he said he had exhausted every possible option available in tipping the scales on Centa Isla's slow doom. The only option he had yet to so much as even humour was a regimented culling, but that would still only prolong the inevitable. He swore when the crown first fell upon his head that such an option would never be explored no matter how many nobles were preferable to it. Once his black-eyed advisor had finished there would be a vote held among the five of them, determining the fate of this wild idea.

"This Obelisk you speak of. We would need to clear a space for something so large to pierce the heavens, as you say?" Marco asked, surprisingly sceptical from a man Grayson had also assumed was very forward thinking and open to new ideas.

"Correct."

"Do we have the space to accommodate-"

Kiara Harrington interrupted him. "Of course we have space. Just look beyond the City Centre; this city is populated by addicts and murderers. Their wretched hovels would not be missed."

The council chamber erupted into debate as Azrael's speech concluded and the strange rock was placed back in its box and sealed. Almost immediately Grayson felt colder, like a cloud had drifted across the sun. As he returned to his seat, Grayson cleared his throat. "My vote is yours, Azrael. Your fresh thinking may yet be the salvation of this city."

Kiara Harrington agreed from the southernmost cardinal. "As is mine."

"This is a matter best discussed with the greater nobility." Marco Barrett declared. "I abstain."

"I also abstain." Theora concurred, despite her intrigue. Grayson had expected this from her, but not from Marco. "Gods forbid the two of us have some common sense."

Grayson had expected this, yet the frustration was still raw. His fists clenched on his pedestal, but he withheld his tongue. As King-Regent, there were no decisions of this scale that he could make alone. Instead, it was for that reason that this Elemental Council existed at all. No decision could be made unless all five of them agreed and these days that was a rare feat. The consequence of an idea failing in these chambers was that it cascaded down to the greater nobility for a more public vote where it would meet its final fate.

They discussed back and forth for a good while longer, making no further progress.

"Is there any other business to discuss?" Theora Ecualire spoke, rising without being first dismissed.

Grayson challenged her. "Somewhere to be, Seat of Water?"

"Someone must prepare for Davin's burial." She gave him a staunch look, as though she knew there was foul play involved. "Before "smithy's lung" gets me too."

Grayson promptly adjourned the meeting. As the servants entered, throwing open the curtains and extinguishing the candles, Grayson could feel Azrael's black eyes boring into him as the Seats departed the chamber, leaving him alone. With no outcome, he now had to prepare to sway the lesser nobility to Azrael's idea in a formal ballot. A difficult feat but worded correctly was not an impossibility. Success here would see the idea come to fruition. For this city and for his family name, he would not be stopped.

—

How many hours had passed? It felt like eternity yet Rissa could not forget the face Kren'shal had given her moments before he was scythed down by Gault and his wicked blade. The image had never left her mind, even as they had dragged his corpse to the edge of the city and flung him into the core of the world. The Omen's body had flapped and flailed in the wind like a broken doll, spraying sinew and viscera until he had burned up in the intense, primal magic of the exposed core. Any trace of her deed had vanished into a small cloud of dust that dispersed with the wind. No evidence. No trace.

Yet Rissa could see his face even now, even as she worked her shift, surrounded by the hedonistic gluttony of a City Centre nightclub. Her mind was still spinning with guilt as she aggressively shook a metal tumbler, pouring the watery contents into a tall glass. Kren'shal's tortured face sought her in the reflection of the watered-down drink and she blinked harshly, pushing the swishing liquid across the counter to a masked patron. She watched, grateful, as they disappeared into the throes of the dancing, writhing bodies taking the rippling visage with them. Deafening music meshed with screams of exult as guttural, rumbling bass and strobing lights only served to amplify the intensity of her thoughts. Before she could get truly lost, the next patron arrived and leaned over the bar to scream slurred orders into her ear through his mask. She didn't understand him, not truly, but nobody cared what they were drinking anyway. Rissa nodded, reminded she was dealing with nobles by how nonchalantly and drunkenly he overpaid several Wreaths. Everybody in Avatar tonight were either nobles, or desperate people just hoping to meet nobles. Masks were offered and encouraged, used to ensure anonymity and safeguard reputation and stature amongst family, friends and fellow nobility.

Avatar Nightclub, owned by nobles for nobles, was located in the beating heart of the City Centre where they could indulge in hedonistic acts of depravity, fulfilling their wildest or darkest desires behind the protection of a mask. Rissa enjoyed her work somewhat, enjoying the carnage a usual night had in store. She had tales innumerable about the wild things she had seen in the short year she had worked here. Joining shortly after her expulsion from Grandmaster, she had gradually begun to enjoy her work, preferring to run her bar alone to stay in control of the standards. The masked guests always intrigued her. On a better day than today, she enjoyed the idle conversation, seeing if she could pick up any suggestion as to what sort of life they led behind their pale disguise. Many here wouldn't know a dose of Synth or a night on the streets if it smacked them in the face. Yet she had come to grimly surmise that in their own unique way; their lives were just as terrible.

The glass in her hand trembled like it was riding the Subrail. It took her a moment to realise it was her who was shaking. Her normally calm nerves were jittery tonight. She tried in vain to put Kren'shal out of her mind yet couldn't. It had been her suggestion to dump his body unceremoniously over the city's edge. She had known his body would disintegrate to dust on contact with the raw magic that the core harboured. Knowing it was her idea made her feel dirty, like she had denied a burial. Rissa hadn't slept since it happened. Once the deed was done, she had left Gault at the city's edge without a word and stumbled home, existing in a twilight haze of disbelief. Her calendar dictated that she had a shift tonight, so she had got dressed and left, jumping on the Subrail's Downtown Line to the City Centre without even stopping to think. Now she was here, seeing the reflection of a dead man in every glass. Even when she closed her eyes his face was burned into her eyelids.

The orders for drinks were relentless. She prepared them with as much precision as possible, trying to control the trembling in her hands. Trying to just get lost in the rhythm of her work, she grabbed two bottles and dual poured them into the metal container before shaking the contents out into an awaiting glass. She lifted it, ready to pass it over a cluster of empty bottles sitting precariously on the edge of the counter when she simply froze. She had been avoiding it as best as she could; the long mirror that ran across the back of the bar. Patrons stared into it endlessly, enamoured by their own image as they waited for their drinks to be made. She only caught an accidental glimpse, but in the glass mirrored wall just ahead of her she saw him. His body was twisted and malformed and his face was expressionless, but the eyes bore into hers. The slash that had severed his head from his body had been stitched back together but the flesh still warped and bled and flapped as though it was caught in the moment where life left his eyes. Rissa jumped. She dropped the clumsy cocktail and it crashed against the bottles, sending them skittling across the counter, splattering the man as though he was a canvas for abstract art.

"Sorry!" She clasped her hands to her mouth instinctively and lunged for a cloth, grabbing several and distributing them to him while drying the counter as best as she could.

"You asinine moron." He blustered and seethed at her, throwing obscenities, embarrassed redness visible through gaps in the mask. "Look at what you've done! Wretch! You'll be fired by the end of the night!"

She continued to dab at the wet splodges on the counter, ignoring his curses. Suddenly he reached across the bar and grabbed her arm. On instinct she swung, whipping him around the face with the heavily sodden bar cloth. The wet rag made a satisfying slap that echoed just momentarily louder than the music. The impact unhinged his mask and it clattered to the floor. His hands flew up over his face and he dived to the ground scrambling for his lost anonymity. Before she could apologise further, hands grabbed her again, this time from behind the bar. They spun her around and Rissa came face to face with her manager who manoeuvred her out of sight. Guilt wracked her as she meekly bowed her head and allowed herself to be banished to the locker room. Told to wait, time felt as though it warped as she paced among the lockers and changing room curtains. Her mind raced as fast as her pulse and she paced up and down, avoiding glancing at the glossy, polished surfaces of the fridges and lockers in case she saw his demonic reflection again.

"Rissa." Her manager appeared after placating the soggy noble, a chronically tired look in her eyes. "What the hell was that!?"

"Sorry." Rissa offered. "He grabbed me and I-"

"They can do whatever they want. You should know this kind of thing by now."

"I know. I'm sorry."

"You're suspended."

"Suspended!?" Rissa's mouth gaped open. "Look, I really need the money."

"You should have thought about that, shouldn't you?" Her manager's temple creased as she rubbed it. "You think you can smack a noble with a wet rag and get away with it? Do you have any idea how much damage control I need to do?"

"No, no. You're absolutely right." Rissa felt her fist clench in frustration. At herself, at the situation she'd put herself in.

Rissa apologised once more before she jettisoned herself out of the back exit, stepping out in the cool air, admittedly relieved to leave the thumping bass and lights behind. Rain fell upon the City Centre and it felt comforting to stand there for a second and feel the rain on her skin. It was a pleasant distraction from her rampant mind. The City Centre was bustling and she had to work up the courage to step out of the alley and into a crowd of bodies. It was like a completely different city. Downtown you could keep to yourself and cross the road without looking. Here - you had to hold your belongings close and your wits closer. If you didn't look before crossing the street you'd be mowed down by a bus or cab. She took a moment to absorb the energy of the city; the bellowing of engines; the chatter of the midnight streets; the smoke that hung in the air from the engines of cars and exhalations of cigars. She had always believed the atmosphere was best enjoyed with a cup of coffee and a roof overhead. There had been a life for her here once upon a time. Her mother had lived in one of the very skyscrapers that loomed so powerfully over her. Rissa wondered what it would be like now, eight years later, had she not disappeared. Could she have lived a life so busy and chaotic that she wouldn't have had time to sit and sulk about it? She remembered a vague childhood spent in a salubrious upmarket apartment with fantastic views. She had tried to find it many times without success. After pronouncing her mother deceased, it had been seized by The Crown, relegating her family to a life in Downtown. Her father had landed on his feet as he always did… but she felt like she had landed and broken both legs.

Traffic ripped through the wide streets. Billboards hung in the air. Everything here fought for her attention. One sign in particular caught her eye. A stern image of King-Regent Grayson Clovis, thrusting an accusatory finger at her from overhead. A sleuth of text told her that it was her responsibility to report any unsanctioned magical acts to the CIPD via a special radio frequency.

Again, she thought of her father. There was a part of her that wanted to speak to him about the events of the last few days in the warped hope that he might help in some way. It wasn't until she was descending into the Subrail did she decide that she would. He'd be on his self-imposed night shift, likely buried in a case or stuck looking deep into the past. She had spent some time at the Compound as a child, visiting her father with wide eyes as he worked. She remembered mirroring his excitement at all the new CIPD patrol cars that had been parked outside, just happy to see him smiling. But that was one of the few good memories there. Rissa had continued her visits involuntarily through her troubled teenage years, each visit escalating the disappointment in his eyes until he could no longer meet her gaze. Every visit had been consequence free thanks to her father. That was the one kindness he had repeated for her, but she had craved boundaries and he had given none. Her cries for attention were silenced with dismissive forgiveness rather than conversation and so she had given up and grown up. They had remained emotionally distant ever since.

The Subrail churned through the deep tunnels. Rissa avoided looking at the reflective windows for fear of seeing Kren'shal's twisted face again. The underbelly flashed by as she was lost to her thoughts. Soon, the grinding of the brakes jolted her awake.

"Now arriving at Downtown Central. Please change for the Coast Line."

With her bag, brick and Conduit back at home, Rissa walked the short journey from Downtown Central to the CIPD Compound. It was a large space, cordoned by a tall, hatched fence. Within, she could see the hustle and bustle as patrol cars constantly arrived and departed from the depot. Entering via the main entrance required a copious amount of form filling, so she approached the compound from the rear and was seconds from climbing to the other side of the hatched fence when a shadow loomed behind her. Fear spiked and she whirled around, finding Gault stood behind her. He looked at her curiously.

"Gault."

"What are you doing?" He asked her. There was a layer of ice in his neutral tone, as though he was frustrated or impatient. There was something off about his presence now that she had watched him butcher and murder.

"What does it look like?" Rissa told him sharply. She wasn't going to be strung along witless any more than she already had been. "I'm getting help."

"No." He took a couple of steps closer, his fingers locked around the hatched steel. "This won't go the way you think it will."

"You don't know that. You've been here five minutes."

"I can know it. And I do." There was a steeliness in his eyes that talked her down as much as his words. "They'll make anybody who believes you disappear."

"No." Rissa had made up her mind. She climbed the steel fence with practised ease and dropped into the Compound, looking at him from the safety of the other side. "You were out of control last night. I don't need your help or your advice."

As she said it, it was like she was acknowledging the fear that trembled her legs slightly as she stood near him. Without her Conduit, she felt vulnerable and was especially wary of his violent potential. But to her surprise he offered no resistance to her damning words, no justification for his intense violence. Instead, his head just bowed slightly, dusty brown hair obscuring any expression.

"Fine. Do as you must."

She left him standing there solemnly and entered the CIPD Compound. The door was unlocked, yet the lobby was empty. She rang the bell and waited patiently, casting her gaze around the interior. It was a solemn, yet stoic blend of dark oak, black steel and crimson upholstery. Portraits were plentiful, framing heroic officers decorated with their accolades. Some frames were old enough to pre-date Reckoning, when the officers had been soldiers, donning steel armour in place of the passionate red uniform they wore today. That was back when the Centa Isla Police Department didn't officially exist and was just a flailing limb of The Kingsguard, the latter now exclusively protecting Monument and the King-Regent's interests. Despite presenting as upholders of the law, Rissa knew that the CIPD were not as far reformed from their roots as they claimed to be. If the King-Regent told them to ignore a crime - they would. Presenting as a modern, slick and lawful establishment, Rissa had seen glimpses of the primitive origins of the CIPD in the public executions and the horrific prison known as The Douldruums that had been built beneath this very Compound, although she had never seen it in person nor would her father even confirm its existence.

Having not noticed it initially, she spied a makeshift memorial at the door, adorned with mementos and photographs. It took Rissa a moment to recognise the face in the photos. The look of youth that had made her think of her father starting out in the force; this was the young officer she had encountered fleeing the sewers. His uniform had been undecorated and she could still remember the glint of fear in his eyes. By the solemn offerings of family photos, childhood toys and sentimental items, Rissa realised that he was dead.

A newspaper trimming, ceremoniously cut out and placed respectfully upon the photographs caught her eye. It pelted a headline that she knew couldn't have been true.

YOUNG OFFICER SUICIDE

A flare of guilt gripped her chest. She couldn't hide from the fact that she had sent him there in the first place. The feeling pressed against her stomach, like a tumour that she couldn't excise. His fear had been well placed, it seemed. His death had likely come at the hands of the Omens, his body apparently never discovered.

"They called off the search parties." A desk attendant appeared and made her jump. An older man, his uniform decorated with medals, yet clearly pushing the age of service and life expectancy. He carried himself with a limp but kept his back tall and proud.

"Oh, that's sad." She gave him a small smile, pretending not to know a thing. "Why?"

"King-Regent's orders." The attendant shook his head. She could see the repressed anger of a life honourably served blazing in his eyes. "Service is tough these days... we're not taking enough care of our young."

"Yeah." In that moment Rissa better understood the reach of the Omens. It was fully possible that Gault was right. Perhaps they had already breached Monument and coiled the King-Regent around their finger? She thought of the family of the young officer, how they may never know peace without the truth that she held yet couldn't reveal. The Omens had made that young man's death appear like a suicide, taking with him any concrete proof that he even existed at all. They were now reduced to memories in the minds and hearts of friends and family.

"Donnel Rawdon, is he here?" Rissa asked. An irrational spike of worry rose into her chest, as if he could have become a target and that his photograph may one day appear on that wall.

The man peered at her with narrowed eyes, as if he'd seen her before yet couldn't place it.

She smiled. "I'm his daughter."

There was a change as the older man's eyes widened and with surprising speed fumbled for the keys and hobbled toward the locked door to the left of the lobby. Rissa felt a pang of guilt, wanting to tell him not to rush, but the door was soon open, and he gestured grandly for her to enter.

"Thank you very much." She gave her politest smile as she entered the officer's quarters, row upon row of compartmented desks stretched far into the distance. They were all empty, save for the distant crackle of radio static coming from further up. She followed the noise slowly, passing by eerily empty blocks filled with papers and typewriters. Some desks were clean, some untidy. Photos of the hole in the road that Gault and the demon had punched into the ground were pinned on walls. As far as suspects or reasoning went, it seemed like they'd got away with it. She found her father's office block, remembering it vaguely from her childhood although it had looked much bigger back then. Now it looked as though her father had been crammed into it, surrounded by stacks of newspaper archive cuttings and a lot of empty mugs. The radio bled static. Not that he had even noticed. He just stared distantly at his own writing.

"Dad?" It felt like she had stood there for years before speaking, anxiety gnawing at her until the word felt comfortable enough to leave her lips.

He looked up and turned, quickly turning off the radio. He made a weak effort to clean his desk and stood up. "Rissa, what are you doing here? It's nearly midnight."

"Where else would I find you?" She tried a smile, though found her lips unable.

"Are you in trouble?" His question was direct, straight to business.

"Not with the law."

"Good. I'm in the middle of something." Despite the way he tried to obscure it under some files, she knew what he was doing. It was the same thing he was always doing. Combing through the past, desperate for answers as to why his wife, her mother, had left them. She spied a newspaper headline about Aryssa Rawdon's disappearance sticking out from under the folder. The announcement of her death had been fairly high profile. Her mother had been an influential noble before she had married into a common family. In diluting the genes of her long-standing generation of water Versorcerers, she had lost a lot of status that day.

"Any luck?" She was genuinely curious. She had fully supported her father's search for a good three, even four years after Aryssa had disappeared. Eight years later, it had become a doomed course of dredging up old memories that needed to be properly put to rest. Yet her father refused to grieve.

"No... But I'm close, I can feel it."

"Can I help?"

"No, no. I'll bring her back to you." He returned to his work. "Go home."

Anger struck her like lightning. She hadn't seen him in weeks, and this was the curt dismissal she received. There was no question as to how she was doing, no interest in her life - nothing. She couldn't help but say something back, despite knowing full well how their vicious cycle always went. "Mom's dead, Dad. Can we just move on?"

It hurt her to say it.

"She is alive." He seethed, pushing the files aside to reveal various articles, letters and documents. "And I'm closer than ever to figuring things out."

"You've been closer than ever for eight years!" Rissa told him the hard truth. "When will it end!?"

"It will end when I find her and bring this family back."

"It's too late for that! I've grown up, Dad!" She gestured wildly to herself, like she wasn't a twenty-year-old woman instead of a bumbling twelve-year-old. "You've given up everything."

He slammed the wall of his compartment and Rissa jumped. Regret flashed across his face for a mere second, only to be replaced by a resurgence of rage. "You kill her memory every time you open your damn mouth! You diminished her accomplishments with every second you were in Grandmaster. Do you have any idea how embarrassing it was for me!?"

"Embarrassing for YOU!?" This had immediately become pointless. Rissa knew she should have walked away the moment he told her to leave. But there was some catharsis in shouting at him at least, like it was a pleasant distraction from everything else going on. "Maybe I'd have done a little better with some support."

"You were a spoiled child." Donnel replied. "You had a roof over your head and food on the table."

Rissa baulked. That was enough. Her anger left her like a plug had been pulled. Her father had a harsh childhood, she knew that. But for him to not even acknowledge the damage he had done to her… it made her sad, like she wanted to cry. Rissa turned her back on him and waved his calls away. She marched out with determined strides, and he didn't follow her, although a part of her hoped that he would.

As she lingered momentarily in the foyer a boy with a flushed, excited face plonked a stack of the early edition of "*City News*" on the reception desk.

"Breaking News today." The red face spluttered in breathy bursts to the old man behind the desk. "Reporters have been working overtime to get this scoop." The thick bundle was folded over and bound with taut string. The old man used the edge of the key on his lanyard to break the string.

"Can I take one?" She asked meekly.

"O-of course." The older officer quickly pushed one across the desk to her.

She knew that he had heard every word she had exchanged with her father. As she left, she deliberately avoided looking at the photos of the deceased young officer and instead focused on the lead story in the paper.

Gault was still outside when she returned. She folded the paper and slid it into her waistband before climbing over the fence out of the gated compound. Tears stung her eyes but refused to fall, giving away her lack of success.

"It's for the best." Were his words, spoken as though to comfort her.

"My mother loved this city." Rissa said slowly. She continued walking aimlessly. "Only she will know why. My father used to as well."

Gault had followed her, walking in her shadow slowly. "What happened?"

"She died." Flatly, she stated the obvious. "Dad was never the same. He'd have listened once upon a time, you know. He'd have done anything to protect me."

Gault went quiet for a while, making her turn around to check if he was still there. When he did speak, it was muted and introspective, the sad smile of a nostalgic memory on his face. "Then go back."

"What?"

"He's family. Don't have regrets." With a small gesture back to the Compound, Rissa realised that Gault wanted her to try again. A bizarre, entire one-eighty from his stance not ten minutes ago. Even if it didn't make sense, she did appreciate it and thanked him with a small smile.

"No, but thank you." From her waistband, she brandished the newspaper. "I got what I needed anyway."

She tapped a finger on the headline and watched him read it.

CLOVIS TO HOST CAMPAIGN TO SAVE CENTA ISLA
NOBLES SENT EXCLUSIVE INVITES BY ROYAL COURIER

The headline stood out like a stain. It dominated the front page of the paper, the rest of the sheet taken up by speculation from tired, hopeful journalists. For the King to summon the nobles at such short notice was unheard of. Something felt off.

Gault squinted at it. "It is due to take place…"

"Tomorrow evening."

"We have to get in there." Gault stated. "An event of this import - The Omens won't keep away."

"Well, we can't just walk in." She was so tired, but the small hits of adrenaline she kept receiving had kept her going so far. Her brain churned for ideas and eventually settled full circle on where she'd thought this night was going to end.

Avatar.

Rissa led Gault through the City Centre. The heartland was just as alive as she had left it mere hours ago. Chaos simmered in the air, carried by the rumbling of engines and the noisy chatter of socialites with nothing better to do than get drunk. The rain came down hard. Pedestrians kept well clear of the flooded roads so as not to get soaked by the stream of traffic that blustered through deep puddles. Gault had been quiet the entire time, but his gaze was everywhere, distracted by the bright lights and extravagance that camouflaged the carnage within.

Having returned briefly to Ocean's View to get her backpack and Grandmaster brick, they reached Avatar just as the great clock adorning Monument approached one in the morning. By all accounts, she should have still been at work at this hour. There was a raucous queue outside Avatar, twisting down the street. The nobility queue was empty, meaning that the clientele they were looking for were already inside.

"You ready?" She asked Gault who stood in the rain, hair drenched down his face. He looked stoic, yet was that the twitch of nervousness upon his face?

"Lead." He told her.

She did so. They darted into the alley adjacent to where the staff entrance was. Rissa knew the code and punched it into the door, peering inside to find the immediate locker rooms empty. She hid Gault inside a changing room while she took a freshly ironed uniform from the rack and quickly undressed in one of the small changing rooms. Dressed in a white shirt with a black waistcoat, Avatar wanted them to look slick and refined. The bass pounded through the walls, and she could feel the wild atmosphere permeating the locker room even now. Nights like these were so often undiluted madness. When working, she usually had to slick her hair back or tie it up. Still soaked from the rain, she found it slicked back fairly nicely, the weight of the water preventing it from springing back up. Dumping her wet clothes into her backpack, she shoved it into her locker. With the brick still inside, she hoped that the radius it emitted would cover enough of the building for her Conduit to pick up if she needed it. She didn't intend to use any spells for risk of setting the magic sensors off but it felt nice to have the assurance.

She rubbed her hands together eagerly. Avatar and nobles went hand in hand. Rissa was willing to bet that a fair percentage of the noble clientele would have received an invite in some capacity to the event that was being held tomorrow. Drunk and vulnerable, Rissa had every intention of ensuring that one of them would have a night they wouldn't remember in the morning.

And that their invitation would find its way into Rissa's hands.

Now changed, she retrieved Gault from the changing rooms and handed him a flimsy, pale mask from an overflowing stockpile. "We'll get a drink in your hand then just act natural."

"Natural?" He clearly had no idea what this involved. He clumsily put the mask over his face. It covered most of his sharp features, leaving his mouth free for drinking, talking and... whatever else the patrons here did. She found his eyes, bright violet, very striking behind the white mesh.

They entered the main room through a heavy steel door. She felt Gault freeze behind her as the dizzy strobe lights and deafening music announced their arrival. Rissa was more than used to it by now, but she still remembered her first time exposed to the sensory annihilation that was Avatar. She waved at him, watching his dark eyes slowly fix onto her, his mouth open and his brow creased with strain. He did not look natural at all. When Rissa stepped behind the bar in uniform and grabbed a tankard of watered down ale nobody batted an eyelid. As she shoved the drink into his hand, his nose curled as he brought the liquid up to his mouth. Once again, she demanded his attention with a wave and over the deafening noise, gestured up above them. Overhead snaked a network of suspended private rooms, connected by steel scaffolding that offered a view into the plunge of chaos below. He nodded. The dance floor was rammed with sweaty bodies, flailing and splashing drinks. They were harmless enough, a shove on the shoulder generally enough to sift your way through, especially if you were a member of staff. They all wore masks of various intricate designs. A small group of socialites clustered in the corner of the main room where decadent sofas enabled anonymous interactions of public intimacy. She pointed Gault toward an ascending set of stairs that had been barred by a cord of luxurious red rope.

"Wait here." She shouted, pointing to the ground beneath them. Gault stood stiffly as she made her way towards a staff exit. She demonstrated some easy dance moves, gesturing for him to pick up the slack. To his credit he did try, his arms floated up and down like he was on strings. He wore a grimace beneath his mask all the while. Satisfied, she left him and disappeared into the staff area for those assigned to tend to the VIP guests. It was the worst shift that everybody dreaded, forced to attend the whims of the wealthiest nobles. A young woman sat smoking a cigarette, rubbing her creased temple. Rissa had seen her before, although had never learned her name.

"Hey." She said casually, "Don't suppose you want to swap roles?"

The surprise on the young woman's face was expected. "You want to swap? With me? To VIP?"

"Yeah. I'm on collection. Losing my mind."

"Oh hell, yes." She rose and came over to her as though she had just saved her life. "Thank you, thank you."

"Don't worry about it. Anything to pass on?"

Her eyes suddenly looked exhausted. The cigarette came back up to her lips for a deep drag. After a long exhalation, she spoke. "There's a handsy prick in Inferno. Tips well though."

She waved her small apron to the jangling of Wreaths. "And there's some drunk in Mountain. Should probably cut him off. Rest of the suites are empty for another hour."

"Sounds like you've had a good night." Rissa smiled at her. "I'll take it from here."

"You're the best, thank you!"

Rissa waved her off, then shut the door, tipping a chair up against the handle to lock it. It felt good to liberate that poor girl, although she would probably end up in trouble once all was said and done. Rissa hoped she'd agree it was a small price to pay for getting away from the grubby hands of the nobility. It sounded like the drunkard in the Mountain Suite was a good target. The clientele had really gone downhill here. Rissa remembered a time where she had got along with many of the patrons and even knew them by name. There was a kindly regular who just seemed lonely whom she had served on occasions. Although, she hadn't seen him in a while, nor any of the nice ones.

She hot footed up the stairs to the VIP rooms, emerging up in the middle of where all four glass VIP suites converged. She could see the aforementioned drunk patron in the Mountain Suite, half-asleep on a pristine leather sofa with a collection of empty beer mugs around him. The handsy one was fortunately occupied, fooling around with some hired dancers in the Inferno Suite.

"At least pull the curtains, man." Rissa grimaced, barring the sight from her memory forever. She moved across the steel walkway, the writhing masses on the dance floor visible through the gaps in the grates beneath her feet. From so high up the bass was somehow even louder, rattling the supports that suspended the walkway overhead. She twisted down a spiral staircase and reached the red rope where Gault was still puppet dancing. She watched the relief flash across his face as he was able to leave and make his way over to her.

"Welcome to Avatar, my lord." She gave him the spiel and grand gesture, conscious that other members of staff could be watching from the various bars that popped up around the place.

"Thanks." Gault poorly played along, although thankfully nobody could have heard a thing they were saying. His ability to perform a convincing part unfortunately rivalled his dancing. Even if they were able to acquire an invitation to the ballot, she couldn't imagine a worse person to put in a room full of nobles. She led him upstairs and across the walkway, gesturing to the drunk visible through the open glass. The suites were hexagonal rooms with windows all the way around. Inside, was a private social area with sound proofing enough to hear only your own breathing if you wished. Gault nodded his understanding, and they entered the Mountain Suite quietly. As they opened the door, the thumping bass invaded the silence and the drunk noble stirred. Rissa closed the door instantly, bathing the suite in a lull of quiet, the bass sounding less like it was outside their door and more like it was several buildings down the road. She could hear her own thoughts just in time for them to start going crazy.

"W-w-what's going on?" The drunk noble sat up, fumbling on the armrest to support himself.

"Just checking in, my lord." Rissa smiled at him, gesturing for Gault to hide behind the sofa as she moved around the room and began to pull the privacy curtains shut. She saw Kren'shal watching her in the reflection, twisted and malformed, yet she held her reaction at bay. "Can I get you anything else?"

"No." The noble tried to stand, staggering. "G-get me a cab."

"I'm afraid there's a short wait for cabs." She lied, pulling the last set of curtains closed in time to see a curious look thrown her way from within the adjacent Inferno Suite. "It's been a busy night."

"Get me a bloody cab." He thrust a finger at her threateningly, although he almost fell over in doing so. "I'll- I'll have your job."

"My lord, you should really sit down."

"Get me home." Repeating himself, the drunk started stumbling toward the door. "O-out of here."

"My lord, please wait." Calling for him, Rissa quickly realised that he wasn't going to come back and so Rissa gave a look to Gault who rose up from behind the sofa, grabbed the man and slammed him into the ground. The noble stopped moving instantly and for a moment Rissa was worried; until a hacking snore came out of his mouth. They lifted the drunkard up onto the sofa and rested a tankard in his hand. Upon searching his pockets, Rissa found a key with a tag to his private locker. Rissa marvelled at their perfect crime as they headed towards the door. Drunk man lost his keys, could it get any more classic?

She opened the door and jumped. A figure waited for her outside. It took her a minute to recognise the man from the Inferno Suite. A face of fury was practically exploding from beneath his mask. "I ordered a drink hours ago. By Reckoning, what have you fools been doing!?"

"A-ah, apologies, my lord." She discreetly looked for Gault in the reflection of the windows around her, finding him magically nowhere to be seen. "Let's get you sorted now."

She stepped out onto the walkway between the suites where the deafening bass returned. Her feet froze suddenly. Inside the Inferno Suite she could see at least two of the handful of dancers from earlier. One of them was bruised and bleeding, smearing blood as they leaned against the glass, comforted by another one. Their eyes met and Rissa felt a silent plea for help in the dancer's eyes.

"I don't like to be kept waiting." His voice came, piercing the bass. With the image before her, his tone carried frightening connotations.

"The Ocean Suite is currently available." Rissa quickly gestured to an empty suite, raising her voice above the music. The drunkard's key was heavy in her pocket, it would be a matter of time until he woke up and if she didn't play this situation correctly there was a very high chance there'd be an unwelcome presence of security swarming the place. "Please get comfortable and I'll bring you some drinks."

She scanned for Gault again but could not see him. How was a man so atrocious at dancing so stealthy? It took her a moment to realise the noble hadn't actually moved, instead he just stared at her expectantly.

"And...?" He asked as if she'd missed something obvious.

"And?"

"You forget yourself, woman. You're talking to a *lord*."

A vein burst somewhere. She felt the comforting weight of her Conduit in her pocket and provided she was still in range of the Grandmaster brick in her locker she wanted nothing more than to scour this man with searing water. Somehow, she scraped a gritted smile together and a dainty, false laugh as she accentuated his title with a dangerously sarcastic tone. "Apologies, my lord."

Seemingly satisfied, the noble ignored her invitation to the Ocean Suite and returned to his preferred Inferno. He sat on the sofa, staring at her while the dancers cowered in the corner. Rissa glanced at them, apologising with her eyes before descending the steps to the staff area. Things were getting messy. She still had the key and could simply loot the drunkard's locker and leave. That was the pragmatic thing to do, she knew that. But it also didn't feel like the right thing to do. Gault was downstairs, waiting.

"Where did you go?" She hissed at him.

"Do I look like a member of staff?" He told her matter of factly. "The key - you have it?"

"I do." She patted her pocket, but Gault detected the hesitation in her. "But..."

"What?"

"There's scared women up there." The look of fear in the dancer's eyes came to her. "They need help."

"This is their job, isn't it?" He seemed confused, edging toward the barred door.

"Well, yes, but-" She cut herself off, unable to fathom a true explanation. She looked at Gault, watching the way he squinted at her, like he couldn't make sense of her thoughts and feelings. Eventually, she saw his face concede. He furled his fist, frustrated at her or himself she wasn't certain.

"His demands?"

"A drink."

"Get it. I'll take it to him." He pulled the chair away, gesturing to the door. "Then get what we came for. Meet me across the street."

She nodded and surged through the door back out into the throes of the dance floor. Perhaps he was trying to please her, to make amends for his actions within the Empty Eyes lair. Nobody had tried to enter the VIP room since she'd locked it, unsurprising, considering the clientele they would have had to deal with. The music surged as the night apexed. Security was out and about, patrolling the floor to break up fights and remove the inebriated from the premises. She would have loved to draw security upstairs and get the noble dealt with, but besides risking her own exposure, she knew that the violent patron could just throw a handful of Wreaths at the problem. Rissa stepped behind the bar again, flashing a strained smile to the frantic barmaids who were overwhelmed by a queue that ran three, four, even five rows deep.

She filled up a tankard with whichever keg was nearest and disappeared back into the VIP service area where she passed it to Gault. "Give me five minutes."

Gault nodded. Rissa felt a twist of guilt for adding unnecessary layers of jeopardy to the mission. Once they had an address for the drunk noble they would then have to break into his house and steal the invite. Any suspicion from anybody, be that Avatar security or the CIPD, could make that final step exceedingly difficult. She returned to the chaos of the dancefloor and made her way toward the exit, taking care to stay as deep in the crowd of bodies as possible. Towards the entrance of Avatar, where the snaking queue had now slithered into the building, there was a guarded area where personal belongings of nobility could be stored. A stocky guy was doubling as a bouncer and a security guard. He saw her coming immediately and raised an eyebrow at her.

"What are you doing here?" He asked, glancing past her for pursuers or for trouble. "Boss said you were suspended."

"I am. I was just leaving." She glanced past him, to the locked door and then had a fake glance worriedly over her shoulder. "There's some trouble at the back bar."

"Noble?"

"No! Some commoner, disturbing the nobility."

"Right." The security guard cracked his knuckles and offered her a smile. "I'll take care of this. Watch the door for a second."

"Thank you so much." She waited until the mass of tangled bodies absorbed him before entering the storage room. Locking the door behind her, she reached into her pocket for the key, feeling her hands shaking with anticipation. The key was tagged thirteen, so she shoved it into the corresponding steel locker and opened it. The smell of aftershave wafted from the open door. She swiftly opened a bag and rifled through it, coming away with a heavy wallet and a set of keys. She hunted for some I.D, finding a driver's licence stuffed into the folds of the faux-leather wallet with the name Graeme Waycrest. She took his I.D for his address and his front door key, shoving the rest back in the compartment and sliding the locker keys beneath the lockers themselves to be found as though they had been dropped.

Rissa slipped out, wishing a silent apology to the security guard for leaving his post unattended. She crossed the dancefloor to access the back of the house staff area. Reclaiming her backpack and the brick within, she swiftly changed back into her casual attire. Slinking out the building through the staff exit, she burst outside and stifled a laugh. That was her job as good as gone, but what the hell. She sprinted down the alley and crossed the street, seeking quiet refuge in a bus shelter across from Avatar. She breathed heavily as she sat and waited for Gault.

From the front entrance, the two bloodied dancers from upstairs suddenly ran out of the building and bolted down the street, swallowed by the hustle and bustle. Gault followed them shortly after, dumping his mask in a bin as he crossed the street. With a brisk pace they walked off, putting increasing distance between themselves and Avatar.

"And?" He looked at her expectantly. She waved the house key and I.D card at him, watching his face soften in relief.

"I see you took care of our friend." She pointed at his bloodied knuckles, purple and swollen from impact.

"He fell on his drink."

She laughed. "Lots of accidents tonight."

Gault grunted, humourless. "Where now?"

Graeme Waycrest's address sat in her hand. She knew the location decently enough and boded well for their chances of finding an invite to the noble rally. He was located on top of one of the tall skyscrapers close to Monument where many important people resided. All they had to do now was break into Graeme Waycrest's apartment and steal his invitation to the rally the next day.

All told, Rissa had enjoyed herself. There was an air of levity in her steps and the permeating fog that had felt like it was constricting her brain had been blasted away. She felt purposeful, like she was making a difference in some way. She had chosen this course of action for herself and that only made her feel more alive. She had been granted many opportunities to turn away, but had forged ahead, nonetheless. Completing the mission made her feel good. Slowly, she realised that at some point in the night she had stopped seeing Kren'shal's face on every surface, but what had changed in her? Rissa didn't know. Deep down, she knew that there was going to be more bloodshed, more violence. Gault had warned her that the deeds would warp her, but Rissa felt a sense of jurisdiction over everything she was doing. She knew who she was and what she was capable of.

This was what she had been waiting for.

4

Judging from the wariness creeping across Gault's face as the rising metallic chamber jostled and jolted, Rissa realised her darkly dressed companion had never seen a lift before. It was all very precarious as the gears clunked and steam hissed, but the doors opened without incident. She could feel his sigh of relief as they arrived on the top floor of a Band A apartment. They emerged to find a fantastic panoramic view of the City Centre, framed by a large window that stretched across the entire width of the spotless corridor. This was like another world. The air inside was fresh; the stale air purified by a whirring filter that pulled the clotted air in and stripped it of toxins. These devices were common in the City Centre, where the stale, industrial air of Forge Town encroached from the east into the delicate throats of the nobility. Every apartment boasted an entire floor to itself, including its own lavish entrance lobby, epitomising grandeur and opulence. It was a life steeped in pure luxury.

Graeme Waycrest's apartment door stood before them. Presumably empty, its owner likely still drooled into his empty cup at Avatar. The key clunked into the lock and the latch clicked. The door opened into a lavish lounge. Her feet were cushioned by a sandy carpet she could have slept on. Automatic lights instantly triggered, bathing the entire apartment in bright light. She froze and waited for cries of intrusion to fill the air, yet they did not. It wasn't a surprise to her that a noble seeking attention at a sleazy venue such as Avatar wasn't married. Striding in with confidence, she kept her voice low just for safety.

"Look for an envelope with a wax seal or the Royal Crest."

Gault nodded and entered. It was deathly silent as they tiptoed around, treading lightly on the carpet, the occasional groan of floorboards disturbing the peace. The apartment cut sharply around to the right, leading into an open kitchen which Gault explored first. Rissa went left, towards another door astride the lounge. She felt like her breathing was far too loud as the door creaked and she peeked in through the gap into some sort of library. Or at least that was her first thought. As she pushed open the door, the obliging light revealed a desk with a pot of ink, a quill and an empty bottle of alcohol. The faint smell of booze still lingered in the air as she stepped inside and sifted delicately through the various papers scattered across the desk, taking care to place them back exactly as she had found them. There was so much paperwork and old letters that Rissa was surprised nobles found any time to enjoy their wealth. An ornately framed photograph on the desk drew her attention and it took Rissa a moment to realise that they did not feature the dreary-eyed Graeme Waycrest. Instead, they depicted a woman, sharp-looking, nose like a battle axe and cheekbones that could cut glass. Pinned beneath the photograph was an opened envelope with the distinctive wax seal of The Crown disturbed upon the parchment. She grabbed it to see a card with gold lettering nestling inside – it was the secret ballot invitation she had been looking for. But it was not addressed to Graeme Waycrest, but rather a Marlowe Waycrest. Her eyes drifted again to the photograph of the important looking lady and Rissa realised that this name was likely the true influencer within this household.

Anxiety built in her stomach suddenly. It was nearly three in the morning and her presumed husband was wasting himself away in Avatar, so Marlowe herself could well be in the building. Rissa's blood turned to ice. Not all Versorcerers were nobles, but the opposite was always true. Harbouring The Algarethan Verse in their blood meant they were dangerous. Especially so in their own homes where magic was mercifully legal when used in self-defence.

Rissa was about to warn Gault when a steely voice echoed from down the hallway.

"Graeme?"

Almost immediately, Gault joined her, slinking into the room like a rodent, his eyes wide. She nodded at him; a wordless understanding that there was someone else in the apartment. If they were discovered, there was no chance of accomplishing their goal.

"Graeme? Is that you?" The voice was getting closer.

Gault closed the door to the office quietly, wincing as the old wood groaned. The automatic lights in the lounge flicked on, spilling a creeping silhouette underneath the door. The air changed and Rissa could feel the hairs on the back of her neck shimmer as the thrum of a Conduit beyond the office door drew nearer. Rissa crammed the card back into the envelope and pushed it into her pocket. She looked around the room, desperately seeking inspiration for an escape. Suddenly, the office was so claustrophobic. If they were caught here it would be a disaster. The only other way for them to get away with this was if…

She watched as Gault's hand fell to Akor'shaki, to violence. She hit him in the shoulder, shaking her head at him as the shadow beneath the door grew larger. He gave her an exasperated look, as though there was no other course of action but to kill the noble in her own home.

There had to be something else. Rissa whirled around the room, feeling the twist of vertigo in her stomach as her eyes fell upon the window. She unlatched it, lifting the bottom pane until it clicked open, allowing the distant throb of bass and blustering rainfall to invade the silence. The city was a dizzy blur of lights from so high up, a fatal fall for noble and commoner alike. Adrenaline surged through her, she grabbed Gault and dangled her legs out of the window, sitting on the windowsill with her heart hammering in her chest. He stared at her like she was insane, but steeled himself for his grim fate like only a man who had resigned himself to death long ago could.

"Graeme? What are you doing in there?!?"

The wind and the rain whipped through her hair and at some point she lost her own breathing to the noise of the elements. As the brass door handle twisted, Rissa plunged from the ledge, dragging Gault with her. They were lost to the rampant elements, tossing and spinning like leaves in a thunderstorm. Her bearings were lost instantly as the world pirouetted, revealing closing glimpses of the City Centre at every spin. She could feel Gault's vice grip on her wrist, squeezing the blood from the hand as death rushed up to catch them with concrete arms. Her weighted backpack did her no favours, pulling her quicker to the ground and destabilising her balance as she spun. As the embrace of buildings cowed them, Gault's grip faltered and he was suddenly sucked into the vacuum of the stormy winds as she continued to plummet.

"Gault!" His name distorted in the wind, and she closed her mind to him, thinking only of her own survival. Her Conduit comforted her, giving her the power and the control to think clearly. She was spinning too chaotically to blast a Geyser beneath her, but there were other ideas tumbling around her mind.

I invoke the Missing Sea. A Vortex; slow my momentum!

She created two linked portals. One atop a passing rooftop; the other directly into the concrete beneath her. As she plummeted, Rissa narrowed her body, straightening like an arrow as she dived towards the foaming Vortex in the concrete. The cold hands of death were cheated as she barrelled straight through it, emerging out onto the rooftop. The sudden inversion of gravity shifted her momentum forwards and she hit the ground like a skimmed stone, bouncing painfully in puddles of water and concrete. She felt her clothes tear and pain wrack her body. Her breath was expelled from her lungs as she crashed into a protruding air vent, indenting the steel with her bloodied form. She lay there for a moment, unsure if she was ever going to get her breath back and as her lungs drew in desperate gasps, she raised a trembling hand and fumbled nervously inside her pocket, her fingers meeting the sharp edge of the crumpled envelope. Despite the intense pain, she managed a wry smile of relief as she found the invitation intact.

"Never again." She tried to sit up, only to slump back into the indent she'd created. The urge to rest her eyes intensified and her entire body was stinging. She could see blood trickling from wounds on her legs where the concrete and stone of the rooftop had scoured the fabric of her jeans and cut deep into her skin. Her lower back throbbed and the pain was growing rapidly with every second from where her backpack had been crushed beneath her spine and the vent. With beleaguered grunts of pain, Rissa managed to remove the straps, anxiously unzipping the pack to find the Grandmaster brick split into two pieces from the impact.

"Gods, damn it." Frustrated, she stared at the two severed fragments in the bag. It wasn't broken, at least not entirely. A completely intact brick afforded her a huge field for magic whereas when split into two halves, they were greatly reduced. But even shattered into pieces, the brick was probably in better shape than she was at that moment.

Suddenly, a shadow fell over her. For a moment Rissa thought it was death, scorned by a denied prize, who had come to watch her fade away. Quickly however, violet eyes and a familiar grim expression told her it was someone else.

"You're bleeding." Gault observed.

"Really?" She couldn't help the sarcasm.

Gault peered into her backpack, his brows frowning upon seeing the broken brick. He glanced into her hand, where the envelope was clasped. "Well?"

She held up her hand weakly and passed it to him, watching with tired eyes as he placed the card on his thigh and smoothed out the creased corner as best as he could. His touch was surprisingly delicate and gentle with a refined poise not befitting of someone with such violent potential.

"Well done." He eventually said, sheltering the invitation from the rainfall and offering her a hand. "You did well."

—

A night of restlessness preceded the day of the ballot. Rissa tossed and turned in her bed. Her body flushed hot, then cold, breaking out into cold sweats that stuck the thin blanket to her skin. Her hand hurt, the scar upon it tingling with strain as though someone pulled freshly at the wound. The bright lights all the way from the City Centre that bled through her drawn blinds stung her eyes. Sleep evaded her when she needed her strength.

Yet when her eyes finally shut, she awoke immediately. But it wasn't her apartment she found herself in, but somewhere else entirely. It was different from her usual wistful dreams of places she would never see. This felt... different. She was aware of herself, yet as her body moved, it felt foreign to her own. To influence her movement was impossible, like trying to stop trembling hands from shaking. Her strides were longer, but she wasn't in control of them. It was as though her vision had been grafted onto someone else.

It was a summer's day suddenly. Rissa could still feel the sun on her skin and the freshest air in her lungs. Tall walls made up of large stone laid brick by brick laddered up around her, forming as though a great fog was peeling back layers of horizon for her to behold. Uneven cobbles rolled out underfoot as she walked down a market street. Stalls sprouted as far as the eye could see, selling crafts, fruits and vegetables, even a selection of fish. As the image completed, the body she had been affixed to marched ahead, uninterested in the stock of food despite Rissa's desperation to investigate. Ahead of them, mantling the horizon of old slate rooftops stood a great castle. It dominated her vision, sprawling out to cast a protective shadow of the populace. Those who looked upon seemed to do so with a smile on their face and light in their eyes. Even from here, she could see the glimmer of armour patrolling the long battlements and movement from within the tall panes of glass that decorated the watchtowers.

People she didn't know smiled at her, waving loaves of freshly baked bread and sewn garments from over the stalls. Their lips moved, but no words came from their mouths. Her nostrils were touched by the scent of the bakery and her stomach churned in desire to tear the hunk of bread to pieces and devour it. Blacksmiths struck iron upon an anvil; Rissa could feel the heat emanating over her body. One of them, forehead wrapped in a sweat-clogged rag turned and waved, brandishing a freshly forged blade, still hot from the fire. Once again, the lips moved but Rissa wasn't privy to what was spoken.

But there was something that shared the horizon with the palace. It stuck out unnaturally against the rest of the castle, looking more like a gnarled branch that twisted up into the air from the courtyard and scratched at the air above it. What was it? But the sight was quickly drowned out by the idyllic sights and smells that she was treated to further down the market. Rissa wanted to see more, to somehow gain control of this body and explore this fantastic, vibrant city for herself. But quickly, she could feel the edges of her vision stretch and warp, as though whatever connection she had formed with this body was being broken. She tried to hang on, to cling to whatever senses she could but the pull was too powerful.

Rissa woke up in her grungy apartment. The scar on her hand burned again and she massaged her palm. Things were just as she had left them. Rising, she ate breakfast quickly. Her body was tired, somehow drained from her dream. She feasted on a small plate of toast with imitation strawberry preserves spread thinly on top, washed down with a large mug of strong coffee. She had offered some to Gault, but he continued to refuse any hospitality from her. She didn't think him intending to be rude; but rather something else that drove him to refuse comfort. Rissa had allowed him to sleep on the sofa of her apartment, although she wasn't certain that he slept at all. When she had doused the lights goodnight he had been sitting in turbulent reflection and by the time she wrenched her eyes open in the morning he had not moved.

They left Ocean's View and walked their regular commute to the Downtown Central Station. By now, Gault had become used to it. Whereas before he had fidgeted and tensed, clinging desperately to the support beams overhead for balance he now stood coolly, adjusting his balance to the warbling of the rails as she did. She felt like a proud parent watching a toddler's first steps.

Before the ballot later that evening they had one stop to make. Rissa didn't own a single piece of clothing that would be considered acceptable at a noble event. Her wardrobe selection was limited to a few pairs of old jeans, several coloured tees, her jacket and the same waterlogged trainers. Suffice to say, old jeans wouldn't cut it in high society. And so, their first destination was Grayson Plaza; an all-purpose shopping centre on the border of the City Centre and the ramshackled streets of Forge Town to the east. Rissa hadn't paid her rent yet, but heading out to the City Centre to buy finery was going to be the nail in the coffin on her apartment. They would seize it within days and that was a lucky estimate, so she had to prepare for the worst. Once they had crashed the rally, she could cover a few days of storage for her few precious items, such as her books that detailed animals and plants of the old-world pre-Reckoning. Any of the others she had resigned to being owned by The Crown once they came knocking. She didn't have a plan in mind for where she would eat or sleep. While still owning a key to her father's apartment, she wanted to keep that as a last-ditch option if all else failed. Maybe she could pick up a thing or two about not sleeping from Gault if they succeeded.

A trip on the Downtown Line then a transfer onto the Blood Line got them to the dedicated Plaza Station. Even as they stepped out of the station and walked through the eastern area of the City Centre, the quality of air felt distinctly inferior. It was thick in her mouth, burning her lungs like she was snorting from an aerosol. She felt the need to clear her throat growing. This was the encroaching industrial smoke that desecrated the City Centre from the neighbouring area of the city known as Forge Town. It was well overdue for the attention of the Wind Versorcerers who frequently blew it back to the edge of the city and made a good load of Wreaths doing so.

Once upon a time, Forge Town was the heartland of trade and industry pre-Reckoning. In the years since, it had been neglected; the tradespeople left jobless due to no materials with which to produce anything. The desolate factories, long abandoned, had stopped spewing the toxic smoke that had ushered in the acceleration of Centa Isla's technology, yet the invasive smog stayed like a virus, spreading and seemingly never truly fading away. The footpaths in the eastern City Centre were empty as people took taxis, buses or just drove themselves, taking advantage of the air filters in the vehicles. There was only one station in the entirety of Forge Town, despite it taking up almost a half of the entire floating city.

Yet only a few paces away from the border stood Grayson Plaza. It was a premier destination for shopping in Centa Isla, named after the newborn heir to the throne upon its construction. That newborn heir now ran the city. It was not nearly as tall as Monument but was easily the widest building in the entire city, spanning the length of several blocks that could easily house a couple of thousand if renovated into homes. Instead, it sat there, blinding everyone with its endless neon lights that pierced the dull fog like the old, fabled lighthouses that would once upon a time guide ships away from crags and stony shores. If you wanted it, Grayson Plaza had it. Multiple stories of shops and trades. Rissa remembered being excited by it as a child, walking the dimly lit hallways, drawn like a moth to the bright lights of the storefronts. In her cynical later years, she surmised that it was all a marketing trick; the dark corridors intentional so that the luminescent storefronts and the stock they sold drew the eye more easily. The nobility claimed it was a measure to save power, but by the neon-lit extravaganza of the exterior, she knew that was a load of nonsense. Bodies poured in and out of Grayson Plaza at all hours of the day. It was a constant wheel of motion. Built so close to the trading area of Forge Town, the presence of the monolithic shopping centre single-handedly killed the careers of many independent tradespeople. Some embraced the neon lights and would bid insane volumes of Wreath to secure a profitable spot inside the plaza whereas others refused, ultimately condemning themselves and their business to a slow death in the throes of the smog.

Smithy's Lung was the condition caused by excessive exposure and inhalation to the century old industrial fumes. It caused coughing fits that progressively grew worse until you were choking up blood from the damage caused by the heaving of the chest. It was a slow, depressing way to go. Deaths were uncommon, yet never a surprise, particularly those weak of body.

The inside of Grayson Plaza was fitted with hundreds of air purifiers. As they entered the gargantuan doors, joining with the stream of foot traffic that surged in and out at all hours of the day, the air felt like a desert oasis after just a short walk outside. Rissa inhaled it in long breaths, already feeling her lungs healing from the damage. Gault maintained his usual reserved demeanour but also breathed deeper, squinting at all the bright lights. He was taking his time adjusting to Centa Isla, it seemed. Packed Subrail carriages, bright lights and vehicle horns had defined much of his time here. It was a sensory assault that she understood all too well. She hoped to one day take him to her scaffolding perch and show him the quiet side of the city.

A large map of the plaza sat at the entrance. They waited patiently for the crowd to disperse before taking a look. Gault baulked at the size of the place.

"Immense." He muttered, eyes following her finger as she traced the various stores, searching for a clothier of some sort. It didn't really matter which one she chose - she was going to be broke after this anyway.

"Alright, follow me." She said, settling on *Royal Threads*, a clothier only a floor up from them.

She led Gault through Grayson Plaza. The halls were as dim as she remembered, making the stores look so bright and interesting that the dumb part of her brain just wanted to wander off and explore. The crowd was dense and full of shoppers, the escalators that led up to each floor rammed with shuffling bodies. There was a restaurant on the second floor where Fire Versorcerers walked among the tables, sautéing expensive food over a flame held in their own palm. The flickering flames mesmerised the eagerly salivating patrons. Rissa had always wanted to eat there! Once all this was over she would indulge for sure and enjoy a hearty meal. The meat was said to actually be real and was freshly frozen from before the Reckoning. Suffice to say, it was the most expensive meal in the city reserved only for those who could afford it. But nobody questioned the price. Savouring every tantalising mouthful, this real meat was a wondrous feast, beyond comparison to the rubbery garbage churned out by Resynthesis and labelled "meat." It had made her ill one too many times for her to continue eating it. The tantalising aroma of the freshly seared venison pleasured her nostrils and made her mouth water as the enticing aromas from the kitchen wafted through the plaza. As she ascended a spiralling stairwell, she felt nervous as *Royal Threads* appeared in front of her. A violet and gold exterior, much like the colours that decorated the standard of The Crown. She could see gaudy dresses displayed in the window, far too revealing or far too obnoxious for her to ever see herself in. A part of her just wanted to chance wearing her ripped jeans and a smart shirt at the event but she knew that if this was going to work she needed to blend in, even if that meant dressing out of her comfort zone. She stepped inside, ignoring the degrading looks from the snooty staff members as she poked around.

Gault pulled out a few pieces for her, showing a surprising interest in glamour for someone dressed so bleary. She turned them all away for their wanton extravagance. Eventually, she found a tidy, navy-blue dress. It was simple and efficient, made from the finest imitation silk that had been put through Resynthesis multiple times to achieve the look and feel of the real thing. She thought it matched her hair well and while a little on the shorter side, a pair of tights would complete the look and conceal her injuries. A glance at the price tag resulted in a sharp intake of breath and she gingerly handed it to the counter and slowly counted out the last of her rent money.

They had plenty of time to spare, so Rissa decided to walk around the plaza for a little bit longer. She had never given a tour before and was enjoying Gault's reactions to the various storefronts. They passed by coffee shops, jewellery stores, restaurants and even a small theatre for muses and artists to express their work. Censorship seemed to dominate much of the performances, topics such as the King-Regent and current affairs seemingly skirted around, but people seemed to enjoy it, nonetheless.

They eventually left Grayson Plaza, plunging back into the toxic air. They took the Subrail back to her apartment to prepare.

—

Her orders were quite simple. Locate the traitorous Brand of the Scout and his new companion and eliminate them. The order came from her brother; Azrael and she knew all too well that a second failure was not going to be tolerated.

Lachesis had found them quickly. Her network of skittering rodents only grew with every sunrise as they carried her Brand of the Watcher's influence into a nest and spread her vision to others. Forge Town and its old streets were highly populated and on the approach to Grayson Plaza, she had felt a twinge in the back of her mind as one of her rodent scouts sought to inform her of its discovery. She had praised the little creature, massaging its brain through the crystal ball she kept in her quarters as reward.

Yet, she did not inform her brother of their location as he may have wished. Instead, she just waited. Galleo et'al was an all-mighty entity, able to contact her and inflict wanton pain via the very Brand that gave her power. But for all of its might, it couldn't read her mind. Insubordination was quickly and painfully dealt with, yet she wasn't foolish enough to truly defy the Dark One. She was just curious. Centa Isla was like no city she had seen conquered before. The towers that reached for the heavens, the lights, the technology. There was more potential here than she had ever seen and in truth, she deemed it a damned shame that it all needed to be destroyed.

Besides, she got to do all of this from the comfort of her luxurious quarters within Monument. As sister to the new Seat of Earth upon the Elemental Council, she had been granted a tremendous view of the city, a four-poster bed and a great, ornate mirror that she had thrown a sheet over. She lounged upon the bed even now, musing over the emptiness of her bespoke wine glass before ringing the servants bell above her bedchamber.

Lachesis smiled. While her brother and the King-Regent were off playing politicians. She had the place to herself.

—

Upon choosing to buy an outfit instead of sending off her rent, Rissa knew her apartment at Ocean's View would soon be seized and re-issued to another. Rissa packed a box. She dusted the old leatherbound covers from her favourite books from her childhood, taking a moment to flick nostalgically through the pages of each one before placing it carefully into the box.

"I loved this one." Rissa had Gault pass her the books down from the shelf as she sat on the hardwood floor. The one he handed her now was a historical counting of the mythical creatures that had once walked the land before Reckoning. She opened the old pages, coughing as a plume of dust exploded into her face. Had it truly been so long since she had read these? The pages had faded slightly, as had the childish scribbles she had written into the margins. Words like "cool", and some awful drawings covered most of the pages. There were so many creatures lost to time that it almost felt like reading pure fiction. She turned idly, smiling to herself. A glimmer of the childlike wonder returned as a small warmth in her chest as she found a page decorated very generously by her childhood crayons. A bear.

Gault was suddenly over her shoulder, squinting down at the book that she had been so absorbed in. "What have you done?"

"Excuse me? I was, like, six." She showed him the bear and all her childish musings. "I guess I was drawn to it or something."

"This... isn't a bear." Gault took the book from her hands with a delicacy that she appreciated very much, letting it sit in his hands. It was like he knew how much these old dusty pages meant to her. The flash of a smile crossed his face. "This is a boar."

"It's a what?" She stood up abruptly, as if he was wrong and looked down at the book. "What's that?"

Gault let out a small laugh. She had no idea what was so funny but was so taken aback by the small snort that he let out that she swore her mind was playing tricks.

"What the hell are you laughing at!?"

He pointed at the title of the page; the word Boar had been scribbled over enough times it had become illegible. A jagged smile tugged at his lips, like his muscles didn't know how to make such a face. "You thought this was a bear?"

A twist of embarrassment crossed her face. She felt her cheeks burn. "Man, how am I supposed to know? Do you see any bears walking around!?"

His small smile faded quickly, replaced by a look of pity that filled his eyes as he looked at her. Dropping down to a deep squat, he took a small pen from her coffee table and gestured it towards the book. "May I?"

"S-sure." She hadn't seen this side of him before. There was something genuine about him as he knelt on the wood floor, tongue sticking slightly out the side of his mouth as he concentrated on whatever he wrote onto the old pages of her book. It was a bizarre interaction, but not entirely unwelcome relief from their impending mission.

"Here." He pulled away, returning her pen to the table. There was a small drawing in the margin of the page where her old crayons hadn't yet claimed. It was a bristly-looking creature, big and shaggy with a small snout. "A bear."

"Didn't tell me you were such an artist."

"They bob for fish at the riverside." He looked at his own drawing, eyes glazing over as if to recall a memory. "They're quick for their size and will attack humans if provoked."

"Sounds dangerous."

"Very." He stood up, seemingly content with himself as he seated himself slowly on the sofa. His violet eyes drifted across her apartment, taking in every dark corner and bit of furniture. When he spoke, it was with melancholy. "You're giving all this up."

"It came furnished." She admitted, sliding the heavy box of books to the front door. "It's been good to me, though."

Gault nodded slowly. "... Thank you."

"What are you thanking me for?" Her tone was full of surprise.

He bowed his head. "I'm not sure."

"I've been waiting for something like this my whole life." Perhaps he felt guilty that she was letting her apartment get repossessed. Perhaps he felt responsible, or that he'd roped her into this dark mission. The reality couldn't have been further from the truth. With the danger they were soon heading into, there was no time for doubt.

"I chose this." She reassured him. "Whatever happens, good or bad, it was my decision. That's all I ever wanted."

"You sound just like an old friend of mine." Gault slowly leaned back on the sofa, resting his neck on the cushion and staring absently at the ceiling.

"What was their name?"

"Kadin Krayt." His voice broke slightly as he said the name, as though it carried with it such a weight of emotion that his body physically reacted to it being spoken. "He was a good person. Thought he was making all the right decisions."

Rissa wasn't sure whether to speak. It felt as though a rare crack had formed in the hardy exterior that Gault presented, so she didn't want to lose this moment with a clumsy question. When she finally did ask, she did so with a gentle tone. "What happened to him?"

He didn't reply straight away. For a long moment Rissa wasn't sure that he had even heard her.

"He died when Galleo et'al arrived." Gault whispered. "With the rest of them."

"I'm sorry." Rissa couldn't comprehend it but apologised all the same. "That must be a lot to deal with."

They sat in solemn silence until Gault spoke again.

"I won't let it happen again." He sat up, his violet eyes blazing with victory fire. "Not to your city."

"You care more than me." She mused, allowing a small chuckle. It wasn't strictly true but was an entertaining thought.

As the evening rolled around, Rissa and Gault made their way back into the City Centre, to the old Guild Hall nestled comfortably beneath the tall shadow of Monument where the event was to be hosted. She hadn't changed yet, her dress folded carefully into her backpack as they loitered a few streets away. Crowds were out in force, chanting protests and vitriol that could be heard several blocks away. In equal measure, the CIPD were out, patrolling the streets and cordoning off huge sections of road around the Guild Hall for the sole use of the nobility. There was twisted excitement in the air. This was the first time that King-Regent Grayson Clovis was leaving Monument for as long as anybody could remember. There was veiled hope that good news would be announced, although Rissa knew better than to believe any word that came from the mouth of the Clovis family.

One thing that she had not expected this evening was to be told the basics of noble etiquette by Gault of all people. As she changed behind a dumpster he stood guard, waffling on about posture and confidence, hand gestures and where to stand in a circle of people. She listened intently but wasn't sure how much she would actually remember. Moreover, she wanted to know how he knew any of this in the first place.

"Where did you even learn this?" She put her thoughts to words, pulling the straps of the dress up over her shoulders. She'd found an old pair of black tights in her drawers at home only to now find them with more ladders than a construction site. Without the funds for some nice shoes, she was stuck with her usual beat-up trainers. She didn't look the part of a noble at all, which only made it all the more important that she actually soaked up Gault's advice.

"A friend of mine worked with the royal family back home." He grunted. "Hard to not pick up a thing or two."

She spun her wheels to recall his name. "Kadin, was it?"

A grunt of confirmation. "He attended all of their political ventures. And there were many."

"Well, I can't think of anything worse." Rissa stepped out from behind the dumpster, pulling at the hem of the dress. She'd slapped some makeup on before leaving, although had found most of her materials crusted and oxidised from lack of use. She had applied some old lipstick to add purpose to her lips and some eyeshadow that she hoped gave her a more striking look than she would have had normally. "I'm dreading this."

"Just keep calm. I'll be waiting for your signal."

"You got it." She assessed her image in a closed shop window. Turning to Gault, she drew her back up and straightened her figure, channelling the vestigial influence of someone who had a steel rod perpetually shoved up their arse. "What do you think?"

"Unconvincing."

"Alright, thanks." She slouched back down. There had been a hope that maybe he'd say something nice. Her makeup had been applied quickly and clumsily, but without being conceited she thought she looked pretty stunning in the shop window. Her blue hair played to her advantage for once, allowing her to play into the expected look of a Versorcerer that would allow her to blend in. "Let's just get this done."

She left Gault by the alley as she crossed over three streets toward the old Guild Hall. It was a gorgeous building, even she had to admit it. Apparently it predated Monument and just about every other building in the entire city save for the old chapel in Forge Town. The historical texts in Grandmaster believed it was the original building that Centa Isla was built around. Of course, it had been maintained over the years, upgraded where necessary to maintain health and safety for practical use but the spirit of it remained. Gorgeous stone spires and stained-glass windows that well encapsulated the freedom of creativity in the days pre-Reckoning. Few who were not nobility ever got to see inside these days which made this doubly exciting. The old building was under heavy watch. The CIPD had built their perimeter directly around the old building, creating a well-maintained queue of invitees. It wasn't just the red uniforms of the law enforcers that stood watch however, but also the radiant golden plated armour of the Kingsguard - the personal military and guardforce of King-Regent Grayson Clovis himself.

If it wasn't serious before, it certainly was now.

Rissa felt her hands go clammy as she approached the taped barrier through a dense crowd of citizens. Barred from going any closer by a CIPD blockade, they chanted vitriol, demanding answers and information on the state of the city. Their voices were loud, raised not just in anger but also in crippling fear. She understood where those shouts really came from. She flashed her invitation to one of the many officers who watched the perimeter. His eyes flashed with recognition, and he lifted the tape so that she could duck beneath.

"Noble whore!" Voices followed her which surprisingly offered her encouragement. If the masses believed she was nobility then that was surely a good omen for what was to come.

As she approached the Guild Hall entrance, the Kingsguard presence multiplied. They stood at the gate, individually assessing a tall queue of muttering, impatient nobility who seemed outright furious that they were not taken at their word for being invited. She took her place at the back of the queue which quickly filled behind her. The line moved slowly, further adding to the vexation of the nobility.

"They're taking our Conduits." Mused one of the voices behind her, slick and regal. "I say, where is the trust?"

Rissa tuned into the various conversations happening around her. It dawned quickly that many of the invited nobility already knew one another intimately. Conversations of old friends and lovers filled her ears. She felt quite isolated, as though standing alone and being quiet was somehow drawing more attention than being already half drunk and boisterous.

"Like I care. I'm just here for the drinks."

"What time does this finish?"

"Our vote doesn't mean a thing."

"Grayson shall deliver us all."

A real mixed bag here. Rissa wiped her sweaty palms on her dress as the queue bumped her closer to the searching Kingsguard. When her turn finally came around, she swore her makeup was dripping down her face like a wax candle. From so close to the entrance of the Guild Hall she could smell the perfume and aftershave drifting out of the lobby. Twin spears fell in front of her, obstructing the entrance. Two Kingsguard knights towered over her. Their faces weren't visible beneath the brilliant golden helmets, but when one spoke his voice was demanding and intolerant.

"Invitation."

Rissa placed the card in his plated hand. It was checked over not by one, but two of the guardsmen. They then searched her with a strange device. It spat small columns of steam as it was waved over her body, seeming to come up inconclusive. As per their plan, her Conduit and brick were currently in Gault's possession.

"Welcome, Lady Waycrest. The Crown recognises you."

The spears lifted and Rissa just smiled at them, not willing to give herself away with some idiotic comment. As she strode through the gates and up the bumpy cobblestone path, she let out a sharp breath of relief. As she entered the Guild Hall, she tried her best to hide her awe as she looked up and around the gorgeous interior. Simple, yet so expressive. Everything felt like it was in the perfect place, making the building look as though it had come straight out of a painting with its ornate walls and beautiful refractions of light that came through the stained windows. The main hall was long, wide and tiered. A staircase on either end of the hall led up to a walkway that skirted the interior of the building. Already, it had been populated by nobles who sipped drinks and looked down at the newcomers, no doubt making unwelcome observations and snarky comments. Servants walked the floor, carrying finger portions of food that she didn't even recognise. Drinks were readily available from just about every orifice of the building, laid out glass by glass on a table with a violet tablecloth that bore the crest of The Crown. Rissa took a glass of wine. Vineyards no longer existed post-Reckoning and so the drink she held was actually incredibly valuable. So much so that she felt a little bit of an impostor even bringing it to her lips for a small taste. She'd never drank wine before; even likely watered down as it was, the taste was sharp and freezing, coursing down her throat like some sort of chemical. For risk of looking immensely out of place, she opted to just carry the glass, rather than drink it. She continued to mill around, honing her hearing the same way she would at Avatar when trying to decipher the orders. Her ears pricked for any bits of gossip as voices bounced off the echoing walls of the old building with its poor acoustics.

Rissa imagined her mother in this very room when she was young. She tried to emulate how she remembered her, walking with confidence and power, an easy smile ready at a moment's notice. She returned her attention to the flutter of conversations going on around her.

"Just kill the commoners. Less mouths to feed." Someone slurred, practically drooling as they spoke. A collection of empty glasses surrounded him. "Resource Crisis no more. Right?"

Rissa glanced at the small group, three nobles total, leaning against a tall table in the back corner of the large hall. Their conversation was morbid, yet curiosity beckoned her close.

"I, for one, don't know why we stopped looking beyond the smog." The second noble wondered aloud, "Are we truly so certain that we are alone?"

"Verscience has been busy, that's why." Spoke the third, an older man. "I can't even get a hold of my grandson for a second. They're working him to the bone."

Rissa's brow crinkled. She knew it wasn't relevant to her task, but she wanted to know more. Approaching the table, she offered a small smile to the trio. She spoke with confidence about something that she had no idea about. "What do you think is beyond the veil?"

One of them, older, shrugged slightly. "Bit of this, bit of that. Who can say?"

She pressed. "Do you think it's possible we're not alone?"

"Once upon a time I maybe could have told you. Back when being nobility used to mean something." To that, the third noble just shrugged, musing fingers through his grey beard. "These days we just settle the worthless debates the King-Regent and his council can't agree on. More of the same today, I'd bet."

By the way they spoke and the respective ages of the group she got the feeling that she was speaking to a different generation of nobility, ones who were used to making a difference and had some degree of disdain for the current state of the city and its new generation of stuck-up nobles. Rissa wished them a good evening and returned to the crowds, intent on avoiding any further distractions. It didn't take her long to spot low riding cloaks that bore the sigil of Grandmaster. The academy professors had gathered, stood in an incestuous circle, disinterested in discussion with anybody but themselves. Curiosity got the best of her, and she approached, curious to see whether she recognised any of them from her time at Grandmaster. The hall was filling up rapidly as she stepped in and around crowds of chattering nobles. She used them as cover to peer in on the Grandmaster social circle. She instantly recognised the High Priestess of Grandmaster, Cordelia Rowe, from her powerful presence alone. Despite her standing as the most powerful Versorcerer in Centa Isla, even she had to have her Conduit taken away. She was older than she looked, Rissa knew that by the sheer amount of years she had been in charge, but her true age was a mystery. Of all the nobility present, she wondered how many had come and gone through the gates of Grandmaster to be here. By the amount of bodies shuffling closer to the congregation of professors, desperate to see if they were remembered, she assumed that this was numerous. So many years on from their graduation, she wondered how apt they would be with magic if a Conduit was suddenly put on their finger. With the heavily policed use of The Algarethan Verse post-Reckoning she imagined they would be extremely rusty if called upon in an emergency. She kept her distance, unwilling to fall into the radar of the High Priestess. As she passed the Grandmaster gathering, she spotted him.

An Omen. The handsome one who she had doused in sewage. She remembered his name as Jace.

Instantly, she averted her gaze, should anyone have noticed her wide look of surprise. Relaxing her expression, she watched him discreetly, touching her glass to her lips. She noted his deep, sandy skin and perfect complexion, the head of oily black hair that fanned like flames with every grand gesture that accompanied his practised smile. More troubling than the mere presence of an Omen was the fact that he wore the academic robes of Grandmaster attributed only to the professors and faculty. How had he managed to ascertain such a role so quickly? Surely it was more than his silver tongue?

Rissa recalled her encounter with him. Had there been a Conduit upon his finger? She couldn't remember seeing one. It was deeply troubling that the Omens were somehow entrenched in the most closeted community Centa Isla had ever seen. Regardless, she already had enough justification to signal Gault ahead of time and so she turned her back to the group and approached the outdoor pavilion, exiting through bespoke doors out into a large garden heavily patrolled by CIPD and Kingsguard. She made her way toward the furthest fence where a clearing of artificial grass separated them from the rampaging public. She wondered if her father was amongst the swathe of officers holding back the repressed rage of citizens left utterly in the dark. Gault had scouted the garden from the surrounding rooftops, it being the only area of the old Guild Hall he could get a clear view at from far away. She scanned those same rooftops now, searching for him, but couldn't see him. There was an ornate white bench, coloured neutral and painfully sterile. She sat upon it and crossed her legs. They had schemed this plan on the go as they made their way back into the City Centre just before the evening had started. If Omens were present, she would cross her legs. If not, she would sit normally. She just hoped that Gault could see her from whichever rooftop he nestled. Nerves pricked her skin. Things were going to get chaotic within the next hour or so. She was unarmed currently, accepting that she wouldn't have made it through the search with a Conduit let alone two chunks of Grandmaster brick. Gault was going to bring her backpack and Conduit which would at least give her a fighting chance.

Attacking Jace would mark them as criminals and as he was now a clearly established and popular member of Grandmaster, the Omen was privy to great protections that Kren'shal hadn't had. But she was ready for this. Rissa had always existed on the edge of the law but had never crossed the line enough to serve any kind of significant time that her father couldn't get bail for. But those had been small crimes, petty thefts, public brawling and unlawful spellcasting. They had all been done not out of malicious intent or even desperation, but more to be put in front of her Father so that he may acknowledge her existence at all. It was pathetic to think about and she felt a blaze of anger that she had ever been so desperate for his affection. What they were about to do was real. This would show him the price of his absence. The officer's daughter; a criminal.

Suddenly the door to the pavilion opened and the noise of the inside spilled out into the outdoor air. Rissa felt a powerful presence approach, turning her blood frosty in immediate recognition of Cordelia Rowe. She lit up an ornate cigarette, dusty auburn hair billowing in the breeze. She stared wordlessly out at the angry mob that had surrounded the venue. Rissa didn't dare say a word for fear of being recognised. Many times she had found herself in the office of the High Priestess, waiting quietly for the penance of her misbehaviour to be delivered, the final one being what removed her from Grandmaster for good.

"Their anger is all too justified." Watching the flashing sirens marshalling the mob beyond the garden, Cordelia took a long drag of a cigarette. "Too many mistakes that they've had to pay for."

Realising she was being spoken to, Rissa kept herself neutral. She avoided eye contact, staring off into the distance, disinterested. "What would you have done differently?"

"What would I have done?" She laughed quaintly. After a smoke, she continued. "It hardly matters now. The cycle is coming to an end."

"Cycle? You mean this event?" Rissa asked. As they spoke, her confidence steadily grew that the Headmistress of Grandmaster had little room in her memory for dropouts. She felt a little bit silly.

Cordelia laughed, so harshly that it was startling.

"Of course not. I mean the cycle of reinvention that this city has been going through for years." She smiled, despite the ominous, doomed words that escaped her lips. "The world ended with the Reckoning. We just live in the ruins thereafter on stolen time."

"You don't think there's hope?"

"Not anymore." She spoke gravely, but her tone betrayed excitement. "And if there was - we do not deserve it. The price for meddling with the natural order is yet unpaid."

"Shouldn't we be trying to prevent that?" Rissa humoured the conversation but was really fully invested in hearing more. There was something in this conversation that unsettled her. Something more than just her concern of being recognised. "So much has been built-"

"This city has always been on a doomed course." She interrupted herself with a curt laugh, raising her wine glass into the sky as a toast to seemingly nobody. "Trying to control that will only come at a cost to you."

Rissa still didn't look her way, yet she could feel the High Priestess's eyes boring into the back of her head. There was an intensity to her gaze that Rissa felt shredded through her facade. Did she know?

"Enjoy your evening. Don't swoon too easily over the words of our King-Regent."

"T-thank you." Rissa waited as the Headmistress took a final draw from what remained of her cigarette and strode away, every movement in her body practised and refined like a well-rehearsed performance. What a tiring way to live. Was everybody here so pessimistic as to the city's future? Rissa thought of her mother, how she had always believed in hope for the future of Centa Isla. With the crowd like she had seen tonight, she imagined her mother must have been a grating figure. Someone who had never given herself up to the rampant nihilism that was rooted so deeply in the nobility. A grim smile crossed her face. Perhaps the nihilism had got to her mother eventually too, enough so to leave a husband and daughter behind without so much as a word. She sat cross-legged for another couple of minutes before heading back inside, suddenly feeling defeated. It was like a cloud had come over her, diluting the scant purpose and blast of colourful emotions, good and bad, that she had felt over the past few days. If the nobility of the city didn't even believe in a future for Centa Isla - then what good was doing all of this? Why not let Galleo et'al claim the place and be done with it? She didn't have an answer just yet but was too entrenched to turn back or change her mind. After several minutes of mindlessly wandering the hall eavesdropping and looking about the place there was a sudden bell that wrenched the attention of the nobility towards the front of the hall where a pedestal had been erected yet was currently unattended.

"Please, be seated. The King-Regent will speak with you all now."

Rissa obeyed, taking up an inconspicuous seat at the very back corner. Rows of chairs had been brought out by servants, the rows steadily getting filled. Surprisingly, it seemed like the attendance was much lower than anticipated. Empty chairs decorated one in every several rows. Of the missing nobles, she wondered what caused their absence. Perhaps an indifference to the wheel of politics - or perhaps an internal protest against the King-Regent's governance? Rissa didn't know. But one thing was for sure. When the King-Regent did reveal himself, those present began to clap.

Something didn't feel right.

—

Gault bided his time. He paced patiently back and forth across the tallest rooftop he could find adjacent to the old Guild Hall. Impatience gnawed at his psyche, carried by the dark wishes of Akor'shaki who swayed erratically at his side.

She'll be killed. The blade's voice sounded in his mind, as though a natural born thought. Telling the difference between them had become difficult lately. "She'll be fine." He muttered.

Are you sure?

He wasn't. Rissa was capable, he knew that, but she didn't understand the true scale of the threat at hand. The rooftop on which he had perched offered an undisturbed view of the pavilion just outside the old hall. They had agreed on a plan, his part in all this now was to just wait.

Just gatecrash the place.

The urge streaked down his spine as chills, enough to make him shudder. But he pushed it down. They had a plan. He was going to stick to it. Once already he had surrendered himself to darkness; not again. Rissa wouldn't trust him a second time and it was her knowledge that had got them this far.

"Ridiculous."

Is it? We do not have time to spend waiting.

He paced quicker, pumping his arms to keep the blood rushing through his body and his brain. This was the first time he had been alone with his thoughts with nothing to do but sit and wait. Rissa had been a welcome distraction to the droning of Akor'shaki that throbbed incessantly in his head.

Gault looked at the guarded perimeter. The soldiers that Rissa had identified as 'Kingsguard' were familiar to him. Looking at them brought him a degree of comfort, harkening his mind back to days gone by, allowing him to find a glimpse of familiarity in the bright lights and deafening noise that was Centa Isla. A part of him enjoyed the carnage, his surroundings finally aligning with the chaos inside his own mind.

Gault. There was a pulsing in his head as his blade sought to contact him, like the first few seconds of a migraine. It went just as quickly as the words were put into his mind.

"What?"

The blade often spoke louder than he, dominating his mind and every effort to shut it out. But beneath the shared space of his mind, Akor'shaki was his ally. It was their shared bargain, their mutual desire to destroy Galleo et'al that granted him strength. His speed, enhanced regeneration and agility were all gifted to him by the dark power that had brought the blade to life upon their union. Without the blade, he was nothing.

She wants to talk.

The wind blew gently, yet the breeze was arctic on his skin and carried with it a deep-rooted chill that scoured at his bones, making him want to curl up into a ball.

"I can't talk now." He fixed his gaze on the pavilion ahead of him, pleading for Rissa to give him a signal so that he may escape what was to come. The dead made their wishes known to him often. They had a right to request it and he had a duty to listen. In order to atone for his failure, he had grown accustomed to it.

You know that's not how it works.

The wind blew again. Colder. He felt frost creeping in the atmosphere around him. He started to realise how quickly he was breathing only when he started to see it in front of him.

"I-I need a minute."

You don't have it. Breathe. Prepare yourself.

His ears twitched. Near or far he couldn't tell, yet there were footsteps. Hundreds, plated, marching in sync like the rhythmic beating of a drum. They travelled below him, and he peered over the edge of the building, seeing nothing but the gathered collective of CIPD and Kingsguard. He recognised the rhythmic marching, but the growing intensity within his skull pushed the memory away with it.

She's here.

The city had frosted over, the rooftops faded blue with the wicked embrace of winter. The lights of the City Centre on the horizon had died, bathing the city in a pitch dark. Soft blue light came from the sky and Gault looked up. Faces had formed in the overcast sky, their faces as thunderous as the black storm that brewed within them. They judged him, no words on their lips but the scorn in their clouded eyes sticking him like daggers. He turned only to find himself surrounded. Faceless figures, twisted and broken, swarmed him. Their bones cracked and snapped as they stumbled in place, barely able to balance on their violated bodies. He remembered them. These were friends and family. Their faces would have been familiar had they not been scrubbed smooth, their defining features scoured away until nothing remained but a flat, fleshy mound that writhed as though they were desperate to scream yet had no mouth through which to do it. They wore clothes he vaguely recognised, although they were ripped and bloodied.

You're alright. Let them know you're sorry.

He obeyed Akor'shaki. They often disagreed, but for these moments where his tortured mind punished him, the blade's faceless voice was often a torch in the darkness. It offered him a guiding light when the cold sunk so deep into his bones that he could barely stay conscious. He made sure he acknowledged every single withered figure, apologising to each with a steeped head. As the animated corpses writhed and lurched, they clumsily parted. A figure emerged from the shadows. Her body was swathed in dark robes and her face obscured save for a pair of ruby lips that scratched maddeningly at a distant memory. The weight on his shoulders was too unbearable and he slouched even lower, the pounding in his head growing and growing until he had nothing but screeching in his ears.

He dared to look back toward the Guild Hall, only for his neck to be swung violently around, throwing him to his knees before the veiled figure.

When she spoke, he knew that he had no choice. The righteous rage of the angry dead bore down upon him with a weight that he simply could not bear.

"Avenge us."

5

Rissa watched as King-Regent Grayson Clovis stepped onto the pedestal to rousing applause. Poor acoustics warped the clapping into an erratic warbling, creating an audible barometer on how the noble crowd perceived him. Some rose, whooping, already drunk whereas others remained seated, arms crossed, and eyes fixated ahead. Like half of the audience, Rissa remained seated, deafened by the vast swathes of bodies that stood cheering in adoration of their ruler.

With arms bulging against his regal shirt, Grayson smiled, gesturing for them to be seated. There was power in his movements; an influence no doubt learned from spending his childhood observing the tyrant who preceded him. As the hall quietened, his expression sobered.

"Thank you for coming tonight. I appreciate this may not be how you're used to doing things. But I assure you, this is of the utmost importance."

He remained on the pedestal yet seemed uncomfortable as though eager to step down. His eyes swept over the crowd.

"As nobility, you understand the truth of this city. The Resource Crisis that steals life from our families with every empty shelf. That knowledge is your burden that you must bear."

Murmurs of agreement broke out, Grayson patiently allowing them to subside.

"Yet I must call upon you once again." He continued, playing to the rampant ego of the half of the room that adored him. "For Centa Isla has found a glimmer of hope in this darkness in which we have found ourselves."

Conversation returned. Rissa heard surprised tones and sceptical words. Once again, Grayson let them slowly dissipate before continuing.

"Many solutions and ideas have been exchanged within these halls." He paused momentarily. "Most of them good, ethical and economic. We haven't had much to work with these past years, yet the amount of ideas we have generated as a society should have put an end to the wretched crisis that hangs over us like a plague."

Grayson paused again. "But it hasn't."

He descended the pedestal, waving away his Kingsguard escort. He stepped among the seated nobility, patrolling. Rissa watched as he focused his attention solely on those who had risen and applauded him on arrival.

"We lost the last of our fertile land five years ago. It's now a graveyard." He said sadly. "My own mother, your queen, is buried there. It is my dream for that graveyard to one day flourish with the life that our dead deserve."

Rissa watched as Grayson breathed in deep, as though to push tears from his eyes. Whether performance or truth, she wasn't certain, but she felt a twinge of inspiration from the way he spoke. His tone was raw and vulnerable, far removed from the cold and guarded tone of his father. Everybody had lost somebody in Centa Isla and he tapped into that like a vein. It was like he knew masquerading as a mighty King was pointless. She remembered much of his father's reign whilst growing up in the City Centre. Downtown was regularly plunged into darkness as the fleeting electricity was redirected to Monument to power his extravagant parties. She had a hazy memory of looking out of the window in her mother's old apartment and witnessing the entire district going dark.

Rissa had never actually seen the new King-Regent in person before. Few ever did. As an absent ruler the rumours were rife that he had descended into madness from spending too much time locked away in his tower, acquiring an unbefitting arrogance from always looking down and never up. But his presence here today proved these rumours greatly false. He spoke well and with intent. It was no wonder that he was so popular among noble crowds. The tainted reign of his father had cursed the Clovis name irreparably and it would take all of his strength to restore its virtue. After warmly shaking hands with clusters of his most avid and loyal supporters, he returned to the pedestal. His voice had a renewed depth of enthusiasm.

"After all our searching for answers, one has fallen miraculously into our hands. We need only to expand our horizons and take it." Grayson raised a fist and punched the air. "Join me, friends, in restoring the element of magic to our tired streets. Join me in basking in unfiltered daylight once more."

His energy intensified. "Join me as we expand this city to the greatness that it once held - only this time, we will learn from previous mistakes."

He gestured grandly ahead of him. Rissa turned and immediately her head snapped back in panic as Azrael walked down the aisle between the two seating areas. Ahead of him, he carried something glowing and vibrant. Its presence reached her even several metres away, filling her with a strange warmth not unlike the soft heat that the Grandmaster brick emitted. Only this was larger, enough to warm the entire room from the chill of Rainsturn that blew beyond the Guild Hall. She wanted to look closer, to touch that presence more to try and understand it, but the feeling of pale, phantom hands wrapping themselves around her throat once again, accelerated her heartbeat and drew blotches of sweat onto her palms. Azrael's black eyes and pale face transported her to the moments in the sewer when she had flitted between life and death as he powered down her magic to a non-existent trickle of nothingness. She hadn't expected to have such an intense physical reaction. It felt as though her brain and her heart were at war, both working on different wavelengths. Her breathing pitched and her lips went dry. She ran her hands through her hair and kept her head bowed low as Azrael passed, trying to blend as much as possible amongst the sea of various hair colours. She stared at the floor, certain that he would be leering over her with his bottomless eyes if she dared to glance up. It was to her great relief that as he passed, his black orbs were too intently focused on the item in his hands to pay attention to her cowering in his peripheral vision.

"In the hands of the Seat of Earth is a stone capable of returning magic back to our atmosphere." Grayson explained as Azrael approached. Once in range, he took the stone, his pupils dilating as he held it firmly. "With this we can create what has been taken from us. Resynthesis will know no limits and no longer will we cower in the face of our stolen potential."

After Reckoning had shattered the planet and left Centa Isla adrift, it was Resynthesis that had rebuilt the city. Rissa understood the subject well enough but had never known there to be a problem with the system. In Grandmaster, she had learned it was the power to create what had been lost. Creating compounds from magic itself that the natural world could no longer offer. But it seemed that the amount of magic in Centa Isla's atmosphere was low. Very low. She'd had no idea, but it explained the closing storefronts and empty shelves.

If before there was uttering, now there was full blown conversation. Questions were hailed at him from all angles, even from those initially disinterested in what he had to say. The King-Regent ignored them all, wincing slightly as the barrage of noise assailed him at once. He waved them down with another powerful gesture. "Peace, friends. You will have answers in time."

Skirting the edges of the seating area, Rissa noticed attendants distributing small cards. They were passed down the row, eventually reaching her. Turning the paper over in her hands, Rissa was presented with two choices.

SAVE.

CONDEMN.

The words were presented as a choice, two unmarked boxes awaiting her decision. The attendants called up each row of nobles in turn, queueing them down the middle of the hall. Rissa watched as they approached a ballot box, pricking their finger and staining the box of their choice with their own Versorcerous blood. Even from several rows back she could still feel the intensity of the strange rock, now strategically positioned by the ballot box to draw votes. She couldn't see what decisions were being made from so far back, but from the revered glances that the nobles afforded the stone, it appeared to be working. Her row was next and she shuffled into the neat line, the queue behind her growing longer, punctuated with muffled voices and nervous coughing.

Rissa looked at her own thumb, soon awaiting the prick of a needle to draw her fraudulent blood to the ballot. How thoroughly were these things checked? As the queue shuffled quickly forward, she debated slinking away into the nearest full aisle. Before she could, Rissa felt a touch on her shoulder.

"Wait..."

She froze. Slowly, she turned, finding a man's face distorted by a bruised welt on his cheek peering at her. It was the aggressive noble from the Inferno Suite gawking angrily at her, finger thrusting toward her quicker than any words could tumble from his lips. "I-it's you! You're just a waitress!"

Attention turned to her as the man continued to shout, waving his arms like a maniac. "Guards, guards!"

"Are you drunk?" She asked the man, desperately attempting to laugh the situation off.

Just as murmurs began to break out. The skylight suddenly shattered and Gault crashed through the ceiling. The cascades of radiant light disappeared as the sickly overcast replaced the ornate view. Gault landed in a shower of glass, moving toward Azrael before his feet even touched the ground.

"ASSASSIN!" Someone cried.

The Guild Hall erupted into chaos. Rissa was barely able to stay on her feet as hordes of panicked nobles all ran for the door at once. Even the Versorcerer's of Grandmaster fled, their Conduits locked away securely. Only Jace remained, fixed in place. Rissa was jostled and barged, falling to her knees where she scrambled away from the fleeing stampede to watch Gault surge toward Azrael as swathes of security instantly blocked his way.

"Gault!" She yelled. He was supposed to bring her Conduit. Where the hell was it? He wore her backpack, rattling the already fragile Grandmaster brick as he battled recklessly with several armoured Kingsguard who put themselves between him and Azrael. No slouches in combat, they put up a strong defence against Akor'shaki as the remaining security force promptly escorted the King-Regent out of the emergency exit. Azrael followed them, fleeing the building. Rissa chased Gault, calling for her Conduit from him, dodging nobles and surging Kingsguard who stayed their blades, unsure whether she was involved or just confused on where to flee. She took advantage of it, gaining ground on Gault.

"GAULT!"

The last of the Kingsguard fell, their radiant golden armour bloodied as they lay in a butchered pile. His face twitched as he turned to face her. For a single moment, there was a flit of recognition that darted across his eyes before a dark cowl of malaise set in. As he sprinted after Azrael, dragging a large portion of the guard force away with him, his arm extended, flinging her Conduit towards her. It landed on the ground a distance away and Rissa surged forward and leaped, twisting out of reach of an onrushing guard as she revealed her alliance with Gault. Her hands fell upon the ring as it rolled aimlessly across the hard floor. As she rose, slotting the Conduit onto her finger, she found herself standing in the tall shadow of Jace who looked down at her with an expression of curiosity. Kingsguard flanked him, ready to apprehend her at the wave of his hand.

"Stop that terrorist." He commanded them after Gault, gesturing to the door. "I'll handle this upstart."

They obeyed without question and much of the old Guild Hall began to clear out, leaving the two of them.

"This place will be swarming with CIPD in seconds." Jace warned her. He held a sword in his hand, the golden hilt indicative that it wasn't his blade; but rather one provided by the security. Most notably, there was no Conduit upon his finger. "We had better make this quick."

"Can't get much quicker than last time, can we?" Rissa straightened out, feeling the comforting hum of her Conduit on her finger. "I thought I smelled sewage - how was your swim?"

Irritation twisted his perfect features. "Good enough to make me realise that mercy was a mistake."

His hands flashed with power suddenly. Rissa felt the primal heat of fire before she saw magic lines of flame snaking towards her. Three in total, they churned with magmatic potential, writhing like tendrils through the air as they whipped at the ground where she had stood seconds prior. She retreated, scrambling across the floor as they pursued her.

I invoke the Missing Sea. Crest - guard me!

Raising a wall of water, two of the writhing masses of flame exploded into steam but one twisted around, coiling itself around her wrist. She screamed. Pain exploded up her arm as the tendril of flame seared her skin. She thrust her arm into her wall of water and blasted the flame away, yet the injury had already formed as a welted, charred ring around her forearm.

"You can use magic!?" She hissed, cradling her arm and she rose to her feet. It shouldn't have been possible. A Conduit was what mediated the magic in a Versorcerer's blood into spells - without it, it should have been impossible.

He gestured to his Grandmaster robes. "You don't become faculty just for being good looking."

With that, he waved his hand and the sword he held ignited. Flames consumed the blade, yet the steel did not temper. He charged towards her and Rissa scrambled to her feet, earning precious seconds to think by Vortexing herself across the long hall. She popped up through the ground a good distance behind Jace, only for him to instantly spin and surge toward her with monstrous speed, flames lapping at his heels as the force of fire propelled him.

Rissa raised another wall just in time and immediately dropped a volley of sharp icicles from the ceiling above him. They struck the hardwood floor harmlessly, exploding into shards of ice as Jace had already manoeuvred around. Rissa moved the wall with him, desperate to keep him at bay as he circled her like she was prey. She couldn't even get a second to think. Was this the true power of The Omens? Had she greatly underestimated their output? The stinging Firelines, the speed of motion from Backdraft, these were all spells she knew from Grandmaster and yet they were happening before her eyes without a Conduit to even enable them.

Rissa turned her water wall to ice and curved the edges around Jace like a cold embrace. She pushed the wall forward, as she had done before in the sewers, forcing Jace backwards. The clashing of steel had her look upwards, to the upper floor where Gault and Azrael had begun to fight. She caught the occasional glimpse of their duel as they dipped in and out of sight over the lip of the walkway. She couldn't tell who had the upper hand, but at this point it didn't matter. Gault had done the very same thing he had done when fighting Kren'shal. It was though a mist descended over him and robbed him of his senses. All he saw were The Omens; nothing else mattered, not even her.

She was on her own, like she always was. That was okay. She only had herself to worry about. The variables were in her control. Her forearm stung with fresh burns but she shoved that pain somewhere distant in the back of her mind and rose as Jace melted through her wall of ice with his blazing sword of wicked fire. The heat melted her magic into puddles, sinking like a stone into the ground as Jace stepped easily through the remains.

Geyser. Keep him away from me!

She pointed her Conduit forward and conjured a concentrated blast of freezing water, as the geyser blasted, her heels squeaked on the wood floor as the force threatened to knock her backwards. Jace vaulted the blast, but she tracked him with it, catching him and throwing him back into the furthest wall where she pushed forward, fighting against the force of her own magic to press him into the wall and crush his bones with the unrelenting force of water.

Already, as she expended her blood, Rissa could feel fatigue's soft touches creeping in behind her eyes. She increased the amount of force, determined to finish this with energy to spare as she heard Jace's drowned screams from ahead of her.

Then, just as victory was in reach her spell ceased to exist and the spell dropped. spilling water harmlessly over the hardwood floor.

Jace exhaled and fell to his knees, alive. What had just happened? As Rissa's mind whirred frantically, she felt the break in the connection between her and her Conduit as the power she felt coursing through her veins disappeared as if pulled through a vacuum.

Of course. The brick. She spun in place, searching for Gault somewhere up on the walkway. There was no sign of him. The idiot hadn't given her the backpack and had now gone so far away that she had lost connection with the bricks. She started running, loosely in the direction she had seen him last.

"Gault!?" She prayed that the training Conduit would burst to life as she closed the gap between them but it remained a silent hunk of useless steel on her finger. "GAULT!? Where are you!?"

She may as well have screamed into the void. All it did was attract the attention of the CIPD and the Kingsguard. They surged into the room from both entrances and immediately fixed onto her, rushing to Jace's aid. Rissa turned and ran; she could feel the trembling of the ground as earth magic sought to trip her up and a torrent of wind that blew strongly against her. She veered away from the gusts, crashing through one of the ornate stained-glass windows, emerging near the pavilion bench that she had sat on quietly not an hour ago. The glass sliced deeply up her exposed arms and she gritted her teeth against the pain as she bolted down the path. She felt uncomfortable in her attire, longing for the protective sleeves of her jacket and the snug fit of stretchy jeans around her legs. As she sought distance, a sudden wall of stone erected itself before her, mountainous and unbreakable. She turned, only to find the CIPD already closing in.

Then her Conduit sprung to life, picking up the signal from the Grandmaster bricks that were suddenly somewhere nearby. "Oh! Yes!"

Vortex. Help me find that idiot.

Using the sightline back inside she had gained through the broken window, Rissa created a Vortex between the walkway and where she now stood. Stepping through her portal, she promptly closed the Vortex before anybody followed. Immediately however, two other Vortexes opened behind her, granting passage to the CIPD. Rissa tried to raise a wall of water in front of them to block pursuit, only to find her connection severed once again. This was infuriating. She might as well have rolled a dice every time she wanted to cast a spell. Where the hell was he?

She ran across the walkway, dipping into the nearest room as they bombarded her from afar with small shards of rocks and ice. She could tell they were pulling their punches, likely due to an innate desire to protect the ancient architecture. She followed a trail of destruction that revealed the collateral damage to Gault and Azrael's fight. There were broken tables and shattered windows, the wallpaper torn and peeling from hundreds of slices missing their mark. At the end of the trail, she found them. Azrael had Gault pinned, laying punches into a body that increasingly had less to give. Gault's arms were raised in desperate defiance, slowly sinking down as every strike knocked another bit of life out of him.

She felt hesitation lock her limbs and for a few long moments she just watched as Gault was beaten within an inch of his life. The feeling of hands around her throat crept in and she found it difficult to swallow. Her mouth felt paralyzed and dry as she beheld the black-eyed man. He looked injured and bled from several deep cuts, but his movements never faltered as the fist came down, spraying up blood every time.

Enough. Rissa forced herself to breathe and with trembling hands, prepared a spell and laid her palm on the ground, willing the location of the coming spell to be directly beneath the pale man.

Geyser. Get his attention.

She knew it wouldn't do anything, but it would hopefully get him away from Gault. Sure enough, the spell didn't even spit an ounce of water, Azrael's presence atop the magic circle that formed was enough to ensure that it ended prematurely. The fists stopped at the very least, leaving Gault a withered mess. The black eyes turned, locking onto her instantly. Fear spiked in her chest and she turned to retreat, only to find Jace blocking the way. He was drenched yet again, but seemingly fully recovered.

"You've done it now." He said.

Just then, Azrael surged towards her, demonstrating surely impossible speed as he landed in front of her with a thud. He was tall and nimble, his shadow towering over her like Monument did to the rest of the city. She backed away, quickly arriving at a wall. Cornered.

In his hand, he held her backpack. From inside, he took the two chunks of Grandmaster brick in one large hand, inspecting them curiously. "Very clever."

He crushed them, fingers straining before finally splitting the concrete into dust that he sprinkled onto the floor before her. Rissa felt her connection sever for good and paralysis took over her body, cowering her in the corner as he closed in. He cornered her and wrapped a hand around her throat. She felt him squeeze with the pressure that had just broken a brick and she felt the bones in her neck begin to warp, seconds from snapping.

"Incoming." Jace said quietly. The Grandmaster lecturer gave her a look that told her she had just been very lucky. The grip around her neck immediately relaxed and she fell to the floor. Azrael also fell to his knees, suddenly clutching his wounds as the CIPD caught up with her and stormed into the room.

"Help me!" Azrael seethed. Immediately he had hands helping him to his feet and his wounds being inspected. The Seat of Earth appeared so weak and vulnerable, a stark contrast from the stone-cold killer who had gripped her just before.

"Wait! Wait!" Rissa was forced to the floor, manacles clapped around her wrists. "He's going to destroy the city!"

The officers ignored her and she realised how mad she truly sounded as they roughly handled her to her feet and confiscated the useless Conduit from her finger. Hoisting her up to her feet to drag her away, Rissa got a glimpse ahead of her only to see that Gault was gone.

Her chest hollowed out. Traitor. He'd left her, after everything they'd done together.

"Bastard." She seethed quietly.

There was relief in the cuffs around her wrists, for the alternative was death. But Rissa couldn't help but feel that a worse fate was in store for her. By all intents and purposes, she would be branded a terrorist, disrupting a rally and attacking the Seat of Earth and a Grandmaster professor.

Creeping dread filled her stomach as the CIPD took her away.

—

King-Regent Grayson Clovis walked the halls of Monument with its violet carpet and dark walls, at every step was a portrait of royalty dating back as far as the history books could go. He thought frequently of these old rulers, of their challenges and conquests. Surely it was he who had been handed the hardest task of them all. What would they have done in his situation? What decisions would they have made? He longed to ask them for counsel as there was nobody in his life who could give him advice. His Elemental Council, Azrael included, had their own agenda and for him to ask for advice would expose his weakness and inexperience that he convincingly concealed behind his charisma and unwavering confidence.

The rally had been a failure. The terrorists who had sought to possibly end his reign had reminded him that leaving Monument carried with it great risk. It seemed that there were those who would not even see his reign begin. There had been a few hundred or so votes still to collect, but he had looked at the provisional results.

CONDEMN.

That had been the box most selected. Despite the wide eyes at the powerful stone that Azrael had carried and the ovation he had received, the votes they had been able to count had still been largely in favour of abstinence and by quite a margin. His gambit had failed to pay off in the face of such selfish greed. There were no risks in that gathering of bloated egos, no drive or intent to change the course of history. Their lack of foresight truly astounded him. Perhaps they believed the population would thin so much that the problem would go away on its own.

If his damned council had only agreed in the first place. Or even better, had he just been King and not been forced to carry the useless label of Regent this would have been done by now. What good was the crown if there were no powers to change with it?

Bristling with anger Grayson stopped. A portrait caught his eye, making his anger bubble further. It was his father: Richard Clovis II, painted at the height of his power. During his fifteen-year reign the quality of life in Centa Isla had nose-dived. Queen Aura Clovis, Grayson's mother died part way through, taking with her the last caring voice for the people. After her death, riots had wracked the streets of the City Centre. Even today, the deepest, darkest CIPD cells were still filled with the life sentences that had been issued. Those prisoners still awaited the scheduled execution for their defiance against The Crown. Grayson could not fathom how so many bodies could be interned in that comparatively small compound, but frankly, he didn't care. The arms that had thrown the bricks that had put his father into a coma had been severed. He had been left to pick up the pieces.

Grayson returned to his personal bedchambers, only to find Azrael waiting outside. The Seat of Earth was injured, bloody bandages wrapped around several deep wounds, his lifeless eyes staring straight at him.

"My King."

"Azrael." He greeted his advisor. "You're feeling better?"

"Better enough to serve, My King."

He could not yet place the true intentions of the man but applauded his commitment. "Then I bid you rest, friend. There'll be time tomorrow to think things through."

Despite his wishes, Azrael didn't move from his door. "We have discussed all there is to discuss. Council chambers, the campaign, the votes. This city doesn't have time."

"Then what do you want me to do?" Frustration marred his voice; he hadn't intended it to.

"Bear the full weight of your crown." Azrael said slowly. It was almost an accusation, as if he wasn't already doing everything in his power. They locked gazes and Grayson felt a creeping chill run up his spine. Without another word, Azrael bowed to him in deep reverence before turning and limping off down the hall.

Grayson entered his chambers and bolted his door. His usually comfortable king-sized bed felt hard and rigid, offering no comfort for his troubled mind. Where he had once enjoyed the space of his giant room he felt so small and so powerless. The great window that offered a view of the city felt exposing, as though others looked in on him rather than the other way around. Feeling caged, he pulled the giant satin curtains closed.

"Bear the weight of your crown."

Such a comment. The meaning was lost to him. Still uncomfortable in his own quarters, Grayson left and wandered the halls. They had not changed much since he was a child. Much like in the council chamber, he had just grown bigger. It had always been his to inherit. The only child; the only heir. But, he hadn't expected to ascend so soon. He had hoped for more time. Time he could have used to get older and wiser. He wished for the Resource Crisis to be over, to have the job of rebuilding as opposed to finding a solution to the impossible. His decisions would decide his legacy and the reputation of the Clovis name. Whether intentional or not, his walk had taken him to his father's chambers. He opened the door, finding one of the attendants he had requested to be present at all times sat beside him. She put down her book as he entered, a look of panic on her face. He calmed her with a smile.

"It's okay." He told her. "May I have some time?"

"O-Of course, My King." She closed her book, scrambled for her things and left the room. Grayson waved her off and locked the door behind her.

"Bear the weight of your crown."

It was a king's duty to sacrifice for his city. It was all becoming clear to him now. His father's reign was coming to a simpering close where his was just beginning. He took a seat on the stool, still warm from where the handmaiden had just occupied it. He took his father's cold, lifeless hand in his own. That hand had once struck servants, ordered executions and commanded the future of the entire city. Now it was gaunt, the lumps of his bone riding the skin as death slowly, painfully, robbed him of life. This was no way for his father to be remembered. He was many things, good and bad, but he was not weak.

A smile crossed Grayson's face. He recalled his childhood spent in this very tower, sneaking around the ancient halls, hiding behind the great curtains as his father received plea after plea from the citizenry and nobility. This was back when Monument was accessible to the average person and the lines of communication between The Crown and its citizens were much more defined. But his father had served his purpose. King Richard Clovis II would be remembered as a greedy, tyrannical ruler who put his self-interest above his reign. Rising from the dead and having a second attempt would not change the past. This city needed someone new, someone with intent and a desire to see this city saved.

Like him. He would restore the Clovis name. He would walk the streets of Centa Isla one day safe in the knowledge that he could close his eyes and not get a knife in the ribs. Better still, the people would cheer him. All he had to do was bear the weight of his crown.

His father looked tired. He slept peacefully, like a corpse. His silver hair was well maintained by the attendants. It grew like vines around his pale, emaciated face, defining the bags beneath his closed eyes. The handmaidens had done excellent work preserving his father's image and he would make sure they were well rewarded once what was to be done was finished. Grayson took a spare pillow from beside where his father slept and felt the soft fabric in his hands. The silk that held these cushions together dated back to days before Reckoning. It was real, tangible and had a consistency that the Resynthesized imitations just couldn't match. More of this was in his people's future.

As Regent-King he was powerless. Relying on rally after rally and councils to get anything done. As King he was undeniable. There would be none who could stand in the way of the salvation of Centa Isla.

Grayson took the silken pillow and pressed it calmly against his father's face.

—

The key to Ocean's View, apartment sixty-five was heavy in his hands. Gault held the key tight as he eased the door open and staggered into Rissa's apartment. The boxes they had packed before leaving for the Guild Hall were exactly as they had left them. He wandered inside, carrying a deep fatigue that sought to drag his eyelids down. His nose bled, leaving a spotted trail of crimson drips as he ascended the apartment block. With the door shut behind him, Gault collapsed on the floor.

He knew what had happened, it had been the same with Kren'shal, only this time there had been true consequences. Guilt tortured his mind, wracking him with an urge to curl up and simper. When the dead of his homeworld came calling, he could do nothing else but answer them. He owed them that much. The spirit of their anger tortured him, seeking to claim vengeance on the Omens who had brought Galleo et'al to his homeworld.

Yet, while he had fled, wounded like some wild beast, Rissa had been caught trying to rectify his mistakes. Worst of all he had been aware of everything that was happening, a prisoner in his own mind who was unable to do anything other than watch his commandeered body chase down those responsible for destroying his homeworld. He had held snatches of influence, but it was never enough. In any case, the spirits who inhabited his body were far superior in combat to what he could manage.

He had become a vessel for those who should have lived instead of him. People who were more talented, smarter, kinder and more deserving of their lives.

You resisted. Akor'shaki berated him. *We had them! Why did you resist her control?*

"I don't know." He laid down on the wooden floor. His body was so tired, bruised and lacerated. He had watched Rissa struggling and had wanted to help. In doing so, he must have momentarily fought against their control and this had weakened his resolve. Perhaps without this moment of weakness, the spirits who dominated him may have defeated Azrael. He wanted nothing more but to close his eyes and disappear into sleep-

No. Gault forced himself to his feet, ignoring the small tears in his flesh as his body screamed for him to lie back down. Rising to full height and gritting his teeth, he condemned himself undeserving of rest for the failure he had committed. It had started to become a habit, his behaviour predictable. Perhaps he was no longer fit to do his work any other way than in solitude. At the very least his failures would then be his alone to bear.

Rissa's flat was going to be seized. She had said so herself while spending the last of her money on clothes to assist him with his doomed mission. The books she had intended to put into storage would also be taken, along with everything else that she held dear. That wasn't fair.

You're better off alone. You can do your work freely, free of attachment and consequences.

He knew. Akor'shaki was right. While often his driving force and motivator, the blade knew his mistakes just as well as he did. When the marching started and the shambling figures of the past demanded revenge, his body became their puppet. The tortured lady who had led them… in life they had sworn an oath together. It seemed however that even in death they were not free from those responsibilities. When she arrived, he could do nothing but remember and serve. Just like old times.

He began to pack another box, taking more of her books from the shelf and placing them delicately inside the packaging. As Akor'shaki granted him power enough for him to heal, he flitted through several pages. So many of the animals considered "mystical" in these books he had seen first-hand. Same in description as his homeworld, only some were named differently. Ducks, stags, eagles, tigers, even the almighty "boar". The recent memory of Rissa's total embarrassment brought a small smile to his face.

Concentrate.

His smile dissolved.

Akor'shaki was always present. Always opinionated. It had felt like an eternity since Gault had been able to think for himself, form his own opinions and react in a way he would consider natural. Everything felt consulted, every thought, word and action appraised by an outside force. It made him feel as though his responses were always a few milliseconds slower than they should have been. The exception to this was in combat. Under threat and filled with adrenaline, he felt the processing power of two minds at once, acting in perfect harmony. He could judge distance, speed and power with nothing but a glance. Akor'shaki understood that which he could not comprehend, lending its knowledge and its intelligence to him for personal gain. Truly, without the demonsteel blade he would be half a man. Identity, control, privacy; they were all chips that he gave away in return for the ability to stand a chance against a cosmic force such as Galleo et'al.

She'd be better off without you. Leave her and forget.

He piled a box up at her door. Then another, and another. Together they were so heavy. Getting them down the stairs would tear the muscles in his arms and legs. But he would do it. He would not let them be taken from her. He felt aimless, content to stumble about the city until it led to another encounter with an Omen. As he descended, slowly, painfully, he played scenarios through his head, what he'd do next, whom he would target, how he should navigate this confusing, sensory city as a criminal charged with regicide? He knew that anything he could think up wasn't going to work. Even with the knowledge of Akor'shaki he knew that without his guide this wasn't going to happen. She knew things about this city he wouldn't discover in his whole lifetime. No, this wasn't going to happen.

Not without Rissa Rawdon.

———

Handcuffed to a table, Rissa waited patiently for questioning. The room was made of reflective steel, a one-way mirror where she knew officers deliberated and discussed her fate, consumed an entire wall. She felt cold, the steel was like ice on her wrists as she tried her bonds, to no avail. She had been in this room only once before, at the pinnacle of her attention-seeking crime spree, she had stolen her father's precious CIPD patrol car and driven it around in the dead of night, crashing it into a lamppost when she took a corner too quickly. They'd questioned her, less interested in punishment and more interested in finding out how she managed it, to prevent something similar ever happening again. Her father had got into a lot of trouble, not her. It had probably set his career back a few years and she regretted it tremendously.

Today, she had the feeling that she would not be getting away with this lightly. Regicide, terrorist, rebel. To name a few, at least. These were not accusations she wanted levelled at her, especially in CIPD custody. People had been executed for less.

A steel door unlocked several times over before swinging open. Her father entered, looking thunderous. He bolted the door behind him before pulling up a chair opposite her. Donnel Rawdon's wrath was not incurred lightly.

"Dad!" She expressed her shock. "Get me out of here!"

"Sit still." He chided, eyes narrowed to slits. "I'm here as your inquisitor, not your father."

"You're kidding me." Rissa tried to get his eyes, but he was too busy sifting through a pile of papers he had brought in with him. "You have to believe me. There's something happening in the city that nobody knows about!"

"And you know, do you?" He didn't even look up. His tone had dropped into cold, hard indifference, like he was humouring a drunkard's rambling. "I have questions for you. Answer in truth and your sentence may be lessened."

"This is insane, dad. They've sent you in here haven't they?" Rissa sought his eyes once more. This time he met her and she felt the piercing gaze of a detective scour through her pupils and begin sifting through her mind. She broke away. "This isn't right. They're testing you! I'm family. They're out of line for this."

She turned to the one-way mirror, certain that there was a gathering of interested parties that were watching. "You hear me!? You're out of line!"

"ENOUGH!" Donnel slammed the table and Rissa felt her heart leap out of her chest. "Sit still and listen."

Wilting like the last flower in the old park, Rissa sat quietly and awaited her questioning.

"You gatecrashed a ballot pretending to be a noble. What for? The attack has been considered a direct threat on the King-Regent's life. Explain your motives." He prepared a notepad and quill.

"I…" Her mind whirled. The narrative had already been set and she hadn't even said a word. "It wasn't an attack on the King-Regent."

"So, you had a target?" Her father jotted down her crime. "If not him; then who?"

Rissa cursed internally. She was nervous, clammy, shaking. Her head was pounding with stress. She needed to calm down and start breathing properly or she was going to bury herself even deeper. To his credit, her father didn't press her as she steadied herself, taking slow, gratifying breaths in through her nose. The air smelled metallic and sterile, free of the impurities of the outside.

"There's something happening in this city. Something-"

Rissa hesitated. All of a sudden, images of the young officer that disappeared in the sewers flew into her mind. She recalled his memorial, rushed and without conclusion, laid out in the foyer of the CIPD Compound without a funeral. She pictured her father's face upon one of the old frames and a shiver ran down her spine. That officer was doubtlessly one of many victims of the Omen's unknowable reach. They had made him disappear, declared suicide, his true fate was a mystery to even his family when Rissa knew full well he had been killed and disposed of. The Omens were everywhere in this city, their influence bleeding from every damned orifice this wretched place had. With the words of the King-Regent weaponised, they could end the career of anybody they so wished then silence them once isolation had taken hold.

What would they do to her father if she set him on their trail?

"Something? Rissa. What something?" Her father seemed genuinely interested. His quill hovered eagerly over the notepad. "Talk."

She couldn't. However much they disagreed, he was still her only family. Strained as their relationship may be, there wasn't even a distant part of her that ever wanted to see him put in harm's way.

"Nothing." She plucked up the strength in her eyes to meet his gaze once more and hold it. The lie she told was for his sake. "Just a protest. About time somebody did something extreme."

Her father wrote it down, but the deepening lines on his face told her that he wasn't truly convinced by what he was writing. His voice was hushed, but she heard him murmuring to himself as he wrote.

"You had an accomplice."

"Did I?"

"Yes, Rissa." His hands heavy upon the papers, sifting through them for descriptions given by several witnesses. "I want you to tell me everything about them."

She felt a small sneer curdle up her lip. The petty side of her practically screeched for her to sell Gault out, to announce his name and where he'd likely go next. His betrayal still stung sore. Yet, Rissa couldn't help but feel that the warning signs had been present. The loss of control he had suffered and the subsequent Empty Eyes massacre as they sought Kren'shal should have been reason enough for her to distance herself from him. But she had pressed on regardless, too excited by the underground war they were waging to pay attention. She shouldn't have even been surprised that he had become so fixated on killing Azrael that he had completely disregarded the entire foundations of their plan. He deserved to be in here alongside her, but then again, who was going to stop the Omens while she rotted in a jail cell?

"I acted alone. I don't know who that was." At the very least, the way he had abandoned her was convincing enough for her statement to be mostly true. Rissa was a good liar. She didn't really know why. Eye contact was never a problem for her.

"I know you're lying, Rissa." She watched her father's brow crease in frustration. "Whatever crowd you've fallen in with. You need to talk or else."

"Don't pretend you know anything about my life." Spite laced her words. "I'm surprised they were able to drag you away from your desk."

"You think I want to be here?"

"You've only ever wanted to be in the past."

"Well, perhaps I'd have found your mother by now if I didn't have to deal with you every five minutes." He seethed at her, the subject of interrogation quickly fading away into their usual collision. "What do you think she'd say if she saw you now!?"

She made a face at him. "'Why did your father abandon you?'"

"To bring our family back together!" He yelled, chair legs skidding against the floor as he rose to his feet. As the rage festered in his eyes, she watched quickly as he mellowed and his gaze averted.

It was cruel. But she was sitting here, bound and cornered. Rissa knew exactly what to say to hurt him.

"I remind you of her, don't I?" She pulled at the cuffs that bound her to the table. "Everything about me just makes you hurt and remember, doesn't it!? There's not a part of me that I got from you."

Hurt flashed across his face but was quickly buried by cold indifference. She watched as her father disappeared, replaced by Officer Donnel Rawdon. He returned to his notepad, scratching down some words before rising and pocketing the pad.

"Perhaps a few nights in The Douldruums will loosen your tongue."

"What?" She had heard of The Douldruums, from her Father mostly. It was the prison that burrowed into the very earth beneath them, spiralling down into isolated layers. The greater the crime, the deeper the time, or whatever he had said to her once. She had heard only stories of those emerging for their executions, cackling and babbling on the verge of madness.

Donnel rose from his seat and unbolted the door, opening it to allow several officers to come in, uncuff and restrain her.

"Dad!" She yelled. "What are you doing!?"

They moved her out of the interrogation chamber. Rissa caught one last look at her father before he disappeared without so much as a second look towards her. Daylight broke in through the window of the compound and for all Rissa knew, this would be the last bit of daylight she would ever see again.

Now, she had no one left.

———

Lachesis stepped into the shadow of the large, concave iron door. She removed her respirator, now free from the clotting smog that swallowed the old factory. The inside of the former workplace was like a crumbling monument, chunks of debris from the degradation and failure to maintain the aged building. Chains hung from the ceiling and menacing hooks rattled as whistling wind blew through the disused foundry. Holes in the tall ceiling leaked light, cascading shallow tunnels of brightness down into the brick, slate and metal interior. The groaning of strained steel from somewhere above and the soft rattling of chains caressed by a strong breeze put her on edge but also provided a degree of comfort, for she knew that nobody would be disturbing them in such a remote location. The edge of the city was so close that she could feel the heat of the core even from inside the building. She had arrived on the outskirts of Forge Town, in an area consumed by the thickest and most lethal of the smog. The damage of the Reckoning had destroyed the area beyond repair, the heat and radiation from the exposed core deeming the outskirts uninhabitable. She was aware of a transient population that still lived nearby, flitting between rubble and surviving on nothing but soups of scrap and waste. They would pose no threat today.

"Of course he chose this place." Jace spoke, lacking subtlety as usual. His voice boomed in the echoing factory, cascading around the place as if hearing him once wasn't already chore enough. He entered in through the same door she had come through, dressed in some gaudy frippery.

"Dressing like that outside the centre. Are you trying to get killed?" She asked him quietly, appraising the outfit he wore. It was distinctly noble, what would have made a perfectly fine shirt had been adorned with several frills and abstract patterns. The absence of enough buttons left it open at the chest, which she admitted that for Jace, was a welcome omission.

"These people barely have food, let alone weapons." Jace observed, glancing out of the large door at the crumbled buildings.

"And if they decided to follow you?"

He strode toward her, flashing an attractive smile as he passed her by. "Then I know you or your little rodents will notice them."

"There's only so much slack they can pick up for you, dear."

Azrael suddenly appeared from nowhere. He did not arrive through the door, but rather stepped ominously out of the darkness, as though he had been there the entire time. "Enough. It's time."

There had been an air of frustration that had followed Azrael since the conflict at the Guild Hall. Now, he bore an aura of excitement. Granted, not everyone could detect this shift in mood, except for her, his sister. There was a levity to his stone-faced expression and confidence in his flat, monotone voice. These were the levels at which she observed and understood the shell that her brother had become. Her part in the King's campaign had been more covert. She had spent the build-up identifying the most susceptible members of the nobility so that Jace's charisma could be put to work to undo their negative perceptions of the Clovis family. It seemed, unfortunately, that it had all been in vain. The egocentric nobility could either not forget the damage caused by King Richard Clovis II or, more likely, they simply didn't care about change as long as they could lead their opulent lifestyles.

"Mires. Come." Azrael stood quietly. There was an unsettling shuffling. From the darkness, a hunched figure emerged, dragging one leg behind him. As he entered the light, his bulging eyes winced.

"I'm here, I'm here." His body jittered and spasmed. There was a decrepit look about Mires. His dark hair was loose, enough to take a handful out with a strong gust of wind. His skin was pale and yellow, pus-like veins protruding dangerously all over his body, as though he was going to explode at a moment's notice. Most strikingly his eyes, Lachesis recalled them once as being green, were now a poisonous red, his pupils permanently dilated from the constant state of adrenaline he needed to be in to stay alive.

"We're ready." Azrael commanded.

"Yes, yes." Mires nodded at them, beckoning them with a trembling arm deeper into the darkness. "But... not here."

Lachesis followed the shambling figure, walking half of her usual speed to not overtake. The darkness clotted the air around them, as though the very building had been cursed for housing Mires for so long. The Brand of the Heretic was one of the Brands she had been deeply relieved not to receive. It absconded the bearer from partaking in the grander strokes of the plan, bringing Galleo et'al closer than ever, but at a cost she deemed far too great. She knew she would soon see the power on display once again. Despite everything, Mires had insisted on spearheading valuable research down here in the derelict factories.

He led them to a rusty, creaking hatch in the ground, grunting and gargling with the effort of pulling open one of the two doors.

"Allow me." Jace took the second and pulled the stiff, rusty door open. The hinges screamed at him, as though hesitant to reveal the dark descent that lay ahead.

Stairs dived into the ground, too dark to see where they led. Distant screams filled the air, chilling Lachesis to her core. She knew what was taking place down here, yet in truth, had wished never to be exposed to it.

"Safe down there- down there." Mires flashed a horrific smile, teeth missing or outright rotten in his mouth. "Come! Ignore the screams!"

Lachesis felt a stab of pity as Mires led them down the stairs. He hobbled, taking one step at a time. It was painstakingly slow, a crippled shadow of the man he had once been. Mires had been an incredible mage once upon a time. She didn't know the full extent of his tale, but in the search for power and the unknown he had dived deep into the darkest arts of his homeworld and by mistake had found Galleo et'al lurking in the black abyss of the beyond. His homeworld had been destroyed by the Dark One and he had gone mad shortly thereafter. The finer details assumed themselves.

Galleo et'al had done something to Mires. There was a bond they shared that ran deeper than the Brands that she, Jace and even Azrael possessed. They reached the bottom of the steel stairs and found themselves in a twisting labyrinthian hall. The cacophony of tortured screams became louder. She was relieved that they meandered away from the horrific noise, down a corridor where they emerged into a small clearing in the pitch dark. As Lachesis's eyes adjusted, she saw what looked like a bed made from dry-rotted wooden planks and a bucket. She wanted to gag yet consigned the demanding feeling in the back of her throat to just a cough. It was like the room of a prisoner, worse, in fact. There was no dignity here.

"The Dark One waits for us." Mires spoke, fear flashing across his crimson eyes, as though a shadow of the man remained trapped and knew what had become of him. "P-prepare yourselves!"

Lachesis tensed as Mires dropped to his knees violently. Jace went to support the shambling body, but Azrael held him back. Power coalesced in the broken body, the already bulging veins warped and pulsed as the skin on his bones literally swam with ripples and tears. His back snapped upwards, the curved spine straightening with a howl of agony as his inverted knees corrected themselves, making noises so horrific that Lachesis cringed. Mires screamed the entire time as his body lifted into the air, twisting and contorting. He screamed until his voice broke and there was simply silence. Then, his body slowly lowered to the ground.

Mires stood up straight as his feet touched the floor. He stretched his body, flexing with full range of motion as his once curved spine had been corrected. The veins that were on edge had calmed and even his hair looked more alive.

Azrael dropped to his knees immediately. Lachesis followed, a hand on Jace's shoulder bringing him down too.

"My Omens." It was with Mires's voice that the words came, although the origin of the voice was certainly not his own. This was Galleo et'al. It spoke through Mires like a spirit at a seance, the grim voice emanating from his hideous monstrosity.

"Appraise me."

"Dark One." Azrael spoke with his head bowed, deep in reverence. "We now have the means to construct the Obelisk."

"Your timeline?"

"Soon. Dark One." Azrael insisted. "The Clovis child has claimed his birthright. I have him in the palm of my hands."

"This pleases me." Mires began to walk, his body moved seamlessly, as though Galleo et'al was the natural inhabitant of his body. "My time is finite."

"I am aware, Dark One. We work as quickly as we can."

"The Brand of the Demon." Galleo et'al demanded. "Where is he?"

"Dead, Dark One. G-" Azrael caught himself and re-postured. "The Brand of the Scout followed us here."

"Akor'shaki may serve him. But that blade is mine." Galleo et'al patrolled slowly up and down the room. "Do not fear the Scout. His weapon will not strike a lethal blow to my efforts. It cannot."

Azrael replied. "I am relieved for that, Dark One."

Lachesis controlled her breathing. There was an almighty presence that had joined them in this room, and it turned her blood to ice. She stared at the grubby steel floor, content to watch Mire's grotesque feet walk back and forth. It was usually Azrael who communed with the Dark One alone, not all of them. She had never seen their black-eyed leader so subservient, not even as a child.

"For the death of the Demon, I shall find you a replacement". Galleo et'al spoke with Mires's voice, the power contained in just the Great One's words clearly damaging the vocal cords of its host as the voice strained yet did not break. It was likely that the damage would be inflicted all at once when Galleo et'al parted with his host. "They will arrive in the days to come. You may not see them, yet trust they work in my favour."

Lachesis felt the irrepressible urge to speak. She looked up. "Dark One. We may not require any reinforcements. As it stands we are-"

Her entire body was on fire. The force of mountains crushed her bones, pressing her into the floor as though trying to push her through the slits between each steel plate. She screamed, that was all she knew to do. Needles skewered her mind and body. The bones that made her were twisted and bent like they were made of rubber. Time interpolated into what could have easily been years. By the time the pain abruptly stopped, she had become used to it, her mind resigned to the rest of her existence spent screaming. Her body shook and trembled, drool and foam unceremoniously pouring out of her mouth like she was some rabid animal.

Azrael was speaking, but she could only hear ringing as her tortured body adjusted to the total pain that had been thrust upon her.

"Perhaps I shall replace your Watcher." She heard Galleo et'al muse.

"I beg you, Dark One." Azrael postured himself before Mires, spreading himself across the mucky floor. "Show mercy. It was a moment's madness."

She didn't die in the seconds that followed; she took it as the mercy so desperately pleaded for by Azrael. She remained on the floor, barely alive as the conversation concluded and by the time she had regained full control of her senses, Mires was once again a hunched silhouette that covered the floor, the Dark One having vacated his body.

As they left the old factory, she couldn't even walk straight. Jace guided her up the steel stairs. He spoke to her, offering words of concern but her hearing was in a state of paralysis. It was only until she was outside, requiring the respirator to breathe, did she begin to recover her lost senses. She was sitting at the edge of the city, leaning against a wall.

Azrael stood ahead of her; hands interlocked behind his back as he stared out over the horizon. As though he knew she had awoken, he turned, lights of the core casting a crimson-orange shadow over him.

"Never do that again." For the first time in an exceptionally long time, she watched anger distort his stoic features. "It was foolish. Do you have any idea how lucky you are?"

He ended the conversation by placing a respirator of his own into his mouth. She didn't have the strength for words. All she could offer was a nod. That seemed to calm him, and the usual indifference returned to his features. Seeming content that she was alive, he walked past her and left, wading deep into the thick blanket of smog, leaving her to recover with the warm heat of the planet's core soothing her aching body.

She hadn't intended to speak but had seemingly done so anyway. She had learned her lesson. However much she had harboured thoughts of sparing Centa Isla, there was nothing in this world that could compare to that pain. Not even the application of her Brand itself.

A moment's madness, indeed.

6

The unshaven stubble on his chin itched. Donnel Rawdon scrutinised an array of papers scattered across his desk with tired, languid eyes. They were old newspaper articles from eight years ago and letters addressed to Aryssa Rawdon that he had already dissected a thousand times. Despite the cynical belief of his daughter, there was absolutely no doubt in Donnel Rawdon's mind that Rissa's mother was still alive.

And he was going to find her.

Aryssa Rawdon had been one of the finest Versorcerers to have ever graced the city. Thanks to the selective, incestuous breeding of a noble family rich with water magic genes, Aryssa was the envy of many. As an influential noble blessed with strong blood and rich magical potential, her insane choice to marry him, a common man without so much as a twinkle of The Algarethan Verse in his eye, was the ultimate sacrifice. She had spoken often about a starched and scratchy childhood with detached and distant parents who had been wed only for their genes, sharing a physical union of the body but not an emotional one of the heart. She had wanted her own marriage to be different. He had never felt as blessed as he had the day their union had been sealed in the old park. That special place had since withered away and been built upon. It was now a graveyard in the smog of Forge Town.

He picked up his favourite photo of the two of them. He looked so young. Donnel tried not to remind himself how long she had been missing. To harbour that thought was to invite a myriad of problems and thoughts that he wasn't ready to address. What would she do if she was here? What would she say to their wayward daughter who lapped at the heels of trouble? Rissa was the spitting image of her mother, yet there was practically nothing resembling him within her. There was a steep distance between them these days, one that Donnel had given up trying to fix. He needed Aryssa; always in tune with her daughter's feelings in a way he could never be and Rissa needed the guidance only she could provide.

The moment their union was sealed and their first child was on the way they had both known that they would all be disowned by the noble world;

banished and stripped of any entitlement for shunning the arranged marriage to a strong and worthy suitor. Donnel cherished her for this sacrifice, of course he did, but he still couldn't shake the unsettling feeling that Rissa's true potential had been diluted by his inferior genetics. Had her father also been a Versorcerer, would things have been different? Would she have been more motivated to study?

He was a workhorse. It was all he knew. The belief that hard work would reap reward had been instilled into him by his late parents and then drilled further by the rigamarole of CIPD training. Give more today and enjoy more tomorrow. Every day he punished himself by working more than he slept, stacking up his entitlement to happiness and wealth. Neither had yet arrived, despite the endless overtime that even at this late hour, found him still seated at his desk long after the bulk of the force had gone home.

A pensive frown created a deep dent between his eyebrows. These late nights were his only time to continue his search. When the day's work was done cleaning up the streets, he would caffeinate himself and sift through the CIPD archives night after night. Officially, the disappearance of Aryssa Rawdon was shelved many years ago, deemed insufficient evidence to accommodate any further effort towards it. Of course, had Aryssa maintained her favourable status within the nobility, there was no doubt that they would still be combing the streets to this day.

He would have to do it alone.

In the year following her disappearance, Rissa would often be here with him, sharing their grief and their hope. This was a time all too brief where they had searched together as a family. As the years droned by, his daughter had been worn down by the plague of pessimism that marred Centa Isla. Not once had he stopped working for the future, whereas his daughter had given up seemingly long ago. She had lasted only two of five years at Grandmaster; a stretch of time that was supposed to be the most lucrative and defining of a productive Versorcerer's life.

This infuriated him. He worked so hard to earn his meagre Band B apartment whereas Rissa, with a fraction of his effort could be living in the City Centre with a lucrative career and pay to match. He knew that finding Aryssa was key to unlocking her potential. She had always been closer with her mother and that was okay, so long as she was happy and achieving.

But these days, his daughter was neither.

Donnel felt his mood sour. He collated the scattered pages related to Rissa's mother and put them carefully back in her case file before lifting a hefty folder from his in-tray. Papers sprawled out vying for his attention, but his focus was lacking this night. It wasn't lack of sleep that hindered his concentration but the very fact that somewhere beneath him, in the horrific prison of The Douldruums was the daughter that he and Aryssa brought into this world together. A daughter now trapped beneath the earth, buried as deep as the dead, in a hell where madness and insanity lay in wait, ready to ambush even the strongest of minds.

It had already been days.

Rissa had begged him for help as they dragged her away. He had never seen such fear in her eyes, and the image replayed on a loop in his brain. What could he have done? She had attempted alleged regicide, then refused to offer an explanation. Imprisonment was a stay of execution for something that could have just as easily seen her head roll on the spot. Any protest from him would have destroyed his career forever, tearing up his exemplary work record and snuffing out his prospects of future happiness. He'd have no archives to aid the search for Rissa's Mother, no income to pay for his apartment and no hope of ever finding lucrative work again. Insubordination would scream out like a blood stain on his record. Actions have consequences. Hadn't he always taught her that? Rissa had made a tremendous mistake, misguided or not.

The conjecture regarding the attack had already hit the papers. The latest issue of The Dawn's Herald, snatched from a pushy street peddler lay on the desk in front of him.

KING-REGENT RESCUED FROM REGICIDE ATTEMPT

Independent journalists scrambled for the story, desperate to be the one to bring the news. There were multiple stories cited, fortunately none of them naming his daughter publicly as an accomplice. Even the number of assailants was inconclusive, some outlets reporting there were upwards of twenty-five terrorists who had descended upon their heroic King-Regent. All it told him was nobody outside the nobility knew a damn thing about what happened.

But he suspected that Rissa had an accomplice. There was one piece of unaccounted evidence known only to him. Footprints. Returning home from work only days ago, Donnel had found footprints in his apartment. One set he had identified as his daughters as the worn tread was similar to trainers that he knew she always wore. The other set was a mystery to him. The prints were larger and more defined, suggesting a male. The treads were deep, as though they were combat or military in origin. He was not as privy to his daughter's social life as he once was, but there were few reasons she would return to his apartment willingly and even fewer with company. He had kept the prints to himself, but when the break-in at the Waycrests' apartment heralded investigation, he had found the very same faint prints pressed into their carpet. What vile crowd has she fallen in with who had the audacity to set up an attempt on the King-Regent's life?

Donnel had kept this information to himself even when asked directly by his superiors. Dishonesty was not in his nature and it troubled his thoughts even now. Deciding he needed some air, he left his cubicle, not realising how late it was. He walked the aisle into the foyer, feeling the cold breeze of Rainsturn blowing in from the open doors. The memorial to the young officer lost in the sewers caught his eye. A short ceremony had been held in mourning, yet the Chief had seemed especially disinterested in any questions and conjecture related to his disappearance. Donnel had seen the young officer a handful of times; always polite, holding doors and respecting the badge. He could never have imagined the internal struggle that kid had been going through to decide he'd had enough. Whatever it was, the same darkness had robbed him of his parents well before he met Aryssa.

Once the show of respect had concluded, Donnel had hoped to be assigned to the attempted regicide, for he believed the Waycrest break in was directly linked. However, his superiors had deemed it a conflict of interest and he had instead been assigned to another case involving recurring disappearances of unmarried Versorcerers and nobles. It was an unprecedented case that warranted his intensity to detail. As he had flicked through file after file of innocent faces, many of them young like Rissa, he took heart that in the very least he now knew where she was. He wasn't sure he could handle losing his only family left.

From his pocket he pulled out his only vice. A cigar made with cheaply made, Resynthesized tobacco. He had tried a "proper" smoke once, from a noble outside of a nightclub where he had served a brief stint as a bouncer in his youth. The cough after the first drag had practically incapacitated him back then. He fumbled in his pocket for his lighter and attempted to ignite the cigar, sheltering from the rain under a curved awning. It didn't work and he cursed, wishing he had been born with the natural flames of a Versorcerer.

The faces of the missing nobles plagued his mind. It was easy to hide a body in Centa Isla. Dumping it off the edge of the city would reduce any life that ever existed into dust. But why? What motive would there be? He felt the warmth of the cigar on his lips and took deep drags, releasing his stress and exhaustion in a long breath, watching as the cold wind grabbed the warmth of the exhaled smoke and carried it away. He would start his investigation tonight and he knew exactly where he needed to go. Allowing himself a couple more drags on his cigar before treading it underfoot, Donnel stepped out into the rain towards his patrol car.

It was another of things he couldn't stand to lose. His pride and joy, his patrol car had been with him when his career had started. It had seen many busts over the years. It was an old thing, running on an old generation magical engine with a Fire crystal for ignition and a handful of Earth crystals to squeeze oil from. He maintained it himself in the CIPD Compound's garage. Donnel had found at a young age that spinning a screwdriver in his hands was a good way to calm his rampant mind and focus on being productive. Had Reckoning not halted the progress of all industry, he would have loved to see what sort of patrol cars would be rolling around the streets now.

However, he was a few feet away when he sensed that something was wrong. It was a cold night, with the summer days of Ashdown a long way off but as he approached his vehicle, his detective's gaze spotted a thin layer of condensation steaming up the window.

Someone was inside.

He veered off casually, rueing the waste of a good smoke and took another cigar from his pack and flicked it between his lips. He ignored his car and continued down the street, his short sword was sheathed at his side, the customary issue weapon for an officer without a Conduit. A discreet check over his shoulder revealed no potential assailant, so he stopped and took shelter beneath a bus stop across the street, lighting his cigar. Deliberately allowing time to elapse, his cigar diminished inch by inch until it burned to a nub that he crushed underfoot. Curiosity nagged at him. Upon returning to his vehicle, he found the windows clear of condensation. Who had he just avoided?

He drew his sword from its sheath. He carefully opened the boot, finding nothing but tools, flashlight, cuffs, spare blade, the like. The hairs on the back of his neck stood on end as his glance was drawn to the roof of the compound, convinced he had seen a shadow flit just out of sight. He stared intently, blinking to refocus his eyes, eventually reconciling himself that it was likely the distant flashing of a coming storm creating shadows in the dark sky. He grabbed the flashlight and switched it on, flickering it over the backseats, before climbing in and slamming the door on the brewing storm. He'd do what he always did, throw himself into his work with a relentless obsession. If Rissa was going to be released from The Douldruums and reform, he wanted it to be into a city without the looming threat of Versorcerer disappearances. With the press of the ignition, the Verscience engine strained and rumbled, the flame crystal within firing as he veered out of the Compound and drove northwest, toward where the grubby streets of Downtown bled into the bustling City Centre.

Downtown was quiet this late in the evening. The windscreen wipers squeaked as they smeared rain and dirt across the window. The dim headlights tried their best in the downpour but barely offered visibility of more than a few feet ahead. He tuned the radio, looking for some ambience to drown out his thoughts only to be met with static. He drove quicker, building up his speed as if to outrun his rampant mind.

He passed a conclave of Synth addicts. Upon spotting a CIPD vehicle, they stumbled into the shadows clumsily. Donnel pretended not to notice them; the number of addicts growing so much in recent days that it had become impossible to arrest them all. At best, the CIPD perpetuated the fear of arrest, forcing scores of addicts to sit in squalor down alleyways, enjoying their exalted visions of a better life in the company of rats. As dark as it was, at the end of the day the problem cleared itself up as exploded corpses were reported appearing in back alleys every single day as overdoses became more and more frequent. To bodies like his and theirs, magic was simply a foreign body that they were not designed to deal with. Donnel found little quarrel with the Synth epidemic. At the very least it kept the population quiet. No crimes could be committed if they were dreaming of being King in a back alley.

The noble disappearances were a city-wide issue. Normally, he'd have no idea where to start but when dealing with crime related to magic, there was always one place Donnel checked first.

The neon skyline of the City Centre loomed as Donnel checked his mirrors and pulled up by the side of the road a few streets down from his intended destination. He left his vehicle, scanning the rooftops as he walked briskly, the distant thunder roaring. As a detective, he had learned to trust his instincts. Those very same instincts spoke to him now, telling him to watch his back. He cut through a quiet backstreet, startling as something rustled, only to find a lone rat skittering through piles of discarded waste. Beyond the alley, a modern and slick building beckoned him from across the street. This was the Verscience Headquarters, modelled similarly to Grayson Plaza. It was angular and alien, seeming abstract and out of place amongst the archaic buildings that surrounded it. Ahead of the entrance stood two stoic Kingsguard, their ornate golden spears were crossed together over the doors. They appraised him as he approached, a grunt of satisfaction from beneath the steel visor came once they acknowledged his badge and the glistening polearms lifted. The double doors slid open automatically with a hiss. Upon entry, the air immediately felt cleaner. Donnel took care to wipe his shoes on the doormat not wanting to tread mud and rainwater onto the spotless, white flooring that stretched out ahead of him. It reminded him of the hospital, so sterile and lifeless, yet futuristic. A clerk at a desk waited for him, Donnel flashed his badge and she smiled.

"How can we help, officer?"

"Syn Counts, please."

"Right this way."

Led through several sliding doors and sterile halls, Donnel peered in through the glass windows of the various rooms and labs. It was quiet this time of night but judging by the slowed state of advancement within the city, this was probably the norm. Since Reckoning, the focus for resources had shifted to survival as opposed to progression.

Entering the Syn Count lab, Donnel was shown a large map of the city housed within a pristine glass case and mounted on a sturdy steel legged table. Lights adorned the map, some areas remaining dark while others were lit up. An illuminated set of digits on a polished steel headboard above the map clicked with each change of number, the machinery clanking with the constant motion of calculations. The room sounded like an old-fashioned typewriter. Donnel marvelled at it. When crime involving The Algarethan Verse was his assignment, this was always the first place he came. Through just data alone you could track the exact movements of a rogue Versorcerer just based on patterns and metrics. It brought a giddy smile to his face, as though he was a child again, disassembling the family radio just for the thrill of putting it back together.

Every light on the map represented a probe that was strategically placed in various locations on Centa Isla. They were constantly recording traces of magic in the atmosphere around them. Despite being battered and assailed by the rampant rainfall, each probe was able to quantify and transfer the data to this table. In another lifetime he would have loved a job here, tracking data and improving the systems with his logical eye for detail.

He observed the lights as they flickered, waxed and waned. Whenever a spell was cast, magic was taken from the atmosphere to help create it. The probes would pick up that change. The light closest to the Guild Hall on the map was dark. But that made sense, considering the amount of Conduits active that evening, leaving the air depleted. Several times a day the workers of Verscience collated the Syn Counts of each probe and calculated an average. This average was what kept them alive. Based on estimation, conjecture and theory, it was believed that if the average Syn Count ever dropped below twenty-five then the core of the planet would implode from lack of magic in the air. Every citizen, noble, king or commoner would be turned to dust before the words "second Reckoning" could even be a murmur on their lips.

The reading for the Guild Hall was currently twelve, understandably low. If the rest of the city was like that, they'd have a problem. Currently, the latest average count had been thirty-three point six, worked out from what Donnel counted as fifteen probes spread out across the city. Downtown had four probes, the City Centre having nine, whereas Forge Town only had two. There was no probe attributed to Grandmaster. Donnel hoped he could locate recent hotspots for magic use and start his investigation there.

Donnel flitted through the last few weeks of readings. Both probes in Forge Town were giving surprisingly low readings compared to normal and were showing a downward trajectory day upon day, dragging the average steadily down with them. A remnant of the old primitive world, Forge Town was like history preserved. No Versorcerers would live there, dwelling in the toxic air. It would be beneath them. For the probes to be reading so low was… well, out of the ordinary. Perhaps the probes needed maintenance, or had been damaged by the turbulent weather? One way or another, it demanded an investigation.

With gratitude, Donnel left the lab and returned to his vehicle. He would patrol Forge Town hoping to discover the source of the declining Syn Count. As the engine started, he suddenly spotted a figure in the rear-view mirror. His eyes widened and he lunged for the door, desperate to escape. A chain snaked around the door handle and slammed it shut.

"Donnel Rawdon." The voice in the backseat was unmistakably youthful but laced with grit and malintent.

Slowly, Donnel raised his hands. Darkness obscured the identity of the figure in the back, but Donnel could feel the press of steel against the back of his fabric seat. One hard push and it would easily skewer him through the foam.

"What do you want?"

"To talk."

"Do I have a choice?"

"No." The voice was reserved. Donnel caught a glimpse of eyes, striking and violet glowing in the shadows. "I want to free a prisoner."

"I don't have that kind of juris-"

"Rissa Rawdon. Your daughter."

Donnel froze. The gears in his brain turned a hundred miles an hour. The description they'd been given for his daughter's accomplice was fresh in his mind, but he struggled to make out any significant details in the dark silhouette on his backseat. The exception were those eyes; unnatural in colour and bright against the darkness like a wild cat pulled from history. His stare was hard and steely, boring into his back, scanning him for the slightest twitch of a muscle. Donnel kept perfectly still.

"Who are you?" Donnel eventually asked.

"An ally."

"You're the accomplice." He surmised, recalling those deep boot prints in his flat and at the Waycrests' apartment. Chances are this was the man.

"She is innocent. Trust me."

At that, Donnel snorted. "Innocent? You both attacked the King."

"We weren't after the King."

"That's what Rissa said." He controlled his breathing. "You attacked Versorcerers and nobles at a private function - that's enough."

There was a pause from behind him. For the first time, Donnel saw confusion flash across those violet eyes. "You don't care about her."

What reaction was expected of him, Donnel wasn't sure. Rissa had committed a crime and was serving her time for it. He cared for her wellbeing, of course he did, but there was nothing he could do to lessen her incarceration. "Of course I care. But her actions have consequences, she's needed to know that for a long time."

"There's bigger consequences if she doesn't get out."

Donnel felt the blade dig deeper into the back of his chair, prodding his lower back threateningly.

"You're not going to kill me. Not if you give a damn about her." He was gaining control of the situation. Donnel could feel the pendulum swinging. He'd have the accomplice in a cell by the end of the night and could get on with his case.

"I'll do what has to be done."

"And getting her out of prison is so important?"

"It is."

"Why?"

Another pause. "I can't tell you."

"Of course, you can't." The engine was still running. "I'm going to start driving back to the station now, you're going to come with me and we can talk there."

His foot slighted on the accelerator and the car trundled softly forward. No blade pierced his abdomen and so he built his speed, gently lowering one hand to the wheel to steer. His uninvited passenger stayed quiet in the back, Donnel kept an eye on him in the mirror, more concerned about him than the empty streets that opened up to him.

"You failed her." When the violet eyes looked back to him, they did with words Donnel hadn't expected. There was an anger in them that was not his own.

"What?"

"Her apartment got seized today. Did you know?"

"Then work and pay rent. That's what I had to do. That's no fault of mine." He spoke bluntly, frankly, it was the truth. "She has always had a room with me. She knows that."

"Do you even know where she works?"

Donnel went blank. For a moment he almost missed a left hand turn on the way back to the Compound. He mulled the question over, keeping his face stoic and reserved. Her job? Had she mentioned it before? She had failed Grandmaster, so it wouldn't be a Versorcerer's employment. What would she make then, surely, no more than two-thousand Wreaths yearly? That should be enough to make her quarterly payments for the year. Assuming she lived in a Band D apartment then-

"You don't know."

"She's an adult. She can do what she wants."

"She works at a place called Avatar."

"Avatar!?" If Donnel had a drink at the time he would have spat it all the way up the inside of the windscreen. To imagine both he and Aryssa's daughter parading about that hovel of wealth and depravity... "What is she doing there!?"

"She doesn't work there anymore. She gave it up. For me."

"And what's so special about you?"

"Nothing." Was the reply. "But my mission is. I need her help."

Donnel pulled over. He snapped the handbrake on and sat in momentary silence. Frustration toiled with him, digging into his psyche like daggers, enough to make him stop for a moment. He had missed much of his daughter's life; of this he was acutely aware. However, he intended to make amends once Aryssa was back in his life and their family was reunited. He protected this thought. It was this thought that kept him going.

"Get in the front seat." Donnel spoke slowly. The Compound was only a few streets away. "If you want to talk, let's do it properly."

There was initial hesitation, but then the back door cracked open and the violet eyes disappeared as a robed torso flashed past the window. Donnel's attention to detail kicked in, noting that he walked with a powerful stride, his oversized robe hiding a strong physique. A silver chest plate protected his heart but it had been scuffed and nicked from battle and judging by his mere presence looming large at his passenger door, he had most likely been the victor. What he hadn't expected was for the powerful figure to struggle with the door handle. He fiddled clumsily with it, making it clunk and clank several times before it eventually opened. He jumped in, swift and agile.

Donnel was taken aback. "You're just a kid."

He looked young, a healthy head of dusty brown tousled hair and a clean, complexion devoid of stubble. His face was defined, cheekbones sharp like a blade's edge. Yet his eyes aged him beyond his years; they were dragged down by deep, dark bags and carried an apathy that should never be present on such a youthful face.

"Gault." The word tumbled, taking Donnel some time to process that it was his name.

"Donnel Rawdon." He introduced himself out of habit, his name already known to the darkly dressed passenger. "Let me get one thing straight. You're a criminal. We're here to talk. As far as I'm concerned, you belong in a cell."

"You know what I want." Gault replied. "Am I wasting my time?"

"Even if I wanted to let Rissa out, I couldn't." He admitted freely, removing his complicity from the table. "She's been admitted to The Douldruums."

His passenger's brow creased. "Where is that?"

Donnel pointed down. "An underground prison. Deep. Nobody in, nobody out."

"How can I get in?"

"In chains. Otherwise, you can't." Even as he spoke, there was something about Gault's violet eyes that resonated with him. There was a hardiness in there, a fire of grit and the undeniable presence of deep-set grief that softened the young man and made him human. Donnel knew because he had seen the exact same look in the mirror thirty years ago when he would grieve his parents.

"How deep you are imprisoned depends on the severity of your crime."

"So, it fills up, what happens then?"

Donnel felt the sudden need to smoke. He rolled his driver's side window down and lit up a cigar, taking a deep, heavy smoke before blowing it all out the window.

"Well, the prisoners with the least severe crime would be transported to the cells above ground."

"Where they can be rescued."

"Well, hypothetically, yes." Donnel released the handbrake and began to move again. He performed a turn in the road and headed back the way he came - away from the compound. Several streets passed him by before he pulled over once again. "There you go."

Gault peered around, then gave him a confused look. "What?"

"Get out, kid." Donnel opened his driver's side door and stepped out, feeling the cool rain on his skin. Turning his back to Gault, he leaned against his car and stared up at the sky, smoking. "I never saw you."

He heard the door open and the heavy thud of boots, but nothing thereafter. Donnel turned to find Gault still present, standing in the pouring rain.

"I can help."

"I told you to go." Donnel pointed to the nearest backstreet.

"I've been watching." Gault didn't budge. "You're looking for something."

Donnel allowed himself a laugh. "You don't even know what I'm looking for."

He watched as Gault's eyes began to glow. As if they weren't bright enough before, now they blazed with energy, piercing the dark with unnatural light. He opened the driver door, moving as though he had been blinded, fumbling with the glove compartment to come away with a small box that Donnel would recognise from a mile away.

Gault opened it and held it out to him. It was a Conduit. Donnel smiled and took it gingerly from its cushioned box, turning the old ring over in his hands. A wave of emotion and nostalgia swept over him, stealing his breath for a moment. A name was inscribed on the inside of the polished steel.

Aryssa E. Rawdon.

He kept his wife's Conduit with him. Their relationship had been so defined by social class that he had often wished they could have disappeared from this city and lived a quiet life away from it all. If they had been able to then perhaps this ring would still be feeling the warmth of her slender finger.

"How did you know it was there?" Donnel asked.

Gault offered him a slight smile. "Let me show you."

———

Rissa was being broken in. The Douldruums was already asserting its oppressive dominance over her mind and her body. It stretched for miles down, dug as deep as the floating mass of Centa Isla would allow without falling through the earth into the planet's core. It was made of mud, stone and chains. So many chains. They rattled all through the confused haze of night and day, accompanied frequently by cries of madness and despair from the deepest levels of the pit.

She was strapped in manacles, tethering her to the muddy brick that made up her square cell. They denied her of agency, with enough slack to barely twitch her muscles before the chain pulled taut. She tested them constantly, certain eventually that the old mud that formed the bricks around her would give way. But from the relentless cries of madness that were carried up to her from the very pit at the bottom of the earth; she knew that they would not.

There were layers to the dungeon, going deeper and deeper. Cascading walkways ran around the perimeter of the prison, patrolled erratically, once, twice or even thrice every hour. Rissa, in need of distraction, had worked this out herself, counting seconds in her head, converting them to minutes and then hours. She was fortunate to be on the top floor but had been told that the severity of her crime would soon relegate her to the deepest cells where the worst offenders were left to rot, bereft of human interaction, air and light. Her skin crawled to hear their dull whimpers, pleading and begging through the earthy acoustics. If the investigation into her and Gault went on, her risk of ending up buried down here grew closer to being a certainty. It was that or execution.

She was already suffering. Her shoulders itched madly from the rough-hewn fabric of the prison uniform, the shackles and chains so tight that they allowed no movement of her arms to scratch them. The more she tried the more they rattled uselessly, as if they were mocking her torture. The garments were scruffy and soiled, reeking of the previous owner's desperate stench.

The air was hot and humid, like sitting in a toxic steam room, where the stagnant air abused the lungs with every shallow breath.

How long had she been down here? Rissa was convinced it had been days. With no sunlight, reference of time or even regular patrols or mealtimes she had no idea. It was all intentional, designed to make her regret everything up to now. She had been fed her first meal of leftovers from failed Resynthesis attempts, her deprived stomach still churned with hunger, unsatisfied with the indistinguishable mush she had been forced to swallow. She had nothing down here. No hope. No future.

Rissa had wondered why, during the spectacle of public executions, there had been no resistance from the guilty, no hollering of final words for loved ones or even curses. Why had they sat there and taken it? Now she knew. The Douldruums annihilated all sense of self, stifling and paralysing the very essence of what made people human, rendering them incapable of any last words of pride, arrogance or passion. This was the death, coming well before the axe even fell. The death of the soul and the spirit.

She had been here, what, four or five days maybe? Already, she felt the madness clawing at her. There had at first been a tranquillity in sitting in silence, staring at the wall, as it almost offered an abstract form of meditation. Patterns had formed on the muddy, damp surfaces and thoughts and memories projected themselves onto the wall to be enjoyed and relived again and again. But eventually, the stale air slowly starved her brain of much needed oxygen. Her weak body held no strength but her stubborn mind did. In a desperate struggle for survival, it awakened painful memories that she had buried away and jolted them out of their deep slumber to keep her senses alert and her emotions alive.

Painful memories shot into her thoughts triggering an emotional explosion on impact. She was at her mother's funeral at the tender age of thirteen, having shouldered the responsibility of organising it while her father combed the streets. The scene played out on the wall in front of her. She closed her eyes to shut it out, but it played on the inside of her eyelids in startling detail. The nobles had come in droves, dabbing their fake tears with dry handkerchiefs. Even back then she had known their presence was a formality and play for status. The nobility had hated her mother. She had always said that wealth was a tool to improve the lives of others, not a means to forgo responsibility.

Rissa wondered if her mother had been here once too. Silenced and shackled like her. It was too painful to imagine such an horrific fate, her mother slowly reduced to a lobotomised, drooling shell of her former self. Her rational brain kicked the thought away with the stark realisation that she could never have been here. Her father would have saved her. She knew that with all certainty. He would have scoured the prisoner's manifest and would have found her immediately. This thought lifted her spirits momentarily.

She heaved on her chains again, spurred on by the cacophony of rattling and the emotions flooding her body. She pulled until her wrists chaffed, irritating the burn on her forearm that was still sore despite being treated at the station. It made her think of Gault, The Omens, all of it. At least down here it was no longer her responsibility. If the city was going to burn, so be it. At least she had tried. She'd be long since insane by the time Galleo et'al's dark shadow blotted out the light.

Her thoughts flitted to Azrael. Her brain enjoyed forcing her to relive the trauma of his cold hands around her throat, pushing on her trachea until the light bled from her eyes. Down here, she couldn't shake the sensation and for a moment her own breath stuck in her throat and she hacked, gagging on the stale air. She never would have defeated him, even with the help of Gault. The speed, the power and the presence of the black-eyed man was infallible. With a wave of his hand, he had crushed her command of The Algarethan Verse. The feeling of helplessness came back to her and she felt tears welling in her eyes.

What had it all been for? Gault, Kren'shal, Avatar, the stolen invite. All of it. Even her years in Grandmaster and youth, what had they all led to? It didn't make sense. All her life she had felt like something was missing, that her soul was a single spark away from igniting into life. It had been her belief that Gault was that spark - his mission and his world, promising new lands to explore and a life beyond the confines of Centa Isla.

Rissa now realised that it was a lie. Everything in her life had been leading to this place. The Douldruums, where the ambitious and the foolish shared a space. She had no control; she never did have. She was a slave to the wicked whims of the world. There was nothing she could have ever done that would have changed that. Her existence was pointless. Down here, in her isolation among the worst the city had ever produced, she realised that she had bloodied her hands for nothing.

———

Donnel veered his vehicle around Forge Town. The rainfall was continuous and rampant on his front window, the noisy wipers struggling to clear the deluge. But at the very least, such violent downpours helped lower the smog that polluted the east district of Centa Isla. The smog rolled at ground level, swallowing the tyres of his patrol car as he churned closer to the rickety cobbled roads.

The discovery of magic had once seen Forge Town thriving at the heart of an exciting and progressive technological revolution. It was a busy and bustling commercial centre with a multitude of trade, tradespeople and markets occupying every building and lining every street. It was now an archaic relic with groaning old buildings with sunken uneven floors. These days, there was no demand for traditional skills such as carpentry, blacksmithing or alchemy. Nor were there the resources. The new doomed generation had little interest in picking up trade skills and Donnel didn't blame them.

Gault was quiet in the passenger seat. His eyes were shut as though in concentration, yet bright violet orbs were still visible darting beneath his thin eyelids. Donnel had decided to humour the young man. There was a desperation about him that he understood all too well. This city liked to take all your cards away until you were forced to go all in and lose. It had happened to his parents, happened to him and it now seemed the same fate was soon to befall Rissa and her companion.

Having explained the missing nobles and Versorcerers, Gault's interest had only increased. They shared words here and there, but they both remained reserved.

Glancing up out the window, Donnel spotted one of the Syn Count probes on a tall building reaching into the sky. Even with the violent weather it remained steadfast with no sign of damage. With only two in Forge Town, they had already visited both and neither were malfunctioning. The sceptic in him believed Gault's powers were all nonsense, yet how had he known exactly where to find Aryssa's Conduit?

"What can you see?" Donnel asked. He watched the young man carefully, watching not just his eyes, but also the strange marking that had been emblazoned over his right eye. They both glowed with the same power.

"Magic." Gault's honesty surprised him. "What you're looking for isn't here."

"Are you certain?" Confusion was his instinct. Perhaps there was a higher population of rogue Versorcerers than he had initially thought. If these Grandmaster bricks were as readily accessible as they had been to them, there was a potential epidemic of illegal magic use forthcoming. The cumulative cost of every little spell sounding a potential doomsday bell for Centa Isla as the Syn Counts dropped lower and lower.

"There." Gault spoke so suddenly that Donnel jumped out of his malaise. The young man was pointing with a gloved finger ahead of them - beyond a block of buildings.

"Alright, kid. Let's see what you've got."

Donnel swerved right and then immediately left, the twisting, unmaintained cobbles of Forge Town slowly destroying the suspension on his precious patrol car. He would tighten up the bolts later. The roads were awful this far east of the City Centre as the further they drove, the more the toxic clotted smog began to roll in around them, devouring the vehicle. Unable to see five feet in front of him, Donnel squinted over the wheel, trusting Gault's thrusted finger to take them to the destination. They suddenly arrived at the end of the city, alerted by a gargantuan sign that declared the end of the road. The sheer drop into the core made his heart lurch. He put the brakes on and rolled to a steady stop - exhaling. "Kid, this is the core."

"No." Gault went to get out of the car. Donnel grabbed him, feeling a flinch travel down the robed arm.

"Wait, wait." Reaching into the glove compartment, Donnel pulled out two respirators. They were portable, adhering themselves to the mouth and nose to filter the toxic air from Forge Town. Donnel demonstrated, hooking the strap around the back of his head. "We're near the old factories. The air here isn't fit to breathe."

He watched Gault hesitate, turning the mask over in his hands. Eventually he obeyed, fitting the mask over his nose and mouth. While not nearly as effective as the air purifiers that had been fitted to the City Centre buildings, the portable editions were convenient but were very much like snorkelling in air. The mouthpiece and invasive tubes made any conversation impossible.

Donnel gestured to leave and they did so, stepping out the car into the smog and the rain. For day-to-day life in Forge Town, you didn't need a respirator. But being this close to the former factories that had vomited endless pollution into the skies pre-Reckoning, they were a necessity. The smog was oppressive and permanent, as though to be a constant reminder of their folly. Wind Versorcerers had tried to clear it with great gusts of hurricane grade wind, yet the smog just rolled back the next day. Guided by Gault's seemingly clairvoyant vision, they waded their way through. Donnel couldn't see more than a few centimetres ahead of himself, his vision dulled like a dimmer switch as though he was wearing a thin fabric blindfold.

Gault led the way with confident strides as though an internal navigation system was guiding him. In the advent of Resynthesis, it had been these very factories that had churned out compound after compound of synthetic substitutes for every conceivable item until the world had consumed itself with its own greed. Donnel ran a hand across the old bricks as he walked, feeling dusty residue come away onto his fingers. The smog obscured the true height of these titanic buildings, the peaks of them visible from some areas of the City Centre, breaking through the clotted smoke as though they were clouds. They were as much a warning for the future as they were a lesson of the past.

Even with the respirator cleaning and filtering air, there wasn't enough to sustain them for very long. As the stale toxins were stripped away, it left less and less clean air to breathe. If they went too far without finding relief, they may reach the point of no return where there would not be enough oxygen to get back to the car. If Gault was truly correct and they were heading towards a tremendous source of magic, it would explain the reason why the kidnapped nobility could not be located. Donnel had heard the factories were labyrinthian, winding beneath the earth where the former factory workers pre-Reckoning would live, eat and sleep between their shifts.

Donnel felt pressure building in his lungs and he gasped for more clean air. He pressed forward, the poisonous fog stinging his watering eyes and burning his exposed skin like a scouring pad was being slowly scraped across his flesh. Then, it suddenly disappeared. The smog ended, opening into a large clearing. Donnel ripped the respirator out of his mouth and broke into a deadly coughing fit, bent double with convulsive spasms. A smoker and a denizen of Centa Isla for what was now pushing fifty years, his lungs were already a cigar away from giving way. Gault had no such problem, he removed the mask and glanced back concernedly at him.

"Are you well?"

Donnel raised a hand. That was the best he could manage between the eye-watering hacking that rattled his ribcage and pounded his head. It subsided and he slumped, groaning. "Fine. Just... need a minute."

"We're close." Gault told him, offering a hand down. Donnel hesitated, then took it, the hidden strength of the young man now fully realised as he easily took his weight with one hand. He wasn't as agile as he used to be.

"Where specifically?" Donnel looked around the clearing. It was a large, presumably circular space surrounded by the smog on the far side and behind them. Up ahead was an entrance to a factory. Gault gestured towards the doors.

"In there." His eyes began to thrum once again with violet power.

Donnel led now, slowly approaching the door, a mixture of intrigue and adrenaline flooding his veins. A van caught his gaze, parked haphazardly a few metres from the entrance. He opened the back door, finding it empty.

"I don't like this."

"I can do this myself." Looking back at the factory, Gault spoke. The answer was swift, convincing and confident. His conviction was clear and in once again seeing unwelcome shades of his younger self, Donnel reluctantly clipped his respirator back to his uniform.

"Fine. You're leading. Someone has to be able to report this back."

"So be it." At that, Gault turned and approached the factory.

Donnel drew his sword and followed. The groaning iron doors were stuck open, the hinges rusted from years of isolation and poor conditions.

There was a burst of violet light. Another glance later and Gault was armed. He gripped a great scythe, once a tool of farmers. It was trimmed with radiant purple energy that sliced brightness into the darkness. It made a soft, silent humming that permeated the area. The light it emitted was comforting in the eerie ambience of the neglected building, which groaned with the strain of age and neglect. Chains rattled, spurred by the hostile wind that drifted in through cracks in the brickwork. The interior had been stripped completely, remnants of old conveyors and Resynthesiser installation fittings protruding with sharp, jagged edges from where they had been forcefully removed.

Gault led him deeper. There was no sign of anybody, let alone several Versorcerers as the young man had boldly claimed. But it wasn't until he stopped, violet eyes downcast, that they discovered a hatch built into the floor. These were the areas beneath the factories he had read about. Together, they pulled open the hatch, finding the hinges surprisingly malleable and cooperative. A deep drop burrowed ahead of them, steep metal steps providing access to great darkness.

It was then that Gault twitched and suddenly looked over his shoulder. Alarmed by his sudden movement, Donnel did so too. "What!?"

A long moment later, Gault shook his head and responded. "It-it's nothing."

"Keep it together, kid." Donnel told him. "You wanted this."

They descended. The flicker of torchlight greeted them at the bottom. As did something else. Distant agonised screams begging for mercy, revealed by the parting of the airtight hatch. They followed the screams through the subterranean halls, the harrowing acoustics reverberating off the steel. They shared a look of extreme concern. Feeling protective, Donnel took the lead, no longer content with letting somebody younger lead the way. He drew his blade as quietly as he could and skulked the corridors, treading the hatched steel floor.

Gault broke away wordlessly, moving away from the screams and disappearing into an adjacent room.

"Kid?" Donnel hissed, frustrated as he followed the young man into a random room. Immediately, the stench of squalor hit him. Gault poked around a small space, staring at a dishevelled old bed and a bucket. "What is this...?"

Gault didn't reply to him. His ears twitched as though he was listening to an unspoken counsel.

"I know..." He muttered quietly. "I know."

"Kid?"

Gault turned and brushed past him. The hum of his scythe drew Donnel's eyes to the miraculous blade. A creation of Verscience, perhaps? Unsettled by the silence of his companion, he followed. The hallway stretched back out ahead and the screams grew louder as they approached. A hard, blind corner awaited at the end of the hall and upon peering slowly around, he was surprised to see the place open into a large, tiered room.

Bodies filled the space, moving, writing, operating panels, all dressed in sterile white robes. Strange devices adorned the centre of the room, pod-like chambers. The screams radiated from inside the sealed pods, the worst of the noise suppressed by the airtight lid that covered it. A network of clear pipes linked them together, pumping thick, viscous crimson liquid into a large vessel at the back of the chamber. The sight of it sent shivers streaking down Donnel's spine.

Blood. Were they harvesting blood?

He retreated, intent on turning to Gault, only to find the young man already passing him, traversing the steel floor with lengthy strides at incredible speed. The scythe scratched noisily against the ground, drawing the attention of the workers in their lab coats. Donnel hissed for him to wait, yet it didn't matter. Their expressions were lost behind their masks as Gault charged them, practically mounting the first one, dissecting the mask to get a look at the face beneath.

"Damn it!" Donnel chased in, drawing his sword. Gault incapacitated the first lab coat, bruises and lumps already starting to sprout on his injured face. Donnel could have sworn he recognised the face from his previous visit to Verscience. What were they doing here? Clapping him in cuffs, Donnel quickly realised he didn't have nearly enough sets for a bust of this size. Instead, he sprinted to the pods while Gault dealt with the panicked lab coats, breaking a leg or ankle like he was breaking biscuits, hindering any attempt at escape up the steep staircase to the surface.

The glass of the pods was thick, but inside Donnel could see the shape of a person inside. Their screams were repressed, sounding as though they were underwater. Donnel tried the sliding pod door only to find it tightly sealed. Instead, he ran to the control panel and surveyed his options, he hit a button that he hoped was a pod release. It did as he had intended and opened the lids unleashing the full intensity of the deafening screams, their voices breaking and wailing with every second. Thick, long needles pierced their skin, incisions at every major artery as their blood was drawn into the massive tank. Donnel felt his legs go weak with revulsion and horror and a slow nausea rising in his throat. He ran over to the nearest pod and desperately looked for a means to shut it down. There were the remains of a woman inside, still alive, yet emaciated and skeletal. If she was a noble once, she certainly didn't look like it now. Her body shuddered and seized, near fatal amounts of blood having been leeched into the awaiting tubes. She looked at him with desperate eyes, relief, fear, sadness, pain, a myriad of emotions all at once. Her pallor turned from pale to grey as death tried to take her - only to return to life a split second later, clinging on to the last remnants of life.

"Kill me." She managed, voice pitched with agony and the repressed urge to scream with lungs that simply couldn't.

"You're okay, just hang in there." Donnel thumbed about the interior and exterior of the pod, finding the chunky cable that powered it and following it to its source to find no plug or socket. He rushed to a fallen lab worker, leg snapped brutally at the knee. Donnel grabbed them, hoisting them to their feet with a scream.

"Shut it down. Now." The lab worker was fearful, Donnel dragged them screaming over to the console and caved in his other leg, pushing his face toward the panel. "DO IT!"

There was hesitation and so Donnel pressed the blade of his sword against the throat of the worker. He felt his captive gasp and with shaking hands, they inserted a master key into the console and powered down the foul devices. The screams, the whirring of machines and the pumping of blood through the pipework all stopped in an eerie moment of calm. Donnel drove his fist so deep into the worker's nose that the lab coat was stained with crimson, the body already unconscious before it even hit the ground.

He set about finding Gault, stepping over a trail of writhing white coats. They were alive but otherwise incapacitated. Eventually he found the young man standing over a prone body.

"Please, please, no!" The body was deformed and hunched. Cowering in the corner of the room, he squealed for mercy. "Spare me! Dark One, please-"

Donnel only arrived in time to watch Gault kick the figure in his malformed skull. His head exploded up the wall. When the young man turned, there was something wild in his eyes that put icy fear into Donnel's chest.

"You can call it in, now."

He would do so. But first, he went from pod to pod, reassuring them that help was on the way, touching their hands or shoulders to remind them of the warmth of humanity. To deliver on that promise he had to ascend to the factory level and exited back through the smog where he seized the radio from his patrol car. With a trembling voice he requested a fleet of ambulances as well as the CIPD and a specialist forensic unit. The survivors needed him so he headed back down to be a comforting presence until backup arrived.

—

Rissa drifted in and out of sleep. The shackles that fashioned her to the wall were beginning to take their toll on her shoulders. She had dropped to her knees as the hours had interpolated, trying to let herself drop off to find some peace in her dreams. She was denied this time and time again. When the swathe of sleep came to claim her, the rattling of her own chains would wake her up. Anger had become her dominant emotion, sitting at the forefront of her mind as tiredness and fatigue wore her down.

More pain wracked her body. It took her a moment to realise it was her palm, where she had been scarred upon touching Akor'shaki for the first time. The wound was mysterious to her. By the time she had got home that same evening the wound had closed and healed, leaving a crease in the palm of her hand that felt numb to the touch. It hurt now, like the wound was being inflicted all over again. She shut her eyes to the pain, desperate to drown it out. Her nostrils twitched, invaded by the strange, pungent aroma of sulphur as the space between sleep and waking were momentarily captured in a strange vision.

A dark temple. Old stone walls and a shower of dirt and dust that cascaded from the ceiling as the earth itself shook. Her eyes adjusted to the darkness, whereas the body she found herself inhabiting moved freely. The floor was close, as though she was dragging herself across it. Ahead of her, a growing light pulsed, spilling crimson power up the black, torchlit walls. Once again,

Rissa had no control over the body she now inhabited. It moved, crawling across the uneven cobbles. Her connection to the legs that hammered against the floor felt stronger than before, enough for her to feel the impact jarring her knees. She clanked with the weight of steel armour, feeling the scratchy leather hilt of a shortsword in her palm.

Ahead of her, the source of the light revealed itself. Screams filtered in through her ears as her senses fully adjusted to the image before her. A young woman, no older than her, floated inches from the ground. Her body was splayed impossibly in more directions than the human body should have ever been able to manage. Limbs snapped and serrated, her veins bursting from the shell of pale flesh that housed them. She screamed all the while, her presence creating a beacon of energy that ascended through the cavernous ceiling and beyond her sight. Standing around her were two familiar figures.

Azrael and Lachesis. They watched quietly as the tortured figure writhed and shrieked as her body was flayed. Cracks formed in her skin as though she was made of clay, her blood on fire in her very body as her cheeks sunk and life drained from her.

Rissa felt a name in her mind as she beheld the tormented, screaming young woman.

Sophia.

Then, the pale face of Azrael turned. Rissa felt the fear of her host in her non-existent form. Rising as Azrael approached, Rissa bid herself to run, standing upon wobbling legs as the Brand of the Knight drew closer. She cursed whoever's doomed story she was witnessing as they raised their sword in opposition, but Rissa winced as it was easily swatted from their grip and a single strike sent them flailing across the room. She somehow felt the impact upon her back, mirrored with the agony of her host, yet held no mouth with which to cry out. As Azrael approached to finish the job, they scrambled away, flitting one last dismal look at Sophia's tortured body before disappearing down a long, narrow tunnel. Rissa could feel their lungs hammering with strain and tears stinging their eyes yet they did not stop. Suddenly, they both emerged from the dark hovel.

The sky was on fire, washed in bright crimson hues that stained the horizon the sickly colour of blood. Rissa found herself in unfamiliar, yet inexplicably nostalgic streets. The twisting tower, like a gnarled branch, brimmed with the same energy that was being harnessed from the fragmented blood of the poor soul Rissa had just watched be left behind.

The eyes looked up and Rissa was forced to follow. Up beyond the fire speckled horizon that saw an entire kingdom aflame. Looming in the sky, large enough to blot out the entire horizon was a great, crimson mass. It was a planet, chunks of dusty earth breaking away from the crumbling monolith, descending upon the city as small meteors. A name forced itself upon her, rattling around inside her head.

Galleo et'al.

She was glad that the body she was inhabiting continued to move by itself for she would have frozen in place, awed and terrified by the presence of such power. She could feel the sheer force of dark power pushing against every cell in this body.

Just then, one of the meteors scorched overhead, crashing through a stone building. It buried a crater into the ground, rising sulphur-stinking smoke from the ruin. From it, a shadow emerged, growing bigger and bigger as it drew closer. The body she possessed could only watch as it stumbled from the steaming crater. Rissa recognised it instantly; it was a spitting image of the very monster she had seen buried in the sewers before it had disappeared into a cloud of ash. Only this one had arms and legs, which made it tower several feet overhead. Quickly, the awe was replaced with fear. It wielded a poleaxe, stained with the blood of previous conquered worlds. Blinkers had been painfully grafted to its leathery face, forcing a pair of stinging crimson eyes to lock onto her.

More bodies rose from the crater. Four legs, wings, twisted shapes of all kinds. The skies overhead were filled with bodies, swarming and flying as the populace of this kingdom were picked like carrion. Horrific demons swarmed her peripheral vision and the arms of her host was barely able to rise as the first of the swings came-

Rissa awoke with a cry.

Shouts from deeper into the prison screamed for her to be quiet. Her hand simmered with hot pain and desperate to scratch it, she pulled at the chains around her wrists until blood leaked down her forearms. Despite the dreariness of her cell and the clotted darkness of The Douldruums, she could still see the bleached crimson spotting her vision and could still feel the sting of sulphur tingling her nostrils.

Galleo et'al and the demonic army that it commanded. She had seen it now. Was this the fate was to befall Centa Isla? If that was to be the case, she hoped to be dead well before then.

7

Noise jolted her awake. With every ounce of energy she could muster, Rissa hauled her aching legs to a standing position. Her shoulders were close to dislocation and Rissa had never experienced such searing pain. She had slept seated, with both arms shackled above her head. Her tired muscles had locked tight; a continuous dull ache now giving way to sharp darting cramps as they begged for release.

Something was happening nearby, but try as she might, she couldn't get a proper look. Shouts and cries filled the arid depths of The Douldruums. She saw hazy movement on the distant walkway opposite her cell - shifting shadows being guided to empty cells. Lots of them. What the hell was going on?

Then, a CIPD officer appeared in front of her cell and opened the rattling steel door. He held no liquid meal for her, spurring a question in her mind.

"What... what's happening?" She put a voice to her thoughts, only to find her own body working against her. Malnutrition and dehydration wore at her consciousness, the tip of her nose was numb and her mouth didn't feel like it was working properly.

The officer sneered at her. "You're moving cells."

"Why?" She muttered weakly.

"Cause there's somehow worse people than you in this city."

The officer unlocked the shackles around her wrists. Having to suddenly take her own weight, Rissa plunged to the floor, her arms failing to support her body as she face-planted the dusty, earthen ground. She felt the blisters before she saw them, horrified to find the flesh around her wrists raw and scoured, fresh blood having leaked down her arms and caked over her shoulders. Her body felt like she had been laid beneath a blacksmith's hammer. Her arms tingled with numbness as her circulation slowly revived itself. The officer called for help and between three of them, they heaved her out of the cell, her feet dragging through the dust. She was moved upwards along the walkway and not downwards into the depths of the prison and the realisation of this flooded her body with relief.

Drifting in and out of a warped fatigue she saw a stream of prisoners being escorted downstairs, some with noticeable bandages or leg casts. They went one by one, several armed officers helping them with their balance before offloading them into various cells, some doubling up by having just one shackled cuff to one prisoner. She watched them through dazed eyes for as long as she could until an iron trap door was opened and blinding rays of daylight entered The Douldruums. She winced as the brightness burned her eyes, forcing them to adjust to the shapes around her. As she slowly recovered from the clotted darkness of the underground, she found that everything popped with a vibrancy and colour she had never been able to associate with Centa Isla before. The air, however stale, was like paradise to her lungs and she gulped greedily as the officers continued to drag her haggard body into her new cell: the short-stay section, a luxury compared to her previous dwelling. The floor was stone but it welcomed in natural daylight through slitted bars near the ceiling. She even had a bed and a bucket. Most joyous of all were that there were no shackles to lash her to the wall. The world seemed fresher and newer. She lay on the bed, splinters digging into her spine, feeling faint spits of rain that had forced their way through the thin bars landing on her pale face. She captured a cold droplet on her finger and touched it to her lips. In her darkest moments, rain had always been her ally, reminding her that no matter what life dealt her, one fact remained. She was still alive.

—

Donnel Rawdon watched as the hunched, twisted body fell from the edge of the world. It twisted through the air, exploding into dust as it approached the core. Mires had been the man's name. Gault had informed him that he had been a man who did not deserve prison, nor did he deserve execution. He deserved to die alone with no trace of his existence ever to be found again. Even as they had loaded the body out of the boot of his vehicle, Donnel hadn't got a proper look at the corpse's face for the imprint of Gault's boot had removed any semblance of humanity from the husk.

It was barbaric and immediately made him realise how much the young man's age had put him off his guard. But even this was no comparison to what he had found beneath that facility.

The CIPD had arrived in droves after his call, detaining over thirty perpetrators. The frantic ambulances had raced the stricken nobles straight to hospital for priority dialysis and magic transfusions and a call for altruism had already been raised among the noble circles as the hospitals were desperate for blood donors. There were people still unaccounted for. Davin Grier, former Seat of Earth among the eight still missing. Based on the timeline of disappearances, Donnel assumed the worst. They had been late. The grim truth was likely that Davin Grier and those who had disappeared so early were already dead, every drop of their magical blood siphoned and the empty vessels that became of their bodies dumped into the core just as Mires had been.

The evil machines that had been draining noble blood had been seized by the CIPD and a full investigation was underway. As far as Donnel could think, surely only Verscience would be capable of inventing such a malicious construct. But what reason could they possibly have to do so?

"I can't believe the depravity." Donnel said, staring out quietly over the smoggy horizon. Chills ran down his spine thinking of the needles that had punctured the flesh of the prisoners. Vertigo kicked in and he turned away from the edge of the world. They had driven a distance away from the factory to dispose of the body, but the thick smog still hung in the air like a curse.

"I can." Gault replied. The young man was still with him, insisting wildly that it had to be him who disposed of the hunched corpse over the rim of the city. Donnel wasn't sure why it had to be him but had respected his decision, nonetheless. His opinion of Rissa's apparent ally had changed drastically since their initial meeting. There was a similarity between them that he hadn't properly picked up on at first. A sense of duty seemed to define both their lives, spurred on by what, Donnel wasn't even sure himself. It was just their nature. Somehow, Gault possessed powers the likes of which the city had never seen. He could track magic like some sort of bloodhound, summon a weapon from seemingly thin air and had an incredible physiological profile that would put anybody in this city to utter shame.

But he was still a fugitive. Wanted for regicide. By all means, Donnel should have clapped him in irons while he stared off into the distance with him. But he didn't. It wouldn't have been imprisonment that would have waited for the young man, but a painful death, likely dissected by the curious hands of Grandmaster or Verscience; whoever got to him first. A magical miracle like him would not long go untapped. Trust wasn't the word that he felt towards Gault, but he couldn't help but in part believe some of what he was being told. Unmistakably, there was something sinister happening in the underbelly of Centa Isla that had been carefully concealed. Gault seemed privy to it and seemingly, so did his daughter. But whenever he dared to raise a question to it, Gault would shut him down with curt dismissal. A desire to protect him or to keep him ignorant, Donnel wasn't too sure, but he didn't press any further. If he wanted to know, he was confident he could figure it out for himself.

With the body of Mires lost to the winds, Donnel returned to his vehicle. "Let's go kid."

"To prison?" Gault asked. It was a loaded question.

"No-."

"Why?"

Donnel blinked. "Why? Because-"

He stopped and thought about it again. He had taken an oath as an officer to uphold the law and shut down criminals. Why wasn't he going to arrest him? The young man was a conspirator in a regicide attempt and had just now murdered an unknown man by caving his face in. Yet, Donnel had a feeling. It was the same feeling deep in his gut that he had always trusted, the hunch that had got him through so many cases and out of dangerous situations. But perhaps most predominantly of all-

"Because I see something in you, kid." Donnel recalled his youth, in his first years in the force. He had been so desperate, so driven and determined to make a career for himself. With long hours, dedication and discipline he had outperformed so many Versorcerers who had held every advantage over him. "Something I had once upon a time."

He spoke of grit: the ability to dig deep under duress and keep going. Where the strength came from he still didn't know, but it was what got him out of bed and through the day. But he had found rolling out of bed harder these days, as though every day Rissa's mother went unfound, his grit eroded away like wispy grains of sand through the window of an hourglass.

"You and I are not alike." Gault's voice was decisive, as though he'd taken one look at him and gleaned all that he needed.

"Perhaps you're right." Donnel stepped away from his car, feeling a swell of emotion deep within his chest. The view was incredible as dawn broke across the edge of the world. The remnants of buildings destroyed by Reckoning surrounded him, many of them bearing names that had been carved into the wall. Names of those who had chosen to jump from this very spot. There was something mystical about becoming a part of the living world. To be reduced to dust and live in the air shared by the ones you loved. It was just a damned tragedy to leave people behind.

Donnel lit a cigar and began to smoke. The tobacco relieved the ache in his heart, steadying his thoughts when emotion dared to challenge his calm logic. "My parents raised me to sixteen. They had lived through Reckoning and had come out the other side."

Gault stood quiet. "What happened?"

"It was my eighteenth birthday. They gifted me everything they had. Every Wreath, even our home." Donnel said quietly. He felt the pain of the repressed memory burning his eyes. "Then they jumped."

He dragged deeply on his cigar, staring up at the clouds that had been decorated with the blush of dawn. His parents had always had wanderlust, the same lust for exploration that had passed him by but somehow found his daughter. Together, his mother and father had been so devastated by the Reckoning and their future of isolation in the barren husk of Centa Isla, that they decided to leave it behind. They had raised him well, teaching him the integrity and the values that still defined him today. Then they had left him. His intended inheritance, their property and savings were seized by The Crown as they sought ways to recover from the disaster and figure out a future.

He traced his hand across the brickwork. Their names weren't listed on the wall. He had searched the perimeter of the city every single day of his twenties, desperate to find the site where they had last visited. He had never found a trace of them. All that was left was a letter that he had found upon waking informing him that he was now alone and entirely independent.

Donnel Rawdon had a record, it seemed, of losing track of the people close to him.

"I lost everybody." Donnel admitted, slumping against the bonnet of his patrol car. "I couldn't do a thing about it."

Gault approached him slowly. He stayed at a distance, but his presence was warm. "You still have Rissa."

He thought of Rissa buried in the dark earth of The Douldruums, lonely and starving. The Douldruums didn't reform criminals. It induced insanity, making them a sad spectacle for a public execution as they babbled and slurred incoherent nonsense as the headsman's axe came down.

"I've failed her."

"There's still time." Gault returned. His words were always few, but they carried such purpose that they didn't need a sentence to work around. Donnel only wished he could be so direct.

Donnel chewed his lip, aware that he was burdening Gault with so many raw emotions. He was just a kid. He regained his composure and abruptly volunteered his hand for Gault to shake. The violet eyes looked confused, then proceeded to slowly shake his hand.

"Thanks for what I think you are about to do for my daughter."

He reached into his pocket and took Aryssa Rawdon's Conduit. The intricacies of the engravings still filled him with awe and his heart ached as he handed it reluctantly over.

"What's this?"

"It's for Rissa."

Gault just looked at him, the silver glimmering in the palm of his hand. Donnel smiled and patted him reassuringly on the arm. Returning to his vehicle hew fired up the engine, only for an idea to flit across his busy, tired mind. He swung open the door and called Gault over. As the young man approached, Donnel offered him the driver's seat.

The next day, Donnel took the day off. He allowed himself a lie in, indulging himself by sitting at the table to drink his cup of coffee instead of on-the-go. These were small changes, but he felt their impact. He savoured the drink, finding a small joy in being able to process the cheap, processed acidity of Resynthesized coffee instead of chugging it down in a matter of seconds behind the wheel of his vehicle.

He didn't wear his uniform either. Instead, he spent the rest of the morning dusting off his old, vintage leather jacket he had worn on his first date with Aryssa. It was an expensive old thing, made from genuine leather in a time where it was still attainable. He put it on, finding it a tighter fit than he remembered back in his prime. He kept it on, leaving it unbuttoned as he glanced in the mirror. He hadn't looked after himself properly since she had disappeared and he was only now fully realising it. The lines on his face had deepened, like great canyons carved into barren earth.

He left his apartment and travelled south. When the body of Mires had been rattling in the boot of his car, Gault had revealed the address of Rissa's apartment. It had always been his intention to visit, but he had never found the time. He followed the address scrawled intricately onto the card by Gault, impressed at his surprisingly eloquent handwriting. Ocean's View appeared before him, crumbling and overflowing with Synth addicts who lay comatose in the alleys and streets that surrounded the place. It both astounded and terrified him that his daughter had lived here. In his pocket jangled the keys to her apartment, seized from her once she had been incarcerated at the compound.

Apartment sixty-five. The stairs went on forever, lined with drug-addled bodies that he had to step over. It was a hovel. The whole building smelled of damp, mould and old stains of viscera decorating the walls around him as he ascended. Rissa's apartment finally appeared, a rental sign showing its availability and Donnel took a moment to catch his breath before clicking the key into the door and stepping in.

The apartment was tiny. Furnished still, yet the identifying features that would have made it Rissa's had already been stripped of the place. The shelves were empty and the windowsills bare. The place reeked of strong, cleaning chemicals. He assumed that The Crown's servants had come already to seize whatever remained of his daughter's possessions. The thought infuriated him, yet his anger dwindled as he realised he had no right to be so upset.

What had he done to help? Nothing.

Donnel looked out at the decrepit cityscape of Downtown and the depressing views his daughter had been forced to tolerate for the past year. The sight made him crumble and he sank down to the hardwood floor and buried his face into his calloused palms. He had never wanted this for his wonderful daughter. The day she had been born in the Centa Isla Royal Hospital he had sworn that he would give her the world. The best view in the city, anything she wanted, whenever she wanted. He had sworn he would spoil that girl. But even that illusion had been shattered when Aryssa disappeared. It twisted his heart so painfully. He had always been so absolute his actions were right and that his energy should go to finding Rissa's mother. But he had been so focused on bringing her back that he had neglected the one thing in this world he still had. How had it taken him so long to realise? He was a bastard and a failure who had no right to call himself a father.

Anger rattled his bones. No matter how much he desired, returning to the past was impossible. But what he did have was a future where he could perhaps help. Rissa was somehow involved in the events that were unfolding in Centa Isla. He sensed it now. It was something deep and embedded, mysterious to him, but seemingly obvious to others.

Something wasn't right. The pods had been delivered into the hands of the CIPD, yet already the case had been closed. Donnel was confused and when questioned, he had been greeted with ignorance. How had there not been a large-scale inquest into the origins of such a horrific device? How could it have been closed so easily?

His radio suddenly crackled, loud in this empty, quiet room. He picked it up.

"Attention Compound. Officer needs assistance!" The voice was panicked, startled, percussed by static interference. "I repeat-"

The voice cut out. Donnel turned the radio off. He stayed there on the ground and sat, his leather jacket crumpling as he shifted.

He sighed. "Good luck, kid."

———

The air in Centa Isla had become thick and humid as dangerously dark clouds leered overhead. The imminent threat of a mighty storm flashed but had yet to deliver on its thunderous promise. Gault knew a storm when he saw one, especially one as ominous as this. Rissa had warned him of the ruinous potential of a magic storm. It was a matter of time until these black skies exploded over Centa Isla and he didn't want to be outside when it happened. On the horizon, the clock face above Monument lit up the darkness, its proud hands showing it was just past midnight. He knew it was almost time.

What are we doing? She is going to reject you.

"I know." He muttered out loud, sounding like a mad man to any who may have overheard him but at this hour his only companion was his shadow. The CIPD Compound sprawled ahead of him, even now at this late hour it was still heavily manned, a likely consequence of the dangerous criminals held within - or rather, beneath its earthly layers. There wasn't a time of day he could spring Rissa from prison that would be easy. But he was confident this was the best chance he would get.

Donnel had told him some valuable information. First, that they would avoid using The Algarethan Verse inside the premises unless absolutely necessary to protect the structural integrity of the building and subsequent prisons within. Once outside it would be an entirely different matter so a quick escape would be crucial.

She isn't going to forgive you. This is wasted time.

"Maybe." Gault watched as another CIPD vehicle burst into life, sirens wailing as it careened down the street of Downtown towards an assumed call. Waiting was becoming intolerable and so he swiftly dropped down from the rooftop. Crossing the street, Gault vaulted the fence at the same point that Rissa had used, taking advantage of a gap in the barbed wire. He entered the deep, wide vehicle depot where a legion of vehicles awaited him. Wielding Akor'shaki like a small letter opener, he slit the front tyres of the vehicles at the front of the arrangement, preventing the vehicles behind from passing. He had

Donnel Rawdon's patrol car, parked and ready for their escape. It had been a surprise parting gift, for sure.

Are you seriously going to try and ride that?

He understood Akor'shaki's apprehension. He had found the vehicles here fascinating but had not yet driven one properly himself. Donnel's advice had consisted of "accelerate and steer".

The father of Rissa Rawdon had surprised him. Stubborn, hard-headed, that much was certain. Yet their interactions had made him distinctly nostalgic for his own lost family. His own father lost before he could-

Concentrate, fool. At the very least don't make me do all the work.

"Right." Gault buried his feelings and left the depot. The air was growing muggier as he approached the compound, entering the front door to find an unattended front desk. Without hesitation he vaulted the dark oak desk and immediately began to flit through the prisoners' manifest, hoping that Rissa had been moved out of The Douldruums to make way for the scores of lab workers who had been part of the heinous blood draining horror. He knew a plot by the Omens when he saw one and the presence of Mires, Brand of the Heretic had all but confirmed his suspicion. Whatever plan they were hatching had hopefully been set back.

The log was overwhelming to read, formatted so tightly together to save paper that he almost felt like he was reading hieroglyphics.

PRISONER #3873 R.R TRANSFER
TO HOLDING CELLS – 24/R 10:34PM

That had to be her.

Attention. Akor'shaki alerted him to the sound of footsteps causing him to look up.

"Wh-What are you doing!?" A mug of coffee dropped from his hand. Hot liquid spilled over the dark floor and the porcelain shattered, making him jump. "You can't be here!"

"Attention Compound! Officer needs assistance!" He yelled into his radio as the sword flew from his scabbard into his hand. Gault observed a Conduit on the officer's finger yet knew with quiet confidence that it wouldn't be used as long as they were indoors. That hand with the conduit instead dropped to his waist to grab a radio. "I repeat-"

Gault vaulted the desk again and kicked the radio out of his hands, disarming the blade from his grip before scooping up and slamming the officer directly through the desk, the wood splintering around his body as he went quiet and still.

You were supposed to hold back.

Panic surged in his chest for a brief second and he searched for a pulse from the body, relief washing over him as he found a steady beat. He wasn't here to kill anybody. Time had made it difficult for him to regulate his own strength. For a long year he had contended with demons upon the very surface of Galleo et'al. There wasn't a day spent there where he had needed to hold back his might. Regardless, he would rather inflict too much damage than too little. The consequences of failure were too catastrophic to do otherwise. Without him, the Omens would add this city to their list of conquered worlds and the dead of his homeworld would no doubt torment him eternally in the afterlife for his failure.

Then, an alarm began wailing.

He whirled around, confused, wondering what triggered it. Two officers entered the room, immediately spotting him and drawing their weapons. Gault rushed them both, using his steel shoulder plate to turn away one of their blades as he speared into the other, driving them to the floor. A forearm across the face rattled the head against the hardwood floor, knocking the officer unconscious before he twisted around, tripping the second officer with a sweeping leg. They were both on the floor and he stepped over them, surging down the hall toward the holding cells.

He could hear the prisoners who were above ground, roaring and yelling, rattling the bars that detained them as the alarm continued to blare. He powered into the short stay holding area where the noise grew louder, almost deafening. They howled like rabid dogs, screaming for freedom, growing louder when he ignored them. He searched the cells, daring not to get too close for risk of a limb flying between the bars and seizing him.

"Rissa!" He called, unable to find her in the madness. He kept looking, dark eyes sweeping the gloomy, dark stone cells until eventually, just as he began to doubt she was even here, he found her. Sat quietly, the antithesis to the raucous loudness, Rissa rested at the back of her cell on an old wooden bed. She didn't look up even when he grabbed the bars.

"Rissa. It's me." He rattled the bars and she looked up, distant. She looked awful, face sunken and malnourished, eyes bloodshot and lacking sleep. Her hair was wilder than usual, matted and unkempt. Recognition flitted across her face and she smiled at him weakly, raising her hand. But she didn't get up.

"Come on. Get up!" He exerted, demanding the strength that Akor'shaki housed to bend the steel bars open. It obliged and he felt the pumping of monstrous might course through his muscles seconds before the metal bent like rubber. The roar of the prisoners pitched in anger, some now begging for freedom as they watched. But, even with a clear exit, Rissa remained seated. Gault stepped into her cell and kneeled in front of her. Her eyes were cloudy and glazed over, staring through him as though he was a spectre or a phantom. Gingerly he reached out to touch her and she didn't move until his hand gently crested her shoulder and she jumped, her eyes widening.

"Gault?"

"You OK?"

The alarms, the shouting from the other prisoners, it was all deafening. She looked as though she had just realised what was happening. She spoke in a whisper like it was the dead of night. "What are you doing here?"

"Getting you out."

Slowly, reality rushed through her. He watched as her face shifted from confusion, then steadily into righteous anger. "You're breaking me out? After you put me in here?"

"I'm sorry."

She flew to her feet with energy that did not befit her sunken frame. It caught up with her quickly and she wobbled, Gault supported her with a hand, but she pushed him away. "No. You left me for dead. I could have been executed here while you... while you..."

She trailed off, blinking. Gault watched her gears turn, like an old clock tower filled with rust.

I told you.

"I'll ask nothing of you ever again. Let's just get you out."

Tears stung at her eyes as she stared at him. She eventually nodded and Gault led her through the gap in the bars and out of the cells, ignoring the deafening cries and rattling bars. Her wrist was shrunken in his hand, small enough to wrap his full hand around. He was gentle, but urgent as he led her out, stepping over the bodies of the CIPD officers he had left on the floor. At this, Rissa suddenly pulled away.

"Did you kill them!?" She demanded.

"No."

She stared at him and lowered herself to the ground, searching for the pulse of one of the officers, seeming content when she found it. Did she even trust him at all now?

Are you going to humour this nonsense? Grab her and get out.

"Can we go?" He couldn't hide his frustration.

She doesn't trust you at all.

"I know." He spoke in response to Akor'shaki and immediately grimaced when she looked at him as though he was insane.

A steady stream of officers arrived and Gault dispatched them all with relative ease. He felt good; limber and quick. His focus was his own and he was careful just to inflict surface wounds or wind them. With the way cleared to the outside, they fled the compound and Gault led Rissa toward their getaway vehicle.

"Get in!" Gault opened the door correctly.

"Let me drive." Rissa headed for the driver's seat, but Gault re-directed her with a curt push.

Assert yourself.

"I know what I'm doing." He got into the car and the ignition surged as he pushed the button. The engine roared into life as the fire crystal ignited. The tyres ground against the tarmac as he accelerated away. CIPD officers poured from the compound in pursuit, preparing magic to launch their attack, but he was already long gone by the time the first spells were cast. Those who sought to pursue found their tyres drained of the wind magic that had filled them.

They drove in silence, slaloming through the twisting streets of Downtown. Rissa sat still, looking out the passenger-side window or ahead of them. She was fidgety. She touched the dashboard absently, her fingers meeting a cigar stub and a film of ash, the familiar smell startling her.

"Gault?"

"What?"

"This... are we in my dad's car?"

"We are."

"How did you-" She cut herself off. "Where are we going?"

151

Gault focused on the road. His hands felt clammy on the wheel as he drove through the city. This hour the roads were deathly quiet, but he knew there was a pursuit mounting. "We'll be there soon."

Rissa suddenly grabbed the handbrake and yanked it upwards, the car screeching with protest as it skidded to a sudden halt.

Gault whirled on her. "What are you-"

"WHERE ARE WE GOING!?" A mix of dread, fear and anger scoured her face. Her voice pitched to a terrified shout.

Gault looked into her eyes, at her pupils wide with fear and panic. The weight of her experience beneath the city showed in the glassy tears that swam across her eyes. He realised in that moment that she was scared - of him. Of his unpredictability, his deadly calm and prolonged silences. She feared the lapses in control he had demonstrated when she had needed him to be strong and stable.

"To Eclipse." He said quietly, recalling the frosty reception he had received from the gold-toothed thug upon returning. "To get your belongings."

She took her hand slowly off the handbrake and turned away from him, gazing out of her side window. Gault continued driving, taking recurring glances in the rear-view mirror which revealed empty roads and no vehicles in pursuit.

"You kept them?" She asked him. Minutes had passed, time dilating into nothing but the road ahead of them. For a moment, Gault was confused, until he realised she was picking up their conversation.

"I did. Should I not have?"

"No, no." He caught her reflection in the window, a weak smile on her face as she stared at Downtown passing by. "I'm glad. Thanks."

"There's also this." Without taking his eyes off the road, he reached into his pocket and pulled out a Conduit. He handed it over to Rissa who took it gingerly.

"This is…" She turned it over in her hands. "This is my mother's Conduit?"

"A gift from your father."

"You've been hanging out with my dad?!?"

"He helped me."

Rissa wore a complicated expression of gratitude and discomfort, yet she held the Conduit tightly. "I find that hard to believe."

Gault felt relief as he started to recognise where he was. Centa Isla was still a maze of nonsensical designs to him, but he had memorised key landmarks such as distinct corner shops, abnormally deep potholes and abstract graffiti, storing a sketchy visual map in his head. He pulled the vehicle up by the side of the road and got out, leaving Rissa sitting in the passenger seat. Donnel had given him instructions on how to mask their disappearance and he intended to follow them. Skirting the patrol car, he ripped off a false registration plate from the front and back of the vehicle, revealing the true one behind it. He ditched the fake plates down a slitted sewer grate before approaching the silent, pseudo-abandoned storefront of Eclipse.

He knocked on the door and repeated the code word he had heard and remembered Rissa saying before. "Only Dawn Will Follow."

There was a long wait, one that Gault had expected. But the door never opened. Furrowing his brow, he turned – straight into the point of a blade at his throat. The hooded face was obscured save for a pair of cunning, deadly eyes. Behind them, other figures searched Donnel's vehicle, apprehending Rissa at knifepoint.

"You think pulling up in that was a good idea?" The figure gestured to the CIPD vehicle. The voice was familiar yet distorted through the thick fabric.

Who does he think he is? Break his neck.

"We're not associated." Gault stated, ignoring the flashes in his head of his hands cracking the hooded figure's neck. "Hard as that may be to believe."

The hood came down and a gold-toothed grin met him. Kenneth Rand, the shopkeeper who had sold Rissa her second Grandmaster brick, acknowledged him. His shaved head was still lumpy from the impact Gault had inflicted upon it. Clumsy stitches held the flesh together. He pulled the blade away and clapped him over the shoulder. "Today, you're lucky."

He waved down the other hooded assailants and they released Rissa and stepped away from the vehicle.

"I'm here to retrieve what I put in storage."

"You haven't forgotten our terms, I trust?"

"I haven't."

Rand seemed content. Gault knew what was coming and he held as still as possible as Rand's calloused knuckles swung around, rattling the very bones in his skull. The arms that had once worked forges tensed from the impact.

"A deal well closed." The dignified front returned; the flesh of his knuckles still raw from the impact. Gault felt a swelling welt forming, only for Akor'shaki's influence to quickly quell the pain.

Are you kidding me?

Rand gestured to the Eclipses who had gathered a few short paces behind him. "Load the boot. I'm due to catch up with an old friend."

Rissa approached as if on cue. She dithered slightly in the cold, even with the protection of his robe. She glanced at both of them, a small smile on her face. "Rand. Good to see you."

"Rissa. You look terrible." The gold-toothed grin returned. "Did you break that brick yet?"

"It lasted all of three days." Despite the fatigue that wracked her, Rissa managed a small, raspy laugh.

Gault left them to it, collecting one of the boxes from the abandoned shop unit as the hooded Eclipse members brought out several boxes of Rissa's belongings. They were as heavy as he remembered. He'd tried to save as much as possible from her apartment, hopefully she would be happy with it. Two went in the boot of the CIPD vehicle and the rest had to sit across the back seat. Rand had given him the address of somewhere they could lay low while the heat dissipated. All that he asked in return was that he lend them his weapon and his services when they next had need of it. He had accepted those terms, mysterious as they were, out of sheer desperation.

With Donnel's patrol car packed, they bid farewell to him and other members of Eclipse. Driving east, he drove onto the raised Bypass lanes that surrounded the City Centre, avoiding Downtown entirely on the way to Forge Town where they ditched Donnel's patrol car at a designated spot and carried the boxes by hand the rest of the way.

They would disappear into the smog of Forge Town and lie low for a while.

———

He saw his home. Sandy dunes and radiant sunshine. A life before Galleo et'al had blotted it out forever.

Jace awoke from a dream. There was a dull, thrumming ache in his head that he continued to nurse with alcohol and sleep. His past had been revisiting him so often these past few nights. Instinctively he reached for his drink, finding only the wispy remnants of strong liqueur pooled at the bottom of the tumbler glass. He rose quietly, careful not to wake the sleeping figure with whom he lay. She faced him, deep in enchanted slumber on the comfort of her bed. She was peaceful, fiery auburn hair draped over the soft silk pillow and her porcelain face pocked with freckles. High Priestess Cordelia Rowe shared his bed. The Headmistress of Grandmaster herself. Her arms were wrapped tightly around his, her fingers resting over the Brand of the Sorcerer that wended up his arm. But this was no romance, no fairytale. This was his charge, his task. Her influence was sizable and he needed it to convince other Versorcerers to vote positively in favour of the Obelisk suggested by Azrael and supported by the King.

She was now an avid supporter and influencer. Although she had admitted to him several times that it wasn't Grayson Clovis nor Azrael that she believed in, but something else entirely. She was a powerful figure here, Jace never quite felt like he had her wrapped around his finger like so many others he had coerced into supporting the Omen's plans.

Jace got out of bed, gently trying to prise his arm from her vice grip. Her pale hands, nails painted a lavish red clung to him, digging into the flesh of his Brand. His mind begged for distraction and he eventually wormed himself away. The floorboards groaned beneath him as he stepped out of the expansive bedroom and out into a wide hallway. Her home was lavishly decorated, entitled as a private residence built in the west corner of Grandmaster. He winded down the stairwell, slipping into a luxury pair of slippers as he shuffled across the impressive foyer and into the conjoined kitchen. He peered through the window, glancing at the stoic Spellguard who stood as still as stone itself outside her door. Of all the things here, they unsettled him the most. They were hulks of armour, designed to protect the academy grounds from threats both external and student disagreements internally. Their might was unquestionable and although he hadn't seen one in action himself, the fear in the student body at so much as a rattle from the armoured body was enough for him to take them at their word. He questioned if beneath that black, bottomless visor they were even human at all.

From the ever-dwindling alcohol cupboard, Jace poured himself a glass of bourbon. This was the real stuff. Preserved over sixty years from before the day of Reckoning. He simply couldn't take a liking to the watered-down replicas served in bars and offered in shopfronts. Part of it was that he had undeniably expensive taste, of that he was unashamed, but it was also for the fact that the heavily diluted liquor didn't get him drunk enough. He shot back a glass, feeling the burn hit his throat and fill his body with warmth. He knocked back one more for good measure, already feeling his mind begin to soften and numb - just the way he liked it.

Just then, a shadow suddenly flashed across his peripheral vision. He whirled, finding nothing but the dark, dim light of the cerebral moon casting its luminescence through the kitchen window.

"Can't sleep?" A familiar, velvety tone turned him around one more time. Lachesis stood in the arched partition that separated the kitchen from the foyer.

"You scared me." Jace told her, the alcohol in the now half-empty bourbon swishing around.

"Poor practice for the professors to get drunk, isn't it?"

"Normally." Jace began pouring himself another drink, this time sipping slowly at the liquid. He shrugged nonchalantly. "They must like me."

"That's good." Lachesis replied, stepping out of the shadows and prying the drink from his hands. "It's time for you to make your move."

"So soon?"

"Things are moving quickly." Lachesis spoke ominously, a hurried tone to her voice that suggested that the timeline they had initially set for their campaign in Centa Isla had been pulled forward. "We need the artefact. Sooner rather than later."

"What about Cordelia?" Jace felt a twinge of concern for the High Priestess. While his intentions to get closer to her had been laced with ulterior motives, the feelings that she had shown toward him so far were clearly genuine and it was his wish to at least honour those.

"What about her?" Lachesis stared at him. She sipped his drink, her lip curdling in disgust. "You do what has to be done."

Jace chewed his lip. His hand was empty, the feeling of a phantom glass pressed between his fingers. An orphaned noble, Cordelia had got to where she was by her own accord and determination. She rose to Headmistress and High Priestess, mothering a daughter who now actually studied under her at Grandmaster. She had taken a special interest in him for his ability to cast spells without a Conduit. While the power was granted by Galleo et'al's Brand of the Sorcerer, it had allowed him to easily infiltrate her personal life.

He just hadn't expected to care so much.

"Don't make yourself a liability." She spoke as though she could sense his turmoil. "You know what will happen."

He did. He knew Lachesis spoke from experience. Galleo et'al had punished her for speaking out and her pain was visible and palpable. Her body still looked tired. He wanted to avoid a similar fate at all costs.

"How bad was the pain?"

"Almost killed me." She replied, a playful smile crossing her face. "Imagine what it would do to you."

Jace felt his brand begin to itch. He ignored it and took the entire bottle of bourbon and took a deep swig.

Lachesis touched his wrist and lowered the bottle away from his mouth. "Sober, if possible, Jace."

"I'll be fine in the morning." He lied. Seeming content with his response, Lachesis disappeared into a whorl of magic through the kitchen window that was slightly ajar. The silent Spellguard outside knew nothing of it. They were attuned to magic in a way few were, but their Brands gave them command of a magic nobody in this city had ever seen before.

Now alone, Jace felt the weight of what was to come heavy upon his conscience.

"Gods, damn it." He cursed, bringing the entire bottle back up with him as he returned to Cordelia's bedchambers.

———

Rissa was feeling stronger. Gault had taken her to a place recommended by Rand; a tavern in the heart of Forge Town's old markets known as The Hound. There, she'd changed out of the soiled prison rags, drank more water than she ever had in her life and eaten the most delicious hunk of stale bread she'd ever tasted.

Her boxes filled the corner of the tavern where they had quietly found unoccupied seats. With cowls thrown over their heads, they waited and rested out of the public eye and the public mind. Rissa made sure that her hair was hidden. Forge Town, located to the east of the centre, was even less friendly to Versorcerers than Downtown. Many of the people here were former tradespeople who blamed The Algarethan Verse and Versorcerers for the death of their trade. And rightly so.

It was a busy night. A lone barman ran the place, serving big, wooden tankards of watered-down ale to rows of patrons who sat on crooked stools at the bar. The whole place smelled of musty wood and stale ale. The tables were splintered and sticky, the wooden stools wobbling with mere days of life left in them. Yet the place felt homely and comforting. Whilst the hearth blazed with radiant fire, a radio, crackling with regular interference, played some ambient, nostalgic music that harkened back to days pre-Reckoning where tavern bands would have played nightly in places like this. A mezzanine ran overhead, revealing a larger, more spacious interior that was yet unused to the public.

She glanced at Gault. They hadn't shared a word since sitting down. There was no malice in their silence, at least not at the moment, but rather there was a shared desire to recharge and put their brain to sleep. He was zoned out as she watched him, a half-empty tankard of water in his motionless grip. He was so still and focused that the surface of the water offered not even a ripple. Rissa wasn't certain where she stood with him. Whether she liked it or not, they were both wanted fugitives within the city and while he had rescued her from imprisonment, he had lost her trust entirely.

If they were going to work together, there would have to be changes. No longer was she going to accept his nonchalant violence. His outbursts of tunnel vision had to be managed and controlled. But it wasn't just him that she needed to work on. Rissa knew that she herself had work to do. If Azrael was going to be defeated then she was going to need to upskill herself. Swordsmanship, martial combat, whatever she had to do to put her reliance on magic in combat to an end. She felt the pressing of her mother's Conduit in her jean pocket. She fingered it comfortingly, aware of the calm she felt with it within reach, but knowing full well that solely relying on it would be a major weakness.

At the very least, progress had been made. The Conduit she now held, while not attuned strictly to her, was authentic and powerful and not limited to restrictive spells that needed a brick lugged around to work. Rissa just had to hope that her genes were similar enough to her mother's for her to use it effectively. She had yet to test it, but she would soon, when she had recovered from the physical and emotional impact of her prison stay.

The radio crackled behind the bar, loudly. The barman fiddled with it, only for the pitch to grow louder until it apexed, resulting in a clear channel.

"This is an emergency broadcast. The Crown will soon speak. Be silent and listen."

The atmosphere changed all of a sudden. An emergency broadcast, sent from the top of Monument, sounded out around the tavern. Those who were talking, went quiet. Those who were standing, sat down. Those who were drinking, lowered their mugs. Broadcasts like these were infrequent and usually of major importance if the whole city needed to know. Rissa hadn't heard one in years, she felt the breath of the entire tavern pitch into silence, only the crackling of synthetic timber from the hearth to be heard until the voice came again.

"This is Grayson Clovis, former King-Regent of Centa Isla."

The voice was unmistakably the same voice she had heard from Grayson at the rally. It was marred by radio static, but his tone was solemn. "I bring ill news from Monument. The King is dead."

There were a handful of cheers from the seated patrons.

"Shut the hell up, you idiots!" The barman roared, cranking the volume up on the radio.

"I, Grayson Clovis, his only son, shall formally take the throne in his absence. With my reign, I bring a promise to you - the people of this great city." There was a break in the transmission. "Better days are coming. For Forge Town, for Downtown, for the City Centre and for all. Please weather the coming storm with proud hearts and strong minds."

Murmurs broke out but were promptly quelled as the barman banged a wooden mallet on the wooden countertop.

"Stay the course, friends." King Grayson Clovis sounded out. "It may get worse before it gets better, but sunnier days are coming. Take care."

The radio buzzed and crackled, then the usual music continued. There was a stunned silence around The Hound, until the first few conversations broke out into a cacophony of uproar and noise. Rissa could only hear pockets of it from patrons sitting closest to her.

"The same tune as his father." An old patron grumbled. "I don't believe a word of it."

"Patricide?" Asked another. "Convenient timing, following the failed ballot, don't you think?"

Across the tavern, things were heating up. Two tall, burly patrons were in each other's faces, arguing over the state of the city.

"People like you are the reason we don't get positive change. Give him a damned chance."

"Open your eyes. His blood is poisonous. The Clovis line cannot save us. May the stones that are thrown end his reign quickly."

There was pushing and shoving, people picking sides. Rissa glanced at Gault and the look he gave shared her sentiment. It was getting rowdy. Signalling it was time they left. They threw a blanket over her stack of boxes and stepped toward the exit for some fresh air. Just then, a patron, violently shoved by another, fell into her. Rissa tumbled to one side, steadying herself on a table as the patron hit the floor. She felt weak as her shoulders heaved with the strain of being asked to support her body. She received looks and in that moment, wondered what was going on until she realised that her hood had been knocked from over her head, revealing a bright head of blue hair for all to see.

"A Versorcerer? Here?" The aggressor revealed himself. Tall, bloated, nose rounded like a boil. His eyes were bloodshot with anger, his speech slurred softly from a night of drinking. He cracked giant knuckles, hands as large as the stool she had just been sitting on. "You haven't timed that well have you?"

His shadow was wide and imposing as he leered over her. His hands were calloused and his skin was leathery and burned from a lifetime of forge work. "Lot of bleeding nerve showing your face around here. Why aren't you cowering beneath the shadow of your tower like the rest of your kind?"

The barman rang the bell for last orders. "That's enough, break it up now."

Rissa put her hands up. She spoke calmly. There wasn't a bone in her body that wanted to fight right now. "I'm not looking for trouble."

"Too late, magic bitch."

"Magic bitch? That's the best you can do?" Rissa felt a surge of anger. Whether the half-baked insult or the threat to her person that irritated her, she wasn't sure. Regardless, she reached into her pocket for her Conduit. Maybe now was a good time to test it after all. It would mean finding a new place to hide once the CIPD swarmed the place, but it was what it was.

Her hand going into her pocket was taken as aggression and the thug swung. Still ailed from her prison time, Rissa's body felt slow and languid, as though she was watching the fist come to break her nose in slow motion but was powerless to move against it.

Gault suddenly stepped in front of her. He moved with terrifying speed, striking upwards with a punch so vicious that it put the burly patron on the floor immediately. It all happened so quickly, so much so that even the aggressor took a moment to process his face mushed against the splintered floorboards.

"What the-" He was on his feet in seconds, only to find Gault waiting for him, seizing him by the shirt and dragging a man twice his size toward the door.

"Get out." Gault shoved him through the double doors and he sprawled on the jagged cobbles that paved the streets of Forge Town.

The barman took advantage of the break in the chaos to sound the bell once again. "We're closing. Everybody out! Out!"

The bell rang in quick succession, reminding the grumbling patrons to down their drinks. Eventually a stream of them shuffled out of The Hound, spilling out onto the street where they loitered. Rissa tapped Gault on the shoulder and he turned.

"Thank you, Gault."

He gave her a small smile, looking pleased with himself.

"Wait. You two." The barman approached them, first stepping past them to put the heavy bolts across on the front door. "I know your faces."

Rissa froze. A shocked glance shared with Gault confirmed their mutual fear that their wanted posters had already sprung up here. She could practically feel his muscles tightening, coiling like a spring. His hand rested atop Akor'shaki's shrunken form. To be recognised so quickly wasn't a good sign at all. They stood still as statues as the barman lumbered around the interior, drawing the curtains on the windows, blocking out the nosy ex-patrons who glared in from the outside. With privacy secured, he approached them, his shadow almost as large as the evicted patron.

"My name is Sheppard. This tavern: The Hound, is my lifeline. I was impressed with what I saw today. How you averted trouble."

"I think I may have brought the trouble to your door." Rissa admitted. Her heart stinging with the last remnants of adrenaline, allowing her exhaustion to creep back in.

"Not at all." Sheppard told her assertively. He walked around his bar and beckoned for them to sit, collecting several empty tankards in one giant hand as he went. "Versorcerers are welcome here. Provided they respect the property, same as anyone else."

Rissa collected a few tankards of her own as she followed, passing them to Gault who seemed confused by the gesture. She glared at him and he promptly took his share over to the bar and placed them down.

"Thank you, both of you." Sheppard smiled through a thick, bronze beard. He took the empty tankards and threw them into a washing up bucket beneath the wooden countertop. He gestured with strong, muddy eyes to the wobbling bar stools and Rissa obeyed, pulling one out for Gault.

"I'll stand."

"Just sit down." Rissa told him. Reluctantly, Gault obeyed. He sat hunched, fingers picking at the splintered wood of the bar.

"I see you've moved yourself in." Sheppard spoke as he ran a soggy rag over the taps on the barrels that lined the wall behind the bar. He gestured with those hardy, steely eyes to the pile of boxes she had thrown a blanket over.

"Sorry about that." Rissa said sheepishly. "I... didn't have anywhere to go."

"That so?" The rag rimmed a tankard, wiping the steel clean. "You need a room?"

Rissa smiled at the offer. "I appreciate that. But we really don't have a Wreath to our name."

"Maybe you don't. But you've got him." The eyes darted to Gault, who seemed confused by the attention.

"What do you mean?" Rissa and Gault spoke at the same time.

"I saw you take down that thug. So did all my regulars." Sheppard nodded, impressed. "You hang around the bar every couple of nights and I'll give you a room in return."

Rissa spoke before Gault had a chance to refuse. "You just got yourself a deal!"

Sheppard smiled. Rissa stifled a yawn.

"It's getting late and you're tired." He observed, flinging the damp rag onto the countertop. "Follow me. I'll show you to your room."

Rissa brimmed with excitement at the thought of a proper bed beneath her aching spine. Perhaps things were looking up.

8

The clashing of swords deafened the muggy, evening air. High left. Low right. Exhausted, Rissa intensified her focus. The heavy swords spliced the air before partnering with split second accuracy. It had been her desire to learn and Gault had obliged. Relentless and full of determination, he had tutored her in the back alleys of Forge Town. After days of gruelling and intense combat training, her backside was a rainbow of pain, with purple, blue and red bruises squatting on top of the fading yellow ones. Every day Gault had knocked her to the ground in repeated succession, thwacking her backside into the unforgiving cobbles. But with a great tenacity of spirit, she had got right back up to do it all over again.

Learning how to move the heavy blade quickly and defend with power had been one of her first lessons in the early days of training. She had felt incompetent and weak, used to carrying the mere weight of a ring on her finger. Just holding the strong sword drained any youthful energy from her weak wrists and biceps. It was like madness. Gault would attack in a pre-rehearsed sequence and her retaliation had as much fight in it as a piece of straw in a hurricane. Patiently, he would start the sequence again, gradually speeding up, and with a stubborn resilience, she eventually gained in both strength and stamina. Soon the muscles in her wrists and arms matched the strength of her shoulders, already strong from hauling round the Grandmaster brick in her backpack.

Inevitably, to increase the level of challenge, Gault would suddenly quicken his speed and her bruises would be greeted by the familiar jagged cobbles. Often, the throbbing welts on her palm flared with pain and the sword clanged its resonance with the floor as it slipped limply from her grip. His swordsmanship was incredible. For somebody who fought predominantly with Akor'shaki, she was stunned and in awe of his enviable prowess with any sword.

Gault had honoured his agreement to be a peacemaker in The Hound and the patrons were unusually timid in his presence, downing their watery beers with an all-encompassing feeling of dread. They side spied him between nervous gulps and on the nights he was present, the atmosphere had become much less rowdy. In return, the barkeep had stayed true to his word and buried away in a converted attic, Rissa was recovering and growing stronger.

The dark heavy clouds hung ominously over the city, yet to unleash the lethal storm that was brewing. As they trained, a radio droned a serious and stern voice which relayed that a severe weather warning was in place. A vicious magic storm, the likes of which Centa Isla had not seen for a good few years was soon forthcoming. There was an element of guilt which she couldn't shake as between herself and the Omens, Rissa had no doubt she had played a small part in the storm's arrival. It was like an immune response from what remained of the planet, seeking to flush the atmosphere with new magic and punish those who recklessly cast spells upon its surface.

The storm had yet to break. According to much of the news that bled in from the City Centre, the populace was on tenterhooks. Preparations for a magic storm were often dependent on the city's rotation around the exposed core beneath them. Their orbit around the fluxing core was how their calendar was built. There were four seasons in the year, each attuned to the elemental magic from the core itself. Rissa had lost track of the date, but knew they were somewhere deep into the ninety days of Rainsturn, the month attuned with the element of Water. Depending on when the storm broke, they could be dealing with torrential rainfall. Or, if the days rolled over too close to the month of Stormsmarch, the attuned month of wind, there could well be a devastating lightning and hurricanes which could finish off the population just as easily as a second Reckoning.

"Rissa." Her instructor spoke to her. His violet eyes watched her darkly as he patrolled, sword gripped loosely in his gloved hand. "Pay attention."

"I am." She replied. The steel in her hands was borrowed from Sheppard, the blade normally stored beneath the bar at The Hound for "security" purposes - an understandable necessity in the wild climate of Forge Town.

"I'm ready."

She was lying, of course. The intensity of the training had now peaked and even her toned and stronger muscles were struggling. In truth, her scabbed palms were bleeding over the leather-wrapped hilt. Her arms were shaking from the strain of even holding the blade up and her wrists, still sore from her imprisonment, had swollen from the strain of taking the force of Gault's attacks head on. The shackles that had scarred her wrists seemed to have left a permanent reminder, a deep-set ring carved into her flesh, intensely itchy and irritated by the swordplay. The itch was intolerable at times and she was grateful for the blustering bouts of cold rain, released by overflowing clouds which cooled her skin and temporarily soothed the pain.

He had assured her several times that this was just part of the process and that he had gone through this level of conditioning too, but at this point, she really didn't care. Her body had been healing slowly since her incarceration in The Douldruums. She had spent the first few days recovering her strength until impatience took over and she insisted she was ready to learn. Sheppard had been kind enough to offer meagre lunches in return for assistance maintaining the beer cellar which Rissa had accepted. She had never lived in Forge Town but was already finding enjoyment from the exchange of favours as opposed to exchange of wealth.

"We do one more. Ready?" Gault took a step toward her and as rehearsed, she redistributed her weight and entered a defensive stance.

"Yeah. Ready."

Gault raced towards her with a speed quicker than normal. They always started with a strike high to the left. Rissa met his steel with her own, feeling the rattling of the bones in her arms as she hardened her wrists to deflect his blow. She knew immediately where to go next and she moved the sword low to the right, catching the second part of the sequence with equal strain. She staggered back with the force of his attack, even knowing that he was not attacking at full pelt. Her weakness irritated her but she forced herself to drag the heavy blade up high to catch the weighty downswing that had so frequently buckled her knees and floored her. She freed a hand and pushed it into the flat of her own blade to better redistribute the force, able to push his swing back. His next swing was always a thrust for her abdomen which needed swatting away. But as Rissa prepared for it, she noticed his body language was completely different. He withdrew, then dropped, swinging low for her legs in a sudden and disruptive change to their strictly rehearsed sequence.

She jumped instinctively, watching the blade whistle beneath her feet as it cut through the air. Before she could even ask him what he was doing, he was attacking again, completing a neat pirouette before swinging hard to her right. She tried to bring the blade up, but the weight of it fettered her into the ground as she landed. Instead, she threw backwards, twisting out of the way of the blade and landing awkwardly on the bumpy cobbles behind her. Gault stopped in his tracks, seemingly content. His sword returned to his scabbard left on the floor beside him.

"You are getting better." He praised whilst nodding his head with approval. "Well done."

"You could have killed me!"

"But I didn't."

He approached her and proffered a hand which she gratefully took, allowing herself to be pulled up to her feet. He took the sword from her and she was grateful for her aching hands to be free of the weight.

"You adapted."

"That wasn't part of the sequence!" She seethed at him, far angrier than she should have been. Where the rage came from she wasn't entirely sure, but it was here to stay for the time being. "You can't just break the pattern like that!"

"Of course I can." Gault replied simply. "Your opponent might."

"We wouldn't have a-" Rissa blustered, unable to fumble words out of her mouth to directly oppose him. She wouldn't have a scripted sequence in a real fight, so what was the point of that stunt!?

"There's always a sequence." He spoke again like he was reading her mind. "Everybody has patterns. Everybody has habits. You need to find theirs and exploit it, while masking your own."

The words didn't feel like his own. They were too structured, too long-winded and too philosophical. She recalled his friend whom he had mentioned once – the only shared memory of his former life.

"A quote from your friend? Kadin, was it?"

"We trained together as knights." Gault spoke slowly, intentionally. "Those words came from our instructor."

"Smart guy."

Gault grunted. Together, they headed back toward The Hound, a street away from the abandoned backstreet clearing in which they trained. The old tavern drifted into view, the creaking sign swinging in the wind and rain.

"So, who was the better out of the two of you?"

"What?"

"You and Kadin. Who was the better fighter?"

Gault smiled softly. His answer was otherwise instant. "Him. Easily."

"He must have been good."

"He was."

They entered The Hound through a side door. It led directly to a staircase behind the bar, a locked door separating them, ensuring they were out of sight from the main tavern. Out of habit, Rissa peered discreetly through the window. It was a quiet night, only one or two patrons present. Gault wouldn't need to be present tonight which was a relief to her as on more than one occasion, on his nights off, altercations had kicked off to the point where

Gault had needed to become involved. For concealment against their fugitive status, he wore a hood and mask, making him look even more intimidating and menacing and it was little surprise that after the first couple of throwdowns the atmosphere had considerably subdued. The presence of the mysterious hooded vanguard watching the place instilled a touch of fear within the regulars and any urge for physical or verbal recourse saw an early exit to continue it elsewhere. Even when Gault wasn't on duty, the idea that he could appear at any moment was enough to keep the peace. Suffice to say that Sheppard, their benefactor and host, was extremely pleased with this mutually beneficial arrangement. Many who lived in Forge Town were former tradespeople. Their bodies usually reflected their hard work and they likely weren't used to finding people who could stand up to them.

With The Hound in good condition for the night, they footed up a twisting, narrow stairwell. The walls were lined with peeling old wallpaper and old paintings, the windowsills adorned with various old pottery, described by Sheppard as "family heirlooms" which Rissa found fascinating. She had spent some time admiring them on their first foray, finding the very existence of these heirlooms as something incredibly special. There was an old bowl, a teapot and most interesting to her: an ornamental flowerpot. It was empty, not a trace of soil in the cracked clay, but its existence inspired wonder in her. What plant had it once held?

There were three main floors to The Hound plus a converted attic, making it much larger than it presented from outside. Their room was the converted attic on the top floor, made accessible via a ladder into a ceiling hatch and could even be pulled up to deny entry. It was the perfect place for two fugitives on the run and they willingly cocooned themselves in the musky attic for hours on end, planning their next steps.

And planning, they most certainly had been.

When they had first been shown the attic, there was little surprise to find it was used to store items from Sheppard's long family lineage. But it was far roomier than expected with an archaic four poster bed dominating much of the space. The mattress had sunken from years of use and a thick column of dust would cough into the air when sat upon. The walls were a mishmash of ugly, test wallpapers, as though the room had been used as a canvas to eventually settle on the final, deep red wallpaper design that was used in the tavern proper.

The ceiling was taller on one half of the room than the other to accommodate the sloped, slate roof that crowned the building. The floor had sunken in where floorboards had rotted and remnants of old threadbare carpet clung to them, nails protruding where the boards had cracked. They learned which areas to avoid as the danger of falling through the floorboards or snagging ankles on rusty nails was an unwelcome one. Everything was a little wonky, the building having sloped softly with age, but was barely noticeable save for on their first night watching a mug of water slide down the coffee table until it spilled.

But it was home enough. At least for now.

They even had a small window that led out onto an extended balcony, offering a short drop out onto the rooftops of Forge Town. She had joked that Sheppard frequently housed criminals, hence the setup. He had laughed curtly but had not denied it. Their host was a hulking shadow behind the bar, yet his voice was soft. She had no doubt his wrath was terrifying, but didn't seem to be won easily.

As the days passed by, they did their best to make the space comfortable and habitable. The thick coat of dust that had blanketed everything had been cleaned and the window to the balcony kept wide open to bring smoggy air into the stuffy old attic. Sheppard had assured them that the levels of smog weren't nearly as bad here as the edge of the city and that her body would adapt in time. Despite the urge to clear her lungs every few hours, the thick air of Forge Town at least carried with it a cool breeze that expelled the dust and rising heat of the building from their room. Furniture had been shuffled around and an old leather sofa, marred with blade marks was the centrepiece of their new home.

But the real work had just begun. From downstairs, Gault had been allowed to take several large chalkboards that Sheppard had used to write up his menus back when there had been enough food to actually serve. In white scrawling chalk, they bore a chronology of all that happened so far and details about The Omens, Galleo et'al and their dark mission. Rissa felt deeply honoured to learn. He had kept her in the dark, intentionally, from their first meeting. Now, it felt like this was an admission of trust and an earnest apology for his failing to keep her from harm. The excitement she first felt when meeting Gault was slowly resurfacing and the regret and misery of The Douldruums was slowly fading. The tingling in her chest reminded her of why she had been so drawn to Gault and his mysterious mission in the first place. The desire she had to take control of her life, to be something more than another headstone of an unfulfilled destiny.

He described to her a design known as an Obelisk. It was a font of great power, constructed intentionally to allow Galleo et'al to locate and attune to it, providing an anchor from which it could pull its planetary mass into orbit above them. The Omens were here to construct one. How they were going to do it she truly had no idea.

She buried herself deep into the sofa and surveyed the boards intensely. Gault was still adding details and underlining key points and circling others. Akor'shaki swayed at his side, defying gravity with its random liquid motion. That weapon was something else. Rissa eyed it from time to time. It was as if it had a mind of its own. Any question she asked about it had been met with curt dismissal, as though he had made a pact to never speak of it. That may well have been true, but she'd never know.

One thing she had not expected to apply was something she had learned in Grandmaster. Algarethan Levels, a short module learned in her first year that described the maximum amount of magic the human body could harbour. As it turned out, on the grander scheme of demons and sentient planets, it was very little. But it was the perfect amount to be transported through time and space without suffering consequences more than a bout of short-lived sickness. Demons on the other hand were practically made from the stuff, the strains of such transport enough to disfigure and maim them. This was exactly what she had seen happen to the demon who had arrived with Gault in the sewers.

He motioned her to come closer and against the better wishes of her tired body, she prised herself up from the warm leather and joined Gault at the chalkboards. He stared at them, deep in introspection. They had united in the past few days and were becoming a formidable team. It had been difficult to convince Gault to strategize as his instincts always seemed to demand motion and action. But she needed to understand the full threat upon Centa Isla. He knew everything - she did not. And she was no longer comfortable in following him around like an unwitting shadow. Not anymore. She had given him an ultimatum – share or be separate. He wisely chose the former and they were equal.

Rissa had a plan for Gault.

He needed to control the dangerous malaise that would overcome him in battle transforming him from what could be a powerful ally to a reckless and wild animal. She truly wanted to consider Gault a friend but frankly, she did not trust him with her life. Not when he had twice metamorphosed into a violent, irrational beast just when she needed him most.

She sidled in next to him and pointed at the map of the city pinned to the board. It seemed ages ago that they had liberated the old map from her father's apartment. They had added their own wild additions to it, drawing in points of interest where they believed the rest of the Omens were located. With Kren'shal and now Mires defeated, there were just three to go. They'd done well all things considered, even if she had played literally zero part in the death of Mires. She had grown quietly numb to the side of her that had once feared taking a life and she attributed this dark shift in mood to her time spent imprisoned.

"So, we know Jace is in Grandmaster." She announced, biting her bottom lip in concentration. "Azrael is in Monument. That just leaves the green one."

"Lachesis." Gault said curtly. By the way he spoke and the tightening of his face, Rissa couldn't help but feel there was something more personal at play.

"You two have history?"

"She deceived Kadin." Gault shook his head with a grimace. "Took advantage of his kindness to slip into the folds of nobility."

"I've barely even seen her."

"That would be by design. She pulls the strings from the most comfortable place in the city."

"She'll be in Monument, then." Rissa chewed her lip absently. The view from their window mercifully put the tower out of sight, but its presence was still felt in the shadow that loomed over the entirety of Forge Town. "But getting inside will be… well, impossible."

"We won't need to." He pointed at Grandmaster, where they knew Jace had become a member of the faculty and now likely resided.

"We'll take out the last of their support. Lachesis and Azrael will have to come out and do the dirty work themselves."

He was referring to taking out Jace next. Rissa had at first marvelled at how the Omen had managed to integrate into the elitist core of the Grandmaster academic staff, which as far as she knew, had been unchanged for over a decade. But after their first fight, he had shown an impossible ability to throw spells without a Conduit, so she knew they would herald him as heaven sent or a miracle birth. Jace was their new protégé and their rare appearance to publicly support him at the Guild Hall was evidence of his exalted and revered status as the new golden boy of Grandmaster.

How they were going to do it, she didn't yet know. But she was going to have to return to Grandmaster. Trepidation gathered in her stomach at the thought of returning to a place that had branded her a failure. Her two years there had been short lived, marred by her terrible attitude and unwillingness to embrace hardship. It was a brutal place to be, filled with deadlines, rigamarole and impeccable standards of education and lifestyle. She just hadn't been ready for it back then. Breaking into the academy of magic was not a feat done easily. But it surely wasn't impossible. Not when bricks from the place were being peddled on the street if you knew where to look.

She fought those feelings of fear, burying them deep down. Instead, she summoned up her excitement at returning for some good old-fashioned revenge. Rissa felt her energy bubbling and her former tiredness was replaced with a sudden whoosh of adrenaline. She fixed Gault in a firm gaze, grabbing the chalk from his fingers. She found a clear space on one of the boards and frantically scribbled.

"Time to kick ass!" She wrote in capital letters before underlining the bold statement with two confident lines.

———

Donnel needed answers. He hadn't expected to be back at Verscience so soon. The investigation into the horrible pods that he had discovered beneath the old factories had been shelved. Any interest in it had diminished to no more than a silent whisper. Those involved had been incarcerated. But who was behind it? And who was the creator of the monstrous machine that had been used to ruthlessly torture and leech blood from the nobility? This information had been redacted on all reports and any mention had been screened from the public. Something was wrong within the CIPD.

For what purpose was the Versorcerer's blood being taken? He had tried to visit the surviving nobles in their hospital wards, only to find all of them stricken in a deep, long coma. There was something wrong, something that stirred his gut and told him to act with care. So, he had returned here, where he believed the cruel machines had their origin. There could be nowhere else capable of such a creation. It was an impossibility. The angular, sterile building seemed more hostile as he approached this time. The soft angles now looked jagged and sharp, the design completely alien to what was considered the norm of Centa Isla. It was a reminder of the city's potential pre-Reckoning and what could still be achieved with the right tools in the hands of the right minds. For many, the potential of magic and science together was frightening but for a long time Donnel never understood the irrational fear of progress that many held.

Now he did.

For all the ingenuity humans possessed to do good, they held equal amounts of genius to create evil. As he approached the doors, he quickly became aware of the silence that surrounded the place. There were guards on duty, Kingsguard, as before. This time they seemed hostile and prickly and he could feel their gaze upon him well before he had even crossed the street. He was appraised and inspected, stripping him down with eyes trained for protection and for scrutiny.

"Officer." One of them greeted him curtly. His arm crested a scabbard, a polished regal blade stored within. This guard was different to the ones he had seen previously. "How can we help you tonight?"

Donnel showed his badge, a lie prepared on his lips. "Syn Counts, please."

They took his badge and turned it over in their hands. Donnel watched the eyes behind the violet and gold helmet narrow as they appraised the integrity of his badge. Seemingly satisfied, they returned it and gestured into the building proper.

"I hope your findings are of use."

"Me too."

Entering through the hissing automatic doors, Donnel left the guardsmen behind and approached the modest but modern front desk where the overnight clerk sat behind a tall stack of paperwork. She peered over as he approached.

"Back so soon. Syn Counts?"

"Actually, I was hoping for a favour." He placed his badge on the smooth, dark surface. "Prototype Gallery. I need access."

"Poor timing, I'm afraid, sir. That area is currently undergoing maintenance." A frown flecked her face, creasing the brow that sat just above her rounded spectacles.

"Maintenance?" He watched her carefully. "Maintenance of what? Haven't all the prototypes been dormant since Reckoning?"

"I can appreciate that line of thinking, officer." She explained. "But I am under strict instructions to keep that area completely cleared for mandatory, essential maintenance."

"Instruction of who?"

"That is none-"

"I'm a CIPD officer, ma'am." He gave her a reassuring smile. "I understand the chain of command."

She hesitated, then finally straightened in her swivel chair.

"Instruction from King Grayson."

"The newly anointed." Donnel mused. "He's not wasted any time, has he?"

"No, sir." The clerk smiled at him. By the bags that pulled at her eyes she was clearly weary from overnight shifts. She was polite but clearly wanted this interaction to end. "Was there anything else?"

"Just Syn Counts then, please."

"Very well." She rose from her chair and collated a stack of paperwork beneath her arm. "Follow me."

Donnel smiled in fake gratitude and followed her through the familiar route. He hadn't come here during the day for quite some time, yet found himself surprised at just how few workers, scientists and Versorcerers there actually were. Perhaps many of those great minds were imprisoned within The Douldruums; accomplices to one of the larger scale busts of his career alongside Gault.

The clinking of the digital Syn-counters met his ears as he entered the familiar room. The clerk bid him good fortune, informed him of the button to press in the event he wanted to leave, and then locked him in. In all truth, he wasn't here to read any Syn Counts. He just wanted to get into the Museum unattended. If there was going to be evidence of the pod's creation, it would be in there.

The door into the Syn Count room was locked magnetically, sealed shut until released by the clerk from the other side. Donnel patrolled the interior, feeling the integrity of the walls and the elongated window that offered a view out of the room and into the hallway. He tapped the glass, feeling it reinforced, the same glass that lined the viewing window of the CIPD's interrogation room and he had witnessed first-hand how difficult it was to break. The walls were metallic white and showed no sign of weakness. He noticed a modern, claustrophobic ventilation shaft that pumped in clean air. Perhaps twenty years ago his leaner body would have fitted inside but there was no chance today.

He had to see the Prototype Gallery. Hearing it was closed by order of the King only made him more certain that there was a grisly truth hidden away.

Donnel observed the fluctuations of the Syn Counts to buy some time and appear convincing. Not that he was here to see it, but the overall Syn count did look much healthier than it did when he had last arrived. Forge Town seemed to be in better health thanks to the large-scale bust that he and Gault had initiated. Staring at it for too long brought about some long-buried feelings of existentialism. They truly did live on the edge of a knife here. The tentative balance maintained by careful management of Resynthesis against the Syn Counts was a war of attrition on the lives of the people of Centa Isla. When enough time had passed, he rang the buzzer and waited, offering a small plea for forgiveness for whoever was listening. The clerk returned and opened the door for him.

"Did you find what you needed, officer?"

"I did, thank you." He smiled. In the next instant, he grabbed her and slung her into the room, slamming the magnetised door behind her. She surged to the door instantly and smashed her balled fists against the reinforced window. He couldn't hear what she was saying through the thick window but bowed his head slightly in apology before he continued down the hall, following signs decorating the wall that labelled the direction of the Prototype Gallery. He moved with swiftness in his step, for it could be only a matter of time until the trapped clerk was discovered.

Arriving at the gallery, Donnel surged through the double doors, relieved to find them unlocked as he stepped into a pitch back room. As if sensing his presence, rows of spotlights activated one by one, a resounding clunk of power as light filled the workshop column by column. The modern, slick aesthetics gave way to what was effectively just one, massive garage. The floors were like sandy stone and the lights were dim, swinging from the ceiling on suspended cables, a far cry from the slick fluorescent light of the rest of the facility. Donnel found himself surrounded by machinations sitting on pedestals all around the expansive interior. Donnel could do nothing but walk and search, trying to find anything that resembled the pod-like device. Every official of high ranking at the CIPD was refuting it ever existed, which had disturbed him. He had been told to forget what he saw. But how could he? It was an image that could not be unseen, forever etched in his brain. He grimaced as he remembered the litany of needles piercing the flesh of those nobles. How many families had been shattered and left in the dark? Any one of the dead could have easily been Rissa. He would never have forgiven himself.

Blurs of abstract metal passed him by every couple of steps. There was a manifest printed on a pedestal in front of each invention, detailing the machine's intention and a wallet of documents, presumably a user manual and specification details. Donnel wished he wasn't here as an intruder as it would have been a childhood dream fulfilled to sit here and comb through every single machine's blueprints. He had to force his mind to focus, looking for shapes similar to the pod-like creation that had housed the captured nobles. The machine itself had been rounded, like the shape of an oval nestled within a tiered, slanted rectangle. It was distinct enough in his mind that he knew he would recognise it instantly.

It was astounding how many new inventions were emerging pre-Reckoning but had to be cancelled. He only allowed himself minimal time to glaze over the details but there were creations that could have changed the world. A prototype magic-lens that could theoretically capture life in motion, a personal radio that had its own private frequency, a modernised typewriter with a digital screen. Reckoning had brought a halt to it all as essential resources were put into the immediate survival needs of the city.

Then he saw it.

It sat innocuously amongst other prototypes as if it wasn't designed for torture and death. He surged toward it, running his hands over the rounded surface as he had when trying desperately to open the door to rescue the victims. This was it. He remembered it hissing with steam as the lid had slid open, but this time there was no decrepit corpse contained within this pod, nor were there tubes and pipes filled with blood being pumped into a tank nearby. It looked innocent with its rounded, chubby features. It wasn't until he cast his eyes upon the blueprints that the true nature of the Magic Extraction Chamber, shortened to the M.E.C, was revealed. He combed through the document, glancing over devilish drawings and text of how to forcefully affix a person to the chamber. Donnel was looking for more than how it worked, he was looking for names, for culprits to whom to extend the long arm of the law to its fullest and most brutal effect.

At the base of the blueprints, he found what he was looking for. The M.E.C was masterminded by Austyn Synner whose scrawl Donnel recognised immediately at the base of the file. A famous and great mind of the city, Austyn was responsible for many of the technological advancements they enjoyed today, such as the very engine that powered his patrol car and much of the genius snake-like Subrail system that spiralled around the limited space beneath the city. Unfortunately, Austyn Synner was dead, evading his charges with an early grave. Donnel recalled the tabloids as the greatest mind in the city had been an early victim of Smithy's Lung from the days when the sheer toxicity of Forge Town's smog was not widely known or controlled.

But there was another name. One who was most certainly alive. While the creation had been masterminded by the late Austyn Synner, the design had been dormant for many rotations. Until recently that is, where resources had been distributed to the project, approved by the Royal Seal of King Grayson Clovis. It had been approved and dated from his earliest days as King-Regent late last year.

"What the hell?" Donnel murmured aloud.

He tore the last page from the blueprints, taking with him the names of those who had funded such a malefic device. Just as he did so, the room suddenly flushed red with flashing lights and a deafening siren began to wail.

He cursed. The overnight clerk had clearly freed herself from her temporary confinement to sound the alarm. Donnel knew he'd soon be contending with the two, perhaps more, Kingsguard who had guarded the door.

His eyes scanned the room for an exit in which to flee but stopped abruptly as something caught his eye. It was just another prototype, just like any other, yet even here in the flashing cascades of red light he swore for a moment that he had seen it once before somewhere. But where? He approached, allocating himself no more than forty-five seconds to inspect the device before he had to run.

Forty-five, forty-four, forty-three…

He grabbed the blueprint and once more cast his eyes across its intricacies. It was a strange looking device and the reason for its jagged, yet aerodynamic design was because it was designed for primitive flight.

THE STEEL WING.

Twenty-nine, twenty-eight, twenty-seven…

Donnel still didn't know why he felt it was familiar to him and continued flicking through all the way to the last page where he found the design was approved by three distinct seals. There was High Priestess Cordelia Rowe of Grandmaster and the now recently deceased King Richard Clovis II. But there was another seal there, listed as the mind behind it that he had never expected to see in a million years.

Aryssa E. Rawdon.

Aryssa E. Rawdon.

He stopped counting and froze. The name hit him like a dagger in the chest. It pierced his heart, striking his lungs with a sudden, long-lost pain and shock. Donnel felt as though he was about to collapse. It was her signature, of that there was no doubt. She strung her words together like they were made of string, conjoined and wispy, written like the stroke of an artist's brush. She had always had much neater handwriting than the scrawl she often made fun of him for having. He could picture her writing, the ink of the quill dancing across the parchment as she would write letters to her noble family and friends. These very same family and friends were still in the city now but they were lost to him. He had subjected all of them to full and intrusive investigations, souring any future contact as they felt humiliated and aggrieved to have been considered suspects in her disappearance. He could find nothing conclusive and his later attempts to apologise were met with icy words, forbidding him to ever contact them again.

With the sudden urgency of escaping over-riding his thoughts, he once again tore the page from the document and fled, bursting out of a sliding set of hissing automatic doors and back into the sterile, glossy halls. His shoes squeaked against the spotless floor as two Kingsguard soldiers closed in to block the hallway ahead of him.

"Hold it right there!" One of them commanded with an outstretched arm, their blades all but drawn from the ornate scabbards.

Donnel could taste fear in his mouth as adrenaline pumped through his body. His mind was awash with emotions of past anguish and the need to escape. He veered off down another hallway and the footsteps that followed him clanked with the dull rhythm of purpose-built steel as the Kingsguard gave chase. Donnel knew he had mere minutes to get out. CIPD response time on high profile locations such as the Verscience were under four minutes. He'd set himself back by staring at his wife's name, losing track of his seconds along the way.

Running at a frantic pace and gasping for breath, he followed the signs directing him back to the foyer. He had looped around the facility once again passing by the Syn Count labs where the door was open but with no sign of the overnight clerk. He surged back into the foyer, only to be cut off by one of the Kingsguard who had broken their rank of two. The clanking of plated armour was so deafening in these ambient halls it could have been two or two-hundred guards chasing him and he would never know.

The sword was fully drawn and Donnel, even from far away, recognised the eyes of a man prepared to kill for his King. He had to escape; he couldn't afford for this grim truth to get buried any deeper. Grit lined his steps as he charged, black boots striking the floor as he slid low, using the polished floor to his advantage to slide beneath the arcing swing of the Kingsguard whose motion and agility was limited by his heavy armour. The clerk hid behind her desk and screamed at him but Donnel was way ahead of her. The double doors screeched as they sought to close in front of him but Donnel slipped through at the smallest possible point and pounded across the street. The moment the nighttime air hit him, he knew that he had irreversibly damaged his career.

The sirens flashed in the distance, twisting between the labyrinthian streets to reach him but at this moment he didn't care. He had followed the oath all officers swore to follow for his entire, almost thirty-year career and had always stayed on the right side of the law. But he now realised that the very establishment still held strong to its origins as a subsidiary of the Kingsguard, despite how they claimed to be an independent body.

The CIPD was now very blatantly in the pocket of the King. And he would have no part in such an injustice.

Donnel stormed to his vehicle and leapt in. He flicked on his sirens, wishing to blend in with the incoming rush of CIPD officers as he careered down the street and as far away from Verscience as he could get. Driving at high speed he risked a glance into his lap where he cradled the two crinkles of crumpled-up blueprints. The name of his wife was still written at the bottom of the parchment. There were no tricks of the mind that had ethereally formed her words in front of him, they were here - clear as day.

The horrors of the Magic Extraction Chamber disappeared deep into the back of his mind. All of it did. As for now, all he cared about was that he finally had something that he had been missing for eight long years…

A lead to Rissa's mother.

—

"These are the decisions only a King can make." Azrael spoke from beside him, still as a statue, his breaths so quiet they were non-existent.

"Indeed." King Grayson Clovis agreed, yet found no such comfort in the words of his advisor. He stood over a table in his chambers where a map of the city had been rolled out. He could see the stretching skyline of the city out of the window ahead of him, putting reality to the lines of roads and rough sketches drawn upon the map. He had everything he needed but the grit to make an agonising choice. The Crown he had inherited so forcefully from his father was heavy on his head, pressing its weighty gold into his scalp.

He opened his mouth to speak. "Is there-"

"No, My King." Azrael proffered him an empty cup, pivoted upside down. "Stay the course."

Grayson took the cup, the stained steel feeling abnormally heavy in his giant hand. Its purpose was known to him, yet he did not wish to use it. The width of the cup represented the rough amount of space that would need to be demolished for a construct, known as an Obelisk, to be built. He had been assured it would save the city, drawing magical earth from the distant lands beyond the stars for their use. The issue Grayson was having was that the cup had an impressive diameter and when placed on the map, wiped out a lot more than he was initially expecting. Countless homes would be lost no matter where it was built, countless lives forced out of their own neighbourhood and into others. It could promote hostility as more mouths would be vying for the little that was available. He placed the cup down gingerly over the City Centre, less out of genuine consideration, but more to recontextualise the size of the construct against the view out the window ahead of him. It was massive, demolishing an enormous chunk of his precious centre. He removed the cup promptly, feeling a shudder run down his spine.

Just then, a knuckle ratted against his door. A welcome distraction from his current charge.

"Enter."

The former Seat of Air, Marco Barrett entered, offering a low bow of reverence to his King. With the Crown now his, he had gladly abolished the Elemental Council, banishing them back to their noble houses. But Marco had expressed a willingness to join him, to advise and counsel and take care of matters unimportant while Grayson could fully attend to The Resource Crisis.

"Have you a moment, My King?"

"For you, friend, of course."

Grayson felt Azrael bristle as he purposefully distracted himself from the decision that lay ahead. In truth, he was glad for Marco's presence as another voice in his ear that wasn't the apathetic tone of Azrael. With a strong hand, he bid Marco rise from his kneeling stance. Indeed, he had come to trust Marco Barrett in recent weeks. Since becoming King, none had shown him the true respect of the title except for the former Seat of Air. It was only he whose ego had not melted by the loss of rank and title following the dissolution of the turbulent council.

Theora, the Water Seat had been as dismissive and indignant of his crown as she always had and Grayson had taken great pleasure in watching the old hag leave his tower forever. Kiara, the Flame Seat had shown him the necessary formalities but nothing more. Her departure was met with equal indifference.

Grayson had been so pleased with Marco's response that he delegated to him the grim, but necessary task of organising his father's funeral. The death of a King was a celebrated event in the annals of Centa Isla's little-known history. Grayson was never a stickler for tradition, but the large-scale event would serve a very specific purpose for him besides honouring the legacy of his father.

"I wish to discuss arrangements for the Wake." Marco spoke slowly, clearly unsure of whether the topic was one that would arouse emotion. It did hurt, Grayson could feel the anguish nestled in his chest. His father was dead and by his own hand no less. The guilt and the sorrow were present, but they were overridden by a great sense of purpose. He now held the power to change this city for the better and no Elemental Council could say anything against it.

His word was ultimately final and if this city was going to survive - it had to be.

"I owe you a debt of gratitude, friend." Grayson felt a smile stretch his face. "It is a grim task I have given you."

"The honour is mine, My King." Returned Marco. "I only wish it were not such a tragedy."

"A tragedy, most certainly. But you handle it with dignity and pride."

"If only I could do more."

"Perhaps you can." Azrael spoke. "Perhaps the Seat of Air may offer his advice on our *hypothetical* situation."

Marco stepped forward. "How can I help?"

"If a piece of the city needed to be levelled...." Azrael spoke without riddle. It wasn't clear from his tone whether it was an exercise or reality, but he handed the cup to Marco and pointed to the map. "Where would you choose?"

Marco approached the table, hovering the cup over the map. His eyes remained cold and impartial as he placed it over Forge Town, pushing as close to the edge of the city as possible.

"The obvious choice is here. Least number of people, least economic resources and least potential for investment." He paused. "But..."

He moved the cup, dragging it across the stained map and up to the north of the city where the most decorated of the nobility lived in their expensive detached houses.

"I'd destroy this."

"Don't you live there?" Grayson asked him, curious.

"I do." The former Seat of Air agreed. "But that's exactly why I'd get rid of it. Per square mile the population density is abhorrently low. The potential homes gone to waste with fake gardens and detached houses is too high for a bloated population like ours."

In truth, Grayson concurred with the assessment. "So, you would rebuild and start again?"

"In this exercise, yes." The Seat of Air concluded. "But by all means, pay me no mind."

"I appreciate your input, friend."

"Anything to be of use, My King." Marco departed with a deep bow, shutting the door behind him.

"The day of your father's funeral shall be a glorious day." Azrael mused as he presented a Verscience blueprint that he laid over the map. "No finer day for the salvation of your city."

Grayson glanced over the document. It was The Obelisk. The paper was thick and heavy, far larger and more intricate than any of the previous creations he had signed off in the past. This was to be the design that would save his city, allowing them to pull tremendous amounts of magic long lost to them from another world entirely. It was a cosmic idea, unfeasible in concept yet entirely made possible by the presence of Azrael and the mysterious chunk of dusty, sulphur-smelling earth that he held as proof.

Grayson had not seen the rock since its presence at the ballot, used as bait to lure in the votes with unfortunately abject results. Upon Azrael's arrival at Monument, they had tested it and found its potential to restore lost magic to the atmosphere, a miracle. They just needed more. With it, they could raise the city's Syn Count out of the precipice of death they found themselves in and freely Resynthesise whatever they needed while also being able to lift the restrictions around magic. It spoke of a brighter future where the name Clovis was praised in history and the name Grayson even more so.

He was proud of the work that had already been accomplished. Even at the immense scale at which the Obelisk was going to be constructed, the reality was it would take just ninety days to bring the project to life once he marked this paper with his seal. The foundations would be raised with the city's finest earth Versorcerers. With all the magic being used, there would have to be a strict curfew on Resynthesis over the next month in order to keep the Syn Counts from dropping lethally low. This would unfortunately mean increased suffering for the populace as already empty food stores would be depleted even further.

But things would need to get worse before they got better. It was that exact sentiment he repeated in his head as he emblazoned the blueprints with his royal seal and bid Azrael and Verscience get to work.

Once alone, he cast his eyes again over the map.

—

Rissa found herself dreaming again. Once again, she possessed a body that was not her own and once again she found herself grafted to their perspective like a third eye. She had grown partly used to these forays now, wistfully wondering if tonight would be the night she visited that strange place.

And tonight it was. As her horizons broadened and her senses bounded to catch up with the shifting surroundings, Rissa found herself beneath the tall palace that had decorated the horizon in her previous visions. Up close it was awe-inspiring; built from solid white slate and handmade bricks it caught the rays of the afternoon sun upon radiant stained glass and beamed it down upon her. She wished to squint against it, but the eyelids of the body she inhabited were already attuned to such brightness, so she had little choice but to simmer beneath the heat.

There was a flash of steel that caught the sun and Rissa felt herself pulled into combat. The body she inhabited was quick, limber, twisting around a courtyard of stone as an opponent stood them up. A tunic of radiant blue decorated the body of her opponent and a restrictive helmet removed much of their identity. A circle of those blue tunics surrounded them, cheering and chanting an intrusive cacophony of names that melted into incoherent noise.

The sword swung and Rissa panicked. This was intense, far more so than her training with Gault. Fortunately, her host was far more composed. They darted backwards, heels spinning in the dirt. She felt the reverberations thunder up their legs and the strain on their arms as the short blades clashed together and riled up the spectators.

"Keep your blade up!" An instructor barked at them, spurring faster motion between the two combatants. She was grateful briefly for this insight into the motions of a trained swordsman. She felt a part of the movements, although having no part in the thought or motion itself, there was a kinetic energy produced by the timing of the swings that she was determined to remember once this dream had passed.

"Kadin! That means you!"

The name flashed in her mind as familiar. The body she inhabited seemed to respond to the words and the legs moved quicker, turning the pendulum of combat in their favour as they drilled the opponent with a flurry of blows that ended in victory when they tripped over their own feet and fell backwards. The crowd cheered, screaming a name that was now familiar.

"Kadin! Kadin! Kadin!"

Rissa knew the name distantly, mentioned by Gault on occasion. Before she could think any further, her host lofted their blade into the sky. In the reflection of the polished steel, Rissa saw the identity of whoever it was she inhabited.

Sharp features, dusty brown hair. The face that stared back at her from the steel was none other than Gault himself. There was only one feature out of place and that was his eyes. Gone were the piercing violets that she was used to. Instead, placid green looked back at her from the reflection in the warped steel. Just as she was about to question it further, she felt her grasp on this reality fraying and just as quickly as she had arrived, she awoke in The Hound once again.

Gault was awake already, standing silently, staring out the window. She had yet to see him truly sleep. The reality of Kadin's identity was a strange lie to be told, but Rissa chose not to pry as to the truth she had just beheld in her vision. He would be suspicious if she suddenly knew something yet undisclosed and would likely only whittle away at their trust even more. Distantly, she hoped he would tell her himself and she could feign surprise.

She glanced at the clock upon the wall. There were a few more hours yet before they needed to leave for Downtown. Some more sleep would do her some good.

———

There was a late-night downpour as Rissa and Gault ventured back into the familiar streets of Downtown. It felt good to be home again, even if she no longer had a true place here to call her own. The rampant rainfall dragged down with it all the smog that had drifted in from Forge Town, smothering the streets in a coat of fog that created nature's perfect foil for her and Gault to move unnoticed. Rissa had found several wanted posters among the twisting streets. Her likeness on each was impeccable down to each looping strand of hair that caressed her face. Gault on the other hand, if that even was supposed to be him, looked nothing like him.

"Who the hell is this?" She laughed as they walked, taking small joy in ripping each poster down whenever they passed one by. She jabbed a finger into the soaked parchment, splitting her sides at the gormless looking drawing of Gault. It was him in abstract, but with a bloated, square chin, sideburns for some reason and an evil smile. Whose account had this drawing come from? And what was with the sideburns? Her stomach hurt from laughing but Gault was noticeably unimpressed.

"Ridiculous." Was all he had to say on the matter, brushing the poster aside when she shoved it into his face. "You need to concentrate."

"I am concentrating."

She took one last look at the imposter on the paper before tearing it up and dropping into a sewer grate like she had done to all the others they'd found.

"Alright, I'm done."

They were heading towards a now familiar place. The Eclipse base, manned by Rand and his golden smile. If anybody knew how to get into

Grandmaster, Rissa had a feeling it might be him. He had sold her a damned brick from the place after all, so she had no doubt there was more going on than petty crime and dodgy dealings behind that storefront.

The Subrail was safe for them to travel. A few test runs had seen a CIPD presence at each station, but once the midnight oil started burning Rissa had found they disappeared entirely. Another thing Rissa had noticed upon her return was that Downtown felt much safer. The once encroaching presence of the Empty Eyes had made wandering out late, especially on a night like this, a dangerous undertaking. But she hadn't even spotted one single eyepatch. There was every possibility they were broken by the death of their pseudo-leader, but Rissa knew that reason lacked merit. In the chaos, a new leader would instate themselves with a display of power and the cycle would go again. They were likely in hiding, pooling their resources and their power to run these streets once again. Now realising that Kren'shal had been in charge longer than previously thought, The Empty Eyes prior encroachments out of their known territory had made sense and Gault had explained that the increase in threat and encroachment would be to likely put pressure on The Crown to take action; distracting attention from whatever plan they were instigating.

"We're close, aren't we?" Gault spoke, still broadly unfamiliar with the landscape of Centa Isla, but experienced enough to know their rough location.

"Very."

They jaunted around a corner, still on a main road. Vehicles surged past at high speed, their headlights refracting in the heavy fog as rainfall rattled against the bodywork.

Sure enough, Gault's navigation was proving much improved as on their next corner off the main road, everything immediately began to degrade. Potholes sunk into the concrete, pooling deep water up to the ankle. Boarded up homes and the distinct stench of wet rotten wood filled the air as the derelict streets opened up ahead of them. Wading through a few more sodden, rain-soaked streets had them darkening the doorstep of the Eclipse storefront once again.

"Only Dawn Will Follow."

The door unbolted immediately and Rand answered in a heartbeat. There was no welcoming grin or a flash of his gold teeth but instead a lip that was curled in rage.

"Get in." He hissed, slamming the door behind them as they entered, bolting it sevenfold. He followed them into the foyer, his fists clenched.

"You are wanted for regicide!? And you've shown up here!?"

"Nobody followed us." Rissa spoke coolly, gesturing for him to bring it down a notch. "I promise."

His seemed to calm, but he peered cautiously between the boarded-up windows, nonetheless. "Well? Is it true?"

"Is what true?"

"What do you think!? Did you actually attempt to kill the King?"

Rissa glanced at Gault. He looked back at her with equal uncertainty. It was a fair assumption to say that the organised street gang had no love for The Crown, but she knew a trick question to ascertain loyalties wasn't beyond Rand. When she spoke, she did so carefully.

"We're just not happy with the direction the city is going."

It wasn't a lie. It wasn't King Grayson they were intending to get, but if that was what was going to get them help then so be it.

"That is fortunate. Us neither."

Her answer clearly pleased Rand as he turned to face her, a big golden grin almost swallowing his face. He stepped away from the window and slid into position behind the countertop. "And for what reason have you darkened my doorstep once again?"

"I'll just come out and say it." Rissa prefaced her wild request. "I need to get into Grandmaster."

"Nothing is ever simple with you, is it?" Rand's brow furrowed, yet to his credit he asked no further questions. "I may be able to help you."

"But...?"

His gold-teeth flashed towards Gault. "But in return, I need an enforcer on some special business."

Gault crossed his arms. "What special business?"

The grin only grew wider. He tapped his nose for secrecy. "I don't ask you questions; I expect the same of you."

"Fine."

Rand held out a hand expectantly. Rissa took it and shook; Gault did the same. Only then, did Rand open the counter and invite them behind for the first time. Rissa had never been this far into the Eclipse storefront, even during the many years she had peddled The Dawn's Herald in the streets. They were led through a set of curtains at the back into an overfilled storeroom, boxes piled high full of illegal wares. They twisted through stacks of crates, many of which Rissa identified as containing Synth, she could see the respirator canisters stacked so high the lids were unable to latch properly. They went further back into the storefront, arriving at a backdoor that led outside into a desolate alleyway that connected the backdoors of several other abandoned buildings on the street. Tarpaulin sheets kept out most of the rain, tied clumsily to the pipework of the buildings above them. Between the rampant wind and the downpour, they didn't look like they would last forever but they were succeeding for now.

A manhole cover that had been secured and bolted from the surface allowed access to the sewers. Gault gave her a soft touch on the shoulder, enough to bring her attention to where he looked. His eyes were fixed skyward, at the decrepit, boarded up windows that looked down into the bottlenecked alley. It took Rissa a moment to notice that there were eyes watching them from between every board that had been hammered across the windows. However many were here with them, there were likely double the amount out in the city right now, working normal jobs, reporting to Rand on the side.

"This feels like a big gesture from you, Rand." She commented idly as they passed through toward the back door of another building at the other end of the isolated alley. It was like an endless stream of doors amongst a sea of buildings. "Never thought I'd ever go through the curtains. Not even back then."

"Consider it an admission of faith." Rand replied. He walked firmly, maintaining his distance with his back turned to her. "Do not let us down."

He led them through the back door and into a room. There was a repurposed round bar table with a map of the city laid out across it. Rand ushered them to gather around the table before unrolling a second scroll and laying it over the map. Gault's eyes narrowed with interest. The second scroll was an intricate, highly detailed layout of the sewer system including every known exit and entrance in and out. Unfamiliar faces filled the room, bodies dressed in attires ranging from noble frippery to transient dregs.

Rand pointed at her. "I can get you in. But it'll be a small window."

Then, he addressed Gault. "But you'll be helping us with our own business. Do we have a deal?"

Gault looked at her and she gave him a shrug. Her going in alone was probably the most reliable plan as she understood the academy of Grandmaster just as well as any of the students there currently. Gault didn't look too pleased with the arrangements, but grunted.

"Deal."

9

A second severe weather warning was announced via the radio just as Rissa and Gault were returning from the Eclipse camp. The tense air was growing thicker and muggier, as though the world itself was begging for a storm to come and clear the air. But by the weather warning that droned on the radio, the storm was going to do more than just lower the humidity - it could well clear out a chunk of the city.

The Hound was busy with trade. People were seeking shelter from the torrid air, keeping their scratchy throats moist with tankards of cool, watered down booze, their dry lungs unable to muster enough oxygen to argue let alone fuel a fight. Disagreements were settled with a wave of indifference and a change of seating as opposed to raised voices and wild fists. There was no need for Gault tonight.

Upstairs, Rissa found herself with little to do but twiddle her thumbs. Their talks with Eclipse had been lucrative and the plan had been finalised in a matter of minutes. The way into Grandmaster would be possible via the sewers, but only when timed with a monthly shipment of food and provisions. It seemed that the students of tomorrow were unaffected by the Resource Crisis while those beyond the academy scrounged. Between the distractions of the lightning and thunder she could slip in unnoticed and from there - somehow find and kill Jace. That final part she was still working on.

But she had to wait. The delivery of supplies was due at Grandmaster in two days.

She had no ill will towards the bearer of the Brand of the Sorcerer. Of them all, he seemed the only one with any conscience. He had thrown her a sword upon their first meeting, unwilling to strike at an unarmed opponent. That very same honour had cost him a dip into the sewage, but his intentions were at the very least noted. It was no surprise that he had swindled his way into the faculty of Grandmaster. Good looks, dulcet tones and the ability to use magic without a Conduit. No doubt the work of Galleo et'al's brandings, but to the wider Centa Isla it would be seen as nothing short of a miracle.

Rissa killed time by doddering around the apartment, making half-hearted gestures to tidy up which amounted to shuffling papers and straightening ornaments. The thick air had depleted her physical energy but her mind was whirling. With wanted posters likely still decorating the streets and the air so uncomfortable, a foray into Grayson Plaza like she'd originally wanted was not a smart idea. It was in their best interest to conserve their energy and stay put at The Hound, to take no risks and simply wait. Even if it was the most sensible plan, her impatience was gnawing at her and she longed to put the plan into action.

Gault busied himself with precious little. His impatience quadrupled hers and the boredom of waiting was consuming him. He paced, eyes darting to the corners of the room as though searching for spies. When he wasn't walking back and forth he was seated, eyes closed in bristling contemplation. It had only been a few hours and they were both losing their minds.

"You hungry?" Rissa asked eventually.

She wasn't, but her idle hands were desperate to be busy. They had access to the kitchen area of The Hound, accessible from their apartment by a backdoor and a set of stairs. They were under instruction to help themselves, but to inform Sheppard of any items consumed. Food was no longer on the menu at The Hound, price hiking on quality ingredients putting that lucrative trade firmly out of reach of Sheppard's meaty fingers. But the cupboards were still laden with wares. Some nights the kindly barkeep would arrive at their door with a stew concocted with a mish mash of ingredients and a synthetic loaf of bread to soak it all up. At the thought of this, Rissa's appetite began to return and the saliva wetting her lips jolted her to quicken her pace towards the kitchen.

"I'll go make us something," she offered.

Gault gave no reply, his eyes closed, refusing to break the concentration of his faux meditation. Yet from the depths of his stomach there was an audible gurgle.

"Suit yourself." she murmured, leaving him in his silent pose.

The large catering kitchen, long since retired from service, no longer proffered the delicious aroma of fresh, home cooking but now stank of old beer that swathed much of the tavern. Rissa busied herself in the cupboards, pleased to find a stash of tinned goods that were difficult to find these days. Anything with a long shelf life was nabbed quickly by bulk-buyers and peddled in the streets of Downtown for a quick Wreath. These days, only non-perishables were Resynthesised and promptly canned. Rissa hadn't seen a proper fruit in a long time.

Rissa pulled her Mother's Conduit from her pocket and held the silver ring up to her eye. This was as good a time as any to try it out. If she was going into Grandmaster then she was going to need it working. As the steel touched her finger, she felt the same familiar rush of power that she had always felt with her training Conduit. That power and that security was familiar and comforting, but Rissa bit it back. If she wanted to beat Azrael, it was going to take more than just The Algarethan Verse. Her spine was relieved to not have to lug a brick around everywhere she went. This mobility would hopefully let her wield a sword at the same time.

I invoke the Missing Sea. Call water, fill the pot.

Testing the limits of the Conduit first with a very light spell, she splashed water into the pot. Beneath the hob, a fire crystal ignited and she brought the water to boil. Using her Mother's Conduit seemed second nature to her, the hug of cold steel feeling snug and comforting on her finger. The water started to bubble in the aged, cast-iron pot and she watched it absently, the ambience of a chatty tavern drifting in through the old, creaking wooden walls. Some water Versorcerers made a career from filling the water bottles that filled the shelves. The pay was average, but the work required little to no qualification or talent. She had applied for a role a few years back, but after witnessing the physical toll on the body of those using The Algarethan Verse all day every day, she had decided against it. The degradation was notable in their sunken cheeks and hollow eyes. Despite providing the liquid of life they were given a lowly status that was on par with the City Centre whores for sharing their genes with the masses.

She dumped some tinned vegetables and stock into the steaming pot and whizzed them around with a wooden spoon. A tin of butter beans and a loaf of defrosted bread and her masterpiece was complete. She brought a bowl and a hunk of bread through to a grateful Sheppard before taking two bowls upstairs. Gault hadn't moved since she had left and she offered him one of the bowls.

His brow creased, feeling the heat coming from the hearty soup just as the aroma reached his nose. his eyes opened. "What's this?"

"Soup."

"I'm not hungry." Even as he spoke, his stomach growled and gargled. He wedged a balled fist into his gut, as though to shut it up.

"But you clearly are." She sat next to him, placing the spare bowl on the coffee table in front of them. She dunked some bread in hers and took a bite. It wasn't nearly as good as she'd hoped but it was edible at least. "Why won't you look after yourself?"

He sat still, staring down at the torn sofa and carpet beneath him. "I…"

Watching him toil, Rissa eased off him. "It's there if you want it, alright?"

"Thanks."

They sat in silence while Rissa ate. The radio crackled with activity, playing some old tavern folk music. It was widely preferable, at least to her, than the bass-defiled noise that Avatar had pumped out while she had worked there. There was the wistful feeling of an era gone by in the merry, jaunted notes of a mandolin. Rissa wondered if this was what it once felt like, sitting in a home not dissimilar in age to The Hound, listening to the music being played live. She envied previous generations for being able to eat from the natural land and walk for miles enjoying nature's bounty without a thought that it would ever not be there. People back then were oblivious to how good they actually had it. She had never run through a grassy field glistening with morning dew or felt the rough bark of an oak tree scratching her legs as she climbed its thick branches.

"Did you ever climb a tree?" The question blurted out before she'd even had a chance to regulate it.

Gault glanced at her. He nodded slowly. "Many times. On the farm."

"Was it fun?"

"For a time." He reminisced slowly, the lines on his face deepening as the gears in his mind turned back like the hands of a clock. "I can't remember when it stopped."

"Probably at the same time jumping in puddles stopped being fun for me." She laughed quietly, then felt another surge of verbal diarrhoea coming that she couldn't stop. "I'm nervous."

"Why?"

She twiddled her thumbs in her lap. "I haven't been to Grandmaster in a long time."

Gault turned his attention now fully to her. "What happened?"

"I studied there for a good two years." She told him, realising in that very moment that she had also kept much of herself a secret. "But I, well, didn't make the cut."

"You're embarrassed about that?"

She felt her cheeks flush slightly. "A little bit. People I was supposed to graduate with will still be there."

"Forget them." Surprisingly, he just smiled at her. "You've done well. You're making a bigger difference than any of them will."

The heat in her face brightened at his overt praise. She dismissed him with a coy wave and turned away. "Thanks."

"I didn't even know an academy of magic could exist." His smile faded. "We never had magic as widespread as here. It was a power that belonged only to the bloodline of the royal family."

"Must've been boring."

"We had war."

"Oh."

Rissa reflected on her own life. She hadn't had trees to climb, that was certain, but Centa Isla's sole benefit was that at the very least it could not go to war with another nation. Unless that war was from within, in any case.

"You were a soldier?" She pried, trying again to peer behind the dark veil that was Gault's background.

He shook his head. "A Royal Guard - much alike those you call Kingsguard here."

"Who was your aide?"

Gault hesitated; she watched his eyes briefly glaze over. "Sophia. Princess of the royal family."

"She sounds nice."

Gault didn't reply. The haze that had washed over his eyes had grown thicker and he averted his gaze away from her, glancing at the ajar door that leaked the muggy evening air into their room.

"Gault?"

She recognised this by now. She had replayed the twitches in his face and the lost look in his eyes over and over while she had been in The Douldruums. He was slipping to that place still undescribed and unknown. There were sounds and sights she could not perceive in the twitches of his ear and darting of his eyes.

"Gault." She said his name firmly. He did not respond.

He rose from the sofa and marched over to the balcony, closing the door suddenly and bolting the latches to shut something out. Panic rose into her chest as she felt the situation slowly spiralling out of her immediate control and into the unknown regions.

"Not now. Not now." Gault whispered. Bizarrely, she didn't feel like he was talking to her.

"Hey! Gault!" She shadowed him as he walked around wildly, twitching and responding. Frustration built in her chest and she stepped in front of him and grabbed his face, regardless of the potential recoil he might have. To his credit, he did nothing - his eyes stared past her, wide with fear.

"Breathe." She told him, sliding her palm beneath his chest plate to where his heart thundered. He fidgeted and shivered as though a glacial storm had just blown in. "Just breathe."

She herself had been an anxious child, always intimidated by the steep shadows cast by the tall buildings of the City Centre. The city had been so giant and scary as a child, but with age came the regression of fear and the rise of apathy and sadness in its place. Controlled breathing helped her to focus on the flow of air that signified life and grounding. She used the same technique her mother used with her when she was young and overwhelmed. It was her hope that this would work now for Gault.

Rissa guided his breathing through the flat of her hand, taking it slowly, counting out loud, her voice calm and reassuring.

"Breathe. Just breathe. Slow."

She had read once of people pre-Reckoning who tamed wild stallions out in the plains by transferring their calmness to the beast. Gault breathed, but his nostrils flared with the strain of keeping to the rhythm of her voice. Rissa could feel his chest hammering against her palm as she brought him down, level by level. His eyes stayed fixed on her through it all and she took his hand and guided it on top of hers.

"You're alright, you're safe."

Recognition flashed across his face and she felt his grip tighten over her hand. He trembled softly; his free hand clenched at his side. Rissa watched his eyes as the glassy haze that signified his absence began to fade away, replaced by his deep, majestic violet eyes with pupils dark and dilated. There was such depth in his glassy orbs that she could swim in them. Several blinks and he was back, his eyes widening as the proximity between them was fully realised.

"Are you okay?" She asked, keeping her voice to a soft whisper. She held her hand on his chest still, feeling the powerful rise and fall beneath her palm. So close to him she could feel his heartbeat reverberating up her arm. It was wild and erratic, like putting your hand over a speaker.

"Your heartbeat is fast."

"That's...normal." He muttered quietly, his words soft and comforting, like a blanket on a cold night. He broke their eye contact to glance at her lips and for a split-second Rissa felt her own heart pound in sync with his. Then he suddenly looked past her, as though someone stood in her shadow and quickly stepped away. His hand fled from her own as he stepped out of reach, a grim expression troubling his face as he turned his back to her. Retreating to the balcony door to unbolt it and allow the city ambience to intrude into the room, he turned back and gave her a small smile.

"Thank you..."

Rissa wasn't sure what had just happened and so stumbled clumsily on her words before finally speaking.

"S-sure thing. Don't worry about it."

She stood in her own embarrassment for a few seconds before eventually shuffling over to the sofa to sit down. In need of a distraction, she tore off a hunk of bread and used it to scoop up several butter beans, grateful that a full mouth made any need for immediate conversation redundant. When Gault returned from the balcony door, he took the second bowl from the table and sat next to her.

"I was one of them." Gault spoke at last. His spoon drifted softly through the surface of the soup. "An Omen."

The revelation came as little surprise to her. Between his Brand, his robe and his apparent history with the Omens who had arrived before him, Rissa had assumed as much, yet was pleased to hear him admit it.

"What happened?"

He went silent for a moment, staring at his reflection in the murky soup. "I was chosen after my world was destroyed. My choice was join or die."

"Do you regret your choice?"

"I don't know." He brought the spoonful of sustenance up to his mouth, then slowly lowered back into the bowl. "It was all too much."

"What did you do?"

"I ran. For a year, I survived upon Galleo et'al's surface. Hunted by demons." He pointed to Akor'shaki at his waist. "The power of Akor'shaki protected me. I hid long enough to come here, to try and prevent further death."

"Then you need to eat." She nudged him softly, encouraging the spinning spoon to be used as intended. "Get some strength."

"My strength isn't my own." His hand dropped to his waist, where he pulled at the hem of his shirt to reveal the mangled wound where Akor'shaki's chain entered his body. "I request my strength and am provided with it."

So that's how he was capable of such feats of strength so frequently. It also explained his ability to heal from injuries so quickly. Rissa played up her reaction, having already seen the injury after he landed in Centa Isla for the first time.

"Stop punishing yourself." Rissa scolded him. "You're trying your best, aren't you?"

He took a moment. His purple eyes were still hazy as the cloud of madness that had gripped him slowly cleared. Eventually, he delicately bobbed his spoon into the soup and delivered himself a sip. He processed it quietly, promptly tearing off a hunk of stale bread. When he ate, she watched his face soften and relax. She knew the meal was mediocre but she had tried her best and food was food after all, there was little room for picky eaters these days.

"Not my best effort. Sorry."

"No, it's good. Thank you." He replied.

There were no further compliments, but the small smile he wore as he licked his lips after the first bite was enough for her. He filled with colour all of a sudden and Rissa realised this was a young man who had starved his body of sustenance for no reason other than self-punishment.

She watched him eat; well aware she was staring. But his focus was tunnelled on the food and not on her. After the first conservative bites had been taken, the meal had now become a feast; the whole loaf dunked in and entire mouthfuls taken on at once. Soup spilled down his chin and onto his lap as he greedily demolished the entire bowl in what could not have been more than a few minutes.

"Maybe I'm a better cook than I thought." She collected his bowl with a small chuckle.

"Well, I don't know about that." His small smile was a relief to see. "I was very hungry."

"Excuse me?" She feigned offence. "Half of it is down your chin!"

He wiped at his chin with his sleeve, turning away in embarrassment.

"Now that you've got your strength back." She laughed triumphantly, gesturing to a twinned pair of steel swords across the room. "It's your turn to help me."

"Training? That's what this was all about?" He went to the balcony and put his hand into the hot and humid air. "It's hardly the weather to stress your lungs with."

"I can't control the weather in a real fight."

"A fair point."

She nodded with a grin, a feeling of unrepressed triumph overcoming her. It slowly dawned that in that moment not several minutes ago she had finally found a way to control Gault's "tunnel vision" and it filled her with a power and confidence that she had not been able to fully realise before now. The remaining time before the storm hit was valuable. If wasted, she may never have another chance to take control of their weaknesses.

Positivity coursed through her veins. Azrael would be put to the sword. Gault's malaise would be managed and Centa Isla would be a city delivered from the brink of destruction. She grabbed a sword and prepared to train.

—

Donnel returned to the Compound. The shine of his headlights banished the darkness that loitered in the dim lights that lit the outside. Gravel crunched beneath the tyres as he brought his patrol car careening to a halt. He sat in his seat for a moment as the engine rumbled and took a moment to behold the document that sat across his lap.

The Steel Wing. A construct that intended to grant prolonged flight, its creation co-signed by his own wife. His eyes had drifted from the road as he drove, greedily absorbing all information the blueprints would glean. He had waited eight years to find a proper clue and he wasn't going to spend a second more waiting. Now back at the Compound, he could cross-reference these dates with what he had already on file and see what came up. Donnel felt his chest tweak with excitement.

But with it, came a spike of anxiety. Seeking the truth was one thing, finding it out was another. Was he going to like what he learned? Was he mentally prepared for an answer he didn't want to find? He thought about how he would tell Rissa, his mind flitting between two entirely fabricated scenarios where her mother was alive and well or long dead. In truth, he had no idea how his daughter would react in either one. He felt their distance more than ever.

He exited his patrol car and entered the Compound, where a veteran officer watched the desk. Donnel didn't know his name; he didn't know many of their names. His mind was fit to burst with cases and memories enough as it was. He gave the man behind the desk a polite nod as he always did, but rather than see it returned, the officer rose to his feet. His plethora of service medals were certainly familiar, Donnel had eyed them up as a youth on the force, certain that he would one day hold the record for most decorated. That hadn't quite gone to plan, all told.

"Officer Rawdon?"

"What?"

As though to double check his own words, the decorated clerk's head bowed to a parchment upon the desk. "You are denied entry."

Donnel blinked. "Excuse me?"

A trembling finger, one moving not of fear but of age, rose to silence any further word from him. The parchment drifted closer to the veteran's face as he read the words out loud.

"For crimes of non-compliance toward the Kingsguard, forced entry to a restricted area and forceful trapping of a member of the public, Donnel Rawdon has forsaken his oath and is suspended from CIPD activities-"

"What the hell is this?" Donnel approached the desk, but the finger rose again.

"-including access to the archives, prisons, armoury, case files and the garage. You are to be suspended without pay for two-hundred days after which you will be enrolled in a training program to-"

"Give me that!" Donnel snatched the paper from the doddering old hands, spinning away to read it. As his tired eyes combed the words, he couldn't believe what he was reading. This was effectively dismissal; directed by an unpaid suspension long enough to force anybody into a new field of work. All his career he had garnered not even a stain upon his badge yet now, after one incursion, he was immediately dismissed so callously!?

"This isn't right!" He spun back towards the desk, slamming the paperwork down in front of the veteran as if he hadn't already been reading from it. Instantly, he regretted his aggression, this veteran deserved more than to work the desks and be shouted at for decisions he didn't even make. "Sorry, I-"

The finger came up again, this time it was softer, accompanied by a pitying smile. "Do you admit to your charges?"

"I do, but-" He thought about his next words. "I had reason to believe information was being withheld."

"It *was* being withheld." The veteran said immediately. "Withheld by order of the King."

"Then-"

"Then nothing. The King's order is final, even to us. You know that."

Donnel took a minute. He felt anger broiling. Even now, years on from the CIPD's separation from the Kingsguard they were still as in the pocket of the acting ruler as ever. Even, it seemed, if it went against the very mantra they were founded upon.

"Those people were being tortured."

"And you rescued them. You did your duty."

He recalled the name of the then King-Regent stamped at the bottom of the Magic Extraction Chamber's design document. Even now, the damning blueprint sat folded in his back pocket, already secondary to the document Rissa's mother's name decorated.

"But why are we protecting those responsible?"

The officer gave him a look that agreed with the statement, but the light shrug of his thin shoulders suggested that there was nothing to be done about it.

"This is bullshit!" Donnel seethed. He turned to leave.

"Wait." The officer spoke suddenly. "I've been asked for your badge."

"My badge-" Donnel breathed deeply, cutting himself off. Reluctantly, he reached into his pocket and took his badge. Turning it over in the flat of his hand, he felt the aged, pocked leather that had been with him for his entire career. It smelled of cigar smoke and was frayed around the edges from years buffering against the inside of his pocket.

Damn it.

He slammed it onto the desk and stormed out of the Compound. He entered his patrol car, still mercifully his.

"GODS DAMN IT!" He screamed, kicking the inside of the vehicle. The suspension bounced under strain.

He felt the blueprints crease in his back pocket as he sat. Furious, he scratched them out of his pocket and dumped them onto the passenger side. He cranked down the window and scrambled in his pocket for a smoke, screaming at his lighter to work until it finally surrendered a flame and he dragged deeply on his vice.

—

The day was finally upon her. Two days had passed in the blink of an eye and Rissa felt rested and refreshed. Grandmaster bound; she couldn't shake the rumbling pit of fear that had taken over her stomach. Anxiety gnawed at her, spurred on by the agonisingly slow passage of time. She had spent the last two days with yet more swordsmanship crash courses and bouts of small meditation sessions to help Gault better ground himself. Things were going well; they had a plan and all that had to happen now was for it to be executed. She had put more time into practising with her Mother's Conduit and had grown in her own belief that she could defeat Jace alone. Ironically, the one time she didn't need Grandmaster bricks to cast spells, she was going directly into the damned place.

She walked with Gault through Downtown, taking the longer route to avoid being recognised as a multitude of wanted posters lined every street. Rissa continued to tear each one down, crumpling it in her fist. The weather warning had put everybody who had a roof firmly beneath it. Those who didn't cowered in back-alleys, reality lost to the embrace of Synth.

"Whoever has the most influence, he'll be with them." Gault talked her through how to find Jace and more importantly, how to beat him. The walk from Forge Town seemed never ending and the air was still thick and heavy. They had set off across the city in the early hours to ensure that they made it to Rand and Eclipse with time to spare.

She nodded absently. Her focus was drifting, pulling her south towards the edge of the city they now skirted. Not far from here was her perch - nestled at the apex of a long-derelict construction site from which she would watch smog drift across the horizon in days gone by.

"Rissa?" Gault startled her, bringing her focus to the potholed tarmac they now walked on. They were far from the main roads and even further from CIPD patrol routes. She hadn't even seen a single wanted poster since coming this far south. Even the Empty Eyes were nowhere to be seen. The place was a ghost town.

"Can we make a quick detour?" She asked.

Gault frowned. "Why?"

"There's somewhere I want to see. One last time." Her words were poignant, but they felt right. It felt as though she was approaching the point of no return. She had steeled herself as best as she could for what lay ahead. Her swordsmanship was much improved, although she had yet to have a blade to call her own. She hoped that her work with Gault had been enough to prevent another incident with his unchecked rage. This was the strongest they could be. If this wasn't enough, then all was doomed.

"Very well." Gault allowed her to lead him off the planned route, drifting through the labyrinthian, crumbling backstreets of Downtown's deep south. They arrived at an old bypass road that ran parallel to the edge of the city, veering off into left hand jaunts onto cordoned off roads and large danger signs warning of the sheer drop into the exposed core of the world. Many of the signs had been broken and vandalised with graffiti, with no effort to maintain or fix them. Rissa pushed her way past one of them, approaching the looming shadow of the tall, rusted scaffolding that she wished to climb. As they drew closer, Gault seemed uncertain.

"What is this?"

Rissa stopped a few metres from the entrance to the boggy, sunken earth. Whatever they had started building here had clearly been abandoned in the wake of Reckoning. The earth magic that had raised the external structure had suffered at the hands of the elements, an unforgiving opponent that had spent its years degrading the once proud structure to a crumbling ruin. All that now remained was the towering scaffolding that had once encased the building in preparation for decorative features or windows to be added. It wobbled in the wind, lacking much of the support it once had, yet still a proud survivor.

Her first steps onto the lower level caused a cascading screech of aged rusty metal that squeaked high above her.

The protests of the steel amplified as Gault warily stepped on, a look of sickly concern on his face. "But... why?"

"You'll see."

She beckoned him to follow and began to navigate the lethal construct. The steel that made the rungs of the ladders were slippery from years of undisturbed rainfall, the once sturdy wooden panels that bridged gaps were rotten and had to be stepped over. Rusty protrusions of jagged steel awaited those not paying enough attention to where they were gripping. She made sure to point out each one to Gault, finding herself still capable of navigating this trembling wreck with her eyes closed. She felt her heart singing with adrenaline. This rush that preceded the calm was what had kept her going so many years.

The higher they climbed, the more unstable it became. It felt like a strong gust of wind was all that it would take to topple the entire thing yet the foundations, mired in the boggy earth beneath them held strong. Eventually, they made it, climbing up through the final gap in the scaffolding to arrive at the very top. It wobbled precariously, although Rissa wouldn't have noticed if Gault hadn't so blatantly struggled to maintain his balance. She had become so used to the waving and trembling of the rusted metal that her body was able to subconsciously and spontaneously adjust her balance. She took Gault's arm and steadied him, allowing him to ease down with her into a low squat. The unusually poor air quality forced them to take shallow breaths and Gault, in particular, began to feel a giddy headedness that contributed further to his lack of balance, so he gripped the metal bars either side of him tightly with both hands.

"Here we are."

She waved an arm up and around her, encouraging him for the first time to take his eyes off where he was putting his feet to observe the breathtaking view of both the city and the horizon. His eyes widened slightly, likely reminding him of the first view of the city he'd had when falling from the sky upon arrival.

"Welcome, to my spot." Rissa smiled at him.

"You used to come here?"

"All the time." She replied, staring out wistfully into the distance. Waves of smog rolled against the horizon like waves upon a forgotten shore. The sunrise burned somewhere beyond, trickling rays of light through the cold murk. "I thought if I looked long enough, I'd see something out there."

He planted his palms on the wet steel beneath him to steady himself. "Did you?"

A laugh escaped from the lips. "Of course not."

Rissa felt a strange feeling of peace. This old, decrepit scaffolding had been here for her during the worst times of her life. When her brain had craved isolation and freedom following the death of her mother, she had found this old place. She was just twelve at the time. To everyone else it was an eyesore but for Rissa it was an escape route to her own private sanctuary. She had felt a strong impulse to climb it, knowing she could do so without incurring the wrath and consequences only a mother would impose out of an instinct to protect. As a child she had imagined she could see the future in the smoggy horizon, always wishing that a shape would flit through the atmosphere and usher in something new and exciting. But it never had.

Ironically, eight years later something had arrived. Gault.

It felt bizarre and surreal that he was squatting next to her on the creaking metal, the wind whistling through his bones, sharing a secret space that had been only hers for years. Rissa hoped she'd be able to come up here again when the deed was done and view the horizon with the knowledge that the future of Centa Isla and her own existence would be safer, brighter and more purposeful.

Rissa reflected on this for a little while longer, silent with wishful anticipation. Within seconds the sky suddenly darkened with the eerie dismal black that comes just before an impending storm. Droplets of rain began to fall and this was the last place she wanted to be if the weather warning was to come to fruition.

"Alright, I'm done."

Despite his best efforts to hide it, she saw the relief flash across his face. She laughed.

"Don't worry, getting down is much worse. And we need to do it quickly in case the storm breaks."

—

They arrived at Eclipse with time to spare. Her legs burned from the walk, an intermittent climbing session only adding to the ache. The heavy rain soothed her limbs and in the far distance a rumble of thunder made its presence known. Storm or no storm, she was ready and raring to go. Rand answered to the usual passphrase and they traced their previous route through the veiled curtain, along the secluded alley and into the war room. They went over the plan one last time, confirming the arrival of the shipment and the fleeting window of mere seconds that she would have to enter without getting spotted. Rand began a stopwatch, the seconds ticking by agonisingly slowly as the minutes began to count down her entry into Grandmaster.

The pit in her stomach grew more nervous as they dropped down into the sewers and began to navigate the slimy underbelly of Centa Isla, guided by Rand and several masked Eclipse members. He lit the way with a torch, flames flickering across the alcohol-soaked rag at the end. Eventually, he brought everyone to a halt.

"Pay attention now." He spoke directly to her, ensnaring her attention with a wave of the flickering torch's flame. "You go to the end of this tunnel and take a left."

He gave her the stopwatch. "When this starts ringing you go. Run. The guard will go to support the convoy and you'll have seconds to pass by unnoticed."

The shiny silver stopwatch reflected her expression, a face lined with stress and anxiety. She watched the hand tick, every second almost too quick for her to manage.

"Get going, kid." Rand waved the torch down the sewer tunnel, sending streams of light scorching down the hall. "Time is wasting away."

Rissa took a deep breath and stepped past the convoy, deeper into the sewers where a warning sign indicated restricted access and threat of prosecution to any unwarranted intruders.

"Rissa." Gault called to her as he pushed his way to the front. As she turned, he gave her a firm yet comforting nod. "You got this."

A smile crossed her face and she nodded back. "Thanks. See you soon?"
"You will."

They held a tentative gaze for a fleeting moment and as Gault turned, Rissa felt the quiet urge to drag him along with her. They had been together for much of this adventure, separated only by her horrific stay in The Douldruums. She didn't have his knowledge to rely on anymore and a part of that made her feel uneasy. At the same time, she was now entirely in her own care, just as she always had been. All that she had to control and overcome were her own weaknesses. A steady, firm confidence brewed within her as she turned and jogged, steady on the slippery surface, deeper towards the entry point. She dug out a copy of the map sketch that Rand had created for her, noting that she was a sharp left turn away from being in the guarded area of the sewers that lay directly beneath Grandmaster. Above her, she could hear the bellow of engines as shadows passed overhead, the underside of the first convoy vehicle, visible through a slitted sewer grate above her. As it passed, the strong aroma of spices briefly replaced the stink of the sewer. The distant thunder of the brewing storm echoed through the tunnels like a stifled roar.

Any nerves were long gone as she crouched silently in the dark corner. Peering out from the shadows, Rissa could see the single guard in question and immediately felt a pit of dread pool in her stomach. It wasn't just any guard, this was a Spellguard. The bulking, armoured frame took up much of the walkway and it stood, stoic as a statue itself. She had only ever seen these silent, ominous guardians standing silently within the halls of Grandmaster. There were no human features visible, only the trembling breaths and spark of light that burned through their narrow, slitted visor. She had never seen one fight but understood on rumour alone that its presence was enough to deter trouble from the peaceful academic halls.

It guarded a strip of fence that stretched across the sewer stream and the walkways, clearly marking Grandmaster's territory from the rest of the city. Any further progress was only accessible from one point only from which the ominous, stoic figure stood guard. Beyond them somewhere, through the labyrinth, was a ladder that led up to campus through a grate. Rissa had been informed it was an access point to the Grandmaster campus, one of only three in the entire city.

She lay in wait, lurking in the dark hollows of the black slated tunnel, the clapping of thunder heralding the next strike of lightning. Through a grate above her, Rissa caught a glimpse of the surface. Due to a gust of unusually strong wind some of the crates of food had been dislodged from the back of a delivery truck and were strewn on the road at the entrance to Grandmaster. Many busy hands tried to reload them quickly to prevent the rain from seeping into the crates and spoiling the wares. She heard a radio cackle through the pounding rain and the Spellguard was ordered to the surface to help his colleague with the rescue mission. It turned with the dexterity of a crane and lumbered down the path, where it ascended the steel ladder cumbersomely. Another clap of thunder roared at exactly the moment that her stopwatch let out its shrill ring.

She ran, knowing that this was her moment.

She pivoted around the corner and sprinted across the walkway, slipping between the blockade and officially taking her first steps into Grandmaster for the first time in two years. She ventured deeper into the sewer network, hoping not to encounter any further guards. The map she held was crude, marked with seemingly nonsensical twists and turns which she followed in a precise and logical sequence. For a moment, Rissa began to worry she had taken a wrong turn, only to stumble upon the unprotected ladder she had been searching for. She hopped up the steel rungs with practised speed and felt her heart hammering in her chest as she gently popped up the manhole cover into Grandmaster.

The thunderous brewing storm of Centa Isla suddenly disappeared as though it had never existed at all. It was replaced instead by the illusory cowl of autumn that perpetually bathed the academy in auburn light. The students here would have no idea of the storm beyond the walls, allowing them to study The Algarethan Verse in peace. She squinted through the raised lid of the manhole resting its weight on both palms. The gothic towers of the main campus building leered at her and Rissa felt her brain bathe her in nostalgia as she immediately recognised where she was. If her recollection was correct there was a twisting, forested walk from the student dormitories to the main campus building where she was now. Rissa slipped from the sewer, carefully sliding the heavy lid perfectly back into place. She ran quickly from the path, disappearing into the sump rushes of fake foliage that had been revived in the spirit of the pre-Reckoning and that adorned much of the campus. Keeping a steady pace, she ducked behind rows of synthetic, rubbery hedges and escaped into the faux woodland that surrounded the student accommodation. On her first day as a wide-eyed and excited eighteen-year-old she had foolishly believed that the foliage in Grandmaster was real. For the first couple of days, she had wistfully believed the illusion until being told that real foliage wouldn't have the same texture as rubber. She had held a disdain for the fake nature ever since, deeming it an abhorrent mockery of what was once so real.

From here onwards there was no real plan. Every decision was now hers to make. Her casual clothes marked her as a clear intruder, so procuring a uniform was her first mission. At least there had been no alarms raised and so she could only presume that her presence was currently undetected. She hid in the obscured treeline, avoiding being in the line of sight from any windows while she gained her bearings. She felt an impending sense of overwhelm fraying at the edges of her vision. Her heartbeat was loud and dominant, overpowering any rational thoughts. She controlled her breathing and fought to regain her lost composure.

Many of the windows of the student accommodation block were closed and the curtains drawn as the students at this early hour were still in silent slumber. Rissa had always preferred to sleep with her window open but she remembered distinctly a thick rubbery branch from a synthetic oak that had pressed itself against the wooden pane, pushing it shut. Opening the window had required brute strength and the attempts had strained the hinges so much that the window no longer closed properly. This memory invited an idea. If she still had her bearings then she was fairly certain her old dorm was nearby.

Grandmaster housed its students in old, three-story buildings with eight rooms somehow crammed onto each floor. The dorms looked exactly the same but were distinguished by signage named after the four elements and the four schools of academia that were studied by the student body: Loyalty, Opportunity, Discipline and Sorcery.

Rissa had been housed in Discipline yet had shared very little in common with the namesake. She was well aware of the irony. Given a second chance now, she often wondered if she'd do better, being a student her father may have been proud of.

She squashed fake branches underfoot while sneaking around the back of the student housing. Closer inspection of the wending lie of trees that twisted over her head revealed a familiar sight. The tree responsible for her damaged window had a very distinct twist in the trunk, an imitation of nature as opposed to anything truly organic, but she had looked at that gnarled trunk every night and was convinced it was that very tree she was staring at now. By that logic, she was outside Discipline, two floors beneath her old apartment. And sure enough, just as it had been two years ago, the thick branch had asserted its strength against the pane and the misaligned window was unable to close and remained slightly ajar.

She just had to get in somehow. And the only way in was to climb the tree. From where the trunk branched she could scoot across the thick branch and reach the top ledge of the window below hers and use it as a foothold. Careful to avoid visibility from the rooms on the ground floor, she studied the tree. The gnarl would give her a natural boost up to the first set of branches. Luckily, she had a good head for heights and great balance but little did she imagine that her first attempt to climb a tree would be the furthest removed from fun that you could ever imagine.

—

Gault watched as Rissa turned the corner and disappeared. Immediately, Kenneth Rand and the rest of Eclipse led him back the way they had come before veering off south down the twisting sewer network. He was unsure where they were going, but Gault knew he was about to have the favour he owed cashed in. The terms of their verbal agreement were to ask no questions so he would do whatever was required of him.

Look at you. A grunt.

With them, they carried several heavy wooden crates. They were long and rattled with the sounds of steel. Crude nails sealed the boxes shut, but their weight was almighty. The other members of Eclipse carried one between them. Gault had one to himself, although he wasn't certain what was inside. Judging by the shape and the weight he would assume weapons, but to what purpose he was not yet sure. Compliance with the agreement was his priority, yet he could not help but harbour questions as to the nature of how Eclipse worked. Kenneth Rand, while clearly the leader of operations, had stated many times that he was not the one in charge of Eclipse. That left but one question remaining - who was? There was enough sway from within the organised gang to have a presence in Grandmaster, which was more than the CIPD and Verscience combined were able to ever get. He left the questions at the wayside, instead trying his best to focus on the mission. Frustratingly however, his thoughts turned to Rissa. Concern ebbed in his mind, distracting and rattling his steely focus.

You don't think she's capable, do you?

He chose not to reply to Akor'shaki. He kept his mouth closed in the presence of Eclipse for risk of looking like a mad man. But even still, he wasn't entirely certain that he disagreed. Rissa was quick and capable, picking up the basic arts of swordsmanship with a speed that would have earned her much praise from his old armsmaster back home. But they were just the basics.

Against Jace, they wouldn't be enough. A few more weeks and he may have felt better against her chances, but their hand had been forced by their strict timeline. Truly, the Omens held every advantage and to him, this felt like a major point in the underground war he and Rissa had been waging.

You trained her as best as you could. Her failure will be her own.

Gault grimaced. He had done his best but knew that her failure would be his. In the event of her defeat and subsequent death, he knew what would happen. He would see her face in the clouds, cruelly amalgamated with the others he had failed, glaring down at him. Her white jacket would be worn among the shambling, jittering corpses that haunted him whenever the oath he had sworn would be called into action. He would weather it as he always did and the fact he had known all of his life would once again be proven true.

You are better off alone.

He was better off alone.

Silence dominated the walk through the tunnels until Rand finally brought the group to a halt.

"This is it." A blade sheathed across his back rattled as he ascended the ladder and pushed the manhole cover aside, scouting the place with a quick sweep before climbing through. "Let's get moving."

The storm had hesitated in the sky, caught between anger and silence. The darkly ominous clouds lingered still, crackling with violent potential. Gault waited at the rear of the group, passing the crates up the ladder one by one until he too was able to climb up, emerging into a section of the street that seemed familiar to him. The air immediately felt less dense and humid and he inhaled slowly in long controlled breaths, his mind calm and his thoughts clear and rational. As the manhole cover was slid back into place, he took a moment to inspect the derelict buildings that surrounded him. There were old apartment complexes that he recognised from his earliest foray into Centa Isla. It only took a few steps toward one of the abandoned complexes for him to recognise it as the Empty Eyes base where he had killed Kren'shal.

The memory was instant. It felt like a lifetime ago that he had come here with Rissa. He had lost control when he had found the Brand of the Demon leading the band of thugs. The will of the dead and the oath he swore had led to the bloodbath that day. It had been so devastating to the Empty Eyes that their activity had barely been sighted outside of their own territory since. He held little regret for the massacre of murderers and thieves but held no pleasant memory of the effect it had taken on Rissa and the way she perceived him. It was the first time that he had seen the destructive potential he harboured affect people he wanted to care about.

Don't be so quick to dismiss the benefits of your malaise.

Akor'shaki made its will known to him yet again as they drew closer. In the arduous year between the destruction of his homeworld and coming to Centa Isla, Gault had survived on the vile, sulphurous surface of Galleo et'al. That very malaise had seen him surrender control of his body and had him awaken in safety from certain death. It was the reason why he was still alive. He never retained memories of how, but all that mattered was his heart had beat for another day.

The time for introspection quickly ended as their small group arrived at the entrance to the seized Empty Eyes apartment block. There was a presence who guarded the door, their hackles raised as they approached.

"I'm here to discuss terms." Rand spoke to them as they approached. The thugs, eye patches in place, steadily surrounded them. They wielded steel pipes and nailed planks of wood.

"You're the Eclipse leader?" One of the women asked. Gault recognised her immediately, her rows of missing teeth a signifier of someone he and Rissa had fought before. She didn't spot him hiding at the back of the group.

"No. But I do speak for the leader." Rand replied.

"Too afraid to come himself?" The toothless smile was cruel and sadistic. There were clearly no lessons learned from the culling of their numbers.

At that, Rand offered a dignified smile. "Too busy, for the likes of you."

The smile became a sneer and the thug waved her pipe for the others to clear a path. "Top floor."

Rand went to proceed, only for the pipe to drop down in front of him.

"You're goin' alone."

"Alone?" The de facto leader snorted. "Preposterous."

"Those are the terms."

"I'll take one person. For insurance. Or we walk."

"Fine. But the rest wait 'ere."

At that, Gault watched as Rand turned and waved him down. He stepped through the stranded Eclipse members, watching as the face of the toothless woman twisted into a furious snarl. "It's you! The bastard-"

"He's with me." Rand silenced her with a calm hand. "Do you want to be the one who ruined this opportunity for your leader?"

Spittle flew from the gaps in her mouth, but she otherwise took a step back. Gault could feel her eyes boring into him. "Watch ya' back."

He picked up one of the wooden crates, feeling the prick of splinters in his fingers as he carried it in pursuit of Rand who was led by a generously armed escort of Empty Eyes gang members. As they ascended the complex, drawing stares of ire, the stripped paint and litter filled interior became distinctly familiar as he recalled striding up these very steps and sending a trail of blood down after him. It was something he remembered vaguely, yet felt dangerously detached from.

They continued to climb until they eventually arrived at a floor just a few stories down from where Kren'shal had resided. The shift in decor was a signifier that they were approaching a space that was a high traffic area. There were empty cans of alcohol and discarded Synth respirators scattered everywhere. The doors to each apartment had been removed and had been replaced by jangling beads and the entire place stunk of urine and watered down booze. Where the paint had fallen from the walls Gault could see cracks and gashes in the foundations of the building.

What a wretched hovel.

Gault found himself in agreement as the Empty Eyes led them into the foyer that divided the various rooms and bid them to wait. They did so patiently. Gault tried to catch Rand's eye, to get a glimpse into his thinking or at the very least some sort of acknowledgement about what they were here to do. He got nothing from the gold-toothed leader and the steely gaze remained fixed on the swaying beads that their escort had just disappeared into.

"The boss is ready for ya'." The toothless smile bid them entry and Gault followed Rand through the shingling beads into a large room. The walls had been knocked through with a sledgehammer, expanding the room into another. Beds, mattresses, authentic animal skin rugs. The room was an eyesore, blending colours and textures into an amalgamation of hand me downs and stolen goods from years of City Centre raids. Bodies littered the room, laid comatose upon the dirty, stained mattresses with a Synth respirator loose in their lips. At the heart of it all was a deep, leather chair. A limber, scarred man sat upon it. A withered woman sat upon his lap whom he shooed away as Gault and Rand approached. She walked away, disappearing among the hazed bodies that filled the room. Gault felt his nose curl at the heavy mix of offensive smells.

"Welcome to my parlour." The figure rose from his deep, leather seat, revealing a size far larger than Gault had expected. He towered over the two of them on tall legs and long arms, a distinct eyepatch over one eye. From his deep, baggy pockets he pulled two Synth respirators. "Please, make yourself at home."

Rand accepted and to Gault's surprise, quaffed deeply on the hazy mist that swirled within the vial. He watched as a shudder coursed down Rand's spine before he offered a puff to him. Gault recalled Rissa's experience and that of the Synth addicts that Ocean's View had courted, then politely raised a hand.

"No fun are you?" The lanky figure approached and the eyepatch leered uncomfortably close to his face. The shadow of the man leaned over him, the stench of alcohol burning on his breath. "Say, you're the one who massacred our people, aren't you?"

How exciting. Akor'shaki trilled.

Those who were conscious in the stinking beds around them stirred and slowly sat up. Weapons were scattered across the floor lazily. Many hands fell upon those blades as members of the Empty Eyes spat on the ground as they stared at him.

"He's my hired protection, I'm sure you'll understand." Rand spoke up, before things could go any further. "That won't be a problem, I assume?"

"A problem?" The man blew hot, rancid air into his face, but Gault remained unperturbed. Then, he smiled a sickly, rot-toothed grin and backed away. "No. He's the reason I'm in a job!"

He laughed manically, then curtly proffered a hand to Rand. "Seth Gore. King of Downtown. At your service."

"I've heard much about you." Rand tentatively shook his hand. "Can we get down to business?"

"There is much to discuss, isn't there?" A deep, guttural chuckle broke out into a hacking, sickly cough that for a minute Gault thought might claim the man. When he recovered, there was a glint of madness in his single eye.

"Centa Isla is due a second Reckoning, no?"

10

The wooden floorboards groaned as Rissa stepped in through the billowing curtains. Bright rays of fake sunlight spilled in through the tall, archaic window. Her shadow cast itself over the endless shelves of books dominating the wall and she felt a sudden irrefutable wave of nostalgia. This had once been her dorm room and she felt a twist of regret that her attitude at eighteen had ended her spell at Grandmaster and seen her dorm replaced by someone else.

She surveyed the space in quiet contemplation. Back when this room was hers, Rissa had left her shelving mostly empty, the lower ones littered with an assortment of useless clutter. But now they were crammed full of meticulously organised study materials, reference books and folders neatly labelled for each term. The floor was bare, no longer functioning as a makeshift wardrobe to be hastily rummaged through every morning. The room was exceptionally tidy and well organised. Despite the familiarity, she felt strangely calm. It was as though the room had stored her in a quiet memory, softly swaddling her in protective linens as though wanting to keep her from harm. She ran her hand over the low set wooden desk; ink stains dotted the surface enhancing its allure in the same way that a spatter of freckles can add beauty to a face. Years of history were embedded in the strong oak and Rissa and the current occupier would be all but brief footnotes in its century old story.

She spotted a journal sitting on the edge of the desk and glided her fingers down the leather cover, lowering her nose to absorb the aroma. It was real, authentic leather from a breed of cow long extinct, making it extremely rare and expensive. Its presence here came as no surprise as many who attended Grandmaster were the spawns of nobility sent to hone their craft before returning to a life of meaningless parlay. Rissa herself would have been no exception had her mother not wed a common man and then disappeared. Her former room was bursting at its seams with an endless array of expensive leather books, a true testimony to the snobbery and overindulgence of whichever noble spawn that resided within it. At least when it was her room it was unpretentious, honest and humble.

She opened the journal, slowly and with the respect it deserved, to find a name written neatly on the inside cover, *Emelia Rowe*. Putting a name to the new occupier brought mixed feelings. Rissa was certain that this old room had much preferred hosting her over this Emelia girl, but then again, she sounded like a maniac attributing thoughts to four walls and a floor. Perhaps it was jealousy that prodded at her. The inhabitant of this room now was clearly a much more dedicated student than she ever was. Beyond the wooden door that led out into the hall, Rissa wondered if the rest of the dorms on this level were still occupied by her former classmates. She hadn't interacted with them much during her time here, save from the occasional foray into the communal area. She didn't have a plan on how to convince them she had returned lawfully.

Memories and regret from the past pulled at her conscience. Rissa knew she was getting distracted, her mind trying to whip her into deep rabbit holes of thought that would lead to nowhere but sadness. And so, she pulled away, viewing the room as just another room – a part of her important mission to find Jace. She had come here for a uniform and so a uniform she would get. The wardrobe hadn't moved from where she remembered it and she was relieved to find two sets of uniforms hung up neatly and pristinely. Rissa couldn't hide the sneer that wanted to twist across her face at the preppy, neat and tidy way the clothes had been carefully positioned on their hangers. They were without creases, organised by blazer, shirt and trousers and a small wicker basket housed an array of neatly coiled ties. Jealousy lurked in the folds of her mockery.

Rissa, like all students, had been given just three sets of uniform upon arrival at Grandmaster, all of which were expected to survive the five years of physical, magical and theoretical study. She remembered within her first few days her blazer had caught fire when someone had tried, without training nor instruction, to skip a chunk of the curriculum and try to cast their first spell. The carnage that followed had left her a blazer and a shirt down for the rest of the year and had incurred replacement charges that she had still yet to pay.

Thankfully, Emelia Rowe's uniform was a good fit, the only part now missing was the shoes. Only one pair was issued per student and as Emilia was presumably in possession of these, Rissa had to settle for her pink trainers that would hopefully not draw unwanted attention. The rest of her clothes she shoved into her backpack. It had been this very old pack that she had hauled her textbooks around in once upon a time.

Rissa appraised herself in a mirror, trying to adjust the awkward tie that seemed to rebel against any attempt to fit snugly in the centre of her collar. She gave up and instead loosened it and let a button down, untucking her white shirt from the black trousers. This was how she had always worn it, unable to comply with the simplest of rules. The deep, black blazer finished it off. Tight around the shoulders and loose around the waist, it kept you warm in the cold days of Rainsturn and provided ample ventilation during the heat of Ashdown. Her disguise worked well. Back then, Rissa had kept to herself most of the time, preferring her own company and avoiding the crowded hallways. At least one action from her past would now hopefully benefit her future.

Rissa left the way she had entered, the final jump down into the overgrowth enabling her to avoid any classmates that might have recognised her. For the first time in two years the tall gothic towers of Grandmaster which led to those hallowed halls would see her return. Students buzzed around in a hive of activity as she walked across the twisting, smooth stone path. Rissa held her breath, convinced she would encounter a familiar face only to find that nobody batted an eyelid towards her. Something rose in her chest as she drew closer to the tall, towering doors held ajar by great stone doorstops, the chalky and historical halls of Grandmaster now just steps away. For a moment she hesitated as she mustered the courage to enter. Her trainers slapped against the marble floor and she marvelled at the great chandelier glistening like a precious jewel from the tall, cavernous ceiling. Bodies shuffled through the halls, a chorus of motion as the footsteps coalesced into a song of urgency and intent. Everybody here believed in themselves, believed in the future they could bring to Centa Isla as the lucky one percent. They all had something that she hadn't those two years ago - purpose. The desire to change the city. Many would be the sons and daughters of nobles; destined to inherit great homes and hold a powerful voice over the decisions that would go on to shape the city, for better or worse. Here, stifled and nurtured by the academy they were blissfully unaware of the awful and progressive degeneration of Centa Isla. They devoured three meals a day, unaware that much of the population starved on the streets just beyond the tall walls that housed them. They studied dusty tomes, while many of Rissa's generation couldn't even read. It was a routine of ignorance, a perfect precursor to noble life.

Rissa merged with the crowd, unable to help herself from glancing upward at the grand staircase that led up to just one of several floors. Classrooms, libraries, silent study areas. You could get lost in this place if you wanted. With no clear direction to start in her search for Jace, Rissa allowed herself to wander. Her legs moved by themselves, twisting and shuffling through packed corridors to the location she had frequented the most when still an academic.

The library. She had spent endless days here.

As she approached the gnarled, wooden archway into the ancient font of knowledge, she noticed the static presence of a Spellguard Knight standing in the darkest corner of the entrance. The light behind its visor burned quietly with ethereal blue power. She felt like it had spotted her, but it offered no movement to suggest otherwise. A hulking figure, it carried titanic grey steel armour on its broad shoulders, treading the line of weight that a human being should be able to reasonably bear. It watched, waited, insurance against trouble or misdemeanour. Even in her wildest youth she had known better than to disturb the guardians of Grandmaster. When incurred, their might was indiscriminate, no matter whose son or daughter you might be.

There were many libraries in Grandmaster, each one attributed to a specific field of study. This library was predominantly history but included all sorts about the world pre-Reckoning. Located on the ground floor, it cleverly created the illusion of reading in a secluded woodland. Large windows with slatted blinds let in large slithers of bright light and the staircase twisted up into cushioned canopies where you could nestle under thick leafy branches and disappear into a book. Rubbery plants draped out of their pots and hung down from window sills, casting waving shadows across the room. At night, candles would be lit, bathing the place in a dim, sleepy light that often found her jolting awake after a peaceful slumber. Rissa felt her heart swell with emotion as she returned to this place so precious in her memories where she would often watch the moon wax and the spectacular sunrises that would bathe the whole library in an orange glow. This magical reincarnation of the natural world which no longer existed, had been Rissa's oasis for the two years she had spent at Grandmaster.

Shuffling sheepishly, Rissa entered the library. Luckily, the librarian had changed since she had last been present. She glanced at the returns desk, now attended by a sleepy old lady whose reading glasses slipped further down her nose each second. Advancing further, she mounted a small set of stairs onto the raised section of the library where shelves stretched in deep, oak rows as far as the eye could see. Ahead of her was a window, casting bright rays across the spines of the polished leather books. Rissa ran her hand across them, forgetting for a moment why she had even come back to Grandmaster. Contemporary history, books of folklore, accounts of old wars fought over land that no longer existed; it was all here. But there was one book that Rissa was desperate to find and her hand darted over the curved, creased leathery spines until she stopped.

Zoology, Astrology & Botany IV. The soft, aged spine felt so familiar to her touch that she knew the book before she had even read the name. It felt heavy with dust as she pulled it from the shelf. Fearing it would disintegrate in her hands; she gently opened the cover to see the most recent reader of her favourite book.

Rissa Rawdon. Rented: 79/A/58. Returned: 89/A/58.
Rissa Rawdon. Rented: 33/L/58. Returned: 79/L/58.
Rissa Rawdon. Rented: 02/R/59. Returned. 34/R/59.
Rissa Rawdon. Rented: 48/A/59. Returned: 67/A/59.

A smile came to her lips. All these years later and it was still only her that was so fascinated. She understood why. It wasn't a book for deep study but was rather a surface level probe of the three declared subjects. Specialists went for more detailed entries dedicated to just one of the fields of astronomy, botany or zoology. But Rissa had adored the variety that the book contained. It was compiled from an old-world author whose name had been lost to history, but whoever they were, Rissa had been so envious of their life. The book was filled with sketches of plants, animals and constellations. Facts, trivia, legends. Whether any of it was true or just conjecture she had no idea, but the chance alone that the world had been so beautiful and full of life had been enough for her to get lost within its pages. She returned the book after a brief moment of hesitation.

Returning to the bustling hallways, Rissa spied a great clock as it ticked deeper into the sixth hour. Breakfast was still up and running at the cafeteria and despite the wishes of her churning stomach, it was unlikely that Jace would lower himself to eat with the students, presumably enjoying his breakfast in private quarters surrounded by opulence. Pushing the pangs of hunger to the distant recesses of her mind, she decided that the bulk of the student body either sleeping in or stuffing their faces was as good of a time as ever to search the classrooms. Her muscle memory snaked her through the halls like an ancient serpent from the very book she had just put away.

Jace would be a professor here at the academy, but Rissa wasn't certain which subject he was teaching. The classrooms of Grandmaster were numerous, cut into deep alcoves in the old building. Searching them all could take her all day, so she needed to make a choice where to start. Discipline, Opportunity, Versorcery and Loyalty were the four schools of education she had been forced to endure during her tenure, each were allocated their own classrooms. Versorcery had been her favourite, the raw practical use of The Algarethan Verse where she actually felt like she was learning. That, compared to Opportunity which consisted of drawn-out discussions on how magic contributed to the running of Centa Isla, had put her to sleep on more than one occasion. Loyalty was some doctrine-filled nonsense with a cursory education in battle tactics, swordsmanship and basic archery. Suffice to say, she did not attend as many as she should have. After that left Discipline, which was understanding how The Algarethan Verse affected your body on a biological level. Boring to her then, but interesting to her now. She had just needed a few more years to realise the value of those lessons.

Of the four, Versorcery seemed the natural fit for Jace. No doubt his Brand of the Sorcerer had awed many of his students and inspired them to push themselves to surpass their teacher. She was close to those classrooms now as she crept through the halls, she wasn't surprised to find most of them empty.

"Damn it!"

A voice came from one of the classrooms. Rissa peeked in through the open door. A young girl sat at the very back of the tiered benches, leering over her desk with her fiery auburn hair clenched between her fists. Immediately, her eyes, fiery and deep locked onto her and a flush of embarrassment darkened her cheeks.

"Sorry." She muttered.

"Don't mind me, you crack on." Rissa stepped into the classroom and nosed around the lecturer's desk at the front of the room. A large chalkboard decorated the entire wall, recently wiped clean from the fresh smears of chalk. "I'm searching for... er, Professor Jace, have you seen him?"

The girl had buried her face into something on her desk. Her eyes didn't even flit up as she spoke. "He was here recently."

Rissa felt her heart lurch. "Where did he go?"

"You're kidding me!" The girl suddenly growled in frustration, entirely ignoring her question. "Damn it!"

Rissa mantled the short run of steps up to where the girl was sitting. As she drew closer, she saw a familiar sight upon her desk. A thick slate, grey like stone, but embossed with abstract shapes and runes. She had used many of these in her time. A wistful wave of nostalgia washed over her and she couldn't help but peer closer, lowering herself onto the desk opposite.

"A Verse Slate." Rissa commented. "Having trouble?"

"That's putting it lightly." The girl groaned.

"What are you struggling with?"

"Everything."

Rissa took the slate, the girl offering no resistance as she spirited it from her table to turn it over in her hands. It was the very basics, a slate that was embossed with the runes of The Algarethan Verse of the fire spell Call Flame. Rissa masked the surprise on her face that a student of Grandmaster couldn't even do the bare minimum. The slates contained an embossed surface that when touched, helped activate the parts of your brain that allowed the spell to be created. Provided you had a Conduit and a purpose for the spell to serve, there should be very little that would prevent this basic spell from happening.

Absently, Rissa ran her fingers across the stone surface. The warbling of the runes beneath her fingers made her body tingle as though her blood was being searched for the means to create fire. However, when none were found, she felt nothing more than that numbness. She had memorised a handful of these back in the day, particularly Geyser, Vortex and Halberd. Those three spells were the majority of her arsenal, although if she had access to the water magic slates again she could try and learn more.

"Show me." Rissa passed the slate back to the girl. "What are you, a first year?"

"I guess." The auburn hair waved as the slate was received. With her palm open and her Conduit glowing with crimson potential, she closed her eyes and ran her fingers over the old stone.

Nothing happened.

"What the-?" Rissa watched. It was a mystery. She held out her hand. "Let me see your Conduit."

The girl obliged and slipped the Conduit from her finger. As she received it, Rissa inspected the bland steel. It was a Training Conduit, the very same design she'd worn for as long while only the crystal embedded within was of fiery origin as opposed to water. The only difference Rissa could find was a name inscribed onto the inside of the steel. She held it up to the dim light radiated from a chandelier overhead.

Emelia Rowe.

Immediately, she realised it was the same name as the girl whose uniform she had stolen and was currently wearing.

"Anything wrong?"

"No, nothing I can see." Rissa mused, promptly returning the ring and straightening her uniform.

"Can you show me how it's done?" Was the dreaded question that came next. "You're a fifth year, right?"

Rissa twitched. Did she look that old?

"I'm resting at the moment. Gotta keep up my strength for the finals."

"Ugh." Just then, Emelia's stomach warbled loudly. The girl clutched her belly, pressing her forearms into her gut.

Seizing a chance to change the subject, Rissa honed in. "You're missing breakfast, you know."

"I can't go yet."

"Why?"

She tapped the Verse Slate. "I have to get this to work. Then I can eat."

Rissa laughed. "Says who?"

Expecting Emelia to have imposed some sort of rule upon herself, Rissa frowned when no such comment was made. Instead, the girl's eyes were downcast. Her fingers ran absently over the runes.

Then it clicked. Emelia Rowe. Could it be?

"Are you...-"

"Yes! I am, okay!?" Emelia buried her head into the desk, only her messy head of auburn hair that fanned like a wildfire visible. "The High Priestess's daughter can't even cast the easiest spell. Laugh it up."

Rissa watched her carefully, not moving from the table opposite the stricken figure. A strange feeling came over her. She found it hard to place at first, but the longer she dwelled on it, the clearer it became. Expectation was never something she had truly had to deal with here. By the time she entered the gates of Grandmaster at eighteen, her mother and her family name were long erased. Her failure here had been a quiet, private affair that only her father had truly given her any grief for. To be the daughter of the High Priestess no less was a pressure she had never needed to contend with. Her apathy and boredom had been allowed to exist because she'd had no pressure to live up to anything. All of a sudden, she felt a great amount of sympathy for the girl before her. If Rissa had a name like Cordelia Rowe to live up to, she would have lost her mind in here long before her second year.

"How old are you?" Rissa said at last.

"Sixteen."

"You're kidding."

Grandmaster wasn't even supposed to be accessible to anybody under eighteen. The Algarethan Verse wasn't supposed to even be attempted until the magic in your blood had aged enough to be stable. This was too much for a sixteen-year-old, for anybody, in fact. She'd have disappeared under this kind of pressure at that age.

"Mother wanted to start my education early." Emelia's words were muffled, buried into her forearms. "But maybe I'm not ready."

"Well, that's for you to tell her." By the fear that crossed the sixteen-year old's face at the mention of standing up for herself, Rissa quickly assumed that wasn't going to be an option. "Look, you need to eat. You paid attention in Discipline didn't you?"

"I know, I know."

"Alright." Rissa thought for a moment. The Algarethan Verse was possible in great part due to concentration and stillness of a rampant mind. "Where do you feel the most relaxed?"

"What?"

"Just answer it, kid."

"I don't know-" Emelia looked out the window. "The lake, I guess."

"So go and eat some food. Then go to the lake, relax, and try again." Rissa hopped from the desk. "If you can't do it there, you can't do it anywhere and it'll be time to tell your mother to shove it. Politely."

Emelia sat for a moment, then pushed the Verse Slate from the table into her bag and slung it over her shoulder. There was a small smile on her face. "Thanks."

"Don't mention it. Now, you mentioned Professor Jace was here?"

"My- the High Priestess borrowed him."

"Any idea where they might have gone?"

"Actually, yes."

—

Gault found Seth Gore an irritating mix of confidence and arrogance. The Empty Eyes leader and self-proclaimed "King of Downtown" had willingly allowed them to outnumber him without surrendering their weapons or insisting bodyguards accompany him. The three of them were now alone in a small chamber nestled adjacent to the cesspit of Synth addicts, their whoops of false euphoria still audible through the thin wall, but their writhing bodies fortunately out of sight.

Rand led the conversation, a negotiation between the Empty Eyes and Eclipse. Coming in, Gault hadn't been privy to the specifics of their meeting today but was quickly gleaning information with every sentence shared. They were collaborating. On what, he was not yet certain, but Gault inferred from their back and forth that any kind of collaboration between the thugs of Downtown had never happened on this proposed scale before. But to what end, he was not yet certain.

"I'm not sure…" The voice was from Seth, animated but after a few seconds of contemplation, it calmed. "We don't like to share our spoils, see."

They were discussing the Empty Eyes and their annual, traditional incursion into the City Centre. It held up their mantra of turning the faith of the people against the King with rampant crime, yet it was painfully clear that many were only in it for a chance to bite back at their oppressors and sow misery across those better off. It seemed that Rand and Eclipse wished to collaborate on this. Gault was surprised, initially thinking the gold-toothed grin of a higher moral development than the common one-eyed thug.

It seemed he had been mistaken.

"You're a crippled force." Rand spoke quietly, yet assertively. "You wouldn't even make it onto The Blades."

"I wonder whose fault this is?" Seth continued to babble his thoughts out loud, rubbing his chin gingerly. Gault felt the single eye of the leader flash to him between his words. "Should we have a little think about that?"

Gault had been told not to say a word. He had no issue standing here quietly, but the urge to replace Seth's misplaced confidence with fear was steadily growing.

Hold your nerve. This bodes to be interesting.

"There is little to think about." Rand replied. He gestured to the thin wall, where the giggles of Synth-addled minds droned through. "Your members are hardly fit for battle."

A gesture from the Eclipse leader saw Gault being asked to bring forward one of the weapon crates. He did so, dropping the rattling wood upon the table that separated them. He tore off the nailed lid in one foul swoop to reveal a small arsenal of polished, steel blades.

"Fresh in from our allies in Forge Town." Rand boasted. "Sharp and pristine."

Seth plucked a blade from the pile and weighed the weapon in his hand. He waved it around manically, before releasing a laugh. "This will do nicely."

"We will arm you. Coordinate our own efforts alongside you." Rand went on. "All you need to do is be ready when we tell you."

This seemed to inflame Seth's anger.

"The Empty Eyes don't take orders from nobody! Why would we take them from you?" He spat the words out.

"Because I know you want the very same thing as me."

Seth remained silent; his face still red from someone daring to tell him he couldn't do as he pleased. Rand responded by pointing a finger out the window behind him to the leering omnipresence of Monument outside.

"Don't you want to see that bastard tower and everything it represents burn to the ground?"

The single eye of Seth Gore flashed with hatred as the lights of Monument darted across his pupil. He went serious, deathly so. Gault wondered what life someone had to lead for such rage to exist. A palpable aura of anger raged through the room, deep controlled breaths flaring the nostrils of the Empty Eyes' new leader.

"And why should I believe a word you say?" Seth's dilated pupil turned now to Rand. "I stand before you - outnumbered and exposed, whereas your leader has not even deigned to show his face."

Gault's ears bristled as he felt floorboards creak beneath his feet. The partitions that separated this room from the Synth-addled repository of thugs were thin, plasterboard walls. He held no doubt that the rotten wood that had held up his barn back home was stronger. All around them, ears pressed against the peeling wallpaper, listening in. There wasn't a word of this conversation that was private. They were ready to defend their leader if so much a glob of spittle flew his way.

"Every word from my mouth, every promise, are *their* words." Rand spoke slowly. "I am merely a vessel."

"What happens when Monument falls?" Seth Gore thought for a moment, then suddenly released a frenzied scream, leaping atop the table and kicking the crate of armaments from their perch. The freshly forged steel clattered and banged as they spilled out over the carpet. Rand flinched and Gault's hand dropped to Akor'shaki as the Empty Eyes leader, madness in his eye, waved his blade toward them.

"And what happens after you slit the throat of King Grayson!? Who will replace him and dictate us once more!? You!?"

"The city will be for the people, led by the people!" Rand matched the wild intensity that had been injected into the room, raising his voice, but never straying into aggression. "A council of those who want to see reform, rather than repression."

Then the pitch was dragged abruptly down, to almost a scarce whisper. "And the riches stored in hoards atop that tower?"

Rand paused. "A conversation, for a later date."

Seth Gore lowered himself to a squat, bringing his gaze directly in line with Rand as a rotten smile stretched across his face. "No. Let's discuss it now."

"To what end? To grant you resources I do not yet own is a waste of both our time."

"Just your word will be enough, then." Seth hopped from the table, blades rattling as the floor trembled from his impact. "I want a seat on the table that will be formed following the death of our good King. I will be the Representative for the Empty Eyes in the new, shiny, Centa Isla."

He cackled with such intensity that his lungs spewed forth another hacking coughing fit.

Rand waited in painful anticipation for it to cease. "And for that, you'll join us?"

"Yes. Most definitely."

Rand looked uncomfortable. He sighed and proffered a handshake, knowing that Seth was no gentleman. After a few awkward seconds staring at the outstretched hand, Seth wrapped a slithering hand around Rand's and shook it softly rather than firmly, creating an uneasy feeling that snarled across Rand's face. There was a small exchange of smiles between teeth golden and rotten.

Seth's smile fell first, into a menacing scowl.

"Now piss off and leave the rest of the weapons at the door."

They were ushered out, promptly and curtly, small shoves in the back as they descended the stairwell, spittle flying onto the floor where they walked, murmurs of "The Butcher" emanating from all sides. Gault knew it was directed at him.

They haven't got all the stains out yet, I see.

Once outside, they rejoined the Eclipse convoy and the weapons were handed over in their entirety. Gault waited until they were a safe distance from the apartment block to question Kenneth Rand for his motives.

"An attack on Monument?" Gault spoke directly in a hushed tone, understanding the severity of what was just discussed. "What madness is this?"

"It's only one tower." Rand replied as they crawled back into the stinking sewer to traverse the city's underbelly once again. "And there are many who have felt powerless for too long under the Clovis family's reign."

There was an intensity in his eyes. "Even those within."

Rand fell silent, making it clear to Gault that their discussion had ended. His thoughts returned to Rissa and the hope he held for her success. There was something brewing under the nose of King Grayson and now it seemed, beneath the attention of Azrael and The Omens too. Most promising of all is that it could quite easily be twisted to his advantage.

He just had to hope it wasn't discovered.

—

Thanks to the emblazoning of his flesh with the Brand of the Sorcerer, every part of Jace's body was sensitive to the magic in the air at Grandmaster and he frequently found himself clearing his clogged throat. For him, attuned so deeply to its ebbs and flows, The Algarethan Verse was like pollen creating an unwelcome allergy that he was forced to suffer. The other members of the teaching faculty weren't so receptive to its presence but neither did they possess the Brand of the Sorcerer scoured down their forearm. It was his gift and his burden, the source of his power and his revered status at Grandmaster. Yet equally it was a scar of cowardice and subservience to a power that had utterly dominated him, causing him to fail those who needed him. Others heralded him a miracle but he simply branded himself a failure.

"We have many artefacts stored here." Cordelia Rowe spoke to him, her words drifting to his ears as she marched purposefully in front of him. "Isolated and controlled. That they may not cause any further harm to the Syn Counts that keep us stable."

From a concealed door within the academy grounds, she had led him down a twisting, burrowing stairwell that speared deep into the remaining underground of Centa Isla. Together, they traversed deeper and deeper into the core's depth, the air thick with heat and magical energy. Jace touched his throat uncomfortably, barely able to swallow his own saliva. A great vault built into the earth appeared down the last set of dusty, stone steps. There was no sign of a lock upon the steel carapace.

He was here because he was trusted. Because he had leveraged the powers of his Brand to appear as an almost godly force to the Versorcerer community. Seeing him, Conduits were suddenly primitive and he was the receptor of great interest of many influential figures, including the High Priestess herself. She had not been shy about wishing to share his genes to create the ultimate offspring. Flattered as he was, he had a feeling they would just as quickly cut him open for research than breed with him.

But he had done as was asked. Cordelia Rowe trusted him and, if not an arrogant assumption, was perhaps even enamoured by him. He enjoyed the attention, yet at the same time felt as though he wilted with every measured glance that studied him. Now he was here to reap the rewards of his conquest.

The Vault. He had heard of it only in whispered passages, rarely discussed outside of staff areas. Following Reckoning, artefacts of magical power that were considered dangerously capable of further destabilising the atmosphere were quarantined below the earth. Only the High Priestess of Grandmaster was ever privy to enter, the means of opening the vault passed down to each successor.

"I hope you can pardon my asking." Cordelia led as they ventured beyond another sealed vault and down a deeper set of stairs, "But as young as you are, how can it be your powers are only just being discovered?"

"It is… beneficial for noble families to have undeclared children." Jace lied. He had been provided a backstory that had been procured and researched by Lachesis, the brains of the entire operation. "They are then not bound by the traditions that most are."

"Traditions such as?"

"Well, this place, for one." He recalled the information he had been drip fed. It was all very dramatic, but he trusted Lachesis unerringly. "My parents didn't want me to be cut open or studied. They wanted me to have a normal childhood."

Cordelia allowed a curt laugh. "Smart parents."

"So, you don't deny I would have ended up in a research lab?" He smiled playfully, staring at her flowing black robe that trailed playfully down the stairs behind every booted step.

"You'd be wasted on an operating table." She replied curtly. "Our children would be the next step in mastering The Algarethan Verse."

"You take what you want, don't you?" He faked a laugh.

"I didn't become High Priestess by playing coy." She turned to look at him. Her eyes were fiery and deep. She put it all into a small, telling smile.

Cordelia took the last step down into the final, cramped vault chamber, the final destination to reach the ornate, stone door. Jace coughed with nervous congestion, the air thicker than ever.

Her Conduit brimmed with power and to her palm, she called the lick of flame. It flickered and she pressed it against the steel door, watching as the flame absorbed itself into the metal. Almost instantly, the metal superheated and it contorted and twisted, malleable as a ball of clay as it formed a neat archway for them to pass. As it did so, Jace felt a rush of magic surge into him and he staggered. It felt for a millisecond that his entire body had been put through a wind tunnel. As his senses climatised to the power emanating from the chamber, his eyes adjusted to the unnatural darkness. Stepping into the room was like wading into the aftermath of a burning building only the smoke was a lingering, thick fog.

Then as Cordelia entered, the fog disappeared. She snapped her fingers and a string of braziers that skirted the chamber lit up one by one in succession to reveal a single glass cabinet in the middle of the room. Inside was a perfect, golden sphere no larger than the palm of his hand, sat on a cushion.

"Is that it?" He lied to present ignorance. The mere sight of the golden sphere sent excited streaks of sheer pleasure coursing up his Brand and down his spine.

"The only one I've allowed you to see, yes." Cordelia replied.

Power. Raw, primordial power.

What was it? He didn't know, nor did anybody in Grandmaster. It predated all records he could find and having asked many questions regarding these artefacts; he had received the same answer each time. Nobody knew. All that was known was that it was incredibly unstable and that it was an unconfirmed factor in the eventual advent of Reckoning that had damned Centa Isla to its fate. For that reason, it was sealed here, buried in the last bits of earth and protected by the secure walls of Grandmaster.

"Why keep it down here?" Jace wondered aloud. "Could it not be used for the good of the city?"

His curiosity was genuine. In his short time in Centa Isla and in keeping intimate company with the High Priestess, he had seen the history of her efforts to address the Resource Crisis herself. Yet now, the solution seemed to be directly in front of him. An immutable source of power that could surely power the city for years to come.

"There was extensive testing done." Cordelia replied slowly. The powerful golden orb reflected in her glassy eyes. "It is a power source, that much is true."

"But?"

"It absorbs magic from the atmosphere in order to compress it into a highly concentrated form." She continued quietly. "It's not buried here just for show. This chamber prevents the artefact from consuming all the magic in Centa Isla. Do you realise what that would mean?"

He did. "With no magic in the atmosphere. That's a second Reckoning, right?"

The face she made confirmed it and Jace felt a small pit of guilt burrow even deeper into his stomach. It was a pity then that Azrael and Lachesis had bid him to steal the artefact. As he prepared his betrayal, he wished for the sting of alcohol to whet his lips. His courtship with the High Priestess was to come to an end. A thousand curses upon him for what he was about to do.

"I'm sorry." Jace whispered. He called powers to his Brand, feeling the lick of fire at his fingertips as he called upon twisting, serpent-like coils of flame with which he sought to bind Cordelia in place. The Firelines wended through the air, wrapping themselves around the arms, legs and torso of the High Priestess. She hissed as the coils of flame seared her skin.

Jace lunged for the cabinet and pressed his palm against the magically tempered glass. He began to Superheat it, pushing immense heat through his palm and watched as the glass melted into a malleable goo that he pushed to one side. He reached for the orb, feeling the power it radiated both taking his energy but also granting it. The skin on his palm flaked and burned as he was inches from touching it.

Then a wall of fire encircled him. Fire scorched his flesh and he cried out as the flames hugged him, contorting to the very shape of his body. His hand, still outstretched towards the artefact couldn't move without burning the tips of his fingers off entirely. He couldn't move his head even an inch, already feeling the painful lash of flame burning the hairs from the nape of his neck. High Priestess Cordelia Rowe stepped into his line of vision, free of his own attempts to ensnare her. Her arms still smoked with fresh burns, but she seemed unaffected.

"I am the High Priestess of Grandmaster." She said softly. There was no rage nor betrayal in her tone, just cold, sinister apathy. "Were you so arrogant to assume you could steal from me?"

She clenched her fist slowly and Jace felt the prison of fire begin to close in around him with the slightest movement of her hand.

"Please-!"

"Quiet." She told him, taking a step closer and putting a delicate finger through her own roaring flames and to his lips. Her Conduit blazed with power on her finger, ornate and decorative befitting her stature within the academy. "I am talking. You must listen."

Jace could do nothing but listen. His arm, still outstretched, was inches from his prize but he knew it was forever out of his reach and that he was likely to die down here in the depths of nowhere. Her power staggered him. Her words had been correct, he had been arrogant to assume she was so smitten with him that he would be allowed into the most sacred vault within Grandmaster. Now he was going to pay the ultimate price.

"The artefact could destroy what is left of this world." She snapped her fingers, drawing his trembling eyes to her. "And you want to steal it?"

She watched for his reaction. Jace offered none, he knew the fear in his eyes was enough. Then, the flames that swarmed him suddenly dissipated. Jace gasped and fell to his knees, scuffing his palms on the floor as he fought for his balance.

"I know the master you serve. A power greater than any I have ever known." She continued, looming over him. Her eyes shone with wistful imagination, but her smile threatened a touch of madness. "I have seen It in my dreams as I scry the night sky. Looming in the dark beyond."

"How do you know?"

"I don't. Not truly. But you will tell me." Her eyes flitted sharply to his Brand. They blazed with a fire he had not seen in her before, simmering and crackling with fanaticism. "There is no end to the Resource Crisis, is there?"

Jace hesitated. "... No."

"Then the campaign, the King, this very artefact." She stripped away his lies, her Conduit still shimmering with potential violence. "It's all for that shape in the stars, isn't it?"

"Yes." Jace nodded grimly. His fists balled. "This city will be destroyed. Whether I get this artefact today or not. The wheels are too far in motion."

"For years I have searched the abyss for this city's salvation. Beyond the limitations of this world, further than any Versorcerer or King has ever been able." Her hand grasped the sphere and she groaned as power that he could physically see coursed up her arm, spooling her hair as though she was standing in a hurricane. She lifted it with strain and placed it squarely into his hands. She smiled madly. "I'll be waiting for your master. Please speak well of me."

Jace felt the impact immediately. Every bone in his body suddenly reverberated, as though he was standing in the deafening boom of a speaker. Just as it began to grow overwhelming and the fear that his bones may vibrate into dust, it all stopped and everything was calm and quiet, enabling him to feel the smooth, perfect surface in his hand and marvel at it. It was taking his magic; he could feel it. But it felt so good. The shape was so perfectly spherical in his hands that it felt unnatural, lacking the rough indents or splayed imperfections that made an object truly beautiful.

"But- what about us?" He stumbled out the words, having realised he had been sitting there staring at the orb in some sort of trance for the last few moments.

Cordelia laughed. Loudly, obnoxiously. She pulled him to his feet with a firm hand around his bicep. Her eyes were frosty with cold indifference. "What about us, my dear?"

"I-."

"As we speak the orb is lowering the Syn Count here." Her urgent words jolted him from his stupor. "The alarms will strike once you reach the surface. Be swift."

Jace started to move. Out of the chamber, back up the stairs. His chest twisted with pain. His relationship with the High Priestess had been borne of the Dark One's mission, but there were times he had forgotten that. Their days together had been pleasant. Walking the autumn campus, discussing the potential of students, eating a packed lunch at the lake. In the evening, they would share drinks and dinner, enjoying intimacy in her private estate at the back of campus. He had intended to betray her the entire time; he knew he had no choice. But, as they had both shared so many moments with each other, Jace had started to care where she clearly hadn't.

Anger replaced his sorrow and Jace sneered to himself. There were strings in play here that only told him he was even more of a dupe than he had first believed. Ultimately it was Galleo et'al who once again was the victor, edging ever closer to claiming this world for itself.

He climbed and climbed until finally, he reached the surface. He burst out of the final door and out into the hallways of Grandmaster and almost immediately alarms began to ring as they sensed the artefact draining magic from the atmosphere. Just as Cordelia had told him.

"Found you." Waiting for him outside was someone he hadn't expected to see. He felt his eyes widen slightly in veiled surprise.

"Rissa Rawdon."

———

Sure enough, Rissa had found him. Emelia's hunch had been mostly correct that her mother would be showing Jace the secrets of the academy. It seemed, the High Priestess was quite smitten with the Brand of the Sorcerer, apparently not shutting up about him even in the company of her struggling daughter.

The deafening sirens had started to blare as something was detected that was out of place. The corridors had spun by as she homed in on the source of the blaring alarms. Rissa had been running against the current, sifting past students who fled the scene as per the evacuation process drilled into every student twice a season. They would all be taken to the training fields out front where a head count would take place while the armoured, titanic Spellguard took care of whatever trouble had arisen inside.

The alarms blared, seeking sources of magic and shutting them down. Her Conduit was dead on her finger. Dread pooled in her stomach at the thought of once again not having The Algarethan Verse at her disposal, not while the alarms droned at least.

It was around a sharp corner that she saw him, hurrying through the halls with something tucked under his arm. Immediately, she felt a wash of power from him; or rather, whatever he carried.

He clocked her instantly. A small smile of recognition flecking his face.

"Don't get in my way." He hissed, raising his voice over the alarms.

"Whatever that is, you're not leaving with it." Rissa frowned, glancing at the orb he clutched so tightly. She could feel the power radiating from it even at a distance.

"And you're going to stop me?" Jace replied curtly. "Get out of my way before we have company."

Their standoff was abruptly cut short as the wooden floorboards beneath them groaned with the strain of a new presence. Rissa turned, watching a jagged, hulking shadow slowly grow itself up the wall ahead of her. It continued to grow in stature, every time she was convinced it had to stop it just kept getting larger and larger. She knew exactly what it was but found herself transfixed as its source was seconds away from rounding the corner.

Rissa laughed. "Is this what you meant by company? Because it's here for you; not me."

She swallowed hard, hoping her words were true as the heavy footsteps grew deafening. The paintings that adorned the walls jolted with every step as the Spellguard Knight lumbered itself around the corner. It appeared slow and cumbersome, but Rissa knew only too well the threat that had just presented itself before them. The stoic guardians of Grandmaster were rarely called upon, but that was because of the sheer fear they instilled in the body of students who were given a demonstration at the start of every new year.

It stood still, a great sword gripped within one giant gauntleted hand. The emblazoned silver armour was fitted with runes of power as the helmet scanned both their faces, appraising the two of them through a slitted visor from which radiant blue power blazed within. The presence alone paralyzed the both of them as to move was to incur its unwanted wrath. Rissa felt its gaze wash over her, the raw power exerted from its visor enough to draw goosebumps to her skin. Its gaze settled on Jace and the golden orb grasped within his clenched fist. A hand came forward, palm open, as if to demand the object be placed in its grip before it was forced to come and take it.

Jace shook his head and gestured to the Grandmaster sigil upon his robe.

Rissa felt its gaze turn to her. Almost immediately, she felt it bristle at her presence, as though it knew she was an intruder.

"I'm a student. I haven't done anything."

The hand fell and for a moment Rissa thought it was going to turn and walk away.

She had been wrong.

It moved with frightening speed. The arm that had once offered a chance to prevent violence rose now with power, a Conduit emblazoned into the finger of its gauntlet revealing itself as a blast of magic coalesced.

Rissa recognised the shimmer of water magic that she had performed herself many times before, only now she was powerless against it with her Conduit locked out by the blaring alarms. But Jace was not; he raised a shield that, to his credit, covered the both of them from the blast of Geyser that came forth. The impact was astounding and Jace's shield was ripped through in an instant, sending the two of them flying down the hall as freezing water surged down the narrow corridors, carrying them with it.

Jace dropped the golden orb watching it swoosh down the hall where it rolled even further away from him. He scrambled to his feet to retrieve it, only for a Vortex to open in the ceiling above him. The Spellguard dropped down, splintering the floor as it landed between him and the artefact. It hefted its blade and swung, Jace was just able to steer the blade away before it had time to slice through his flesh and bones. However, there was no time to dodge the armoured boot that pummelled into his stomach, sending him into an agonising back flip that left him screaming in pain. He lay there writhing and the blue visor creaked as it twisted to look at her.

Rissa put her hands up. "Hey, I'm with you."

It didn't seem to care. Whether it knew she was an intruder or that she simply wasn't adhering to the evacuation procedure, it didn't matter. The mighty blade rose again and Rissa turned to run, only for a Crest of surging water to rise ahead of her. The Spellguard gestured closer and the water moved to its instruction. Rissa tried to push desperately against the water, feeling the ripping current tearing at her uniform yet the integrity of the spell was far too strong. The ribbed, black blade was inches away from staining these sacred halls with her guts and in an instant, Rissa had only one chance to escape. She sprinted sideways, throwing herself through the last ornate glass window between her and the Spellguard.

Just as she climbed to her feet, shrugging stained glass from her shoulders, a gauntleted hand followed her and seized her by the scruff of the neck. She screamed, the steel felt like ice to the touch as she was dragged back into the halls and slammed violently into the ground. There was no mercy in that lifeless visor as the blade rose gently, ready to be pressed into her chest. Just then, a swathe of Firelines wrapped themselves around the joints of the armour, seeking to restrict the movement of the stoic knight. This seemed to draw its ire and with one robust motion, it snapped the lines that bound it with a wild swing of its sword arm. Fist then outstretched, it immediately fired a volley of razor-sharp Icicles toward Jace who managed to evade their whistling touch with a tidy pirouette, the impact shattering the walls where they landed.

Rissa rose to her feet, clutching the back of her neck where the icy touch had seized her. She had always wondered how powerful the guardians of Grandmaster were, having only been warned of them from campus legend. She had never expected, nor truly desired to experience it firsthand.

"Destroy the alarms!" Rissa yelled to Jace. "I can help!"

"Patience, please." The moment Jace landed he was already besieged. The Spellguard, without so much as moving from its position, used a Vortex to plunge its blade into the floor beneath it and out of the wall where Jace landed. With impressive agility, the Omen twisted out of the way.

As Rissa could only spectate, sitting in what was hopefully a blind spot behind the Spellguard, an idea formed in her mind. Recalling her first encounter with Kren'shal, she understood the ramifications of a limb not being fully clear of the portal once it closed. Rissa waited until the Spellguard sought to plunge its blade through time and space once more and then struck. She threw her entire weight behind the armoured beast, driving her knees into its back as she mantled her arms onto the grooves of its shoulder plates. It toppled yet didn't completely fall until Jace launched cables of flame up through the Vortex, clearly clued into what she intended to do, and pulled. The Spellguard heaved with strain, steel groaning as though its pain was voiced through the armour. Then it toppled, its torso toppling part way through the Vortex where Jace was already waiting for it on the other side.

His blade came down hard with speed and accuracy, driving the blade into the narrow slit where the armour allowed the elbow to bend. The strike hit and Rissa was surprised to see the armoured knight actually falter as its arm fell loose, clanging to the ground with the weight of the plates of steel. With the access to its Conduit severed, the Vortex closed and cleanly severed the Spellguard in half. The light beneath the visor disappeared and the husk slumped, both halves on either side of the hall.

Rissa fell back and for a moment, she shared a look with Jace that questioned whether whatever he was doing was really worth all this. A deep, steady shrug of an expression crossed his face and he rose, having successfully retrieved the mysterious golden orb. He wasted no time and sprinted off down an adjacent corridor. Scrambling to her feet, Rissa dragged herself up and pursued him, storming down the corridors. Jace was unbelievably fast. On the straight lengths of corridor he would surge forwards, leaving a trail of fire in his wake. To keep up she took the corners at full speed, crashing a shoulder into the wall to try and maintain her momentum. She followed him through Grandmaster, pushing and thrusting herself past dazed students who hadn't had time to question why one of their teachers was pelting at full speed through the halls.

"Outta the way!" She cried, twisting through a tangle of bodies who had initially stepped aside for Jace to pass and had since regrouped. They were holding her back and she gulped with frustration as she chased the flash of his coat tails whizzing around the distant corridor. Slaloming through two more winding halls, Rissa found herself bursting from one of the side entrances onto one of the several practice fields filled with students lining up in formal queues.

Spellguard swarmed the perimeter and their hollow helmets turned to look at her as she surged out of the building, pointing wildly at Jace who was crossing the field just beside them.

"It's him! Stop him!"

They didn't seem interested and had instead identified her as an aggressor, lumbering with clanking strides to block her path with their swords splayed. Behind them, Jace was putting distance between them as he scorched a blazing trail of fire across the field, scorching the artificial grass as he went. As she approached, she felt the tingling of her Conduit on her finger and realised she had finally left the radius of the sensors and could once again freely use her magic.

I invoke the Missing Sea. Vortex, help me catch up!

Instantly she Vortexed herself behind the two Spellguards, busy casting spells in an attempt to subdue her. The colours that burned through their visors were an ephemeral turquoise and dusty brown, signifying the knights were attuned to Wind and Earth, respectively. She felt a sudden blast of strong wind, seeking to bring her back into their clutches while the earth itself sought to bind itself around her ankles, tangling them with strong stemmed weeds.

She freed herself by prizing her ankles free, escaping through another Vortex, diving swiftly through the void putting space between herself and the repressive wind.

Ahead of her, Jace was approaching the giant wall of Grandmaster. He raced to the base of the wall and then surged upwards in a spiral of flame. Rissa could hear the confusion from the gathered students and faculty as one of their own crested their protective wall and took a solitary look back before disappearing into the illusionary bubble that created the idyllic weather here.

Halberd - strike him with ice!

Spinning around her arm like a barrel, Rissa launched a volley of icicles in a vain attempt to slow him down but it was to no avail. They tapered off without even reaching the top of the wall, exploding harmlessly against the polished marble surface. She struck her fist in frustration against the smooth surface. When she turned, she found herself approached by three Spellguard Knights, on high alert with the realisation she was an imposter.

Just as she prepared to surrender, a sudden wall of flame rose up between her and Grandmaster's guardians. Rissa winced as the flames lapped and roared with such untamed ferocity. For a moment, she thought Jace may have been somehow responsible but quickly realised that wasn't the case.

"I can do it! Look!" Emelia Rowe emerged from the edge of the lake; a large smile stretched across her face. She screamed at the Spellguard Knights, as if trying to address her mother through them. "Shove it, mother! Are you seeing this!?"

Rissa didn't waste any time.

Geyser! Create me a cloud of mist.

Mist exploded from the flames as she cannoned them down. As the mask fell over her, she fired a Vortex blindly up to the top of the wall and portalled herself through the ground. Emerging at the top of the wall where the illusionary shield met the old stone, passing through was jarring, as wind and rain immediately assailed her. The sun disappeared and the blackest clouds clotted the sky and cast everything in near pitch darkness. But, she was sharp enough to spot Jace almost immediately, mantling over rooftops with a distinct trail of flame visible during his short bursts of acceleration.

She slid part way down the slant of the wall before kicking her heels to propel herself into the air, twisting as she broke her fall by blasting a Geyser into the nearest rooftop as she approached to give chase.

As if reacting to their presence, the heavens above her opened and several streaks of lightning illuminated the black sky. Her autumnal oasis was gone. Replaced with a raging storm that surpassed any she had ever seen in Centa Isla.

A Magic Storm on the eve of Rainsturn and Stormsmarch. A storm of water and thunderous winds.

11

Leaving the illusion of Grandmaster's eternal autumn in her wake, Rissa pursued Jace across rooftops, derelict buildings and multi-story car parks, tailing the flickering trail of his elusive flames. Rain pelted down so hard that it was blinding, the heavens all but open to allow all the pent-up magic to thunder down upon the population who cowered in their homes. The air was thick and lethal with violent potential. Rissa expected a strike of lightning to hit her at any second. But the fear was buried behind Jace and his dark, robed silhouette that threatened to disappear into the stormy darkness. With the artefact tucked tightly on his person, he abruptly fled the rain-slicked rooftops of Downtown, descending to street level to bash through a door and seek refuge from the relentless forks that stabbed the dull air in bright succession.

Rissa knew she had to catch him quickly. This was a plan in the midst of execution and it wouldn't be long until the Brand of the Sorcerer was met with reinforcements that would make his escape truly impossible to prevent. She tracked his path onto a lower rooftop, immediately bouncing off it, feeling her ankle threaten to twist as she propelled herself from the slippery surface and down into a backstreet, kicking neatly off the wall to land in a tidy roll through a dark puddle. Having gained several precious seconds, the trail of his robe was inches from her grip as she followed him into an office complex.

Storming through a prestigious and modern interior, she lost ground on the stairs as the Omen took each step three at a time. Rissa was desperate to get a shot at a spell, but found the twisting, sharp turns impossible to line up a proper angle. Her hamstrings roared with pain as she chased him, pounding up the polished stairs. Even as he slipped out of sight on every floor, Rissa knew that if she couldn't see him, she could still somehow sense him; or rather, sense the golden orb that he carried. It radiated such a mass of power that it called out to her like a light in the blackest void of the abyss. The potential of it evoked curiosity and intrigue but equally a healthy dose of fear that pleaded with her to end the pursuit. She wished Gault was with her with his inhuman speed and agility and impressive weaponry of Akor'shaki. Every floor she scaled revealed a greater view of the City Centre to the north and Downtown to the south. The clouds looked blacker and the lightning more ferocious the higher she went. The Magic Storm was wreaking havoc on the city. She could see immobile headlights lining the flooded streets bringing the city to a standstill.

Relief flooded through her when Jace stopped climbing and glided across a freshly mopped hall towards an empty office. The staff were likely home, sheltering from the storm following a severe warning, leaving them the entire block to play with.

Rissa surged into the office, finding Jace staring out the window at the end of the room.

"Come on! Where are you?" She heard him mutter, pressing his hands against the freshly swabbed glass.

With Jace distracted at the window, she surged up behind him and summoned power to her Conduit without a second of hesitation.

I invoke the Missing Sea. Geyser, take him by surprise.

A column of water blasted toward him with force enough to send him flying through the window. Jace turned immediately, receptive to the danger and twisted out of the way with milliseconds to spare as her Geyser shattered the window allowing a way in for the pounding rain and torrid wind. In the carnage, Rissa watched as the orb slipped from Jace's grip. He frantically tried to grab it, but gravity was already pulling him onto his backside. The artefact hit the floor with a resounding, deep thud. Out of instinct, Rissa lunged for it and wrapped her hands around the strange artefact. Immediately she felt reverberations fly up her arm and through her body, rattling her skull as though it was in a blender. She tried to let go but couldn't, her grip was drawn to the artefact as though her body was trying to meld with it. The wind and the rain that buffeted in through the shattered window felt no stronger than the breath that would blow out a candle. Her lungs felt clear and strong, as though she hadn't just run up several flights of stairs to be here. It was unnatural, like breathing pure oxygen through a tube like those in hospital about to lose their battle with Smithy's Lung. She was so distracted that she didn't see Jace until he surged into her view, wielding a wicked blade with the intent to kill. There was no mercy in his eyes, only frustration and anger. She dodged it, twisting backwards out of reach, edging dangerously close to the broken window. She fought for her balance as Jace prepared himself for another attack. She cradled the artefact, scanning the streets below for a place to escape. Jace, realising her intentions, immediately forced her away from the area with a wall of twisting flames that flared across the gap in the window. Jace lunged again and she dodged his deadly blade, preparing another spell.

Crest. Keep that blade at bay.

"No weapon for me this time?" She asked through gritted teeth, raising a wall of water between them that caught Jace's blade before it pierced her heart. He was riposted by the surging stream and thrown off balance enough for Rissa to push the wall toward him. With a wave of his hand, he sent a curtain of flames toward her spell, the impact of the warring elements causing an explosion of thick steam. Using the mask of smoke to cowl her next spell, she lined up her Conduit to where she had last seen the Omen's silhouette.

Geyser. Find him!

From her Conduit burst an intense column of water that hurtled through the mist and the smoke. She heard it connect with Jace and he cried out in pain as he was flung across the room, crashing through an office desk. His blade clattered to the ground and Rissa scooped it up as she retreated through the cowl of steam, emerging into the hallway with the artefact still in her hands.

Rissa felt her mind spinning in her skull. She needed to destroy the artefact before it could be put to any use. Placing the perfect sphere upon the floor, she held it beneath her shoe as she raised Jace's discarded blade, moving her foot at the last moment as she brought the sharp steel down upon the prismatic surface. The blade bounced harmlessly away and she felt powerful reverberations spinning up her arms. She struck again and again, the artefact tumbling across the floor with each strike.

"Damn it!" She picked up the sphere, finding not even a scratch upon it.

Before she could decide what to do next, she became aware of a presence over her shoulder and she whirled around.

"You have something that doesn't belong to you, dear." Lachesis stood behind her, arms clasped calmly over one another. Dressed in crimson, noble frippery, she looked more ready for a party than a fight.

"I won't give it to you!" Rissa turned to run, only for her blood to turn to ice in her veins. The elevator dinged and from it, emerged Azrael. He wore a shirt with frilled cuffs, unbuttoning the sleeves and rolling them to his elbows as he approached. She could already feel the phantom hands grasping themselves around her throat and Rissa suddenly found it hard to swallow.

"You don't even know what it is, do you?" Lachesis asked from behind her. When Rissa turned, it was a look of mercy that was being offered by the green haired Omen. Her hand, nails manicured a toxic green, was outstretched as if to take all her problems away. There was a veiled kindness in her green eyes that urged her to surrender, like her death was going to be too hard to watch.

"What the hell is this thing?" Her words croaked from her dry throat, her grasp on the orb tightening.

Rissa watched as Lachesis shared a long look with Azrael. The green-haired Omen then spoke.

"An artefact from your very own Grandmaster." Lachesis explained. "It's a power source. But without being put to use - it consumes."

The storm that raged just moments ago had suddenly quietened. The pelting rain was now a light shower and the screaming wind dropped to a whisper. In the dense silence, Azrael's boots clapped against the hall as he walked towards her. His black eyes were fixated not on her, but the orb, as though she were a mere pedestal for it to be taken from. The Conduit on her finger blazed with power, yet the agony of knowing it was of no use around the pale Omen tormented her. She didn't even have a sword with her.

"Every second it spends out here is a second closer to a second Reckoning." Lachesis spoke with urgency behind her, proffering her hand once more. "You don't want that do you?"

Would a second Reckoning even be the worst fate in store for Centa Isla? The implosion of the core was darkly preferable to the clotted shadow of Galleo et'al and the demonic armies it commanded. Rissa wasn't certain, but what had become clear was the presence of the magic storm. It was like an immune response to the presence of the artefact, warning them of the kind of instability that could end them once and for all

"Now hand it over."

Rissa debated handing it over there and then. But, she realised why the storm had become so quiet. It sought the artefact itself, which meant their building was now the epicentre of the storm. Through the tall windows she could see the black clouds writhing in the smoggy sky, curling around the skyscraper like a serpent. The artefact had drawn the full intensity of the magic storm like a magnet, which meant-

There was a noise so deafening that it was as though the sky itself had clapped in her ear. The entire building trembled, the roots of it pulled from the earth. It wasn't until Rissa glanced out the window to see the paved roads of the City Centre rising up to meet her, did she realise that the earth magic that made the foundations of the building had been completely eroded by the blast of magic fuelled lightning. It was like Azrael's powers in the hands of the heavens and as a consequence, the building had lost its spine. A huge chunk of ceiling fell, separating her from Azrael and Lachesis as the skyscraper started to collapse both inward and outward. She quickly lost her footing on the polished floor and as the entire building began to topple, a smashed window quickly beckoned her to a deathly plummet.

Rissa felt her calves burning as she fought the incline, dodging chairs and desks as they fell from the office block. Just then, she felt a presence over her shoulder and Azrael appeared behind her. He could have taken the artefact from her then and there, but for some reason he didn't. For the first time Rissa saw a moment of hesitation distort his countenance which she used to immediately put distance between them; turning and stumbling as quickly as she dared down the slanted hall. Her mind burned with adrenaline as she lunged for the stairwell, literally sliding down the first couple of steps. She had to get out of this building before it became her tomb. The collapse would no doubt devastate a huge chunk of the City Centre.

Where was Gault? She needed to get his attention.

Just then, a shadow flitted in her periphery and a boot suddenly planted itself into her side. Rissa grunted as she was launched into the wall at the base of the stairs, the orb bouncing from her grip and continuing its descent. Lachesis quickly passed her with an unapologetic smile and with terrifying alacrity, she wended between the banister of the stairwell like a serpent, easily catching the orb and twisting herself acrobatically up to her feet.

Rissa swept the rubble from the once-polished floor and planted her hand into it.

Come churning Maelstrom, scourge of the ocean. Don't let her get away with stealing from me!

A torrid whirlpool of deep water formed at the base of the stairs, immediately entrenching Lachesis's feet in its vicious current, sweeping her to her knees as it pulled her towards the apex where Rissa had already begun to prepare her next spell.

Just then, Azrael dropped through the ceiling, crashing down with rubble and flames in his wake. He plunged his hand into the water that bound Lachesis and immediately it disappeared, fizzling out into a vapour that the wind instantly expelled. Lachesis scurried away and for a moment, Rissa was left to face Azrael alone.

"You don't want to touch the artefact." She spoke as the very realisation dawned upon her. His hesitation was born of fear that his powers may nullify the orb forever. It was a curious fact and she intended to use it to her advantage. "You're scared of destroying it, aren't you?"

"It will end up where it needs to be regardless."

Before she could reply, the building violently heaved. The entire structure began to separate and Rissa dropped to her knees, clinging to the railing as wind and rain besieged her. The entire building began to split from the top down. Azrael grunted in frustration, sliding into the wall, allowing Rissa her opportunity to bypass him. Lithely, she slipped between the railings out onto the perilous drop between the stories and took advantage of the building's steepening inversion to hop down a flight of stairs that were still intact, catching a glimpse of Lachesis's green haired trail a few stories beneath her. She finally caught an angle from which to attack only for it to be blocked by a crumbling wall.

"Damn it!" She cursed, watching the opportunity pass her by. The air above suddenly became hot and she glanced upwards, just in time to see a wave of searing flame descending upon her.

Crest. Protect me!

She had little time to articulate the nature of her spell, only its existence. A wall of water apexed over her, protecting her in the foaming shadow of a great, cresting wave. The flames struck it and she heard the searing hiss.

"Nice reflexes." Jace descended the stairs behind her, wind and rain sticking his oily locks to his scalp. He looked grim and tired, but his teeth flashed a hollow smile all the same. "You'd have made a good Omen."

"I'd rather die."

At that, Jace smiled. "I thought that too once."

Then the final sinew that held the two splitting chunks of building together finally snapped. Rissa felt it separate as the wall opposite her suddenly tore away, revealing with it the skeleton of the rest of the building as they fell in opposite directions as though repelled by a magnet. On that distant side, she saw Lachesis, falling with the half of the tower that was bound for the City Centre while she plummeted towards Downtown.

Vortex. Get me over there.

She created a sloshing portal of seafoam beneath her, mirroring it to the rapidly distancing stairwell that Lachesis descended.

"NO!" Jace lunged for her, but it was too late.

Haphazardly, Rissa dropped into the portal and popped out on the other half of the building. The world was spinning and she hadn't realised how perfect her aim had been until the second Vortex spat her out directly on top of Lachesis. They collided, violently winding her and catching Lachesis unawares. In the carnage, the orb broke free as the two tumbled down the stairs, clinging to the railings to prevent themselves from sailing off the edge of the building. But there was nothing to prevent the artefact from doing so. Rissa was only able to watch as it bounced down the stairs and rolled out of a window, disappearing over the edge.

"No!" Rissa got to her feet first, her muscles screaming at her to stop. It felt as though she had been struck with an anvil but she sprinted nonetheless for the window as Lachesis rose to stop her, dark crimson blood pouring down her forehead.

"You little-"

The wind consumed the last of her words as Rissa leaped from the window, twisting into a deep dive as she plunged from the crumbling building. The winds whipped at her, throwing her about as she fought to reclaim her bearings as she plummeted among the falling rubble. A glimpse of gold betrayed the artefact's location as it dropped like a stone through the atmosphere. She twisted her body after it, spiralling like a falling star in pursuit of the prize. Destroyed remnants of the building fell with her, jagged chunks of rock whistling past her head. Just when she was within reach, lightning clapped again, so close to striking the golden orb that it almost hit her. With the city rushing up to meet her, Rissa realised she wasn't going to catch it in time.

"Damn it!" Rissa twisted in the air, forced now to concentrate on landing safely.

Geyser! Break my fall!

She pivoted in the air and, relying on her tried and tested method, blasted a current of water into the ground beneath her, immediately taking the momentum out of her landing. Moments later, the two halves of the building crashed down, demolishing a huge chunk of the City Centre in an explosion of earth and flying objects. Rissa buried herself into the ground, nestling behind a scattered pile of rubble. As the impact reached her, it brought a torrent of sharp, jagged and blunt objects that flew overhead and destroyed everything in their path. When the second half of the building hit, a terrifying shake rocked Centa Isla. Rissa felt gravity pull her backwards as though she was cresting a steep hill. Parked cars on the street began to roll towards her, forming a small avalanche of rubble and vehicles as the floating city began to tilt precariously from the weight of the impact. She scrambled for cover, sprinting across the street and into a nearby storefront where she dived to the ground as the tremors and lightning strikes continued. When she lifted her head, she saw a mother and a child cowering behind the counter, parental hands pressed softly against the child's ears as their cries were lost to the deafening noise from outside.

"Just a storm. That's the worst of it now." Rissa tried to reassure them with a steady smile. She just hoped she was telling the truth. Deciding that they were safer inside than out, Rissa left the family hiding in the corner. Upon stepping out into the ruined streets, she coughed as dust and concrete blew through the thick air. Her arms burned and she shook the lingering magic residue from her hands and wrists which tingled with a creeping numbness from casting one too many spells.

Scattered down the street she saw dusty faces, destroyed homes, limbs trapped beneath rubble and people crushed in their own cars. The city always in motion had come to an abrupt halt and it was a frightening sight.

Suddenly, she spied Jace running across the street, clutching the orb tightly to his chest. He was headed for the Subrail tunnels.

Path of Frost, slow him.

Rissa planted her palm firmly into the earth, slickening the ground beneath him into a sheet of ice. His footing went immediately and Rissa heard a curse break from his lips as the orb slipped as he sought to break his fall. It rolled across the bank of ice and down into the deep stairwell of a subway station. Rissa sprinted after it, skidding down the hand-railing only for a wall of fire to rise in front of her. She yelped and jumped from the railing, crashing into the wall to avoid entering the searing flames. He overtook her and she grabbed his ankle as he passed, dragging him down onto the jagged steps. He landed with a crunch, compressing his arm against the angle of the steps, screaming in pain. Water surged down the stairs from the raging storm outside, carrying them both down to the bottom where they slipped and skidded on the cobbled floor. Alarms blared within the underground station, the occupants long-since evacuated. Yet the carriages still ran, pounding through the platform even now at breakneck speeds, throwing up billows of water onto the platform as they passed. The ground quaked and dust rained from the ceiling above as another ferocious blast of frustrated lightning sought the artefact.

"You're going to destroy the city! Stop this!" Rissa hissed.

She beat Jace to the artefact, scooping it up in her arms as her body screamed for rest. She tried to put some distance between the two of them, going as far as she could before her back was mere inches from a pounding carriage that was surging through the platform. The force of it billowed wind through her air and freezing water drenched her back.

"It's already going to be destroyed." Jace spat back. "Does it really matter how?"

"Let me take it back!"

"I'm sorry." Jace shook his head tragically. When he moved towards her, he did so gingerly, his right arm grotesquely mangled from his fall. "It's no use."

From the stairs behind him, Azrael and Lachesis arrived. There was no lightning strike to save her this time. They arrived at the platform covered in dust and rubble, yet clearly no worse for wear.

"Kill her." Azrael commanded. He approached with intent, as though he'd do it himself if it wasn't done before he reached her. They approached and Rissa almost toppled backwards into the carriage when a shadow passed over her, ushering her forwards and away from the tracks. A grey coat, streaks of violet and a great scythe rose before her.

"Gault!" She yelled, unable to hide the relief that fell over her as the final carriage disappeared into the dark tunnel beneath the city. He gave her a small smile, revealing a concealed sword beneath his robe that he then handed to her.

"You found me!"

"You destroyed an entire building." He said dryly.

"The *storm* destroyed the building." She took the blade he offered, the leathery hilt providing a feeling of comfort and security akin to how she felt with a Conduit safely on her finger. She then realised, as a chill coursed down her spine, that Gault was face to face with three Omens. It was clear that he was already warring with external forces even now.

"Will you be okay?"

He turned and offered her a reassuring smile. He touched a hand to his chest and breathed deeply. The slight curve in his lips held no promises, but he was already doing better than usual. That was going to have to be enough.

"They want the artefact."

"I know." Gault turned to face the encroaching trio. "It's a power source for the construct that will bring the end of this city."

She knew he was referring to Galleo et'al.

"Then what do we do?"

Gault thought for a moment. "Take it to the edge of the city. Throw it off."

"Will that work?"

"I don't know."

The underground station chamber rumbled again, heralding the arrival of another carriage.

"Go." Gault commanded, ushering her less than gently toward the oncoming carriage. "Don't stop."

"Good luck." She said to him as the headlights of the carriage blazed through the dark tunnel, thundering into the station without any intention of stopping. Rissa ignored the burning pain in her fingers as she pressed her palm into the ground beneath her.

Vortex. Get me on that carriage. Alive preferably.

The frothing portal opened and she connected it to another portal on the ceiling over the tracks. She stared down waiting for the carriage to pass beneath her. Her brain ached and she started to feel dizzy with the wait, staring at her own reflection in the infinite mirror that tunnelled below her, her anguished face reflecting her suffering.

The carriage blazed through the station and Rissa felt it billowing her hair. She held her breath in silent prayer and dropped through the Vortex, emerging from the ceiling and falling. She held the artefact as though it were her own child as she struck the steel of the carriage's rooftop, bouncing painfully on the surface. The image of Gault engaging with the Omens was ripped from her vision by a steep curve in the tunnel. Wind blustered into her eyes, making it practically impossible to see what was ahead of her. Rissa lay low and outstretched, clutching the artefact under her as the roof of the tunnel caught the splayed edges of her unzipped jacket which flailed in the wind. This was horribly narrow, more claustrophobic than the city had ever felt and she despised every second of it.

The nearest edge of the city? Her mind thrummed with stress and adrenaline as she tried to steady her thoughts. While she had barely any time to get her bearings, she knew she had boarded this carriage at Austyn and was currently eastbound towards Bladepoint Station. If the carriages were still running by the time she arrived there, she could jump on the Downtown Line and get as close to the edge of the city as possible.

Her mind refocused. She'd get to the edge of the city, throw this thing from it and hope it wouldn't blow up whatever was left of Centa Isla. It was a plan at the very least, albeit one formed from chaos. She just hoped that Gault was doing okay-

Then a hand grabbed her leg. The touch was cold; as though a vat of ice had been thrown over her. She felt the chills immediately, coursing up her leg like electricity. There wasn't a part of her that needed to look back to know that Azrael had joined her. She shook off his clasp and scrambled to her knees, careful not to scalp herself on the stone tunnel overhead. Twisting, Rissa turned herself around to come face to face with the black-eyed Omen squatting atop the carriage, the lack of light in his eyes concealing him in darkness, only the flitting lights that passed overhead revealing his otherwise silent presence.

There weren't any words to be shared that wouldn't be swallowed by the wind, but Rissa understood loud and clear that her life was in danger as he edged slowly towards her.

Then, she remembered his reaction to the artefact in the building before it had crumbled. The hesitation she had seen in his face, could it be?

"You want it?" She shouted over the scouring winds, holding the artefact towards him, she found power in his reaction. He recoiled, like a roach shrivelling from the light of a candle. Maybe she, didn't even need to throw it over the city after all, not when she could just get Azrael to touch-

The brakes screeched unexpectedly and Rissa felt the full force of momentum billow into her chest, immediately sending her tumbling backwards. She clutched the artefact as tightly as she could, using her free hand to scramble for purchase on the ribbed rooftop. With the brakes on full force, Azrael surged towards her and speared viciously into her, tipping her onto her back. His clenched fist moved to strike her and she twisted out of the way, the force of his punch shattering the weak carriage plating, sending them both crashing through the ceiling into the carriage where passengers began to scream and panic. Rissa was unable to keep the artefact from slipping from between her fingers as the forceful landing dislodged it from her grasp. She found herself pinned, unable to avoid the death blow that was about to come from the Omen. Before he could strike, Azrael was suddenly grappled by several passengers.

"Stop!" One of the bystanders shouted, combining strength with other fearless passengers as they wrestled Azrael out of nothing but common decency.

"Leave her alone!"

It brought enough time for Rissa to scramble away, diving onto the artefact just as one of the bystanders was about to bend down to touch it. As she rose to warn them, Rissa watched as Azrael splintered one of their throats with a lethal strike. The passenger dropped, clutching his shattered trachea as Azrael promptly drove another's head through one of the passenger windows, glass digging fresh into the skull as he pulled them back in and slung their bloody corpse across the floor.

"No!" Rissa fought back tears. She tore her eyes from the mangled dead as the body with the broken neck finally stopped fighting and lay still. "You're a monster."

"No more interference." He hissed to the rest of the carriage, pulling his deep, black hood over his face. Before he approached, his eyes flitted to a bystander who cowered in their seat, turning almost as pale as the Omen himself.

"Your gloves." Azrael put his hand out menacingly and Rissa watched as the man, clearly of noble descent, swallowed and surrendered his gloves to Azrael who promptly snapped the black leather over his hands. A small smile crossed his face.

"That's better."

Rissa felt a pit form in her stomach as she backed away. The carriage had gone silent now as Azrael approached her. The carriage jostled aggressively as the brakes screeched, forcing Azrael to cling to the support beams. Rissa was at ease with the seismic movement beneath her, this shaking being merely a fraction of the challenge faced by maintaining balance on the old scaffolding in her secret perch. She pressed up against the door between the carriages, the chaotic activity having already attracted eyes from the neighbouring compartment. Rissa could see a mixture of concern and terror on the passengers' faces. She frantically slammed the button until the doors hissed open with a billow of steam, only for passengers from the next carriage to block her entrance with their tightly huddled bodies.

"You stay where you are!" One of them yelled, a dishevelled, tired looking man in a suit. He spread his arms wide, many behind him nodding in agreement. "We don't want any trouble!"

She fully understood their reaction, having watched the savage slaughter of two passengers. But it sure as hell didn't help her right now.

"Just get out of the way!" Rissa hissed, she shoved herself at the crowd, only to be bounced back into the carriage for a second time. She went for her

Conduit, more than prepared to bully her way but Azrael was now behind her. He spun her round. His gloved hands, still cold through the faux leather, grabbed her fist and ripped the orb from her grasp, dispersing her with a curt kick to the stomach that sent her flying into the cradling arms of the passengers who this time chose to catch and support her.

A small smile crossed his face.

A crackling voice droned through the carriage. "Due to structural damage, this carriage will now terminate at Bladepoint Station. Please take care."

The screeching of the brakes climaxed, then the carriage came to a metal crunching halt, jostling the carriage aggressively as water spilled in through the shattered roof and painted itself up the outside of the windows. Even as she recovered, Azrael was already out the doors and surging toward the stairs.

"Damn it." Immediately after leaving the carriage, Rissa found herself treading in water. It took her a moment to realise that the station was partly flooded, a thin layer of liquid pooling across the platform. From the stairs ahead of her, water surged down from above ground like the phenomenon of the waterfall she had seen in books. What in the hells was happening above ground? She ran for the stairs and was immediately crushed by a wave of water that almost swept her off her feet. Digging her heels in, she powered through, managing a glance up through the deluge to see Azrael storming up the stairs and out onto the street. Rissa almost immediately stumbled over as she emerged from the subway. It was pitch black and even the lights on Royal Crescent were out. Water scoured the City Centre, washing rubbish and rubble from the collapsed building all across The Blades. The downpour was relentless. The sewers were flooded, bubbling water and sewage out of the foul-smelling drains. She could barely see five inches ahead of her for the torrid rainfall, the flashes of violent lightning doing little to light the way for her. When she lost her footing again, she was initially confused until she saw the familiar sight of a car, driverless and door swinging ajar, trundling through the deep water as if possessed.

"Oh no."

The city was tipping. The weight of water was pooling so heavily from the wreckage that it had caused the floating city to tilt due south, explaining the surging water in the Subrail below.

Then, through the downpour, she glimpsed a set of headlights and felt the skin-tingling presence of the artefact heading towards them. The lights stayed still for a moment, then began to move, carefully traversing the deep water slower than she was sure they would have liked.

"Oh no you don't." She wasn't going to let them get away so easily.

—

Be more aggressive!

Gault ignored the demands of the weapon that he wielded. Its voice was growing, mimicking his voice, yet the longer he resisted the urge to surrender to its whims, the more it distinguished itself from him, taking on a voice far louder than his own internal monologue. He buried the voice deep, focusing instead on the threats before him as Lachesis bore down upon him with dauntless, flashing steel. She was not as proficient with the blade as Jace, for her skillset lay elsewhere. But it was her speed and trickery that made her just as lethal.

And she talks too much.

"Come on, Gault." She goaded. "Is this truly all you have?"

Their fight had taken them out of the Subrail and on to the streets. Jace was long gone, ordered to flee in further aid of their dark mission. Gault had sought to destroy him, but the dancing blades that Lachesis wielded had denied him a killing blow. That missed opportunity only added to the voice that was beginning to reach a crescendo.

Do not let her escape too.

Gault buried the voice once again, focusing on his striking. He had put Lachesis on the defensive, the billowing storm that hailed around them working to his advantage as the watery mire removed an aspect of her agility from their fight.

You know who this is, don't you? What she did to us?

He knew. There was never a day he wouldn't replay that day over and over in his head. Gault could feel himself slowly slipping, every strike of the steel reverberating through his bones, shaking loose the desire to surrender himself to the growing loss of control that was mounting within him. He grew in his aggression, kicking up spools of water as he drove through the flooding to press her further. It filled him with dark joy to see her usual look of poise twisted into strain and threat.

And you won't stop until she is silent.

He kicked her away all of a sudden, sending her flying into an empty, trenched vehicle.

"You tricked me!" Gault seethed at the Omen, the spittle flying from between his lips absolved into the hammering rain. He had to break his own momentum just for a moment of respite.

"I did." Lachesis pulled herself out of the wreck. "And it was easy."

"You took advantage of me. Of Sophia."

"Two bleeding hearts." A curt shrug came his way, poisonous green hair darkened by the downpour. "You were made for each other."

"Don't act like you never cared." Gault could feel the vignette of guilt encroaching his vision, threatening to rob him of his senses, as a frigid chill blew in with the storm. "You should have come with me. Atoned for the death you caused!"

"Death I caused?" They stalked one another, moving in a steady circle. The sleet of rain made it difficult for Gault to even see her as she slipped in and out of the darkness. "It was you who picked me, a beauty in rags, from the street that day."

"Stop it." He felt his mind pulse with strain.

"Did it feel good to have me fawning over you? The princess too?"

Gault pushed a hand into his chest and dared to close his eyes, feeling the unrelenting rain soak him wet through until his hair clung to his head in soaked strands. With eyes still closed he could hear the distinct pinging of raindrops against his steel shoulder-pad. He breathed deep, in and out, just like Rissa had shown him. He felt his soggy boots in the sodden streets, up to his ankles in freezing water; the billowing breeze on the back of his neck and the numbness as the hairs on his skin stood on end as thunder roared overhead. It was a sensory nightmare. Yet this mindfulness helped him feel calmer, the lurking darkness repelled for another few precious moments.

"A new trick?" Lachesis dusted herself off from the indent she had left in the side of the vehicle. "And who taught you that?"

Gault ignored her. He wielded Akor'shaki anew, his trusty weapon now feeling unusually heavier in his hands, as if it was offended by his denial of surrender. He swung with force, cleaving the vehicle in half, boot to bonnet, as Lachesis performed a spry backflip, evading his strike with nimble precision.

"The artefact is already in our hands." She goaded him into pursuit which he gladly obliged, lunging over the wrecked vehicle with a wild swing which she diverted away with her twin blades, burying Akor'shaki into the water. He wrenched it out with a cry of strain, spraying her with freezing water and using the distraction to swing for her throat. She dodged, but not before Akor'shaki tasted the supple flesh of her cheek, drawing a great satisfying line across her porcelain features.

I want more.

"Did it like it?" She hissed, crimson trickling down her cheek.

I did.

"It can't hear you." Gault lied, refusing to allow her a second longer to poison his mind with her words. He waded towards her, only to feel the city suddenly teeter as though balanced on the point of a needle. Traffic moved, although there were no drivers behind the wheel as the phantom cars rolled down the rapids towards them. Gault shrunk Akor'shaki to allow him to properly roll, narrowing avoiding the churning wheels as his face submerged into the arctic depths. In this moment he was again able to focus his mind as empty vehicles whooshed past him. The cold felt good, like a reset to his thoughts.

Just then, Lachesis laughed. Gault felt a spike of rage as he rose to address her, but upon reaching for his weapon all he found was the rapidly extending chain of Akor'shaki trailing out behind him. The rage fell into his stomach and turned to dread. In its shrunken form, Akor'shaki had tangled in the suspension of the passing vehicle as it built up speed due to the tipping city, which could only mean one thing.

"We'll see you soon. With any army." Lachesis gave him a coy wave and Gault lunged for her, desperate to bury her face into the water, only for the mystic chain to reach its limit, pulling at his insides like a phantom limb and whisking him from his feet. He watched between droves of water as the green-haired Omen turned and left, likely going after Rissa who was already outmatched by Azrael.

The vehicle ahead was building up speed, dragging him through the shallows where sharp rubble and washed-up items lay invisible at the bottom, striking him across his entire body as he was violently pulled along. He couldn't get his bearings for a second, his face submerged and breath snatched from him by the freezing cold as he was towed helplessly along by the rampaging set of wheels. Gault tried to dig his heels in, to offer some resistance alongside the water but the pooling rainfall had created a stream, adding to the speed and momentum the car was gathering as it washed down the street.

You fool. We were so close. We tasted her!

He had no reply and wouldn't have provided one even if he could. He desperately willed the blade to untangle itself, but it couldn't obey. He choked and gagged through the overflowing sewage and rainfall, catching a brief glimpse of where the road was heading.

No Man's Land, where the city ended and the void began.

With the city inverted so terrifyingly, he could already see a chunk of the planet's core peering up over the horizon of the city. It rippled and coursed with radiant blue hues, like a raging ocean in a prism. Yet it was hot, so hot. Vapid, humid heat that heated the very water he was being dragged through. It was ready to take him, suck him under with its hot breath and turn him into the very same dust that had become of Kren'shal, Brand of the Demon and Mires, Brand of the Heretic.

Gault, Brand of the Scout, was likely soon to join them. Reduced to dust in the wind. Another particle whipped up and scattered by the Magic Storm. A life dimmed forever. For a moment, he stopped struggling, quietly content with his fate. It felt good not to struggle, peaceful to not resist. There would soon be an end to his turmoil and his struggling, a means to lift the weight of guilt that had weighed him down for so long. He should have died with the rest of his people and not been unfairly spared while everyone else was culled. He wasn't a hero. He was merely a puppet in the hands of a greater tool. Akor'shaki. The very same tool that now dragged him to his death. Everything good he had done; he had done with the power bestowed by the blade. His contribution had been nothing.

Yes. This was it. A deadly calm washed over him, the water no longer causing panic nor strife. He got his head firmly above the flood allowing the image of the core of the world to sear his pupils. He did not even attempt to look away.

Then his calm was broken. He felt cold, so very cold once again. Even through the raging thunder, the crashing of water against homes and hearths, he could hear marching. The distinct, heavy footfalls of a legion of armoured dead. They sought him, yet he did not see them.

But he did see her.

She stared at him through the back window of the vehicle that towed him to his doom. Her mangled face stared him down, cold, calloused palms pressed sternly against the glass. There were no words for him, but once again her gaze was enough. Hard, glassy eyes, still emerald as they were in life, only diluted and tired. Disappointed, even.

Let me in.

His heart twisted to see her here, just as it did every single time he laid eyes on her. In life, she had been so beautiful. Even now, skin sickly blue and divine features twisted, pale jaw hanging by loose sinew she still carried the aura of divinity and royalty that she had possessed in life. Now she was the one possessed by him. Her spirit, captured and held in a moment he would forever see in the darkness behind his eyelids. Watching her tortured body pleading with him to give in to the rampant malaise that festered within him made him weak of spirit, body and mind.

Let me in.

Gault wished a silent apology and final farewell to Rissa for failing to adhere to her guidance and allowed the creeping dark to clot his peripheral vision. It was an easy thing to do, the path of least resistance to allow Akor'shaki to possess his body once more, having a greater affinity with itself as a weapon than he ever could. It was what she would have wanted. An end to eternal suffering that she and the citizens of his homeworld all went through.

Well done.

Suddenly out of nowhere a vehicle pulled across the stream, battling the surging current of the slanted city streets. It drove perilously, windows cracked and its body scuttled with dents and scrapes. It pulled out dangerously in front of the rampaging vehicle that towed Gault to his doom. It was a CIPD patrol car, albeit mangled and struggling as the exhaust spat water and smoke. The wheels spun, kicking up great columns of water as the driver deftly spun the car around, putting the driver's side furthest from the incoming collision before suddenly applying the brakes.

Gault braced himself, throwing his arm up over his face predicting the violence of the impact. The momentum behind the sudden stop was not enough to slow Gault as he dug his heels into the bedrock of concrete, straining as he took as much speed out of his descent before colliding with the back of the runaway vehicle, indenting the back as he spilled out into the water, grateful to be still alive.

Free me!

Without missing another beat, Gault dived beneath the car, fighting the water rushing behind him to stay in one place as he sought the entanglement of Akor'shaki beneath the car, finding it coiled around the suspension. He fiddled with the blade, finding the chain thrice wrapped around the steel, Akor'shaki's shrunken blade threading itself immortally through one of the chain links. Enough tinkering and it came loose. Gault retreated, emerging just in time to see the driver's side door open.

"Get in, kid!" Donnel Rawdon shouted over the wind and rain, pointing to the backseat behind him. The passenger side had caved in by the impact and was a twist of crushed and mangled metal. Gault didn't need to be told twice and waded through the water, throwing open the backdoor, diving in and closing it behind him before too much water could flood in.

"Thank you." He said, breathless, his lungs and throat aflame from forced water intake.

Donnel looked at him in the rear-view mirror. "Where's Rissa?"

"With the artefact."

"Artefact?"

Gault grunted. "Long story."

He shut his eyes, feeling a fleeting spectre of the pain he had felt as the demonic Brand had been seared across his left eye. He called upon the power from the Brand of the Scout, granting him the magic-seeking sight that inadvertently almost blinded him. The world was awash with blinding colours, the storm skies were still filled with pent up magic that heralded the storm was yet to ease up. But the artefact, a beacon of light from even so far away, it nearly blinded him. He would have hurt his eyes less staring into the core of the planet. But at the very least, he knew that wherever the artefact was, Rissa would be there too.

Gault pointed due east, requesting the battered engine fight against the current.

"Drive. I'll guide you to her."

———

Rissa was quickly realising that in the overbearing presence of water, her own water spells were diluted and less effective. Any wall of water she tried to raise ahead of the vehicle was promptly broken down and amalgamated by the floods. Any Vortex in the floor beneath her was filled with water until it became impossible to traverse. Instead, she had been forced to rely on her limited arsenal of ice spells that she now wished she had decided to delegate more time to in Grandmaster. She pursued the car as best she could, following its lights in the heavy rain, cutting through what backstreets she could recognise amidst the rubble of devastation. It was a harrowing sight, seeing the streets that had raised her desecrated and destroyed. The only small ironic joy she could take was that Ocean's View had now become its namesake again. Assuming that was, that the building still stood and had not been struck into dust and rubble by the storm overhead. The lightning was frustrated, swirling about the sky in a dark spiral, the air crackling with anger as it continued to seek the artefact.

Rissa saw the headlights veer off in the distance, departing The Blades to surge down the similarly flooded inner ring of the city that housed Monument itself. Rissa knew her shortcut, wading through a backstreet that ran roughly parallel to the curved road into the City Centre, intersecting onto the pavement alongside it. She hopped on top of some buoyant dumpsters, stepping over bins and swinging on ventilation pipes to keep herself from being mired by the flooding. There was a sharp corner which she turned nimbly, just in time to see the vehicle she was pursuing trundle past. She was so close. The immeasurable weight of water that had tilted the city had been tipped from the edge and so the balance of the city had been levelled once again. The sudden motion rocked her, sloshing the water around in the alleyway like shaking a bottle of water. The car seemed undisturbed, but otherwise began to pick up speed as the incline it had battled subsided and the engine purred, gravity no longer an enemy. Rissa twisted around the corner, plunging her soaked shoes back into the cold water.

Halberd, forged in the frigid deep, thrust from the cold dark. Dismantle the wheels, let me catch them!

Ahead of her, parallel to the space the vehicle was just passing, Rissa summoned a barrage of jagged, ice spears. They flew towards their mark in a compact formation, sharp enough to pierce steel. Azrael flew out the window, clinging to the strap of the seatbelt as he put his body between the spell and the nearest back wheel. The spears struck his hand as though they had struck lava, turning into sizzling, harmless water in impact.

"Damn it." Rissa hurried in pursuit as the car gained distance. As a last ditch, she plunged her hands beneath the water and pressed her palms hard into the floor.

Path of Frost. Claim this world in your arctic glory. Freeze this entire street!

She felt a chill akin to plunging her entire body into a vat of iced water as the power surged from the magic circle beneath her. Rissa watched as the water ahead of her began to freeze over, granting her enough time to pull herself out of the flood and begin to chase the vehicle, following the ice as it froze the entire street ahead of her, allowing her part-run and part-skate towards the vehicle as ice began to form. Her arms stung with returning fatigue and she shook them frantically, desperate to restore the feeling to her fingers as she wrapped a hand around the hilt of her sheathed blade.

Azrael appeared out the window once again. But Rissa had expected him to. She leaped, finally drawing the sword from her back as she surged towards him, intent on severing his arm clean from its shoulder. He pulled away at the last moment and she claimed nothing but air. The car ground to a halt with her spell undisturbed, the seconds allowing her to catch a glance inside the vehicle, seeing the artefact stored on the back seat, sealed within a strange, translucent container that seemed to be containing its almighty power and drawing the ire of the storm away. That glance was all she was afforded as the door of the vehicle flew off the hinges towards her. She dodged it, pure adrenaline twisting her body out of the way of the spinning steel as it lodged itself into a building behind her.

At the sight of her holding a sword, a sheet white brow lofted, betraying a fraction of emotion over his stoic and pale face. "Your form is poor."

"Come on, I learned this just for you." She sneered at him, immediately going on the offensive. Her shoes skidded on the ice as she attacked, intent on keeping Azrael's hands as far away from the icy floor as possible.

The pale Omen maintained his composure as she approached, his swing hard and steely, much like Gault's. It felt strangely familiar to cross blades with him, the reverb of steel stinging her arms as their swords met. This would be her triumph. Azrael may have immunity to her magic but not to her sword. She had been forced to adapt, to learn new skills and break her reliance on magic alone. This was her moment.

She swung low, intent still on keeping him and the car trapped within the ice. With every swing, every step and every second she fought for balance, Rissa could feel the spell zapping her energy. Maintaining the integrity of the magic circle beneath the ice was steadily taxing her and her movements became slower. Her ability to premeditate counterattacks and evade an injury was hindered.

But she didn't stop.

She was going to win.

With the shadow of Monument over them, she wasn't about to let them get away and have in their hands the means to summon their dark God. This fight was her last stand, not just for her, but for Centa Isla. Gault was nowhere to be seen. Frustration burned at the back of her mind, where the hell was he when she was doing so well?

Azrael was a hard opponent to read, even on slick ice he was still and static, moving only when demanded. He did not directly attack her, but she could see that he was watching her just as much as she watched him, his sword moving to counter each of her strikes. But just as the thought crossed her mind, something in her next attack felt wrong. There must have been a sign of desperation in her movements, something weak, something holding her back. Whatever it was, Azrael had noticed it before her. Rissa watched, mid-combat, as a small smile crossed the gaunt, sickly face. Her instincts screamed at her to pull out of her next swing, yet with her arms numb from magic and her body so cold and tired, she couldn't muster enough energy to do it.

He riposted her, swatting her clumsy strike away. She cursed herself, planting her feet dangerously on the terrain. She was ready to counter, watching his blade carefully to make up for her amateur mistake.

But it wasn't his sword that came for her. But his fist. A pale knuckle piled into her face with enough force to snap her neck. She staggered, her entire vision going black for a painful second until she felt the slit of steel pierce her gut and then twist painfully. She gasped, feeling numbness spreading through her body.

"You can't just break the pattern like that!"

She had seethed at Gault that night, her body sore from repeated failure. *"Of course, I can."* Gault had replied. *"Your opponent might."*

The ice beneath her fell away, her mind immediately surrendering the concentration needed to maintain the spell. Water swallowed her lower body as she dropped to her knees. The pull of the blade from her abdomen felt hot and painless, yet the trickle of hot blood down her stomach was like magma against the cold water in which she knelt.

What an idiot she had been. To think she could cover her flaws so easily. Magic was her crutch; it always had been. The confidence she had held strutting about Downtown in the dark was only ever present because The Algarethan Verse gave her the edge over the common thug. It was nothing but a lie and now it had been broken down piece by piece by the pale hands of Azrael.

"No…" Her hands came away crimson. There were spots in her vision and despite her best efforts, it became difficult to take a full breath.

Azrael kneeled before her, ensnaring her gaze in his black eyes.

"Admirable effort. Die proud."

The driver's side door opened and Jace emerged. He had forgone his Grandmaster robe, his mangled arm curled up at his side. He watched her wordlessly, mouth stretched into a grim, thin line.

"Get back in the car." Azrael ordered, not yet finished with his blade that dripped still with blood.

Her blood.

As the stained steel rose, blazing headlights caught themselves in the reflection.

12

Gault clung to the backseat as the mangled patrol car swerved and ploughed through the streets of the City Centre. Donnel drove quickly, blinded by rainfall, yet guided by a knowledge of the city that surpassed even his daughter. He took corners before they even appeared, wrenching the wheel around with one hand resting on the gear lever. Beneath them, rising water lapped and gurgled under the wheel arches. Elemental crystals embedded within the engine fired at full capacity, powering the patrol car through the deep flood. Suddenly, just ahead of them, a car rolled into view with a glaring set of headlights illuminating the streaks of torrential rain in the full beam. Gault instantly recognised the pale figure who stood in the downpour.

"That's them!" He yelled.

It took Gault a moment to wrench his eyes from Azrael but beneath him was Rissa, part submerged and clutching her stomach as a pool of crimson water lapped against her waist.

You're too late. Avenge her!

Gault ground his teeth anxiously. Donnel slammed the accelerator to the floor and the car surged forward, throwing Gault backwards. Donnel had Azrael in perfect position as he sped forward but the pale man, looking almost translucent in the flare of headlights, vaulted out of the way moments before impact, fumbling his sword into the murky water.

"Get her in the car. Now!" Donnel called, swinging the vehicle to make a physical barrier between Rissa and her attackers.

Retreating, Azrael leapt into the back seat of his own car, the artefact now contained within a clear container that seemed to neuter the aggravating effects it had on the storm. In an instant, the car roared off, unable to reach any significant speed as its weak engine struggled to muster enough power to combat the fast-flowing torrent. Gault launched from the patrol car and frantically scrambled towards Rissa who remained in a kneeling position, the water still sloshing around her waist.

It's all your fault.

"Rissa." He hissed, dropping immediately to his knees. She didn't look at him, her dim, tired gaze was fixed ahead of her with a vacant expression. Water streamed down her pale face, diluting the blood dripping from her nose. Gault followed her arms, both of which were fixed at her side, palms collated over her abdomen just beneath the water's cloudy surface.

"Rissa."

She's not going to make it. Go after the Omens.

"No!" Gault snapped at the cruel urge that Akor'shaki instilled within him. Instead, he gingerly raised her to a standing position and moved her hands away from her stomach to reveal a deep, twisted slit, oozing thick globules of blood.

Fine. Pressure. Now. If you want her to live.

"Pressure." Gault muttered out loud. He felt his hands tremble as panic began to grip his mind and his thinking slowed to a crawl. He steadied his breathing and tore a split from the robe, wrapping it around her abdomen, tying it as tightly as he could over the wound. He lifted her gently, feeling her body stiffen and resisting movement as he hoisted her from the water and lifted her into the backseat of the CIPD vehicle. As her torso creased with the pressure of the movement, the white shirt darkened with crimson and her face grimaced in pain. Instinctively, she shielded the wound with her hand.

"Has she-" Donnel stepped around the front of the vehicle, his hands on his head. Gault nodded and he surged forward, pushing him out the way as he cupped his daughter's head in his hands. "R... Rissa. It's me."

Her eyes stayed glassy and unfocused, her chin dropping unsupported to stare at the floor. Donnel checked the tightness of the tie. His eyes were wide and fearful.

"I'm taking her to the hospital."

"She's still wanted for regicide, she'll be-"

"Like I give a damn." Donnel went to move around the vehicle to the driver's seat, only for Rissa to grapple at his sleeve. He turned attentively, stooping low in the water to hear her.

"No." Rissa murmured. "Go after them."

"But-"

"I'm okay." Her voice was hushed, over the storm, practically silent. "Hurry, Dad. Please."

Gault watched as Donnel's face twisted in crisis. Eventually, he rose and slammed the car door.

"Get in." He said. "You watch over her."

Gault obeyed, jumping into the backseat as the wheels churned and the elemental shards spat their combustive song as the engine jostled into life and accelerated down the street. Rissa sat beside him, becoming paler by the second as they roared towards the shadow of Monument. Donnel's patrol car, holding a staggering five crystal engine, quickly brought the lights of the fleeing vehicle into view.

"What do you want me to do?" Donnel called out. Gault caught his gaze in the rear-view.

"Get me close." His hand fell to Akor'shaki. "I'll take care of them."

Barriers were in place, protecting entrances to apartment blocks, shopfronts and any buildings of high esteem or rank. There were many silhouettes who sought asylum several stories up. They watched curiously from the window as they pounded through the streets. The car ahead defiantly pulled away, twisting down sharp turns and taking unexpected, wild manoeuvres as the tall shadow of Monument grew ever closer.

"We're running out of time." Gault said.

"I'm doing my best, kid. Sit the hell down."

It took Gault a moment to realise Rissa was trying to get his attention. She pulled at his arm with increasing strain until he finally came to her attention. Her hand came up, revealing her Conduit that still gleamed with potential.

"Let me help."

"Just rest." Gault waved her down, but she stubbornly raised her arm higher.

"You trust me, don't you?" Her voice was quiet, but despite her clear and growing weakness, she still seemed capable.

"I do."

She gave him a small smile, but at that moment couldn't meet his eyes. An expression he had seen in his own reflection many times crossed her face. Guilt, or some form of it. But it was gone as soon as he thought he had noticed it, replaced by an expression of strain as she forced herself to sit up from the slouch the rocking vehicle had slumped her into.

"Then get ready."

Her arm, trembling with effort, lifted itself to the window. Whether intentional or not, she murmured something and winced as her Conduit brimmed with magical power. A line of magic flashed into the sky. A Vortex appeared high above them, projected onto the face of a tall building that was coming up ahead. Gault opened his mouth to ask her what she was up to. But then, she turned to him and aimed her Conduit directly onto the back of the seat behind him.

"What are-"

A Vortex appeared behind him, foaming and swirling like a maelstrom. The wind and the rain surged into the car from outside, freezing water and frigid wind streaking up his spine. The vehicle rocked from the force and Donnel yelled something illegible as he tried to steady it. Once the shock to his system abated, Gault then understood what she had intended for him to do.

"Don't let it take over." She spoke to him quietly. Even through the noise and the splashing water, he understood. "You're better when you're you."

"You can trust me." He watched her face carefully as the words rolled from his lips.

Her eyes flitted weakly to the side. "Just go."

She doesn't trust you to get this done.

With a forced smile, Gault let himself drop backwards into the Vortex, leaving the pang of sadness at her response behind and felt his perspective twist and distort as he emerged - backwards - out of the Vortex on the face of the building. The wind and rain threatened to relieve him of his senses but he focused on the headlights that now flashed on the street below him.

Gravity granted him power as he fell. He twisted his body around and bid Akor'shaki answer his summons. The blade obeyed, but once again it felt heavier in his hands. He hurtled down towards the vehicle, bidding the dark power of Akor'shaki now to reinforce his legs moments before he crashed into the bonnet of the fleeing vehicle. It sank immediately beneath his weight, the engine exploding in puffs of smoke. In that moment, he saw that it was Jace behind the wheel, face still distorting into an expression of shock as the vehicle's back wheels lifted from the tarmac as it began to flip. The front of the vehicle crumpled beneath him as it snapped into a jagged angle.

Kill them!

Gault swung, high and wide as the vehicle body shunted over his head. He sought Azrael in the backseat, Akor'shaki's violet-trimmed demonsteel scouring through the steel frame in search of prey only to find nothing but empty space. The back window shattered as Azrael launched himself from the wreck. The artefact was with him. The white hair billowed in the storm as he landed neatly ahead of the carnage and immediately began sprinting away towards the shadow of Monument and Gault knew he had to catch him.

Wait! Pay attention.

He felt Akor'shaki pulling him towards the vehicle, ushering him to seek out the Brand of the Sorcerer who was in there, injured and weak. Jace would be the easiest kill he would ever claim. Yet…

Kill him. What are you doing?

It would come at the cost of Azrael escaping. Already, the pale Omen was disappearing into the rainfall. The artefact was likely the final piece of their plan and knowing what was at stake, Gault knew that he couldn't let him get away. He resisted the summons of his blade and pounded down the street after Azrael. Without a sword with which to defend himself, Gault only needed to catch him. He called upon Akor'shaki for power, to embolden his legs with speed, only for there to be a long spell of silence before he felt the power finally granted.

You should not have done that.

Droning directionless in the air, Gault suddenly heard the clapping of steel marching in his ears. Footsteps of thousands, refusing to be drowned by the percussive rainfall. They were so close to him that for a moment he was convinced he was about to be trampled over. He knew what this was but knew that he couldn't stop chasing.

You've angered them.

Ahead of him, he saw the twitching silhouettes of the dead writhing in the rainy dark alleys. They leered at him as he passed, cowled by the clotted darkness of the lightless streets. The cracking of their bones pierced his ears, somehow audible through the rampant rain. Gault gritted his teeth. He could feel the pounding of strain in his mind and behind his eyes, spraying the edges of his vision with murky blackness.

Gault watched as a tall shadow suddenly built itself up alongside Monument, laddering up the horizon as though a thousand years of construction were happening within seconds. It was a tower just as mighty as Centa Isla's own, but pointed and royal, nostalgic to the distant part of him that still associated with his past. It stood proudly on the horizon, bearing stained glass windows and hand-crafted brickwork just as he remembered it. Just as he questioned the reality before him, the tall, proud spire suddenly began to crumble into arid dust, disappearing over the lip of the buildings that leered overhead. Just as he blinked, it was gone.

"Focus." He told himself. He pushed his hand into his chest and tried to control his breathing but found it difficult as he needed the thrust of an adrenaline surge to keep up with Azrael. He could feel his own lungs heaving as his body fought the impossible battle between the release of adrenaline and its peacemaker.

She wishes to speak with you.

"I need time." He hissed.

Ahead of him, Azrael ran down an alleyway, leaving the sprawling main roads behind. Gault followed him, crashing into the furthest wall as he struggled to control his own momentum. Rain pounded down, crashing into fire escapes and pipework as flooded dumpsters spilled water out into the alley.

The intense cold had already set in and Gault couldn't tell if it was the water itself or the presence of the past that chilled him so vehemently. His numb legs and frozen joints dragged through the icy floodwater, his teeth chattering and clicking loudly.

You can't run from her. You swore an oath, didn't you?

An illegible whisper in his ear made him jump. Panicked, he glanced over his shoulder to find nothing but the claustrophobic walls leading to the empty entrance behind him. Sophia was waiting for him when he turned around. The withered husk suddenly stood in the path ahead of him. Her scream was haunting, piercing his very soul with her grief as her jaw unhinged itself to stretch wider than should ever be humanly possible. Gault twisted around her, feeling the billowing of her torn dress against his cheek as he lost his footing on the slick floor to come crashing down into the dirty water. He pulled his head up from beneath the flood, feeling water streaming down his face.

"Just leave me alone!" She was gone when he looked back, but the cold and the distant marching were as present as ever. The shambling dead filled the alley behind him, casting their contorting and seizing shadows up the wall after him. He felt like he was going insane. Why was this happening? He was only trying to prevent another world from meeting the same fate as his home. "Isn't this what you want!?"

Darkness tortured his vision. He rubbed his eyes with his sleeves, no longer able to see Azrael ahead of him. He rose, feeling the weight of water trying to drag him back down into submission.

She wants you to go back. Kill the Brand of the Sorcerer.

"NO!" Gault snapped. He staggered against the wall, feeling his brain pulsing from the strain of tainted memories. He was tired of their taunts. Rissa still did not trust his ability to control himself and think rationally and he couldn't fail her again. Futile or not, Gault blindly continued his pursuit, the alley opening into a flooded clearing. Within it, someone was waiting. The marching was growing deafening and the cold that chilled his body to the core intensified.

"Sophia! I-" Gault spoke without realising it. A head of green hair emerged from the darkness, jolting him back to reality.

"Not quite." Lachesis replied. She normally carried twin blades, but held only one this time, the scar on her cheek was now a line of dried blood. "Flattering, I will say. I didn't realise you saw me that way."

"Get out of my way." Gault wrapped a hand around Akor'shaki, finding the blade all too willing to obey him as it exploded in size. "I don't have time for you!"

"Then you'll have to make some." She blocked the exit, where Azrael had fled. Even from here, nestled deep in the alcove of two tall buildings, the presence of Monument could still be felt in the deep, dark shadow it cast to the darkest corners of the city.

Let her in. Do not deny her revenge now.

Gault sensed a shadow behind him, a writhing silhouette cast by the flashing of lightning in the sky. There was a presence over his shoulder that moved exactly as he did, always lurking in his peripheral vision no matter how he moved. Freezing breath frosted down his neck and the wretched breathing of tattered lungs warped in his ear.

"Leave me alone." He whimpered as a concussive ringing in his ears began to rob him of his senses.

You know what you must do.

Desperately, Gault slipped his hand beneath his chestplate, feeling the pressure of his own palm against his rampant chest. He breathed slowly in and out, desperate to calm the turmoil. He took himself through the steps Rissa had taught him, desperate to stay in control.

"You know I can't let you do that." Lachesis stepped towards him, swinging her blade towards his throat. Forced into battle, Gault swung Akor'shaki and parried. His swing was clumsy and misguided, his depth perception was completely wrong and for a moment, Gault was convinced that Lachesis was wearing a look of pity as she circled him like a deerstalker would hunt its prey. With only one blade to contend with, Gault knew he should have been at a distinct advantage.

Quickly!

Gault swung for her again, the reach of the weapon was wide and he didn't lack power, but Lachesis stepped easily out of the way as the blade scoured the brickwork of the alley, kicking up sparks.

Silence her forever.

He tried for the kill again, almost stumbling over his own feet as he pitiably tried to skewer her on the sickly curve of Akor'shaki's blade. It was the same as before, her lithe frame slipping out of reach at the final second.

NOW!

Gault yelled in frustration, his body began to move by itself, desperate, so desperate and so hungry to see her blood litter this flooded alley. He swung repeatedly, unable to feel his own arms as they moved without his consent. The entire time he could feel the icy breath on his neck, the shadow over his shoulder. His attacks grew with speed and vigour, his cold heart found enjoyment in the frightened strain that began to etch across Lachesis's face.

The ringing in his ears, the rain, the cold, the breathing, the marching, the thunder and the lightning. It was all too much. Gault watched as pale hands came over his shoulders, twitching and writhing as they fell slowly over his eyes, flesh peeling on the palms.

It all went dark.

Well done. Now rest.

Gault wished Rissa a silent apology as he felt himself become a prisoner in his own mind. He had tried his best; he was just too weak. As he always was.

He felt happy in the darkness. Free of torment and guilt. Vengeance was taking its course, free of his intervention. Whether his intentions had been good or bad, the damned had only ever wanted one thing. Revenge. It seemed he was not worthy of providing it.

Pain suddenly shocked him to life. His eyes opened, the malaise over his body suddenly lifted and what he had done in the time he was under the influence revealed itself. Lachesis was down, part-submerged beneath the flood water. The pity on her face had transformed quickly into a look of pure fear. In his hand, he held Akor'shaki yet lacked the strength to properly manoeuvre the blade to finish her. It was then that he noticed what was wrong.

A blade had pierced him from behind. The pointed steel tip protruded from his stomach and was promptly removed. He felt his knees go weak. Stepping out from behind him, Azrael revealed himself, dragging the tip of Lachesis's second blade through the water, staining it murky with Gault's own blood.

The artefact was no longer in the pale Omen's possession, but from the small smile of satisfaction he wore, it was likely exactly where he wanted it to be.

"All is as it should be." He said quietly. His footsteps, silent as a wraith even in the floodwater, carried him past Lachesis. He handed her back the sword and placed a pale hand upon her shoulder as he hoisted her to her feet. "Finish him. Return to the tower."

Azrael didn't once look back as he disappeared down the alley, falling into obscurity beneath the looming shadow of Monument.

"When you're losing control…" Lachesis stepped between him and the view of the tower. She wielded just one of her blades, the pointed tip scratching the steel of his chestplate. "Who do you see?"

"Everyone." Gault murmured. "Her."

"For what it's worth." Lachesis offered a thin smile. "She never blamed you."

Never blamed him? Then what was the twisted vision that tormented and controlled him? Just as Gault wished to think about it more, her blade pierced him and he felt his mind wash with pleasant numbness. Tiredness swept over his body and he fell backwards crashing into the water. Icy wetness filled his ears and flitted over his flickering eyes as he struggled to keep them open.

"None of them blamed you." Lachesis stared down at him. "I hope they're kinder to you in death."

Above him, the skies continued to flash with rage. The water in his ears deafened any sound and for a moment he felt a strange peace as familiar faces manifested themselves into the clouds, each of them staring down with apathy and malice.

He could be with them now.

—

The intensity of pain nearly rendered him unconscious. As the car had flipped and been cleaved into two pieces, Jace's arm, already shattered from a violent fall down the Subrail stairs, had been pinned for several agonising minutes beneath his body. And now he lay trapped, part-drowning beneath the flooded streets as he fought to free himself from the wreckage. Yet despite his current adversity, they had been victorious. The blue-haired girl, Rissa, as applause-worthy as her efforts had been, had failed and by now the artefact would be in place. Azrael would surely return to help him and if not he, then Lachesis would return to reward him for his hard work of liberating that artefact from Grandmaster.

As the water pooled around him, Jace had to keep telling himself that he was valued enough to be saved and that they would not just leave him alone to die. Yet, the longer he lay here, slowly losing feeling in his limbs, the more he began to worry that he had been left to his fate. Or worse, presumed dead in the carnage. His one working arm was pinned beneath the floods. His fire spells were neutered by the oppressive waves, leaving him kicking and struggling beneath the metal. There was every possibility that he could just drown here, a pathetic, gargling death, fit for the coward that he was.

"Damn it!" He bucked, kicking his legs out with what little mobility they could render. His thoughts flitted to Cordelia. Had Galleo et'al and this grim mission not existed, there could have been a life for him in this city. He could have done a lot of good, perhaps helped resolve the Resource Crisis. If he had only chosen to be brave, to take risks. Just as it had been in the many worlds he had been sent to conquer before this, he had allowed the hard choices to pass him by. Perhaps there would be more opportunities for him to squander on worlds beyond Centa Isla. But right now, he knew that without help to escape, he wouldn't see another sight besides the inside of this damned car. Panic caused him to make another flurry of hopeless flailing as his legs writhed and kicked and he yelled until his throat hurt. The water was rising, welcoming the nape of his neck and the back of his ears to their freezing embrace. It was now a possibility that his grave would be under the flooded streets of Centa Isla.

"Help!" He screamed pathetically, his jostling movements sending the vehicle out of position, putting yet more weight on his shattered arm. "Someone!"

There was a notion in his mind that he couldn't shake. The feeling that he had played his part. The Brand of the Sorcerer held little use in Centa Isla now that the means to power the Obelisk was in the hands of the Omens. Deep down, he knew that they were not coming back. The stay of execution he had earned for himself by betraying, cheating and lying on world after world had finally come to an end. He just wished he could have faced his inevitable demise with more dignity. Snot and tears streamed down his face as he felt the water level rising further, taking his nose and mouth briefly beneath the flitting waves that raged through the city. He burst free, crying and spluttering, the tendons in his neck taut as a bowstring as he fought to stay above the crashing waves. "Please! Azrael! Cordelia! Someone-"

He went under again. This time it felt final. He prayed silently beneath the dark water for the water to lull and offer him respite to take some gasps of air. He held his breath, desperate not to allow the dirty water to enter his lungs. His heart raced as it tried to return the last of the oxygenated blood to his lungs. He had played his part all too well. A pawn, destined to fulfil the needs of others. He kept his eyes open, knowing that he had mere seconds left before he would drown, cold and alone.

Then a silhouette flitted above the shimmering waves.

Jace dared to feel the lurch of hope in his chest as he puffed out his cheeks, feeling the invasive water seeking to drown his lungs in its freezing embrace. A strong hand groped beneath the water and shifted the crushing mass of steel that had entombed him. Jace felt the freedom immediately as the hand came now for him, grasping him by the collar and pulling his head out of the water. He spluttered and coughed, his vision blurred and dark as he grasped the arm of the dark shadow of his saviour.

"Azrael! Thank you-" As his vision was restored he could see that it was not Azrael who had saved him, but someone else, someone unfamiliar.

"Good night, kid."

A fist piled into his face and the world went silent and dark.

—

Donnel pulled over and tapped the steering wheel nervously. On the back seat his passengers had become unresponsive. On his passenger side was a locked black case that had bobbed around the wreck of the car they had pursued. His gut told him it was important, yet he had yet to find the time to figure out the combination.

An enormous crowd had gathered at the gates to the Centa Isla Royal Hospital. People were screaming, shouting, begging for help for their loved ones. But the gates to the hospital remained curtly closed, the entrance guarded by a legion of Kingsguard who forcefully shoved back anyone who sought entry.

"No, no, no…" Donnel stepped out of the car, running up to the back of the crowd. He put his head in his hands as he felt his heart sink into his stomach. Swathes of people stood there, ankle deep in floodwater holding bodies in their arms. Family, friends, children. They all cried the same desperate tears as they gathered in droves outside the hospital gates, denied entry by the forces of The Crown.

"What's happening here?" Donnel pulled at the closest person whose arms weren't full.

"They're not letting us in." It took Donnel a moment to notice the man had been stabbed. A large, jagged pipe had been driven through his shoulder, the pipe itself stopping him from completely bleeding out. Blood both fresh and dry covered his overalls. He looked like a shopkeeper, wearing a name badge that was so covered in blood it was illegible.

"They won't treat us. None of us." Donnel could see swathes of people, carrying or supporting their injured loved ones. The air was filled with their painful wails.

"But why?"

"They sold out." A weak sneer crossed the man's face. "Nobility only. Priority care."

"You're kidding me." Donnel stared back up at the guarded gates, the Kingsguard growing in aggression as they were forced to make examples of those who grew too incensed. They maimed people, striking joints with the blunt steel shafts of their polearms.

"It has all gone to hell." The reply came weakly. "My store was robbed the moment the flooding started. The badges were nowhere to be seen."

"I'm sure-" Donnel stopped himself. His urge to protect the integrity of the CIPD was instinctual. But, he knew better now. Knew that they were corrupt, just as much in the pocket of the nobility as the hospital. He had two lives in his care and a hospital that had closed its doors and refused to help. His patrol car was attracting attention as other desperate people made their way towards him, hoping to find an officer who could help them. What could he do? Donnel leapt back into his vehicle, swinging it around aggressively, forcing the crowd to disperse. He could see the shopkeeper's harrowing face in his mirror, dripping with disappointment.

"Damn it." He cursed out loud, feeling an enormous sense of helplessness.

Donnel focused on Rissa, glancing in the rear-view mirror. He felt his hands shaking as he reached into the back with an exhaled sigh to check his daughter's pulse. It was present but fading slowly. Her eyes fluttered open at his touch.

"Dad… are we there?" She spoke weakly, her skin paler than he had ever seen.

"Not yet. You just rest." He replied with a grimace, feeling the faux-leather steering wheel pressing against his palms as he gripped it tightly. "I need to try somewhere else."

Gault lay beside his daughter, bleeding into the jacket Donnel had tied around his torso to stabilise his wounds. The kid had practically no heartbeat save for a pulse that beat once every twenty or so seconds. For all Donnel knew he was driving a corpse in his back seat. The only hint of life came from the weapon that hung at his side. Donnel had seen that scythe grow miraculously to the size of its wielder. It was impossible, yet even now, it was thrumming with energy. To even hover his hand over the steel chain was like thrusting his hand in a furnace. He didn't know what was happening but he knew it was keeping Gault alive. How he had even located the kid was miracle enough. Pressing on her palm, Rissa had known exactly where to find him. It defied belief, yet she had guided him as close as the patrol car could get, allowing him to find the young man dying in an alley. His mind was being pushed to its limit today and he was beginning to realise that not every phenomenon had a logical explanation.

As he sat there, feeling the strain of his thoughts compressing his skull, Rissa spoke.

"… Sheppard."

He turned, peering at her in the backseat. "Who?"

"The Hound. Forge Town." Her eyes drifted closed only to intermittently snap open as she tried to pull her body upright and failed each time. "Map."

A map. Donnel fumbled in the glove compartment, sifting through spare cigarette boxes, cuffs and Aryssa Rawdon's old Conduit box. He found the parchment folded up at the back, crusty with dried coffee stains.

"Show me." Donnel urged his daughter and watched as she raised a trembling arm. Blood smeared on her hand, she pressed a finger of crimson onto the old parchment before pulling away.

Donnel looked at the print, embedded deep within the labyrinth of Forge Town and knew roughly how to get there. He slammed the ignition, firing the flame crystals beneath the bonnet and spun the patrol car around, the engine started to seize, spluttering with the death throes of a fading machine as it hauled itself through the streets.

"Come on, baby!" Donnel goaded it, thrusting himself forward in his seat as though it was somehow going to propel the car forward. To its credit, it continued to splutter, dragging along on what was likely two slow punctures and multiple dents. Donnel felt a rush of pride. Beside him, cars surged through the water, sending columns of water up around them. Many of them drove towards the hospital and Donnel tried to warn them by flashing his lights, but they continued, unaware of their impending disappointment. There was no help for the citizenry in their time of need and Donnel couldn't help but feel that if the city recovered from this storm, there would be a reckoning waiting for The Crown, spurred by the rage of the people who were denied care for their loved ones in a time of crisis.

He glanced in the rear mirror at his daughter, her head leaning silently against the window. Her mouth hung slightly open, her skin looking paler than it had when he had last checked just seconds ago. Was he going insane? His sweaty palms slipped on the steering wheel as he forced himself to breathe to retain his composure.

"Rissa." He called her name and felt panic rise into his throat with every second passing that she didn't respond.

"... Yeah?"

"You're in uniform." He was referring to the Grandmaster blazer that he had never had a chance to see her in before. "It suits you."

"Thanks."

He allowed a moment to pass. There was a strange tightness in his chest, like his body was grieving lost moments. He had been so excited for Rissa's graduation, to stand outside the gates of Monument as they cracked open enough for the students of tomorrow to return to the folds of the city, educated, indoctrinated and ready for a career. Being denied that had hurt him, perhaps more than he had cared to admit.

"I intended for your mother to be present when you graduated." He spoke quietly, eyes flitting to her pale form in the mirror. "I wanted to see your face when the family was back together."

"Not this, Dad, not now…" In the backseat, he watched her face twist in discomfort.

"I just want you to know having the three of us back together was all I ever dreamed of." He felt a lump in his throat. "I've missed a lot because of that dream, I realise that."

"You have." Rissa spoke harshly, but her tone softened quickly. Whether it was the lack of blood that was pulling the anger out of her or a genuine desire to forgive, he wasn't certain. "But thank you for being here. Saving me."

"Saving both of you if I have it my way."

She laughed, then by the look on her face, regretted it. "Sure."

They drove in silence. He spent more time watching his daughter than the road. She was fading, he could see it by the way she could no longer support herself, leaning her head against the window as the stormy city passed them by.

"I think I'm close to finding her."

"Dad-" It took her a moment to even fumble words.

"I have one more lead. This is it." He took a deep, resolute breath. "After this, I'm done, whatever happens."

He meant it. This final lead was the closest he was ever going to come to finding out what fate had befallen Rissa's mother. If this went nowhere, he was out. If Aryssa wasn't coming back then Donnel would just have to do the work of two. He was no stranger to overexertion.

When he looked in the rearview mirror, he saw hopeful blue eyes, forced open and staring at him. She was the spitting image of her mother.

"… Promise?"

"Promise."

A weak smile crossed her face as her head slumped back against the window. Her features dropped as consciousness left her and Donnel felt fear spike in his heart. He put his foot down, consuming the tarmac beneath rattling wheels.

"Come on…!" He willed his patrol car forward. If it would make it to Forge Town he'd never ask anything of it again.

To distract himself, he played with the radio, greeted only by crackling static on most frequencies. Noble vistas and flooded faux-gardens flashed by as he drove up a steep bank onto the Royal-Mage bypass. He was finally able to shed the water weight and increase his speed. These bypass roads ran around the edges of the City Centre, offering entrances and exits at all four cardinals.

As the bypass road took him curving between the City Centre and Grandmaster, he continued onward instead of exiting into Downtown. The road remained elevated enough to avoid the flooding but provided a view of the damage that had truly been done to the city. On his left, the City Centre was in shambles. Barricades had been erected by Earth Versorcerers to stop as much carnage as possible but it had only done so much. Entire streets were flooded, claiming the ground floor of most buildings. Many of them were storefronts, their already dwindling stock of food now in the water, sloshing down the street among the sewage.

There had only been one building that had collapsed during the chaos, but it had split in half during its descent, blocking two main roads that led into the City Centre from the west. It had taken businesses, apartments and a still indeterminate body count along with it. It was a profitable time, it seemed, to be an Earth Versorcerer. There were several working to reinforce damaged structures with their magic, but there weren't nearly enough, nor could there be. It was all so reckless; every spell cast edged the Syn Counts down into the precipice of disaster ever closer and the damage was simply too much. Were they even looking at the Syn Counts while they did this? But of course, the City Centre had to be maintained. Donnel doubted very much that Forge Town or Downtown were receiving this level of immediate treatment.

The radio crackled to life for a moment and he jumped, having grown comfortable with the warbling interference that fizzed in the air. He rapped a knuckle against the old radio, hearing it crackle and jump before spitting out a barely legible transmission.

"--no word from - - - at this - - - are an unconfirmed number of - - -"

"Come on!" He hit it again, then bashed the roof of the car to jostle the likely damaged antenna into life. The static blustered before changing into a different channel entirely.

"--we have just witnessed was on a scale the likes of which hasn't been seen since Reckoning." A commentator warbled over the radio. "If you ask me. This is a sign."

Another host spoke, female. Likely a reporter. "A sign of what?"

"Intervention." The commentator replied. "Our lack of faith has put us here, on the precipice of extinction and famine. At the mercy of the elements and the whims of dictators."

"I-I'm certain this has no correlation with the good work of King Grayson." The reporter sounded nervous, a weak chuckle crackling through the radio as she sought to quell any talks of insurrection.

"It has everything in correlation." The voice returned, doubling down. "Men who parade as gods will find their empires crumble. Unless they-"

The radio cut off into a dead transmission. Donnel wasn't convinced it had been an accident either. The plug had likely been pulled from somewhere the moment that conversation began to descend into slander upon the King. Donnel searched the nearest frequencies but couldn't find a hint of the troubling discussion. Centa Isla had stomped out any mention of deities and worship many years ago. The old chapel in Forge Town was all that remained of that era of civilisation and had been derelict following the reformation of the city after Reckoning. Nowadays it had been lost to the encroaching smog, a death wish for any who ventured so far out. The degradation of the city and the slow death of resources, rising costs and a dissolution of freedom and quality of life had smothered any idea of a greater being ever having the best interests of the people at heart. There was something ominous about what that brief conversation had heralded. He had never turned his thoughts or wishes to any godly forces. It was never something he had considered. He had never found the time. Yet if any were now listening, he just hoped they would save his daughter and return her mother.

The bypass allowed him to exit just before Forge Town and he did so, bringing his patrol car slowly down the incline and back into shallow water, quietly apologising to the old engine. He fumbled the map over the dashboard, keeping one eye on the road as he traced a trembling finger over the old parchment. He felt eyes upon him through hastily drawn curtains as families, tradesmen and whoever else called the narrow, cobbled streets of Forge Town their home, glared with contempt. CIPD rarely travelled this far east. When on patrol, he had been encouraged to avoid these parts of the city where they were seen as an offshoot of The Crown and in that respect engendered hostility, hatred and rage.

As he turned down a cobbled street he spied a sign swinging from an ornate, old building. He gasped with relief as the words: The Hound came into focus. The door was open, water having seeped into the ground floor. Donnel didn't have a frame of reference for what it looked like before, but this place looked storm damaged. He pulled up outside.

Gently, he checked Rissa's pulse to find the steady ticking of life. He cradled his daughter in his arms. She was so light that it terrified him.

Leaving Gault strewn across the backseat, Donnel entered the derelict old tavern. The tilting of the city had displaced tables, overturned stools and thrust barrels of beer from the shelves, where they had split all over the floor, wasting what was no doubt years' worth of stock.

"Hello?" Donnel called out warily, feeling the sinking of the flooded wooden boards beneath him as he entered. "CIPD. I'm coming in."

No response. He waded deeper. There had been some futile attempt to stop the water flooding in by using overturned tables to block entrances. The place stunk of damp and mould already. A large, framed portrait of the tavern's namesake had fallen from the wall and the bottom part was submerged, the ancient oils smudging and smearing across the old canvas. There was more than just financial loss here, Donnel could feel the history in this old building. Every lick of paint, every candle that had been lit. Every scratch on the bar; the creaks in the stools. This was heritage, a reminder of Centa Isla's recent past. Now destroyed.

He heard a creaking from upstairs. Senses sharp, Donnel glanced toward a narrowed set of carpeted stairs. The bottom few steps were submerged, the crimson carpet stained a swampier, darker shade before returning to a pleasant, deep red. The stairs cut sharply around a blind corner. Wary of who may have taken residence in the wake of the storm, Donnel softly cleared the bar of scattered tankards, rags and loose Wreaths to lay Rissa on top of it. He checked her pulse one last time and tightened the bandage he had tied across her abdomen. It was thickly stained and wet with blood, badly in need of changing. Her breath was faint against his hand, but she was alive.

"Hello?" He called out to the stairs, to whatever had made the floorboards creak above him. "I've got injured. I need help."

Nothing. Water sloshed noisily beneath his feet as he approached the stairs, mantling the first few steps to get himself out of the water. There was a thick silence through the tavern, the creaking of old, rotting wood creating an eerie ambience. Donnel clenched his fists, taking the blind corner of the stairs with a sudden burst of speed as he threw his arms up in front of his face to protect himself. But there was no ambush, nor was there anybody.

He rose to the first floor. It took Donnel a moment to notice there was a silhouette in the room closest to him. It was a large, hulking back that was turned to him, seated on the bed in silence. Deep, powerful breaths came from the figure, the floorboards groaning as it heaved with his size.

"Are you Sheppard?" Donnel called out quietly, standing in the doorway. "I-"

"Is that your car outside?" The figure shrugged toward the window on the other side of the room. Donnel peered at it, seeing the headlights of his CIPD vehicle catching on the pooling water.

"Yes, but-"

"Get. Out." The figure didn't turn, but Donnel could see the defined muscles clenching across his arms and upper back through his tight, beer-stained shirt.

"I will. But my-"

With terrifying speed, the figure rose and stormed toward him. Donnel barely had time to identify any features before large, calloused hands grabbed his collar and shoved him backwards out the room. "I said - LEAVE!"

Stopping himself before he toppled backwards down the stairs, Donnel dug in his heels. "Easy, friend. I'm Rissa's father. My daughter, do you know her?"

Sheppard had to dip beneath the door frame slightly as he exited the room. His puffy, watery eyes glistened with emotion. They warily looked him up and down, but Donnel didn't feel like he was truly being seen.

"How dare you come here?" Sheppard sniffed, wiping his eyes, in doing so replacing the sadness with a sudden mask of rage. "Puppets of The Crown are not welcome."

"This is yours, isn't it?" Donnel gestured to the building around him, desperate to placate the fury that he was facing. "I'm sorry, for what you've-"

Sheppard released a cry of both sorrow and anger. His giant fists clenched and in the next moment, Donnel was facing a swing. Donnel ducked and grappled at the large bartender's waist, shuffling behind him to tighten his arms around his neck and restrain him.

"Easy! Stay down!" Donnel squeezed, feeling the meaty fingers picking at his hands to try and loosen his grip. The smell of alcohol was heavy in the air. The man was clearly intoxicated. He didn't budge and felt weakness begin to spread through Sheppard's large body. But then, he did something unexpected. Heaving himself forward with powerful legs, Sheppard threw them both from the top of the stairs. Donnel let go and twisted up to protect himself as he struck the angular wooden steps several times before landing at the base of the blind corner leading back down into the main tavern. Sheppard landed shortly after, the floorboards screaming as his powerful mass landed upon them. Donnel rose first, seeking again to grapple only for a rising fist to rattle his skull and send him stumbling back against the wall.

"Get out! GET OUT!" Sheppard raged; his hands poised to clutch Donnel's throat. Donnel immediately felt the squeeze, digging his fingers into the powerful wrists to try and break the hold, to no avail. He instead kicked, fighting for his breath as he piled his boots into Sheppard's knee repeatedly until it buckled. With a cry, the bartender's balance shifted and Donnel took advantage, throwing himself down the next set of stairs and bringing his opponent with him.

There was a great splash as Sheppard landed first, face disappearing for a moment beneath the water as the whiplash of landing snapped his neck back. Donnel mounted him immediately, piling his knuckles into the shimmering face beneath the water until the giant hands that grabbed at him weakened. For a moment, Donnel felt like a teenager again. He briefly returned to the Downtown alleys from his youth, scrapping for his life against the other kids his age in sewage puddles and rubbish piles. And it took him a moment to remember that he was no longer that impulsive, wild boy.

He withdrew immediately, pulling Sheppard's collar up to yank his head from the water just as his breath began to bubble up to the surface. Blood streamed down his face, but the cold dip seemed to have sobered him up. Donnel dismounted the hulking figure and warily lowered a hand down, watching the glazed eyes of the bartender register what was happening. There was a long strand of silence, then his hand took his and Donnel grunted as he heaved the man to his feet. They were both drenched through, but at the very least on more agreeable terms than they had started.

Sheppard dusted himself down, spraying water as he ran a hand through his hair. He clearly had utter contempt for the CIPD and everything it stood for.

"You don't fight like the usual lapdogs."

"I'm not here as a lapdog. I'm here as a father."

Sheppard's gaze suddenly looked past him, toward the bar where Rissa still lay. His eyes widened with genuine concern and he went over to her, taking a small piece of smashed glass and holding it to her mouth. He seemed genuinely relieved to see the glass mist over. He took her wrist and felt for a pulse, before untying the bandage at her waist and removing the blood-soaked robe. He grabbed a bottle of strong spirits from a shelf and poured it over the wound, watching as red blood streaks eventually became clear and the wound itself was clearly visible. He soaked a bar towel with the alcohol and placed it firmly over the wound.

"Can you help?"

"I can stitch her up. But it won't be conventional." Sheppard nodded, a grim smile crossing his face. "I think I still have alcohol left."

"You'd better." Donnel headed towards the door. "There's one more."

Sheppard moved suddenly, gently lifting Rissa from the table and heading towards the stairs, blood still streaming from his nose. He had an air of leadership about him and had clearly formulated a plan. "Bring them. Find me upstairs."

"Copy." Donnel hurried outside. But before he opened the backseat to retrieve Gault, he felt an urge to double check. Moving around the back of the vehicle, he glanced up at the windows of The Hound to ensure that he wasn't being watched and softly opened the boot. A body lay motionless, a cloth bag secured firmly over the head. He had cuffed the arms together, showing no regard for what was clearly a broken limb.

This person was going to be the missing piece to whatever blight was afflicting this city. A link to the storm, Grandmaster, the Magic Extraction Chambers and the missing nobles. If he were lucky. Perhaps even his wife. He would interrogate him later and try to piece together the puzzle, perhaps even crack the lock to the black case.

A grimace formed on his face as he slammed the boot shut. As he gathered Gault's lifeless body and carried it inside, he could not distract his mind from the dark thoughts of what he was going to do to his new prisoner. To solve the puzzle would be a bonus. But revenge was higher up on his list.

Nobody harmed his daughter and got away with it. Nobody.

13

As Jace slowly regained consciousness, a pounding in his head accompanied blurry vision that slowly became sharper and clearer with every blink. The sudden sensation of water caused him to buck instinctively, his mind flashing back to the drowning death he had almost faced beneath the crashed vehicle. Yet as he moved, the sudden stretching of his broken arm crippled him with agonising, darting pain and he quickly realised he was strapped to a low backed chair. Strong ropes bound his legs while his arms were tied behind him at the wrists. His hands were pressed palm to palm and were submerged in a bucket of icy rainwater, which once again denied him from using his fire magic.

Azrael had abandoned him. Lachesis had abandoned him. He had been left to drown, under the rising flood water, trapped amongst the mangled wreckage of a car. Bitterness sat heavy in his throat and the hopeless reality of his situation washed over him like a second layer of pain. For as long as he remembered there had never been true camaraderie amongst the Omens. There existed just a shared purpose and a singular goal over which they complied with or faced death. Their Brands allowed each of them to play a part, but those roles were so isolated and individual, void of any synergistic properties. Friendship was never a precursor to success. So, what naive part of him had believed they would return?

There had only been one saviour from beneath the cold dark and he was standing a few feet away, tall and broad shouldered, leaning against a wooden table. Having seen him before from beneath the flitting of murky water, the blurry shape was now in full and clear focus. Wispy trails of smoke rose from a pile of discarded cigarette butts that had pooled at his feet. There were several buckets of water on the table with him. His intentions seemed as murky and dark as the water that had almost claimed his life.

"You're awake. Good." The man's voice echoed in the dark chamber. A single bulb, struck by a fire crystal, flickered weakly as it cast the room in a dim light.

"Who are you?" Jace straightened his spine, channelling the arrogance and fury of a Grandmaster professor, ignoring the pulling of his shattered arm as he sought to make himself as tall as possible. "I'm a professor of Grandmaster. There's been a mistake!"

"I'm aware of who you are. And what you are." Donnel approached, lowering himself down to his level. "But that doesn't win you any favours with me."

"Don't talk down to me." Jace continued to play his character. "You don't know a thing."

"Maybe not right now." The man rose. "But I will."

Reaching into his pocket, the man brandished a crumpled, torn piece of parchment. Thrust into his face, Jace's eyes adjusted in the low light to the scratched handwriting, trying to make sense of it. It was a blueprint for some sort of rudimentary glider called 'The Steel Wing', nothing more than a dream behind a quill that he had never seen before in his life. There were three seals emblazoned upon it.

"The hell is this?"

"A blueprint. Signed off by your High Priestess." The man's finger pointed to the name Cordelia Rowe who had signed and sealed the bottom of the document. "What was this project? Was it ever completed?"

"I don't even know what that is."

A fist piled into his stomach. Jace squawked as he felt the balled knuckle twist into his gut, forcing him to spew spittle and air from his already tired lungs. The heavy hand grabbed him by his hair and hoisted his head up to once again behold the document.

"Look again."

Through watery eyes, Jace squinted. Some sort of machine, capable of intermediate flights. It was signed by the High Priestess, but also another. Aryssa Rawdon, the name was familiar and he quickly realised why.

"Rawdon?" The name fizzled on his tongue for a moment until he realised the correlation. "Wait, are you-"

Donnel Rawdon's knuckles collided with his jaw and the chair rocked as whiplash rocked his body.

"Stay on track."

"Look... I don't know an Aryssa Rawdon." Jace hacked a gob of blood out onto the floor, already feeling another one coagulating in the back of his throat. "... I've only been there less than a year. She was never mentioned and whatever that blueprint is for, I've never seen it in my life."

Donnel crouched in front of him. Jace watched as the aged lines on his face deepened with rage, his lips thinning and eyes blazing with anger and fury. He pulled away suddenly, roaring with rage, kicking one of the water buckets he had prepared, sending it spilling across the stone floor.

Jace felt a sting of fear as the powerful figure immediately turned and got back in his face. Spittle flew from his mouth as he shouted. "My wife! I know she was in there! TELL ME!"

"S-Show me it, again!" Jace hissed, desperate to buy himself time.

The document was raised to his face again. Jace could already sense the swelling welts forming on his cheek. It began to obscure his vision as he looked desperately for something that could grant him some favour with his captor. His hands felt cold and numb as they sat in the bucket of water behind him. Any attempts of a spell would cause it to bubble and steam, not only denying him the spell but also alerting his aggressive captor to his attempts to escape. He held off, hoping instead to make himself useful.

"How long ago was this?" Jace feigned interest, frantically scouring the paper for anything he might be able to offer.

"Forty-eighth. Ashdown. Fifty-two years after Reckoning." Donnel replied instantly, a glint of madness in his eyes as he read the contents of the page from memory. "Eight years ago."

"I… I honestly don't know." He braced as he spoke, the expected outcome coming true as Donnel struck him again. Once, twice, a third time. Enough to spin his head and invade his vision with black spots. Jace prayed to fall unconscious, but a bucket of freezing water caused him to scream as his entire body suddenly shivered.

"Okay. Let's try another angle." Donnel seethed. He pointed now at the bottom of the blueprints, where a name Jace was intimately familiar with resided. "Cordelia Rowe. Tell me about her."

"She's the High Priestess."

"Try again. Something useful."

"She wanted….to…." His mind spun rapidly. "She… has been searching for a means to save the city. For quite some time, she said to me."

He left out her apparent allegiance to Galleo et'al. That rabbit hole was not one that he wished to dive into.

"Meaning?"

"Like I'd know! She probably built your blueprint if she'd thought it would help!"

He watched as Donnel mulled it over, the acuity of a detective hard at work. He seemed relatively satisfied. Then, he got closer, squatting down to his level. "Whatever you stole from Grandmaster. Was that somehow part of it?"

"That…" His tongue twisted in his mouth. "Is complicated."

"You seem to think this is a conversation. Let me assure you it isn't." Donnel rose up and paced about the room. "I'd implore you to recall that my daughter may die because of the carnage you have wrought. Lives have been shattered; the city has been levelled."

"I-"

"When you want to tell me it's complicated." Donnel got in his face, blazing intensity amidst a terrifying deadly calm. "You should think again."

"I… don't know. But it's nothing to do with that blueprint, I promise you!"

He braced for the hit and it never came. Until he dared to open his eyes, then a fist drove into his stomach. Then his face. The world flashed black for a split second, the impact feeling numb on his face as he was struck repeatedly with no time to recover in between. He felt dizzy and sick, his stomach was heaving with strain and he coughed up globules of blood.

"You're lying."

"I-I'm not!" He was. There was no honourable desire to protect his mission, but instead just immense fear. A fear that Galleo et'al could do far worse to him from across the cosmos than this officer could do to him now.

Or so he thought.

The flickering bulb revealed the shining sting of steel as a small knife was brandished from the officer's boot. "There's a question I've always wanted to ask."

When Jace didn't reply, Donnel grabbed his hair and yanked his head up aggressively, pushing the steel softly against his cheek.

"Tell me. What good is a Versorcerer with no hands?"

"They would need a career change that's for sure." Jace laughed nervously, his lips swelling up and his teeth coated in blood. His face was bruised and his vision hazy. Humour was all he had left.

Donnel huffed in amusement. A small smile crossed his face. Then, his expression amalgamated into a sudden snarl as he quickly drove the blade of the knife down behind Jace's back and under the icy water until it made contact with the flesh midway down the back of one of his hands. Jace screamed, but Donnel wrapped a firm hand around his mouth and he yelled into the calloused palm.

"Tell me what I need to know. Or I take this one first."

Donnel's hand came away and Jace's scream tailed off into a hoarse whimper. Tears streamed down his face at the contemplation of having his hand hacked off. Not being able to see his hand or the blade intensified his fear. The blade pressed deeper and firmer and he felt a sharp stab of pain as his flesh was sliced. His hands were too numb to sense the thick trickle of blood seeping downwards thick and fast from the deep wound. He could not see the water in the bucket as it grew darker and redder but he felt the difference in temperature as the warm blood travelled down his fingers.

"It's…"

Donnel's raised the blade as though to slice into the wound a second time but with greater force. Jace saw blood glistening on the tip. Jace felt urgency pump into his voice.

"It's for an Obelisk!"

"What the hell is that?"

"It's… a construct." Jace watched the hand on the blade, steady, practised hands twitching on the dagger's hilt, ready to cause him further agony at so much as a slip of the tongue. "Uh, designed to… to… pull."

"Pull? Pull what?"

Jace spoke quickly. "A great evil. Its name cannot be spoken-"

"Ridiculous." Donnel sneered. He toyed with the bloody weapon, wiping the crimson liquid on his sleeve. "If that's all the good you have to say, then I will end it."

Jace's head pulsed. His body was in so much pain that wanted desperately to just lose consciousness. His black strands of hair, matted with sweat and dirt were pulled once more, yanking his throat up into the point of a blade that flitted around his throat with the terrifying precision of a steady hand.

"W-wait!" Jace spoke as loudly as he dared, feeling the prong of the dagger sticking the lump in his throat. "Please!"

"Last chance."

"I-I can get you into Grandmaster! You can look around for yourself." He maintained unwavering eye contact with Donnel Rawdon, watching as they narrowed in suspicion of his claims.

"And how exactly will I do that?"

Were his arms mobile, Jace would have gestured grandly. Instead, the best he could do was encourage Donnel to look with his darting, fearful eyes to the black case, squatting on the table, adorned with the prestigious branding of the Grandmaster Crest.

"My robe case. Unlock it. The combination is four-seven-three..." His aching mind whirled, desperate to find the final number as the dark eyes watched him expectantly. "-eight!"

He watched in silence as Donnel used his thumb to move the solid golden lock to the desired code. The secure fasteners flicked open and he tentatively stepped back before raising the lid, half expecting a trap of some sort. Instead it contained an immaculately folded Grandmaster robe. Perfect and pristine. The silky material was embossed with an ornately stitched logo and the words: Professor.

"Look. You wear it. Put the hood up, stick out your chest and look important. That's good enough for most students to not ask questions." He spoke breathlessly. "Faculty might have something to say, but you can avoid them, right?"

The reality was that Donnel Rawdon would never set foot in Grandmaster. You needed more than just a robe to open the gates to the sacred grounds of the academy. Besides, with the imminent Obelisk bringing Galleo et'al into orbit, there would be no closure for anybody, not for Donnel's missing wife, not for this city. And certainly not for himself.

The blade withdrew from his throat and Jace breathed a deep, guttural sigh. Blood rose into his throat like bile and he hacked it up. Donnel looked dark as he approached. The flash of the blade returned and Jace cowered as he thought he was facing certain death, only for the knife to slash the ropes that bound his arms and his legs. Jace didn't rise straight away, his body too tired and injured to do anything other than sit and be grateful.

"Get out of here." Donnel pointed to the stairs that descended out of the dark, grungy attic room.

Jace didn't move. Or rather, couldn't. With his hands free of the icy water, he brought them round to his lap. The full extent of the deep gash on his hand became apparent as it continued to bleed out. He tried to discreetly seek magic, only to find himself unresponsive. The blood that was still gushing from the wound was laced with fiery orange streaks. He could only watch as it left him, demanding his body's attention. There was no blood that could be spared for spells. He clasped his hand to the wound and pressed it as firmly as he could but it refused to abate.

"You're not killing me?" There was no desire to tempt fate, but more a genuine curiosity. "But you said yourself-"

Donnel growled as he soaked the blade in one of the several unused buckets of water, drying it on his sleeve. He sheathed it into his boot and drew back a thick curtain draped across a small window. Daylight spilled in, enough to make Jace cover his eyes.

"You'd like that wouldn't you?"

Jace grimaced but was too weak to reply. He just sat there, squinting through the gap in the dirt-smeared window. It looked almost heavenly out there, the squalls of the storm seeming now so far away.

Donnel grabbed his keys and cigarettes off the table and slammed the case shut before grabbing it tightly. Within seconds he had descended the stairs.

"Get gone." He shouted, the wind carrying his voice up the stairs to the attic. "Seek attention for your wound."

Jace dragged his body to its feet and began to drag himself down the stairs. He emerged into a ruined building, flooded and stinking of damp and mildew, causing him to cough up yet more blood. The door to exit was open and he stumbled through the ankle deep water and out into the street, surprised to only find a light drizzle coating the city. It was worlds apart from the hammering downpour that had accompanied the storm. The sky, from what he could see through the smog over Forge Town was a lighter grey, the clouds having relieved themselves of magic at long last.

On the horizon, Monument leered over the old, industrial town. Had Azrael succeeded? Was the Obelisk imminent? The only thing that burned more than his questions was his body. He didn't know the answers and for a moment, he feared that he never would. His head felt light and dizzy and darkness was falling across his vision. His legs gave way and he lost his balance and was already unconscious by the time he hit the concrete.

—

The storm had ravaged Centa Isla. The tall spire of Monument revealed the full extent of the damage and Grayson Clovis felt an increasing sense of unease. Bedlam ruled the streets and stirred up chaos in ways that he could never have imagined. The magic storm, one of the worst ever recorded, had destroyed much of the foodstores that Centa Isla had been counting on. He sat alone in his quarters, the upturned cup and map of the city yet untouched. The destructive decision he had still yet to make had been covered by a pile of reports that he now sifted through.

A report from the CIPD Compound detailed the extent of the flooding. Much of the Compound itself had been spared, however the vehicle garage had collapsed to a strike of lightning, damaging many of their vehicles beyond use. Most notably, was the detailed description of The Douldruums. Water had seeped into the underground prison, flooding most of the lowest level. Those clapped in chains below had been sentenced to a drowning death most unwelcome. Their bodies had yet to be recovered as the floodwater currently had no means of draining.

Verscience were reporting a Syn Count anomaly. Many of their probes had been damaged, rendering much of the city completely dark as to the amount of magic left in their atmosphere. The metres that still worked declared that the rush of power from the magic storm had actually increased the Syn Counts, almost as though the world was issuing a desperate last minute immune response to prevent itself from overloading into a second Reckoning. Grayson could make little sense of it all but was counting on the closing words of assurance that he had been given that at least for now, they were stable-ish.

Regardless of any potential good the storm had done for the atmosphere; the damage was insurmountable. With many food stores destroyed, the city now had to ration, and he had included himself in that. Grayson's stomach gurgled and writhed. He had given much of his allowance to his servant staff, grateful for their unerring support and loyalty. Soon, the city would unite to revere and celebrate him for saving the city from the precipice of doom. He, The King, would make history for being the ultimate saviour of Centa Isla. This moment of desperation and hopelessness would only make his rise sweeter.

Yet before that, buried beneath the pile of reports, was the map of the city and the upturned cup. The decision on what part of the city to demolish to construct the Obelisk. It had troubled his sleep and filled him with trepidation and uncertainty. Should he demolish the wealthy suburb to the North, the history of Forge Town or the squalor of Downtown? The wrath of the nobility would be fearsome, where the meagre anger of those in squalor would be easily squashed, making it the path of least resistance, even if it was not the moral one. In truth, Grayson didn't want to tarnish the crowning act of his reign with so much death and displacement. The history books may look unfavourably upon him for that.

He pondered over the Obelisk dilemma. He was hesitating, he knew it full well. The Crown upon his head was heavier than ever and every time he stopped looking ahead, he felt the grip of panic in his chest. This was the final decision to make and he had to get it right. Was there a third option he was missing?

"My King?" Marco Barrett's deep voice stirred him from his thoughts. Grayson focused on the reflection in the window, not the carnage beyond it. He saw himself, looking tired and the former Seat of Air standing before him.

Marco pulled out a chair and removed a gold embossed parchment from a file. It was the final plans for the funeral of his father. Even the devastating impact of the magic storm, would not impact the predicted thousands who would line the streets. There would be no finer time to address his people than then - to show them the fruits of his hard work and usher in the salvation of the city.

"I had some thoughts about security." Marco spoke as though to continue a conversation he had rehearsed over and over in his own head. "If you would entrust me with such."

"Of course."

"There'll be many who are angry. A descent into rioting is wholly possible, especially after the storm." Marco unfurled a map of the City Centre, drawing a finger around the perimeter of Grandmaster and the surrounding streets. "We'll close the main roads, create a bottleneck where you will deliver your words. Line security between yourself and the crowd, as many shields deep as we can spare."

"Thank you."

"We're practically there, My King." Marco smiled up at him. "I need to confirm a date."

A date. His timeline had narrowed since the storm had ravaged much of whatever food and willpower the people of Centa Isla had left. The food shortage was dire, power equally so. As he understood, there were entire blocks of Downtown that were in pitch darkness. But this decision had to be right. If he were to decide a date, then he would first need-

A slow, stoic knock rattled the door to his chambers.

"Enter."

The door swung open and Azrael entered, wearing fresh robes and clutching the clear box containing the glossy, golden orb. It looked entirely ordinary. But Grayson understood it was anything but. He held out his large hand, awaiting to receive the box in his grip. He noted the hesitation on Azrael's face in the split seconds before he dutifully complied. The orb was lighter than he thought. He dared not break the seal but admired it from behind its glassy shield.

"This is it?"

"Yes, My King." Azrael stooped down to one knee. "The salvation of this city. In the palm of your hand."

For an object so surprisingly light, it was in fact heavy in his hands. The weight of responsibility weighed on him daily and it was moments like these where he felt it the most. His time following King-Regent had given him a surprising amount of empathy for his father. Leadership was difficult for many, impossible for some. And with so much at stake... he was better off not thinking about it, staying isolated in his tower and doing what had to be done. That was what his father would have done, a pragmatic and direct approach. But Grayson had held two voices in his ear growing up. His Mother, ever the philanthropist, had held other ideals.

She had urged him as a child to see beyond the skyline and get amongst the city streets, to see Centa Isla in motion; to witness the day to day, even if ugly, or unpleasant. When she had died as a victim to the stones thrown by the very people she had cared so much for, Grayson made sure not to forget her lessons of kindness, no matter how much he wanted to hate them all back.

"What's our timeline?" Grayson asked.

Azrael bowed his head, resting a pale fist into the ground beneath him. "With aid of earth Versorcerers, the Obelisk can be raised in fourteen days."

"Then... the eighteenth upcoming." Grayson spun the date out loud, then looked at Marco who sat patiently. "Can you work with that?"

"I can work with anything you desire, My King."

"Then proceed." He couldn't hide the smile from his face as everything started to fall into place. The eighteenth of Stormsmarch would be a historical day for Centa Isla. The day the Clovis name was restored to its former glory and the Resource Crisis was finally ended.

"My King." Azrael interrupted his triumphant, rampant thoughts. "Did you make your decision?"

His decision. What part of the city should be destroyed for the Obelisk to exist?

"I have not." He admitted. "But... you will know by sunrise tomorrow."

"As you wish, My King. But do not-"

"Yes, yes. Leave me." Grayson waved his hand swiftly with an air of impatience. He watched as Azrael rose slowly and obediently left the room. Marco Barret followed, offering a deep bow before shutting the door behind him.

There was but one thing left to do, but Grayson knew that he could not tell a soul. He waited patiently in his chambers for the cowl of night to darken the streets of the city. Opening his regal, expansive wardrobe, he rooted around at the back until he felt the familiar, tattered grey robe. It had been previously worn by Azrael upon darkening the doorstep of Monument for the very first time. Grayson had humoured the grandiose claims of the pale man only because he had seemingly single-handedly subdued his legion of Kingsguard who were on patrol beyond the courtyard. The robe still bore the cuts from the blades. Did he entirely trust the pale man? No. But Centa Isla had long since exhausted all options available and Grayson had been willing to take a chance on a miracle.

The robe didn't quite fit him. Azrael's lithe physique had made the robe look baggy, where Grayson found his biceps bulged in the sleeves and the frayed knot that tied the rope above the chest looked as though it was ready to explode under his duress. Still, he wore it. The hood was cavernous and covered even his spiked head of earthen royal hair. He appraised himself in the mirror, looking more like a drifting transient than a King.

It was exactly as intended.

He slipped on a pair of black gloves, wearing his Conduit discreetly beneath and peered through the door to his quarters. He had given his stewards the evening to themselves, much the same for his personal Kingsguard protectors, playing up his desire for privacy in this difficult time. They had obliged readily, allowing him now this moment of silence to slink from his quarters toward the service elevator at the end of the long, decorated hall of Monument. The floorboards groaned beneath his weight as his feet padded across the plush violet carpet. One of the heavy portraits that adorned the walls was a portrait of his father. His dark eyes seemed to follow him, his silent stare, even now, a menacing reminder of his harsh judgement and constant disapproval.

He opened the hatched elevator door and stepped inside, selecting the third floor. He felt the coil jostle as the lift began its slow, noisy descent as it rattled down the floors. These lifts had never failed, but he couldn't shake the unease from the perpetual jittering and jostling. When it finally stopped, his tense body relaxed and he let out a long deep breath. The third floor of Monument was where the stewards and cleaning staff were housed, alongside their brooms, brushes and whatever else they used to buff the carpets. There were also large waste hatches, used to transport rubbish and laundry from the tower. Where they went beyond that, Grayson didn't know.

But he was about to find out.

Demolishing part of his city was a decision his father would have made from his armchair with a glass of whiskey. But not him. He had to see for himself, if for no other reason than to be different from his father. He had to see the people whose lives he would disrupt, even if it was all for the greater good. Grayson opened the hatch, wide, but barely wide enough for him.

Claustrophobia spun his head into a panicked dizziness but he fought against it and swung his legs into the hatch, allowing it to slam shut behind him as the twisting darkness of steel absorbed him. Stagnant air raced up his nostrils and his thighs stung as they whacked in echoing thuds against the inside of the steel pipe. For a moment, he thought it would never end until the pipe rudely spat him out, his backside pummelling into several bulging sacks of rubbish that had miraculously cushioned his fall. The King of Centa Isla promptly picked himself up and dusted down his grey robe.

Now he was alone. Unprotected. Far removed from his bubble wrapped existence in his protective tower. This realisation caused a wave of anxiety to engulf him. Now he was amongst it, the good and the bad. It was not conflict he feared, but the truth. His royal blood was more than a match for any who would seek to harm him. There had been no cause for him to use his Conduit in many years, yet his grasp of The Algarethan Verse was as strong as it had been the day his tutor had left his quarters and returned to Grandmaster for the last time.

The reality of what he was about to find frightened him. His view atop Monument had offered only a bird's eye view of the carnage, but he had only biased accounts of what life was really like for his citizens. He crouched low, using the bags of litter as cover as he watched as a small patrol of two Kingsguard circled Monument's perimeter. It was gratifying to see them still vigilant, not a word shared between them in line with the oath of allegiance demanded of their role. The obedience and conformity of these soldiers would be repaid in kind once The Resource Crisis was resolved.

His exit was swift.

Magic sensors adorned the outside of Monument's courtyard, sensing even the slightest touch of magic. All except for his. They had been calibrated to ignore his royal bloodline, which allowed him to easily reach the tall, spiked walls that separated the tower from the rest of the city. He removed the glove on his right hand, allowing his palm to touch the cobbles beneath him.

I invoke the Shattered Mountain. Raise. Spirit me over this wall that I may see my kingdom.

A pillar of earth rose up beneath him, elevating him into the air. A knee-buckling drop later and his feet were firmly on the open streets of the City Centre. As soon as he landed, his eyes were blasted with bright light as the traffic rumbled through the beating heart of the city. After days of roads being impassable, the city was moving again, the tenacious spirit of survival unquenchable. The floating nature of the city had for once served them well. Once the rain had subsided, the sewers cleaned themselves out as streams of floodwater were ejected out into the core of the world. The roads had soon followed but while the flooding had dissipated, the damage had been done. Now, the city was back to work, busy streams of people trying to earn an honest Wreath amongst the destruction and debris.

The thick, unfiltered air forced itself into his lungs, making him dizzy at first until he adjusted his breathing to take shallow breaths. Over the roar of engines, he could hear the pulsating rumble of music, the bass pounding as though the city had its own heartbeat. He had felt this beat as mild reverberations on the glass of his window in Monument and it was curiosity that now pulled him towards the throbs. The nobility was renowned for their parties and it seemed, even in times of crisis, the lust for hedonistic pleasure still reigned supreme. Alcohol had never wet his lips, though his father had claimed that it soothed his nerves, but his mother venomously declared it a poison and forbade him to go near it.

Squinting into the bright neon lights, he realised that only a handful of the letters held their illumination and that he was now outside a venue called Avatar. He grasped the bar on the door and before he could change his mind, a loud group of drunks pushed past him and the full blast of the bass intensified in his ears. He was jostled in by the eager queue that followed and thrust amongst the warmth of moving bodies and boozy breath. A small smile crossed his face and he felt curiously excited; an emotion he had been bereft of lately.

"Wait. Stop there." An imposing, broad figure stepped in his way, a bottleneck forming in the narrow corridor that led to one of the main dance floors. "No hoods."

Grayson peered past the security guard. He saw flashes of writhing shapes dancing in the pulsing light and he longed to be part of it. Even in a time of crisis, these people had nothing to worry about. The end of the world wasn't pinning down their shoulders. The reputation of their family was irrelevant and they were not given difficult choices like he was. He wanted in. But he knew, as his hands reached for his hood to reveal his face, that it was an impossibility. The King of Centa Isla would be recognised immediately and in that moment, he would have traded all his riches to be someone else for just one night.

No.

His hands fell uselessly to his side. "Apologies. My mistake."

His wealth and status allowed him many things, but disappearing into a crowd like this was not one of them. There was too much at stake, too much work to be done.

No matter how easy or tempting, Grayson would not be like his father, shirking his kingly duties to get drunk and enjoy the numb touch of his concubines.

The air outside felt much more agreeable after the hot stuffiness of Avatar and Grayson knew that his aimless wandering had to come to an end. He had a new objective he needed to fulfil. A rank of drivers for hire had snaked themselves outside the club looking to pick up the last Wreaths of the night by transporting drunken, tired nobles back to their homes.

He ratted on one of the windows, watching as a tired looking woman wound it down.

"Where to?" Her gaze was foggy, the bags beneath her eyes dominating her face. She chewed gum apathetically, wearing a lazily done up shirt and crooked cap.

"Forge Town. Graveyard."

"I don't drive that far out, pal."

"Then get me as close as you can." Grayson opened the back door and manoeuvred himself into the back of the cab, careful to keep his hood from falling.

"You hiding from someone? You a criminal?" Apathy laced her voice. Tired eyes watched him through the back window, suspicious and judgemental. The car didn't move.

"No."

"You been in Avatar, then? Indulging yourself?" An accusation, laced with amusement.

"Excuse me?"

"Come on. I hear it all the time." A sardonic smile flashed across her face. "We're all gonna starve anyway, right? Who gives a shit?"

"W-We'll see." Grayson wanted this conversation to end. He sat silently, part wanting to get out of the car and just walk. This wasn't what he had expected from his foray into the city. "Will you just drive?"

She turned around, throwing an arm over the torn, ripped fabric seat. "Yeah… it's payment up front."

"Payment?" Grayson patted himself down. There wasn't a Wreath on his person. "Look, it's urgent."

"That sucks."

Hissing in frustration, Grayson removed just one of his black gloves, keeping his Conduit still concealed beneath the other. He offered it to the driver who looked at him as though he had just defecated in the back seat.

"It's authentic leather. Worth far more than a trundle into Forge Town."

She took it, running her fingers over it as though to convince him that she could interpret the difference. He could tell by her age that she would likely have never seen the real thing.

"Damn nobles." A sneer crossed her tired face, but she took it anyway, shoving it crudely into the aptly named glove compartment. The car pulled away from the roadside, merging chaotically into traffic as horns blared and insults were thrown. They didn't share another word all the way through the City Centre. He occasionally thought he caught her looking at him through the rear-view mirror. The roads began to clear out as they passed Grayson Plaza, the intense lights of the trading hub had not been shut down, even when parts of the city were without power. Upon hearing the behemoth shopping centre had been named in his honour by his father, Grayson had felt nothing but shame. The bright lights and overpriced commerce went against everything that he wanted his name to be synonymous with.

He cowled the bright neon lights by putting a hand upon his head. As they drove, the air bellowing in through the open windows had deteriorated in quality, so much so that Grayson found himself disguising deep coughs. As if sensing it as well, the driver cranked a handle, bringing all the windows up in the vehicle.

"Do you have filters?" Grayson asked, coughing abruptly as they careened closer to Forge Town. The roads emptied rapidly, the density of the footpath diminishing into beleaguered, single digits.

"*Do I have filters?*" The driver let out a sharp, cynical laugh. Then, the vehicle pulled over. "What do you think? Just get out. This is as far as I'll go."

"Thanks." Grayson opened the door and stepped out, throwing a hand over his mouth and nose. He could see the thick, dense smog in the far distance, swallowing the horizon in its choking wake. This was just the encroaching remnants of the old industry boom and he felt as though he could barely breathe. Ruin. What was it like further in?

Before closing the door, Grayson turned to the driver. "Where is the cemetery from here?"

"Just shut the door."

He sighed and did so, wincing as the car's wheels spun aggressively before disappearing around the corner, likely on its way back to the relative comfort of the City Centre.

Adjusting his hood, Grayson ventured further into Forge Town. There was a specific reason he sought the cemetery, not just that it was near to a part of the city he was bordering on demolishing, but a reason more sentimental. He couldn't shake the growing cough that wracked him as his unaccustomed lungs rapidly expelled the stale air. A part of him was embarrassed, as he watched an older man, weight planted firmly onto a steel cane, hobble down the street opposite completely silent. These people were used to it. Their bodies had grown accustomed to the clotted air and stale sky whereas he, having enjoyed a lifetime privilege of filtered air, was now struggling to adapt.

His respect grew for the people of Forge Town, whose trades would have once been valued and revered. The years pre-Reckoning had seen the demise of their artisan practices with the advent of Resynthesis that rendered their services obsolete. There was no going back now. Forge Town was a museum relic and with the worsening air quality, would soon be uninhabitable. A sad, but irrefutable fact. Grayson may have been a child born of the modern world, but he had inherited his mother's empathy and respect for all the generations living and breathing on Centa Isla.

He escalated to a brisk walk, ignoring the burning harassment of his lungs. The streets were quiet, laced with a doomed silence. Homes were still flooded, forcing people to live upstairs. Grayson could see the candle lights flitting through curtains above him, while the sickly smell of wet rot did little to ease his struggling breaths. Virtually every house here would have to be rebuilt. Would it be worth it? It was an entire third of the city waiting to die.

To his surprise, he found the cemetery signposted. A hunk of wood, scratched with a blade, pointed the way past derelict storefronts. There were dormant forges with flames forever extinguished. Taverns, quiet and empty. He had heard of the boisterous nature of Forge Town but this was nothing like what he had been told. The shops that had dared to remain open had been looted, their shelves messy and bare.

Just ahead, old, black iron fencing gave way to a cemetery. While once upon a time it had been one of the last parks Centa Isla could boast, the grass had since long withered and the entire cemetery had been paved with cobblestone. The bodies were incinerated, and for the nobles who could afford it, their ashes were entombed within the very headstones themselves. Everybody else? Grayson didn't know. Perhaps they were flung unceremoniously from the edge of the city, to become one with the wind and rain that fell perpetually upon Centa Isla.

Grayson felt the weight of time as he entered. A sea of headstones sprawled out ahead of him, darkened by the rain. Some were tall and imposing, others scratched into the very stones beneath his feet. Each name that he read filled him with a wistful sorrow, the lives of people whom he would never meet, yet were beloved enough to be laid to rest here, in this place of respect and silence. A tall block of stone had been raised, thousands of tiny names scrawled upon its surface. These were the dead of the Reckoning, who had been lost when the land shattered and a lucky fragment of Centa Isla was left adrift. The names were endless and these were only the nobles. Countless others had perished without so much as a memory to tie them to this place.

Grayson didn't notice straight away, but there were others here. They knelt in the shadows, hands pressed hard against the stone tablets, placing soft kisses on the weather ravaged stones. Many powerful, wealthy families had been buried here and it seemed a paradox of values that the nobles who would never dream of inhabiting Forge Town during their living days, were at peace with having their ashes spend eternity here. It was testament to the names that decorated the headstones.

Grayson could tell the age of these rocks from just looking at them. Some were weathered, whilst others were new and unblemished. There was one name in particular which he searched for. He knew nothing of the headstone that bore her name, only that it was old. His eyes scanned across the stones, many of the names were those who he recognised as nobles, the same surname appearing on a succession of graves, as whole generations of families lay side by side in their privileged and pricy plots.

But how many were not here? How many names had been too poor to be properly remembered? Was wealth what ultimately defined the worth of a person? Grayson knew the answer, but it didn't matter. In his father's Centa Isla and all the versions prior to that, it seemed the answer had historically been *yes*. There would be hard work ahead to turn the deep-set traditions and cultures around, but he would make sure that there was due respect for all those who died within his kingdom once the Resource Crisis was resolved at long last.

Suddenly, his thoughts were disturbed by an angry altercation taking place within the silent, solemn grounds. There were raised voices and the sounds of crumbling earth. The other grievers raised their heads, being unduly disturbed during their time of remembrance and Grayson felt anger flicker in his mind.

He strode forward towards the noise, tracking it to a large, ornate-looking tribute. It was made of stone, yet sculpted into the image of a blooming flower, long lost to time. The enchanting statue began to quake and a chunk of its beauty fell away in a clump of dishevelled earth.

"Hey!" Grayson stormed around the back of the statue. Behind it, four young men, masked and hooded beat at the stem of the memorial with steel pipes and splintered wood bludgeons. "What are you doing?"

"Join in, buddy." One of them sneered, face twisting into anger behind the thin cloth that covered his face. "There's plenty to go around."

He struck again, the rusted pipe he wielded reverberating with the impact as the memorial rocked and reeled.

"This isn't how-" Grayson approached them, only to come to an abrupt halt. There was a name carved into the base of the flower.

Aura Clovis.
Beloved Queen. Beloved Mother.
17AR – 50AR

This was his mother's grave. Her beloved ashes had been raised into this very flower that was now being desecrated by the people whom she had encouraged him to respect and value. Fury and rage struck through his veins with the intensity of lightning.

How dare they?

"You just gonna stand there?" The faceless hood spoke again. They all raised their makeshift weapons.

Grayson stepped forward. He took the first hood by the throat and wrung his neck in his hands. The snap resounded through the cemetery as the body hit the floor.

"What-" The second one started to speak but Grayson had already grabbed him. He had always been strong. At birth, he had been a large, healthy baby, inheriting genes of power and strength that he had grown into. Growing up, he had been a spoiled, tempestuous child whose instincts had been only to hurt. It had been his mother, Aura Clovis, who had stopped him from trying to harm the stewards who had sought to care for him and her nurturing touch had given him the temperance he tried hard to respect today.

But kindness and respect for others had to be reciprocal. And today they had dared to disrespect his family legacy. He tried to avoid staining the stone flower with blood, but there was only so much he could do as the second body dropped in a neat pile at his feet. The other two had bolted. The grievers whom he had not intended to disturb also fled, screaming. But his focus was on the two desecrators, their makeshift weapons discarded as they sprinted for the exit. Grayson felt his Conduit pulsing with energy on his finger and he tore the remaining glove from his hand and planted it firmly into the ground.

I invoke the Shattered Mountain. Create for them, their Tomb.

He exhaled as he felt the magic from his royal bloodline travel down his arm, leaving his body as it disappeared into the auburn magic circle he created in the ground. Seconds later, the two fleeing perpetrators screamed and Grayson rose, slowly approaching them as the eternal grasp of earth encased itself around their legs. It froze them in place mid-sprint, the grasp of eternity snaking up their legs and torso.

They screamed and begged him for mercy, but Grayson saw no humanity beyond those masks. They had chosen to come here today to destroy the grave of their former Queen. His mother. He just watched as their earthen prisons contorted to their bodies, travelling up their writhing chests and throats. It was a sharp pang of satisfaction Grayson felt as he heard the hitch of their final breaths as the prison of stone covered their noses and mouths, leaving only a terrified gaze darting in their wet eyes, that moments later were entirely consumed by hollow stone. He stretched out his arms and placed the open palm of one hand on the first statue and the other palm on the other stone-bound form. Their eyes were dark, hollow pits and the contortions of their mask twisted into a shrill scream that looked haunting.

Dust. Remove these vermin from my city.

Their bodies turned into a shower of dust before his eyes, peppering the ground with earth as the wind caught their essence and carried them off into the sky. Satisfied, Grayson returned to the statue, tearing a chunk from his grey robe and dabbing it into a puddle. With it, he wiped at the base of his mother's memorial, cleaning the splatter of crimson from the weathered grey stone. He had learned much here today. By coming here, he had done as he had intended. There was little doubt in his mind what he was going to do next.

His focus had been kindness where it should have been strength. He had initially seen the two as both sides of a coin, but he saw now that was always the case. How many days had he lost simply deliberating on the ethics and morality of his actions when he could have already been part way to the salvation of his city - saving millions for the price of hundreds?

"Perhaps I have been too considerate." He spoke to the stone flower as he wiped the last of the crimson speckles from its damaged exterior. From the ground, he picked up the pieces of earth and stone that had fallen and amassed them together in his hands.

Raise these broken pieces whole again.

Her headstone was instantly restored, forming, fresh new earth that would remain so long as he wished for it. It was as good as new, if not better. He kissed two of his fingers and placed the warmth that sat upon them on her name.

He remained there in quiet meditation, expecting the flashing sirens of the CIPD that never came. As the threat of dawn broke, Grayson stole his way back to the familiar plush opulence of Monument, but he had been forever changed. Upon returning to his chambers, he sought the upturned cup and slammed the surface upon the squalor of Forge Town.

True conviction, the strength to do what had to be done. Separate from kindness, from morality. This was the vigour that now ran through the royal veins of King Grayson Clovis, pushing him to his next decision with an intensity he had never experienced before.

The Obelisk would rise from the dust of the past.

14

Something bizarre was happening to her. Rissa felt weightless, like she was floating. She tried to open her eyes, as though to wake herself from a nightmare, only to find them already wide open and staring into an empty void of blackness. In a state of sheer panic, she tried to flap and flail her legs and arms but they remained eerily still. Her mouth tried to scream but produced no movement or sound. Fear gripped her tightly. Was she dead? Her mind spun with questions. But there were no answers.

Her legs began the motion of walking, yet she had no control over her muscles or felt any sensations in her arms nor legs. There was a deep, unnerving silence in her body, not even a thud of her own heartbeat. The darkness here was worse than The Douldruums, where at least the digging pain from the harsh metal restraints and the audible growling of her empty stomach was a reminder that she was still alive. Here she had nothing - *was* nothing. Just a spirit in the dark. A floating mass of energy. There was no horizon, no gravity, nothing. Just an unfathomable feeling of walking forever on the same spot. Her steps quickened to a run and yet there was no pounding beneath her feet, no stale air flying through her lungs, no magic in her veins. She was powerless. It was worse than any night in The Douldruums could have been.

Then, a merciful spot of colour appeared on the horizon. As Rissa squinted at it, she watched as it began to grow. It was green, blue and brown, culminating into a splodge of unintelligible shapes like the drawing she would have done as a child. But as it grew, it also grew out of its vague image, expanding into something Rissa thought she would never see in her lifetime.

A field. Green, as far as the eye could see. A blue sky came down to meet it, forming a sunset that stretched into eternity as the two colours met. As she floated towards the image, it continued to grow and expand, consuming the dark void in a wash of colour and vibrancy. The splodges of brown grew into a great wooden structure Rissa recognised as a barn and from behind it appeared rough-hewn fences built by hand. It was as though she was there; yet absently not. A breeze blew through the meadows, wafting the tall grass and rattling the old fences, yet she didn't feel it. A blazing sun beat down in the sky, searing the earth dry, but she could only feel cold. She knelt to touch the grass, only to find her knees wouldn't truly touch the ground, hovering tauntingly just above the first blade of green. She lowered a hand to the floor, desperate to finally touch this evergreen wonder of nature she had been wishing for her whole life - only to find her spectral hand disappeared into the earth. Disappointment wracked her and she tried several more times in vain before distraction pulled at her attention. Movement, growing closer, storming down the path of dried mud that led towards her. Rissa couldn't believe her eyes as the shapes drew closer, eventually forming into yet another sight Rissa thought she would never see.

Horses.

Two of them, cantering down the old path. In their wake, rolled a regal-looking carriage, like the cars that rumbled through the deluge of Centa Isla, only silent. The passengers inside were barred by a drawn set of curtains. Armour decorated the pulsing muscles of the steeds and Rissa reached out to touch them as they passed, but her disappointment was confirmed as they galloped right through her and continued down the dried-up road. They approached a small farmhouse. It was built primarily from stone but boasted intricate wooden supports and a panelled roof for cover. The door opened and Rissa squinted at the figures who emerged. There were four in total, yet only one of them was properly visible to her. The rest wore a strange cowl of static that distorted their image as though she was staring at them from underwater. No matter how many times she rubbed her eyes, it was like a smudged fingerprint on glass that she couldn't remove.

The one she could see, however, she somehow recognised instantly.

Gault.

His name came to her lips and she tried to speak, but it emerged only as energy. He was young here, far younger than she knew him now. Yet his sharp nose, tousled head of brown hair and distinct stride that he still had to this day immediately tripped recognition in her mind. He left the old stone home, embracing the smudged memories as he bid them farewell and walked up the slab-paved path toward the carriage and entered as the doors swung open for him.

Then it all went black. The colour left without so much as a warning, plunging her once again into total darkness. She waited patiently and within moments a new canvas of colour once again began to shapeshift.

A kingdom made from cobblestone and slate appeared. She stood in the shadow of an impressive castle, its tall spires and beautiful stained-glass windows still constructing itself before her as the memory formed. It looked

like something that had leaped out of one of her books in Grandmaster. But…
she recognised it, didn't she? It took her a moment, but as a courtyard grew at
the base of the stone castle, she remembered it from her otherworldly visions
that she had been granted while she had slept and slipped away to that
unfamiliar world.

A drip feed of sound came to her ears as she heard the unmistakable
clashing of steel. Figures duelled, shadowed from the beating sun by the tall
battlements that loomed overhead. They wore radiant blue tunics, silent words
boomed at them by a drill instructor whose words she was not made privy to.
But she had seen this before too. A circle of trainees surrounded the combat,
among them, Rissa picked Gault once again from the crowd. He looked older.
He had put on muscle, standing tall and stoic, his strong gaze fixed on the
conflict. She still found herself unable to get closer, but even from here Rissa
could see that his eyes were not the radiant violet she had come to grow
accustomed to, but a natural green. As she wondered why, she watched those
green orbs flit away, his entire body turning with them as another sound made
itself known to her ears.

The sounds of the steel gave way to a rhythmic, deep marching that she
could feel pulsing through her ethereal bones. Marching up the wobbly,
cobblestone road was a legion of blue tabards and steel helmets. People hung
from the windows, cheering and hollering as this vaunted legion stormed the
streets in their rhythmic sequence. Rissa searched for Gault in the madness
and found him applauding with wide eyes and a big, silly grin on his face. She
had never seen him express himself anything like this. The sight made her feel
happy. That pleasant warmth that managed to permeate her spectral form
lasted all the way up until the vision faded and the darkness returned.

Why was she able to see visions from Gault's life? It was like she was
looking into a kaleidoscope of his most treasured memories; each turn
showcasing a vibrant moment of his life. Rissa felt a sudden voyeuristic guilt,
as though she were intruding where she did not belong, trespassing over his
memories without his consent. But why?

The colours returned once more and she wondered which of his memories
would be re-enacted this time. She gasped as the most gorgeous sunset she had
ever seen burned out of the darkness. The light was blinding, but Rissa didn't
need to squint. Instead, she was able to watch as rolling green meadows
blanketed the horizon. With the tall shadow of the castle behind her, Rissa
watched as Gault materialised on the grassy mound, then a picnic basket,
then…

Someone else. A woman. They had their backs to her, staring at the setting sun. Rissa fought for motion, yet frustratingly found herself suspended above them, stuck in the shadow of the castle from which they had barely escaped. Who was it? Rissa waited for something else. Their jaws moved, yet Rissa was not given access to their conversation no matter how hard she strained to hear it. Then, as if able to sense her frustration, the girl in the memory turned around. For a moment, Rissa thought her sharp, royal gaze was staring directly into her, but quickly realised her gaze was drifting up the spires of the castle, a forlorn expression flitting her face. She was gorgeous! Sharp, regal features, blazing blonde hair and eyes as fiery as the core of the world itself.

Gault just stared ahead, oblivious to the pale fear that washed across the girl's face. Rissa waved her arms at him, frustrated. Yet by the time he had bothered to notice, she had already turned around. As the colours began to fade, Rissa watched as they wrapped their arms around one another in a long, deep embrace as the rays of the setting sun blessed them.

As the last of the picture faded, Rissa was granted a single word from the vision, her own voice ringing through her head as though she had known the answer the entire time.

Sophia.

The name was familiar. Rissa recalled it from Gault's own explanation of the royal princess whom he had aided as Kadin Krayt. She had still not been told the truth. Then, everything began to speed up. She found herself barely able to keep up as a flurry of memories began to cycle through in front of her. The sun gave way to the moon, then the moon waxed for the sun to rise. Days were passing by in a blur.

She watched years of life happening before her. And she could not slow it down. The memories would intermittently freeze for a second, a few words hovering in the air momentarily before the flashing whirlwind of moments continued. It was as though a spectral entity flitted through a catalogue of moments, indecisive in what it wished to show her. Rissa tried to tell it all to stop, immediately sensing the impending doom and final futility of it all. When the accelerated speed of time paused once more, a face dominated the vision and it belonged to somebody she had not expected to find so deep in his memories.

Lachesis.

She spoke to Gault cordially within the exquisitely decorated halls of what Rissa assumed was the castle. She caught only the small exchange of a smile until time ripped her from the moment again, sending her tumbling through time and space. Her translucent body flipped and spiralled, as though being disrupted from the moment.

The next vision she had seen before. Although not entirely. The city that had looked so gorgeous in the light of dawn was now cast in a deep, menacing red. She had seen this picture before, but from a perspective she hadn't realised had belonged to Gault. From her elevated view of the city, now cast in a blanket of flames, Rissa could see the true extent of the carnage. The silhouette of Galleo et'al was fully realised, sitting in orbit and blotting out the sky as monsters rained from its crumbling mass. It broke away before her eyes, sending meteors of destroyed, cursed earth crashing down, destroying the stone spires that had cast a protective shadow over the city.

Shadows stalked the streets. Inhuman beasts, skewering fleeing civilians upon their axes and pikes. Rissa understood what she was looking at, having seen them clearer in Gault's visions. These were demons. The same threat that loomed for Centa Isla.

You stand in defiance of our Bargain.

Another thought intruded her mind. She didn't understand its origin, but the thought was… her own?

I had hoped for us to be allies. Now, you are an obstacle.

Rissa felt darkness creeping into the vision. But it wasn't the landscape itself that was changing; but her. She looked down at her body, finding her legs and arms starting to slowly fade out of existence. What was happening to her? She tried to speak but found herself again without a voice.

I am sorry that it came to this. Truly.

As she panicked, the vision changed once more, this time into a dark, grim chamber. Power warbled in the air and the howl of demons flitted into the cavernous underground from above. The ground trembled and red dust hailed from the ceiling. In the centre, a familiar sight appeared. Akor'shaki, in full form, suspended over a violet trimmed altar. As Rissa felt her form disappearing, she watched as Gault appeared from the shadows. He looked tired, gaunt and forlorn. There was grit in his eyes, yet his stride betrayed his fatigue and tiredness. He reached for the suspended Akor'shaki, only for a force of violet power to expel itself from the blade and repel him. Rissa watched as he skidded across the ground, nursing an arm burned with dark power. He gritted his teeth and approached again; the tears of pain that stung in his eyes buried beneath what Rissa knew was a mountain of guilt. He tried again, reaching out toward the weapon. Rissa watched as the loose chain that swung from Akor'shaki sought him out, winding itself softly around his arm as though to test the waters of his spirit.

She wanted to see more. To understand how he worked, how everything worked, yet as Rissa fought for spiritual consciousness, she felt the pull of sleep washing over her as her spectral form continued to fade away. Before she fully disappeared, she heard the binding words that Gault spoke as he communed with Akor'shaki for the first time.

"Destroy Galleo'et al, at any cost."

She saw the chain recoil like a striking serpent and then spear into him. He buckled. Rissa understood it as the creation of the bond between boy and blade that he still carried to this day, the bargain that he had made with Akor'shaki that would grant him the power to avenge his homeworld. This was the final vision she was granted before total darkness overcame her. Immediately however, a blurry light appeared, becoming brighter and clearer until a new image came into focus. What opened up before her was a sight much more familiar than she had expected. It was the interior of The Hound.

She was in her own bed. Yet something was wrong. Her darting eyes took in the space around her, but her body refused to move. Her connection to her limbs felt like they had been severed, yet her body continued to breathe and her heart continued to beat.

She comes for you.

Her own thoughts invaded her head, yet Rissa knew instantly they were not her own. She tried to move, to speak and open her mouth. Her Conduit sat quietly on the bedside table. She would have to do nothing more than shift her arm to be within reach of it, yet she could not move.

Then, the window creaked open. Rissa watched as a shadow drifted in. She could feel the cold air blowing on her skin, yet still she could not wake fully. A dangling, pale arm leered in through the billowing curtains, fingers bereft of nails fumbling on the wooden floor for purchase as a head followed, a mane of rotted auburn hair, falling out in viscous clumps of matted blood and ooze as the sickly figure pulled itself into her room. An unhinged jaw swung loosely, flashing rotten teeth and decayed gums as the withered corpse crawled slowly, erratically, towards her.

Fear would have paralysed her if she wasn't already immobile. She wanted so desperately to move, to flee, to at the very least defend herself from the horror that approached her. The deranged figure offered no information, declared no intent, she just approached. First crawling on the creaking old floor, the sharp crackling of bones ringing through the airy room as she rose onto trembling legs releasing a horrific, throaty death rattle as she neared.

Hands from the grave crested the bed and Rissa could only watch in sheer horror as the figure slowly mantled up and leered over her body. Rissa's wide eyes flitted with fear as a flash of recognition coursed across her mind at the glimpse of the dead woman's pale face.

Sophia. The name was at the front of her mind. It was her, wasn't it? This was the Princess Sophia who she had seen sharing a sunset with Gault just moments ago. Yet she had seen her before then. She had appeared in her visions as a tortured, broken body whose skin had split like clay as Azrael and Lachesis had watched. That same twisted body was before her now, unhinged jaw clicking as her shambling arms approached her, was a shadow of that person. A torn silk gown clung to her scorched, serrated flesh. The hands that approached her were scarred, deep cuts wending all the way up her arm. Even as those hands approached her throat, Rissa's mind was invaded with the cruel and agonising torment this girl had endured before the mercy of death claimed her. Yet it seemed that there would be no rest even in death.

The touch was cold as ice as the hands of Sophia wrapped themselves around her throat. Rissa wanted to struggle, yet her fingers wouldn't so much as twitch but lay pinned to her side. She could only watch as the jaw unhinged itself and opened impossibly wide, a scream of utter suffering and rage expelled into her face. Then, the haunting figure of Sophia disappeared.

Rissa awoke suddenly with a strangled, rasping gasp. Adrenaline pumping, she found she was still unable to breathe. Choking for breath, she sat upright, gasping and spluttering. Instinctively, her hands went to her throat and her numb fingers met the sensation of hot steel coiled tightly around her throat. Rissa flung her legs from the bed, feeling the popping of fresh stitches on her abdomen. The chain was so tightly wound that she couldn't even get her fingernails beneath the interlocking steel. She rose onto wobbly, fading legs, finding the scalding steel chain wrapped also around her left arm. She followed it, the twisting trail leading to Gault. He lay beside her, unconscious, yet the chain at his waist was active, simultaneously glowing and vibrating with its own dark life. It didn't take her long to realise that the chain around her throat was Akor'shaki.

"Akor'shaki?" She croaked, feeling the life being squeezed from her body by the demonic blade. She felt the point of the scythe as she explored around her throat, coming away with a bloodied finger as she sought to pry it from her. Her head was full of the faceless words she had found at the forefront of her mind in the swathe of memories. They spoke in her voice, yet were vapid and emotionless, as though her corpse had been raised and made to speak.

You stand in defiance of our Bargain. You are an obstacle.

Rissa dropped to her knees, drool pouring from her restricted throat as her eyes fluttered as though to close. She wasn't an obstacle, was she? She was helping Gault to remain in control of himself, to help stop Galleo et'al. How could she be an obstacle?

Her fingers were so numb that she was no longer certain she was even fighting back anymore as she slumped over. She was too weak to fight back. Yet… she couldn't accept this. Something surged within her, the pure desire to survive. Finding strength in her legs, Rissa pulled herself from the floor and threw herself over Gault's unconscious body. She slipped her hand beneath his chest plate, feeling the freezing, scarred skin of his chest beneath the palm of her hand. She held it there as blackness poured in the edges of her vision, her face turning as purple as the blade that choked her.

"Come on!" She spluttered.

She felt a single beat of his heart. The rise and fall of his chest in those precious seconds. Whatever it was, it was just enough. For a moment, the control Akor'shaki had waned briefly and Rissa felt the nudge of loosening chain links around her throat. She dug her hands beneath the chain and wrangled it, untangling the mess of evil hatched steel from her body. Even as she fought again for air, she didn't stop moving, coiling the chain around her hands and wrapping it tightly around the legs of the bed and securing the blade beneath a pile of dusty old books. She wobbled to the window and slung it open, grateful for air as she collapsed, the raspy rising and falling of her chest hammering in her ears.

As the adrenaline faded from her body, her abdomen screamed for attention and she curled up on the hardwood floor, running her finger across the rough, erratic stitching across her stomach. Some of the wound, which had been scarring over, was now open and raw, the tips of the split stitches sharp to the touch and excruciatingly painful. It made her skin crawl to feel her skewered flesh that had been pulled tautly back to form the shape of a large cross. By fortune or fate, she had survived. Rissa ground her teeth, resisting the dark urge to tear the stitches from her body. Her efforts to learn swordsmanship had not been enough, all of the falling and getting back up, the calloused palms, the sore backsides and the long nights. All to just lose again. Was Azrael truly unbeatable? Was he put in this city to remind her that she would always be weaker? Rissa wasn't certain, but now, she didn't even know if she could fully trust Gault. A twist of guilt hit her as the thought crossed her mind. It wasn't entirely him that she distrusted, but now his blade. It was the unfortunate truth that more often than not, it was Akor'shaki who seemed to be in more control than him when it mattered. Akor'shaki had tried to kill her, yet she had survived yet again. Like a rat in the grand machine.

Just then, footsteps hammered beneath her and the hatch into the attic was thrown open. Sheppard appeared, his eyes wide.

"You're awake! Are you okay?"

"Sheppard? I'm... fine enough, I think." She took a moment to process the bearded barman. He looked tired and thinner, much of his mass having fled his body since she had last seen him. "Are you?"

"I'm fine, thank you." Closing the hatch behind him, Sheppard had to bow his head to avoid bumping it on the angular ceiling. He took a steady seat upon the sofa, groaning as he did so. "The storm took its toll."

"You've been taking care of us, haven't you?" Rissa glanced back at Gault's comatose body. "Thank you, really. But you shouldn't have. You have a business to run."

At that, Sheppard laughed, but grief pulled at the edges of his mouth. "I did."

"Oh no, did the storm-"

"Yes." He stared at the wall of his precious tavern. "Suffice to say, we won't be needing the bouncer anymore."

"That's terrible. I'm so sorry."

"I'm just pleased you're both safe."

Rissa sat in a mournful silence. "How did you end up owning the place?"

"It belonged to my father." Sheppard rumbled. His hands combed through his scruffy beard. "He died of course and it was passed down to myself and my sister."

"You had a sister?"

"Barely." A twinge of anger throbbed upon his forehead. "She left to train with the CIPD. Led a bust on this place a few years ago when I used to offer sanctuary to those with the coin."

"Isn't that what you're doing now?"

"Sure is. Except you don't even have the coin." He laughed, rising to his feet to lay his hands upon the old walls. "This place has always been here for the people. Respect the property and it respects you."

"This place gives you purpose." Rissa smiled at him. "I'm glad you have that in your life."

"Well… If you call stress purpose, then I suppose so." Sheppard smiled at her, rising to his feet and making his way back to the hatch. "Oh, your father came to visit."

"He did?" She could remember fragments of her bumpy ride here. He had spoken of the past as he normally had, only it had been different. One last lead before he gave it up and returned to her as a fatherly figure. "What did he want?"

"He left you these." Shepherd gestured to a small open box in the corner of the room.

Peering inside, Rissa found a spare change of clothes, a sword and a handful of Wreaths.

"Thanks, Sheppard. For everything."

"Don't mention it." He left, closing the hatch behind him. "We'll see the dawn yet."

As the adrenaline faded fully from her body, Rissa found overwhelming tiredness come over her. Her healing had been interrupted and her body forced to move. She had no idea how long she had been unconscious for, nor what day it was. A look out the window revealed nothing changed on the Centa Isla skyline. The demands for sleep were deafening and so Rissa heaved herself up on the sofa, plumping a cushion to rest her head upon as she tried not to further stretch out her painful abdomen. Nothing else mattered to her right now, except sleep.

—

When Jace awoke, he was surprised he had done so at all. Fully anticipating death, he instead found his body entirely mobile and much to his surprise, fairly comfortable. He lay on a filthy, foam, pock marked mattress, which felt like an oasis compared to the chair and water treatment he had endured at the hands of Donnel Rawdon. He glanced down to find his hand bandaged and poking out from a crudely fashioned sling and the sharp whiff of strong antiseptic tingling his nostrils. The remnants of medicinal stings were still throbbing on his face and his grimace served only to aggravate his injuries. Jace felt gratitude for there being no mirror as he had no appetite to view the smorgasbord of bruises, lumps and bumps that no doubt blemished his complexion.

The windowless room was brusquely decorated with a small, stitched carpet and an old dressing table with a scratched mirror. As he moved the mattress wobbled upon the handmade, rickety bed frame. Someone had made a proud effort to fashion the space into a semblance of a bedroom. He could feel the wind beating against the bricks that supported the roof over his head but with no ventilation, the air was thick and stuffy. Begrudgingly, his tired, aching body obeyed his command to rise. He swung his legs over the bed, knees knocking as he fought for balance. The door to his room was, to his surprise, unlocked and he opened it gingerly, wincing as the groan of the rusty steel hinges announced his presence.

He emerged into an even smaller space than he had expected. To call it a home was somewhat of an overstatement. The roof over his head was covered in tarpaulin, held in place by crude shards of steel that had been hammered into the rotted wooden framework. Here and there, holes had been patched up to keep out the rain. There was a window, but it was locked shut, the trim sealed with crude tape. Smog clung to the streets beyond, mixed with the evening rain and these elements had taken their toll. Water dribbled in from the overburdened tarpaulin, trickling in through weakness in the taped-up window. Whether the flooding from the storm had caused the damage, or this was how it always had been, he wasn't certain.

Jace could scarcely believe he was thinking this, but the room he had woken up in had been nicer. Hells, even the attic room with Donnel had at least been dry and the water deliberately put into the buckets, rather than drip-dripping into them from the roof.

The floor was partly stone, re-laid crudely by hand. There were remnants of a respectable wooden floor, the planks that were lucky enough to be fully sheltered from the drips, in moderately good condition. There were more rooms yet unexplored, an archway that descended a stairwell into what looked like a dingy cellar. Auburn lights danced on the walls down there, the distant and soft crackling of protected flame stirred up feelings of safety and warmth that made him lumber towards it.

"You're awake, lad."

Jace jumped. Whether his senses were diluted and still recovering, or someone had successfully snuck up on him he was not yet certain. But upon turning, he saw a figure sitting quietly in an armchair, tucked in the furthest corner of the room out of the way of the leaky drips.

"Where am I?" The room was dark. The man lit a candle inside a metal lantern and held it up in front of his face. The flickering light revealed a tired, old man. He sat in his armchair, still as a statue, watching.

"Forge Town. The furthest outskirts. You're safe, boy, you have my word."

"Your word doesn't mean a thing to me."

"Aye." The wick eagerly consumed a globule of wax and in a moment of bright glare, Jace caught a flash of sadness on the wrinkled, sunken face. "Words don't, these days."

Jace chewed his lip. He looked down at his bandaged hand in the sling. A pang of guilt rocked him. "Why did you help me?"

The old man looked confused. "Because you asked me to."

"I did?" Jace didn't remember. He had stumbled from that basement and roamed the streets like a stray until his legs no longer worked and his body gave way. He had thought it was the end. The guilt melted into gratitude and he realised there were words that needed to be said. "Thank you. For helping me."

With a grunt, the elder lifted himself from his chair and approached. He walked with a striking limp, one half of his body seeming much more mobile than the other. A hand was thrust towards him, palms gritted and calloused. "Stanwyck."

Jace slowly reached out and took Stanwyck's hand. They shook and Jace felt reassurance radiating from the old man's firm, yet respectful shake. Even in his age, there was power in his movements that suggested a previous life that had been much more grandiose.

"Jace." As he spoke, Jace looked around the hovel that Stanwyck called home. "This is your home?"

"Aye." The old man let out a guttural chuckle, followed by a brisk cough. "Has been for eighty years."

Eighty years? Surely not. Jace's time in Centa Isla, when not overindulging in alcohol and noble parties, had been intensely educational. He had learned the history of the city, of its plight and its people, in order to fit in convincingly. His understanding of history was cursory at best, but even Jace knew that to be eighty years old was...

"You're... pre-Reckoning?"

An amused smile crossed Stanwyck's face, as though he enjoyed the disbelief that was so blatant. For over twenty years, Stanwyck would have seen the world before it was ravaged, half a lifetime for many living today.

"Aye lad and I've got another in me yet."

The average life expectancy in Centa Isla was late fifties with thuggery, suicide, starvation and Smithy's Lung top of the list for premature deaths. Jace marvelled for a moment, staring at a man who by all accounts was an anomaly in this city. This was just another life about to be ruined by the work of The

Omens. This humble hand-built abode had sheltered this proud man and his family for decades but it was now a weathered patchwork of repairs with scraps of foraged wood and metal. It had miraculously survived a planet-cracking cataclysm to face certain annihilation in all but a matter of weeks.

To Jace's surprise, another voice reverberated through this crumbling home. It belonged to an elderly lady, her voice cracking as it pitched as high as she could muster. "Stan!"

Stanwyck smiled at him, gesturing towards the room he had woken up in. Jace realised now that it was the master bedroom, the nicest room in their home and they had given it freely to him. "Get some rest, lad. I'll bring you some dinner."

"Dinner?" Jace was confused, he felt his brow furrowing deeply over his eyes. "But, the Resource Crisis, aren't you rationing?"

"Nothing new out here, son." The old man hobbled towards the cellar. "We were struggling well before the crisis."

Jace followed the man, stepping down several sunken wooden steps. Rounding a narrow corner, the cellar opened out into what looked like a makeshift kitchen. The source of the flames he had sensed earlier was revealed, crackling and simmering beneath a large cookpot. Within, the warm smell of a stew wafted. Jace breathed deeply of it, feeling his stomach twisting in hunger.

Stanwyck conversed with somebody, another elder. A lady, old but having aged perhaps more gracefully than her counterpart.

"Jace, this is Celia - my wife."

"Hello, dear." Celia smiled at him. Her eyes looked tired, yet her pupils locked onto him and Jace felt as though she appraised him in an instant. He sensed that even though her words and actions were friendly, they were so because she had searched him for malintent already.

"Hello." Jace bowed his head slightly. "What are you cooking?"

"Just an old classic." She waved him away, stirring the broth with a wooden ladle. "There's plenty to go around."

That was an understatement. As Jace neared, the scope of the cooking became clear to him. The cookout was enormous, more akin to a cauldron. The soup inside was enough in quantity to feed an army.

"It's ready?" Stanwyck asked.

"Yes."

Jace watched, confused. Stanwyck handed the lantern to him and approached the cauldron, gripping the handles with his calloused hands. In that moment, he caught a glimpse of the man's impressive muscle mass, retained even in age, bulging against the baggy sleeves of his tunic. The cauldron lifted from the ground and Jace immediately felt like he was in the way as Stanwyck began to move it towards the stairs.

"Can I help?" He asked uselessly, forced back up the stairs as the cauldron approached. He dangled the lantern lower so that the steps were clearly visible.

"Nay, lad, nay. Just light the way." The strain in the old man's voice was palpable. Jace did what he was asked and retreated further up the steps. The show of strength on display was incredible.

As he reached the top, the grunting grew louder. There was a sudden thud as the base of the cauldron hit the ground, searing against the stone section of the floor.

Celia's voice shouted from the cellar. "Are you okay?"

"Aye...!" Stanwyck shouted back. He nursed his back, one hand still wound so tightly around the handle that his knuckle had gone white. "Just... a moment."

"I can help." Jace stepped forward, only for a hand to shoot out and block him.

"Keep back." Stanwyck murmured, waving him away as he stretched out his spine. "It's always the same point. Just a tweak, it'll pass.."

A flush of relief fell through Jace. He'd offered to help, but there was every likelihood that he wouldn't even be able to so much as budge the cauldron. What this man was doing at eighty-something years old was astounding.

Jace looked to the window, not wanting to scrutinise the man while he recovered. With the storm having cleared the sky, it was a rare cloudless night. The sun had set and its luminescent kin had risen into the sky and it looked magnificent. So close to the edge of the city as they were, there were no skyscrapers to blot out this view. For a moment, Jace was lost in that tranquillity and he just stood there, squinting into the silver shine of the moon. Such peaceful calm was a rarity of late. But then, sudden movement withdrew him from that trance. He sharpened, eyes narrowing to slits as he peered through the window at the smoggy streets. Shapes were drifting slowly across the street towards the house. At first, there was one. Then two. Then more than he could count on two hands. They flitted in the cover of the smog and dwindling light, approaching from all angles.

Jace pulled away, instinctively reaching for his weapon only to find it long abandoned. He looked within, feeling the fiery call of magic still pumping through his blood. So long as he was able, Stanwyck and Celia would fall under no harm, not after they had shown him kindness the likes of which he had never seen in this city so far.

"Beware, friend." Jace spoke to the old man, not taking his eyes from the flitting shapes beyond the veil of glass, smog and rain. "There is movement outside. Shadows."

"Aye. Don't worry about them." Stanwyck nested again into an impressively agile squat as he sought to lift the cauldron from the ground. Even as he did so, Jace could hear the clicking of weathered bones and the muted grunts of a man desperate to hide his growing fragility.

Casting a final sweeping stare out the window, Jace stepped back, placing the lantern on the floor. He took one of the pot handles with his non-injured hand. "Two, three, lift!"

He felt as though his hand was going to fall from his wrist, but the cauldron lifted from the uneven stone floor. His fingers screamed for release as he allowed Stanwyck, now bearing only half the weight, to lead him through the groaning old home and toward the front door. Jace wished to warn him again of the figures, but his lungs were at full capacity as he channelled deep, belated breaths through his flaring nostrils with every knee jerking step. He was never physically strong, not truly, yet he surprised himself now with the power which he was exerting from a body that had seen much better days than recently.

How she got ahead of them, Jace didn't know but Celia was suddenly at the front door, holding it open as the cauldron was shuffled hastily outside. The crisp air was cold, laced with a thickness that could only be attributed to their proximity to the worst of the smog. In fact, Jace could see it, skirting the furthest edges of Forge Town like a predator. It seeped into his lungs even now, lesser in form, but still as thick as the hot, arid air of Galleo et'al's planet surface. Immediately fear seeped in with it, thoughts of Smithy's Lung, a lung disease that he had yet to see firsthand but had heard enough horror stories about to harbour a fear. Quickly, his rational mind set in and quelled the harm. He was in the presence of an eighty-year-old lifting three times his bodyweight. If he was okay, then surely he would be too.

"Anywhere here, lad!" Stanwyck grunted and the two of them lowered the searing cauldron down onto the ground. A waving shadow sheltered them from the drizzle. Jace looked up, finding a long sheet of tarpaulin suspended over the front of the home like a canopy. Beside them, just next to where they had placed the cauldron was an old, chipped wooden table. Celia followed them out, bearing with her a tall stack of clunking wooden bowls which she laid out.

Jace searched for the shadows, finding them now in great numbers as they crossed the road toward them. Whether Stanwyck sensed his tension, or just got lucky, the calloused hands fell onto his shoulder.

"At ease, kid."

Jace stood there as the shadows emerged from the fog as… people. The radiance of the moon revealed sunken cheeks and tired, gaunt bodies. They wore multi-layered clothing, tears and rips in the fabric at every stitch. Their hair was matted and clumpy, yet tired eyes dragged into the depths of hell by deep, bruised bags lit up at the sight of the cauldron.

Stanwyck and Celia took a ladle and began serving up portions of the thick, hearty soup in the wooden bowls. With words of gratitude on their lips, they accepted the bowls and began to drink slowly, moving away to gather in small groups among shelter. The soup had a warm aroma in the chill of the night and soothed the minds and souls of those around the old home, himself included. As more and more gathered and were fed, Jace just watched. It took him a moment to notice a young girl was staring at him, waiting patiently in line despite the thundering of her stomach. When she received her bowl, she smiled at him.

"Thank you!"

She left before he could reply. Not that it mattered, there were no words that Jace could find, so he just stood there until the right words came to his lips.

"… You're welcome."

The hungry and the grateful came in droves, grateful for heat and sustenance, devouring bowls and returning them neatly without so much as a drop left in the smooth wooden surface. These were the people who populated the outskirts of the city, Jace had never given them thought. What had been made of those who had lost homes and property in the wake of Reckoning? Who had been too slow to adapt to the rapidly shifting climate of the city? These were the forgotten people. Yet not by everybody, not by Stanwyck and Celia.

He took a ladle from Celia, bidding her speak to the people who she had been holding strained conversation with while serving. She left with a small smile, leaving him to serve up bowl after bowl, many of which were second helpings. Jace scooped up the final remnants, scraping low down into the cauldron to rescue the hearty chunks so as not to waste a single morsel. Seeing the empty vessel made him feel warm, igniting a small fire in his chest that he hadn't felt in many years. He felt… good. It was a feeling he didn't want to drink away.

He sat down, putting his back to the old stone wall that held up the hovel that Stanwyck called home. The old man appeared beside him, lowering a steaming bowl of soup.

"Saved you some, kid."

"Thank you, sir." He wasn't certain why he threw such a title in there, but there was something that radiated from the man that simply felt like it deserved it. Regardless, he quickly discarded the thought as the warm soup trailed down his throat, filling his body with the warmth only a nourishing meal could provide.

"Sir?" Stanwyck chuckled, coughing abruptly. "Many years since I was called that."

Jace wiped his mouth before looking up, coming away with greedy splashes of soup on his arm. "What did you do...for a living?"

"Hardly matters now." The man's dark eyes looked up at the dark tower of Monument. "No use looking back."

Jace sighed, envy in his breath. "I don't know how you do it."

A grunt was the reply. The old man stood there, watching as the masses ate, sheltered from the drizzle. "Let me show you something."

Jace followed quietly as Stanwyck entered his home, lifting the lantern off the serving table. They passed through the main room and back down the creaking stairs into the basement. A hatch that Jace had failed to notice previously, was concealed in the back corner by a small, stitched carpet. Sweeping the fraying linen aside, Stanwyck grappled with the steel latches that bound the old wood and grunted as they demanded yet another burst of his strength. Eventually they gave up their resistance and the hatch was lifted, revealing a small set of stairs that led deeper underground.

"Where are we going?"

He was offered no reply as Stanwyck simply gestured for him to descend. Reluctantly, Jace obeyed, dismissing the distrustful instinct that pricked at his thoughts. The second set of stairs led into pitch darkness. It wasn't until Stanwyck followed with the lantern did he see what was hidden beneath the old hovel.

Planters. Soil. Jace thought it first a trick of the dim, flickering light until it dawned upon him that it was not. He moved closer, stooping to one knee. The stone floor beneath him had been partially removed, creating a thin aisle that was flanked by... fertile soil. Within that dark, damp earth were green stalks that sprouted. Jace recognised them immediately.

"Potatoes?" He spoke in awe. "How?"

There was no fertile soil in Centa Isla. The smog and the construction of an industrialised city had seen to that. All farmland was either destroyed by Reckoning or spent the last sixty years decaying to the point of non-existence. This was truly a miracle, a one-of-a-kind discovery.

One that could save the city.

If an old man could grow vegetables in his basement, what could the combined minds of the city achieve? This was… nothing short of a revelation.

"You wanted to know how I do it." Stanwyck grumbled. "Here it is. Hope."

Jace hovered a hand over the soil, looking first to the old man for permission to lay hands upon his precious crop. A curt nod granted his request and Jace felt damp, clumpy soil slip beneath his fingernails as he dug a small, careful hole at the base of the stalk. Sure enough, the rough skin of a potato greeted his fingers and a smile stretched across his face.

"This is… a revelation." He whispered as he gently re-buried the potato beneath the earth. "Do you know what this means? For the city? For everyone?"

"Aye, lad." Stanwyck looked at his crop with a glimmer in his eye.

"We have to tell-"

"No." Stanwyck was firm and sudden.

"What?"

"This city has given us nothing." As he spoke, Jace could see distant, repressed anger clouding his eyes. "This is all we have. To feed us, to feed those who struggle here with nothing but the clothes on their backs and the shadow of their homes to sleep in."

Dropping to his level, Jace saw the intent in Stanwyck's eyes. "The Crown will seize this place in a heartbeat. The food will go to the fat and nourished, leaving us exactly where we started - with nothing."

Jace understood. He did not deny the old man's claims because he knew that they were true. As quickly as awe and excitement had filled him, he all too suddenly felt it replaced by guilt and by dread. Despite Stanwyck's wishes, this discovery was enough to save the city. Not just from the Resource Crisis, but also Galleo et'al. If he simply told the King of existing fertile soil then his need to rely on the construction of the Obelisk would be null and void. The young faces he had taught at Grandmaster would live full lives in a city with a future and Stanwyck and Celia may become legends as the cultivators of a new tomorrow.

And he may even have a place in all of it. Somewhere.

He knelt there, staring into the dark soil. Eventually, he rose, ready to leave. "Thank you for showing me that."

Stanwyck just grunted.

Then there was a crash. So loud, so deafening that the very ceiling above them spit dusty earth. Screams followed; the churning of magical engines filled the air. Jace shared a single look with Stanwyck before they both sprinted back up the stairs, speeding through the main room and out the front door. From out of the dark, they were blinded by bright headlamps from numerous vehicles, slowly moving in succession towards them.

Jace watched as a bulldozer ploughed through the old ruins, scattering the ragged denizens to the shadows as what was left of their hovels was crushed beneath tracks and rollers. Dust hung heavy in the air as the old, derelict homes were reduced to nothing but a memory by a legion of rollers. The smoke that churned from their funnels was visible all around him.

Jace was paralysed as the cauldron tipped from the rumbling of the earth. The little girl who had thanked him so earnestly wept alone, an orphan to the chaos that had people running for cover. There were those, emboldened by the hearty stew who sought to prevent this carnage. They approached the rollers with words of warning and despair. When ignored, those who sought to climb the vehicles were blasted with magic from a small accompaniment of Kingsguard Versorcerers. The starved bodies hit the ground, some seared by flames, others punctured by jagged stone.

The crushing of earth turned his attention to Stanwyck's home. Jace could see a spout of smoke approaching.

"The crops." He whispered. Whirling, he surged around the back of the home to see a roller directly approaching. He threw his hands up, waving desperately for the destructive vehicle to stop its course, the harsh headlights illuminating his frenzied gesticulations. The driver behind the wheel wore a grimace, the kind of look Jace had seen many times before in the mirror. It was the desperate look of someone who was doing what they had to do to survive.

"STOP! STOP!" Jace waved desperately, feeling the heat from the headlamps warming the night air. It was clear that he would become collateral if he did not move.

He dropped to his knees, pushing his palm deep into the ground.

I will not let them destroy this city's last hope.

A great wall of flame surged from the ground before him, curving in a protective arc around the back of the home. These people didn't know what they sought to destroy. They truly had no idea that the possible salvation of the city lay beneath the earth they sought to flatten. He had to stop them - to make them see sense, even if it meant that Stanwyck would lose his hope.

Just as his spell was cast and the brakes screeched on the destructive construct, Jace felt a presence. It sent a streak up his spine, settling in his mind. He felt suddenly the presence of another, a presence so thick that it made his head throb with strain.

Step aside, Brand. You meddle with the design.

Jace knew it immediately. He felt the Brand of the Sorcerer on his arm ache and throb with pain as he was contacted by the dark god whom he had sworn to serve. There were no further words given to him, but he didn't need them. Jace knew he had a choice. Lower the barrier or suffer the wrath of the Dark One.

"Damn it." Jace closed his eyes shut, squeezing them so tightly as though it would make the presence go away. But it didn't. The fear clotted his heart, the fear of punishment, pain and torment that came with disobedience. He had seen what had become of Lachesis for merely speaking against the addition of another Omen. That had been enough to guarantee his service.

And so, he dropped the barrier. With the falling flames, also went his self-respect. This was the life he had chosen. There was nobody to blame but himself. As the fire disappeared and he took a subservient step to the side, he felt his lips dry up as the roller once again continued its progress.

He licked his dry, parched lips, unable to watch the carnage. He needed a drink.

"BEGONE!" Stanwyck's voice made him look up. Surging around the back of his home, the old man moved with the agility of a man half his age. The hobble remained, but it was purposeful. In his hand he wielded a sword, rusted and blackened with age.

He leapt on the machine and sought to drive his sword through the screen. The driver dipped down beneath the wheel as the glass smashed. In response to the immediate threat, Jace watched as a Versorcerer, royal violet robes dusty from the chaos prepared a spell. Bright white light burned on his Conduit as a magic circle formed in the palm of his outstretched hand. A Wind Versorcerer.

Jace gritted his teeth. It felt as though the world was moving in slow motion as his Brand immediately allowed him to process what was happening. By the speed at which this Wind Versorcerer spun his magic, Jace knew he was highly advanced. Judging by the force used by the others he had seen; it was going to be something lethal.

Stanwyck wasn't going to see it coming. The blast of wind would be sharp, like an invisible blade, enough to serrate his head from his shoulders. It would be a quick death, over before he knew it. A death in defence of his home was noble, more than many got these days.

Jace watched as the magic circle consumed oxygen as the spell manifested in a white crescent. In that instant he held out his hand on instinct, a single word crossing his mind.

Flare.

He created an ember in the palm of his hand, watching as it travelled directly into the pocket of oxygen-less space directly where the Wind spell was being created. Once it arrived, Jace felt the seconds pass... then there was a great explosion of force! A backdraft obliterated the Versorcerer who had been none the wiser. The violet, charred robes waved, lifeless as the dead body crashed the machine into a tower of rubble where it lay whirring with spinning tyres.

It had been too easy. He wasn't the Brand of the Sorcerer for no reason. But no sooner had he acted did regret wash through him. He felt the pressure in his mind begin to multiply, feeling as though his skull was going to crack from the force. Galleo et'al's displeasure coursed through him as agony.

So be it. Suffer well for your interference. We will speak further upon my arrival.

The Brand on his arm went from ache to agony as it felt as though the flesh on his bones was being slowly peeled. Jace screamed immediately, regret mixed among the pain as he fell to his knees. His entire body felt flayed, like his organs had been set on fire and a thousand pins picked at every painful nerve on his body.

He prayed that the mercy of unconsciousness would once again save him. He watched as a column of water blasted Stanwyck from the machine as its progress continued. Jace watched the stone walls of Stanwyck's home crumble. The potato crop was soon to become buried in a grave of rubble.

Despite the pain, he felt a tremendous sense of intolerable loss. What a fool he was. Why had he even tried? He saw a beleaguered, drenched Stanwyck hobbling towards Celia, her shoulders rising and falling with heart wrenching sobs. As the old couple hugged each other tightly, he felt a flood of emotion that carried him back into the black abyss.

15

Lachesis watched from across the room as her crystal ball flared and pulsed with power. Her aid was sought, yet she had no intention of providing it. Her network of enchanted rats who fed her information, were desperately fleeing the outskirts of Forge Town, terrified as their burrows collapsed around them. They had served her well, keeping her well informed from their vantage points on the squalid streets whilst she relaxed in the comfort of her opulent quarters. Their loss of life was collateral damage and she would not stoop so low as to mourn vermin. So, she sat there in silence, contemplating as her network of spies fled the steamrollers of the demolition crew. They would be replaced. There were plenty more rats, roaches and spiders who lived in the dark underbelly of Centa Isla whom she could enchant as her next army of informants.

In a previous conquest, she had once created a network of birds, who scouted the skies and reported back to her. Centa Isla had offered her no such luxury and so upon her arrival she was forced to root through garbage and filth to find the first little rat to bless with her power. It had returned to its den and spread her influence exponentially throughout the city, infecting thousands of rats with her insidious enchantment.

In truth, she knew exactly where Gault and Rissa lay asleep. She knew they had survived their injuries, hiding in the smog and history of Forge Town. The old building they called home was filled with eight-legged friends who she used to keep an eye on them. Gault would squish one here and there, his paranoia spurring him to seek every inch of their attic home, but spiders were always plentiful. She even knew of Donnel Rawdon's doomed mission into Grandmaster and his subsequent interrogation of Jace. Admittedly, she had lost The Brand of the Sorcerer since, but knew he had earned his rest having completed his part of the mission. It would have been so blissfully easy to materialise herself within the attic of The Hound and slit Gault's throat while he slept. Yet, she didn't...

She liked to keep the pieces on the board, so to speak.

For how much longer however, she wasn't certain. As for why, her rampant mind kept pulling her back to the same thought. A distant feeling that she was

319

missing an opportunity. With the King making his decision on where to construct the Obelisk and the machines already flattening the desired land, the remaining days of the once great kingdom of Centa Isla were dwindling in number, taking with it her opportunity. Could she allow it to pass her by? She felt her perfect row of pearlescent teeth grinding against one another and she grimaced in annoyance. Heretical thoughts spun often around her mind these days. Initially, they had started as little more than a lingering thought, quickly extinguished as her reality kicked in. But lately they had loitered, festering in the darkest recesses of her mind until they dominated her waking hours and invaded her nightly dreams. There was an intense desire to make her stand here. To break the strings that puppeteered her and end Galleo et al's chaotic crusade across the stars. Even now, such thoughts were cloaked in danger for she knew that the pain it would inflict upon her for such heresy would be incomprehensible.

Yet there had been no pain. No comeuppance for harbouring such treachery. For now, The Dark One didn't know.

Where it had once seen everything, sensed every touch on her skin and breath on her lips, now it couldn't. Or, even if it still could, it was distracted. The plight of Galleo et'al was known to her. It was a maw of raw, demonic and godly power that decayed every second that it didn't spend consuming planets. Its lifespan was limited, yet it reset the grim countdown with every planet core that it absorbed. And with every consumption, it grew stronger and stronger. Yet the Dark One had made an enemy of time itself, the hands of fate constantly ticking precious seconds closer to the day that the epicentre of the vile planet would run out of worlds to consume and die, quietly and alone in the empty, dark beyond.

But that did little to provide her comfort. What use was the Dark One's demise if she, nor the rest of the universe, would be alive to relish it? Pressure weighed upon her. If not Centa Isla, then where? Where was a stand going to be made? Would it be too late when she finally decided that now was the right time?

The truth was blasphemous, but she had spared Gault's life even at the request of her brother that he be slain. Gault was wild and deeply disturbed, wracked by what seemed to be a malady of the mind that held him back just as much as it propelled him forward. But, deep down she knew his conviction would be the key to Galleo et'al's demise, were such a thing possible. She had struck him, but deliberately not lethally. His wounds had likely already healed from the dark power that his blade bestowed. Once upon a time, Akor'shaki had been meant to be wielded by the hands of her brother but upon looking at how the influence of the weapon had twisted The Brand of the Scout, she was quietly grateful it was stolen away. The last thing her brother needed was another voice in his head.

Lachesis looked at the mirror, the glass obscured with an intentionally draped silk sheet. Quietly, she rose and sauntered over. touching the silver, ornate frame whose flowing design felt like the waves of an ocean beneath her fingers. Then she grabbed the sheet and tore it off.

She saw herself, but not in an empty room.

Bodies. Piles upon piles of naked, bloody corpses surrounded her. They trapped her, the congested dead heaped together in an inhumane pile. Discarded limbs protruded from the stinking mass of flesh. Flies buzzed in her ears and the stink of carrion drew maggots that slithered on the floor around her feet. Rotting flesh and steaming innards defiled her nostrils. Sick rose to her throat and she gagged, throwing the sheet desperately over the vile scene-

-and then she threw up, splattering the bedsheet. Fatigued, she stumbled backwards plonking down upon the mattress. From a flask, she took in water gratefully, washing her mouth and throat. From her bedside table she took a perfume bottle and doused herself in a floral lavender scent, desperate to spare her nose from the lingering stench of rot. But it had served its purpose. If Centa Isla fell, the pile of corpses would grow, those that died while she delayed her stand would find her in every reflection. Obscuring the mirrors would not alter the future. If the body count continued, it would not be long before her own reflection would avoid looking her in the eye.

Decisively, she rose and left her quarters, leather boots soft underfoot as she strode through the halls of Monument. She smiled at passing servants of whom she had grown quite fond of and headed towards the lavish quarters of Azrael several floors higher than her own. His door carried a plaque carved with the prestigious title of the now redundant Seat of Earth. She knocked politely.

"Enter."

Azrael stood at the end of the room; hands clasped behind his back as he overlooked the city. On the distant horizon of Forge Town, clouds of smoke and dust rose up like a pillar into the sky as the land that would hold the Obelisk was flattened and readied.

"Brother." She cleared her throat, unfurling an intricately woven blanket-topper from the bed and throwing it over an intricate glass mirror that towered beside the bed. "I wish to speak."

"Then do so carefully."

He turned as she approached him, wary of her vague reflection in the window. She focused on Azrael, on the still, vacant expression he wore as he stared out over the city.

"There's no going back. After this."

"I know."

Lachesis chewed anxiously upon her lip. Her words would need to be careful and deliberately vague just in case they were being listened to. She had learned the hard way what dissent against Galleo et'al entailed and her body still burned with the pain even now.

"So... what do you think?"

"I'm not sure what you mean."

Lachesis waited for him to give her a sign that he understood. His dark eyes looked expectantly at her and she had to swallow the words she wanted to say to avoid them explicitly tumbling into the air.

"You know what I mean."

He moved closer, casting his black eyes over her. As she felt them drilling into her, she remembered what they had looked like as children. Green, radiant green, much like her own. "I think you should concentrate. The final day is almost upon us."

"We can do it here, brother. Centa Isla can-"

He was upon her in an instant. His pale palm sealed her lips and his sheet white hair, once auburn, became dishevelled as he thrust forward. Those black eyes demanded absolute silence. She pushed his arm away, but kept her mouth closed. Meeting his stare, Lachesis sensed a conversation lying trapped between their glares.

Azrael was not going to budge. Those eyes were as black as he was stubborn and a distant part of her was relieved that not every part of him had been lost in service of the Dark One. Her brother had always been stubborn and for most of their life growing up on the run it had availed them well. But not this time. Lachesis was certain; Centa Isla was capable of what she needed, but without Azrael... it would likely never be possible.

Eventually, she felt herself concede. Breaking his gaze, she slinked towards the door. "We may never get a better chance."

"You say that every time." He shut her down, branding her little more than a crazed schemer with his tone.

"Maybe." Her teeth clenched in her mouth. "But this time... I..."

There was something here. Something in Centa Isla that she hadn't seen across the countless worlds they had conquered in the Dark One's name. It was difficult for her to put into words, even more difficult when she had to speak in abstract.

"Forget it. Rest well, brother."

She felt his dark eyes watching her as she approached the door to leave.

"Sister." His words pulled her back into the room. She turned, surprised that he would seek further audience. When she faced him again, his stiff demeanour had softened somewhat, as though he had finally realised he was talking to his baby sister and not another soulless savant.

"You are right to question things. To challenge." He spoke softer. "But this is our path."

"But- "

"A path on which we- *you* are safe. Healthy. Alive." He put any further dissent to bed with his next few words. "Just as mother and father had wished."

Lachesis wondered how he lived with it. The death, the carnage, was there no part of him that screamed to be free of the cycle of deceit and manipulation? Perhaps there was not. Perhaps the black eyes had bleached her brother's soul beyond the point of empathy. Of all the Omens, it was Azrael who had been chosen to descend into the heart of the Galleo et'al's dusty planet surface to commune with the Dark One itself. A different man emerged from the squalid earth that same day, forever changed.

"Quite right, brother." She smiled at him, masking the sinking in her chest. Their own home seemed such a vapid, distant memory that she was surprised he recalled it at all. The memory of her parents and her youth were nothing but a haze, a version of herself that she liked to keep separate from who she was today. It seemed her brother had little problem with his decisions and frankly, she envied him for it.

She departed his chambers. For a moment she lingered there, grip resting on the handle. What she felt from Centa Isla was hard to explain, but despite the hardships, struggle and misery that plagued this city there was something that toiled in the air around her. It was a latent energy of some kind, whether anger or grief or something else entirely, it was palpable to her. It alone wasn't enough, but combined with the magical might of Grandmaster and the coercion of the Omens, maybe it could have been.

She removed her hand from the door. Cursing her brother's stubborn ignorance. Not that it mattered now anyway. There would be another world and another one after that to try again.

—

Days passed. Rissa had lost track of how many. She dived in and out of fever, running hotter than the summer storms of Ashdown and colder than the most frigid night of Rainsturn. The wound on her abdomen would feel better one day, only to be at its worst the next. Treated with alcohol saved from the bar and stitched with old thread that had once been used to repair the crimson curtains, it wasn't a surprise that she was having so much difficulty healing.

She nourished herself with rationed soup and stale bread, collected and prepared by her and Sheppard in The Hound, which had become more of an infirmary than a tavern. The old, respected interior was so flood ruined it could no longer operate commercially. When able, Rissa would help make stews out of whatever food scraps the injured would bring in return for treatment and shelter. Those whose homes had been destroyed in the storm had found solace here. For how long they could last, Rissa was never sure.

This very evening Sheppard had warned she was doing too much, trying to take over every job and spreading herself too thin until nothing got done. She'd been banished upstairs now, feeling weaker than ever. Rissa dragged her painful body to the balcony to watch as the mysterious, foreboding construct continued to take shape on the horizon, feeling helpless as it grew in stature at the close of each day. The Obelisk. No sooner had the dust settled on the demolished chunk of Forge Town had Earth Versorcerers moved in to raise the skeleton of the doomsday pillar.

Through it all, Gault had yet to wake. Each evening Rissa secured the knot on Akor'shaki, only to find it loosened on every morning inspection. Gault's heartbeat had stabilised and his breathing had returned to a rhythmic consistency. In his catatonic state he looked peaceful, even his injury had fully healed, yet he would not wake. She had spoken to him, read him stories from her old books, pleaded with him to wake up, even allowed a handful of palm to strike his cheek, yet he never roused.

There was a futility and curse in the knowledge that whatever dark shape was forming on the horizon was going to destroy everything. At the very least those who dwelled now in the walls of the old tavern could find peace in the ignorance. She was not afforded that luxury, cursed with the knowledge of everything she'd experienced within the last rotation, yet was not strong enough to act. Her sword gathered cobwebs in the corner of the room, and when she lifted her Conduit off the bedside table a perfect clear dust free circle had formed. Her fingers had slipped many times from just the weight of a soup ladle, so swinging a heavy sword in her current state was out of the question. It dampened her spirits beyond what a hot bowl of nourishment could save.

Yet again, she stood on the balcony, watching as the ominous shape in the distance grew. It had started as nothing more than a sprout on the horizon but had grown exponentially in the days that had followed. There had been smoke and ash that billowed through the city, much of it still clung to the windows, tainting them with a murky haze. It only made the air thicker, but by now she was used to it. The storm had at the very least purged the air and blasted the smog back to the edge of the city. Smithy's Lung was no longer the threat it once was as a result. Older, unhealthier people than her were in this tavern and they seemed fine.

Even still…

The truth. Even now the words burned in her throat. The rancid truth of what dark fate beheld the city once the Obelisk was completed. It encased her tongue like a vice, unable to be spoken out of guilt. The people here deserved hope, deserved a chance to believe that the food they ate and the wounds they mended would buy them a future. Galleo et'al's looming presence was her burden and her responsibility. A small handful of those who had stumbled upon The Hound had hailed from the distant edges of Forge Town, speaking of their homes being either destroyed or seized. They said that spectators and reporters had arrived en masse yet had been turned away by a fierce force of Kingsguard who had locked down the area night and day where the Obelisk grew and were repelling any attempts to seek questions.

A radio broadcast from Monument a few days ago had tried to quell the growing unrest over the silhouette that grew on the horizon. The King spoke of history, of the struggles that had pervaded the city since the Reckoning. But he also spoke of hope and the future that lay on the horizon. He kept it brief, preaching vague well-rehearsed platitudes, committing to a date on which he would publicly address the entire city on the eighteenth of Stormsmarch. The funeral of his father, King Richard Clovis II.

That day was tomorrow.

Rissa knew that the crowds would gather in full force at the base of Monument to await the word of their King, hopeful for an announcement of good news. What lies would he unknowingly tell? He had clearly been cleverly duped to unwittingly lead Centa Isla into a trap. Rissa had felt nothing but dread as his animated euphoria about its future had crackled through the old radio. Everybody was talking about it. It was painful to hear their excited conversations about hope and deliverance, so Rissa returned to Gault's side, grateful to hear only the muffle of conversations and listen instead to the steady rhythm of his breath.

Had she given up? Rissa wasn't certain. The thought of death was no longer so terrifying. Her eyes were heavy despite resting and her energy levels had stooped so low that she only wanted to sleep. Apathy clung to her like a depressive cloud, stifling her words with negativity and dissonance as it threatened to absorb her completely. The reality was simple, as unchanging as the passage of time - they had failed. She had failed. Every trial, every challenge that they needed to succeed, had gone wrong. To be facing the end with two out of five of the Omens dead was a feat and even then, she had contributed to just the one. She wished that she could have felt prouder about herself, to be ready for the demonic army she had seen in her dreams annihilating the city with fire, steel and shadow. But she wasn't proud, not even slightly.

"What am I doing?" She stepped in from the balcony and closed the door, catching her own pale reflection in the glass. She stood there, useless, waiting for the end of the world. Gault continued his slumber, likely never to wake, not even to feel a demonsteel axe roll the head from his body.

As she stood there, wishing the time away, Rissa felt the floor tremble slightly. Raised voices rose through the old building, spurring her to exit the attic, quietly stepping down the wooden ladder to better hear what was being said. She crept, carefully planting her feet on the carpet, hearing the quiet groaning of the old floorboards. She had come to understand this old building intimately, knowing what step creaked the loudest, where the ground sank with age. She used that to her advantage now, creeping through the corridor and down the stairs where she could peer through the box window between her and the tavern proper.

Sheppard stood in the ruins of his tavern. Between the narrow glass she could only see him, he moved his arms powerfully, backing his muffled words. Even from here, Rissa could see that the tavern owner had lost much of the mass that he had carried when he first offered his room to them. His cheeks had sunken, eyes tired and beleaguered. The shirt that had once hugged his wide shoulders had begun to hang loosely over him. He claimed that it was just the weight of time that withered him away, but Rissa knew he'd been giving his rations to those who needed it more. A figure stepped into view alongside him, Rissa recognised the flash of gold immediately.

"Rand?" She opened the door and stepped out. As the wooden hinges creaked, it revealed the tavern was fuller than she had realised. There were no patrons on the other side of the door however, but a legion of eyepatches and hoods. Rand's face turned to her and his dry lips parted, revealing a row of gold teeth.

"There she is!" Rand gave her a wave. "Just who I was looking for."

"What are you doing here?" She stepped fully out of the door now, she gestured to the small legion of thugs that had amassed themselves in the tavern, so numerous that they spilled out through the front door into the streets.

"Quite simple." Rand replied. "We're here to rally the troops."

"I hope you don't mean me."

His eyes blazed with purpose and intent. "The city is on the precipice of change. There is a part for you if you are willing to play it."

"My part in what?"

"You heard the recent announcements, I'm sure."

"You mean the King's funeral?"

Rand smiled at the date. "Indeed. Our benevolent King may finally show his face in public. This is an opportunity not to be missed lightly."

Rissa felt a twinge of intrigue. There were machinations brewing beneath the shadow of Monument, Gault had said so plainly after he had acted as enforcer for Rand and Eclipse. But to what end?

"Friends!" Rand turned to address the large force of thugs that had spilled into the tavern. "Busy yourselves. Close the door behind you."

Rissa watched as the crowd began to depart. She realised quickly that there were more than just Empty Eyes thugs and masked members of Eclipse present in their ranks. There were citizens. Suits, top buttons undone. Tradespeople, wielding tools of their craft as a weapon. The more she looked the more she saw. Shopkeepers, homeless, Synth addicts, renegade CIPD Officers, socialites, barmen, waiters, journalists and even the occasional glint of a noble. They all left in droves, shutting the door at Rand's command. What was this?

Rand pulled up a chair and sat in it, hearing the squelch of a damp cushion beneath him. "Join me."

Rissa did so, giving Sheppard a reassuring smile as she sat opposite the Eclipse spokesman.

"What's going on?" She asked. "That's... a Downtown army."

"Not just Downtown." Rand smiled. "There's more. So many more."

As he spoke, floorboards creaked around The Hound and many of the beleaguered bodies of those who had been housed beneath Sheppard's roof emerged. They came down the stairs, dragging injured legs and tired eyes.

"Arm yourselves outside, friends." Rand spoke as if he knew each of them by name. That may as well have been true for they smiled at him. "Take food and water, fuel yourself for the blush of dawn is soon upon us!"

Sheppard smiled proudly. Many came and thanked him for his aid and his piety, leaving small gifts on the bar beside him. Wreaths, trinkets, heirlooms. They acted as though nothing they owned mattered, like the rising of the next dawn would be a new world.

"Rand, what is this?"

"Reckoning, my dear, in the truest sense. A pity your violent friend cannot join us. His power would have been a great asset." Rand watched as the newly anointed departed the tavern. He gave them a charismatic wave. "We are all Eclipse. The hands that have toiled for endless nights just to survive reign after reign of arrogance and oppression."

"Nobody here said a thing."

"We were sworn not to." Sheppard spoke up. "I didn't mean to deceive you."

"You're in on this?"

"I am." A proud smile stretched the beard across Sheppard's face. "If not a tavern, this place can be a fortress. So long as it serves a purpose, I can too."

Rand's golden smile only grew. "We work in the shadows of the tower they built to oppress us. But now, the embargo is broken. The Eclipse is upon us and only dawn will follow."

He rose grandly from his chair and proffered his hand to her. "Join me. I had wished to leave with your companion, but I can make do with you."

Rissa's mind spun. Impossible, yet here it was. Outside this very tavern, the citizenry of Centa Isla had gathered under a single banner. Deliverance: the promise of a new dawn that had been heralded now by the Eclipse. This was lightning in a bottle, powerful enough to strike her languid heart into action, feeling it pounding in her chest. Every beat was adrenaline, hope, a second chance to stop the Omens by removing the source of their influence. Monument and King Grayson.

"So much for you being a journalist."

At that, Rand laughed. "Every copy sold, a Wreath to the cause."

"You're welcome for my part in that, by the way." Rissa rose and clasped her hand around his. "I'm not at full strength yet, but I'll help you."

"And we are all the merrier for it." Rand rose and together, he led them onto the streets of Forge Town. The streets were filled with bodies, many of them armed with weapons, where others wielded makeshift arms crafted from pipes or planks of wood. Yet for all the tension, anger and anticipation in the air. It was so quiet. There were no torches, no drums of war, no chants of battle, just silent anticipation. Food, weaponry and protection was available readily for those in need, incentive enough for many to join the ranks. At the behest of Kenneth Rand, bodies began to pour into The Hound, building up a staging area. Sheppard remained and upon sharing a knowing glance, Rissa felt safe knowing Gault wouldn't be discovered as long as he was present.

Monument leered on the horizon, the eastern clock face creeping with the passage of time. It was a prime spot, one long stretch of road that led all the way onto Monument's doorstep. The road was used in the past to transport goods in and out of the city centre but now ran all the way up to the edge of the city where an endless horizon waited.

Rand led her through the gathering force, towards a seized storefront where a war table had been erected. He bid her look at the table.

"What you see here is only half of the force."

"You're kidding."

"We are many, but few of our number are Versorcerers." He gestured to Downtown on the map, where their forces gathered at the base of The Blades, ready to storm up the throat of the city and into Monument. Attacks from the south and the east formed the main thrust of their plan. "Your presence is valued."

"So, the King dies, what then?"

Rand smiled. "We celebrate."

"And then…?"

"Well. That decision is not mine to make."

Rissa sighed. There was every chance it was going to be one evil for another in Centa Isla, but whatever the alternative, it was surely better than annihilation. She wished Gault was awake, his input here may have given her a clearer direction than to just go with the crowd, but she'd have to trust her own judgement from now on.

"The King will speak at seven. Dawn will be breaking, just as poetically as he intends it to be."

"What then?"

"Then we attack." He spoke as if it was the most obvious thing in the world. There was little plan or coordination in play here, but Rissa understood why. They had an army of grievers, addicts and workers. Their prowess for tactical decisions on a battlefield was non-existent. But using their rage, using their hatred, was the key that was going to bring Monument crumbling down.

"I can work with that." Rissa blew air. "I suppose I'll go and get ready."

"You should. Then eat, rest. Be at your strongest." Those were the last words that Rand had time to give her, for an eager queue that had gathered outside the war tent demanded his attention. They were called in one by one as Rissa was leaving, her ears catching the first reports from the City Centre as the roads were getting closed in preparation for the funeral and subsequent speech. Her stomach churned with anxiety, yet her chest fluttered with excitement. She felt strong, a phantom strength perhaps while the adrenaline lasted, but in that moment, the fatigue and malaise that had previously consumed her had disappeared.

The tavern had been transformed so quickly into a base for triage and first aid. Blankets had been laid across rows of tables, holding the injured and the unconscious in the absence of support from the Royal Hospital. There were even Midwives, their own enclave forming in the furthest corner of the main building. This was an army, but it represented more than a force of war and reckoning like Rand claimed. This was a collective of those who had suffered the consequences of Centa Isla's decline, forced to sacrifice and endure without hope. But the choice to be here, prepared to give birth on what could amount to a historic day for those who called this city home, told her that there had been hope present for much longer than she had realised. Perhaps she just hadn't been willing to see it, nor inclined to search for it. The desire for better days was a wish so powerful that it had kept the populace alive even in their darkest hour.

Rissa went upstairs, politely stepping aside as people ferried medical goods, blankets and cushions out of the various rooms. She waited until the hallway had been vacated before pulling down the hatch to the attic and promptly pulling it up behind her.

Gault lay as dormant as she had left him. She approached and took a seat upon a stool that hadn't moved from his side in several days. Quietly, she watched his chest move. In his peaceful sleep, he looked so unburdened. In waking, there had always been a heaviness to his face, as though the weight of his problems and his guilt was dragging down his flesh. He looked free here, lips pursed as funnels of air came and went. He looked younger and Rissa realised that she didn't even know his age. There was so much that she still didn't know despite her intrusion into his memories. Were they even friends? Even allies?

"You think you get to sit this one out?" She stared daggers into him. "You think that's fair?"

He didn't respond. Her mind began to pulse with strain, warbling and reverberating around her skull as though her brain was overheating. The pain spread quickly, throbbing in her temples as she watched not even the flit of recognition cross his face. Rissa felt a sudden surge of anger.

"WAKE UP!" She grabbed his shoulders and violently shook him. "WAKE UP, DAMN IT!"

Overwhelm gripped her heart, feeling like a thousand coils of barbed wire pressed against it with every beat. This wasn't her fight. It never was. She'd stumbled blindly into this underground war looking for something to distract herself from her vapid life. Now she was here. Alone. The only one in the entire city who knew the consequences of failure, who understood what had to be done for the city to be saved. And she wasn't telling anybody. Why? Was she stupid? Was she so virtuous that the burden could only be carried by her and her alone?

No.

Rissa remembered the memorial to the young officer who she had sent to die in the sewers when she had first met Gault. The messages and gifts left by family had made her realise then and there why she couldn't simply report what was happening to the CIPD. The Omens made people disappear, had a say in every decision that cascaded down the ranks of the city. And now, if she were to start spurting out everything she knew about a cosmic force coming to destroy everything would she even be taken seriously? She wouldn't have believed it herself had Akor'shaki not invaded her mind with the information she needed to believe the truth.

Her thoughts fell to the treacherous blade. The coiled chain of Akor'shaki was still wound up tightly around the bedposts, undisturbed since this morning when she had secured the bonds. Perhaps it was for the best that she was alone. There should have been trust between her and Gault by now. But she didn't possess it. Whether it was Akor'shaki's influence over him that prevented that wall from coming down, she didn't know, but she had trusted him before and ended up imprisoned. He'd saved her, that much was true, but the damage had been done. Rissa had tried her best to control him, she truly had, but so long as Akor'shaki desired her death, Gault was not someone she could trust with her life.

Making up that absent trust had been difficult. She had done her best to make herself as strong as possible in the face of an enemy who had crushed her defining powers with a wave of his pale hand. And now with their one chance to make things right again she was on her own.

Yet despite all the risk. She didn't want to be alone.

She cried, burying her head onto his stomach. With a clenched fist, she slammed her hand into his chest-plate over and over. "Please! Please! I can't do this on my own!"

He still did not stir and she felt a part of her freeze over. The last of her tears dried and she rose, wiping her puffy eyes. She stared at him with an emotion that she didn't intend to creep in.

Disgust.

"Leave it all to me, then." She took her sword from the corner of the room and removed the cobwebs with a brush of her hand. The steel felt heavy. Then, she lifted her mother's Conduit, blowing the dust from the old silver before slipping it over her finger. Immediately, the emotion disappeared as endorphins washed through her. Guilt lingered, but she forced it back. Having her mind clouded and unfocused wasn't going to do her any good.

A glance out the window showed Monument's clock face. Eight PM. It would be less than twelve hours until the city would shake from the conflict. The second silhouette drew her eye. The Obelisk had grown rapidly over the last few days and had ceased to grow any higher. It could well have been finished or perhaps put on hold for the funeral of the old King. Rissa wasn't certain.

She put her ear to the attic floor, listening for movement beneath her. Finding none, she lowered the ladder, taking one last hopeful glance at Gault before disappearing, sealing him above the hatch.

The time for a final attempt to save Centa Isla had come. Fit to fight or not, she had to do her best, but this time without the presence of Gault at her side.

—

King Grayson Clovis felt his nerves twisting in his gut. He breathed slowly, and deliberately, keeping at bay the looming nausea that lurked in his throat. He could hear the crowd even from the top floor of Monument. There were chants, yells, cries and pleas, absolved into one horrific droning song whose noise carried through the quiet halls of his tower. They sang for answers which he would soon be providing. The curtains in his quarters were drawn shut. Grayson struggled to look upon the crowd at this moment in time.

The preparations were complete. The body of his father had been incinerated by Fire Versorcerers; the ashes now placed in an ornate urn that was to be raised among earth to form a statue in a celebration of the Clovis line. It was more than his father deserved, but Grayson intended to honour him in accordance with tradition. Greener pastures lay ahead and a new era would begin, with him at the helm. He had to remind himself of the grim truth that it was he who snuffed the last life from his father's lungs. The realisation of the truth came in infrequent bouts, bringing with it washes of guilt and grief that he had no choice but to bite down. For the good of the city, he had been offered little choice.

The King of Centa Isla stared at himself in the mirror. His servants had provided the finest frippery for such an event. A grand, violet doublet with flared sleeves and tassels around the collar that made his neck itch. The entire outfit felt dated, slipping into the distant obscurity of time with every day that passed. He undid the string that held the collar together, allowing it to drift casually out. He felt more comfortable, like the sort of the King he wanted to be. Traditional, yet informal. A smile crossed his face. This was the real start of his reign.

A knock at his door. Grayson glanced at the timepiece that clicked on the wall of his quarters. Fifteen minutes until he was due to speak. He just wanted to be out there, amongst it all. The adrenaline might at the very least quell his nerves.

"Enter." He bid his voice to be strong.

The former Seat of Air of the dissolved Elemental Council entered. Marco Barrett bowed. "My King, are you well?"

"A nervous wreck." Grayson admitted with a wry chuckle. He had come to enjoy the company of the ex-Seat. His work to organise and coordinate this entire event had allowed him to better understand his advisor. "This will take some convincing."

"You wouldn't be here if you didn't know what to say, My King." Marco approached, a reassuring hand dropping onto his shoulder. "Tell them what you've been telling us. The hard work to make it happen is done. This is the easy part."

"Perhaps. Thank you, friend." He had been putting off looking out the window, content enough with the noise to paint his picture. But he felt emboldened by the words of his advisor and dared to step toward the window. His breath pitched as he parted the curtains and looked beyond the glassy veil. A sea of torches stretched down The Blades, as far as the eye could see. The streets were crowded. People stood on cars, filling up the rooftops. Those at the front pressed against the Kingsguard blockade he had set up around the pedestal from which he would speak. But in seeing it, Grayson no longer felt apprehension, but responsibility. His people deserved answers. After today the shape of the Obelisk that grew on the horizon would become a shadow of fortune, rather than fear.

He descended the tower, musing on the choice words he was going to use as the elevator clunked and rattled its way toward the ground floor. The cacophony of demanding voices grew louder and louder, peaking as the ding of the elevator reaching its destination was drowned out by the noise. Marco attended him, living in his shadow silently. Grayson stepped out into the foyer and could well have sworn that the walls were shaking. A legion of Kingsguard greeted him, offering a salute.

"Are you ready, My King?" One of the soldiers asked him, pauldrons decorated with the insignia of a commander.

"I see no reason to delay them further." Grayson held his voice firm, falsely puffing out his chest as though to instil deeper confidence. His father had never once expressed any sentiment resembling nerves, at least not outwardly. Grayson almost felt inferior but had to remind himself that he was nervous because he cared, where his father would have likely been drunk or just didn't give a damn.

Just then, he felt an absence. It took him a moment to realise that Azrael was nowhere to be seen. He was used to his stoic advisor blending into the background, but it wasn't usually out of his sight. He put words to his concern. "Where is Azrael?"

The commander shrugged. "Unsure, My King. I thought he attended you."

"No." Grayson chewed on the word, unsure. The clock struck the hour and he knew he had little time. "Send a man. Seek him. I want him by my side."

"At once, My King." The commander grunted, slamming the base of his spear against the ground in salute. He pulled a soldier aside, promptly removing him from the formation and filled his place by tightening the rank. The soldier surged off into Monument.

It was no desire to share this moment with Azrael that spurred Grayson to seek him out, but a dapple of mistrust. It had lingered within him from the first second they had formed their fragile alliance. Their relationship had always unsettled him, Azrael holding power due to the promise of salvation for the city. Azrael dangled this promise like bait, forcing Grayson to fight for scraps of control among it all.

"You've worked for this, My King." Marco spoke behind him. "Don't let your nerves ruin the moment."

Grayson felt a small flush of warmth in his chest. Kind words, indeed. Necessary besides. He turned to his advisor and gave him a nod. "Gratitude, my friend. We shall celebrate when this is over."

"FORM UP!" The commander slammed the base of his spear into the ground again. The ranks of Kingsguard copied, facing the door as they filled in around where the two men stood. "FORWARD MARCH!"

Grayson moved, surrounded by the rattling of plate armour as the wide doors of Monument were thrown open by his attendants. The noise that had been confined to outside the tower blasted in - almost tempestuous enough to throw him from his feet. His eyes struggled to focus on the writhing mass of bodies that stretched eternally ahead of him. Whether they jeered or cheered he couldn't tell, all sound and motion had blended into a dizzying warbling of noise. It felt as though the entire city had come to life and stood before him. He kept going only because his marching legion forced him along. They escorted him out the gates and onto a large, stone ramp leading to a podium. Kingsguard Versorcerers awaited, their fingers twitching with spells ready at a moment's notice. Grayson admitted to feeling comfort from their presence. No projectiles had been thrown which already made him more popular than his father, yet that could change were his words not appropriately chosen.

He stood in front of a pedestal draped in silk that was embossed with the royal emblem. His guard force returned to the base of the ramp, ready to protect him on the return trip back to the safety of Monument. The commander and Marco rose with him. At the top of the small set of stairs, a Wind Versorcerer awaited, bowing politely in his presence, ready to project his words upon the wind itself to reach even those who could not see him from the bottom of The Blades. Grayson returned the nod, indicating that he was now prepared to address the population.

The Versorcerer's eyes blazed azure and Grayson felt the air around him tighten and focus as the spell was put into place. He had been assured that he would not deafen himself, nor would he even hear the echo of his own voice. All that was asked was that he paced himself to allow the winds to carry his words before continuing.

"Good people of Centa Isla!" He began, feeling the constricting and loosening of the breaths that left his lips as his words were magically launched down The Blades for all to hear. He controlled his breathing but found it surprisingly easy now that he was up here. The chants had ended, the rambunctious street had gone quiet. "I thank you for gathering here before me. These have been uncertain times, truly, some of the worst put to text. But...!"

He paused, allowing his words to travel. In that space between his next sentence, he took in the faces that decorated the street. There were few nobles, likely too afraid to mix so intimately with the masses. Those that were present looked tired, beaten, deprived and hungry. A twinge of disgust that he sought to repress flooded him. Even as he stood up here, the images of his mother's grave being defiled lingered.

"I stand here today to celebrate and mourn the life of my father!" He heard jeers and slander from the crowd. Grayson chose to ignore them for their opinions were likely all they had left. "He was not a popular figure. Yet the past retains its importance for our future."

He cleared his throat. "My mother died in a moment just like this… A brick thrown by the hands of those she wished to protect. I know, you may not have felt her love, but it was there. I promise. I commit this moment to her also."

With a wave of his hand, Earth Versorcerer's emerged at the base of Monument. Four of them in total. Their Conduits blazed as they spun The Algarethan Verse together, raising a statue on the spot that bore the resemblance of his father in his prime. A powerful, imposing figure, not the gaunt husk that had rotted in bed for the last days of his reign. Weaved in amongst the very stone itself were his ashes.

There was no applause as the statue of his father formed, but Grayson had expected that. This moment was his to indulge in after all the sacrifices he had made. He looked upon the likeness of his father and allowed himself a satisfied smile of absolution before returning his attention to the crowd.

"I thank you for witnessing my grandstanding." He allowed a small chuckle to echo out to the masses before looking to the Obelisk, throwing a grand gesture toward it. "I mark this day. The death of a King, but the rise of a civilisation once again!"

The crowd thrummed with energy and anticipation. Grayson allowed himself to indulge in it before continuing.

"That construct is an Obelisk. Where we have struggled to find resources from our own means, we have found a solution… out in the very stars that visit us every dark." He looked at the construct. Finished in all its glory. It was not a pretty thing, jagged and twisting into the sky like a gnarled branch of an old tree. But it was going to save him, save everyone. "With this, we can restore the magic we lost to Reckoning. Undo the work of our foolish ancestors whose consequences we have borne for so long!"

"You will have questions and they will be answered. But..." He smiled, raising his hands to the people. "The Resource Crisis is over!"

Now, The Blades erupted. Torches flew into the air, car alarms wailed as they were trampled upon as people jumped and cheered. The animosity was gone and Grayson could only feel smug about it all. It was fickle, all of it. But this was exactly what he had wanted, to be loved, to be cheered and cherished by the people whom he served. Yet that was no longer the case, it seemed. He felt no satisfaction from their joy. He couldn't put the image out of his mind. The steel and the wood that struck his mother's grave. The greed, the opulent parties that spat in the face of philanthropy. Was there anything truly left to save? Had he made the right decision? Centa Isla had a long way to go before he could call it a city he was proud of ruling.

For now, he had taken a first step toward correcting the curse of his family name. That was what mattered now. The Clovis line would-

The briefest surge of light on the horizon distracted him. It was gone before he could even question if his mind played tricks. The Obelisk, did it just-

"My King." Marco spoke from behind him.

"Yes, friend?" Grayson turned, grateful-

A dagger slipped between his ribs and twisted cruelly.

"Only dawn will follow."

16

The embers from hastily lit fires crackled and hissed as makeshift tents sprang up like mole hills around the walls of Monument. Tired, excited eyes peered at the guards who were proudly putting the finishing touches to the podium in readiness for the royal address. Seven in the morning was the time chosen to allow the normal working day to continue afterwards. The race for the best vantage point was underway and Rissa found herself much further down The Blades than she'd expected. She was among the first batch of Eclipse renegades ordered to assemble in inconspicuous clumps near the tower. More would follow, arriving in scattered groups from Downtown to the south and Forge Town to the east. Each passing hour drew more and more spectators and the streets were soon heaving with bodies. People pushed forward, aggressively seeking a spot on the front row, which incited small skirmishes of violence. It never lasted more than a few swings before faceless hands reached from among the bodies and pulled them apart. Rissa felt uneasy as she was barged and jostled by the sweeping crowd, feeling an overwhelming claustrophobia creeping in. Even Akor'shaki's chain around her throat was just about preferable to this. Frustration began to bubble as she was pushed forward by a surge in the crowd. A look over her shoulder revealed a growing mass of bodies as far as the eye could see.

Who amongst this crowd was with Eclipse and who wasn't she couldn't tell but her stomach churned with the promised chaos. Once the fighting began she'd do well to avoid being trampled, let alone stopping any sinister plot. Envy was the emotion she felt towards those savvy business owners who ran a storefront on The Blades. They took payments of Wreaths in return for roof access, lining their pockets while allowing those with enough jangling coins to spectate without the constant succession of pushes and shoves. Rissa had little of any value except for a Conduit which hugged her index finger tightly. She could have moved it on for a handful of Wreaths, but she sensed it would be proving very valuable in what was to come.

The air was thick with anticipation. Voices muffled into a drone but some conversations were distinguishable. One woman prayed to the skies for a final hope for Centa Isla whilst another berated the King and cast scorn upon his reign. Opportunist pickpockets dipped their sly fingers into handbags or jackets, moving nimbly through the surging crowd. Rissa interlocked stares with one of them, their guilty hand sunk into the pocket of another like a child caught in the biscuit tin. Her stare said it all and the thief relinquished his hand and disappeared, rewarding her silence with a parting flit of gratitude in the form of a wry smile. Sirens flashed at the front of the mass as the crowd were marshalled by a combination of the CIPD and the Kingsguard, using tall shields to push back those who were arrogant enough to encroach on royal grounds. Their presence was, to all purposes, a false sense of security, as should the crowd become aggressive and unruly, their weak line of defence would be no match. Unfortunately for them, Rissa knew that was to be the case. She glanced at the clock as it rapidly approached the hour. The old hands clunked with the weight of time, bringing the city ever closer to change. The pit in her stomach grew with every passing minute. Her ears were filled with the droning of the crowd, their words no longer intelligible among the growing unrest, as though every minute added to the growing tension bubbling within a simmering cauldron of mania.

The hand struck the hour and the King of Centa Isla strode up to his podium. Rissa felt the energy dissipate and a wave of subdued calm engulfed the crowd. He spoke of family, heritage, the struggles of the people and most of all - the future. Rissa stood for the first time without being jostled. It was a sobering conversation and the tension was palpable, so thick in the air that it may as well have been the smog that had drifted in. The tensions rose as the statue of Richard Clovis II was unveiled, the legion of Kingsguard and CIPD at the front of the pile intervening as people threw themselves towards the monument of their tormentor. But it was soon quelled by Grayson's words as he gestured toward the looming shadow of the Obelisk on the horizon.

As he spoke, Rissa wished for ignorance. The crowd around her responded positively to the shadow of their potential saviour, the excitement and buzz was electrifying in the air, causing the hairs on her arms to prickle. Yet she could feel only dread for she knew what the promised salvation truly entailed for these people. For her father. For her.

"The Resource Crisis is over!"

The words came with a reverb. The billowing wind magic that funnelled through the street carried with it the promise of a tomorrow. And The Blades erupted. Hands flew into the air and lungs were tested as they screamed and yelled their relief into the sky. The hard times were over, it seemed, yet Rissa knew they were just to begin. She felt like a spectator, as though she was back in another vision. She stood amongst a sea of flailing celebratory limbs as she waited quietly for the signal to come.

Then, a flash caught her eye. Few others may have spotted it, their faces buried in the shoulders of their friends and loved ones. The Obelisk flared for a moment, a blinding light that burned for no longer than a half-second, lighting up the horizon. Rissa stared at it, waiting to see if it would happen again, but it didn't. Dread pooled in her stomach, what was-

Screams came from the front of the crowd. Rissa leaped into the air, seeking to catch a glimpse of the podium from the tall heads in front of her. There was no sign of the King.

Then, there was a great explosion of magical fire in the sky. A flare; the signal. There was hesitation, born of the good news they had just received. But then the first people started to yell and charge towards the front, the rest followed.

"Only dawn will follow!" The shout echoed through the crowd. Rissa felt her breath hitch and adrenaline spiked as she surged through the bodies. Many stood confused, seeking shelter and cover from the sudden chaos whereas the rest knew their task. Rissa moved with the masses, pushed along by eager arms in her back. But, just as she sought to break away from the surge and seek high ground, there was a change in the air. Her senses diluted and she slowed to an eventual halt. People surged past her, their shoulders colliding with hers, but she barely felt it. The Blades had descended into carnage as the first wave of rebellion hit the Kingsguard blockade.

Yet Rissa was distracted. The air was thick, the stinging smell of sulphur invaded her nostrils. She had both seen and felt this before and it took her a moment to recall from where.

Her visions.

She looked up at the Obelisk on the horizon, horrified to see that the light had returned. Her arms hung helplessly at her side as the assault on Monument intensified. Citizens surged past her, wielding their trade tools and torches. One of them even stopped in front of her, yelling encouragement in her face. She didn't hear them, nor did she even look their way. Her heart felt as though it was missing beats as she stared, the light intensifying all the while. Bodies already lined the streets and courtyard beneath Monument. The carnage was indiscriminate; dead Kingsguard entombed within their golden armour, fallen CIPD officers and just as many rioters. Even as the overwhelming number of citizens pushed the blockade further and further back, there was a word that invaded her mind, yet this thought was distinctly her own.

Pointless.

Her head began to pound, like an alien pressure was compressing her skull like a nutcracker. The air thickened even more and the smell of sulphur intensified to an overpowering burning that scoured the back of her throat, causing her to gag. A look at the Obelisk revealed a beam of light that had begun to burn from the top of the structure. It fished through the clouds, disappearing into the limit of human perception as it soared upwards, beyond the city and into nothingness like a line cast into the great dark beyond. Nobody else seemed to notice. Perhaps it was the adrenaline that pulsed through them, somehow enough not to notice the atmospheric changes

Then, a wave of power reverberated through the city. The entire foundations shook as the floating city warbled like a plate balanced on the tip of a spear. The skies themselves heaved with strain as though birthing a monster. A mountainous crackle thundered across the atmosphere, like a thousand distant mountains had shattered. The bones in her body rattled as a great, crumbling mass lurched into orbit and blotted out the sky. A swathe of deep crimson bathed the city, casting bloody shadows through the City Centre as the light was swallowed and replaced by the tormenting visage of Galleo et'al.

The Dark One had come.

Its titanic body was a half-crescent as it disappeared beneath the horizon. The heat that it radiated made her insides burn with infernal fire, yet she had never felt as cold as she did in the presence of such evil. No sooner had It leered over the city did the first pieces of its withering shell break away, soaring down from the atmosphere like meteors. The fighting stopped; the city delved into a terrified silence as the first chunks of the ancient planet crashed into the courtyard of Monument, levelling the freshly raised statue of the late King. It exploded, digging a great crater into the hollows of the city as it steamed and boiled with atmospheric heat. Rissa watched as the smoke and ash cleared.

People started screaming and Rissa could only barely see the distant shadow of a horrific creature that emerged. The severed limbs of those who stood too close spilled into the air. But she didn't need to see it to know what it was, nor did she need to see to know that many, many more were following. The sky was alight with falling stars, hundreds, perhaps thousands of Galleo et'al's army fell at once, disappearing over the tall buildings only to rise up as a plume of smoke. The assault on Monument ceased as rioters and defenders alike ran. Dark shadows chased them, twisted, demonic beings that had evaded Rissa even in her visions. The ones she did recognise were just as destructive and malicious as she had witnessed, striding through the crowds, trampling with their gore-stained plate boots and cleaving limbs with demonsteel poleaxes.

She wanted to fall to her knees, but shock and horror kept her standing. She had seen this in her visions so vividly, yet it failed to compare to seeing it happen to her city. Her home. Chunks of skyscrapers came away as the meteors crashed through them, bringing entire streets down upon those who dared flee. It was happening so quickly. It was a wonder no world had ever stood a chance. Fire crossed the sky as Downtown and Forge Town were peppered with craterous impacts as the demon's presence stalked further into the city. Rissa watched with terror as one sailed through the air towards the domed shield of Grandmaster. The crumbling earth spun with the weight and fury of its descent, yet upon striking the shield - it disappeared into nothing but dust, scattered immediately to the violent winds that blew through the city.

"Grandmaster..." Rissa realised it all too slowly. She shook her head, forcing the stagnation that had begun to set into her bones. She whirled toward anybody who would listen, thrusting a finger toward the domed academy. "GRANDMASTER! GET TO GRANDMASTER!"

Some listened, redirecting their scrambling panic west, others ignored her, screaming as they disappeared into dark alleys where monsters already prowled. Their screams were short lived as their gored carcasses splattered the walls like grisly art. Rissa turned her back and ran, breaking from the carnage that had become The Blades.

As the street population surged west, Rissa found herself unable to follow them. On her finger, her Conduit felt heavy, as though burdened by the weight of responsibility. Her gaze pulled back, towards Forge Town in the east where the dominating shadow of the Obelisk rested. It was the source of all of this. She knew better than anybody else here what its purpose served. With that lone knowledge, came the dreaded responsibility of action.

She grimaced, realising what she had to do. Her legs heaved with protest as she turned in the street and moved against the crowd, heading straight towards the horrific demons who hunted them.

—

Gault felt a powerful sensation course through his veins. His muscles contracted in his body, the pain enough to pry his heavy eyes open as he took a long, conscious breath that broke into an aggravating cough.

We have not failed yet. Get up.

"What's happening?" Even as he spoke, visages of terrible memories filled his mind as the burning of sulphur attacked his nose. The curtains to his chambers were drawn, but a blazing crimson presence sought to burn through the thin fabric, casting a volcanic streak of dark power that ran across the room. A dark power that he recognised all too well.

You know.

"No." Gault moved from the bed. His body was tired and his joints were wracked with numbness from lying sedentary for days. With legs that wobbled with every step as his body got used to functioning again, he staggered to the window and threw open the curtains, wincing as the blazing image of Galleo et'al sat on the horizon. He dropped to his knees, fingers trailing down the glass. A great fire blazed through much of the City Centre. It spread rapidly, bringing with it a distant cacophony of screams that chorused through the city, diluted by the sealed window. A surge of anger rushed through him. He had slept like a child while Galleo et'al had arrived? How could he have let this happen?

Stop. Free me. This can yet be prevented.

Free? Gault touched his abdomen, first finding the wound that he had sustained fully healed. The flesh was new, soft to the touch and unscarred by a life of combat and squalor. Next, he found the chain of Akor'shaki loose and trailing. He followed it, finding the coil of his weapon snaked around the bed stand and pinned beneath several heavy books. Rissa's books.

She sought to bind me. The words of the blade hissed in his mind as he unbound it, as though it had read his question before he had even begun to ask it.

We have no time for this. The city burns.

There was noise beneath him. Floorboards groaning beneath weight that it was not built to carry. Gault shook the fatigue from his arms and approached the hatch, opening it slowly. He lowered himself down, feeling the strain on his unused biceps. He held his breath as he planted his boots down softly on the old carpet, offering a quiet prayer to the floorboards to remain silent as he sought the source of the noise downstairs. He kept low, the howl of the chaos outside bleeding in as he peered between the wooden slats that held the wooden railing together.

It took him a moment to notice a woman crouched behind the bar. She held a child in her arms, her hand collapsed tightly over the child's mouth. She had noticed him already, seeking to snare his attention with her eyes. He allowed the mother to guide him, gesturing with the flits of her eyes towards the entrance to The Hound that lay outside his field of vision. It didn't take him long however until the source of their silence revealed itself. A slim, hound-like creature padded into the old tavern. Gault recognised it instantly. Canine in appearance yet deviating horrifically from tradition with a serrated jaw that went as far back as its neck, giving it a jaw span that could consume and crush a humanoid head with a single bite. On its back, lay four dormant limbs, curled up in silence, waiting for their turn to carry the demonic body forward should it be overturned.

A Hound of Xer.

He didn't need Akor'shaki's encyclopaedic wisdom. He knew it already. He had dealt with hundreds of these monstrosities while they had stalked him across the surface of Galleo et'al's crumbling wastes for an entire year. They were trackers, capable of sniffing out magic entities, sources and traces of spellwork. But what hounded Gault the most was their ability to gather reinforcements. With their terrifying jaw span came the ability to release a horrific shrill that would serve as a beacon of interest for other demonic forces to zero in on. Their weakness was their remaining senses, sight and hearing. Both of which Gault intended to take advantage of.

The Hound of Xer drooled molten spittle as it moved slowly through the tavern, the liquid sizzling on the wooden floor. It sought the woman and her child, likely having tracked them here for an easy feast. It approached them slowly, detecting the intricate traces of magic that had been Resynthesised into the clothes they wore. Gault rose slowly, stepping up onto the railing. He stretched out Akor'shaki's chain and leaped, landing directly atop the demon and coiling Akor'shaki's chain around its titanic maw. It immediately tried to shrill, but he tightened the chain around its jaws and dug Akor'shaki's shrunken blade clean into its neck, claiming vital arteries as it spat and gargled bubbling, demonic blood over the woodwork.

It died pathetically and Gault rose, beckoning for the mother and child to emerge from their hiding.

"Thank you. Thank you so much." Tears surged down her cheeks as she shepherded her youngest from hiding. "Has Reckoning come again?"

"Worse." Gault told her. He pointed up to the mezzanine, where the attic hatch remained open. "Shelter up there. Close the hatch, draw the curtains, use no magic and let nobody in."

"Thank you."

Gault smiled as the mother ushered her child up the stairs to safety. He deserved no such thanks. He had allowed this to happen, drooling over a pillow like a sleeping infant while the city ended around him.

Accept their gratitude. Even if we have only prolonged their deaths.

Gault stepped out of The Hound, closing the doors behind him. Unfiltered by the dusty old window, the sight of Galleo et'al in orbit flared horrible memories of his past failure, of his burden that he still bore. If he could not have revenge on this day then he at least wanted death as a final release.

There will be no such quick death for you. Akor'shaki's intrusive thoughts blended with his own. *The torment of a traitor will be eternal. Or as long as your mind and body can last.*

Gault grimaced. Ahead of him, the once omnipresent shadow of Monument looked diminutive with the mass of Galleo et'al dominating the crimson horizon. His gut lurched as he saw a second, unfamiliar silhouette, one that had not been present before, twisted into the air like a necrotic limb reaching for the heavens, bearing a shimmering light that connected to the Dark One. An Obelisk of the very same design that had risen over the royal palace back home.

It has brought the Dark One here.

It was gargantuan in comparison to the Obelisk that had brought Galleo et'al to his world before. Why the enormity in size, Gault did not fully understand, but what was clear was that it may pose his only chance of repelling this invasion.

"Will destroying it be enough?

Do you think I have all the answers? I know as much as you.

Breaking into a sprint, Gault surged through the desolate streets of Forge Town. The carnage had not yet reached The Hound, the scouting demon within was proof of that much, but it didn't take long until he found many of the old buildings sunken and aflame. Many of the old walls had been caved in by poleaxe or by the thrown bodies of their owners, the corpses still nestled within the old brick. Their skin was blue from asphyxiation, the red coils of strain around their necks granting him all the information that he needed to understand just what foul creature had dropped these people to their deaths.

Scarr'dath. Above you.

Gault looked up and saw its slimy, slithering shadow wending through the sky toward him. A vaguely humanoid shape twisted in the air overhead, arms bearing sharp claws. Yet, it became serpentlike just below the shoulders and its bat-like wings carried the demon toward him. The leathery appendages tucked into its scaly body as it dived down. Its tail, rounded like a noose, sought him, desperate to squeeze the life from his body as it lifted him into the air. However, the Scarr'dath didn't know that he knew exactly what it intended to do. At the last moment, Gault swerved, grabbing onto the tail of the creature and digging his heels into the ground. He strained, keeping it at arm's length while it hissed and spat, wings flapping viciously as it sought to twist its limber, vaguely humanoid body back to bite and claw at him.

Gault drove a fist into its snarling face, mantling Akor'shaki's chain around its throat as he planted a foot into the noose-like tail as though it were a stirrup. He planted his other foot upon its spine, feeling the jagged ridges of its bones digging into his boot as he bid the demon fly, yanking the chain as though to tame a wild beast. It did his bidding, climbing shakily into the air as its wings flapped with thunderous might. As he rose, the carnage revealed itself to him fully. He was mere streets away from the bulk of the demonic forces in Forge Town. Their shadow of death passed grimly over the district, invading homes and slaughtering those within, street by street. Gault urged his mount forward, billowing under the shadow of Galleo et'al's might as he neared the Obelisk. As he neared, he could see a thick cloud surrounding the structure. Quickly, he realised that it was a cloud of fellow Scarr'dath, protecting the Obelisk and circling its light like moths around a flame.

Screams reached his ear, even from this height. Desperate cries for mercy, echoing through the streets. The sound made him physically reel. It reminded him so closely of his own home, and the perpetual screams that had filled the streets as the city died.

Focus on the Obelisk.

Gault felt his attention being pulled forward, to the shadow of the Obelisk that grew closer and larger on the outskirts of Forge Town. The screams started to disappear, dulled as though he had put his head upon a pillow.

Focus. She has made you a bleeding heart.

He did as Akor'shaki bid him. It was the pragmatic thing to do-

The wind whistled and Gault flinched as the dull glimmer of demonsteel flew over his shoulder. A great poleaxe, thrown from the city below separated the head of his Scarr'dath from its body. The wings stopped pumping and Gault felt the rush of vertigo as his demonic mount suddenly plummeted from the air. He yanked at the chain, pulling the corpse into a dive down towards the street where the screams were coming from.

Don't break your legs.

"That'll be up to you!" Gault hissed, feeling the rush of monstrous power course through his veins as the cobbles of Forge Town raced up to meet him. Hulking figures stalked the streets below, waiting for him to arrive. Gault rode the dead Scarr'dath as close to the ground as he dared before leaping, taking the rest of the fall upon reinforced legs. As the decapitated body stained the old stone roads beside him, four hulking figures turned their large torsos towards him.

Dom'inari.

The grunt of Galleo et'al's forces, the Dom'inari were not to be trifled with. Their bodies towered over him, their width stretching the entire narrow street. Their prey sought shelter within a nearby house, the grey, leathery fists of the Dom'inari seconds from tearing the walls down.

There were horse-like blinkers grafted to the flesh around their eyes. They were simple beasts, incapable of perceiving too much information at one time, but once their focus was upon him, they would seek him single mindedly, an unstoppable drone of power and martial might. Their demonsteel poleaxes absorbed light as their skull adorned halberds were reared in his direction.

Gault willed Akor'shaki to expand and the blade grumbled but obeyed. There was the faintest light of recognition in the black eyes of the monstrous creatures before it was replaced by a hood of rage. They roared at him, jagged rows of teeth and tongues as black as tar.

Gault leaped into the air, disappearing from the head of the group's field of view. He sought to drag Akor'shaki down its back and split the foul spine in half only for it to whirl violently and dangerously with a backhand that caught both him and one of its own kin. Gault felt the air expel from his lungs as he crashed into the nearest wall. He rose quickly, rolling as the thrust of a spear sought to skewer him. He followed the poleaxe, swinging Akor'shaki, missing the flesh and the eyes but close enough to sever the blinders from its leathery face. Immediately, the Dom'inari staggered with sensory overload and Gault took advantage to drive his curved blade through its gullet before any aid could arrive.

Three remain.

"I know." Gault hissed. A poleaxe drew dangerously close to splitting his stomach open but he managed to swat the lunge aside with Akor'shaki before darting in on the demon and severing the arm at the elbow. It roared and Gault saw the swelling of its eyes as pain wracked its body. It didn't rest for long and immediately swung with its final arm. Gault braced Akor'shaki and cut directly between the onrushing knuckle, blood spilling over him as he sliced deep into the forearm. The hand split into two dangling chunks and Gault ripped his blade from it and put the demon out of its misery.

Two now.

Gault saw one, but not the other. It took him a moment to realise he was already standing in its towering shadow. A great hand grabbed his head and he should have died then and there as the demon squeezed his head like a grape. But Gault felt a power surge bestowed by Akor'shaki in a moment of dire need. It was strength enough for him to grip the mountainous index finger with both his hands and force it open. He escaped, but a hammering fist in his back sent him reeling to the floor where the second Dom'inari stalked, ready to spear him like a fish floundering out of water.

A solid oak chair crashed against the thick skull, splintering immediately into shards of damp wood. It may as well have been made of paper, yet it served well enough as a distraction. The blinders whirled, seeking the source of this outrageously futile attack. Gault searched also, spotting the cowering silhouette of a ragged man disappearing into the shadows of a nearby home. He surged upwards, his arcing blade sticking the Dom'inari through the stomach as it twisted up and out, swiping the pulsating heart of the demon clear from its chest. Its hollow eyes watched as its own heart stopped beating, the trunk-like legs giving way shortly after.

One remains. Be swift.

He charged it, sliding to the scratched stone as an air-splitting swing of the poleaxe roared over his head. Leaping on its chest, he drove Akor'shaki through its throat and rode the body down to the cobblestone where the cavernous rise and fall of its chest came to a steady halt.

"Thank you, thank you!" A shape emerged from the old home. A tired man, young-looking, but with features dirtied and aged by poverty. "We're treating the wounded. They'd be dead if not for you."

Gault raised a brow. "They don't normally leave wounded."

You're wasting time.

"There were worse monsters than these already roaming the streets." The man pointed behind him, at the Obelisk. "Levelled our homes to build that thing. Some salvation."

"I need to get over there. Any suggestions?"

"The sewers. Those fiends are down there though. I can hear them scratching at the stone beneath us." A small look of hope crossed his face. "You look like you can handle yourself fine though."

"Thank you." Gault bid the man enter the home. "They can sense magic. Use none. Lay your dead by the entrances, the smell may mask the rest of you."

A grim task, but the young man nodded. He blockaded the door and drew the curtains. Gault could hear the faint muffle of him dragging bodies towards the door.

Approaching the nearest sewer grate, Gault hailed the blade at his side. "You've been quiet."

It stirred. Its tone disapproving. *I'm letting you concentrate.*

"About time."

He tore the grate from its resting place at the side of the curb, the smell of sewage and grime blasted the sulphur from his nostrils. The darkness beneath the city was an ominous jet black, yet down he dropped dauntlessly, leaving the gruesome carnage behind him for a few precious moments.

———

Standing on top of one of the few skyscrapers that still stood tall, Lachesis observed the onslaught with a sober countenance. A great fire raged through Centa Isla, consuming the city and bathing it in chaos as it spread with unrelenting ferocity. With the dark shadow of Galleo et'al sat in the sky, the flames took on a crimson hue like dancing waves of blood through the ravaged streets. It had been less than an hour and already the city was coming to its knees. Perhaps she had been right to hold her tongue after all, to wait until a better opportunity to one day make her stand.

Yet, there was one victor among the chaos. Grandmaster. The academy of magic stood proud, defiant against the Dark One who leered in the sky overhead. She had not made contact with Galleo et'al, yet Lachesis could feel its frustration permeating the atmosphere. Chunks of scorched earth fell from the crumbling surface, only to explode into ash upon striking the domed barrier. She was impressed but knew it would not last. No force in the universe could survive the purging force of Galleo et'al and its demonic hordes. It would be but a matter of time until the walls crumbled and the Versorcerers within were slaughtered.

She could feel a change in the air from so high up. It was slight, barely even noticeable, yet she had felt it many times before. The air felt thinner, as though a layer of it had been stripped away. This was, at least as she knew it, the first stages of Galleo et'al consuming the core of this world. Without the core, magic would cease to exist, taking with it everything that kept the city of Centa Isla alive. It was doom twofold, a fate that the people here did not deserve, but...

That was just how it was.

Those lucky few who impressed the sweeping presence of Galleo et'al may well become Omens, replacing the dead Kren'shal and Mires in their ranks for the next incursion. And so, the cycle would continue, subservience or annihilation. It was only she who had not been given a choice.

Cupped in her hands, her scrying orb was quiet. Her network of gutter spies had dwindled rapidly and she had felt each tiny loss as a twinge in the back of her mind, as though a fraction of herself she had shared with another had perished along with it. The degradation was something she had grown used to across so many campaigns, yet she couldn't help but address the small pockets of darkness she felt inside. It was more than just a missing memory, or apathy towards things she may have once cared for, but something more. She felt the Brand of the Watcher on her back sing with power. This was the price of her powers it seemed, the degradation of the self until nothing remained but the same subservient husk that her brother had become.

She lowered herself, dangling her legs over the edge of the building as she watched the chaos. A job well done; she supposed.

—

Jace had played his part as well as he could, yet as he ran now through the fires of Forge Town, he felt no joy. On their previous conquest when the Dark One had arrived to blot out the stars, he had spent the day of invasion drinking in an isolated basement. The cool liquid had absolved him of his part in summoning the chaos, helping drown out the screams that had roared above ground. When he had woken up the next day, he was back on Galleo et'al's powdery surface as though nothing had happened. Now his lips were parched and his body was desperate to offer his guilt-ridden mind absolution. Yet he held no drink in his hands, but instead a blade. His body still glowed with pain, but he dragged his weary self through the flaming streets.

Demons scourged the area around him, but Jace felt little fear from the Dark One's spawns. They addressed him with reverence as he passed, bowing their heads of various shapes and malformations in a show of absolution. The Brand of the Sorcerer thrummed down his broken arm, responding to the presence of the demons. It was how they identified him as a master. A preferred alternative of course, to being victim to these mindless monsters, but it weighed no less heavy on his conscience as he watched the demons stalk and kill while he walked freely.

He sought Stanwyck and Celia. If this city was going to burn, Jace intended to make sure that at the very least the people who did right by him were going to survive the night. It was a small mercy, but it made him feel like he was doing the right thing. That would have to be enough.

He was given pause from his frantic search when he stumbled upon a row of four familiar corpses. But they were not human bodies, they were demons known as Dom'inari. He approached and laid a hand over one of the deceased, finding their typically steely flesh flaky and brittle, a strong gust enough to scatter them to the wind. They were fresh enough kills, the bodies of demons turned to ash once life had been snuffed from them. If they were able, they would return to Galleo et'al where they would be given new life. Otherwise, they were gone for good. Jace surmised it was a matter of time until these demons stalked the streets anew. But what intrigued him the most was who it was that killed them. It was no easy feat, typically an impossibility by native civilians. To do so, was a guarantee of being offered the chance of becoming an Omen for there hadn't been many humans who had slain a demon.

Jace had, of course. A proud moment, but also his worst curse.

A smell curdled his nose. Death, rotting corpses. Flames caught his attention as he noticed a pile of bodies being burned at the doorstep of an innocuous hovel. Jace understood their intent well enough, to mask the smell of their blood with something strong and malodorous. Once again, a demonstration of knowledge that none in this city should have possessed. He approached the old home, immediately finding signs of ill fate. The door had been bashed off its hinges and the windows and surrounding walls had been caved in. Bodies lined the interior, the attempts to repel the demonic forces clearly not enough. The blood that covered the floor and walls was fresh. He entered the old hovel, immediately feeling disgust at the sheer amount of carnage. Bodies of the dead piled up in the room, bloody stains smearing the wall in some sort of sadistic decoration. These were children, families, injured, none were spared the unprejudiced wrath of Galleo et'al, yet there was something truly grim about the scene that played out before him. Worse still, Jace recognised many of the pale, stricken faces that lay before him. He had served them soup not a day previously. His heart sank into his stomach as he laid eyes on the little girl who had thanked him in earnest. Her words had touched him, made him feel gratified for the first time in a long time. Now, much of her had been splattered up the wall against which her body lay. Her eyes were shut, her mouth locked open with a cry that had been silenced by whatever foul instrument had punctured a hole in her stomach. There was a time, perhaps two or three invasions ago the sight of such violent, cruel chaos would have stirred his stomach, yet he had become desensitised to it now. It was the expectation that everybody he met would end up this way, yet for others it hurt that much more. He thought of Stanwyck and Celia - were they still alive? The old floorboards groaned beneath him as he advanced. Each room he peered into was an identical story to the last, a tale of tragedy and death. He took in each silent face, hoping he would not find them among the deceased.

As he ventured into one of the rooms, a shadow passed behind him and Jace jumped, startled. A tall, dominating shadow clotted the doorframe, spilling its broad-shouldered bulk into the room with him. A Dom'inari. It watched him with those pitiless, black eyes. As they flitted to the Brand, Jace felt his arm tingle and the Dom'inari bowed its head in quiet reverence, blowing a strong guttural breath from its upturned nostrils. Scars decorated the demon's flesh, the blinkers that had been grafted to its head partly broken. There was an age to this demon, a likely veteran of many frontiers. It could well have been present when Jace's own homeworld fell. One scar in particular stood out to him. Deep, grievous scars darted across its chest, twisting and curling in a pattern of deadly accuracy that only the deftest of swordsmen could have done.

Then, it left. The lumbering footfalls were heavy and languid, making Jace wonder how he hadn't heard it skulking about before. It lowered its mass, taking away more of the shattered door frame as it left, returning to the blaze of chaos that Forge Town had turned into.

With one last room to go, Jace entered. Something cold gripped his chest as among the bodies, still laid out for makeshift triage upon blankets and old cushions, was Celia. Her entire lower body had been cruelly mangled, yet her face betrayed no such pain. Her eyes were open, staring blankly up at the ceiling with her mouth gently agape as though lost in a thoughtless dream.

"No…" Jace stepped over equally crippled bodies, kneeling at her side to gently close her eyes. Such a kind, altruistic soul, she deserved a better fate than this. They all did. These people were survivors; their homes levelled for the Dark One's grand design, to end up slaughtered on triage beds. Yet there were likely those who had survived, Stanwyck it seemed may even be among them. The window in the back room was shattered, but not taking the entire wall with it like the bulk of a Dom'inari would have done. The shards of glass had exploded outwards, littering the cobblestone outside, meaning whoever left had done so seeking to leave rather than enter. As for the others, dignity in death was all he could afford them now. Rising, Jace unravelled the makeshift sling that supported his shattered arm and winced as it sought to support itself. He called upon his Brand, seeking avenging flame to burn the bodies to whatever afterlife may await them.

Put these souls to rest.

A cowl of fire surged from his open palm. Jace grimaced as pain spiked through him, having to support his broken arm while the spell took place. He blanketed the room in flame, igniting the dead. Retreating from the building, Jace torched everything in sight and stepped back to watch as the old hovel burned like the fires of a ceremony he had witnessed on other worlds. Stepping back out into the aura of Galleo et'al spurred him to look up at the Dark One. He wondered if it even noticed him, or if it was too busy consuming the core of the world to care what its thralls were up to?

Like it mattered. Centa Isla would be nothing but a memory by day's end, yet he owed it to Stanwyck and Celia to try and do the right thing for those who had taken him in at his darkest hour. Moving around the burning hovel,

Jace picked up the trail of shattered glass, finding thin traces of blood coating the jagged shards, the trail ran east, towards the untouched silhouette of Monument before running cold. But it was good enough. He advanced, pushing through the chaos. Even with the trail of blood exhausted, Jace found something new to follow - the corpses of Demons. It shouldn't have been possible, yet here it was. Expert strikes cleaved the demons. The spike of a blade pierced the cavernous space where the heart should have been, yet finding none, it had gone for the throat and claimed the Dom'inari's life. There was learning here, evidenced in every demonic body that he passed, humanoid or otherwise, taking no more than one kill to identify the weakness in the physiology of each one. For a mortal to claim so many demons during invasion; these were the portends of a future Omen. The trail of carnage led him through what looked like an old battlefield; the bodies of civilians seeking survival decorated the floor. Their bodies were hours old, well-trodden territory for the wave of demons that washed through the streets, it seemed. Yet there were now new corpses, some civilians, likely among the group that escaped the old hovel, but many were demons - felled by the same, clean strikes to the jugular as those he had passed previously. As he crossed the old battlefield, things started to take a turn. The bodies of civilians increased, many of the faces left intact were recognisable to him as ones he had served soup to just a day ago.

And so, it didn't take him long to find what remained of the surviving party. Or rather, the sole survivor. The roads of Forge Town twisted and curved erratically and upon rounding one of those corners, Jace saw Stanwyck. He rested, seated upon an overturned wooden crate with the tip of his longsword buried into the ground as he supported himself upon it. Before Jace could even speak, Stanwyck had spotted him, the aged eyes snapped to him and he could feel them assessing him for threat. They relaxed when recognition crossed his face.

"Jace." The old man pushed himself from the crate. "What are you doing here? It's not safe."

"You're alive." Jace approached, unbelieving. "All of the bodies, did you-"

"I couldn't protect them." Stanwyck hissed. For the first time, Jace saw beneath the hardy exterior to find a stoic man finally broken. "I couldn't protect their homes. I couldn't protect my wife."

"You can survive this." Jace urged him. "It will be over soon."

"It was over long ago, lad." Stanwyck shook his head. "This is just... the work of the Gods."

"You're closer than you think." Jace pointed to the sky; to the looming shadow of Galleo et'al. "You've slain so many demons, It will favour you. All you need-"

"Is that what you did, lad?" Stanwyck's dark eyes looked at his Brand. "Seek favour?"

Jace found it hard to reply. "I... did."

He was expecting rage. Anger. To be skewered on the spot for the death he had brought to Stanwyck's home, his family and his community. Yet, there was none of that. Perhaps the old man was simply too broken to feel rage, or too kind. Instead, a trembling old hand fell upon his shoulder.

"There's still goodness in you." Stanwyck looked tired, his smile curving only on one side of his face. "Whatever this God has made you into. You are better than that."

"No. I chose this. All of it." Jace felt tears daring to sting his eyes. He bit them back. He had no right to cry before a man who had lost everything. "I deserve your hatred."

"Because death was your alternative?" Stanwyck removed his hand, pressing it against the wooden crate to support his failing body. "I've seen enough war to know what such fear can do to people. Good people. Wanting to live isn't a sin."

"But at the cost of so many. It can't be right." Jace wanted to change the subject, feeling the guilt weighing too heavily upon him. "What were you? Before Reckoning?"

The old man humoured him.

"Commander of the Kingsguard. The very first." Stanwyck's arm twisted into a salute of reverence, a closed fist pressed into a palm, then held over his heart. "Stanwyck Bowers."

Jace couldn't believe it. What could have gone wrong in life for a man of such a station to end up relegated to the scraps and dust of a city.

"Then, Celia?"

"An assassin of Kings." A wide, yet strained smile stretched across Stanwyck's face. He looked happy to recall the memory, more than ever with his wife now deceased. "A very good one too. Nearly got the better of me."

"I'm sorry-"

"I know, lad." The smile faded as quickly as it had come. "But she understood the value of her life. She stayed while I fled with as many as I could gather."

"Noble."

"Very. There comes a time, where we must weigh the worth of our life against others. It must be impartial, unbiased, which isn't always easy." Stanwyck raised his greatsword, balancing the weight across his open palms as he offered it out. "That's the righteous thing to do."

The weight of life? Before Jace could ponder it further, there was a guttural growl over his shoulder. Jace whirled in time to see a Dom'inari surge forward. It passed him by, as narrow as the width of a needle and seized Stanwyck. His sword clanged to the ground as the old man was caught off-guard, his body lifted from the floor by a single, leathery hand.

"NO!" Jace called upon flame, only to feel the powers of his Brand nullified. The permeating aura of Galleo et'al flared, as though to tell him it was watching. Stanwyck groaned and writhed in the vice grip of the demon, the crunching of rib and spleen deafening as life was squeezed out of him. "Put him down! Please!"

He sought to dominate the Dom'inari, to leverage the power of his Brand to make it recognise and serve, yet his Brand remained powerless. Gritting his teeth, Jace seized the greatsword from the ground, burying his screams of pain as his broken arm shared the weight of heavy steel. He charged toward the Dom'inari, only for his mind to be pierced once again by a thousand needles.

Enough.

The sword fell from his grip as his entire body was paralyzed, forcing him to his knees.

"No-!"

"It's alright, lad…" Stanwyck spoke weakly to him, breathless from the chunks of bone piercing his lungs. Blood flew from his mouth as he spoke, the light leaving his eyes as he forced a small smile across his aged face. "…You're a good kid."

The light left his eyes and the corpse of Stanwyck Bowers slumped over the hand that crushed him. Recognising death, the Dom'inari released the body, allowing the broken husk to crumple against the cobblestones.

"DAMN IT!" Jace screamed, slamming his broken arm repeatedly into the floor. Tears streamed down his face. He was helpless. A helpless failure, doomed to watch those who did right by him die.

The Dom'inari turned to him. When its titanic form shifted, crunching the stone beneath its plated feet, Jace recognised it. The scars that danced across the chest immediately made it familiar to him. It was the very same demon that had slaughtered the old hovel.

Then Jace realised. It had followed him.

Rage clouded him, the sheer anger unlocking a memory he had sealed away beneath days of copious drinking. The scars on the chest; the ones dealt by a master swordsman. They were inflicted by him. Many years ago, during the invasion of his homeworld when he had earned the favour of Galleo et'al by defending his home from harm. He had felled many demons that day, fighting dawn to dusk until there was nothing left but a decision. Join or die.

Whether this demon sought vengeance for the day it had been reborn and slain several times by his hand, he didn't know. But there was something sinister in those vapid black eyes that incited further fury deep inside him. He had never known such insidious intelligence from these mindless monsters before. He wished to rise, to skewer the creature on Stanwyck's blade and inflict scars so deep that its entire body may become a tapestry of his hatred. Yet, he could not. The Brand of the Sorcerer, for all that it had given him, was also how Galleo et'all took away his will when he needed it most.

As the Dom'inari walked away, leaving him a sobbing, seething shell of a man; Jace eyed the keen, well-maintained edge of Stanwyck's blade. The weight of a life. The words had bounced around his head since he'd been told them. What was the value of his life? Had he lived beyond his means all these years, drinking on stolen time while entire planets burned for his involvement? He knew the answer yet felt nothing but further disgust and self-loathing upon admitting it.

The weight of a life. Jace had once believed his own life in service of Galleo et'al was beyond redemption, beyond the salvation of what any one act could achieve. But as he lay here, helpless before those who had helped him, he realised that this transient moment was truly where he was worth the least.

He took the blade of Stanwyck Bower's and laid his shattered, Branded arm over the concrete. He held the blade overhead and levelled it against the flesh of his Brand, prepared to come down with the full force of his anger.

A voice thrummed in his head. Invasive, dominant.

Consider the consequences, Brand.

Jace pushed the voice out his head before it could paralyse him - and brought the blade down with all the force he could muster.

17

Donnel Rawdon adjusted the lens so that the ivory walls of Grandmaster came clearly into focus. The ornate detail seemed close enough to touch. He yawned so widely his jaw clicked and his eyes began to water. The strap supporting the heavy binoculars left a deep red indent across the back of his neck, a friction burn from carrying the weight of them for several hours in succession. His backside was numb and he had to stand and shake his feet periodically to avoid getting pins and needles. He lit a cigarette and exhaled a gush of warm smoke out of the open window and into the cold, night air. He could not remember when he had last endured an all-night stakeout. In the first flush of his career, he had earned an enviable reputation for his stakeouts. The ability to fixate on his intended target with intense concentration had enabled him to bust some of the earliest Synth peddling rings within days of the drugs hitting the streets. It launched his career. Yet, as the years had passed, his body had started to resist the all-nighters and he had been forced to accept his best days were behind him. But now he was back and so was the impressive concentration and focus from his glory days. To find Rissa's mother, it seemed even the hands of time could be wound back.

One last try. He had promised Rissa that if this led nowhere, he'd never look again.

If the truth of what happened to Aryssa lay beyond the domed veil of Grandmaster then he was going to get inside and confront the High Priestess. He just had to bide his time and work out the best point of entry. He had heard from Rissa about the surreal existence beyond the walls that mirrored the world pre-Reckoning; of the blue skies and eternal autumn season, where students could feel the dappled sunlight on their skin and sit in a faux woodland to study. Sealed away in this oasis, the children of tomorrow were absolved of the horror that existed beyond its walls. Only those with The Algarethan Verse in their blood could enter its gates, and in the sixty years since Reckoning, nobody of non-magic descent had ever entered.

He poured a mug of strong coffee from a flask and took a couple of sips. He'd sold his old apartment and many of his belongings, buying instead an unfurnished apartment as close to the academy as possible. Here, he could stake out the ivory gates for as many nights as he could stay awake. If there was so much as a murmur of weakness within those walls he would be the one to find it. He manoeuvred his sparse breakfast towards him, an old tin of Resynthesised meat and hard-boiled eggs. The taste was nonexistent, like spinning rubber around his mouth but what nutrients were to be found would fuel him enough to stay awake. With each passing hour his eyes burned with the desire to sleep, yet the thought of missing even a twitch upon those white walls was enough for him to stave off fatigue. His new apartment was drab and dreary; a dark empty room filled with old boxes he was too sentimental to part with. All of them belonged to Aryssa. His only possessions now were the clothes on his back, his radio, the case housing Jace's Grandmaster robe and the leather jacket that Aryssa had bought for him. He kept it wrapped snugly around his shoulders, providing him warmth as the thunderous season of Stormsmarch retained the chill of Rainsturn.

Sitting here, alone, he found it difficult to stop his mind from wandering. He had been more focused in his youth, always looking ahead for opportunity. These days, he found he could only look back. But the past was his strength, his conviction. Donnel freely allowed the memories to swallow him, the ache in his heart providing the strength to keep his eyes open another hour. In this semi-slumber his tired brain fired up precious memories from the past, projecting them in full clarity upon the white walls of Grandmaster. He saw himself looking healthier and happier, walking with his wife and daughter through the old park, or the three of them celebrating Rissa's birthday. Flashes from the past tormented him in a frenzy of frozen frames. He blinked away the images and finished the last dregs of his coffee.

He sought his noisy timepiece out of his pocket. The clock had not long since struck the hour of eight and he had gleaned nothing noteworthy from his nocturnal surveillance. He decided to turn on his radio to hear the King's Funeral Speech but then decided against it, wondering whether the King was as corrupt as the CIPD and somehow involved in what Rissa and Gault were trying to prevent.

Grandmaster remained an impenetrable fortress. Still suspended from active duty, he was unable to access any records or known data on Cordelia Rowe. Her signature burned at the bottom of the strange document, alongside that of his wife. Just what plan had they come up with? Moreover, why hadn't he known?

But something interrupted his introspection. It happened so quickly that he barely had time to comprehend what was happening before him before explosions and screams filled the streets. Heat washed over the city and a crimson hue bathed those white walls in the colours of gore. Unnatural chills rattled his spine and he rose from his chair, feeling the sedentary strain of his stakeout in his aching knees. He grabbed the black case and fled down the stairs out of his apartment to the ground floor, finding the streets filled with screaming. Before he could pull someone aside and demand answers, the sky was set on fire as great shards of earth struck the city. He felt the ground beneath him tremble. One of the meteors struck the great shield that crested over the academy, exploding into a shower of dust and ash that scratched at his throat as he breathed.

A second Reckoning? The overwhelming carnage carried him forward with a tidal wave of bodies that had already begun to swarm around the ivory walls of Grandmaster. There was chaos and alarm. Desperate pleas hollered from their mouths, begging for entry and asylum. Cursing, Donnel spun around and down the long barrel of the street ahead, he saw the flickering of flames and the leering, lumbering shadows that it carried with it. In the sky overhead, an impossibility presented itself before him. An entire crumbling planet loomed, absorbing the horizon in its infinite mass. His mind was tired, and for a split second he thought he was experiencing an hallucination or a night terror but the intense smell of scorched flesh and sulphur caused him to violently heave and Donnel quickly realised this horror was reality.

Even amidst this chaos, his brain sought logic. The cover-ups, Rissa's arrest, Gault's presence here – it had all been an alert to a sinister plot to destroy Centa Isla and yet he had refused to acknowledge it. The greatest threat the city had seen since the Reckoning itself and he had ignored it. He glanced up at Monument, which stood untouched on the horizon, a reeking testament of corruption at the highest level. Everywhere else was carnage. But in that madness there was a hidden element. One that made his lips dry and his eyes widen.

Opportunity.

He had spent years protecting these streets which were now awash with ash and blood as horrific creatures stalked them like something out of a story book that he once read to Rissa. But he could only think of one thing. One truth.

One last lead.

As the monstrous demons approached the crowds, the screams grew to a cacophonous madness of desperation and wailing. Donnel reached for his weapon but wondered what good it would do as the silhouettes only seemed to grow larger and larger as they approached. There was a dark anticipation to their march up the Path of Discipline, as though there was a desire to relish in the screaming and the fear before the slaughter started. Just as it looked as though the massacre was set to begin, a deep, guttural groaning came from behind him. Donnel feared one of the creatures had slinked to attack him, until he turned to see a great light burning through the slit between the closed gates of Grandmaster. There was another groan and then the heaving of great mass as the gates slowly began to open and a stream of bright sunlight cast rays of yellow-orange into the grey, bloodied streets. It was so bright, it was blinding, Donnel could only make out enough to see tall, broad silhouettes emerge from the gates of the academy, bathed in radiant light. They were towering knights, features lost behind deep black helmets whose eyes blazed with the power of magic. He understood them to be Spellguard Knights, dredging up a distant memory of Rissa trying to explain them to him, just before she was expelled.

A voice came with them, carried by the wind itself. "Enter! Asylum awaits you!"

Donnel took a sharp intake of breath and pushed his way to the front, ignoring the jostling crowd as the humble citizens of Centa Isla poured into the sacred grounds of Grandmaster. The Spellguard Knights surged forward, creating a perimeter of protection around the open gates ready to combat the approaching horde of creatures. He didn't see the outcome, for he was shepherded into the courtyard of the academy where tents had been erected. Versorcerers approached the masses, bidding them to stay calm. Donnel didn't hear them, nor did he wish to, for he was engrossed in the wonder of being in Grandmaster for the first time.

It was a glorious building, abstract yet simple, layered with brickwork and incredible sculptures chiselled from the old earth itself. He could see in the flawed stone and layers of cement that this building was older than anything in this city and the work put into maintaining it was nothing short of miraculous. The rays of faux sunlight bathed the spires in a holy radiance, but before he could appreciate the illusionary weather, it disappeared. The dome that ran overhead, providing the illusion of such pleasant days became translucent, allowing the crimson grime and murk of Centa Isla's current reality to wash through the courtyard. There were gasps and wails as those within beheld the red planet in their orbit for the first time.

Another meteor struck the surface and Donnel watched as ripples of strain cascaded down the dome, forcing small cracks to appear in the magical surface. In response, the front doors to the academy were thrown open and several

Versorcerers emerged, wheeling a large device in front of them. They stopped in the middle of the courtyard and hooked needles from it to their veins. As their blood began to flow through the pipes and into the machine, a great beam fired into the air and layered the shield above them with renewed strength, sealing the cracks that had threatened to form.

"Are you injured?" It took him a moment to realise a Versorcerer was speaking to him. With a mass of fiery auburn hair, she looked young. Much younger than Rissa had been when she'd first been enrolled.

"I'm fine. Thank you."

She gave him a smile before moving onto somebody else.

The city was burning and facing destruction and his daughter was out there somewhere, amongst the flames. Distantly, the father in him was screaming for him to find her. Yet, equally, the detective in him remained focused on one objective. The open doors to Grandmaster beckoned him, heralding secrets that he had to discover. He could feel the weight of his yearning spurring him onwards. Years of research had darkened the edges of his eyes and it was all for this moment. The Versorcerers of Grandmaster, both student and staff, were busy hooking themselves up to the device in order to reinforce the dome. This was his chance.

One last lead.

He slinked into the fake foliage and opened the case. He slid into the Grandmaster robe and raised the hood, leaving the black case hidden in the foliage. He straightened his posture and matched the accelerated walk that many of the roaming Versorcerer's carried, heading straight through the front door. Nobody batted an eyelid. He may as well have worked here all his life. He was perhaps among the first of commoners to set foot in Grandmaster since the beginning of recorded history and yet this meant nothing. His focus was High Priestess Cordelia Rowe and her office.

"Aryssa..." He muttered, feeling a cool, deadly calm come over him. He was walking through the halls that his wife and daughter had crossed many times. "I'll find you."

The world could well be about to end, but he would know the truth. He did not know where the office of Cordelia Rowe was to be found, but navigating the intricate marble floors of Grandmaster proved a much easier task than he had first anticipated. He mantled stairs that curved upwards through a grand foyer. It seemed to be law that the quarters of important people were always on the top floor. By the third floor, the halls were completely empty. Donnel allowed himself a glance out the window, revealing the sprawling courtyard that was growing in bodies. These old walls seemed to bring silence to the chaos outside, but the fires that engulfed the city flickered all the same. His thoughts fell again to Rissa, out there somewhere, but just as quickly he buried them. He was here for both of them. They both deserved answers. She'd be okay, the young man would keep her safe. He felt his brows crease as he searched for the young man's name, only to deem it irrelevant. A determination took over, a thick clot of focus honed from years of detective work. It stripped away information that wasn't relevant to his immediate case. Right now, only one thing mattered. Eight years of searching had him venturing up yet more flights of stairs until he reached the top floor. Two rows of stairs converged at a single, ornate wooden door. Steel flourishes decorated the panelled wood, proudly gesturing toward an engraved plaque.

High Priestess Cordelia Rowe.

It seemed the entirety of the top floor was dedicated to her office space. Donnel was uncertain how to approach. He tried the handle, finding it predictably locked. He had brought his lockpicking kit with him; yet found the door bizarrely bereft of any conventional lock.

"Versorcerers." He cursed under his breath, seeking a weakness in the hinges or the handle itself. No doubt there was a spell or Conduit that unlocked the door, but he sure wasn't going to know how. So, he reared back, edging the final step to gain as much distance as possible before charging the door and driving a stern boot into the space just above the handle. The ornate wood buckled under his powerful stride and immediately splintered, putting him already one foot into the office. He tore the rest of the wood away and stepped inside, dusting himself free of splinters and shavings.

One last lead.

The inside was not as large as he initially believed. It opened into an office, the entire room jutting out and in again as though shaped like a diamond. Bookshelves lined the wall, reaching to the tall ceiling, with ladders on rails to reach them. Donnel stepped inside, feeling the crunch of paper beneath his feet. He glanced down, finding a folded note on the floor just behind the door, as though it had been slipped through. He unfurled it in his hands, realising that a thick layer of dust had coated the letter. How long had it been sitting here?

Mother,
I need to talk to you about my future. It's important.
Where have you gone? When you read this, please come and see me.
Love you.
Emelia

The note suggested much, but Donnel did not find himself privy to the details. He understood that the artefact Jace had stolen originated from here. Had the High Priestess locked herself away in shame? If that were the case, why was her office empty? Donnel cast the note aside. So long as she was not returning, he didn't care. The promise of her absence stirred a tingle in his fingertips, excited at the prospect of rummaging through every drawer and cabinet, he started at the desk, skimming a stack of papers with his analytical eyes. He searched for words that matched the blueprints he had committed to memory a thousand times over. Nothing. He pulled out the deep drawers, just finding student files working alphabetically A through Z. Abandoning that, he sought the bookshelves, mantling the ladder to sift through the weathered, leathery spines in search of glory. Time twisted and knotted, becoming a blend of disappointment as every nook and cranny that dared to contain a piece of paper was turned inside out. His frustration grew with every failed search and he stood in the middle of the room, cursing how close he had come to finding out the truth. In rage, he slammed his fists on the desk and-

Hollow? Calm washed through him immediately as the realisation widened his tired eyes. He ran his hands over the dark oak desk, knocking again as though to confirm his suspicion. Sure enough, the sound rang hollow beneath him. He fingered the edges of the wood, searching for a latch or button, skirting around the desk until he found a small latch fit for a finger far daintier than his. He swiped a quill from the desk and used it to pry the latch free, revealing a hidden compartment that contained just one thing.

A small brazier.

He took his lighter and struck it several times, the tiny fire crystal within spitting at the edge of exhaustion. Finally, it caught and he lit the brazier. A deep, groaning came from behind him. He watched as the rows of bookshelves that lined the walls began to shift. They edged across the room, crunching the splintered wood of the front door as they came together to ultimately block the exit. But, behind him, in the space that had been freed was another door. Donnel opened it, relieved to find it without a magical lock and stepped into a dark chamber. Red light spilled in, a crimson spotlight that shone through a shattered skylight. The shards of glass crunched beneath his feet as he entered, his eyes adjusting to the darkness. A strange object sat in the centre of the room, directed up at the skylight. Donnel glanced at it, feeling the long tube-like nozzle squeak as the hinges that supported it allowed it to move up, down and side to side. It apexed in size as it went, culminating in a large glassy eye that looked up - through the skylight and at the dark shadow that hung over the city. Donnel peered through the other end, almost losing his breath as his vision was magnified to such a detail that he could make out the cavernous craters that dotted the planet's exterior... and the horrific, giant shapes that marched across it. He pulled away, shaken and quickly resolved to continue his search before whatever roamed that surface found their way here. He sifted through drawers and lockers, finally, falling upon a collection of journals whose spines had been written over by ink and quill. A glance across them seemed to detail various projects that had been overseen by Cordelia Rowe. They were all attempts at finding solutions to the Resource Crisis, all resulting in failure. But there was one that caught his eye.

Beyond the Veil on Wings of Steel.

A grandiose title, perhaps that was what caught his eye. Or rather, it could have been the very mention of the name of the construct that decorated the blueprints. Donnel felt drawn to it. His hands caressed the spine and he felt the old leather sink beneath his grip as he drew the journal steadily from the pile. He opened it, refusing to so much as blink away from the words within, even as dust wafted up into his face. He read, frustrated as he found nothing but abstract ramblings, yet didn't stop for fear of missing an important detail. The scrawl was barely legible, written with daft flicks and loops, but he persevered. It talked of conjecture regarding what may exist beyond the veil of smog that pervaded the city. A theory was presented, speculating on the idea that there could be surviving remnants of Reckoning besides themselves. It was a bizarre theory, daring to find hope from the hopeless in defiance of the punishment that humanity had been issued. Yet, as Donnel read on, it wasn't an impossible thought.

Feeling around for a surface to sit upon, he kept his eyes fixed on each page. The rambling went from theory to practice, journalling her meeting with the now deceased Austyn Synner, one of the city's greatest minds, to create a means to test her theory. On the next page, Donnel found a sketch, upon comparing an exact replica to the blueprints on the design document.

His heart raced. He'd found it. Reading on, he flicked through early design trials and mistakes, searching for his wife's name written amongst it all.

Then, he found her name buried in a passage.

-our minds are alike in our assessments. This city cannot be saved without risk. This alliance of magic and machine shall seek the very borders of our new world. Aryssa Rawdon will be our wings, her bravery our salvation. Like me, she is a visionary. She understands this city cannot last on its current means. This is what must-

He stopped reading for a moment, feeling a tightness grip his chest. Seeing her name in this journal made the likelihood of her surviving seem hopeless and for the first time his mind questioned whether she was alive. Had Rissa's mother really sacrificed her life to go on a futile and experimental mission? Had she been prepared to never see her husband or daughter ever again?

The pages that followed detailed her preparation and the final stages of testing before her flight. An aerodynamic glider that, when piloted, was capable of sustained flight, the Steel Wing had been modified in testing enough to venture far out into the smog. A Vortex would be used to link the Steel Wing, allowing Aryssa to stay in contact with Centa Isla as she steered the glider. It would also serve as her escape if things went awry. Donnel thumbed through, no longer interested in the conjecture but now desperately vested in the outcome. He thumbed through quicker and quicker, until the journal suddenly ended half-way through.

"What?" He said aloud. He kept going, certain it was a test of his dedication. But the blank pages ran all the way to the end of the leather that bound it. "What!?"

He backtracked, finding the last page to have been stained by ink. It held only one thing, a large sketch, scrawled quickly and clumsily: decorating the page with accidental splodges of ink. It was the perspective seen through a Vortex, a spell Donnel had seen Rissa cast many times before. Within the foaming mass of magic was a vision; a horizon that he could have seen in an art gallery. It looked like mountain peaks, several of them, decorating a foggy horizon. There was a footnote, scratched at the bottom.

The Vortex suddenly closed. Aryssa Rawdon failed to return. This was the last image I could make out. Drawn from memory.

Failed to return.

An emotion began to surface as he absorbed the words. What was this feeling? It was like a dying fire, trying to ignite itself again with flickering embers at the base of a fire pit. Failed to return was *not* death. Yet it was not life either. He should have felt relief, closure on a chapter in his life that had burdened him for so many years. Yet he felt nothing. There was no relief or freedom from this endless search; only the uncertain words written in front of him. Donnel realised that he may never truly rest until he had the body of his wife in front of him; dead or alive.

She was alive. He had come too far for her not to be. The erratic sketch of those distant mountains inspired him to start dreaming of a world where his wife roamed beyond the city, free of the famine and the suffering. She was alive out there. Perhaps she even sought to return? Desperate to see him again?

Desperate, even, to see her daughter?

Rissa's face flashed across his mind. He had held her cold body, pale and lifeless. Those hungry blue eyes were dim and vacant. He had left her in trusted care, but what had become of her now?

"What am I doing?" He dropped the journal, the leather striking the wooden floor with a thud. He staggered backwards, crashing into the great scope and knocking it to the ground.

He had a tangible lead on Rissa's mother. He'd finally found out, after so many years of searching. He should have felt the rush of triumph and the glory of success yet he did not. He felt only guilt. For years he had just wanted to reunite his family and return to the days of old where they had been together. But, even as he stood here with the answers he had sought, he realised the true cost. He'd been an absent father; so, lost in the past that he'd missed his own daughter growing up.

A memory dredged itself up. Its unwelcome presence weighed heavy. For a moment, he was eighteen again, waking up in the morning to a rolled-up note from his parents. They had taken their own lives, unable to live with the world post-Reckoning. He had cried all day, curled up in a house that was now his, but would never feel like home again.

He had just wanted Rissa to have her family back together.

Tears stung his eyes as he tore the page from the journal. Rissa had to know. Even if the city was going to end. She had to know. It was the least he could do to pay back the childhood she'd had taken away. His daughter deserved closure more than he ever did. Donnel gently placed the page in his satchel and fled the office, a glance through the window reminding him of the ongoing brutal annihilation of Centa Isla.

What was he doing? Rifling through the past while his daughter was out there. He bit down hard on his own lip, drawing blood. On the horizon, a strange machination connected itself to the planet in the sky. If he knew his daughter, she'd be amongst the worst of it. He just hoped his car would survive the trip.

—

King Grayson Clovis woke in and out of a feverish sleep. During his moments of lucidity, he wailed out loud before sleep ripped him back into its dark embrace. His time spent awake lessened as the pain of his infected wound intensified. The sharp dagger of betrayal had ruined everything. A blinding crimson light bled through his heavy drapes, stinging his tired eyes with its permeating presence. He was flush with heat, in a bed soaked in his sweat yet no attendants had come to see him. Had he been forgotten so quickly?

Marco Barrett. He cursed the name through gritted teeth, writhing alone in his bedchambers while his city suffered a fate unknown. In his restless sleep, he dreamed increasingly surreal visions of his city in the throes of a nightmare. The CIPD Compound burned, terrifying silhouettes storming the depths of The Douldruums to slaughter the remaining mad bound within their cells; the Guild Hall, ornate windows caved in and monuments levelled. Even Grandmaster was besieged by monstrous figures. The City Centre all but burned, yet his tower remained untouched. He could not fathom why.

Then, he woke. Sweat dripped down him, soaking his hair to his face. He sought to sit up, desperate not to revisit these nightmarish visions. His open wound was still seeping and the bedsheet had stuck to the oozing liquid that had now dried to a thick crust. He screamed as it tore itself loose. His mind was abuzz, impossible to silence. He pushed his face into his palms and cried. How had this happened? How had he not realised? Reaching to the bedside table, he jangled the bell for his attendants. Nobody came. Frustrated, he rang again and again until finally he snapped and launched the bell across the room in anger, immediately regretting stretching his wound causing a searing pain that sent him crashing back into the headboard.

"Why!?" He spat into the air. No reply dignified him, as he had expected, but the release of rage had quietened his mind enough to hear the noise of the city below. It didn't sound dissimilar to when he had prepared for his grand speech not... hours ago? He sought his timepiece in the darkness yet couldn't read the hands through his hazy vision. Perhaps his crowd still waited for him?

Ignoring every part of his body that was telling him to rest, Grayson ushered himself out of bed, throwing the heavy duvet from his person and swinging his legs over the bed. The stab wound had penetrated deep into his back but there were several areas of pursed flesh that stained his vest with crimson streaks. This was more than betrayal, this was... hatred? He didn't realise how weak he truly was until he sought to put his weight upon his legs and they gave way. His body crashed to the carpet, causing him to scream as his injuries were further aggravated. But he had to see his public; he could hear them screaming for him beyond the drawn curtains. He would not let them down a second time. Dragging his husk across the floor, smearing the violet carpet with blood, Grayson clawed himself to the curtains and forced himself to kneel. With the last of his strength, he pushed the heavy drapes aside... and his eyes widened.

Centa Isla burned. His city, his legacy. Everything he had worked to save was aflame, crashing down among a shower of meteors and carnage. A cry of despair caught in his throat, emerging as nothing more than a pathetic whimper. Fresh tears flowed down his face. His father; murdered by his hand - for this? Homes levelled and families displaced, for it all to burn anyway? If such a thing was recognisable, Grayson swore madness was taking hold. He felt a pressure in his head and a strong irresistible urge to-

Behold.

He looked up, his chin snapped upwards as his teary eyes transfixed themselves upon what could only be described in that moment as a crimson planet that stained the horizon with its permeating hues. But there was something more there, something powerful, a presence.

You have been found wanting.

The thoughts were his own, yet distinctly not. His body suddenly felt cold and tired, yet his head pounded with heat.

The grip of death takes hold, young King. The heartache; too great.

Sure enough, Grayson could feel it. The dread in the back of his mind that told him that his body was failing. His wounds, untreated, were taking their toll upon him. Perhaps the blade that had stuck him could have been poisoned, affecting him with this malaise-stricken vision of chaos.

But it is not over.

Visions rushed into his mind, the force of which was enough to throw his head back and glaze his eyes over. He saw himself: healed and triumphant. He looked strong, healthy, his eyes glowing with a radiant power that was beyond what his bloodline could offer him. Markings covered his body, brimming with such potential power that he felt as though he could create mountains and rivers. Yes… this was what he wanted. To be free of the manipulative whims of Azrael and the traitor Marco Barrett; free of the deception and the forced hands. With this power, he could simply rebuild what Reckoning took. He would create new earth, new oceans, new life with the wave of his godly hands. No longer would he be at the mercy of schemes and machinations. Any who sought to deceive him would simply disappear in a blaze of fire. There was hope yet.

"What must I do?" King Grayson muttered weakly, pressing a clammy palm against the window. The vision of the crimson planet splayed between his fingers, as though multiple eyes watched him; preyed on him.

Accept my gift.

Then, Grayson felt himself become weightless.

———

Gault could feel the might that radiated from the very tip of the spire that anchored Galleo et'al to the city. The Obelisk dominated the sky. Rising from the sewers, a trail of demon bodies lay behind him as he ran down the twisting streets of Forge Town. But the path ahead was only going to get tougher; or rather, what was left of it. What had once been paved cobblestone roads, laid by hand years ago had now become a mire. The earth had sunk and twisted, corrupted by the dark power that radiated from the Obelisk that had turned all the land around it into a bog. The moment Gault laid boots upon the desecrated surface it sank beneath him, as though seeking to pull him beneath its shifting surface.

Press on. Together.

Gault waded through. A small army of demons protected the Obelisk; yet the mire worked against them. A legion of Scarr'dath picked at him from above, seeking to snare his throat while he contended with the foul earth and monstrous shadows on the ground. Gault used the towering Dom'inari to his advantage, using their overwhelming mass to shelter himself as he stuck them with Akor'shaki.

He could feel the excitement that radiated from his blade into him; the prospect of victory, of delivering a hammer blow to the Dark One who had defiled his home. Their vision was one. For the first time in a long time, Gault felt himself and Akor'shaki truly align, like the fire in the sky during the moments of an eclipse. Every step was amplified, backed fully by the powers bestowed upon him from wielding the demonic weapon. He tore through the sludge as though it were rainwater gathered in a pothole, ripping through demons on his way towards the Obelisk in a haze of violet and steel. All the while, the voice in his head warned him of trouble, like eyes in the back of his head, allowing him to respond to attackers he should never have seen coming. They were truly a formidable team like this.

But, as he swatted the last of the Scarr'dath from the sky, cleaving its slithering body into two twitching halves, he realised that a uniquely human shadow waited at the base of the spire. Gault ground his teeth.

Azrael.

The pale man struggled through the mire. It seemed not even Azrael could truly contend with the pallid earth beneath them. "Far enough, I think."

Standing beneath the shadow of his overlord, Azrael was bathed in crimson shadow. He nursed a sword, sheathed at his hip. Any injuries or wear he had sustained in retrieving the artefact from Grandmaster had all but healed, leaving him sharper than ever. He had left behind the lavish cloth of the nobility and had returned to the simple, tattered grey tunic that he had likely arrived in. Gault couldn't help but wait to feel the pull of madness, the call of Sophia in his peripheral vision. Yet, nothing happened. He found himself fully in control of his senses and his purpose. It was unusual, but an entirely welcome change. Control coursed through him; granting him renewed confidence that he would not become such easy, supple prey as he was the last time they had met.

Focus.

Akor'shaki felt good in his hands. Loose. He prepared himself for combat when a familiar voice called to him.

"Gault!"

"You're here?" Gault turned, awed to find Rissa standing behind him. She was ankle deep in the mire, bruised and bloodied; yet alive.

Focus.

"Of course I'm here." She came closer yet remained well out of reach. "We have to stop this."

Gault gestured to Azrael, who seemed unperturbed by the balance of power shifting against him. "Then we take him together!"

"No." Rissa's answer came as a surprise. It was shocking enough to draw his gaze back to her to see a look on her face that he hadn't yet seen. She eyed him with as much trepidation as she did Azrael. He felt a twist in his heart. What had he done to-

Focus!

He willed the blade into silence. He needed to think. Needed to share the company of his thoughts and his alone-

FOCUS!

"Silence!" He snapped out loud, well aware that he must look quite the fool. The embarrassment stood little chance against the flood of anger that flowed through him.

"Gault." Rissa called his name and the lull of her voice snared him. He looked up, her blue eyes blazing with diluted trust. "The artefact. Go and stop this. Destroy, remove, do whatever you have to do."

"What about-"

"I'll take care of him." She looked at Azrael, eyes narrowing to lethal slits. "What is this, round three?"

"Four." The black eyes simmered with idle challenge. "There will not be a fifth."

Let her throw herself upon the Omen's blade. With her borrowed time, we can end this.

Gault gritted his teeth. He couldn't just leave her... could he? He looked at her again, only to find she had coldly turned herself away from him, focusing intently upon the still figure of Azrael who had yet to even draw steel.

"Take care." He bid her, before turning and running beyond Azrael's vigil. The pale man moved to stop him, only for the flash of steel to force him to turn. Gault heard the first blades clash as he surged toward the Obelisk and ascended a slope of pure, black stone that led him out of the mire and up towards the twisting, erratic structure. Dom'inari guarded the entrance, their demonsteel spears seeking to spear the heart out his body. He cleaved them down, advancing to the stairs that spiralled up into the narrow, claustrophobic black walls.

Light felt swallowed inside the Obelisk, only the dim glow of Akor'shaki kept him from tumbling from the increasingly narrow stairwell. He took the black stone several steps at a time, feeling the air clot and writhe in his lungs as he approached the tip of the spear. Demons crowded the stairs, their laboured breathing and crimson eyes giving them away as they sought to oppose every determined step toward the top of the spire. Every step brought more slaughter, splattering the black walls with sizzling demonic blood. Blades caught him as he battled up against forces that leveraged their high ground against him. His robe tore, blood leaked, but he did not stop. It felt inevitable now as he looked up through the spiral above him to see a bright crimson light.

We are close!

Spurred on by Akor'shaki's will, Gault ascended in a flurry of steel, sending demonic corpses tumbling from the stairwell as he paved his way to the top. As he reached the pinnacle, the Obelisk stretched up around him into some dark canopy. In the centre, sealed within a pedestal built from the black stone that built the tower itself, was the artefact. It took him a moment to truly recognise it for the former innocent properties that it had possessed had been twisted and corrupted. The smooth, rounded shell had now become erratic and strained; glassy pustules having formed across its surface. There was something else present, something that Gault recognised instantly from the long year he had spent crawling amongst it. A dusty chunk of barren earth that he recognised as a part of Galleo et'al's crumbling mass itself.

It serves as the source. Telling the orb what to seek.

Gault grabbed it; only to feel the scouring of raw magic flay the flesh from his palms. He screamed and pulled away, immediately feeling Akor'shaki pump him with power to heal over his grievous wounds.

"What do I do?" He asked.

Destroy the orb.

"Rissa said she tried that-"

Not with me.

The will of Akor'shaki thrummed up his sword arm. Gault took a deep breath and held the point of the blade inches from the glassy surface. He looked up through the top of the Obelisk, where Galleo et'al's lethal form leered overhead. It was not death for the Dark One, but it would be good enough. The power contained within the artefact was so much so that if this worked, Gault knew that he surely wouldn't survive. He cast one last look at Centa Isla from atop the Obelisk, allowing himself a small smile, safe in the knowledge that he had done as well as he could have.

With a snarl, he raised Akor'shaki and brought it down upon the artefact. As demonsteel cracked the magic within, an explosion ripped through him.

—

Round four. "There will not be a fifth" as Azrael had so expertly put it. As it so happened, Rissa agreed. Her mind flitted back to their first encounters, how outmatched she had been; lucky to leave with her life on each occasion. Every time they met she had improved, yet it still hadn't been enough to win. That had to end now. Rissa found relief in seeing the back of Gault as she sent him and his cursed blade into the heart of the Obelisk while she alone contended with her fate. Without the threat of Akor'shaki turning on her again and the destruction of the Obelisk delegated, Rissa felt like she could truly concentrate on this fight. She would win this time and Azrael would fall under the shadow of his dark master.

Sludge clung to her shoes as she pushed herself forward through the mire, meeting blades in a fierce duel. Her Conduit sat heavy on her finger, although she knew that it would see very little use. The torrid conditions dragged them both down, heavy footfalls marring much of their encounter. Rissa swung for his legs, seeking to take advantage of the sinking mud that accosted them. But Azrael was quick, pulling himself away at the last moment. She led with a thrust, seeking to stick the pale stomach on the tip of her blade. His steel swatted her away and she felt his cold hands seize her wrists and his leg tangle with her own. She fought for balance, but her own momentum was twisted against her as she was flung to the floor. The mud absorbed the impact, but clumsily stuck itself to her clothes as she immediately had to scramble away from a fatal blow.

Freezing sludge seeped down her back and clung to her wild strands of hair as she scrambled to her feet in time to meet Azrael's follow up. There was an element to his game here that she had yet to have encountered, grappling. She liked it. It showed his back was against the wall that he'd try so hard to end this fight quickly but failed. Rissa weaved a barrage of kicks into his legs as they duelled. Their blades were dragged to and fro as they held each other's force at bay, steel scratching against one another as they fought for the front foot. Beneath them, the arid mire shifted and gurgled, slowly becoming treacherous. He threw an elbow into her and for a moment her vision flashed as she staggered backwards. In the haze that returned, she raised her blade just in time to parry Azrael's follow up. She forced his blade into the dirt and delivered a hammer blow of her own to his nose. She felt his features crunch beneath her fist as blood exploded down his pale face. Her knuckle throbbed with pain, but she could only imagine that he felt much worse. He staggered back but Rissa pressed her advantage, digging her sword deep into the mud as she advanced, flicking up a splash of sludge into his eyes on her way to deliver a clean cut up his midsection. Blood soaked into his tunic and for a single moment, rage flashed across Azrael's features, seeping into his movements as he swung aggressively towards her.

"You will not stop what is to come." He hissed.

Rissa knew she had him on the run. It was clear that he was distracted. His black eyes flitted to the spire of the Obelisk, likely already planning his steps once she was a bleeding corpse face down in the dirt. But with every passing second that she demanded his attention, she could feel cracks in his composure slowly begin to form. She slipped herself into those cracks, desperate to shatter the stoic image of Azrael that had tormented her so many times. Perhaps she was too eager, too keen to exploit the blood that he freely bled. When their blades next met, Rissa felt the full force of the Brand of the Knight as the impact of his swing sent reverberations up her arm. Her wrists, still weak from days in shackles, gave way. Even the calluses on her palm couldn't keep her sword in her grip as it slipped from her hand and disappeared beneath the murk below. Before she could reclaim and rearm, she was afforded no time to even attempt to reclaim the leathery hilt, forced to tumble away as Azrael split the air she had just occupied moments prior. He came for her again and she weaved a spell quickly.

I invoke the Missing Sea. Geyser, mask me!

The blast of water had no effect as she'd expected, but it did create a weak blanket of condensation that she used to quickly disarm the Omen. Her hands sought to control his wrist and she delivered a swampy kick to his midsection, managing enough force to separate his cold grip from the hilt. His blade fell too into the mire, disappearing beneath the sluice. But Rissa had given up on trying to fight blade to blade. She swung for his jaw, seeking to spin the tormenting tongue around his head. Azrael's arms came up and stopped much of the force before he grabbed her and drove his knee into her abdomen. Rissa gasped as she felt her stitches buckle and pop, but she slipped out of his follow-up, disappearing into his shadow to drive her foot into the back of his leg. Azrael buckled and she mantled him, coiling her arms around his neck and snaking her legs around his torso. She fell back, dragging him down into the mud with her as she sought to squeeze the life from his body. His pale fingers picked at her arms, desperate to worm their way between them. She resisted, feeling him splutter for breath as she only tightened her grip. Despite all her weight dragging him to the floor, Azrael managed to sit up. His hands, accepting of her vice grip, moved to the mud itself to steady himself as he rose up onto trembling legs. He reached over his shoulder for her and seized her by collar and hair. With an almighty heave, Rissa felt herself thrown from his back and into the dirt where she tumbled. Before she could so much as rise, he strode toward her and punted her in the gut, sending her further apace. Rissa felt the air leave her body as she fought to stand. His right hand whipped her face and she slumped back down, feeling the hot dribble of blood running down her nose

"This ends now." His cold hands grabbed her collar and hoisted her up. A scuffed fist reared back and hammered towards her. Twisting her face out of harm's way, Rissa felt the full force of the strike blow past her ear. She tried to wriggle free, stopping into the dirt and delivering a vicious uppercut that rattled the chin of Azrael enough to send him staggering backwards. They traded blows, wobbling on tired legs and slipping in the bog. Rissa's legs screamed for rest, the muscles in her calves trembling as they fought for control of not just combat but their balance. Much to her frustration, Azrael was adapting better than her, seeming to float through the mire. He drifted towards her, darting away from her clumsy punches. With a sweep of the leg, she was on the ground, mud filling her ears and plastering her hair. Cold hands clasped themselves around her throat and once again she felt herself pulled back to that first encounter. His black eyes bore into hers, lifeless as the day she had first seen them. Her death would be nothing to him, little more than dust in a hurricane of apathy. She tried to kick, but the mud sapped her strength, rendering her helpless. She felt death creep into every breath as her lungs heaved and warbled with strain. Blackness ebbed into her vision and she raised her Conduit in protest only for Azrael's nullifying touch to quieten the magic in her veins. She had never felt so helpless.

Then, there was the roar of an engine and the flash of headlights. A CIPD patrol car dived into the mud, immediately spinning its wheels in the murky swamp. A figure flew from the driver's seat.

"Stay away from my daughter!"

Azrael suddenly disappeared. Hands reached from behind him and dragged him from her. Rissa's head spun as oxygen surged into her grateful lungs. She scrambled to sit up, watching with wide eyes as her father hammered fists into the pale Omen.

"DAD!?" She yelled. Mud slipped and slithered beneath her as she fought for balance. As she hurried closer, she could only watch as Azrael recovered from the ambush and parried his strikes. In one swift motion he pushed her father back, scooped the glint of steel from beneath the mud and drove the blade through his chest.

Rissa screamed. Donnel wobbled on unsteady legs, his hands cradling the hilt of the blade that pierced his chest before it was ripped free. He turned to look at her, words on his lips that he couldn't manage as he toppled backwards.

Rage filled her. It coursed through her heart and down her arms, begging release. Rissa allowed it, feeling the burning numbness in her fingertips as she blasted Azrael with the rage of a thousand tempests. A cannon of water, scalding, constant. She wanted him to feel the flesh peel from his bones. The water struck him, dissolving into harmless condensation upon contact with his hand. But Rissa didn't stop; but doubled down. She felt the ground beneath her sink and contract as the force exerted by her sent her sliding back. She wished for more, expelling every ounce of magic in her body to crush Azrael beneath the force of the tides. The ground beneath him began to waver, spiralling down like a great sinkhole until the ground, weakened already by the vile presence of the Obelisk, gave way. There was a short cry as Azrael disappeared beneath the mud as the ground itself sank, crashing mud and rubble into a great crater that only grew and grew.

Raw magic poured from her mouth and nose like smoke from a dragon's maw. Her raging body trembled with overloaded magical might. Then, it all faded; replaced by a feeling far worse.

Dread.

Mud seeped through her fingers as she sought her father's still body. Panic and bile rose in her chest all at once as she slipped in the mire, ignoring the faceful of filthy earth on her way towards him.

"DAD!" Her hands sought his wound. It was deep and cavernous, bearing the same signature wound-opening twist that Azrael had dealt to her. "No. NO!"

"Rissa…" He spoke quietly. She cradled his head, refusing him to die with his head in the dirt. "My daughter…"

"Dad. It's okay." Tears stung her eyes and she could feel her mouth stretching into a sob but she bit it all back. "Can you get up? Let's-"

His hand found hers. Mud pressed in between their palms, but Rissa felt the warmth of his touch slowly fading.

"I promised... I'm sorry..." He spoke slowly. His eyes were already fading. "Our family..."

"Our family? What? Dad, stop talking, just try-"

"Your mother... she-"

"Not now, Dad. Please, not now." She tried to move him, but she could feel him resisting her. His arms reached out, energy rapidly fading as he sought her attention.

"Your mother..."

"I DON'T CARE ABOUT HER!" Rissa felt something catch fire in her chest. Rage rose to the surface, unstoppable as the rising of the tide. Immediately as the anger had arrived, it went. She calmed, her heart breaking in a thousand places as she watched hurt dapple his eyes with tears. "I just want you, Dad! That's all I've wanted..."

"I'm sorry..." Donnel choked out the words, a blanket of blood spewing from his mouth as his pierced lungs fought for breath. "I missed... everything."

Rissa began to cry, no longer able to deny the weight that was building in her eyes. Her hands were slick with her father's blood. It just wouldn't stop, no matter how much pressure she pressed into his wound. Eventually, his hand came across and pushed her efforts away. She wanted to be strong but just couldn't find it within her and she sobbed loudly into his chest but that same hand lifted her chin to look at her. There was a small smile on Donnel's face; forced, but a smile, nonetheless. "I'm so proud of you. Of whom you've become."

"Dad... Please, no..."

Donnel pressed a folded piece of bloodied parchment into her jacket pocket to shield it from the squelching mud. Rissa kept his eyes fixed on her. In his dark eyes she saw tears, washing down his cheek as the last light began to fade from his eyes. "You deserve... closure. We both... love you..."

Rissa watched as the light left her father's eyes. As the last flicker faded, she felt herself trembling, no longer able to fight back the grief that had boiled within her. She cried, hideous and ugly, throwing herself over his bleeding body as she screamed into his chest.

From the sky, she heard the screeching of demons. The Scarr'dath that had patrolled Monument had turned their attention here. Their shadows passed over her and she threw herself over her father's body as their talons raked down her back.

"Stop it!" She begged, clutching her father so tightly that they may never be able to separate them. "Stop! Please!"

Just as they began to swarm her, picking at her body like vultures, a tremendous explosion from atop the Obelisk rocked the very ground itself. The Scarr'dath immediately dispersed, screaming and hissing as though wracked by a sudden pain.

Rissa looked up; her vision blurry from tears as the dominating shadow of Galleo et'al disappeared. Its crimson mass catapulted out of the atmosphere, gone from sight within milliseconds.

The Scarr'dath fell from the sky, their wings crumbling to ash as their proximity to the Dark One was taken away. Their bodies writhed in the mud as they slowly went still.

Everything was quiet.

They had won?

Rissa looked down at the still and silent body of her father. The father who had given his own life to save hers. She gave a harrowing scream into the air.

This was far from victory

18

Gault awoke in shallow water. His eyes burned as blazing white light bleached his vision. He sat up slowly, raising a hand from the shallows to cover his eyes only to find it immediately dry. Everything was so quiet, yet his ears were still ringing from the deafening chaos that he had just beheld. He felt calm, his airways clear and his heart steady in his chest. A tranquillity spread through him, tingling his fingertips with peace.

Eternity stretched all around him. A blanket of water that stretched into a blazing white sky flecked with the auburn radiance of the morning sun. The rays were warm on his face and Gault closed his eyes, welcoming the soft heat that spread across his tired features.

"Kadin Krayt." A cacophony of voices called to him, manifesting in the very air around him. He pulled himself up, the water rippling in response to his movement as he looked down at his own reflection. The person who looked back surprised him. It was him, of that there was no doubt, but there were key features missing. The Brand of the Scout had disappeared, leaving not even a scar. With its departure, his eyes had returned to their natural green. He smiled, his face clean and eyes free of the heavy bags that had marred them.

"Kadin Krayt!" The voices came again. Their voices were many, indistinguishable from the collective. But their tone was different to what he had become used to. Gone were the venomous, spit-laden words. Instead, they sounded... pleased?

Gault turned around, seeking the source of the voices. Behind him, tall walls skirted the horizon's sunlit edge, disappearing as far into the distance as he could see. Ahead of him were gates, wide open - a field of green and oak fences. Home. Figures waited for him, their hazy bodies featureless so far away. Feeling compelled, Gault approached the figures, rippling his reflection with every step in the shallow water.

"Kadin Krayt!" They called again. Their arms hailed him, beckoning him closer. As he approached, their faces were fully realised.

He saw his sister, mother and father. They stood together, their hands resting happily on the shoulders of his sister. She had grown up, here, in this nameless place. Their faces welcomed him home. The more he looked, the more faces he recognised. The Bladesmaster who had taught him swordsmanship, the sun-toasted faces of the local bakers, the knights who he had trained with growing up. Nobles, beggars, villagers, tradesmen. It was a pantheon of the people he had known in life as Kadin Krayt. But there was one face out of them all who he was most shocked to see.

Sophia. Seeing her put a streak of cold into his sun warmed body. He had become so used to her twisted, tortured visage that seeing her now put him on edge, as though he was facing some sort of trick. The fate she had suffered, her royal lineage used to power the Obelisk that destroyed his home, was not one that should have left her so happy and pleased to see him.

Yet here she was. As Gault approached, the smile on her face widened. Her arm lifted slowly, her upturned palm waiting for him to take it.

"It's good to see you." The words that came from her mouth were friendly, genuine, void of the insidious threat of failure. For a moment, in the face of the Sophia he remembered, all memories of her twisted visage were washed away in a sea of joy.

"You too." It was as he spoke that Gault realised he was free of influence. Free of Akor'shaki's scathing intent wiggling in the back of his mind. The sudden freedom spurred more words from his mouth, words that were undeniably his own. "I'm sorry. Sorry, for everything."

Her royal bloodline had been used to power the Obelisk that had destroyed their world. As her sworn aide, to apologise felt good. It was more than he deserved. The prospect of her answer twisted in his stomach, tying his body into knots that he could not wait to be released.

Leaning back to appraise him up and down, the tug of a smile crossed Sophia's face. She opened her mouth to speak-

But there were no words.

"Sorry, what?" Gault squinted and leaned in, watching the curve of her lips form unintelligible words. "What? What are you saying?"

It was then that he realised that the gates and the people before it were getting further away. The shallow water beneath him behaved like an unnatural current, simultaneously pulling him back and pushing them away. He tried to run, to keep up with Sophia and hear the words that he was so desperate to hear, but she was only getting further away.

"Sophia! Wait, please!" He sped up, but found his body inhibited. Without the power of Akor'shaki to bestow its dark power upon him, he was no match for the growing current that washed him away. He fell as the water turned murky, deepening like the step that bordered the beach from the ocean. As he fought to keep his head above the water, he watched as the gates disappeared into the horizon. Suddenly he was pulled under. Gault held his breath, kicking his legs and striking his arms in a desperate attempt to rise. Chains coiled themself around him, snaking up his leg and pulling his arms to his side as he sank like a stone into the abyss below. His lungs burned and his cheeks felt as though they were going to burst as he struggled and writhed in vain. Beneath him, scouring the darkness of the ocean away was a violet light so bright that-

Gault woke. It was not water that he lay in this time, but rubble. It took him a moment to get his bearings. He was buried, piled upon him was dark, black stone.

The Obelisk.

Get up.

Gault felt Akor'shaki's familiar cold power course through him, providing enough power to his starved lungs to push up; up through the pile of rubble that buried him. He burst from the surface, gasping greedily for the stale Forge Town air. The sky was clear, the dark shadow of Galleo et'al was gone... they had done it.

Yet...

"You... I was-"

You died. I prevented it.

"Prevented it?" Confusion and anger spiralled interchangeably through him. "You... had no right! I saw them, I saw-"

No. Galleo et'al still lives. Our work is not finished.

"I gave my life!" Gault yelled into the air. "It was my choice. You had no right to take that from me!"

If the blade could sneer, it would have. *Of course it was my right. Your life is my life; we are one and the same.*

"You're a parasite." Gault hissed.

That grants you strength. Purpose. Without me you were nothing. I am only doing as you told me to.

"Told you to? What are you talking about?"

Destroy Galleo et'al, at any cost. These were the words; your words, that founded our bargain. We may have defeated the Dark One, but it is by no means destroyed.

Their bargain. Made in a moment of madness and desperation. He had never realised it would bind him so fiercely. Gault seized the chain that hung at his waist, hoisting Akor'shaki up to his eyeline to dangle before him. There was no breeze, yet the tiny scythe warbled and waved with life.

"Then our bargain is done."

If it could have laughed, it would have. *You are a fool. I was destined for the hands of Azrael and instead, I have been stuck with you. Twisted to your blind desire for vengeance. I am you. The bargain is you. I am merely an adhesive to the strongest desire you felt upon laying your hands upon me. But let me make one thing clear. I have always had your best interests in mind.*

"My best interests?" Gault knew the words were true, his memory of the day he made his bargain were hazy, marred by dehydration and desperation. Yet there was something afield that did not feel right. Akor'shaki had taken his hatred and guilt and weaponised it. Made him an unstoppable force of regret and rage that would not rest until Galleo et'al was dust upon the stars for what he had done to his home. "Then…"

You were always so slovenly. So, in need of the whip to get anything done. We would spin our wheels in the mud for eternity if not for my intervention.

"Intervention?" Gault felt his body trembling even as the dark depths of the manipulation he had suffered began to dawn upon him. "Sophia… the others… It was you…"

I only sought your strongest motivator. She always lit a fire in you.

"You bastard!" Gault pulled at the chain, feeling it unspooling around his insides. He kept going, desperate to be free of the cursed blade that had poisoned his mind with visions and twisted control of his own body from him. All the horrific sights he had plagued with had been nothing but a manifestation. His thoughts and memories, stolen and tortured into motivating him into surrendering control of his body to the blade.

Cease this tantrum. Without me, your Brand will connect you to the Dark One once more. He will kill you. It was not a lie when I said I had your best interests in mind. Your goals are mine. We work best when we are aligned; you saw that yourself just.

383

He felt the limits of the chain approaching. With it, came a growing discomfort. He had never found just how far the chain ran. "Aligned to what? Single-minded destruction without regard for anyone else?"

Precisely.

"Then we can never be aligned!" Gault suddenly found the end of the tether. He felt his entire body jolt, as though his spirit had momentarily been fractured from his body. He sought his wound, finding the chain unable to budge any further. But still, he pulled, desperate to free himself.

Separate us. We both die.

"Fine."

Like this? Wallowing in pity in the rubble of your greatest work? You are alive, ready to throw a second life at the forces of the Dark One that still roam this accursed city.

Gault felt his efforts slow. He had expected to feel better about a victory over the Dark One, yet he had found his triumph sufficiently diluted. His moment had come and it had passed. Galleo et'al was gone and he had retained his life for another use. There were people here he needed to thank, to aid.

"Rissa."

A distraction. She sought to sever our bond.

One thing was clear now. His voice and Akor'shaki's were separate, distinct. It was as though the part of him that the blade embodied had fully separated itself, no longer trying to blend into his thoughts as though they were his own. It was relieving but felt now as though a parrot lived on his shoulder, squawking madness in his ear.

"She helped me resist your control! You couldn't abide that, could you?"

It hardly matters. A bridge burned already; I fear.

Gault felt a stab of anxiety. There was something he was missing from Rissa. There was a fresh boundary between them, whether set by her or him he had never been certain. "What did you do?"

Akor'shaki offered him nothing but silence.

"Bastard!" Gault slung the chain downward, smashing the scythe into the ground where it harmlessly wound back up into his body, returning idly to his hip. He felt the anxiety return. "... What did you do?"

Mantling up the remains of the Obelisk, Gault surveyed the mire that had become the outskirts of Forge Town. Loose stone that was slowly evaporating before his very eyes spilled down as the magic that held it together began to dissipate with the destruction of its foundation. Soon enough, the rubble would be gone, only the swamp remaining. There. Among the dark ooze and black rubble, a head of blue hair stood out like a sore thumb, she rested where the base of the dark construct had been. Still.

Gault felt his heart hitch. He surged down the rocky mountain. "Rissa!"

She did not respond. Gault feared death, until he got closer.

Rissa lay over a body, the corpse was entirely recognisable. The eyes were still open, staring blankly up at a sky free of evil. Donnel Rawdon. At the edge of the mire, Gault spotted an abandoned CIPD vehicle, its bonnet splattered with blood and dissolving demonic limbs.

"Rissa-"

"This needs to end." She spoke without looking up, face buried in the bloody chest of her father. "This has to end."

"It has."

"No." She shook her head, lifting herself up slightly to look at the silhouette of Monument, as untouched as the day it was built. "Not while the Omens live."

She's right, for once.

Gault shut the words from his mind. "It will take them years to rebuild. You have time to grieve-"

"NO!" Her fists drove into the mud around her as she sat up, knees buried in the murk. "There isn't any time. Can't you feel it?"

Gault remained still and silent for a moment, seeking whatever vague feeling she was describing, but ultimately coming up blank. "No."

"The city is reeling. There will be a response." She rose, running her muddy hands through her hair. When she turned to him, her eyes were puffy and her cheeks were streaked with mud and tears. "I'm not waiting. There won't be a better chance. He will pay."

Gault watched her. Her expression was like nothing he had seen from her before. Anger eroded her, like the tide against a cliff. But it was not blind rage, but a pitch perfect focus.

"Then let me help."

"No." She whirled on him, her face twisted with rage. "You keep your distance."

"I'm in control, trust-"

"I said keep your distance, Kadin." She spoke his name with a sneer, her sharp eyes watching his face for his reaction. "You didn't even tell me your real name."

He didn't need to ask how she knew. The answer swung at his waist. Just how entrenched was the influence of Akor'shaki in their relationship?

"But... I need a favour from you." Her eyes warbled with grief but thrummed with magic potential, her face was strong and stoic.

"Anything."

She pointed indifferently to the body of her father. "Take him away from here."

"Where to?"

"I don't care." Her response was so frigid that he felt a chill down his spine. "Just not here. Not in the dirt."

Without another word, she turned and trudged through the swampy murk, towards a great sinkhole that had formed nearby. It ran deep, crashing into the sewers below. He didn't follow her. He wasn't sure what to say. Beneath him was her one request. The body of Donnel Rawdon was still warm, Gault identified his wound immediately and felt sorrow at the man's fate. The blade that had pierced his chest and lung, the cruel twist of steel to widen the wound and ensure death was a trademark he recognised all too well.

Azrael.

The air crackled with energy. Even as Rissa marched for revenge, Gault sensed her intuition was correct. Without Galleo et'al to empower the demonic army, they would quickly be overrun by the rallied survivors of Centa Isla. The people's response would be quick and lethal, spurred by the swinging of the momentum finally in their favour.

He glanced up at Rissa's head of navy hair as it disappeared beneath the earth. There were few stronger opponents than Azrael that Gault could think of to bear a strong grudge against. She would need his help, whether she desired it any longer or not.

Kneeling in the dirt, Gault scooped up Donnel's body. He felt the rush of Akor'shaki offering strength enough to move the body with ease, but Gault denied it, burying that power where it belonged. He wasn't going to rely on it for every little inconvenience anymore. Donnel's body would be moved with the respect it deserved. For now, Gault could conceive no better place than the vehicle the man had loved so much in life.

Rissa was right. This wasn't over.

—

Lachesis watched as the carnage unfolded across the city. Her network of critters shared with her their vision of death, allowing her to track the invasion practically street by street from atop her rooftop perch.

Downtown burned, the streets finally cleansed of the Synth-addled dregs in a wash of fire and demonsteel. The tall tower blocks crumbled as shards of earth crashed through them, killing the denizens within and around. The CIPD Compound was culled, the force dispatched and the mad prisoners within The Douldruums purged by the indiscriminate wrath of the Dom'inari. The sewers were flushed out, blood bursting through the drains as Hounds of Xer stalked the pitch darkness, dragging away those who sought only to hide. Storefronts were destroyed, hideouts were ransacked and the derelict buildings finally collapsed in on themselves as the city wobbled with the strike of every earthen meteor that hit it.

The scorched earth of Forge Town had become a wasteland. The grim influence of the Obelisk turned much of the outer edge of the cobblestone district into nothing but a marsh as the demonic power took its toll on the land.

Only Grandmaster offered resistance. The shields that the Versorcerers had erected and the stoic, inhuman knights that protected the gates had been able to stave off the invasion. But she could see the academy from her perch. Cracks were formed across the shield and the amount of demons that swarmed the gates was only growing moment by moment. It would be just a matter of time. Even still, she had all but confirmed her suspicions that Centa Isla wouldn't be entirely annihilated. Even unprepared, there were pockets of resistance that had cropped up through the city, although they were not to last.

Then, the unthinkable happened.

The Obelisk exploded. Bright white lights flared in the distance and Lachesis could not believe what she was seeing. The sky reverberated with the pulse of magic might and just as quickly as the sky had caught fire; it dimmed.

And Galleo et'al was gone.

But she felt him immediately. The Brand of the Watcher on her back flared before she could even comprehend what had happened. The rage of the Dark One filled her body, the brand burning hotter than the day it was scorched onto her flesh. She screamed, collapsing onto the rooftop from which she had wished to watch the events unfold. Her mind spiked and her entire blood ran as hot as molten lava. She lay there on the floor, desperate for the pain to pass, entering her mind sanctuary of a youth well lived back home.

Then, the pain had ended. She could still feel the anger, singing her skin like the spitting fires of a forge, yet it was weak. So very weak. The Dark One was exhausted, after taking its rage out upon its subjects, there was only a single command it made.

Return to the tower.

Monument stood tall on the horizon. It had been left entirely untouched by the army that had surged through these streets. Lachesis suspected that it had been an intentional decision that had been willed into the demonic masses. She had watched from her perch as the flames had coursed through the city, spreading exponentially like a match dropped in a jungle. The destruction had been indiscriminate and Lachesis had felt a pang of sorrow upon watching the prospect of Centa Isla come undone. And yet here it was culled, destroyed, yet still very much the victor. She sought her network, commanding their vision to her own as she found herself scampering through the ruins at street level. Already, the people were fighting back. Without the crimson shadow of the Dark One to empower them, the demonic hordes were quickly losing their power. Their leathery flesh was becoming flaky and brittle, breaking away in dusty clumps upon the smallest of impact as they were returned to their dark master piece by piece. Somehow, the Obelisk had been destroyed. She knew not how such a feat had become possible, the bog that had become of the once cobblestone streets making it impossible for her skittering network to get anywhere near. But she had her suspicions. Even still, she had thought it impossible.

Lachesis had always preferred to watch the destruction than partake in it. Her work was complete and there was little joy to be found in indulging in it further. Although this time, it seemed her presence may have been needed. No doubt the pain she had been filled with had been a recourse of her choice to stand by and let the chaos run its course. Not that she'd expected things to turn out the way they did.

Galleo et'al was weak. She could sense it. Yet, even in its current state it could probably claim her life with a single thought. And so, she obeyed the bidding it had given her and sought out Azrael, seeking his Brand with the powers of the Watcher. She saw his aura, dim and fading, trudging through the bowels of the city itself. She attuned herself to his Brand and numbness came over her, spreading rapidly through her arms and legs until it reached her head and her vision blacked out, returning with her limbs a second later in the dark, dingy underground. As her senses returned, she was blasted with the stench of sewage.

Azrael rested against a nearby wall. He was bloody and bruised, belly cut open like a pig and an arm that had been bludgeoned out of shape. Rubble still fell from him, clinging to his torn tunic as dusty black ash that had already covered the floor.

"Brother!" Upon seeing him, she hurried over and knelt at his side. "What happened to you?"

Azrael flexed his broken arm. A horrible crackling came as he twisted and clenched his shattered fingers. No pain passed across his face. "I failed."

"You-"

"And where were you, sister?" His black eyes turned to her, simmering with accusations. "Where were you, as I defended the Obelisk alone?"

"I'm sorry." She reached for his injuries, but he swatted her away. "I... didn't think this was possible."

"They should be dead. I told you to kill them." Azrael hissed.

Before she could reply, there was a flash in her peripheral vision. Streaks of blue lit up the dark tunnel moments before a column of water lurched through the narrow sewers. Lachesis shoved Azrael against a wall and pressed herself equally against it. She could feel the stinging edges of the blast scratching at her back. It ended and footsteps hammered through the echoing tunnel. Swiftly, Lachesis seized Azrael, coiling her hand around his wrist and concentrated on her scrying orb stationed in her quarters within Monument. As she felt her body begin to dematerialise, the numbness spreading down her arm and into Azrael, she turned around as the jagged point of a sword flew towards her throat. Blue eyes, burning with fury and a cry of anger-

Lachesis screamed, clutching her throat as she appeared in her quarters. She brought her hands away, finding nothing. Immediately, she calmed. She had been seconds from death. Instantly, she sought her brother who rested weakly against her wardrobe.

"Brother, are you-"

There was a thud from the hallway outside before Azrael could reply. They both shared a cautious glance, turning just as the door opened.

King Grayson Clovis stepped in. For a moment, Lachesis thought the King had made a miracle recovery, only to quickly realise there was much more at play here. Across the King's handsome features, a Brand had been scalded. The pattern was murky and his flesh still sizzled from the sizzling heat of the cruel instrument that had branded him, but she would recognise that mark anywhere.

The Brand of the Heretic. The very same mark that Mires had worn that allowed him to surrender his body to the voice of the Dark One.

"My Lord." Lachesis dropped to one knee immediately, keeping her wide eyes fixed firmly on the carpet beneath her. Azrael copied her seconds after, likely realising what fate had befallen the King of Centa Isla.

"Attend me on top of the tower." The voice was Grayson's, yet it was backed by a dark, throaty reverb that crackled the air with power. Whether the Dark One had possessed the corpse of the King, or was simply controlling him, she did not know. But as the awkward body shambled a hand into its pocket and brandished an ornate crimson vial, she could tell that there was a contingency plan taking place. "Imbibe, Knight."

The vial rolled across the floor. Azrael took it immediately.

"Watcher." The King's voice called to her and she felt her heart jostle with fear. She looked up, terrified as the former King manoeuvred clumsily towards her. The Dark One was clearly new to this body, for its movements were hesitant, like a toddler learning its first steps. "I expect compliance from you."

"Of course, My Lord."

Without another word, Galleo et'al marched the body out of the room and disappeared into the hallway.

"Brother-" Lachesis turned to Azrael, only to find him glugging down the contents of the vial without so much a second thought. She sought to proclaim but found herself mute as he suddenly rocked with pain. His eyes bulged from his sockets and drool oozed from his mouth as his entire body seemed to become locked in stasis. She watched as the wound on his belly healed over. The bruises faded and the shattered bones in his body snapped back into place. Yet, for all the miracles she was witnessing, there was something deeply disturbing happening within her brother's body. She could see the veins pressing against the prison of his flesh, coursing bright red with vile power. His eyes warbled and chunks of white hair fell from his scalp in terrifying clumps. Blood oozed from his nose and he spat, sending several bloodied teeth flying from his gums. The empty darkness in his eyes grew, taking over even the whites of his eyes in pitch black.

Then, he went still. Slowly, a crimson colour filled his eyes, painting his iris the colour of sickly blood. He licked his lips, coming away with bleeding gums and a tongue seared by whatever foul liquid he had imbibed. He had changed, yet upon rising, did so with so much power that his very body trembled with might.

"Brother?" Lachesis asked quietly.

"... Pure demon blood." When he spoke, he did so through a throat seared by the toxic gore of demonic armies. His eyes were sharp and terrifying, filled with such evil that even she felt afraid. Lachesis had often thought the day light returned to her brother's eyes would be a good one. It seemed she had been wrong.

"Come, sister." His hand fell to her, now missing several fingernails. "There is much work to be done."

She took his hand and could feel the power in every twitch of his body as he hoisted her up. Without another word he departed, bound for the elevator that led up to the throne room. She joined him, moving in silence as they entered the clunking lift and arrived in the vast space. It was quiet in Monument now. Where once these halls had been filled with Kingsguard, nobles and servants alike, it was now derelict. As they walked through the empty chamber, the throne itself caught her eye. It was an ornate, golden seat, cushioned with violet fabric and eloquent drapes that spilled down the side of it. The crest of the Clovis family adorned it.

She imagined herself sat upon it. A leader. Beloved and worshipped by all for saving the city from the designs of evil. An amusing thought, quickly quelled by the sight that awaited her up the steel service steps that led up to the roof of Monument. As they arrived, Lachesis beheld Galleo et'al as it puppeteered the body of King Grayson Clovis. It stood in the centre of the flat roof, surrounded by Magic Extraction Chambers upon which she had seen Mires take a keen interest before his death. There were four pods in total, each one occupied by a body she had seen pass through these halls before.

The Elemental Council. Kiara Harrington, the Seat of Flame. Theora Eculaire, the Seat of Water and the traitor Marco Barrett, the Seat of Air. Their bodies were confined to the claustrophobic interior of the pod as their magic was harvested. Their screams threatened to burst free from within. The oldest of them, Lady Eculaire, seemed to have already succumbed to the pain, yet the Magic Extraction Chamber was indiscriminate in taking her cold blood for its own. Their pods all connected to a steel tank that was rapidly filling with crimson.

"My Lord." Azrael arrived before the avatar of Galleo et'al and dropped down to one knee in reverence. Lachesis promptly did the same, trying to drown out the screams from the two surviving Seats.

"As you surely see, I have a contingency." Galleo et'al spoke, already seeming more in control of the King's powerful form. "Protect me at all costs."

"What will you do, My Lord?" Lachesis asked.

At her question, Galleo et'al brandished a shard of pocked, ashen earth from the King's pocket. It was the Dark One's mass itself, some of it having survived its fiery descent to the surface.

"This body houses immense power. An impressive lineage runs in these veins." He spoke quietly, stretching the King's face into a cruel smile. "His blood is not as potent as the princess, but he may work where the Obelisk no longer can."

"Will that work?" Lachesis watched grimly as The Dark One sought to use Grayson Clovis as a makeshift Obelisk to once again blot out the skies with its form.

"For your sake, I do hope he endures." Galleo et'al turned away and approached the tank of blood. "Now, affix me to this infernal machine."

He gestured to the steel tank, where an array of large needles extended from its exterior. Azrael rose immediately, taking up the needles and connecting Grayson's puppet body to the tank. Lachesis copied him, finding it terrifyingly easy to find the bulging veins of the King's powerful body.

"Protect me at all costs. I must not be interrupted."

"Of course, My Lord." Azrael bowed. "Is there anything else?"

"Yes." Grayson gestured towards the Magic Extraction Chambers. Three of them were occupied, sapping the blood from its hosts. But one of them was empty, missing the Seat of Earth who Azrael had replaced at the beginning of this long campaign. "I require four. The tank will run empty before I am able to summon myself."

Lachesis was confused, until she felt the Dark One's gaze fall upon her, spearing through the auburn eyes of the King. "... but My Lord-"

A hand fell upon her. Pale, fingernails missing. She couldn't believe it.

"Brother! What are you doing?"

His crimson eyes avoided her as he dragged her towards the empty machine. Lachesis kicked and screamed, but his new infernal power was undeniable. This was to be her fate? Leeched of her vitality to allow the Dark One to return once more? She sought her crystal ball; sought to transport herself to it once more-

Pain coursed through her. The eyes of the King glowed red with power and Lachesis felt her Brand strike like a match, crushing her mind as though it was trapped in a vice. She screamed, helpless to resist as Azrael lowered her into the machine and quietened her writhing by binding her limbs in leather straps.

"BROTHER! Please!" She shrieked as the needles pierced her skin one by one. She could feel the icy, sterilised steel deep in her veins. Try as she might, she could not ensnare his gaze, even as he brought the lid down around her. It hissed, sealing her inside with nothing but her own words for company as the pod descended into silence. But as soon as it activated the silence was replaced with harrowing screams.

—

Only dawn will follow. The mantra carried by the leaders of Eclipse had survived the demon invasion, survived the slaughter and the death, even if its progenitor did not. The words had gained new life, shared and carried forward by all of those who had survived. The fightback seemed to have come from Grandmaster, driving up the Path of Discipline back towards Monument, slaying the vastly weakened demons along the way. The city was emboldened, Gault could feel it in the air, hanging in the atmosphere like gas fumes ready to explode with the strike of a flame.

He had lost Rissa. She was able to traverse the city far quicker with her Vortexes than he could on foot. Refusing to use the enhanced leaps and bounds that Akor'shaki granted him did little to speed him up.

You're sulking. Use me.

Permitting himself a breather, Gault stopped. The Blades was a wash of corpses. Many of them, he darkly recognised. The golden teeth of Kenneth Rand were stretched into an eternal grimace, yet the uprising he had fathered was very much alive. He had fallen to demons, yet his intent lived on in those that marched over their corpses to storm Monument for the final time. There were other dead present, corpses piled up at the gates like bags of sand. Within them, Gault saw Sheppard, a gaping hole in his chest where a demonsteel pike had punctured him fatally. There were few in Centa Isla who had extended him true kindness, but the heart that had beat within the chest of the stoic bartender was one that he would not soon forget.

Gault watched the frontline of Centa Isla's vengeful survivors arrive at the gates. There were nobles, synth addicts, Empty Eye thugs, Versorcerers; just about everyone who called this city their home who had somehow survived. They marched down The Blades, parading severed limbs of demon and Kingsguard alike as they swarmed the gates of Monument that had been sealed shut. It did not take long for the gates to be under siege as battering rams created from Earth magic struck at the steel hinges. The spells were created by nobles, finally donning their dusty Conduits. At the steps of the tower, demons roamed the courtyard, greatly weakened, yet still more than capable of demolishing the most eager of the frontline. Among them were a scattered force of Kingsguard, clearly confused to be standing among demons in defence of their King. Gault felt a pang of sympathy for the twisted, confused loyalty that would have led them this far. Had this been the kingdom he had taken an oath to protect back home, he too may have been so loyal as to stand among monsters in defence of Sophia and her family.

Just then, the sky was struck with crimson once again and Gault felt his heart lurch in panic as he looked upward to see a beam of power rise into the sky from the top of Monument. He recognised it instantly as it drove up out of the atmosphere, fishing once again among the stars for the Dark One's return.

Fortunate that I saved your life now, isn't it?

"Spare me." He hissed. The sudden reemergence of Akor'shaki's voice, now distinctly separate from his own, jolted him from simply staring up at the coming chaos. He sprinted towards the gate of Monument, coiling his legs like a spring to launch himself up over the tall wall. Upon doing so, he rose only a fraction of his usual height into the air and crashed into the wall, landing abruptly on his backside.

He could feel Akor'shaki laughing at him. Without the blade he was truly useless.

Ready to accept my power again?

"Fine."

As he spoke, Gault felt the swell of power wash through him and he leaped, easily mantling the wall and surging into the courtyard where he crashed into an unsuspecting demon. As its flaky head rolled, so too did the gates finally give way to the vengeful masses. The steel hinges buckled and the great gates toppled to a roar of insurrection. Bodies poured in, meeting the Kingsguard and vastly weakened demonic forces in a mangle of combat. Even in its malaise, the remaining Dom'inari culled ranks with great swings of its demonsteel poleaxe. Limbs flew into the air, immediately stripping away momentum and energy from the rampant crowd. Gault charged for the remaining demons and began to rip through them in a flurry of Akor'shaki's steel. With every monstrous body that crumbled into dust after death, Gault listened as the crowd rallied.

You are wasting time.

He ignored the strained words. This was an important moment for the people of Centa Isla. Their rage and their vengeance would help bring Monument down. Gault watched as the bulk of the Kingsguard either surrendered their weapons to the masses or retreated into the tower as their demonic allies were felled. Those who stood to the end were buried in their armour, trampled and stuck with daggers and jagged pipes as the charge led up the stairs and into the carpeted foyer of Monument itself where a second wave of security waited for them. Gault looked for faces in the seething masses that surged through the courtyard and through the great doors into Monument. He sought Rissa among the blurry faces, yet didn't find her among the grieving and vengeful. She had to be here, yet he couldn't find her anywhere. It wasn't until he looked up, did he receive his answer. A body flew through one of the towers middling floors, shattering the window along with a blast of water. It was a Kingsguard soldier, dragged screaming by the weight of his armour towards the ground, landing with a metallic clang. Many cheered up at the figure who peered down from the broken window before closing in on the terrified guard. She loitered for a moment, seeming to enjoy the cheers before disappearing inside.

Gault stared up at her, then glanced toward the nearest stairwell. Within Monument's foyer, a legion of Kingsguard had formed a chokepoint at the first set of stairs into the tower. They bore great, tall shields and long pikes, sticking those who dared to charge them in the gut and using their corpses to create obstacles. Behind them, two Versorcerer's disrupted the masses with spellwork, creating earthen barricades and whirlpools of water. Gault wasn't sure even he could have influence against such a force, yet he couldn't stay here and wait. Instead, he coiled Akor'shaki's chain and spun the loose blade like a grappling hook. With a grunt of power, he launched his blade up to the shattered window, willing Akor'shaki to find purchase within the halls within.

I'm secure.

He half expected the words of the blade to be a lie and for the grip to fail as he ascended the face of Monument. To its credit, it held. All the way up as he dragged his body up through the window and into the velvet-lined halls of Monument. They were not as he had expected. From the outside, the tower presented as a fortress; its leering shadow a reminder to all beneath it of just who ruled over them at all times. Inside, it took on an unexpectedly warmer tone. The floor beneath the royal violet carpet was laid from planks of darkened oak and dim chandeliers that lined the long halls provided scatterings of low light that cast a sleepy spell over the entire place.

Yet he knew there was to be no rest here, not until whatever machination was taking place atop the tower had been quelled and the threat of Galleo et'al had been all but removed from this city. He sought stairs, bounding up flight after flight of the empty halls. As he ascended, he ran into a member of the Kingsguard. He braced for battle, but quickly noticed that behind the helmet were a pair of wide, fearful eyes. The knight held his spear with trembling arms, his back turned now to a window that showed a menacing view of the legion that was descending upon the tower. He was terrified. Gault lowered his fists, as did the Knight. In truth, a kill may have been a mercy compared to what the crowd would do to him, even after death. Already, he could see the armoured bodies at the base of the tower being strung up; severed heads wobbling on steel pipes at the base of the tower they had sworn to protect. It was barbaric. Without a word between them, Gault left him to cower in the corridor. From the floor, he took up the discarded blade of the Knight.

What are you going to do with that?

"I don't need you." He clutched the blade in his hand, recalling the old lessons beneath the shadow of the palace back home. It felt heavy and his grip pined for the hilt of Akor'shaki, but he pressed that down. The blade was rotten and he was done relying on it.

See how long that lasts.

As he climbed, he caught up with Rissa. She leant against a wall, resting. At her feet were two armoured bodies, drenched. As he approached, she quickly sniffled and dried her eyes, pushing herself as though to move again.

"Rissa. Wait." He dropped, finding a pulse on the writhing bodies as their waterlogged armour clunked with their strained movements. For a moment he thought she had killed them.

"They're fine. Don't act like a saint now." Rissa smiled falsely at him. "I asked them to let me through. They didn't."

It took him a moment to realise she was nursing an injury. Her abdomen, where Azrael had stabbed her during the storm. Fresh blood stained her shirt.

His face darkened. She was acting well beyond her means of combat surging in here alone. She was going to end up dead well before she could seek any kind of vengeance. Gault could feel his breathing quicken and his heartbeat faster.

Like looking in a mirror, isn't it?

Gault found himself agreeing. Following the destruction of his home, he could remember the rage and the hurt as fresh as the day it was dealt. The fires had consumed him for so long. Even now, they dimmed but were never truly sated. They likely never would be. Irritating as the fact was now, if he had not been granted power from Akor'shaki, he would have died upon Galleo et'al's surface well before the first week, let alone first year. Rissa would likely find no such luxury. He had to choose his words carefully.

"You're hurt."

"Just overstretched." She turned her body away from him, seeking to continue towards the next stairwell.

Gault grabbed her arm. "You need to slow down. We can work-"

"NO!" She yanked herself free, face twisting in pain as she aggravated her open stitches further. The pain melted away to anger, plastering deep lines across her face as she practically spat with every word that followed. "You stay away from me! Both of you!"

Even if he had seen them coming, the words hit like a blade to his heart. The seed of mistrust had been sown from the very beginning, from the moment he lost his mind to Akor'shaki's influence at the Guild Hall and had ruined their plan. She had been kind to him, pleasant even and they had shared a living space for days at a time. She had even sought to help him with his condition, but even through all that he had never found a way back through that wall she had raised. She didn't take betrayal lightly and it seemed that for Rissa, forgiveness was a mountain. And every lapse of control he had suffered was a landslide of progress taken back.

"I'm in control." He spoke quietly to her raised voice. He raised Akor'shaki's shrunken form, dangling it harmlessly in front of him. He watched her eyes snap warily to the blade, her body shying away from its presence as though it was poison. "I am sorry for everything."

Rissa looked from the blade to him. Her eyes narrowed. Then, tears shone in the dim light. Her face failed to hold onto the rage and it all melted away as she suddenly broke into a grieving mess. She collapsed on the carpet and wailed.

"Gault... He's gone...!"

He felt his chest twist in pain as he watched her grieve. Even still, he stood there, paralysed as she wept, darkening the violet carpet with her tears.

Comfort her, idiot. At the very least get an ally out of this.

"I know, I know." Gault dropped down to her level, feeling a gnawing anxiety at how she'd react to his touch. His hand fell on her shoulder and he half expected her to wheel away, lashing out and rejecting his comfort. Yet, she didn't. As his hand fell upon her shoulder, she instead sank into him. Her head burrowed into his shoulder that wasn't guarded by steel. As she sobbed uncontrollably, her hands pulled at his sleeve, clenching the old fabric tightly until her knuckles bleached white. Her body trembled and her voice was hoarse and cracked.

"He's gone!" She yelled, her voice muffled by her proximity to his shoulder. Just as the words came out, she cried even louder. "My family-!"

Her sentence never found its conclusion, the thoughts ahead of the words too much for her to not wail. He could feel her body sinking, forcing him to take her weight. His arms came around her back and he held her silently, unsure of what to say in the face of such grief.

Silence is best. Do not ruin it with your flapping gums.

How Akor'shaki knew how to be so tactful when he himself did not, irritated him. Had the blade not said itself that everything it knew, it knew from him?

Eventually, Rissa grew still. Her grief satiated for the moment. Gault remained present while she gently pulled her head from his shoulder and swiftly wiped over the surface with her sleeve before he had a chance to see anything. She hid her face, hands frantically working to regain her composure. When she was able, she looked him in the eye, breathing in deeply. Her eyes were puffy and red, warbling still from repressed tears.

"Sorry." She eventually murmured. The flush of embarrassment darkened her cheeks "That was... well, there's... more important things to do, isn't there?"

"No. There isn't." Gault just smiled at her, as earnestly as he could manage. "Take as much time as you need."

"I'm ready." Was her reply. For a moment, her eyes caught the two dead Kingsguard and for a moment, it looked like she was going to explode again.

To her credit, she held it all back. "These deaths.... Dad's death ...needs to count...for -"

She cut herself off, swallowing hard. Promptly, she gestured to the stairwell behind her with determined eyes. Her intentions were perfectly clear.

19

Rissa felt a shift in her mood. The raging fire of her anger had quelled to hot embers that burned with an eternal constancy. Her desire for revenge was now the stronger emotion - focused onto a single point.

Azrael had to die.

Rissa was certain that once the pale one was skewered upon her blade, her mind would clear and clarity would be the reward. Until then, her thoughts were dominated by him. She pictured him dying, blood spewing from his mouth as she lopped the head from his shoulders. The cruelty and excess were pleasing; this single thought allowing a state of deadly calm as the usual hubbub of her mind was dominated by a solitary obsession for justice. She had felt like this since reuniting with Gault.

Did she trust him? Like it mattered. If he lost control again she didn't care, so long as it was directed at Azrael. Whatever pieces remained of their relationship she could salvage once the deed was done. As they ascended higher into Monument, the past weighed heavily upon her. She had wrongly assumed she had always been in control. From her first involvement in Gault's doomed mission. She had naively held onto the idea that she could opt out at any time and that she was in charge of where she was heading. That notion had now been turned on its head and she felt less pressured by her own self-imposed expectations and was experiencing a completely new feeling wash over her.

Freedom?

It was a strange liberty of sorts. The separation from the anxiety that had controlled her life all these years. It made so much more sense to her now, but the cost of her knowledge was too great. Her response to Azrael's immunity to her magic had been to learn to use a sword. Her response to Gault's bouts of tunnel vision was to try and fix him. They were different problems struck with the same brush that she had used to paint all her problems in life.

Control. Was she a control freak? Was she so arrogant that she couldn't trust somebody else to do an important task? She didn't know. But she understood herself a layer deeper than she had before all of this. With that feeling, came a strange resolve, a relief from a weight that had dragged her down for so many years.

She was free now. Any desire she had to control her life had gone. In grim terms, she'd given up. In brighter terms, she'd let go of her fear and simply embraced the chaos that defined Centa Isla. Her efforts to create a life of significance and meaning in this city had been akin to a balloon surviving in an ocean of pins. All that remained was to let it burst. Yet there was something new stirring deep within her; a violent maelstrom of emotion that churned her stomach and weighed heavy in her heart. It filled the void that fear had once dominated. It was a dark desire for cruelty, for revenge.

She pushed the memory of her father down, deep into the pit of her mind where everything she didn't want to confront was buried. While that dark space had once held the direction her life was heading, it was empty now. All her problems seemed pathetic in the face of true loss. Rissa rued all the time she had lost with her father. After all these years they had started to finally mend the wounds her mother's disappearance had driven between them. Yet now, it didn't matter. The dream Donnel Rawdon had held so stubbornly of reuniting their family was truly dead along with him. She was orphaned; both her parents lost to Centa Isla's marred history of self-destruction.

So be it. She would have revenge, then she would figure things out. Rissa was no stranger to being alone.

Her deep thinking had gratefully distracted her from the ache in her calves from running up so many flights of stairs. But they ended the moment she reached the last step. She glanced out a window, immediately feeling a rush of vertigo at the sheer height. Never, in her wildest days of leaping from rooftops with Vortex's beneath her had she ever had so much as a churn in her stomach from the height. Yet this was truly something else. She could see all the way down The Blades to Downtown. Ocean's View, her old apartment block was out there somewhere. It seemed a lifetime ago that it was once her home, milling the days away with the moans of Synth addicts on her doorstep. The city was so insignificant from here. It was no wonder that every King had been an arrogant fool. The flames of the rebelling populace were little more than kindling, washing through the city in a wave of light. She wondered for a moment, as she stared at every little flicker across the cityscape. Who were those people? What were their problems? Who had they lost? She wondered if her feelings were more important than theirs. That her loss was greater than anything they could ever feel. Then again, what did it matter? She watched those little fires move through the tiny streets. She would never know their names, nor would they likely ever know hers.

"Rissa." Gault's voice distracted her and she jumped slightly.

"Yeah?"

"Focus."

"I'm here." She wrenched herself from the window and looked at Gault. He gestured down the long stretch of hallway ahead of them. At the end, it expanded out, revealing a large set of steel doors.

As they approached the door, ornate markings embellished the surface. She didn't care to read them, but they certainly looked important. Gault reached it ahead of her, planting his palms into each of the steel surfaces and grunting as he pushed, the doors groaning with effort as their hulking forms churned open. Inside, a vast room awaited them. A violet carpet led from the doors all the way to the end where it mantled a set of stairs to a golden throne. A wall ran across the left-hand side, adorned with paintings and huge framed portraits of Kings and Queens long past. On the right, was a breathtaking view of the city, framed by an entire wall of glass panes.

Inside, a lone figure waited for them. Pale, sickly, yet changed. But he could have worn a wig and a mask and she'd still recognise him. Those dark, vile eyes. Yet even from afar she could see there was something different about them. A crimson glaze lurked within the mire. He stood healthy, hale, a far cry from the retreating form that had skulked into the darkness of the sewers.

"Azrael!" She hissed his name like a curse. Her sword had flown into her hands before she'd even had a chance to process it. "You'll pay!"

Beside her, Gault brandished a blade of his own. She was surprised to not find the familiar violet arc of Akor'shaki in his hand.

Azrael seemed entirely unphased. His voice carried much further than it should have, as though carried by an unseen power. From his back, he brandished a greatsword. It towered over him, yet he balanced the blade with ease in his hands. "Your father died for your failure."

Rissa felt a throb of anger dilate her vision. Before she could move, Gault did. He charged forward, blade ripping into the violet carpet as he closed the distance in seconds. He swung and Azrael's greatsword rose in response, steel clashed, kicking up sparks as they traded blows in quick succession. Rissa followed, flanking Azrael wide. Even with his back to her, she could sense his dark eyes tracking her movements and sure enough, just as she stepped within reach of his greatsword he whirled, slicing open the air above her head as she dropped to the ground. Her weapon was the shortest of the three and while Azrael focused primarily on Gault, he warded her efforts away with violent, zoning arcs that began to frustrate her. She wanted badly to feel his flesh peel beneath her sword, yet she couldn't so much as get close.

"You should have fought me like this at the Obelisk." Azrael spoke. If his movements were fast before, now he had delivered several powerful swings in the space between lightning and thunder. Gault kept up but could do very little to break his guard. "Your father might have lived."

He spoke with his back to her, which only further aggravated the fury that was quickly growing inside her. Worse still, she knew that he was right. Her Conduit burned with potential, yet she knew its use was pointless. She dared to approach him again and barely raised her sword in time to guard as Azrael whirled on her. She pushed her palm into the flat of her blade just to stop her guard from being smashed straight through. Even then, her trainers burned against the carpet as she was pushed backwards against his swing.

Gault surged into the air, coming down upon Azrael who quickly twisted aside as he cleaved up yet more of the carpet. He surged after Azrael, who after neatly evading, began an offense of his own upon Gault who seemed to be caught in the transition between offence and defence. His blade staggered many of the blows that came, but Gault was quickly sent scrambling backwards as the greatsword sought his heart. Rissa stepped in and Azrael's attention snapped onto her, allowing Gault to regain his footing. The greatsword sought her, but Rissa ducked, channelling every second of training she had spent falling on her backside. She was barely able to come out of her dodge before the blade came around again, manoeuvred expertly back towards her. She jumped, planting a foot on the flat of his blade to push it into the ground and open up his guard. Her first swing drew blood as it slit a gash in Azrael's retreating cheek. She couldn't help the spike of joy that followed his blood decorating her blade. Gault sought to finish the Omen, but Azrael twisted away and drove a violent knee into Gault's over-extended form. In a flash, Azrael was seconds from killing him, but Rissa was faster.

I invoke the Missing Sea. A Vortex, prevent his demise!

The patterns of The Algarethan Verse danced across her mind. Where he ended up she didn't care, so long as it wasn't beneath the sharp edge of Azrael's blade. Gault fell through the floor into her Vortex as the blade whistled through the air. He was spat out behind her as she allowed the portal to seal itself shut.

There was a lull in combat, a palpable pause. Rissa used it to regain her breath and her composure.

"And where is your trusty blade, Gault?" Azrael jeered. "Do not tell me you have forsaken your only chance at victory?"

"I don't need it." Gault hissed back. His eyes were dark and determined, but Rissa could tell from just his tone and tense body that he was wondering how true his own statement even was.

"Come then. Prove it."

Needing no further invitation, Gault charged. Rissa followed him, determined to not be lost this time in the frenzy of battle. Azrael stood them both up, wielding his greatsword as though it was a feather, somehow always finding an answer to the flurry of attacks that was thrown at him. Rissa would go low, seeking to sever a leg or slice an artery yet he would always find a way to parry even when Gault was attacking at the same time. He was good before, but never this good. Alone, she would have died within seconds, it was Gault's proficiency with a sword that was keeping them in this fight and even he was struggling. As though sensing her doubt, Azrael bore down on Gault and locked blades, sending him crashing into the stairs at the foot of the throne. Gault rolled as the blade came down and cut into the stairs, retreating up to the throne as Azrael advanced. Rissa followed him up, sticking her blade into Azrael's back only to find it didn't even slow him down.

"What!?"

A backhand caught her and everything pulsed black for a split second as she hurtled through the air and crashed to the floor before the throne. Her blade was still buried into the Omen's back, leaking black blood onto the carpet.

"Demon blood!" Gault hissed as he ducked beneath another swing. Azrael's greatsword flew over his head and rattled against the golden throne. Taking advantage of the jarring vibrations that travelled through the blade and into the Omen, Gault sought to drive his sword through his heart but Azrael was just able to push a hand into the flat of the blade and re-direct it into his shoulder. He laughed as the blade pierced him and drove his fist into Gault's stomach, smashing his head into the golden throne with a resounding clang before hurling him to the base of the stairs where Rissa recovered.

Gault hissed, clutching his head as he writhed on the floor. His eyes flashed violet before he snapped them shut, a wide grimace spreading across his face.

"A good effort. Let it be said." Azrael wiped the throne where Gault's face had bloodied it before slowly descending the stairs towards them. "The weak and the vengeful. Roles swapped, it seems."

Rissa ignored him and reached out for Gault. His hand lashed out at hers, striking her away. For a moment, he opened his eyes and Rissa recognised instantly what was happening. She had seen him lose control enough times to know what the warning signs were. Yet, here, he resisted it so strongly that blood began to trickle down his nose. All the while Azrael stalked closer, his greatsword scratching the wood as he neared.

Rissa reached out for him again. Slowly. Her hand fell on his shoulder and his wild eyes darted wildly as he fought for control, locking onto her for a split second. She needed his power, needed his focus. The time for damage control had long passed. With her smile, she willed him to go wild, with her eyes she apologised for the coldness she had given him.

"It's okay." She told him. "I trust you. You got this."

She watched him surrender. What looked like relief crossed his face moments before she watched the mist and the haze descend over him. His veins thrummed with violet energy as Akor'shaki's dormant form seemed to drift into his open palm. As his fist closed around it, not a second later it burst free, exploding with power as it grew to full size. The scar on her hand burned as Akor'shaki steered Gault's body into combat.

Azrael seemed momentarily caught off guard. He raised his greatsword, but the steel still embedded in his shoulder greatly hindered his movement and he was barely able to deflect the first strike. Akor'shaki came around again with lightning speed, targeting the same area twice.

"My Lord - grant me strength!" Azrael blustered as the keen edge of Akor'shaki stole strikes on his flesh, drawing black blood that oozed out of him. Rissa just watched, unwilling to put a third blade into the mix lest she fall victim to Gault's rage. Instead, she had a front row seat as Azrael's guard finally failed and his arm was severed from his body, the greatsword flying into the air with it. A scream escaped his lips, not pain, but grief, failure. But death did not follow as she thought it would, even the Omen wore a look of aggrieved confusion as Akor'shaki's blade didn't immediately pierce his chest.

"Gault?" She asked warily.

His eyes turned to her, clouded still by the mask of vengeance. He seized Azrael by his brittle, white hair and pulled him forward, pinning him on his knees before her. Rissa felt the scar on her hand flare once again and a voice rang in her mind.

Reward. For holding sweet Kadin back no longer.

Rissa looked upon the bleeding, beaten body of her father's killer. A dark delight rushed through her, yet it was tempered by a strange feeling that she couldn't place. As she pulled her oozing blade from his back and levelled it against his chest, she couldn't help but feel there was a part of her that she wasn't going to get back once the deed was done. But this was revenge, wasn't it? This was what she had wanted. What she had needed to move on.

I will change my mind.

She didn't expect Azrael to be staring straight at her. Their eyes met for a moment as she pressed the sharp tip of the sword over his heart. Much to her surprise, the Omen wore a small, weak smile. The darkness that had filled him was rapidly leaving through the wound where his arm had once been and she could see the blackness leaving his eyes and his dark veins sinking back into his flesh.

"What are you smiling at?" She sneered at him.

"My freedom. At long last."

His words enraged her, threatening to remove the satisfaction of her revenge entirely. "There's nobody waiting for you, monster."

As though sensing her anger, Akor'shaki ripped the hair back, pushing Azrael's chest out and into the tip of her blade. He grimaced as it pierced a layer of his skin.

"I hope my death grants you what you seek, Rissa Rawdon." Azrael looked longingly at the steel pressed into him. "But do it quickly. Before My Lord does it for you. He does not tolerate failure."

Rissa found herself hesitating. Her palms were slick on the leather hilt.

Kill him. Before the Dark One takes your choice away.

"I-" She felt tears stinging her eyes. She saw her father in the back of her eyelids every time she blinked. His face was solemn, as still as it was after the last breath had left his body. He wouldn't want her to do this. She wasn't a killer, not-

Azrael's heart suddenly fell upon her blade. Rissa screamed and dropped the weapon, the hilt embedded into his chest as he fell backwards, staring up at the ceiling as blood clogged his throat. His eyes ensnared hers as the life left his body.

"Save... my... sister-"

The black eyes somehow got darker. There was a gurgle as the last bloody breath of the Brand of the Knight finally fell.

Well done. I will return him to you now.

She dropped to her knees, paralysed by shock. Beside her, the malaise faded from Gault's eyes and she watched him as his dark eyes processed the scene before him. The sword, the hands that had killed him.

"It's done then." Gault said quietly. He stared at his own hands, brow creasing in thought.

"Yeah." Her hands trembled in her lap.

"Does it feel...-" Gault started to speak, his eyes widening in vested interest, only to go silent.

The dead body of Azrael was before her, a complete vengeance for the death of her father, yet she felt... nothing different. The anger and grief within her were just as present as it had been before.

"I... I don't know." She ripped her eyes away from his body and pulled her blade from his skewered corpse without a second glance. "Let's go. We can finish this, can't we?"

"I hope so."

—

Beyond the throne room was a door. It led into an unfinished section of Monument, construction likely having frozen from the days just after Reckoning. It was a twisting, hollow labyrinth of scaffolding and steel steps that spiralled upwards to the top of the building. Had it been completed as planned, no doubt it would be a glorious ascent to the greatest height the city had to offer, but in its current form, it was a walk of darkness towards the light that awaited above.

The crimson light.

Gault heard Rissa behind him. They hurried up the steps in silence, yet where before Gault had enjoyed his own thoughts and opinions, he was once again graced by the presence of Akor'shaki who had been all too smug about being responsible for victory over Azrael. The impact to his head had shaken his will and Akor'shaki had decided then and there to make a play for control. Gault had resisted, if only to keep his word to Rissa.

At least now you see.

The steps went on forever, yet he knew that they were getting closer to the top as the smell of sulphur grew in potency. As he emerged into the freshest air the heights of Centa Isla had to offer, a drizzle of rain had begun to pour, slickening the steel steps beneath his feet. The air tingled with potential disaster as he arrived atop Monument. The peak of the spire pierced the heavens themselves, removing the rest of the city entirely from view beneath the thick clotted smog that hung in the air beneath them. He breathed deep, taking in the freshest air his lungs had breathed in a long time. Awaiting them was a visceral sight. Gault immediately recognised the magic-siphoning pods that he had discovered as he had killed Mires beneath the old factories. New bodies were sealed within, screams muffled by the airtight seal that trapped them.

Stood with his back turned, arms raised to the heavens as his skin pulsed and warped with the same energy that had coalesced around the Obelisk. King Grayson Clovis stood on top of his tower, a crumbling chunk of Galleo et'al's earth clutched within his fist as he fished through the stars for the rest of it. Gault was certain of what was happening, although he had never believed it possible. Spoken in Centa Isla's plainest terms, there should not have been a human alive strong enough to bear the brunt of such power. His body should have turned into sludge, like the earth beneath the Obelisk. His mind should have melted into his skull and his veins should have exploded with the coursing strain that blew through them. A memory sent a chill down his spine. That was exactly what had happened to Sophia.

Yet, King Grayson Clovis remained intact. A human Obelisk, intent on drawing the rest of Galleo et'al's crumbling form back into orbit once more. Needles pierced his flesh, linked to the pods that extracted the blood from the four trapped prisoners and delivered their power directly into him.

"STOP!" Gault sprinted up the last set of stairs, calling Akor'shaki to grow into his hands as he charged.

Beware!

He ignored the blade and charged, leaping high into the air to split the King's spine straight down the middle as he landed.

King Grayson turned and revealed a thrumming Brand seared across his entire face. The Brand of the Heretic. "You are too late."

The Conduit around his finger thrummed with earthen might and Gault felt a pillar of earth shoot up into his gut, compressing the air from his lungs. He flew backwards, landing jarringly as Rissa rushed up alongside him. King Grayson turned to address them. His chest and arms were lined with needles, feeding the dark ritual that he was performing.

"What's happening?" Rissa asked. She held her sword firm, but he could see her arms trembling.

"Galleo et'al." Gault replied, not taking his eyes from the Brand that had surrendered the body and mind of Centa Isla's King to the whims of the Dark One. "He's nothing but a puppet."

"As are all of you." Grayson Clovis's voice spoke to them, yet it reverberated as though gravel spun in his throat. "None more than you, Scout."

With powerful hands, Galleo et'al began to rip the syringes from the King's body, discarding them to the ground. All the while, the screams from the pods continued, filling the vat with blood, ready for the summoning to continue. The shard of Galleo et'al's earth, was clasped tightly in one hand and in the other, his Conduit brimmed with lethal potential.

Rissa cast a spell, priming a chamber of jagged spikes of frigid ice that rotated around the circle of magic that blazed from her Conduit. She fired them towards King Grayson, their course direct and true as they split the wind itself to seek his heart. As the shards connected, they exploded into a crystalline shower of ice that cascaded harmlessly to the ground. Behind the veil, Grayson stood untouched. His shirt had been torn to pieces, revealing a freshly inscribed Brand emblazoned across his chest.

The Brand of the Knight. Azrael's powers were also his own.

"You're joking." Rissa groaned in frustration, throwing her head to the sky.

A laugh burst from Grayson's lip, spurred by the Dark One's amusement.

Let me take over.

For the first time since their dark union, Gault agreed. This was no time to be precious, not with so much at stake. "Fine. Take over."

He felt his vision darken as he began to disappear from his own body to the plane of darkness where he was forced to reside while Akor'shaki controlled him. Just as his vision began to fade, he caught the first moments of combat where his body surged forward and spun the blade like it was an extension of his own body-

Grayson caught the staff of the blade. Upon his cold touch, Gault felt his entire body turn to ice and from his place of willing surrender he was pulled forcefully back into his body where he retained full control just in time to feel the weight of Grayson's power seeking to tear the blade from his grip. He planted his feet, head spinning with the vertigo of being thrust back in control of his body.

Something is wrong!

Gault didn't know what was happening. He felt a throbbing in his skull, like a blade was dissecting his brain cut by cut. It was pain enough for him to scream, dropping to his knees as he felt his grip on Akor'shaki failing.

Beside him, Rissa charged in, seeking to disrupt whatever malaise he had been inflicted with, only for Grayson's Conduit to flash with power. Seconds later, her advance came to a whimpering halt. Stone had seized her legs, encasing them solid like the masterwork of a statue. Yet it did not stop, the creeping earth spread quickly up her legs like a disease, petrifying her gradually in the terrified stance of a helpless young woman. Rissa tried to raise her Conduit, only for the stone to spread down her arm and into her fingers.

"Gault!" She cried out, arching her head upwards as though to take a final breath as the cursed stone encased her entirely, leaving her as still as death itself. Her features were preserved, strands of hair crystallised, screaming mouth filled with earth.

All the while he could do nothing but scream as he felt a part of him being forcefully vivisected and removed.

Gault! Do not let-

Akor'shaki went silent. It was not like before, where his blade had disappeared from his mind but had preserved its protection. Gault felt cold, empty. Akor'shaki shrunk as Grayson released his grip and the weapon fell lifelessly to the floor. No colour surrounded the blade, no heat came from its touch. It hung from his waist now like a necrotic limb.

"What a fascinating experiment." Galleo et'al laughed again, a cruel mask of amusement plastering the King's tormented face. "Akor'shaki was my design. Did you truly think to use it against me?"

"What did you do?" Gault asked. Weakness overcame him and he could feel his body... changing. The dark power he had been bestowed, the heightened senses, all of it was fading. He felt like a child again, training in the courtyard with a wooden sword.

"I removed its presence. You must be grateful."

Gault slammed his fists into the ground, he tried to rise but felt his Brand flare with a wave of Grayson's large hand. He realised then, that he had no protection from the irrefutable wrath of the Dark One. With a wave of his hand, Gault felt pain like he never had before. It coursed through his entire body, setting his blood on fire and warping his bones to their breaking point. Gault cried, feeling tears coursing down his cheeks as the agony continued. He sank into the ground as his mind was ripped to pieces and reassembled each time.

"Thanks to you I will think twice before inheriting the vengeful into my cloister."

Gault had given up. He wished for death. Between torments, he would see the petrified figure of Rissa staring at him. He had failed her, failed this city. No matter how many civilians stormed Monument, no matter how much ground they won against their oppressor, they would be flushed out and culled once the Dark One's shadow blotted out the sky yet again.

"Everybody is vengeful." A voice that Gault didn't immediately recognise sizzled through the air. "Even the cowards."

Grayson's face fell for a moment. Seeking the origin of the voice, he turned, only for the flash of steel to slice the arm from the King's body. As the muscular appendage flopped to the floor and muddy blood spilled, the light of the Conduit faded.

The spell that held Rissa broke and the earth crumbled from her like hardened mud. She dropped to her knees, coughing and gagging, hacking up clumps of dirt.

With the distraction so too came the end of Gault's pain as Galleo et'al's host turned its attention to someone else. It took him a moment to recognise the slick head of black hair who had arrived.

Jace. He was without one arm, yet wielded an old, rustic sword with his free hand. Gault realised the arm that was missing was the very limb that had held The Brand of the Sorcerer.

"You forsake your gifts?" Grayson seethed with the rage of the Dark One. "You will be tormented in the pit for eternity.

"Hopefully not." There was a flash of steel. The cables that connected the pods to the vat were severed, spilling the flow of blood across the rooftop.

"That's enough." Enraged, King Grayson swelled. Another Brand burned through his clothes, revealing itself on his thigh. The Brand of the Demon. Kren'shal's twisted powers. From the wound where his arm had been severed, a black mass of flesh burst and coalesced into a mangled claw-like arm that was more akin to the Dom'inari than a human. It was large and cumbersome, giving the King double the reach as wicked claws burst from the fleshy fingers. With it, he surged after the former Omen, striking him with a violent backhand that sent him hurtling into one of the pods.

Gault struggled to his feet, moving to help Rissa stand as she continued to regain her breath.

"What do we do?"

"The pods." Gault looked around. With the vat leaking, the pods needed to be destroyed for this scheme to end. He sought the magic with his spectral sight, finding a high concentration around the back of the devices. "Around the back. Shut them down."

Rissa nodded and sprinted behind two of the four pods, powering them down. The blood-siphoning ended and the lids opened with a hiss, revealing two deceased members of the Elemental Council, Theora Eculaire and Kiara Harrington. Their bodies were sunken and pale, their proud lineage used to fuel the doom of their city. The other two pods were a battlefield as Jace evaded King Grayson's wicked claws, narrowly moving his body from being diced up by the powerful new limb.

Gault ran into the combat. For once, he held no intention to fight. His body felt slow and cumbersome, like he bore weights attached to each of his limbs. Was this truly how he had felt before Akor'shaki's bargain? His heartbeat was wild in his chest, rather than controlled. His head pounded with bloodrush; his legs ached with strain where they normally never did. He dived behind one of the pods and powered them down, pulling out the cables, plugs and tubes that adorned the back of the device for good measure. The supply cut off with a whimper and the lid lifted, revealing another vampiric corpse. This one belonged to Marco Barrett, the true leader of Eclipse who was now dead along with his visions of a new city. Over his head, Grayson's monstrous form lunged and he heard Jace cry out as he was launched across the roof. He landed with a tidy roll. Gault crept to the next pod and tore yet more cables away, relieved to hear it power down. Within, he was surprised to find the body of Lachesis. She lived yet was extremely weak. Her chest rose and fell, her throat scratchy and hoarse as she pushed out beleaguered breaths. Gault pulled the needles from her body and lifted her from the machine, laying her out on the floor.

"... Gault." Her eyes fluttered sleepily. He didn't know what to think without Akor'shaki spurring him on, or how to feel. Apathy filled him where he surely should have felt rage? It was through him that Lachesis had gained a foothold within his homeworld. So why did he not want to close those viperous eyes forever?

"Gault." She said again, sitting herself up weakly against the pod. "Azrael... is-"

"He's dead."

He watched as pain crossed her face. It was grief and pain, compressed into a single second that passed all too quickly. To his own surprise, he found no joy in her suffering.

"He was a stubborn fool."

She eyed Jace who fought against King Grayson and his demonic arm. Rissa had joined him, but even together they were constantly on the back foot, evading rather than attacking.

"You can't win. Not without Azrael."

"We have to-

"Idiot. Silence." She touched Akor'shaki weakly. "You've lost its protection and its power. You don't stand a chance. Neither do they."

She groaned as she raised her hand. Her eyes glowed green and an ethereal mist manifested between her fingers. "I can protect you."

"Why would you?"

"Because I know you can win. But not here, not now." She tried to sit up. "I can protect you from its torments, disguise you as another one of my fold."

The power she had used on rats and roaches she now sought to use on him. He understood that it granted her vision through them, adding them to her network of spies from the shadows. With her mark upon him, he may be disguised from Galleo et'al's influence. Potentially being observed at all times by Lachesis did not fill him with his glee, but equally being subjected to the torment he had experienced earlier again filled him with even less.

"So be it."

She flashed her hand at his face and the mist sought him. It circled his head, tingling his eyes enough to water as they entered. He felt the presence in his head. With it, came the desire to push it away. He resisted the natural urge and allowed the mist to take root within his mind. He could feel it behind his eyes, lurking wordlessly until the sensation disappeared.

"Good. Now come with me." She moved around the back of the pod and tried to remove a panel, her trembling fingers failing to get any purchase on the steel. "Help me."

Gault removed it for her, revealing a chamber within that housed the elemental magic crystals that powered the machine. Lachesis removed the air crystals, leaving only the fire crystal to bear the weight of operation. Immediately, it began to rumble with instability.

—

Jace tumbled against the concrete of Monument's spire. He had mere seconds to react as King Grayson was already bearing down upon him. The Brand of the Heretic thrummed with energy and Jace was all too aware of what grim fate had befallen the former King. It pained him to see what had become of Grayson. They had interacted sparingly, little more than acknowledgements passing the hallways of Monument and exchanging pleasantries at the rally. He seemed like a genuine person. More than could be said of many of the rulers he had encountered throughout the various worlds he had visited. A pity, that this was what became of people who wanted to change the city for the better.

413

He was unbeatable. The incestuous bloodline of a royal family pledged to earth magic, the Brands of multiple Omens and the cruel whim of Galleo et'al itself all powered the King's body beyond mortal limits. But Jace had to remind himself that this was not about victory. This was about who he was, who he had wanted to be. Courage had always evaded him throughout his life, robbing him of a chance to better himself until he had given up entirely. He didn't enjoy admitting it, but he had envied Gault. Envied the courage of someone who would break away from the throes of a god and openly defy their unbeatable will. Now, Gault had been stripped of the power he had achieved through his bargain and cowered behind the pods.

But that was okay. Jace had come here to die doing the right thing. Even now, as he narrowly twisted his body out of reach of Grayson's demonic arm, he knew that he only delayed the inevitable rush of the afterlife that reached for him. His severed arm tingled with a phantom's touch, the cauterised wound still causing him great pain as he fought.

The very blade in his hand reminded him of why he was here. His fiery eyes flitted to the hilt; the name inscribed upon its steel a reminder of the kindness he had not deserved.

Stanwyck Bowers.

He would repay that favour now. Not just to the memory of a friend, but to the entire city who had suffered from his inaction.

Rissa Rawdon fought alongside him. He guarded her where he could, goading Galleo et'al into pursuing its traitorous coven. Her sword blows did little to slow the march of a puppet who felt no pain. It was a moment of weakness when Jace felt his tired body fail him, rendering him too slow to dodge the swing of the clawed hand that whipped across his body and sent him crashing to the floor.

"Leave him alone." Rissa put her body between them.

Just then, Grayson's body stammered and trembled as if hit by lightning. He staggered and dropped to his knees for a moment. Rissa looked confused, as if she'd done something to cause this. In the moments she had spare, Rissa hurried to him and helped drag him to his feet.

"Didn't think you had this in you." She said to him, a wry smile on her face.

He returned it. "I'm not convinced either."

Then, King Grayson's face looked up at them. But it truly was him, even if just for a moment. His face twisted as though just registering all of the pain inflicted upon him at once. Tears streaked down his face and Jace found his eyes locking with the confused King as he spoke words free from Galleo et'al's influence.

"What is happening? What have-" The mask had slipped for a moment. Mid-sentence, the will of Galleo et'al dominated the King once more and his expression immediately turned to apathetic fury.

The King's beaten body glowed once more, this time his human arm. Another Brand blazed up his arm and Jace recognised it instantly. Unmistakably. The Brand of the Sorcerer. His powers.

Dread filled him. The entire world seemed to slow down.

"Move!" He dropped Stanwyck's blade and pushed Rissa. She hadn't taken two steps back before a magic circle appeared in the ground beneath her and a spear of earth surged upward, piercing straight through his body as he pushed her to safety. The jagged earth ripped through his insides, lifting him from the ground as he sunk down the thickening mast of earth. He ground his teeth, feeling numbness spill through his torso.

So, this was it.

Rissa turned to exact payback, only for Grayson's demonic form to strike her, sending her soaring through the air, colliding with the pods with a sickening crunch. Jace tracked her, his vision already failing. Before Grayson's silhouette obscured his sight, he saw a familiar head of green hair lurking behind the pods.

Lachesis. He sought her, reaching out through whatever astral plane existed in this world. She saw him and for a moment, their eyes met across the rooftop. She smiled at him and he felt his quieting heart lurch for a moment.

In her smile, he saw pride. She had always been good to him. Always sheltered him, protected him from the hardest choices. He offered her a weak wave, only for the visage of Galleo et'al, speaking through Grayson to step between them. But there was something else there that he hadn't expected to see.

Comfort. Her smile was warm, like a bowl of soup on a cold night. As it crossed her face and promptly faded, he realised that she had a plan. She always did.

"Death is too good for you, Brand."

Jace felt blood trickling out of his mouth, pooling in the back of his throat. With precious few breaths remaining, he allowed himself to smile at death.

"I couldn't agree more."

The pods began to hiss and black smoke began to billow from them. The smoke travelled through the network of pipes, leading into the vat of blood, creating an arid smell of impending chaos.

Grayson picked it up immediately, his possessed neck practically wringing as he whirled on the source. He spotted Gault, crouched behind the last of the four pods, his hands frantically buried in the back of the machine. Immediately, the puppet King surged towards him but Jace was quicker. With the last cry of energy, he wrapped his free arm around the King's throat and pulled him close. The strength he was faced against was enough to tear his body apart, but Jace held himself together with nothing but sheer will.

"No! No!" The first of the pods exploded, bathing the rooftop in fire. The rest quickly followed, exploding in sequence until the vat of blood itself exploded. Flames ripped through the rooftop and Jace felt the familiar searing of flame touch his skin. Grayson writhed in his arms and he held on for as long as he could until life finally left him.

Jace was the name he had been given as an Omen.

Omar Jahn was the name he died with. His true name, one that he had never been able to face since his home fell.

The last words of Stanwyck accompanied him to the grave.

"You're a good kid."

Hoping that was true, he silently wished everyone the best.

———

The first explosion rocked Monument itself.

Rissa searched frantically for Gault among the flames. She saw him, desperately seeking shelter from the raging inferno. She could sense the rampant fire magic coiling through the air, ready to ignite and destroy most of Monument at any moment. Their eyes met and she saw the relief in his green eyes as she hurried towards him.

She took his hand and together they threw themselves from the top of the tower, propelled by the ripples in the air as Monument's peak exploded with an earth-shattering wave of power, magic and noise. The entire tower rocked beside them as the city tilted from the strain. Huge chunks of Monument broke away, nearly striking them as they fell through the blanket of smog and down to the city proper where the rush of the city rose to welcome them.

Rissa gripped Gault until her knuckles were bleached. Gravity assailed them and the wind harassed them, threatening to tear their grip from one another. For the first time she saw fear in his eyes, locked onto her in hope that she wouldn't let them down. As the city rushed to meet them, Rissa felt anxiety clawing at her. Of all the leaps of faith she had performed with a Vortex to catch her, this was the first one to have someone else's life attached to it. She focused.

I invoke the Missing Sea. A Vortex. Please, save us.

Upon the first rooftop they soared past, she opened the first Vortex. As the ground rushed up to meet them, she coiled her body around Gault's, making them as narrow as possible as she opened the second Vortex beneath them. They soared through the ground, bursting up from the rooftop with the momentum of their fall still behind them. Gravity sought to catch up with her whims and their ascent was quickly inverted back to a fall. Her stomach hurdled and flipped as they fell again, this time back through the rooftop and down onto the path where their descent had slowed enough for them to land safely, knees jarring still from the impact.

Rissa looked up as the explosion on Monument sent plumes of black smoke into the sky. Shards of the tower still fell around them, showering them with flaming shards of Monument. Even now, it was still the largest building the city had to offer yet seemed oddly humbled in its current state.

A roar filled the streets. It took Rissa a moment to realise it was cheering. All down The Blades and the Path of Discipline, both paved with bodies of human and demon alike. They cheered almighty as Monument exploded. In the windows as high as part-way up the tower, citizens cheered and jeered, asserting their ownership over the shadow that had towered over them for so long.

A victory it may have seemed. But Rissa knew better. The grim expression Gault wore told her that this was far from over. The plan may have been foiled, but the Dark One was still out there, undeniably seeking entry to Centa Isla for dark revenge.

But she wanted to be sure. So, to Gault she turned. "Is it over?"

He looked up at the tower. His eyes were green, just as she had first seen in the visions of his past. It seemed, for good or ill, he was free of Akor'shaki, even if the lifeless blade still hung from his hip.

"I...-." He pressed a hand to his head for a moment. The green in his eyes intensified, almost unnaturally. He looked at her, the green power dissipating like powder from his eyes. "I... don't know."

20

Days had passed and Centa Isla was a city in unprecedented chaos. Once the thrill of watching Monument explode had faded, angst and uncertainty had trickled down the spine of the entire city. Shockwaves surged down the dusty streets like palpitations as more of Monument continued to break away over the days that had followed.

There had been no word from King Grayson who had been confirmed to have survived the ordeal. He wordlessly fled the tower, surrendering the throne room to the rebels who had looted and pillaged every orifice of the tower. It was chaos. The remnants of Forge Town were little more than headstones for the honest trade for which it was once renowned and Downtown had become a war zone for gangs. The Empty Eyes, led by the surviving Seth Gore, reigned supreme, yet many more middling gangs had risen up as the people had sought allies and power in a rapidly shifting climate. The City Centre had been picked clean, most of the nobility slaughtered. The gates of Grandmaster had closed once again, flushing those without magic from their sacred grounds like a disease. They had taken in the scientists of the abandoned Verscience lab, before sealing themselves away beneath the familiar dome for good while the city destroyed itself.

But none of that mattered to Rissa. While it pained her to see what had become of her home, today was a more important event.

Donnel Rawdon's funeral. It was a private, quiet event. She and Gault were the sole two in attendance. She had found a spot on the edge of the city she believed he would have found significant. His body was before her, having been unceremoniously waiting in the back of his vehicle at the ruin on the Obelisk where no soul seemed to have visited since.

Her father had been wrapped in an old blanket Gault had found along the way. His pale face had been concealed beneath the dusty fabric but even then she couldn't find the strength to look at him. Instead found herself staring at his CIPD vehicle. His precious car had found enough life to bluster its owner to the edge of the city before its engine failed for good. It waited behind them, headlights broken, windows smashed and marred with dents and damage.

"I'm sorry." She spoke absently, sharing the edge of the city with Gault.

"For what?" He replied. Gault looked weaker than ever, his complexion pale and his now green eyes cloudy and faint.

"For not trusting you." She started, then pivoted direction. "You were trying your best and I gave you a hard time."

"You were only doing what you thought was right."

"I was trying to control you. To take care of everything myself." She clenched her fists. "My father is dead because of that."

"I wish I'd known him better." Gault had coaxed stories of her childhood out of her and had sat in patient silence as she had regaled him with such. At first, she had been unwilling, but grief had gradually loosened her lips into spilling everything she could remember about him during her childhood.

The stories had ended quicker than she had expected once her timeline of memories surpassed her thirteenth birthday. The same year her mother had disappeared. Now, she sat in silence, unsure of what to fill the silence with.

"Your parents. Did you ever get to grieve?" She asked him.

"I... no." Gault admitted. "But this isn't about-"

"Just humour me." She interrupted him abruptly, fidgeting as the chill of the evening blew down the edge of Downtown. "I... I don't really know what I'm supposed to be doing."

He softened, a strained smile crossing his face. "Well. You should tell him something."

She looked at the shape of his body beneath the blanket. Her mind warped and forced her to look away. "I... there isn't enough time in the world."

Gault gestured around them. The edge of the city was silent, spared of the chaos of the City Centre and surrounding region. "Sure, there is."

Rissa still couldn't manage. This had been her idea. It seemed like the right thing to do. But now that it was happening, it all felt too soon, too forced. But that was life, wasn't it? A rush of events that you were never prepared for. Control was nothing but an impossible mercy granted by the universe to prevent you from going mad. It wasn't right that it had taken all of this chaos and death for her to realise that.

Gault rose from the perch of rubble he had sat upon to hear her tales. Silently, he walked past her and approached the blanketed body of her father. He dropped to his knees before him, bowing his head in quiet reverence.

"You raised a wonderful daughter. You know that too, don't you?" The question was rhetorical. Obviously. The answer was lost to the winds that blew across the edge of the world. "Perhaps you didn't see it right away, but she's everything you would have wanted her to be."

Rissa choked back tears. Gault balled a fist into his palm and pressed it to his chest. It was a familiar gesture, another of the things she had seen while intruding on his past during the visions Akor'shaki had subjected her to.

"What is that?"

"Respect." Gault replied. He rose politely, dusting down his leggings. "A gesture of it, at least."

"Akor'shaki granted me visions of your past." Rissa admitted. "Yet, there's so much I don't know about you."

"I'm sorry you never heard it from me." He turned and smiled at her. "I'd like to put that right."

Since Akor'shaki's influence had seemingly left him, there was something different about her companion. His demeanour had changed completely. Whereas before he was as tightly wound as a coiled spring, he seemed to have let go of so much of his tension and his rage, showing just how much of it was unnaturally riled up by his blade. Beneath it all there was a respectful, quiet young man who had a good heart. Even with these changes, she could see in his eyes that he was struggling with the fallout of everything. His brave face was for her when she needed it the most. In reality, at least physically speaking, he was weaker than ever. If the Dark One ever returned, they knew that they would not stand a chance.

"Come on." He burst her bubble of thought with his words.

"What?"

"It's your turn." Gault gestured to her father.

Water rushed through her yet again. Not magic, but tears. She held it back once more, feeling the warbling strain behind her eyes that was desperate to get through. Rissa denied it. She didn't want to grieve. Didn't want to go through the pain all over again, to think of the memories they had missed all these years broke her heart into a thousand pieces.

"I'm not ready."

"You won't get another chance." Gault told her. His voice was firm, yet kind. "Don't add another regret to the pile."

She wiped her eyes with her hands. Groaning. "You're harsh, you know that?"

"It's the truth." His eyes went glossy for the first time since they'd turned back to their natural colour. "It's the one thing I wish I could have done with my family."

Was she being selfish? Putting off her grief before someone who had never had that chance? She didn't know, but the thought was enough to move her into action. She pushed off from the wall that had taken her weight for the past hour and approached her father. She couldn't look at him and instead, she cast her gaze out to the horizon. Things were going to get harder. This was her chance to see her father off with security. She wanted him to know that...

"Dad..." She began, feeling her own voice breaking in her throat as she lowered softly to her knees. She reached for the shape beneath the blanket, feeling his hands cold beneath the old blanket. "I want you to know..."

Her voice was paralysed within her throat. Everything was starting to hit her all over again. His dream of seeing their family reunited, the dream she had never even given much thought, was suddenly an unbearable image branded behind her eyelids. She couldn't escape it. The sadness he must have felt in his final moments, knowing that all that he worked for all these years had amounted to nothing.

She felt Gault beside her, his hand warm on her shoulder. With his presence, she pushed the words out.

"I want you to know I'm going to be okay! Please don't worry about me!" Her throat was like a clogged drain. The block had been removed and the words poured through like a surging current. "It's your turn to rest. Finally, your turn! You worked so hard!"

Was there more to say? She felt words pooling that hadn't been through a filter, but let them out, nonetheless.

"But you weren't always good to me." Her hand pulled away from him. "You were fixated on her. On mother. You weren't there when I needed you. I grew up alone and I blame you for that."

She felt tears trickling down her face. Finally, she pulled her gaze painfully from the horizon and forced herself to look at him.

"But you were my dad. And I loved you. This city wasn't good to us. We Rawdon's should have stuck together. Maybe things would have been better." She leaned down and rested her forehead against his. It was cold, but she could feel him somehow, a joyful spirit in her chest that brushed against her heart and added a new, warmer tone to the icy grief.

"Love you Dad. All the best."

With that, she rose. Her chest was fuller, her spirit brighter than when they had started.

To Gault, she turned. "I think I'm ready."

He nodded. In his arms, he scooped up her father's body and laid it across the backseat of his beloved vehicle. With broken doors taped shut, Rissa moved around to the back of the vehicle and together; they began to push.

The misshapen wheels of the car rolled slowly towards the edge of the city. It was as good of a funeral as many in Centa Isla got. Once they approached the core of the planet, all matter would break down and they would become one with the world. There was a comfort in knowing that if she ever needed her father again, he would be all around her. The car moved slowly; Rissa could feel not just her weakness but Gault's too. A shadow of his former self, she could see the strain plastered silently across his face as he tried to move the car. Rissa felt strength from within, like her father was with her, lending his strength to the effort as the car's front wheels hung over the edge of the city.

All it took was one last effort and it went. Rissa stumbled to the edge and looked over, ignoring the whoosh of vertigo as her father sailed over the cliff and fell. It felt like an eternity as the shape of the car got smaller and smaller until suddenly it exploded into a magical blast of dust once it got too close to the core.

Then he was gone. Rissa stayed at the edge, watching for a little bit longer in case he came back. But he never did. When she pulled herself from the cliff, Gault greeted her.

"I'm here." He said quietly.

"I…" Before she could even find her words, Rissa began to cry. Her guard was down and tears spilled from her eyes before she could even stop them. Her body went so weak that she sank and Gault eased her down, pulling her in for a warm embrace. Whereas before his body had felt cold to the touch, there was now a human warmth in him that spread through her as she coiled her hands around his neck and bawled into his chest.

An eternity could have passed and she never would have realised. Gault was as still and stoic as the earth itself until she finished and pulled away, drying her eyes desperately. There was still one last thing to do.

From her pocket she brandished a small blade. A letter opener, nothing more, found within the ruins of Forge Town. She approached the brick wall that she had first leaned upon and searched its scratched surface. Names decorated it, so many names. All of them carved by the people who had chosen to end their lives at this very cliff.

There was a reason she believed it would be significant to her father, for she had found something that he never had. Down near the bottom, where the brick met the dirt, were two names.

Balor Rawdon
Amy Rawdon

He had never talked much of his youth, but Rissa understood much from her mother before she disappeared. His parents had taken their own lives here once he had turned eighteen and was old enough to take care of himself. He had searched for the spot where their names rested for his whole life yet had never found it.

In truth, Rissa had found their names long ago. Exploring the dangerous perimeter of Centa Isla had killed many days of boredom in her youth. It was a nasty secret that she had kept from him and she would regret it for the rest of her life. She had held every intention to tell him, but... it never came up. She just hoped this offered a little bit of closure.

With the letter opener, she carefully carved a name into the brickwork beneath the two names.

Donnel Rawdon

"Hey, Gault?" She spoke quietly, staring at the freshly scratched words.
"Yes?"
"Could I... get a minute?"
"Of course." She heard him hurry away, disappearing deeper into the city.

With a small smile she waited patiently until she was sure she was alone. Tears fell and would not stop and her nose sniffled with grief. She reached into her pocket for tissues, but her finger encountered something sharper than tissue. It was a scrap of parchment folded in two, charred and a little crispy from the explosion. How had she missed this?

She hadn't even read it. But she knew it was from her father.

Her fingers trembled as she peeled at the roughly folded page, slowly opening it up to find a large drawing with some text scrawled beneath. The frothing edges of a Vortex framed the image, but what was inside made Rissa dredge back to her Grandmaster days spent reading of the past. Jagged triangles were seen from inside the Vortex, they looked to her like mountains. As her eyes slowly widened, she looked to the text at the bottom.

The Vortex suddenly closed. Aryssa Rawdon failed to return from her
voyage. This was the last image I could make out. Drawn from memory.

What? Voyage? What was this handwritten scrawl all about? She read it again, as though it was going to reveal hidden words that she had missed the first time. Nothing appeared and she cursed aloud.

"Voyage? What are you talking about!?" She whirled, holding up the paper to the light. As she turned, she placed the image of the mountains on the foggy horizon. The gears in her mind dared to turn. Could it be…?

She painfully fished up the memory of her father's last words. He had mentioned her mother several times, each time she had silenced him. Was… this blasphemous document trying to say that her mother was alive? Is that what her father had been trying to tell her?

He must have been so excited. The thought broke her heart all over again.

Her mother may not be dead, it dared to seem. But then where was she? Beyond the smog, beyond the veil that had trapped them there? Was there more to this post-Reckoning world than everybody believed?

She thought about it for a moment. Then, she suddenly scrunched the paper up in her hands and went to launch it over the edge of the city. She hesitated, arm trembling with the strain. Instantly, she yelled and undid her work, squatting and resting the paper on her knee to unfurl her damage with her sleeve. What was this feeling? There was something mixed in among the confusion that she couldn't shift. It interacted with her grief and the maw of anger that still stirred deep within her in a way that was deeply unsettling.

Her father had died to try and reunite their family. All the while, her mother was off exploring lands unknown? Making herself a part of such a dangerous voyage without so much as telling her family of her intent? Donnel Rawdon had given his life to find her, to try and bring her back. All that searching and grief wasted when all they would have needed to be a functional family was a little bit of notice!?

Rage coursed through her. Anger at such idiocy, such wasted time. The fury in her was stirring. Aryssa Rawdon had abandoned her family to chase the horizon. For what? For the good of exploration? For the fun of it? Rissa didn't give a damn about herself, she'd have got on with life either way. But for her father? It wasn't right… her dad had committed the rest of his life to finding her.

But one thing was clear. She could be alive, maybe Donnel had been right all this time. It was her father's will that she follow up on this, Rissa could sense it. If there was more to this world than Centa Isla, she would find it. And if her mother was there…

"I'll find her dad." She held the piece of paper to the sky, as if he was watching. She wondered what to say next, wondering what to do if she did see her mother again. Then, the answer came to her.

"And I'll make her pay."

—

Gault shivered. He waited patiently in the shelter of some derelict building while Rissa had a moment alone.

His body ached, sore from the damage it had been inflicted over the course of his long campaign. While he had healed most of the damage with Akor'shaki's help, it seemed that some of the damage remained a part of him that he hadn't been aware of before. His joints ached; from all the impossible heights he had fallen from. His shoulders were strained and swollen from swinging Akor'shaki at inhuman speeds.

But most strangely, he felt empty. The limp chain of Akor'shaki still ran through him. It still ended within him, adhered to his very soul as promised, but he couldn't feel a thing. It was so quiet in his head that he didn't know what to think. What lesson was he supposed to have taken from all this? The blade had proven its point that he was strongest when not in control, but now that revelation had been for nothing. He was alone again, utterly himself, whatever that meant. Without his power, what was he? If Galleo et'al came again, he would stand no chance. If he looked a thug the wrong way, would he be able to defend himself? It was the whim of Lachesis that kept him from being tormented for fun by the Dark One and he didn't even know if she was on his side. She had contacted him several times already, willing him to hide and lay low.

While she had survived the explosion, it seemed so too had King Grayson's possessed body. He kept that from Rissa for now, wishing her to grieve and find closure before discussing what came next for them.

But there was something that came along with his weakness. The moment the thought crossed his mind he retched, curdling over onto his hands and knees as he vomited a thick globule of blood onto the ground. His tongue burned with the taste of copper and he went to wipe his mouth only for another surge of crimson to force its way out.

He felt so weak. Weaker than he ever had before. Once Galleo et'al had regained its composure, he held no doubts that it would return to claim Centa Isla once again. Gault had no idea how he was going to stop it.

He looked up to the evening sky. Was this the price of his bargain forcefully ended by nothing more than a touch from the Dark One?

What was next for him? Was there a life for him here, in this ruin of a city?

—

Lachesis stood in the ruins of the throne room, looking out through the shattered window at the ruins of civilization. The explosion had rocked the tower, taking the roof over the throne room with it. Even now, rain drizzled in, dampening the carpet and softening the fine wood beneath. The frigid wind of Stormsmarch blew in the first snow, the season now in full swing as she was chilled to her core. Despite the damage, the golden throne had remained intact until the fury of the citizenry had reached it. Graffiti, cuts, dents, the throne had been all but defiled as Monument had been ransacked.

The tower was no longer inhabitable, not for royalty in any case. The King of Centa Isla now sat beneath the earth, deep in the sewers that ran beneath the city. He was there now, comatose, Galleo et'al's malevolent will having temporarily departed from his body. Considering the damage he had sustained; it was quite the surprise that the young core had a pulse at all. He woke only when Galleo et'al's domination returned and his limbs were moved like the strings of a puppet. The days of his reign had been spent rallying what scattered forces of loyal Kingsguard remained and still wished to serve him. The alternative was death.

Lachesis felt pity for the King. Behind those eyes there was no doubt the spirit of Grayson Clovis sealed within, a prisoner in his own body and a channel for the evil that had destroyed his city.

She departed the throne room, returning to her old, ransacked quarters. The Dark One had plans for Centa Isla, had plans for the body of Grayson Clovis. But she was not yet privy as to what those were. The city still thrummed with chaos. Magic use was rampant, crime was a guarantee and murder just as likely. There was a power struggle in place. From Galleo et'al's first invasion, much of the Dark One's dusty surface had broken away to carry the demonic hordes down to the surface. The magic present within those chunks of earth was immense and in part, had already seemed to restore the balance of magic in the atmosphere. The people scrambled for it, to sell, to trade, to study. The Versorcerers of Grandmaster and the great minds of Verscience had come together, sealing themselves within the walls of the sacred academy away from the pillage and chaos. No doubt a new age of technology would be coming with their union.

And so, the Resource Crisis had ended. The King, in that regard, had been true to his word.

Certain that she was alone, Lachesis attended her scrying orb. It was with her protection that Gault was free from Galleo et'al's reach. It seemed her duplicity had been so far unnoticed by the Dark One who, as far she could tell, had assumed Gault's death within the explosion to be the reason why it could not trace the Brand of the Scout.

Yet, it was not Gault she sought. For a time, Lachesis had assumed herself the only Omen alive, yet it seemed that was not the case. After being painfully promised reinforcements when Mires had surrendered his frail body to Galleo et'al, she had watched the sky every night for their arrival. She never saw them. When the magic storm had raged through the city, she must have missed the arrival of the Dark One's promised reinforcements as when she reached into the darkness of her orb to seek another Brand, she found one. But it was far, far away. Much further than the confines of Centa Isla. Her green eyes flitted to the window, to the smog-clouded horizon that obscured it. There was another Omen out there, fulfilling the Dark One's desires that she was not privy to. She didn't know how to feel about that.

Indeed, Galleo et'al had grander designs in motion. She would be on the winning side regardless. Yet, Lachesis couldn't help but grieve the loss of her brother and most importantly, the wealth of information that had been lost with him. Azrael had been the most trusted of Galleo et'al's Omens. Loyal to the end, even if it had meant betraying his own sister. The demon blood had twisted his mind, of that there was no doubt. The brother she knew and loved died the moment that foul liquid entered his system. But he had been privy to meetings with the Dark One that no mortal ever had. If there was a weakness to be found, then her brother would have known it.

She had fashioned the demonic blood vial into a small necklace. As kin, they had no possessions to call their own save for the clothes on their backs. This was not the reminder of her brother that she might have desired, but it was something. It sat around her neck, resting against her heart, a grim reminder of what reward true loyalty entailed.

Lachesis sighed, easing her aching body down onto her bed. It had been days and she had yet to still feel entirely whole after her ordeal within the pod. Her fingers and toes were numb and she found herself feeling haggard and drowsy from the simplest use of her powers. Galleo et'al had kept her around even after betraying her. It was testament to the power of the Dark One, or perhaps its arrogance. Lachesis was yet unsure which but had every intention to find out.

There was no end in sight to the chaos or the death, but Lachesis held onto a sliver of hope. Galleo et'al had been thwarted twice already. That was more than had ever been known.

Yet, this was not over.

~~~THE END.~~~